Andrew Clark, John Aubrey

Brief Lives

chiefly on contemporaries, set down by John Aubrey between the years 1669 and

1696

Andrew Clark, John Aubrey

Brief Lives
chiefly on contemporaries, set down by John Aubrey between the years 1669 and 1696

ISBN/EAN: 9783337423056

Printed in Europe, USA, Canada, Australia, Japan

Cover: Foto ©Andreas Hilbeck / pixelio.de

More available books at **www.hansebooks.com**

'Brief Lives,' chiefly of Contemporaries, set down by John Aubrey, between the Years 1669 & 1696

EDITED FROM THE AUTHOR'S MSS.

BY

ANDREW CLARK

M.A., LINCOLN COLLEGE, OXFORD; M.A. AND LL.D., ST. ANDREWS

WITH FACSIMILES

VOLUME I.   (A -- H)

Oxford

AT THE CLARENDON PRESS

1898

Oxford
PRINTED AT THE CLARENDON PRESS
BY HORACE HART, M.A.
PRINTER TO THE UNIVERSITY

PREFACE

THE rules laid down for this edition have been
fully stated in the Introduction. It need only be
said here that these have been scrupulously followed.

I may take this opportunity of saying that the
text gives Aubrey's quotations, English and Latin
alike, in the form in which they are found in his
MSS. They are plainly cited from memory, not
from book: they frequently do not scan, and at
times do not even construe. A few are incorrect
cementings of odd half lines.

The necessary excisions have not been numerous.
They suggest two reflections. The turbulence
attributed to Sir Walter Raleigh seems to have made
his name in the next age the centre of aggregation
of quite a number of coarse stories. In the same
way, Aubrey is generally nasty when he mentions
the noble house of Herbert, earl of Pembroke, and
the allied family of Sydney. There may be personal
pique in this, for Aubrey thinks he had a narrow

escape from assassination by a Herbert (i. 48); perhaps also there may be the after-glow of a Wiltshire 'feud' (i. 316).

The Index gives all references to persons mentioned in the text, except to a few found only in pedigrees, or otherwise quite insignificant; also to all places of which anything distinctive is said.

ANDREW CLARK.

January 4, 1898.

CONTENTS

————

VOLUME I

FRONTISPIECE: JOHN AUBREY, AETAT. 40.

PAGE

SYNOPSIS OF THE LIVES . . . . ix–xv

INTRODUCTION 1–23

LIVES:—**Abbot** TO **Hyde** 24–427

VOLUME II

FRONTISPIECE: AUBREY'S BOOK-PLATE.

LIVES:—**Ingelbert** TO **York** 1–316

APPENDIX I:—AUBREY'S NOTES OF ANTIQUITIES . 317–332

APPENDIX II:—AUBREY'S COMEDY *The Countrey Revell* . 333–339

INDEX 341–370

FACSIMILES . . . . *At end.*

    I. Castle Mound, Oxford. Riding at the Quintin.

   II. Verulam House.

  III. Horoscope and cottage of Thomas Hobbes.

  IV. Plans of Malmsbury and district.

   V. Horoscope and arms of Sir William Petty.

  VI. Wolsey's Chapel at Christ Church.

SYNOPSIS OF THE 'LIVES'

IN the text the Lives have been given in alphabetical order of the names. This was necessary, not only on account of their number—more than 400—but because Aubrey, in compiling them, followed more than one principle of selection, writing, first, lives of authors, then, lives of mathematicians, but bringing in also lives of statesmen, soldiers, people of fashion, and personal friends.

The following synopsis of the lives may serve to show (i) the heads under which they naturally fall, (ii) their chronological sequence.

The mark † indicates the year or approximate year of death ; ‡ denotes a life which Aubrey said he would write, but which has not been found ; § is attached to the few names of foreigners.

BEFORE HENRY VIII.

WRITERS.	MATHEMATICS.	CHURCH AND STATE.
Poets.	John Holywood (†1256).	S. Dunstan (†988).
Geoffrey Chaucer (†1400).	Roger Bacon (†1294).	S. Edmund Rich (†1240).
John Gower (†1408).	John Ashindon (†13 . .).	Owen Glendower (†1415).
Prose.		William Canynges (†1474).
Sir John Mandeville	ALCHEMY.	John Morton (†1500).
(†1372).	George Ripley (†1490).	

HENRY VIII—MARY (†1558).

WRITERS.	MATHEMATICS.	CHURCH AND STATE.
Sir Thomas More (†1535).	Richard Benese (†1546).	John Colet (†1519).
§Desiderius Erasmus	Robert Record (†1558).	Thomas Wolsey (†1530).
(†1536).		John Innocent (†1545).
		Sir Thomas Pope (†1559).
		Edmund Bonner (†1569).
		Sir Erasmus Dryden (†1632).

ELIZABETH (†1603).

WRITERS.

Poets.

Thomas Tusser (†1580).
Edmund Spenser (†1599).
Sir Edward Dyer (†1607).
William Shakespear
(†1616).

Prose.

§‡ Petrus Ramus (†1572).
John Twyne (†1581).
Sir Philip Sydney (†1586).
John Foxe (†1587).
Robert Glover (†1588).
Thomas Cooper (†1594).
Thomas Stapleton (†1598).
Thomas North (†1601).
William Watson (†1603).
John Stowe (†1605).
Thomas Brightman
(†1607).
John David Rhese
(†1609).
Nicholas Hill (†1610).

MATHEMATICS.

James Peele (†15..).
Leonard Digges (†1571).
Thomas Digges (†1595).
John Securis († . . .).
Evans Lloyd († . . .).
Cyprian Lucar († . . .).
Thomas Hoode († . . .).
‡ Thomas Blundeville
(†16..).
Henry Billingsley (†1606).
§ Ludolph van Keulen
(†1610).
John Blagrave (†1611).
Edward Wright (†1615).
Thomas Hariot (†1621).
Sir Henry Savile (†1622).

CHEMISTRY.

Adrian Gilbert († . . .).

ZOOLOGY.

Thomas Mouffet (†1604).

ALCHEMY AND ASTRO-LOGY.

Thomas Charnocke
(†1581).
John Dee (†1608).
Arthur Dee (†1651).

STATE.

William Herbert, 1st earl
of Pembroke (†1570).
William Cecil, lord Burgh-ley (†1598).
Robert Devereux, earl of
Essex (†1601).
Sir Charles Danvers
(†1601).
George Clifford, earl of
Cumberland (†1605).
Thomas Sackville, earl of
Dorset (†1608).
? Sir Thomas Penruddock
(† . . .).

LAW.

Sir William Fleetwood
(†1594).
William Aubrey (†1595).
Sir John Popham (†1607).

COMMERCE, ETC.

Sir Thomas Gresham
(†1579).
John Davys, capt. (†1605).
Richard Staper (†1608).

SOCIETY.

? . . . Robartes († . . .).
Elizabeth Danvers († . . .).
Sir John Danvers (†1594).
Richard Herbert (†1596).
Edward de Vere, 17th earl
of Oxford (†1604).
Sir Henry Lee (†1611).
Silvanus Scory (†1617).
Mary Herbert, countess of
Pembroke (†1621).

JAMES I (†1625).

WRITERS.

Poets.

Francis Beaumont (†1616).
John Fletcher (†1625).
Arthur Gorges (†1625).

MATHEMATICS.

Edward Brerewood
(†1613).
John Norden (†1625).
Edmund Gunter (†1626).
Thomas Allen (†1632).

CHURCH.

Richard Bancroft (†1610).
John Overall (†1619).
Lancelot Andrewes (†1626).
George Abbot (†1633).
John Davenant (†1641).

JAMES I (†1625) *continued.*

WRITERS.

Poets.

Fulk Greville, lord Brooke (†1628).
Michael Drayton (†1631).
George Chapman (†1634).
Ben Jonson (†1637).
George Feriby (†16..).
‡Benjamin Rudyerd (†16..).

Prose.

Henry Lyte (†1607).
Richard Knolles (†1610).
‡Richard White (†1612).
Thomas Twyne (†1613).
Thomas Coryat (†1617).
Sir Walter Raleigh (†1618).
John Barclay (†1621).
William Camden (†1623).
Nicholas Fuller (†1624).
John Florio (†1625).
Francis Bacon (†1626).
John Speed (†1629).
Thomas Archer (†1630).
John Rider (†1632).
Isaac Wake (†1632).
William Sutton (†1632).
Philemon Holland (†1637).
John Willis (†16..).

MATHEMATICS.

Robert Hues (†1632).
John Speidell (†16..).
‡Thomas Fale (†16..).
‡Thomas Lydiat (†1646).

ASTROLOGY.

Dr. Richard Napier (†1634).

STATE.

Everard Digby (†1606).
Thomas Overbury (†1613).
‡James I (†1625).
William Herbert, 3rd earl of Pembroke (†1630).

LAW.

Sir Thomas Egerton, lord Ellesmere (†1617).
Richard Martin (†1618).

MEDICINE.

... Jaquinto (†16..).
William Butler (†1618).
Francis Anthony (†1623).

COMMERCE, ETC.

Thomas Sutton (†1611).
John Guy (†1628).
John Whitson (†1629).
Sir Hugh Middleton (†1631).
William de Visscher (†16..).
Edward Davenant (†16..).

INVENTORS.

William Lee (†1610).
... Gregory (†16..).
... Ingelbert (†16..).
... Robson (†16..).

SEAMEN.

Walter Raleigh (†1617).
‡Thomas Stumpe (†16..).
Roger North (†1652).

SCHOOLMASTERS.

Alexander Gill (†1635).
Martin Billingsley (†16..).

MISCELLANEOUS.

Charles Hoskyns (†1609).
Richard Sackville, 3rd earl of Dorset (†1624).
Sir Henry Lee (†1631).
Simon Furbisher (†16..)

CHARLES I (†1649).

WRITERS.

Poets.

Hugh Holland (†1633).
George Herbert (†1633).
Richard Corbet (†1635).
Thomas Randolph (†1635).
John Sherburne (†1635).
Sir Robert Aiton (†1638).
John Hoskyns (†1638).
Philip Massinger (†1640).
Charles Aleyn (†1640).
Sir John Suckling (†1641).
William Cartwright (†1643).
Henry Clifford, earl of Cumberland (†1643).
George Sandys (†1644).
Francis Quarles (†1644).
William Browne (†1645).
Thomas Goodwyn (†16..).
William Habington (†1654).
John Taylor (†1654).
Sir Robert Harley (†1656).
Richard Lovelace (†1658).
John Cleveland (†1658).
Gideon de Laune (†1659).
James Shirley (†1666).

Prose.

Gervase Markham (†1637).
Robert Burton (†1640).
Sir Henry Spelman (†1641).
W. Chillingworth (†1644).
Rob. Stafford (1644).
William Twisse (†1646).
Degory Wheare (†1647).
Edward, lord Herbert of Chirbury (†1648).
§Joh. Ger. Vossius (†1649).
Abraham Wheloc (†16..).
Theoph. Wodenote, sen. (†16..).
§René des Cartes (1651).
... Gerard (†16..).
‡Samuel Collins (†1651).
§Jean L. de Balzac (†1655).
John Hales (†1656).
James Usher (†1656).
Joseph Hall (†1656).
William Harvey (†1657).
Robert Sanderson (†1663).
Sir Kenelm Digby (†1665).

MATHEMATICS.

Henry Briggs (†1631).
William Bedwell (†1632).
Nathaniel Torporley (†1632).
Henry Gellibrand (†1637).
Walter Warner (†1640).
William Gascoigne (†1644).
Charles Cavendish (†1652).
Henry Isaacson (†1654).
Edmund Wingate (†1656).
William Oughtred (†1660).
Franciscus Linus (†16 .).
John Tap (†16..).
John Wells (†16..).

CHURCH.

Richard Neile (†1640).
George Webb (†1641).

STATE.

George Villiers, duke of Buckingham (†1628).
Sir Edward Coke (†1633).
William Noy (†1634).
Richard Boyle, 1st earl of Cork (†1643).
Lucius Cary, earl of Falkland (†1643).
Henry Danvers, earl of Danby (†1644).
Robert Dalzell, earl of Carnwarth (†1654).

LAW.

Sir Henry Martin (†1641).
David Jenkins (†1663).

MEDICINE.

Sir Matthew Lister (†1656).

ART.

Inigo Jones (†1652).

SOLDIERS.

Charles Cavendish (†1643).
Sir James Long (†1659).
Sir Robert Harley (†1673).
Sir William Neale (†1691).

SCHOOL AND COLLEGE.

Alexander Gill (†1642).
Ralph Kettell (†1643).
Hannibal Potter (†1664).
Thomas Batchcroft (†1670).

SOCIETY.

Elizabeth Broughton (†16..).
Venetia Digby (†1633).

MISCELLANEOUS.

Elize Hele (†1633).
John Clavell (†1642).
? ... Cradock (†16..).

COMMONWEALTH.

WRITERS.	MATHEMATICS.	STATE.
Poets.	Richard Billingsley	Sir John Danvers (†1655).
Thomas May (†1650).	(†16..).	Thomas Chaloner (†1661).
Katherine Philips (†1664).	Samuel Foster (†1652).	Sir William Platers
George Withers (†1667).	Lawrence Rooke (†1662).	(†16..).
John Milton (†1674).		James Harrington (†1677).
Andrew Marvell (†1678).		Henry Martin (†1680).
		Sir Henry Blount (†1682).
Prose.		SOLDIERS AND SAILORS.
Clement Walker (†1651).	SCIENCE.	Robert Grevill, lord Brooke
John Selden (†1654).	John Wilkins (†1672).	(†1643).
Walter Rumsey (†1660).		Robert Blake (†1657).
Thomas Fuller (†1661).		George Monk (†1671).
William Prynne (†1669).		Thomas, lord Fairfax
		(†1671).
		LAW.
	ASTROLOGY.	Henry Rolle (†1656).
	Nicholas Fiske (†16..).	MEDICINE.
		Jonathan Goddard (†1675).
		SCHOOL.
		Thomas Triplett (†1670).

CHARLES II (†1685) AND JAMES II.

WRITERS.	MATHEMATICS.	CHURCH.
Poets.	Christopher Brookes	Herbert Thorndyke
Alexander Brome (†1666).	(†1665).	(†1672).
Abraham Cowley (†1667).	William Neile (†1670).	William Outram (†1679).
Sir William Davenant	Lancelot Morehouse	Peter Gunning (†1684).
(†1668).	(†1672).	Thomas Pittis (†1687).
Sir John Denham (†1669).	Richard Norwood (†1675).	
Samuel Butler (†1680).	Isaac Barrow (†1677).	STATE.
John Wilmot, earl of	John Newton (†1678).	Sir Robert Moray (†1673).
Rochester (†1680).	Francis Potter (†1678).	Sir Edmund Bury Godfrey
John Lacy (†1681).	Sir Jonas Moore (†1679).	(†1678).
Martin Lluelyn (†1682).	‡Richard Alcorne (†16..).	Sir Thomas Morgan
Edmund Waller (†1687).	‡Henry Bond (†16..).	(†1679).
Thomas Flatman (†1688).	Michael Dary (†1679).	John Birkenhead (†1679).
‡Sir George Etherege	William, lord Brereton	William Harcourt (†1679).
(†16..).	(†1680).	Robert Pugh (†1679).
Henry Vaughan (†1695).	Edward Davenant (†1680).	§Jean Baptiste Colbert
John Dryden (†1700).	Richard Stokes (†1681).	(†1683).

CHARLES II (†1685) AND JAMES II (*continued*).

WRITERS.

Prose.

Peter Heylyn (†1662).
James Heath (†1664).
Sir Robert Poyntz
            (†1665).
Thomas Vaughan (†1667).
George Bate (†1668).
John Davenport (†1670).
Vavasor Powell (†1670).
Samuel Hartlib (†1670).
Edward Bagshawe (†1671).
Edward Hyde, earl of
    Clarendon (†1674).
Sir William Saunderson
            (†1676).
John Ogilby (†1676).
John Tombes (†1676).
Thomas Whyte (†1676).
Silas Taylor (†1678).
Thomas Stanley (†1678).
John Cecil, 4th earl of
    Exeter (†1678).
Thomas Hobbes (†1679).
... Barrow (†168.).
... Munday (†16..).
Joseph Glanville (†1680).
Thomas Jones (†1682).
William Stafford(†1684).
Edward Lane (†1685).
Thomas Pigot (†1686).
Richard Head (†1686?).
Sir William Dugdale
            (†1686).
Isaac Vossius (†1688).
Robert Barclay (†1690).
John Rushworth (†1690).
Fabian Philips (†1690).
Samuel Pordage (†1691).
Elias Ashmole (†1692).
Anthony Wood (†1695).
Henry Birkhead (†1696).
John Aubrey (†1697).
William Holder (†1698).
Richard Blackburne
            (†17..?).
Thomas Gale (†1702).

MATHEMATICS.

Sir George Wharton
            (†1681).
Thomas Merry (†1682).
John Collins (†1683).
William, lord Brouncker
            (†1684).
John Pell (†1685).
Nicholas Mercator (†1687).
Thomas Street (†1689).
Seth Ward (†1689).
John Kersey (†1690).
John Wallis (†1703).
‡John Flamsted (†1719).
‡Isaac Newton (†1727).
Edmund Halley (†1742).

SCIENCE.

John Willis (†16..).
John Graunt (†1674).
Robert Boyle (†1691).
Sir Edward Harley (†1700).
Robert Hooke (†1703).
Sir John Hoskyns (†1705).

STATE.

Anthony Cooper, earl of
    Shaftesbury (†1683).
Sir Leoline Jenkins
            (†1685).
‡James, duke of Monmouth
            (†1685).
Sir William Petty (†1687).
Thomas Osborne, earl of
    Danby (†1712).

LAW.

Sir Matthew Hale (†1676).
George Johnson (†1683).

MEDICINE.

Thomas Willis (†1675).
Baldwin Hamey (†1676).
Sir Richard Napier (†1676).
Henry Stubbe (†1676).
Thomas Shirley (†1678).
Sir Edward Greaves
            (†1680).
Sir Robert Talbot (†1681).
William Croone (†1684).
Daniel Whistler (†1684).
Christopher Merret
            (†1695).
Walter Charleton (†1707).

ART.

Samuel Cooper (†1672).
Wenceslaus Hollar
            (†1677).
Sir Christopher Wren
            (†1723).

SCHOOL.

... Webb (†16..).
Thomas Stephens (†16..).
Arthur Brett (†1677).
Ezerel Tonge (†1680).

COMMERCE, ETC.

Sir Edward Ford (†1670).
Thomas Bushell (†1674).
William Marshall (†16..).
Robert Murray (†1725).
James Bovey (†....).

CHARLES II (†1685) AND JAMES II (*continued*)

WRITERS.

Prose.

‡Sir Edward Sherburne
(†1702).
John Evelyn (†1706).
John Philips (†1706).
John Hawles (†1716).
William Penn (†1718).

ASTROLOGY.

John Heydon (†166.).
John Booker (†1667).
William Lilly (†1681).
Henry Coley (†1695).
Charles Snell (†16..).
John Gadbury (†1704).
John Partridge (†1715).

SOCIETY, ETC.

Lucy Walters (†16..).
Sir Walter Raleigh (†1663).
Eleanor Ratcliffe, countess
of Sussex (†1666).
... Berkeley (†16..).
... Curtin (†16..).
Dorothy Selby (†16..).
Anne, duchess of York
(†1671).
Cecil Calvert, lord Balti-
more (†1675).
Sir Thomas Billingsley
(†167.).
Richard Sackville, 5th earl
of Dorset (†1677).
Charles Pamphlin (†1678).
Sir Francis Stuart (†16..).
‡... Aldsworth (†16...).
Sir Robert Henley (†1680).
Sir Thomas Badd (†1683).
... Ralphson (†1684).
Charles Howard (†17..).
Willoughby Bertie (†1760).

AUBREY'S PERSONAL FRIENDS.

I. OF THE OLD SCHOOL.

Isaac Lyte (1577–†1660).
Thomas Tyndale (1588–†167½).
James Whitney (1593–†166.).
William Beeston (....–†1682).
Deborah Aubrey (1610–†168¾).
Edmund Wyld (1616–†16..).

II. CONTEMPORARIES.

Anthony Ettrick (1622–†1703).
William Morgan (1622–†....).
Ralph Sheldon (1623–†1684).
William Radford (1623–†1673).
Theophilus Wodenoth (1625–....).
George Ent (....–†1679).
John Sloper (....–†....).
Richard Kitson (....–†....).
Sir John Dunstable (....–†....).
Thomas Gore (1632–†1684).
Jane Smyth (1639–†16..).
Thomas Deere (1639–†16..).
... Gwyn (....–†....).
... Yarrington (....–†1684).

AUBREY'S 'BRIEF LIVES'

— ◦◦ —

INTRODUCTION

I. ORIGIN OF THE 'LIVES.'

AUBREY sought and obtained an introduction to Anthony Wood in August 1667. He was keenly interested in antiquarian studies, and had the warmest love for Oxford; he had been a contemporary in Trinity College with Wood's brother, Edward; and so was drawn to Wood on hearing that he was busy with researches into the History of the University of Oxford.

Aubrey was one of those eminently good-natured men, who are very slothful in their own affairs, but spare no pains to work for a friend. He offered his help to Wood; and, when it was decided to include in Wood's book short notices of writers connected with Oxford, that help proved most valuable. Aubrey, through his family and family-connexions, and by reason of his restless goings-to-and-fro, had a wide circle of acquaintance among squires and parsons, lawyers and doctors, merchants and politicians, men of letters and persons of quality, both in town and country. He had been, until his estate was squandered, an extensive and curious buyer of books and MSS. And above all, being a good gossip, he had used to the utmost those opportunities of inquiry about men and things which had been afforded him by societies grave,

like the Royal Society, and frivolous, as coffee-house
gatherings and tavern clubs. The scanty excerpts, given
in these volumes, from letters written by him between
1668 and 1673, supply a hint of how deeply Wood's
Historia et Antiquitates Universitatis Oxoniensis, published
in 1674, was indebted to the multifarious memory and
unwearying inquiries of the enthusiastic Aubrey.

Dean Fell's request that Wood should notice Oxford
writers and bishops in his *Historia* had suggested to Wood
the plan of, and set him to work upon, the larger and
happier scheme of the *Athenae Oxonienses,* an 'exact
history of all the writers and bishops that have had their
education in . . . Oxford' since 1500. He engaged his
friend Aubrey to help him in his undertaking, by committing to writing in a more systematic way, for Wood's
benefit, his multitudinous recollections of men and books.
He was dexterous enough to supply the additional motive,
that, after serving his friend's turn, Aubrey's collections
might be gathered together, preserved for a while in some
safe and secret place, and, when personal feelings were
saved by lapse of time, be published and secure their
writer a niche in the Temple of Fame.

It was now by no means easy for Aubrey to undertake
any extensive, and especially any connected work. Being
by this time bankrupt, and a hanger-on at the tables of
kindred and acquaintances, he had to fall in with his
patrons' habits, at the houses where he visited; to sit with
them till they wearied of their carousings in the small
hours of the morning; and to do his writing next forenoon,
before they had slept off their wine.

Still, his interest in the subject, and his desire to help
his friend prevailed; and we soon find him thanking Wood
for setting him to work. March 27, 1680[a]:—''Twill be
a pretty thing, and I am glad you putt me on it. I doe
it playingly. This morning being up by 10, I writt two
⟨lives⟩: one was Sir John Suckling[b], of whom I wrote

---

[a] Letter of Aubrey to Wood: MS. Ballard 14, fol. 131.
[b] MS. Aubr. 6, fol. 110, 110ᵛ.

a leafe and ½ in folio.' May 22, 1680[a] :—' My memoires of lives' ⟨is now⟩ ' a booke of 2 quires, close written : and after I had began it, I had such an impulse on my spirit that I could not be at quiet till I had donne it.' Sept. 8, 1680[b] :—' My booke of lives . . . they will be in all about six-score, and I beleeve never any in England were delivered so faithfully and with so good authority.'

Aubrey, therefore, began these lives[c] on the suggestion of, and with a desire to help Anthony Wood.

Among the lives so written were several of mathematicians and men of science. And another friend of Aubrey's, Dr. Richard Blackburne, advised him to collect these by themselves, and add others to them, with a view to a biographical history of mathematical studies in England. To this suggestion Aubrey was predisposed through his pride at being ' Fellow of the Royal Society,' and for some time he busied himself in that direction[d].

In the same way, although the bulky life of Thomas Hobbes[e] was partly undertaken in fulfilment of a promise to Hobbes himself, an old personal friend, the motive which induced Aubrey to go on with it was a desire to supply Dr. Blackburne with material for a Latin biography, *Vitae Hobbianae Auctarium*, published in 1681.

These matters will be found more fully explained in the notices which Aubrey has prefixed to the several MSS. of his biographical collections, as described below.

II. CONDITION OF THE TEXT OF THE 'LIVES.'

Few of the 'Lives' are found in a fair copy[f]. Again and again, in his letters to Anthony Wood, Aubrey makes confession of the deficiencies of his copy, but puts off the heavy task of reducing it to shape.

---

[a] Aubrey to Wood, in MS. Wood F. 39, fol. 340.
[b] Ibid. fol. 347.
[c] Composing MSS. Aubr. 6, 7, and 8 (part i.).

[d] Writing MS. Aubr. 8 (part ii.).
[e] MS. Aubr. 9.
[f] The lives of Isaac Barrow, and of (Serjeant-at-Law) John Hoskyns, may serve as specimens of a fair copy.

His method of composition was as follows. He had a folio MS. book, and wrote at the top of a page here and there the name of a poet, or statesman, or the like, whose life he thought of committing to paper. Then, selecting a page and a name, he wrote down hastily, without notes or books, his recollections of the man, his personal appearance, his friendships, his actions or his books. If a date, a name, a title of a book, did not occur to him on the spur of the moment, he just left a blank, or put a mark of omission (generally, . . . or ———), and went on. If the matter which came to him was too much for the page, he made an effort to get it in somehow, in the margins (top, bottom, or sides), between the paragraphs, or on the opposite page.

When he read over what he had written in the first glow of composition, he erased, wrote alternatives to words and phrases, marked words, sentences, and paragraphs for transposition, inserted queries: unsettled everything.

If later on, from books or persons, he got further information, he was reckless as to how he put in the new matter: sometimes he put it in the margin, sometimes at a wrong place in the text, or on a wrong leaf, or in the middle even of another life, and often, of course, in a different volume.

And there, as has been said, the copy was left. Very seldom was a revised copy made.

To the confusions unavoidable in composing after this fashion, must be added the unsteadiness consequent on writing in the midst of morning sickness after a night's debauch. One passage, in which he describes his difficulties in composing, explains, in a way nothing else could, the frequent erasures, repetitions, half-made or inconsistent corrections, and dropping of letters, syllables, and words, which abound in his MSS. March 19, 168$\frac{9}{1}$ [a]; 'if I had but either one to come to me in a morning with a good scourge, or did not sitt-up till one or two with Mr. ⟨Edmund⟩ Wyld, I could doe a great deal of businesse.'

[a] Aubrey to Wood, MS. Ballard 14, fol. 129ᵛ.

III. AIM OF THIS EDITION.

In presenting a text of Aubrey's 'Lives,' an editor, on more than one important point, has to decide between alternatives.

1. Shall all, or some only, of the lives be given?

It is plain, from a glance over the MSS., that many of the lives are of little interest; in some cases, because they contain more marks of omission than statements of fact; in other cases, because they give mainly excerpts from prefaces of books; and so on. A much more interesting, as well as handier, book would be produced, if the editor were to reject all lives in which Aubrey has nothing of intrinsic value to show.

2. In the lives selected, shall the whole, or parts only, of what Aubrey has written be given?

Many sentences occur, which declare only Aubrey's ignorance of a date, or a place, or the title of a book. In other cases, dull and imperfect catalogues of writings are given. The omission of these would be a service to the whole, like the cutting of dead branches out of a shrub.

3. In constituting the text, how much, or how little, notice is to be taken of the imperfections of Aubrey's copy?

The simplest, and, from some points of view, the most effective, course would be to treat Aubrey's rough draft as if it were one's own, rejecting (without comment) one or other of two alternatives, supplying (without mark) a missing word or date, omitting a second version (though having some minor peculiarities) of a statement, and so on. In this way, with a minimum of trouble to the editor, a smooth text would be produced, which would spare the reader much irritation.

4. How far is the text to be annotated, the editor supplying Aubrey's abundant omissions, and correcting his many mistakes?

In respect of all these questions, the aim of the present edition, and the reasons for the decision taken in each case, can be stated very briefly and decidedly.

1, and 2. This edition seeks to give in full all that Aubrey has written in his four chief MSS. of biographies, MSS. Aubrey 6, 7, 8, and 9.

The entire contents of these MSS. will thus be placed beyond that risk of perishing, to which they must have remained liable so long as they were found only in MS., and they will, for what they are worth, henceforth be accessible to all.

Some things in Aubrey's writing offend not merely against our present canons of good taste, but against good morals. The conversation of the people among whom Aubrey moved, although they were gentry both in position and in education, was often vulgar, and occasionally foul, as judged by us. I have dealt with these lives as historical documents, leaving them, with a very few excisions, to bear, unchecked, their testimony as to the manners and morals of Restoration England.

3. This edition seeks to present faithfully Aubrey's text as he wrote it, neglecting only absolute minutiae.

(*a*) A plain text is given of what Aubrey wrote, taking, as seemed most convenient, sometimes his first version of a sentence or a word, sometimes his alternative version. The rejected alternatives are given in the textual notes, as 'duplicate with'; and occasionally the erasures, as 'substituted for.' Many of these notes are very trivial; but their presence, which after all gives little trouble, provides a complete view of the MS. text. I believe also that in this way I have preserved for the collector of words some quaint forms and expressions for which he will thank me, and provided the student of English style with some apt instances of the way in which terse native words have been replaced in our written language by feebler latinisms.

(*b*) I have been careful to give, in every case, Aubrey's own spelling, with or without final or medial 'e,' with single or double letters, 'ie' or other diphthong where we write 'ei,' and the like. The English of Aubrey's age is so like our own that it is not unimportant to mark even its minor differences.

All merely artificial tricks of writing (wch for which, and the like) have been neglected.

(*c*) Where a date, a word, or a name has been inserted, the insertion is enclosed in angular brackets ⟨   ⟩. Where it seemed requisite to mark that a word or phrase was added at a later date, or by another hand, square brackets have been used [   ]. The use of these symbols, borrowed from Vahlen's edition of Aristotle's *Poetics*, has been censured as pedantic, but I know of no clearer or shorter way of making plain in a printed text just what is, and what is not, in the MS. text.

(*d*) Punctuation is generally absent in Aubrey's text, as might be expected, and where it is found, it is often misleading. The points and marks in this edition are therefore such as seemed to make the meaning clear to myself, and therefore, I hope, to others.

(*e*) As regards the order of the paragraphs, Aubrey's text has been given, where convenient, sentence by sentence, and page by page. But I have taken full liberty to bring into their proper place *marginalia*, interlinear notes, *addenda* on opposite pages, &c. In some cases, indeed, to give in print the MS. text sentence by sentence is to do it injustice. In the MS., the difference of inks between earlier and later notes, the difference of pen-strokes (on one day with a firm pen, on another with a scratchy quill), and similar nuances, impress the eye with a sequence of paragraphs which in print can be shown only by redistribution. For example, I claim that the life of Milton, in this edition, is, from its bolder treatment, truer to the MS., than the servile version in the old edition.

4. As regards notes and explanations. Aubrey's lives supply an inviting field for comment, correction, and addition. But, even so treated, they will never be a

biographical dictionary.　Their value lies not in statement of bibliographical or other facts, but in their remarkably vivid personal touches, in what Aubrey had seen himself and what his friends had told him.　The notes therefore seek to supply no more than indications of outstanding features of the text, identifications of Aubrey's informants, or necessary parallels from his letters.

IV. Description of the MSS.

MS. Aubr. 6: a volume chiefly of folio leaves; written mostly in February 16$\frac{79}{80}$; now marked as containing 122 leaves (some pages blank), but having also a few unfoliated slips.　Aubrey's own short title to it was:—

'Σχεδιάσματα. Brief Lives, part i.,'

and, in his pagination, it contained eighty-six leaves. A rough index of its contents, by him, is found as foll. 8–10: and there he gives the names of several persons whose lives he intended to write, but has not included in this volume. Some of these are found elsewhere, especially in MS. Aubrey 8; but a few [a] are not discoverable in any MS. of his biographical collections—e.g., Richard Alcorne; ⟨Samuel⟩ Collins, D.D.; Richard Blackbourne, M.D.; ⟨John⟩ Flamsted [b]; Sir John Hoskins; James Rex; James, duke of Monmouth [c]; Peter Ramus; Benjamin Ruddier; captain ⟨Edward⟩ Sherburne; captaine Thomas Stump [d]; Richard White.　Possibly Aubrey never wrote the missing lives; but it must be remembered (1) that he cut some leaves out of his MS. himself (see in a note to the life of Richard Boyle, earl of Cork); (2) that Anthony Wood cut out of MS. Aubr. 7 forty pages at least, containing matters 'to cut Aubrey's throat,' i.e. reflections on politics, where the lives of James R. and Monmouth may well have been.

[a] In this edition, some notes about some of them have been brought in from Aubrey's letters, and his 'Collectio Geniturarum.'

[b] Aubrey notes 'Mr. ⟨Edmund⟩ Halley' as the person to ask about Flamsted.

[c] Aubrey adds the reference 'vide libr. B.': see Macray's *Bodleian*, p. 366.

[d] The adventures of Captain Thomas Stump in Guiana are recorded in Aubrey's *Natural History of Wilts.*

One point about this MS. which deserves mention is that, in these lives, Aubrey, in his hope to supply data for crucial instances in astrology, is careful to give the exact nativity wherever he can. His rule is thus laid down by himself in MS. Aubr. 6, fol. 12ᵛ, in a note attached to the nativity of his friend Sir William Petty :—

'Italian proverb—

" E astrologia, ma non é Astrologo,"

i.e. we have not that science yet perfect; 'tis one of the *desiderata.* The way to make it perfect is to gett a supellex of true genitures ; in order wherunto I have with much care collected these ensuing ª, which the astrologers may rely on, for I have sett doune none on randome, or doubtfull, information, but *from their owne mouthes* : quod N. B.'

Another point is, that Aubrey very frequently gives the coat of arms, in trick or colour. In some cases, no doubt, he did this from having seen the arms actually borne in some way by the person he is writing about; but in other cases he merely looked up the name in a 'Dictionary of Arms,' and took the coat from thence, thus nullifying his testimony as to the actual pretensions to arms of those he writes about. All coats he mentions have, however, been given in the text or notes.

Prefixed to the volume ᵇ are two notes in which Aubrey explains its origin and destination.

(A)—MS. Aubr. 6, fol. ° 2 :—

'*Tanquam tabulata naufragii,*

Sum Johannis Aubrii, R.S.S.

Febr. 24, 16⅞⅞.

My will and humble desire is that these minutes,

ª i. e. the schemes of nativity given at the beginning of many of the lives in MS. Aubr. 6. MS. Aubr. 23, 'Collectio geniturarum,' drawn up by Aubrey in 1674 to be deposited in the Ashmolean Museum, is an earlier contribution to the 'supellex.'

ᵇ In fol. 11ᵛ Aubrey's book-plate is pasted on.

° In the top left corner, ' 1s. 4d.' is written. Possibly the price of the original paper-book.

which I have hastily and scriblingly here sett downe, be delivered carefully to my deare and honoured friend Mr. Anthony à Wood, antiquary, of Oxford.—

Ita obnixe obtestor,

JO. AUBREY.

Ascenscione Domini,
    correptus lipóthymiâ, circiter 3 P.M.
        1680.'

(B)—MS. Aubr. 6, fol. 12:—

'To my worthy friend Mr. ANTHONIE à WOOD,
        Antiquarie of Oxford.

SIR!

I have, according to your desire, putt in writing these minutes of lives tumultuarily, as they occurr'd to my thoughts or as occasionally I had information of them. They may easily be reduced into order at your leisure by numbring them with red figures, according to time and place, &c. 'Tis a taske that I never thought to have undertaken till you imposed it upon me, sayeing that I was fitt for it by reason of my generall acquaintance, having now not only lived above halfe a centurie of yeares in the world, but have also been much tumbled up and downe in it which hath made me much* knowne; besides the moderne advantage of coffee-howses in this great citie, before which men knew not how to be acquainted, but with their owne relations, or societies. I might add that I come of a longaevous race, by which meanes I have imped some feathers of the wings of time, for severall generations; which does reach high. When I first began, I did not thinke I could have drawne it out to so long a thread.

I here lay-downe to you (out of the conjunct friend-

---

* 'Much' substituted for 'so well.'

ship[a] between us) the trueth, and, as neer as I can and that
religiously as a poenitent to his confessor, nothing but the
trueth: the naked and plaine trueth, which is here exposed
so bare that the very *pudenda* are not covered[b], and affords
many passages that would raise a blush in a young
virgin's[c] cheeke. So that after your perusall, I must
desire you to make a castration (as Raderus[d] to Martial)
and to sowe-on some figge-leaves—i. e., to be my *Index
expurgatorius*.

What uncertainty doe we find in printed histories?
they either treading too neer on the heeles of trueth
that they dare not speake plaine, or els for want of intelligence (things being antiquated) become too obscure and
darke! I doe not here repeat any thing already published
(to the best of my remembrance) and I fancy my selfe
all along discourseing with you; alledgeing those of my
relations and acquaintance (as either you knew or have
heerd of) *ad faciendam fidem*: so that you make me to
renew my acquaintance with my old and deceased friends,
and to *rejuvenescere* (as it were) which is the pleasure of old
men. 'Tis pitty that such minutes had not been taken
100 yeares since or more: for want wherof many worthy
men's names and notions[e] are swallowd-up in oblivion;
as much of these also would [have[f] been], had it not been
through your instigation: and perhaps this is one of the
usefullest pieces[g] that I have scribbeld.

I remember one sayeing of generall Lambert's, that "the

---

[a] Aubrey cites in the margin:—

> 'Utrumque nostrum admirabili modo
> Consentit astrum.
>
> Horat. lib. 2, ode 17:
>
> Nescio quod certe est, quod me tibi temperet, astrum.
>
> Pers. *Sat.* v. *v.* 50';

and adds the date in the margin '1665'; but according to Wood, 1667 was the date of their first acquaintance (Clark's Wood's *Life and Times*, ii. 116).

[b] Dupl. with 'hid.'

[c] Subst. for 'girle's.'

[d] Matth. Raderi 'novi commentt.' were published in 1602, and later editions.

[e] Dupl. with 'inventions.'

[f] 'Have been' is scored out.

[g] Subst. for 'things.'

best of men are but men at the best ": of this, you will
meet with divers examples in this rude and hastie collection. Now these *arcana* are not fitt to lett flie abroad, till
about 30 yeares hence; for the author and the persons
(like medlars) ought to be first rotten. But in whose hands
must they be deposited in the mean time? advise me,
who am,

Sir,

Your very affectionate friend
to serve you,

JOHN AUBREY.

London,
June 15,
1680.'

MS. Aubr. 7: a folio volume of twenty-one leaves
(several pages blank), of which two[a] only belong to the
original MS.

The original title may be conjectured to have been :

'Σχεδιάσματα. Brief Lives, part ii.,'

and it possibly contained some letters, like those in the
preceding volume, which made Wood think it was given
to him.

On fol. 1, is a note describing the make-up of the
volume :—

'Aubrey's Lives: fragments of part ii.—These scattered
fragments collected and arranged by E. M. Sep. 1792.'
A note (in Dr. Philip Bliss's hand?) says that E. M. is
Edmund Malone.

In this, as in the other Aubrey MSS., Dr. Bliss has
made several slight notes, both in pencil and ink, with
a view to his edition.

The mutilation of the MS. was the crime of Anthony
Wood, to whom it had been sent. Two conjectures may
be hazarded—either that Wood did this in order to paste
the cuttings into his rough copy of his projected *Athenae*,
and so save transcription; or, more probably, that he was

---

[a] Foll. 47, 48, in the original (foll.
10, 11, as now foliated). The rest are
scraps: fol. 8 is a paper, bearing date
'London, March 12, 168⅘.'

so thoroughly alarmed by the threat of Lord Clarendon's prosecution of himself (Clark's Wood's *Life and Times*, iv. 1–46), that he destroyed the papers containing Aubrey's sharp reflections on various prominent personages[a]. But whatever the pretext, Aubrey was, naturally, very grieved at his unjustifiable conduct. In a letter to Wood, dated Sept. 2, 1694 (MS. Ballard 14, fol. 155), he writes:—

'You have cutt out a matter of 40 pages out of one of my volumnes, as also the index. Was ever any body so unkind?—And I remember you told me comeing from Hedington that there were some things in it that "would cutt my throat." I thought you so deare a friend that I might have entrusted my life in your hands and now your unkindnes doth almost break my heart.'

When Aubrey had the volume back in his own hands, he wrote in it[b] the following censure:—

'Ingratitude! This *part the second* Mr. Wood haz gelded from page 1 to page 44 and other pages[c] too are wanting wherein are contained trueths, but such as I entrusted nobody with the sight of but himselfe (whom I thought I might have entrusted with my life). There are severall papers that may cutt my throate. I find too late *Memento diffidere* was a saying worthy one of the sages. He hath also embezill'd the index of it—quod N. B. It was stitch't up when I sent it to him.
Novemb. 29, 1692.'

MS. Aubr. 8: a folio volume, containing 105 leaves: it contains two distinct MSS., bound together.

The first part of the MS. (foll. 1–68 in the present marking) might have been entitled:—

'Σχεδιάσματα. Brief Lives, part iii.'

---

[a] See, e.g. in the life of David Jenkins, from a letter of Aubrey's, the expressions which brought Wood into court and expelled him from the University.

[b] Fol. 2, in the present marking.

[c] I have little doubt that the substance of all the missing pages is incorporated into the *Athenae*: cf., e.g. William Penn's life here by Aubrey, and the notice of Penn in Wood's *Athenae*.

On fol. 1 and fol. 3, the short title actually written by Aubrey is :—

Pars '♄' iii^{tia}

1681

i.e. the symbol for Saturn, the patron of antiquarian studies, and Aubrey's monogram. On fol. 4 Aubrey has a very elaborate title, showing the destination of the MS. :—

'Auctarium vitarum a ⚇ collectarum, anno Domini 1681.

Tanquam tabulata naufragii.

John Aubrey, R.S.S.

Le mal est que la vive voix meurt en naissant et ne laisse rien qui reste apres elle, ni formant point de corps qui subsiste en l'air. Les paroles ont des aisles ; vous scavez l'epithete * qu'Homère leur donne, et un poëte Syrien en a fait un espece parmy les oiseaux ; de sorte que, si on n'arreste pas ces fugitives par l'ecriture, elles eschappent fort vistement à la memoire.

Les Oeuvres diverses du sieur de Balzac, page 43.

. Ornari res ipsa nolit contenta doceri.—HORAT

For Mr. Anthony Wood
at
Oxford.'

A slip by Anthony Wood, pasted here, shows that Aubrey recalled the MS., probably to make additions to it :—

' Mr. AUBREY,

I beseech you as you have been civill in giving this book to me at Oxon in Sept. 1681, so I hope when you have done with it you'l returne every part of it againe to your servant,

ANT. WOOD.'

As originally made up, this 'Auctarium' contained

---

* Aubrey quotes in the margin :—ἔπεα πτερόεντα.— HOM.

four leaves at the beginning (for an index [a]), and leaves foliated 1–38 (of which 12 and 13 are now [b] missing).

The second part [c] of the MS. extends over foll. 69–103 in the present marking.

Aubrey, on fol. 69, writes the title :—

'An Apparatus for the lives
of our English mathematical writers
by
Mr. John Aubrey, R.S.S.
March 25, 1690.'

As originally made up, this treatise consisted of one leaf (for an index [d]) and pages marked 1–46 (of which pp. 31–38 are now missing).

The history of this treatise is fully set out by Aubrey in some notes in it and in the other MSS. :—

1. It was suggested by Richard Blackburne.

MS. Aubr. 7, fol. 8ᵛ:—'Dr. ⟨Richard⟩ Blackbourn would have me putt out in print the lives of our English mathematicians together.'

2. It had been partly anticipated by Selden and Sherburne.

MS. Aubr. 8, fol. 70 :—'My purpose is, if God give me life, to make an *apparatus*, for [e] the lives of our English Mathematicians; which when I have ended, I would then desire Mr. Anthony Wood to find out one that is master

---

[a] Dated 'July 1ᵐᵒ, 1681'—MS. Aubr. 8, fol. 5. In this index the names of some persons occur for notice, of whom no account is found here or elsewhere:—e.g. '. . . Aldsworth ; Richard Blackbourne, M.D.; Sir George Etheridge; Isaac Newton.'

[b] There are now several inserted papers and slips. The two last leaves of the MS. as now made up (foll. 104, 105), belong to neither section of it, but have been brought in from elsewhere, possibly from loose Rawlinson papers.

[c] Anthony Wood has marked it as

'G. 10' of his *Athenae* Collections (see Clark's Wood's *Life and Times*, iv. 232), thus showing that he looked on it as his own property.

[d] In this index or on blank pages in the treatise, some are mentioned for their lives to be written, of whom no account is found here or elsewhere in the biographical collections :— e. g. Mr. ⟨Thomas⟩ Blundeville ; ⟨Henry⟩ Bond; Mr. Robert Hues; Mr.⟨Thomas⟩ Lidyate ; Mr. . . . Phale ⟨i.e. Thomas Fale⟩; Edmund Wingate.

[e] 'For' subst. for 'in order to the writing.'

of a good Latin stile, and to adde what is[a] already in his printed booke[b] to these following[c] minutes.

'I will not meddle with our own writers[d] in the mathematicks before the reigne of king Henry VIII, but prefix those excellent verses of Mr. John Selden (with a learned commentary to them) which are printed before a booke intituled ⟨Arthur⟩ Hopton's *Concordance of yeares*[e], scilicet:—

.   .   .   .   .'

MS. Aubr. 8, fol. 69:—'Sir Edward Shirbourn, somewhere in his translation and notes upon Manilius, has enumerated our English mathematicians, and hath given short touches of their lives—which see.'

3. The first step towards it would be to pick out the mathematicians from the lives already written by Aubrey.

MS. Aubr. 6, fol. 51[v]:—'I would have the lives of John Dee, Sir Henry Billingsley, the two Digges (father and sonne), Mr. Thomas Hariot, Mr. ⟨Walter⟩ Warner, Mr. ⟨Henry⟩ Brigges, and Dr. ⟨John⟩ Pell's, to be putt together.—As to the account of Mr. Hariot, Mr. Warner, and Mr. Brigges, I recieved it from Dr. Pell.'

MS. Aubr. 9: a folio, containing fifty-five leaves, and in addition several printed papers.

The title is found on fol. 28 (as now marked) of the MS.:—
'Supplementum vitae Thomae Hobbes,
Malmesburiensis,
16$\frac{79}{80}$

HOBBI[f] jucunda senectus,
Cujus erant mores qualis facundia, mite
Ingenium.—   JUVENAL, *Sat.* IV. v. 81.

Extinctus amabitur.—
                    HORAT. *Epist.* I. lib. 2.
I. A.'
I. A.=Aubrey's initials.

---

[a] 'Is' subst. for 'Mr. Wood haz.'
[b] *Hist. et Antiq. Univ. Oxon.*, 1674.
[c] 'These following' subst. for 'my.'

[d] Aubrey queries 'Is John Escuidus mentioned among them?'
[e] Lond. 1616.
[f] Written at first 'Venit et Hobbi.'

The reason for this title was that Aubrey intended his Collections to be a sort of commentary on Hobbes' short Latin autobiography, which was in the press in Febr. 16$\frac{79}{80}$, and was published in Nov. 1680 (Clark's Wood's *Life and Times*, ii. 480, 500).

But Anthony Wood (MS. Aubr. 9, fol. 28) objected:— 'What need you say Supplimentum?' *sic* 'pray say the life of Thomas Hobbs.' And Aubrey, in obedience to this, changed the short title on fol. 30 (see the beginning of the life); and on the parchment cover of the MS. (now fol. 1) wrote :—

> ' The life of
> Mr. Thomas Hobbes,
> of Malmsbury,
> by
> Mr. John Aubrey,
> Fellow of the Royall Societie,
> 16$\frac{79}{80}$.'

Aubrey set about this Life of Hobbes immediately after Hobbes' death, partly as a tribute of respect to his friend's memory, but apparently also in fulfilment of a promise to the deceased. The preface [a] is as follows:—

' LECTORI.

'Tis religion to performe the will of the dead; which I here [b] dischardge, with my promise (1667) to my old friend Mr. T⟨homas⟩ H⟨obbes⟩, in publishing [c] his life and performing the last office to my old [d] friend Mr. Thomas Hobbes, whom I have had the honour to know ⟨from⟩ my child-hood [e], being his countreyman and borne in Malmesbury hundred and taught my grammar by his schoolmaster [f].

Since nobody knew so many particulars of his life as

---

[a] MS. Aubr. 9, fol. 29. Aubrey notes in the margin :—' The ὕλη of the preface to the life written by Mr. H. him selfe in ⟨the⟩ third person '; intending I suppose to consult it in re-modelling his own draft preface.

[b] Subst. for 'now.'
[c] Subst. for 'setting forth.'
[d] Subst. for 'honoured.'
[e] Dupl. with 'pueritia mea.'
[f] Dupl. with 'having both the same schoolmaster.'

myſelfe, he was willing[a] that if I survived him, it should
be handed to posterity by my hands, which I declare and
avow to do ingenuously and impartially, to prevent mis-
reports and undecieve those who are scandalized by . . .

One sayes[b] that when a learned man dyes, a great
deal of learning dyes with him. *He* was 'flumen ingenii,'
never dry. The *recrementa*[c] of so learned a person are[d]
valueable†. Amongst innumerable observables
of him which had deserved to be sett downe,
these few (that have not scap't[e] my memory)
I humbly offer[f] to the present age and
posterity, *tanquam tabulam naufragii* ‡, and
as plankes and lighter things swimme, and are
preserved, where the more weighty sinke and
are lost. And[g] as with the light after sun-sett—at which
time, clear[h]; by and by[i], comes the *crepusculum* ; then,
totall darkenes — in like manner is it with matters of
antiquitie. Men thinke, because every body remembers
a memorable accident shortly after 'tis donne, 'twill never
be forgotten, which for want of registring[k], at last is
drowned in oblivion. Which[l] reflection haz been a hint,
that by my meanes many antiquities have been reskued[m],
and preserved (I myselfe now inclining[n] to be ancient[o])—
or els utterly lost and forgotten.

For that I am so minute, I declare I never intended it,
but setting downe in my first[p] draught every particular[q],
(with purpose, upon review, to retrench[r] what was super-

Margin notes:

† We read that an earthen lamp of a philosopher (quaere nomen) hath been sold for . . . .

‡ Vide Erasmi *Adagia* and quaere Dr. ⟨Richard⟩ Bl⟨ackburne⟩.

[a] Dupl. with 'desired.'

[b] See in the life of Selden.

[c] In a marginal note Aubrey re-marks 'meliorate this word.' Another note is 'Quaere of the preface of this Supplement,' i. e., I suppose, ask some one's opinion whether it will do or not.

[d] Dupl. with 'will ⟨be⟩.'

[e] Dupl. with 'slipt.'

[f] Dupl. with 'dd' i. e. dedicate.

[g] Subst. for ' But for that the *recrementa* of such a person are valueable.

It is with matters of antiquity as with the sett . . .'

[h] Subst. for 'good light.'

[i] Dupl. with ' so many degrees, etc.'

[k] Dupl. with ' entring.'

[l] Subst. for ' This.'

[m] 'From oblivion' followed; scored out.

[n] Dupl. with ' growing.'

[o] Dupl. with ' *senescens*.'

[p] Dupl. with ' rude.'

[q] Dupl. with ' thing.'

[r] Dupl. with ' cutt off.'

fluous and triviall), I shewed it to some friends of mine (who also were of Mr. Hobbes's acquaintance) whose judgments I much value, who gave their opinion: and 'twas clearly their judgement [a], to let *all* stand; for though to soome at present it might appeare too triviall; yet hereafter 'twould not be scorned [b] but passe [c] for antiquity.

And besides I have precedents of reverend writers to plead, who have in some lives † recited things as triviall [d], nay, the sayings and actions of good woemen.

† Dean Fell hath recorded his mother's jejune sayings and actions and triviall remarques of Dr. Hammond in his life, written by him.

I am also to beg pardon of the reader for two long digressions, viz. Malmesbury and Gorambery; but this also was advised, as the only way to preserve them, and which I have donne for the sake of the lovers of antiquity. I hope its novelty and pleasantness will make compensation for its length.

Yours [e],

I. A.'

In MS. Aubr. 9, fol. 28^v are two letters by Aubrey, asking advice in connexion with this life.

i. *Aubrey to Anthony Wood.*

'To his honoured friend Mr. Anthony à Wood, Master of Arts, at Merton College in Oxon.

Deare friend!

I have hastily writt this third draught, which I hope is legible: I have not time to read it over. Pray peruse it as soon as you can, for time drawes on. Dr. Blackburne and I will be diligent in it and will doe *you* all the right [f] your heart can wish. I thought together with this to have sent you the transcript of Mr. Hobbes' life revised by himselfe but am prevented by hast, and 'tis the last day of the terme. I will send it suddenly.

[a] Dupl. with 'sense,' 'opinion.'
[b] Dupl. with 'slighted.'
[c] Dupl. with 'goe.'
[d] Dupl. with 'meane.'
[e] Subst. for '*Tuus*.'

[f] In connexion with the controversy originated by Dr. Fell's excisions in Wood's notice of Hobbes in his *Hist. et Antiq. Univ. Oxon.*, 1674, see Clark's Wood's *Life and Times*, ii. 291.

My service to Mr. Pigot. I am, Sir, your affectionate friend and servant,

Jo: AUBREY.

London Feb. 12,
16⅞⅞.

Why might not his two sheetes *Of heresie* be bound up with this to preserve it and propagate trueth?

I know here be severall tautologies; but I putt them downe thus here, that upon reviewe I should judge where such or such a thing would most aptly stand.

Why should not Dr. Blackbourne in the life of Mr. H. written by him selfe quote that of A. Wood in the margent for a blindation, because there are in great part the very same words?'

ii. *Aubrey to Richard Blackburne.*

' Dr. Blackbourne!

Pray advise me whether 'twould not shew handsomest to begin with a description of Malmesbury, and then to place Mr. H. pedigre?

But, with all, should not

"Thomas Hobbes was borne at Malmesbury, Apr. . . . 1588ᵃ"

be the initiall and, as it were, textuall, line?

Shall I in the first place putt Mr. H. life donne by himselfe? (If so, whether in Latin, or English, or both?) Or else, shall I intersperse it with these animadversions?

I could begin with a pleasant description of Malmesbury, etc., (all new and untoucht) 14 leaves in 8vo, which his verses will lead me to, and which Ant. Wood seems to desire.

Pray be my Aristarchus, and correct and marke what you thinke fitt. First draughtsᵇ ought to be rude as those of paynters, for he that in his first essay will be curious in refining will certainly be unhappy in inventing.

Doctor, I am your affectionate and humble servant.

J. A.

ᵃ MS. has '1688,' by a slip.   ᵇ Dupl. with 'sketches.'

I will speake to Fleetwood Shepherd to engage the earl of Dorset to write in the old gentleman's praise.

Should mine be in Latin or English or both? (And by whome the Latin, if so?) Is my English style well enough [a]?'

Other MSS. A few additional lives, and portions of lives, of persons mentioned in these four biographical volumes, have been brought in from letters by Aubrey in MS. Ballard 14 and in MS. Wood F 39 and F 49.

Three lives, in fair copy, by Aubrey, are found in MS. Rawlinson D. 727, foll. 93–96, and have been given here. They were formerly in Anthony Wood's hands : see Clark's Wood's *Life and Times*, iv. 192, note.

MS. Aubr. 21, a volume made up in the Ashmolean library from siftings out of Aubrey MSS. and papers ; MS. Aubr. 22, a collection of grammatical tracts, brought together by Aubrey with a view to a treatise on education ; MS. Aubr. 23, a volume of 125 leaves, dated on fol. 8 as ' Collectio geniturarum, made London May 29, 1674,' but on the title as ' 1677 : for the ⟨Ashmolean⟩ Musaeum ' ; MS. Aubr. 26, ' Faber fortunae,' i. e. projects for retrieving Aubrey's fortunes —— have yielded additional matter.

V. THE OLD EDITION.

The pith of these lives was extracted by Anthony Wood, and incorporated in his *Athenae*, vol. i. in 1691, vol. ii. in 1692, and the 'appendix' left in MS. at his death (published in the second edition of the *Athenae* in 1721).

The MSS. of Aubrey's 'Lives' were placed in the library of the Ashmolean Museum, in the personal custody of the Keeper, Edward Lhwyd, in 1693. Aubrey, writing [b] to Thomas Tanner, intimates that his MSS. will show how greatly Wood's *Athenae* was indebted to his help, and

---

[a] Anthony Wood has jotted here ' 'Tis well.'

[b] Aubrey's letter, dated June 1, 1693, is found in MS. Tanner 25, fol. 59.

makes a special request that Wood shall not know that they have been placed in the Museum.

Beginning[a] on Sept. 16, 1792, Edmund Malone made a transcript of 174 lives from the three MSS. (MS. Aubr. 6, 7, 8), with notes, with a view to publication. The first volume of this contained folios 1–152, forty-four lives of poets and sixty-eight of prose writers. It is now in the Bodleian, by the gift of C. E. Doble, Esq.; but mutilated, folios 126–152 having been torn off from the end of the volume. The second volume, containing folios 153–385, sixty-two lives, was MS. 9405 in Sir Thomas Phillipps' library, was mentioned in *Notes and Queries* (8 S. vii. 375), and has recently been bought by the Bodleian.

Some years later, James Caulfield, of London, publisher, arranged for the issue of a select number of biographies from Aubrey's MSS., illustrated by engravings from originals in the Ashmolean and elsewhere. They were to appear under the title of 'The Oxford Cabinet'; and one part, 32 pp., a very pretty book, was published at London in 1797. This part contains the lives of William Aubrey, Francis Bacon, John Barclay, and Francis Beaumont, with engravings (inter alia) of Aubrey's drawings of Verulam House, and Bacon's fishponds. At this point the Keeper of the Ashmolean, at Malone's instance, withdrew the permission which had been granted to Curtis to transcribe for Caulfield. The reason given was that Curtis had taken away papers and title-pages from Oxford libraries, and was not to be trusted in the Ashmolean— see Macray's *Annals of the Bodleian*, p. 273.

The dates, however, suggest that Malone's action may have been in part inspired by a wish to keep the course clear for his own project. The transcription made for Caulfield, although not always accurate in point of spelling, is by no means badly done: certainly it is much better than that which was made for the later issue.

In 1813 appeared '*Letters written by Eminent Persons . . . and Lives of Eminent Men by John Aubrey, Esq. . . .*

[a] Malone's note in Mr. Doble's MS.

from the originals in the Bodleian Library and Ashmolean Museum : in two volumes.' The editors are said to
have been Dr. Philip Bliss and the Rev. John Walker,
Fellow of New College.

The *Lives* by Aubrey occupy pp. 197–637 of Volume II.

Dr. Bliss's interests were bibliographical, and he was not
careful * to collate with original MSS. either the printed
text of earlier editions or transcripts made for himself.
As a result, that issue of Aubrey's Lives, although making
accessible the greater portion of what is interesting in
the originals, is marred by many grave blunders and
arbitrary omissions.

A comparison of a few pages of Dr. Bliss's edition with
Aubrey's MS. copy suggests a troublesome question in
English textual criticism. If two eminent Oxford scholars
in the beginning of the nineteenth century could thus
pervert their author's meaning, can we have trust in the
earlier redaction of greater texts, such as Shakespeare ?

---

* I have shown this as regards the text of Anthony Wood's *Life*; and I hope some day to show it in the much more important matter of the text of the *Athenae*.

THE 'LIVES'

—٭—

George Abbot (1562–1633).

* Archbishop Abbot was borne in the howse of old Flemish building, timber and brick, now an alehouse, the signe 'Three Mariners,' by the river's side by the bridge on the north side of the street in St. Nicholas parish on the right hand as you goe out of the towne northwards.

** Old Nightingale was his servant, and weepes when he talkes of him. Every one that knew, loved him. He was sometimes cholerique.

He was borne the first howse over the bridge on the right hand in St. Nicholas parish ⟨Guildford⟩. He was the sonne of a sherman ᵃ. His mother, with child of him, longed for a jack, and dream't that if shee could eate a jack, her son should be a great man. The next morning, goeing to the river, which runs by the howse (which is by the bridge), with her payle, to take up some water, a good jack came into her payle. Which shee eat up, all, her selfe. This is generally recieved for a trueth.

His godfather and godmothers sent him to the University, his father not being able.

---

* Aubrey, in MS. Wood F. 39, fol. 223 ; Sept. 16, 1673.
** Idem, ibid., fol. 221 ; Aug. 10, 1673.
ᵃ *Sic*, substituted for ' cloth-worker.'

Sir Robert Aiton (1570–1638).

*** Sir Robert Aiton [1], knight ;—he lies buried in the south
aisle of the choire of Westminster abbey, where there is
erected to his memory an elegant marble and copper
monument and inscription—viz.
This long inscription is in copper :—

M. S.

Clarissimi, omnigenaque virtute et eruditione (presertim poesi)
ornatissimi equitis, Domini Roberti Aitoni, ex antiqua et illustri gente
Aitona ad Castrum Kinnadinum apud Scotos oriundi: qui a serenissimo
rege Jacobo in cubicula interiora admissus; in Germaniam ad impera-
torem imperiique principes, cum libello regio regiae authoritatis vindice,
legatus; ac primum Annae, demum Mariae, serenissimis Britanniarum
reginis, ab epistolis, consiliis, et libellis supplicibus; necnon Xeno-
dochio S'ᵃᵉ Catharinae praefectus; anima Creatori reddita, hic, depo-
sitis mortalibus exuviis, secundum redemptoris adventum expectat.

> *Carolum* linquens, repetit *Parentem* ;
> Et valedicens *Mariae*, revisit
> *Annam* ; et *Aulaei* decus alto *Olympi*
>   Mutat honore.

Obiit coelebs in Regiâ Albaulâ, non sine maximo bonorum omnium
luctu et moerore :

> Aetat. suae LXVIII, Salut. humanae MDCXXXVIII.

Hoc devoti gratique animi testimonium optimo patruo, Jo. Aitonus,
M.L.P.

In white marble at the bottome of the monument :—

> Musarum decus hîc, patriaeque, aulaeque, domique
> Et foris exemplar, sed non imitabile, honesti.

His bust is of copper, curiously cast, with a laurell held
over it by two figures of white marble.

That Sir Robert was one of the best poets of his time—
Mr. John Dreyden sayes he has seen verses of his, some
of the best of that age, printed with some other verses—
quaere.

He was acquainted with all the witts of his time in
England. He was a great acquaintance of Mr. Thomas
Hobbes of Malmesbury, whom Mr. Hobbes told me he
made use of (together with Ben Johnson) for an Aris-

---

* MS. Aubr. 6, fol. 116.

tarchus, when he made his Epistle Dedicatory to his translation of Thucydides. I have been told (I think by Sir John himself) that he was eldest brother to Sir John Ayton, Master of the Black Rod, who was also an excellent scholar.

Note.

[1] Aubrey gives in trick the coat:—'. . ., on a cross engrailed between 4 crescents a rose,' with the motto

'Et decerpta dabunt odorem.'

He encircles the coat of arms with a laurel wreath, as is his custom when it is a poet whose life he is writing.

Aldsworth.

* . . . Aldsworth, mathematical boyes.

** Memorandum :—the patent for the mathematicall blew-coate boyes at Christ Church in London was dated '19th August in the 25th yeare of the reigne of king Charles the second' ⟨1673⟩.

Thomas Allen (1542–1632).

*** Thomas Allen, Trin. Coll. Oxon.—Elias Ashmole, esqr., ⟨has⟩ the MSS. of Thomas Allen's commentary on the second and third bookes of Ptolomey's Quadripartite ᵃ.

**** Thomas Allen—vide Anthony Wood's ⟨*Hist. et*⟩ *Antiq.* ⟨*Univ.*⟩ *Oxon.*

Mr. Thomas Allen [1] was borne in Staffordshire.

Mr. Theodore Haak, a German, Regiae Societatis Socius, was of Glocester Hall, 1626, and knew this learned worthy old gentleman, whom he takes to have been about ninety-six yeares old when he dyed, which was about 1630 (vide).

The learned ⟨Edmund⟩ Reynolds, who was turned Catho-

† Memorandum the Latin verses made on their mutuall conver-sions—which insert.

Bella inter . . . plusquam civilia fratres.

lique † by his brother the learned Dr. ⟨John⟩ Reynolds, President of Corpus Xti Colledge, was of Glocester Hall then too. They were both neer of an age, and they dyed both within 12 monethes one of th'other ˣ. He was at both

---

* MS. Aubr. 8, fol. 5 : in the index, as a life to be written.

** MS. Aubr. 7, fol. 6.

*** MS. Aubr. 8, fol. 14ᵛ.

ᵃ MS. Ashmole, 388.

**** MS. Aubr. 6, fol. 95ᵛ.

their funeralls. Mr. Allen came into the hall to commons, but Mr. Reynolds had his brought to his chamber.

He sayes that Mr. Allen was a very cheerfull, facetious man, and that every body loved his company, and every howse on their *Gaudie-dayes* were wont to invite him.

His picture was drawne at the request of Dr. Ralph Kettle, and hangs in the dining roome of the President of Trin. Coll. Oxon. (of which house he first was, and had his education there) by which it appeares that he was a handsome sanguine man, and of an excellent habit of bodie.

There is mention of him in *Leicester's Commonwealth* [a] that the great Dudley, earle of Leicester, made use of him for casting nativities, for he was the best astrologer of his time. He hath written a large and learned commentary, in folio, on the Quadripartite of Ptolemie, which Elias Ashmole hath in MS. fairly written, and I hope will one day be printed.

In those darke times astrologer, mathematician, and conjurer, were accounted the same things ; and the vulgar did verily beleeve him to be a conjurer. He had a great many mathematicall instruments and glasses in his chamber, which did also confirme the ignorant in their opinion, and his servitor (to impose on freshmen and simple people) would tell them that sometimes he should meet the spirits comeing up his staires like bees.

† J. Power³.
‡ Kington (S. Michael, Wilts).

One† of our parish‡ was of Glocester Hall about 70 yeares and more since, and told me this from his servitor. Now there is to some men a great lechery in lying, and imposing on the understandings of beleeving people, and he thought it for his credit to serve such a master.

He was generally acquainted, and every long vacation, he rode into the countrey to visitt his old acquaintance and patrones, to whom his great learning, mixt with much sweetnes of humour, rendred him very welcome. One time being at Hom Lacy [b] in Herefordshire, at Mr. John

[a] By Robert Parsons, S.J.　　　　[b] i.e. Holm Lacy.

Scudamore's (grandfather to the lord Scudamor), he happened to leave [a] his watch in the chamber windowe— (watches were then rarities)—The maydes came in to make the bed, and hearing a thing in a case cry *Tick, Tick, Tick*, presently concluded that that was his Devill, and tooke it by the string with the tongues [b], and threw it out of the windowe into the mote (to [c] drowne the Devill.) It so happened that the string hung on a sprig of an elder that grew out of the mote, and this confirmed them that 'twas the Devill. So the good old gentleman gott his watch again.

Sir Kenelm Digby loved him much (vide Sir K. Digby's Life ⟨p.⟩ 69 [d]), and bought his excellent library of him, which he gave to the University. I have a Stifelius' Arithmetique that was his, which I find he had much perused, and no doubt mastered. He was interred in Trinity College Chapell, (quaere where: as I take it, the outer Chapell.) George Bathurst [4] B.D. made his funerall oration in Latin, which was printed. 'Tis pitty there had not been his name on a [e] stone over him.

*) Thomas Allen. . . . left the house [f] because he would not take orders.

Queen Elizabeth sent for him to have his advice about the new star that appeared in the Swan or Cassiopeia (but I think the Swan), to which he gave his judgment very learnedly.

He was great-uncle to Mr. ⟨Henry⟩ Dudley, the minister of Broadhinton in Wilts ⟨1665⟩.

Notes.

[1] Thomas Allen, of Staffordshire, aged 17, was elected Scholar of Trinity, June 4, 1561, and Fellow, June 19, 1564. His retirement to Gloucester Hall was no doubt to avoid the Oath of Supremacy imposed by Elizabeth on members on the foundation of the Colleges. Edmund Reynolds, in the same way, retired to Gloucester Hall, vacating his fellowship in Corpus Christi College.
[2] Edmund Reynolds died Nov. 21, 1630; Thomas Allen died Sept. 30, 1632.

[a] Dupl. with 'forgett.'
[b] i. e. tongs.
[c] Subst. for ' to have drowned.'
[d] i. e. fol. 99, of MS. Aubr. 6.

[e] Subst. for ' the.'
* Aubrey in MS. Wood F. 39, fol. 142ᵛ: Oct. 27, 1671.
[f] Trinity College.

³ This will serve to show how imperfectly the names in the Matriculation-register represent those who actually studied in Oxford. The Matric. register gives ' *Zachary Power*, e com. Wilts.,' as matriculating at Gloucester Hall, Nov. 3, 1609: but omits his elder brother John Power (mentioned in MS. Aubr. 3, fol. 48, as being 40 in 1624, when Zachary was 32).

⁴ George Bathurst, of Ga(r)sington, Oxon, aged 16, was elected Scholar of Trinity June 6, 1626, and Fellow June 8, 1631 ; B.D. 1640. His *Oratio funebris* on Allen was publ. London 1632.

Charles Alleyn (obiit 1640?).

* Charles Alleyn, who wrote the Battailes of Agencourt, Poitiers, and Crescy, was usher to Mr. Thomas Farnaby.

Lancelot Andrewes (1555–1626).

** Lancelot Andrewes¹, lord bishop of Winton, was borne in London ; went to schoole at Merchant Taylors schoole. Mr. Mulcaster² was his schoolemaster, whose picture he hung in his studie (as Mr. Thomas Fuller, *Holy State*).

Old Mr. Sutton, a very learned man of those dayes, of Blandford St. Maries, Dorset, was his school fellowe, and sayd that Lancelot Andrewes was a great long boy of 18 yeares old at least before he went to the university.

He was a fellowe⁵ of Pembroke-hall, in Cambridge (called *Collegium Episcoporum*, for that, at one time, in those dayes, there were of that house . . . bishops).

The Puritan faction did begin to increase in those dayes, and especially at Emanuel College. That party had a great mind to drawe in this learned young man, whom if they could make theirs, they knew would be a great honour to them. They carried themselves outwardly with great sanctity and strictnesse, so that 'twas very hard matter to——as to their lives. They preached up very strict keeping and observing the Lord's day ; made, upon the matter, damnation to breake it, and that 'twas lesse sin to kill a man then . . . Yet these hypocrites did bowle in a private green at their colledge every Sunday after

* MS. Aubr. 8, fol. 42ᵛ.   ** MS. Aubr. 6, fol. 27.

ᵃ Elected Fellow in 1576.

sermon; and one of the colledge (a loving friend to
Mr. L. Andrewes) to satisfie him one time lent him the
key of a private back dore to the bowling green, on
a Sunday evening, which he opening, discovered these
zealous preachers, with their gownes off, earnest at play.
But they were strangely surprized to see the entry of
one that was not of *the brotherhood*.

There was then at Cambridge a good fatt alderman
that was wont to sleep at church, which the alderman
endeavoured to prevent but could not. Well! this was
preached against as a signe of *reprobation*. The good
man was exceedingly troubled at it, and went to Andrewes
his chamber to be satisfied in point of conscience.
Mr. Andrewes told him that ⟨it⟩ was an ill habit of body
not of mind, and that it was against his will; advised him
on Sundays to make a more sparing meale, and to mend
it at supper. The alderman did so, but sleepe comes
upon ⟨him⟩ again for all that, and was preached at.
⟨He⟩ comes againe to be resolved, with tears in his eies;
Andrewes then told him he would have him make a good
heartie meale as he was wont to doe, and presently take
out his full sleep. He did so[a]; came to St. Marie's[b],
where the preacher was prepared with a sermon to damne
all who slept at sermon, a certaine signe of *reprobation*.
The good alderman having taken his full nap before,
lookes on the preacher all sermon time, and spoyled the
designe.—But I should have sayd that Andrewes was
most extremely spoken against and preached against for
offering to assoile or excuse a sleeper in sermon time.
But he had learning and witt enough to[*] defend himselfe.

His great learning quickly made him known in the
university, and also to King James, who much valued
him for it, and advanced him, and at last[c] made him
bishop of Winchester, which bishoprick he ordered with
great prudence as to government of the parsons, pre-

---

[a] Subst. for 'he followed his advice.'
[b] 'To St. Marie's' subst. for 'to church.'   [*] MS. Aubr. 6, fol. 27ᵛ.
[c] In 161⅞.

ferring of ingeniose persons that were staked to poore
livings and did *delitescere*. He made it his enquiry to
find out such men. Amongst severall others (whose names
have escaped my memorie) Nicholas Fuller (he wrote
Critica Sacra), minister of Allington neer Amesbury
in Wilts, was one. The bishop sent for him, and the
poor man was afrayd and knew not what hurt he had
donne. ⟨He⟩ makes him sitt downe to dinner; and,
after the desert, was brought in in a dish his institution
and induction, or the donation, of a prebend : which was
his way. He chose out alwayes able men to his chaplaines,
whom he advanced. Among others, ⟨Christopher⟩ Wren,
of St. John's in Oxon, was his chaplaine, a good generall
scholar and good orator, afterwards deane of Winsore,
from whom (by his son in lawe, Dr. William Holder)
I have taken this exact account of that excellent prelate.

His Life is before his Sermons, and also his epitaph,
which see. He dyed at Winchester house, in Southwark,
and lies buried in a chapell at St. Mary Overies, where
his executors . . . Salmon M.D. and Mr. John Saint-
lowe, merchant of London, have erected (but I beleeve
according to his lordship's will, els they would not have
layed out 1000 *li.*) a sumptuose monument for him.

He had not that smooth way of oratory as now. It
was a shrewd and severe animadversion of a Scotish lord,
who, when king James asked him how he liked bp. A.'s
sermon, sayd that he was learned, but he did play with
his text, as a Jack-an-apes does, who takes up a thing and
tosses and playes with it, and then he takes up another,
and playes a little with it. Here's a pretty thing, and
there's a pretty thing!

* Bishop Andrews: vide the inscription before his
Sermons.

Notes.

[1] Aubrey gives the coat :—' See of Winchester; impaling . . ., 3 mullets on
a bend engrailed and cottised . . .,' ensigned with a mitre or, and encircled by
the Garter motto.

[2] Richard Mulcaster, Head Master of Merchant Taylors' School, 1561–1586.

* MS. Aubr. 8, fol. 9.

Francis Anthony (1550–1623).

* Dr. [Francis[a]] Anthony, the chymist, Londinensis, natus 16 Aprilis, 1550, 1[h]. P.M., Virgo 0° 3′ ascend.

Quaere A⟨nthony⟩ W⟨ood⟩ if of Oxon or Cambridge[b].

Scripsit 2 libros, viz.:—*Aurum potabile*, and his *Defense* against Dr. ⟨Matthew⟩ Gwyn (who wrote a booke called *Aurum non Aurum*). This is all that Mr. Littlebury, bookeseller, remembers.

He lived in St. Bartholomew's close, London, where he dyed, and is, I suppose, buried there, about 30 yeares since[1], scil. 1652.

Vide his nativity in Catalogue[2].

He had a sonne who wrote something, I thinke (quaere Mr. Littlebury); and a daughter maried to . . . Montague, a bookeseller in Duck-lane, who in Oliver's time was a soldier in Scotland.

Notes.

[1] Wood notes here 'so that by this reckoning,' i. e. if born in 1550 *ut supra*, 'he was 102.'

[2] i. e., I suppose, in MS. Aubrey 23 (Aubrey's *Collectio Geniturarum*), where at fol. 121, among nativities from Dr. Richard Napier's papers, is:—'Dr. Anthony, Londinensis, who made *aurum potabile* at London, natus 16 April, 1550, 1[b] P. M.'

Thomas Archer (1554–1630?).

** Mr. Archer, rector of Houghton Conquest, was a good scholar in King James's (the 1st) dayes, and one ⟨of⟩ his majestie's chaplains.

He had two thick 4to MSS. of his own collection; one, *joci* and tales etc., and discourses at dinners; the other, of the weather. I have desired parson Poynter[c], his successor, to enquire after them, but I find him slow in it. No doubt there are delicate things to be found there.

* MS. Aubr. 8, fol. 21[v].
[a] Added by Anthony Wood.
[b] He was M.A., Cambridge, 1574.
** MS. Aubr. 8, fol. 1[v].
[c] Thomas Poynter, rector of Houghton Conquest, Beds., 1676–1700.

John Ashindon (obiit 13— ?).

* Johannes Escuidus[a], Merton College :—Elias Ashmole, esq., hath the corrected booke by the originall MSS. of Merton College library, now lost, which is mentioned in Mr. William Lilly's almanack 1674, a folio.

Amongst many other rarities he haz a thin folio MS. of Alkindus in Latin.

** Johannes Escuidus:—Summa astrologiae judicialis, in folio, Venetiis, 1489.—It is miserably printed, he sayes there ; and that he was a student of Merton College Oxford.—Mr. Elias Ashmole has the booke.

Elias Ashmole (1617–1692).

*** Memorandum—the lives of John Dee, Dr. ⟨Richard⟩ Nepier, Sir William Dugdale, William Lilly, Elias Ashmole[b], esq.,—Mr. Ashmole haz and will doe those himselfe : as[c] he told me formerly but nowe he seemes to faile.

Deborah Aubrey (16$\frac{0}{1}\frac{9}{0}$–168$\frac{5}{6}$).

**** Mris. Deborah Aubrey, my honoured mother, was borne at Yatton-Kaynes, *vulgo* West-Yatton, in the parish of Yatton-Keynel in com. Wilts., January 29th 1609[d], mane.

In a letter from my mother, dated Febru. 3[d], 16$\frac{7}{8}\frac{9}{0}$, she tells me she was seaventie yeares old the last Thursday [29 Januarii]—quod N. B.

Her accidents.

My mother was maried at 15 yeares old.

She fell sick of a burning feaver at Langford, Somerset.

---

* MS. Aubr. 8, fol. 14[v].

[a] John Ashindon (or Eastwood): see Brodrick's *Memorials of Merton College* (O. H. S.), p. 200.

** Aubrey, in MS. Wood, F. 39, fol. 229 : Sept. 22, 1673.

*** MS. Aubr. 6, fol. 10[v].

[b] In MS. Ballard 14, fol. 19, 20 is an autobiography dictated by Ashmole to Robert Plot, to be sent to Anthony Wood, Dec. 29, 1683.

[c] Added later by Aubrey to his note.

**** MS. Aubr. 23, fol. 81[v], 82.

[d] 16$\frac{0}{1}\frac{9}{0}$.

I.   D

She was taken on the 6th June 1675 ; feaver there againe in July 1675.

She was borne Jan. 29th, morning, scil. the day before the anniversary-day of the king's decollation.   She was 15 yeares old and as much as from January to June when she was maried.

She fell from her horse and brake her . . . arme the last day of Aprill (1649 or 50) when I was a suitor to Mris Jane Codrington.

Lettre, Aug. 8, 1681 :—she was lately ill three weekes and now her eies are a little sore.

Memorandum : 6 Januarie 168⅔, my mother writes to me that she is 73 yeares of age.

Note.

She died at Chalk in Jan. 168⅘, and was buried at Kingston S. Michael; so in a letter by Aubrey to Anthony Wood, May 11, 1686, in MS. Ballard 14, fol. 139.

John Aubrey (1626–1697).

⟨These autobiographical jottings are found in MS. Aubr. 7, fol. 3-5. They have been printed, with a few slips and slight omissions, in John Britton's *Memoir of J. Aubrey*, London, 1845, pp. 12-17. Aubrey (fol. 3) directs that the paper is 'to be interposed as a sheet of wast paper only in the binding of a booke'; and appends to this direction the motto :—

> 'I presse not to the choire[a] . . .
> Thus devout penitents of old were wont,
> Some without dore, and some beneath the font.
> Mr. Thomas Carew.'

Aubrey gives (fol. 3) an (incomplete) drawing of his own horoscope, on the scheme :—

'♈ natus 162⅔, March 11th, 17^h 14' 44" P.M. . . .[b] (tempus verum), sub latitudine 51° 30'.'

In MS. Aubr. 21, fol. 110, is Charles Snell's calculation of Aubrey's nativity, on the scheme

'Sunday, 12 Martii 1626, 5^h 13' 40" A.M., natus Johannes Aubreius, armiger, sub polo 51° 06'.'   The astrologers of the time used sometimes the English, and sometimes the Italian, enumeration of the hours.⟩

---

[a] 'Nor dare I' followed, scored out.   [b] Astronomical symbols omitted.

* I. A[a].

His life [b] is more remarqueable in an astrologicall respect [1] then for any advancement of learning [2], having [c] from his birth (till of late yeares) been labouring under a crowd of ill directions: for his escapes of many dangers [3], in journeys both by land and water, 40 yeares.

He was borne (longaevous, healthy kindred [4]) at Easton Pierse [5], a hamlet in the parish of Kington Saint Michael in the hundred of Malmesbury in the countie of Wilts, his mother's [6] (daughter and heir of Mr. Isaac Lyte) inheritance, March the 12 (St. Gregorie's day [7]), A.D. 1625 [d], about sun-riseing, being very weake and like to dye that he was christned before morning prayer.

I gott not strength till I was 11 or 12 yeares old; but had sicknesse [e] of vomiting [8], for 12 houres every fortnight for ... yeares, then about monethly, then quarterly, and at last once in halfe a yeare. About 12 it ceased.

When a boy, bred at Eston, an [f] eremiticall solitude. Was [g] very curious; his greatest delight to be continually with the artificers that came there (e. g. joyners, carpenters, coupers, masons), and understood their trades.

1634 [h], was entred in his Latin grammar by Mr. R⟨obert⟩ Latimer [9], rector of Leigh de-la-mere, a mile's fine walke, who had an easie way of teaching: and every time we askt leave to *goe forth*, we had a Latin word from him which at our returne we were [i] to tell him again—which in a little while amounted to a good number of words. 'Twas my unhappinesse in half a yeare to loose this good enformer by his death, and afterwards was under severall dull ignorant rest [k]-in [k]-house teachers [10] till 1638 (12 [l]), at

---

* MS. Aubr. 7, fol. 3.
[a] Aubrey's favourite way of writing his initials. Ⱥ is his favourite monogram.
[b] Dupl. with 'This person's life.'
[c] Subst. for 'being.'
[d] i. e. 162⅘.
[e] Explained in the margin as being 'the belly-ake: paine in the side.'

[f] Subst. for 'a place for solitude like an ...'
[g] The notes slide from 1st to 3rd person.
[h] Subst. for 'at 9,' scil. years of age.
[i] Subst. for 'must re⟨peat⟩.'
[k] Reading doubtful, blurred.
[l] i.e. at 12 years of age.

which time I was sent to Blandford schole in Dorset (William Sutton [a], B.D., who was ill-natured).

Here I recovered my health, and gott my Latin and Greeke, best of any of my contemporaries. The [b] usher [c] had (by chance) a Cowper's Dictionary, which I had never seen before. I was then in Terence. Perciveing his method, I read all in the booke where Terence was, and then Cicero—which was the way [d] by which I gott my Latin. 'Twas a wonderfull helpe to my phansie, my reading of Ovid's *Metamorphy* in English by Sandys, which made me understand the Latin the better. Also, I mett accidentally a booke of my mother's, Lord Bacon's *Essaies*, which first opened my understanding as to moralls (for Tullie's *Offices* was too crabbed for my young yeares) and the excellence [e] of the style, or hints and transitions.

I [f] was always enquiring [11] of my grandfather [g] of the old time, the rood-loft, etc., ceremonies, of the priory, etc. At 8, I was a kind of engineer; and I fell then to drawing, beginning first with plaine outlines, e.g. in draughts of curtaines. Then at 9 (crossed herein by father and school-master), to colours, having no body to instruct me [h]; copied pictures in the parlour in a table booke——like [12].

Blandfordiae, horis vacuis, I drew and painted Bates's .... (quaere nomen libri [13]).

I was wont (I remember) much to lament with my selfe that I lived not in a city, e.g. Bristoll, where I might have accesse to watchmakers, locksmiths, etc.   ⟨I did⟩ not very much care for grammar. ⟨I had⟩ apprehension enough, but my memorie not tenacious. So that then [i] was a promising morne enough of an inventive and philoso-phicall head. ⟨I had a⟩ musicall head, inventive, ⟨wrote⟩ blanke verse, ⟨had⟩ a strong and early impulse to antiquitie (strong impulse to ♄ [a]). ⟨My⟩ witt was alwaies ~~working, but not adroict for verse.~~ ⟨I was⟩ ex⟨ceeding [b]⟩ mild of spirit; migh⟨tily⟩ susceptible of fascination. * My idea very cleer [c]; phansie like [d] a mirrour, pure chrystal water which the least wind does disorder and unsmooth—so noise or etc. would [e].

** My uncle Anthony Browne's bay nag threw me dangerously the Monday after Easter [f], 1639. Just before it I had an impulse of the briar under which I rode, which tickled him, at the gap at the upper end of Berylane. Deo gratias!

*** 1642, May 2 [d], I went [14] to Oxford.

Peace [g].

Lookt through Logique and some Ethiques.

1642, *Religio Medici* printed, which first opened my understanding, which I carryed to Eston, with Sir K. D. [h]

But now [i] Bellona thundered, and as a cleare skie is sometimes suddenly overstretch⟨ed⟩ with a dismall [k] cloud and thunder, so was this serene peace [l] by the civill warres through the factions of those times; vide Homer's Odyssey.

In August [m] following my father sent for me home, for feare.

In February . . . following, with much adoe [n] I gott my father to lett me to beloved Oxon againe, then a garrison pro rege.

---

[a] i. e. to Saturn, patron of antiquities.

[b] Margin frayed.

* MS. Aubr. 7, fol. 3 [v].

[c] In the margin Aubrey writes 'Tacitus and Juvenal,' perhaps meaning that he read these authors now, before going up to Oxford.

[d] The sentence stood at first :— 'Phansie like a pure christall mirrour.'

[e] Scil. 'disorder my phansy.'

** MS. Aubr. 23, fol. 2.

[f] i.e. Monday, April 15.

*** MS. Aubr. 7, fol. 3 [v].

[g] Aubrey intended to write a fine sentence, parallel to what follows, describing the quiet of Oxford before the outbreak of the great war.

[h] Sir Kenelm Digby's 'Observations on *Religio Medici*,' publ. in 1643.

[i] Dupl. with 'now did Bellona . . . .'

[k] Dupl. with ' black.'

[l] Dupl. with ' one.'

[m] Dupl. begun, but scored through 'J.' i. e. July.

[n] Dupl. with 'importunity.'

I gott Mr. Hesketh, Mr. Dobson's man, a priest, to drawe the ruines of Osney 2 or 3 wayes before 'twas pulld downe [15]. Now the very foundation is digged-up.

In Aprill I fell sick of the small pox at Trinity College; and when I recovered, after Trinity weeke [a], my father sent for me into the country again: where I conversed [b] with none but servants and rustiques and soldiers quartred, to my great griefe (*Odi prophanum vulgus et arceo*), for in those dayes fathers were not acquainted with their children. It was a most sad life to me, then in the prime of my youth, not to have the benefitt of an ingeniose conversation and scarce any good bookes—almost a consumption. This sad life I did lead in the country till 1646, at which time I gott (with much adoe) leave of my father to lett me goe to the Middle Temple, April the 6th 1646; admitted . . .

24 June following, Oxon was surrendred, and then came to London many of the king's party, with whom I [c] grew acquainted (many of them I knew before). I loved not debauches [d], but their martiall conversation was not so fitt for the muses.

Novemb. 6, I returned to Trinity College in Oxon again to my great joy; was much made of by the fellowes; had their learned conversation, lookt on bookes, musique. Here and at Middle Temple (off and on) I (for the most part) enjoyd the greatest felicity of my life (ingeniose youths, as [e] rosebudds, imbibe the morning dew [f]) till Dec. 1648 (Christmas Eve's eve) I was sent for from Oxon home again to my sick father, who never recovered. Where I was engaged to looke after his country businesse and solicite a lawe-suite.

Anno 165–, Octob. . . . , my father dyed, leaving me debts 1800 *li.* and bro⟨thers'⟩ portions 1000 *li.*

[a] Trinity Sunday, 1643, was June 4.

[b] Subst. for 'was faine' ⟨to converse⟩.

[c] Dupl. with 'renewed' ⟨acquaintance⟩.

[d] i.e. though my friends were not debauchees, yet their conversation was not improving. For the low tone which grew up among Oxford scholars from contact with the garrison, see Clark's Wood's *Life and Times*, i. 129.

[e] Subst. for 'like.'

[f] 'Dew' is subst. for 'and sp⟨irit⟩.

Quid digni feci, hîc process. viam? Truly nothing; only umbrages, sc. Osney abbey ruines, etc., antiquities. *Cos*, a wheatstone, *exors ipse secandi*, e. g. ⟨my⟩ universall character[a] ⟨: that⟩ which was neglected and quite forgott and had sunk had not I engaged[b] in the worke, to carry on the worke—name them[c].

He began to enter into pocket memorandum bookes philosophicall and antiquarian remarques, Anno Domini 1654, at Llantrithid.

Anno 16— I began my lawe-suite on the entaile in Brecon[16], which lasted till . . . , and it cost me 1200 *li*.

Anno —— I was to have maried Mris K. Ryves, who died when to be maried, 2000 *li*. + [d], besides counting care of her brother, 1000 *li*. per annum.

Anno —— I made my will[17] and settled my estate on trustees, intending to have seen the antiquities of Rome and Italy for . . . ⟨years⟩, and then to have returned and maried, but—

Diis aliter visum est superis,

my mother, to my inexpressible griefe and ruine, hindred this[e] designe, which was[f] my ruine.

* My estate ⟨was of⟩ value 100 *li. fere* + Brecon.

Then debts and lawe-suites, *opus et usus*, borrowing of money and perpetuall riding. To my prayse, ⟨I had⟩ wonderfull credit in the countrey for money. Anno . . . sold manor of Bushelton in Herefordshire to Dr. T⟨homas⟩ Willis. Anno . . . sold the manor of Stratford in the same county to Herbert ⟨Croft⟩ lord bishop of Hereford.

Then anno 1664, June 11, went into France. Oct. . . . returned. Then Joan Sumner.

---

[a] i.e. my character throughout my life was that I discharged the function of a whetstone.

[b] Perhaps scil. 'others.' He set other people to work to record matters and so rescued them from oblivion.

[c] The people he set to work.

[d] i.e. her portion was to be more than £2000, and her husband was to be guardian of her brother's estate (during minority?) which was worth £1000 a year.

[e] Subst. for 'my.'

[f] Dupl. with 'was procatractique cause' ⟨of my ruine⟩.

* MS. Aubr. 7, fol. 4.

* Memorandum. J. Aubrey in the yeare 1666, wayting then upon Joane Sumner to her brother at Seen in Wilts, there made a discovery of a chalybiate waters and those more impregnated than any waters yet heard of in England. I sent some bottles to the Royal Society in June 1667, which were tryed with galles before a great assembly there. It turnes so black that you may write legibly with it, and did there, after so long a carriage, turne as deepe as a deepe claret. The physitians were wonderfully surprized at it, and spake to me to recommend it to the doctors of the Bath (from whence it is but about 10 miles) for that in some cases 'tis best to begin with such waters and end with the Bath, and in some *vice versâ*. I wrote severall times, but to no purpose, for at last I found that, though they were satisfied of the excellency of the waters and what the London doctors sayd was true, they did not care to have company goe from the Bath. So I inserted it last yeare in Mr. Lilly's almanac, and towards the later end of summer there came so much company that the village could not containe them, and they are now preparing for building of houses against the next summer. Jo⟨hn⟩ Sumner sayth (whose well is the best) that it will be worth to him 200 *li.* per annum.   Dr. ⟨Nehemiah⟩ Grew in his History of the Repository of the Royal Society mentions this discovery, as also of the iron oare there not taken notice of before——'tis in part iii, cap. 2, pag. 331.

** Then lawe-suite with her[a]. Then sold Easton-Peirse [18], and the farme at Broad Chalke. Lost 500 *li.* (Fr. H.) + 200 *li.* + goods + timber. Absconded as a banishd man.

Then

In monte Dei videbitur[b].

I was in as much affliction as a mortall could bee, and never quiet till all was gone, ⟨and I⟩ wholly[c] cast myselfe on God's providence.

* MS. Aubr. 7, fol. 5ᵛ.
** MS. Aubr. 7, fol. 4.
[a] Joan Sumner.

[b] Gen. xxii. 14.
[c] Dupl. with 'submitted myselfe to God's will.'

Monastery[a].

I wished monastrys had not been putt downe, that the reformers would have been more moderate as to that point. Nay, the Turkes have monasteries. Why should our reformers be so severe? Convenience of religious houses—Sir Christopher Wren—fitt there should be receptacles and provision for contemplative men; if of 500, but one or two[b]. 'Tis compensated[c]. What a pleasure 'twould have been to have travelled from monastery to monastery. The reformers in the Lutheran countrys were more prudent then to destroy them (e. g. in Holsatia, etc.); ⟨they⟩ only altered the religion.

But notwithstanding all these embarasments I did *pian piano* (as they occur'd) take[d] notes of antiquity; and having a quick draught, have drawne landskips on horseback symbolically, e. g. ⟨on my⟩ journey to Ireland in July, Anno Domini 166–.

⟨The⟩ earl of Thanet[e] ⟨gave me⟩ *otium* at Hethefield.

⟨I[f] had⟩ never quiett, nor anything of happinesse till[g] divested of all, 1670, 1671 [19]: at what time providence raysed me (unexpectedly) good friends—the right honourable Nicholas, earl of Thanet, with whom I was delitescent at Hethfield in Kent [20] neer a yeare, and then was invited . . . ; anno . . . , Sarney ; Sir Christopher Wren ; Mr. Ogilby ; then Edmund Wyld, esq., R⟨egiae⟩ S⟨ocietatis⟩ S⟨ocius⟩, of Glasely-hall, Salop (sed in margine), tooke me into his armes, with whom I most commonly take my diet and sweet *otium's*.

Anno 1671, having sold all and disappointed as afore-

---

[a] i. e. Aubrey then wished he could have withdrawn into a monastery.

[b] i. e. had been left.

[c] ? i.e. the advantages of the Reformation in England have drawbacks in the disadvantages of losing monasteries.

[d] 'tooke' in MS.

[e] Nicholas Tufton, 3rd earl. In MS. Ballard 14, fol. 99, April 23, 1674, Aubrey mentions a project for his advantage :—' The earl of Thanet would have me goe to his estate in the Bermudas.'

[f] The paragraphs following repeat, with some enlargement, the statements already made.

[g] Dupl. with ' till all was sold.'

said of moneys I received, I had so strong [a] an impulse [b] to (in good part) finish my [c] *Description of Wilts*, two volumes in folio, that I could not be quiet till I had donne it, and that with danger enough, tanquam canis e Nilo, for feare of the crocodiles, i. e. catchpolls.——And indeed all that I have donne and that little that I have studied have been just after that fashion, so that had I not lived long my want of leisure would have afforded but a slender harvest of . . .

A man's spirit rises and falls with his [d] ⊗: makes me lethargique.

* ⟨My⟩ stomach ⟨was⟩ so tender that I could not drinke claret without sugar, nor white wine, but would disgorge. ⟨It was⟩ not well ordered till 1670.

☞ A strange fate that I have laboured under never [e] in my life to enjoy one entire monethe † or 6 weekes *otium* for contemplation.

My studies (geometry) were on horse back ‡, and ⟨in⟩ the house of office: (my father discouraged me). My head was alwaies working; never idle, and even travelling (which from 1649 till 1670 was never off my horsback) did gleane som observations, of which I have a collection in folio of 2 quiers of paper + a dust basket, some wherof are to be valued.

His [h] chiefe vertue, gratitude.

Tacit. lib. IV § xx :—Cneus Lentulus [i], outre l' honneur du consulat et le triumphes de Getules, avoit la gloire d'avoir vescu sans reproche dans sa pauverté, et sans

Marginal notes:

† Once at Chalke in my absconding Oct. anno . . . at Weston [i] . . . anno . . .

‡ So I got my Algebra, Oughtred in my pocket, with some [g] information from Edward Davenant, D.D., of Gillingham, Dorset.

---

[a] Dupl. with 'great.'

[b] Aubrey adds a reference :—'vide Camden's divinum instr.'

[c] One volume is now MS. Aubr. 3; the second is lost.

[d] Aubrey's symbol for 'fortune' or 'wealth.'

* MS. Aubr. 7, fol. 4ᵛ.

[e] The marginal note names two exceptions.

[f] i.e. Ralph Sheldon's (Anthony Wood's friend): Aubrey was there in 1678, Clark's Wood's *Life and Times*, iii. 420.

[g] Dupl. with 'a little.'

[h] In these paragraphs Aubrey jots down his opinions as to his own character.

[i] TAC. *Ann.* iv. 44.

orgueil dans son' opulence où il estoit parvenu de puis par de voyes legitimes.

⟨I was⟩ never riotous or prodigall ; but (as Sir E. Leech said) sloath and carelesnesse [a] ⟨are⟩ equivalent to all other vices.

My fancy lay most to geometrie. If ever I had been good for anything, 'twould have been a painter, I could fancy a thing so strongly and had so cleare an idaea of it.

When a boy, he did ever love to converse with old men, as living histories. He cared not for play, but on play-dayes [b] he gave himselfe to drawing and painting. At 9, a pourtraiter [c] ; and soon was . . .

Reall character, ⟨things [d] that⟩ lay dead, I caused to revive by engaging 6 or 7 . . . *fungor vice cotis*, etc.

Wheras very sickly in youth ; Deo gratias, healthy from 16.

Amici.

A⟨nthony⟩ Ettrick, Trin. Coll.

M. T. [e]—John Lydall.

Fr⟨ancis⟩ Potter, of 666 [f], C lettres [g].

Sir J⟨ohn⟩ Hoskyns, baronet.

Ed⟨mund⟩ Wyld, esq. of Glasley Hall, quem summae gratitudinis ergo nomino.

Mr. Robert Hooke, Gresham College.

Mr. ⟨Thomas⟩ Hobbes, 165—.

A⟨nthony⟩ Wood, 1665.

☞ Sir William Petty, my singular friend.

Sir James Long, baronet, of Draycot, χρονογραφία etc.

Mr. Ch⟨arles⟩ Seymour, father [h] of the d⟨uke⟩ of S⟨omerset⟩.

---

[a] Dupl. with 'negligence (lachesse).'
[b] i.e. school holidays.
[e] Subst. for ' drawer.' See *supra*, p. 36.
[d] See *supra*, p. 39.
[e] ! acquaintance begun at the Middle Temple.

[f] i.e. who discovered (in his own opinion) 'the number of the beast.'
[g] i.e. Aubrey had a hundred letters of his.
[h] 'Father' is written, as frequently in Aubrey, in a symbol, viz. ⌐ᵤ

Sir Jo⟨hn⟩ Stawell, M. T. [a]
Bishop of Sarum ⟨Seth Ward⟩.
Dr. W⟨illiam⟩ Holder.

Scripsit [b].

'The [c] Naturall History of Wiltshire.'
These 'Lives' (pro AW [d], 16$\frac{79}{80}$).
'Idea [e] of education of the noblesse,' in Mr. Ashmole's
     hands.
item, 'Remaynders of Gentilisme,' being observations
     on Ovid's *Fastorum.*
memorandum, ' *Villare Anglicanum* interpreted.'
item, *Faber Fortunae* (for his own private use).

I. A. lived most at Broad-chalke in com. Wilts ; sometimes at Easton Piers ; at London every terme. Much of
his time spent in journeying to South Wales (entaile [f])
and Hereff⟨ordshire⟩. I now indulge my genius with my
friends and pray for the young *angels.* Rest at Mris More's
neer Gresham College (Mrs More's in Hammond Alley
in Bishopgate Street farthest house [g] ♂ old Jairer (?)
taverne).

⟨I⟩ expect preferment ⟨through⟩ Sir Ll. Jenkins [h].

* It was I. A. that did putt Mr. Hobbes upon writing his
treatise *De Legibus*, which is bound up with his *Rhetorique*
that one cannot find it but by chance ; no mention of it
in the first title.

** I have writt ' *an Idea of the education of the Noblesse*
from the age of 10 (or 11) till 18 ': left with Elias Ashmole,
esquire.

*** 1673 [i], die Jovis [k], 5to Martii, 9 [h] 15' + P. M.   J. A.

---

[a] See note on p. 43.
[b] See Clark's Wood's *Life and
Times*, iv. 191.
[c] Now MS. Aubr. 1 and 2.
[d] The monogram of Anthony
Wood.
[e] This is now MS. Aubr. 10.
[f] i.e. on business of the suit concerning the entail : *supra*, p. 39.

[g] This symbol is for 'opposite to.'
[h] Sir Llewelyn (*or* Leoline, from
the Latin form) Jenkins, Secretary of
State 1680–1684.
* MS. Aubr. 7, fol. 5.
** MS. Aubr. 7, fol. 5^v.
*** MS. Aubr. 23, fol. 97^v.
[i] 167$\frac{2}{3}$.
[k] i.e. Thursday.

arrested ⟨by⟩ . . . Gardiner, serjeant, a lusty faire-haired solar fellow, prowd, insolent, et omnia id genus.

* March 25, 1675, my nose bled at the left nostrill about 4ʰ. P. M. I doe not remember any event [21].

** July 31, 1677, I sold my bokes to Mr. Littlebury, *scilicet* when my impostume in my heade did breake.

About 50 annos ⟨aetatis⟩ ⟨I had⟩ impostume in capite.

*** Captain . . . Poyntz (for service that I did him to the earle of Pembroke and the earl of Abingdon [22]) did very kindly make me a grant of a thousand acres of land in the island of Tobago, anno Domini 168⅚, Febr. 2ᵈ. He advised me to send over people to plant [23] and to gett subscribers to come in for a share of these 1000 acres, for 200 acres he sayes would be enough for me. In this delicate island is *lac lunae* (the mother of silver).

William Penn, Lord Proprietor of Pennsylvania, did, ex mero motu et ex gratia speciali, give me, (16—) a graunt, under his seale, of six hundred acres in Pennsylvania [24], without my seeking or dreaming of it. He adviseth me to plant it with French protestants for seaven yeares *gratis* and afterwards ⟨they are⟩ to pay such a rent. Also he tells me, for 200 acres ten pounds per annum rent for ever, after three yeares.

**** John Aubrey [25], March 20, 169¾, about 11 at night robbed and 15 wounds in my head.

January 5ᵗʰ, 169¾, an apoplectick fitt, circiter 4ʰ. P. M.

***** *Accidents of John Aubrey* [26].

Borne at Easton-Piers, March 12, 162⅚, about sun-rising : very weake and like to dye, and therfore Christned that morning before Prayer. I thinke I have heard my mother say I had an ague shortly after I was borne.

1629 : about 3 or 4 yeares old, I had a grievous ague.

* MS. Aubr. 23, fol. 2.
** MS. Aubr. 23, a slip at fol. 103ᵛ.
*** MS. Aubr. 26, pp. 9, 10.
**** MS. Aubr. 23, fol. 103ᵛ.
***** Aubrey in MS. Rawl. J. fol. 6 (No. 15041 in Summary Catal. of Bodl. MSS.), fol. 30.

I can remember it. I gott not health till 11, or 12 : but had sicknesse of vomiting for 12 howres every fortnight for . . . yeares ; then, it came monethly for . . . ; then, quarterly; and then, halfe-yearly ; the last was in June 1642. This sicknesse nipt my strength in the bud.

1633: 8 yeares old, I had an issue (naturall) in the coronall suture of my head, which continued running till 21.

1634: October [a]: I had a violent fever that was like to have carried me off. 'Twas the most dangerous sicknesse that ever I had.

About 1639 (or 1640) I had the measills, but that was nothing : I was hardly sick.

1639: Monday after Easter weeke my uncle's nag ranne away with me, and gave a very dangerous fall.

1642: May 3, entred at Trinity College, Oxon.

1643: April and May, the small-pox at Oxon; and shortly after, left that ingeniouse place; and for three yeares led a sad life in the countrey.

1646: April ——, admitted of the Middle Temple. But my father's sicknesse, and businesse, never permitted me to make any settlement to my studie.

1651 : about the 16 or 18 of April, I sawe that incomparable good conditioned gentlewoman, Mris M. Wiseman, with whom at first sight I was in love—haeret lateri [b].

1652 : October 21 : my father died.

1655: (I thinke) June 14, I had a fall at Epsam, and brake one of my ribbes and was afrayd it might cause an apostumation.

1656: September 1655, or rather (I thinke) 1656, I began my chargeable and taedious lawe-suite about the entaile in Brecknockshire and Monmouthshire.

This yeare, and the last, was a strange year to me, and [c] of contradictions ;—scilicet love M. W. [d] and lawe-suites.

1656: December : Veneris morbus.

---

[a] Subst. for ' Mich:' (aelmastide).   [c] i.e. a year.
[b] Letalis arundo: VERG. *Aen.* iv. 73.   [d] i.e. Wiseman, *ut supra.*

* 1657: Novemb. 27, obiit domina Katherina Ryves, with whom I was to marry; to my great losse.

1658: . . .ᵃ

1659: March or Aprill, like to breake my neck in Ely minster, and the next day, riding a gallop there, my horse tumbled over and over, and yet (I thanke God) no hurt.

1660: July, August, I accompanied A. Ettrick into Ireland for a moneth; and returning were like to be ship-wrackt at Holy-head, but no hurt donne.

1661, 1662, 1663: about these yeares I sold my estate in Herefordshire.

. . .ᵇ: Janu., had the honour to be elected fellow of the Royal Society.

1664: June 11, landed at Calais. In August following, had a terrible fit of the spleen, and piles, at Orleans. I returned in October.

1664, or 1665: Munday after Christmas, was in danger to be spoiled by my horse, and the same day received laesio in testiculo which was like to have been fatall. Quaere R. Wiseman quando—I beleeve 1664.

1665: November 1; I made my first addresse (in an ill howre) to Joane Sumner.

1666: this yeare all my businesses and affaires ran kim kam. Nothing tooke effect, as if I had been under an ill tongue. Treacheries and enmities in abundance against me.

1667: December —: arrested in Chancery lane, at Mrs. Sumner's suite.

⟨166⅞⟩: Febr. 24, a.m. about 8 or 9, triall with her at Sarum. Victory and 600 *li.* dammage, though divelish opposition against me.

1668: July 6, was arrested by Peter Gale's malicious contrivance, the day before I was to goe to Winton for my second triall, but it did not retain me above two howres; but did not then goe to triall.

1669ᶜ: March 5, was my triall at Winton, from 8 to 9,

---

* Ibid., fol. 30ᵛ.   ᵇ ? 166⅞.
ᵃ Two initials obliterated.   ᶜ i.e. 16⅚.

the judge being exceedingly made against me, by my lady Hungerford. But 4 of the Venue (?) appearing, and with much adoe, gott the moëity of Sarum, verdict viz. 300 *li*.

1669 and 1670: I sold all my estate in Wilts.

From 1670, to this very day (I thanke God), I have enjoyed a happy delitescency.

1671: danger of arrests.

1677: later end of June, an imposthume brake in my head.

Laus Deo.

* Memorandum :—St. John's night, 1673, in danger of being run through with a sword by a young . . .ᵃ at Mr. Burges' chamber in the Middle Temple.

Quaere the yeare ᵇ that I lay at Mris Neve's; for that time I was in great danger of being killed by a drunkard in the street opposite Grayes-Inne gate—a gentleman whom .I never sawe before, but (Deo gratias) one of his companions hindred his thrust.   (Memorandum : horoscope . . .ᶜ)

Danger of being killed by William, earl of Pembroke, then lord Herbert, at the election of Sir William Salkeld for New Sarum.

I see Mars in . . .ᶜ threatnes danger to me from falls.

I have been twice in danger of drowning.

Notes.

¹ This beginning of Aubrey's autobiography is explained by Henry Coley's judgment on his nativity, found in MS. Aubr. 23, fol. 104, on the scheme 'J. A. natus 162⅘, March 11th, 17ʰ 14′ 44″ P.M., sub latitudine 51° 30′.'

'The nativity,' Coley says, 'is a most remarkable opposition, and 'tis much pitty the starres were not more favourable to the native.' Coley goes on to state that the stars 'threaten ruin to land and estate ; give superlative vexations in matters relating to marriag, and wondrous contests in law-suits—of all which vexations I suppose the native hath had a greater portion than ever was desired.' Aubrey must have been only too glad to have authority for attributing his failure in life to the stars, and not to his own ill-conduct.

* Ibid., fol. 31.

ᵃ ⌗ ; a symbol I have not found elsewhere in Aubrey, as indicating a person.

ᵇ Aubrey adds : 'vide Almanac: 'twas that yeare I went to Hethfield.'

ᶜ Some astrological symbols follow.

¹ In MS. Aubr. 7, fol. 3, in jottings at the side of his horoscope, Aubrey suggests that his failure in this respect was due to defects of his upbringing, not of natural ability.

'Ἐὰν ᾖς φιλομαθής, ἔσῃ πολυμαθής. By *pian piano* I might have ⟨attained to learning⟩; though ⟨my⟩ memory ⟨was⟩ not tenacious, ⟨yet I had⟩ zeale to learning, and ...ᵃ extraordinary, ...ᵇ; ⟨but I was⟩ bred ignorant at Eston.'

² Henry Coley, in his 'Observations upon the geniture' of Aubrey, MS. Aubr. 23, fol. 105ᵛ, finds that the stars show that he 'will be in great danger between the years of 40 and 50.'—On this Aubrey remarks :—

'Much about that time the native was several times in danger of expiration, as,

first, by the e⟨arl⟩ of P⟨embroke⟩;

2, a bruise of the left side;

3, a narrow escape of falling downe stayres; and,

lastly, as dangerous a fall from a horse;

besides the accident of sowneing, cum multis aliis.

1668: the native was in no small trouble, at least received disparagement, by an arrest, and other untoward transactions.'

³ In MS. Aubr. 3, fol. 62 sqq., is a notice of Aubrey's family and of Kington St. Michael.

The pedigree is :—

William Aubrey, LL.D.
|
John Aubrey (3rd son)
|
Richard Aubrey *m.* Deborah,
(only son)   daughter of
                    Isaac Lyte

John   William   Thomas
(our author)

See in 'Wiltshire: the Topographical Collections of John Aubrey, corrected and enlarged by John Edward Jackson,' Devizes, 1862.

In MS. Aubr. 23, on a slip at fol. 47, Aubrey notes his father's christening :—'Richard Aubrey, July 26, St. Anne's day, christened A.D. 1603.'

MS. Aubr. 23, fol. 83, notices Aubrey's brother William :—'My brother William Aubrey's scheme by Henry Coley.—Natus Mr. W. A. March 20, 164⅘, at 11ʰ 30′ P.M.'

MS. Aubr. 23, fol. 119ᵛ, is the back of an envelope (seal, a pelican feeding her young) addressed to Aubrey's third brother:—'to his very loving freind Mr. Thomas Awbrey at Broad Chalke give these.'

⁵ In MS. Aubr. 8, fol. 8, Aubrey notes:—

'John Aubrey ⟨was⟩ borne in the chamber where are on the chimney painted the armes of Isaac Lyte and Israel Browne.'

MS. Aubr. 17 contains several of Aubrey's drawings, in pencil and water-colours, of the house and grounds at Easton-Piers.

In MS. Aubr. 3 (his 'Hypomnemata Antiquaria'), fol. 55 sqq., is Aubrey's

---

ᵃ One word I cannot decipher.   ᵇ Two words I cannot decipher.

description of Easton-Piers. It is printed in J. E. Jackson's Aubrey's *Wiltshire Collections* (Devizes, 1862), pp. 235 sqq.

[6] In MS. Aubr. 23, fol. 8, Aubrey notes :—'*ex registro Kington St. Michael in com. Wilts* : June 15, Richard Aubrey and Debora Lyght maried, 1625.'

[7] Aubrey in a marginal note seeks to bring his birth-day into connexion with the Roman Quinquatria (March 19). The note is : 'Quinquatria : feast dedicated to Minerva' (dupl. with 'Pallas').

[8] In MS. Aubr. 23 (his 'Collectio geniturarum '), fol. 116, 117, are letters from Charles Snell about Aubrey's nativity and accidents. Snell there enumerates Aubrey's :—

'Sicknesse att birth ; ague and vomittings aboute 5 or 6 yeares old ; issue in his head ; small-pox ; amours with madam Wiseman[a] ; selling away the mannor of Stratford, etc. ; haesitating in his speech.'

Snell gives this advice :—

'If the haesitation in your speech doth hinder, gett a parsonage of 4 or 500 *li.* per annum, and give a curat 100 *li.* per annum to officiate for you.'

The letter is dated from 'Fordingbridge ; 12 August, 1676.'

Aubrey, in his letters to Anthony Wood, several times touches on the idea of his taking Orders. MS. Ballard 14, fol. 98 :—'I am like to be spirited away to Jamaica by my lord ⟨John⟩ Vaughan, who is newly made governor there, and mighty earnest to have me goe with him and will looke out some employment worthy a gentleman for me. Fough ! the cassock stinkes : it would be ridiculous.'—April 9, 1674. MS. Ballard 14, fol. 119 :—'I am stormed by my chiefest friends afresh, viz. Baron Bertie[b], Sir William Petty, Sir John Hoskyns, bishop of Sarum[c], etc., to turne ecclesiastique ; "but the king of France growes stronger and stronger, and what if the Roman religion should come-in againe ?" "Why then !" say they, "*cannot you turne too ?*" You, I say, know well that I am no puritan, nor an enimy to the old gentleman on the other side of the Alpes. Truly, if I had a good parsonage of 2 or 300 *li.* per annum, (as you told me) it would be a shrewd temptation.'—Aug. 29, 1676.

[9] Aubrey notes in the margin, (1) 'T. H.' (in a monogram), i.e. that this Latimer had been schoolmaster to Thomas Hobbes, and (2), 'delicate little horse,' to indicate that he did not walk the mile to Leigh-de-la-mere like a poor boy, but rode his pony there like a fine gentleman. John Britton has mis-read the note, and made it a description of Mr. Latimer's appearance, 'delicate little *person.*'

In MS. Aubr. 3, fol. 109, Aubrey gives this inscription as on a stone 'under the communion-table' in the church of Leigh-de-la-mere :—

'Here lieth Mr. Robert Latymer, sometime rector and pastor of this church, who deceased this life the second day of November, anno domini 1634.'

And then Aubrey notes :—

'This Mr. Latimer was schoolmaster at Malmsbury[d] to Mr. Thomas Hobbes.

[a] See *infra*, p. 52.
[b] Vere Bertie, Baron of the Exchequer, 1675-78.
[c] Seth Ward.
[d] 'At Malmsbury' is scored out, and the following substituted :—' In a private schoole at Westport, next to the smyth's shop as is (now, 1666) opposite to the . . . (an inne).'

He afterwards taught children here ᵃ. He entred me into my accedence. Before Mr. Latimer, one Mr. Taverner was rector here, who was the parson that maried my grand-father and grandmother Lyte.'

¹⁰ In a marginal note (MS. Aubr. 7, fol. 3), Aubrey excuses his father's neglect of his education on the plea that he himself grew up illiterate. The note is :—

'My grandfather A⟨ubrey⟩ dyed, leaving my father, who was not educated to learning, but to hawking.' See in the life of Alderman John Whitson.

¹¹ In the margin Aubrey notes :—

' ♄ : strong impulse to ♄.' This means I suppose that the position of Saturn at his nativity gave him a bias to the study of antiquities.

¹² This means, I suppose, that the copies he made sufficiently resembled the pictures on the parlour wall. A note in MS. Aubr. 8, fol. 6ᵛ, perhaps refers to his own skill in drawing, 'As Mr. Walter Waller's picture drawne after his death ; è contra, I have done severall by the life.' Walter Waller was vicar of Chalk, where Aubrey lived : see in the life of Edmund Waller.

¹³ Possibly 'The mysteries of nature and art, viz. . . . drawing, colour-ing . . . ," by J[ohn] B[ate], Lond. 1634, 4to.

¹⁴ Here (fol. 3ᵛ) in the margin is written :—' Vide Pond,' referring perhaps to a pocket almanac, in which Aubrey had marked the date of his going up to Oxford. See Clark's Wood's *Life and Times*, i. 11, 12. In a letter from Aubrey to Anthony Wood, of date Feb. 21, 16⅞⅞, in MS. Ballard 14, fol. 127, is this interesting note :—' At Trinity College we writt our names in the Buttery-booke, when we were entred.'

Aubrey cites in the margin (MS. Aubr. 7, fol. 3ᵛ) :—' HORAT. *Epist.* 2ᵈ.' (i. e. *Epist.* ii. 2. 45) :—

    ' Atque inter sylvas Academi quaerere verum.
    Dura sed emovere loco me tempora grato.'

¹⁵ In MS. Wood F. 39, fol. 183, Aubrey, writing on Oct. 19, 1672, tells Anthony Wood, ' yon must not forgett that I have 3 other faces or prospects of Osney abbey, as good as that now in the Monasticon. They are in my trunke yet at Easton Piers.' Ibid., fol. 190ᵛ, on Oct. 22, 1672, he says, 'I will bring you about March my two other draughts of Osney ruines, one by Mr. Dobson himselfe, the other by his man, one Mr. Hesketh, but was a priest.'

Note that in MS. Wood F. 39, fol. 200, is a drawing (from memory) by Aubrey of the stone-work which crowned the great earth-mound of Oxford Castle.

¹⁶ In a slip at the end of MS. Aubr. 26 (Aubrey's *Faber Fortunae*, in which he entered schemes by which he hoped to 'make his fortune'), is this note :—

' I have the deed of entaile of the lands in South Wales, Brecon, and Monmouthshire, by my grandfather, William Aubrey LL. D., which lands now of right belong to me. Memorandum :—Mr. David Powell, who liveth at . . . (neer Llanverarbrin neer Llandvery, as I remember), can helpe me to the counterpart of this deed of entaile in Wales—quod N. B.'

    ᵃ i. e. at Leigh-de-la-mere.

[17] In MS. Aubr. 21, at fol. 75 is part of a draft of a will by Aubrey, probably the one mentioned here (Ralph Bathurst became 'Dr.' in 1654) :—

'Item, my will is that my executors buy for Trinity Colledge in Oxon a colledge pott of the value of ten pounds, with my armes theron inscribed ; and ten pounds which I shall desire my honoured friends Mr. Ralph Bathurst of Trinity College and Mr. John Lydall to lay out upon mathematicall and philosophicall books.

Item, I give to the library of Jesus Colledge in Oxon my Greeke *Crysostomus*, Bede's 2 tomes, and all the rest of my bookes that are fitt for a library, as Mr. Anthony Ettrick [a] or Mr. John Lydall shall think fitt, excepting those bookes that were my father's which I bequeath to my heire.

Item, I bequeath to John Davenant of the Middle Temple, esq., a ring of the value of 50*s*., with a stone in it.

Item, to Mr. William Hawes [b] of Trinity College aforsaid a ring of the like value.

Item, to Mr. John Lydall [c] of the Colledge aforesaid a ring of the like value.

Item, to Mr. Ralf Bathurst [d] of Trinity College aforesaid a ring of the like value.

Item, to Mris Mary Wiseman of Westminster, my best diamond ring.'

[18] On a slip at fol. 101 of MS. Aubr. 23 is the jotting :—' Eston-pierse : possession given, 25 March, 1671, P. M.'

[19] In his retirement during this year at Chalk, Aubrey tried his hand at play-making. Writing to Anthony Wood on Oct. 26, 1671, MS. Wood, F. 39, fol. 141[v], he says :—

'I am writing a comedy for Thomas Shadwell, which I have now almost finished since I came here, et quorum pars magna fui. And I shall fit him with another, *The Countrey Revell*, both humours untouch't, but of this, mum ! for 'tis very satyricall against some of my mischievous enemies which I in my tumbling up and downe have collected.'

Of the first of these comedies, the autobiographical one, I have found no trace : of the second, satirizing the men and manners of Wiltshire, a very rude draft is found in MS. Aubr. 21.

[20] In MS. Aubr. 23, fol. 113 is a note (dated 167⅔) from Henry Coley, addressed :—

' For his much honoured friend Mr. John Aubrey, at the right honourable the earle of Thanet's house at Hethfield in Kent, these present.'

The letter states that the writer has forwarded letters to and from Aubrey ; and concludes : 'you are much wanted at London, and dayly expected, and therefore I hope you will not be long absent. Interest calls for your appearance.'

[21] i. e. which followed after this bleeding. Bleeding at the nose was thought ominous : see Clark's Wood's *Life and Times*, iii. 289, note 1.

[a] Anthony Ettrick, 'of Berford, co. Dorset' : matric. at Trinity College in 1640, and was afterwards called at the Middle Temple.

[b] William Hawes, of Byssam, Berks, aged 16, was elected Scholar of Trinity College, Oxford, June 5. (Trinity Monday) 1640 ; President in 1658.

[c] Of Uxmore, Oxon, aged 15, elected Scholar of Trinity, June 4, 1640.

[d] Of Hoothorpe, Northants., elected Scholar of Trinity, June 5, 1637 ; Fellow, June 4, 1640 ; President, 1664.

[21] In MS. Aubr. 26, p. 17 is this note:—'The earle of Abington to buy of Captain Poyntz the propriety of the island of Tobago, now regnante Gulielmo III.'

[23] Aubrey before this time had planned to retrieve his ruined fortunes by colonial schemes: e g., MS. Aubr. 26, p. 46:—'1676: from Sir William Petty—(in) Jamaica 500 *li*. gives 100 per annum: take a chymist with me, for brandy, suger, etc., and goe halfe with him.'

[24] In consequence of this grant, Aubrey seriously thought of emigrating. MS. Aubr. 26, p. 14:—

'Mr. Robert Welsted, goldsmith and banquier, saies that Mr. John Evelyn's bookes are the most proper for a plantation. Also Markham's husbandry and huswifry, etc. This is in order for Mr. W. Penn and myselfe.—Also let him carry with him Mr. Haines booke of Cydar Royall, which method will likewise serve for other fruites—it is by distillation. Quaere of Mr. Tyndale's at Bunhill, who makes severall sorts of English wines and cydars. Memorandum the great knack and criticism is to know when it comes to its sowrenesse; it must not be vinegar for then nothing will come—quod N. B.'

[25] This is noticed on a slip (fragment of a letter, '8 March, 169¾' from Edward Harley) at fol. 113 of MS. Aubr. 23:—'J. A. vulneratus die 20 Martii inter 10 et 11 horas Londini. Deo gratias.'

[26] This paper was acquired by Rawlinson in July ... 1746 (ibid. fol. 31ᵛ). There is an inaccur te copy of it in MS. Ballard 14, foll. 158, 159, which has the note:—'1754, June 11, transcribed from a MS. in Mr. Aubrey's own writing in the possession of Dr. Richard Rawlinson.'

William Aubrey (1529-1595).

* William Aubrey[1], Doctor of Lawes:—extracted from a MS.[2] of funeralls, and other good notes, in the hands of Sir Henry St. George, . . .[a], marked thus ♡. I guesse it to be the hand-writing of Sir Daniel Dun, knight, LL. Dr., who maried Joane, third daughter of Dr. William Aubrey:—

William Aubrey (the second son of Thomas Aubrey, the 4th son of Hopkin Aubrey, of Abercunvrig in the countie of Brecon, esqre) in the 66th yeare of his age or thereabouts, and on the 25th of June, in the yeare of our Lord 1595, departed this life, and was buried in the Cathedrall-church of St. Paul in London, on the north side of the chancell, over against the tombe of Sir John Mason, knight, at the base or foot of a great pillar standing upon the highest step of certain degrees or

* MS. Aubr. 6, fol. 19ᵛ.

[a] The blank is left for his official title, viz. Clarencieux King of Arms.

staires rising into the quire eastward from the same
pillar towards the tombe of the right honble the lord
William, earle of Pembroke, and his funeralls were performed the 23d of July, 1595. This gentleman in his
tender yeares learned the first grounds of grammar in
the College of Brecon, in Brecknock towne, and from
thence about his age of fourteen yeares he was sent by
his parents to the University of Oxford, where, under the
tuition and instruction of one Mr. Morgan, a great learned
man, in a few yeares he so much profited in humanity
and other recommendable knowledge, especially in
Rhetorique and Histories, as that he was found to be
fitt for the studie of the Civill Law, and thereupon was
also elected into the fellowship[a] of All-soules Colledge
in Oxford (where the same Lawe[b] hath always much
flourished). In which Colledge he ernestly studied and
diligently applied himselfe to the lectures and exercise of
the house, as that he there attained the degree of a Doctor
of the Law Civill at his age of 25 yeares, and immediately
after, he had bestowed on him the Queen's Publique
Lecture of Law in the university, the which he read with
so great a commendation as that his fame for learning
and knowledge was spred far abroad and he also esteemed worthy to be called to action in the commonwealth. Wherefor, shortly after, he was made Judge
Marshall of the Queen's armies at St. Quintins in France.
Which warrs finished, he returned into England, and
determining with himselfe, in more peaceable manner
and according to his former education, to passe on the
course of his life in the exercise of law, he became an
advocate of the Arches, and so rested many yeares, but
with such fame and credit as well for his rare skill and
science in the[*] law, as also for his sound judgment and
good experience therein, as that, of men of best judgment,
he was generally accounted peerlesse in that facultie.

[a] William Aubré was elected into a
Law Fellowship at All Souls in 1547.
[b] i.e. a number of the All Souls

Fellowships were set aside for 'legists,'
i.e. students of Civil Law.
[*] MS. Aubr. 6, fol. 20.

Wherupon, as occasion fell out for imployment of a civilian, his service was often used as well within the realme as in forrein countries. In which imployments, he alwaies used such care and diligence and good circumspection, as that his valour and vertues dayly more appearing ministred means to his further advancement. In soe much that he was preferred to be one of the Councell of the Marches of Wales, and shortly after placed Master of the Chancery, and the appointed Judge of the Audience, and constituted Vicar Generall to the Lord Archbishop of ⟨Canterbury⟩ through the whole province, and last, by the especiall grace of the queene's most excellent majestie, queen Elizabeth, he was taken to her highnesse nearer service and made one of the Masters of Request in ordinarie. All which titles and offices (the Mastership of Chancery, which seemed not competible with the office of Master of Requestes, only excepted) he by her princely favour possessed and enjoyed untill the time of his death. Besides the great learning and wisdome that this gentleman was plentifully endowed withall, Nature had also framed him so courteous of disposition and affable of speech, so sweet of conversation and amiable behaviour, that there was never any in his place better beloved all his life, nor he himselfe more especially favoured of her majestie and the greatest personages in the realme in any part of his life then he was when he drew nearest his death. He was of stature not taull, nor yet over-low; not grosse in bodie, and yet of good habit; somewhat inclining to fatnesse of visage in his youth; round, well favoured, well coloured and lovely; and albeit in his latter yeares sicknesse had much* impaired his strength and the freshnesse of his hew, yet there remained there still to the last in his countenance such comely and decent gravity, as that the change rather added unto them then ought diminished his former dignitie. He left behind him when he died, by a vertuouse gentlewoman Wilgiford his wife (the first daughter of Mr. John Williams of Tainton in the countie of Oxford, whom he

* MS. Aubr. 6, fol. 20ᵛ.

maried very young a maiden, and enjoyed to his death,
that both having lived together in great love and kindnesse
by the space of 40 yeares) three sons and six daughters,
all of them maried, and having issue, as
followeth †.

His eldest son Edward, maried unto Joane,
daughter and one of the heires of William
Havard, in the countie of Brecon, esqre.

His second son Thomas maried Mary the
daughter and heire of Anthony Maunsell of
Llantrithed, in the com. of Glamorgan, esqre.

His 3d son John, ‡ being then of the age
of 18 yeares (or much thereabouts), was maried
to Rachel, one of the daughters of Richard
Danvers of Tockenham, in com. Wilts, esqre.

His eldest daughter Elizabeth, maried to
Thomas Norton of Norwood in the countie of
Kent, esqre.

His 2d daughter Mary maried William Herbert of
Krickhowell, in the countie of Brecknock, esqre.

His 3d daughter Joane maried with Sir Daniel Dun,
knight, and Doctor of the Civill Lawe.

His 4th daughter Wilgiford maried to Rise Kemis of
Llanvay, in the county of Monmouth, esqre.

His 5th daughter Lucie maried to Hugh Powell, gent.

His 6th and youngest daughter Anne, maried to John
Partridge, of Wishanger, in the countie of Glocester, esqre.

Of every of the which since his death there hath proceeded a plentifull issue.

(Additions by Aubrey.)

Memorandum :—he was one of the delegates (together
with Dr. Dale, &c.) for the tryall of Mary, queen of Scots, and
was a great stickler for the saving of her life, which kindnesse was remembred by King James att his comeing-in
to England, who asked after[a] him, and probably[b] would

Marginal notes:
† Vide pedegre.
‡ John Whitgift, archbishop of Canterbury, was his guardian, and the doctor's great friend. I have heard my grandmother say that her husband told her that his grace kept a noble house, and that with admirable order and oeconomie; and that there was not one woman in the family.—Vide the archbishop of Canterbury's case in Sir Edward Cooke's *Reportes* where he is mentioned.

---

[a] Dupl. with 'for.'   [b] Dupl. with 'some thought.'

have made him Lord Keeper, but he dyed, as appeares, a little [a] before that good opportunity happened. His majestie sent for his sonnes [b], and knighted the two eldest, and invited them to court, which they modestly and perhaps prudently, declined. They preferred a country life.

You may find him mentioned in the History of Mary, queen of Scotts, 8vo, written, I thinke, by ⟨John⟩ Hayward; as also in Thuanus's *Annales*, which be pleased to see [3] and insert his words here in honour to the Doctor's *Manes*. Dr. . . . Zouch mentions him with respect in his *De Jure Faeciali*, pag. . . . ; and as I remember, he is quoted by Sir Edward Coke, Lord Chief Justice of the King's Bench, in his Reports, about the legitimacy of the earle of Hertford.† Quaere if it was Edward the father [4], or els his son William, about the mariage with the ladie Arbella Stuart?

† Memorandum: Mr. Shuter, the proctor, told me that the Doctor appealed to Rome about the earle of Hartford's suite, tempore reginae Elizabethae.

* [Johannes [c] David Rhesus M.D. makes an honourable mention of him in his Welsh grammar in folio, pag. . . . ; as also in his preface.]

** [*Linguae Cymraecae institutiones accuratae*, J. David Rhoesus, folio, London, 1592, pag. 182 (quaere if he is not mentioned in the Welsh preface) :—

Caeterum nunc et propter eorum authoritatem et quod huic loco inter alia maxime quadrent, non pigebit antiquissima Taliessini [5] Cambrobrytannica carmina subjungere, furtim (quae mea est audacia) et eo nesciente, a me surrepta, et clanculum calamo commissa, ex ore, vesperi fortuitò juxta proprium ignem pro solito in sua cathedra considentis, et haec una cum aliis carminibus memoriter, et non sine delectatione quadam decora, proferentis, ornatissimi et doctissimi viri domini Gulielmi Aubraei, Cambrobrytanni ab illustrissima Aubraeorum familia oriundi, linguae Cambrobrytannicae peritissimi eximiique patriae suae decoris et ornamenti, Juris utriusque Doctoris celeberrimi, ac regiae majestati à Supplicum Libellis constituti Domini, et amici

---

[a] He died more than seven years before James's accession.

[b] ' 2 eldest ' is written over as a correction.

[c] This sentence is scored out on fol. 21; perhaps that the following paragraph, on fol. 21ᵛ, may be inserted.

* MS. Aubr. 6, fol. 21.

** MS. Aubr. 6, fol. 21ᵛ.

optimi perpetuoque colendi, nobisque amicis jam strenuas et auxiliatrices manus porrigentis, qua citius et magis prospere elucubrationes hae ad nostratium et aliorum utilitatem proelo committebantur.

Carmina vero sunt hujusmodi.

* Memorandum:—old Judge Atkins [a] (the father) told me that the Portugall ambassador was tryed for his life for killing Mr. Greenway in the New Exchange (Oliver's time), upon the precedent of the bishop of Rosse (Scotch) by Dr. W. Aubrey's advice. Memorandum:—Dr. Cruzo [b] of Doctors Commons hath the MSS. of this bishop's tryall.

** *De legati deliquentis judice competente dissertatio*, autore Richardo Zoucheo, Juris Civilis professore Oxoniae, Oxon 1657, 12mo, pag. 89 :—

Quarto, quod cum episcopus Rossensis, legatus reginae Scotorum, multa turbulenter in Anglia fecisset ad rebellionem excitandam et ad Anglos in Belgio profugos ad Angliam invadendam inducendos, Davidi Lewiso, Valentino Dalo, Gulielmo Drurio, Gulielmo Awbreio, et Henrico Jones, Juris Caesarei consultissimis, quaestio proposita fuit *An legatus, qui rebellionem contra principem ad quem legatus est concitat, legati privilegiis gaudeat* et *An, ut hostis, poenae subjaceat*, eidem responderunt, ejusmodi legatum, jure gentium et civili Romanorum, omnibus legati privilegiis excidisse et poenae subjiciendum.

*** He was a good statesman; and queen Elizabeth loved him and was wont to call him 'her little Doctor.' Sir Joseph Williamson, Principall Secretary of Estate (first, under-Secretary), haz told me that in the Letter-office are a great many letters of his to the queen and councell [c].

He sate many times as Lord Keeper, durante bene placito, and made [d] many decrees, which Mr. Shuter, etc., told me they had seen.

Vide Anthony Wood's *Hist. et Antiq.*: he was principal of New Inne.

Memorandum:—the *Penkenol*, i.e. chiefe of the family,

* MS. Aubr. 6, fol. 20v.
[a] Sir Edward Atkins, Puisne Justice of the Common Pleas, 1649.
[b] John Cruso, LL.D., Caius Coll., Cambr. 1652.
** MS. Aubr. 6, fol. 22.

*** MS. Aubr. 6, fol. 21.
[c] Here followed, 'which Mr. Shuter etc. told me they had seen': scored out, as belonging *infra*.
[d] Subst. for 'gave.'

is my cosen Aubrey of Llannelly in Brecknockshire, of about 60 or 80 *li.* per annum inheritance; and the Doctor should have given a distinction; for want of which in a badge on one of his servants' blew-coates, his cosen William Aubrey[a], also LL. Dr., who was the chiefe, plucked it off.

The learned John Dee was his great friend and kinsman, as I find by letters between them in the custody of Elias Ashmole, esqre, viz., John Dee wrote a booke *The Soveraignty of the Sea*, dedicated to queen Elizabeth, which was printed, in folio. Mr. Ashmole hath it, and also the originall copie of John Dee's hand writing, and annexed to it is a lettre of his cosen Dr. William Aubrey[b], whose advise he desired in his writing on that subject.

He purchased Abercunvrig (the ancient seate of the family) of his cosen Aubrey. He built the great house at Brecknock, his studie lookes on the river Uske. He could ride nine miles together in his owne land in Breconshire. In Wales and England he left 2500 *li.* per annum wherof there is now none left in the family. He made one Hugh George (his chiefe clark) his executor, who ran away into Ireland and cosened all the legatees, and among others my grandfather (his youngest son) for the addition of whose estate he had contracted with . . . . for Pembridge castle in the com. of Hereford, which appeares by his will, and for which his executor was to have payed. He made a deed of entaile (36 Eliz., 15⟨94⟩) which is also mentioned in his will, wherby he entailes the Brecon estate on the issue male of his eldest son, and in defailer, to skip the 2d son (for whom he had well provided, and had maried a great fortune) and to come to the third. Edward the eldest had seaven sonnes; and his eldest son, Sir William, had also seaven sonnes; and so I am heire, being the 18th man in remainder, which putts me in mind of Dr. Donne,

> For what doeth it availe
> To be the twentieth man in an entaile?

---

[a] William Aubrey, Student of Ch. Ch. in 1580; D.C.L. 1597.
[b] See *infra*, p. 61.

Old Judge Sir ⟨Edward⟩ Atkins remembred Dr. A. when he was a boy; he lay at his father's house in Glocestershire: he kept his coach, which was rare in those dayes. The Judge told me they then (vulgarly) called it a *Quitch*. I have his originall picture. He had a delicate, quick, lively and piercing black eie, fresh complexion, and a severe eie browe. The figure in his monument at St. Paules is not like him, it is too big.

Heroum filii noxae: he engrossed all the witt of the family, so that none descended from him can pretend to any. 'Twas pitty that Dr. Fuller had not mentioned him amongst his Worthys in that countie.

When he lay dyeing, he desired them to send for a *goodman*; they thought he meant Dr. Goodman, deane of St. Paules, but he meant a priest, as I have heard my cosen John Madock say. Capt. Pugh was wont to say that civilians (as most learned an⟨d⟩ gent.) naturally incline to the church of Rome; and the common lawyers, as more ignorant and clownish, to the church of Geneva.

Wilgiford, his relict, maried . . . . Browne, of Willey, in com. Surrey.

The inscription on his monument in St. Paul's church :—

Gulielmo Aubreo clara familia in Breconia orto, LL. in Oxonia Doctori, ac Regio Professori, Archiepiscopi Cantuariensis causarum Auditori et Vicario in spiritualibus Generali, Exercitus Regii ad St. Quentin Supremo Juridico, in Limitaneum Walliae Consilium adscito, Cancellariae Magistro, et Reginae Elizabethae à supplicum libellis: Viro exquisita eruditione, singulari prudentia, et moribus suavissimis qui (tribus filiis, et sex filiabus e Wilgiforda uxore susceptis), aeternam in Christo vitam expectans, animam Deo xxiii Julii 1595, aetatis suae 66, placidè reddidit ;

Optimo patri Edvardus et Thomas, milites, ac Johannes, armiger, filii moestissimi, posuerunt.

* This Dr. W. Aubrey was related to the first William, earl of Pembroke, two wayes (as appeares by comparing the old pedegre at Wilton with that of the Aubreys); by Melin and Philip ap Elider (the Welsh men are all kinne);

* MS. Aubr. 6, fol. 21ᵛ.

and it is exceeding probable that the earle was instru-
mentall in his rise. When the earl of Pembroke was
generall at St. Quintins in France, Dr. Aubrey was his
judge advocat. In the Doctor's will is mention of a great
piece of silver plate, the bequest of the right hon[ble] the
earle of Pembroke.

. . . . Stephens, the clarke of St. Benets, Paules Wharfe,
tells me that Dr. W. Aubrey gave xx*s.* per annum for ever
to that parish.

* Vide the register of St. Benet's, Paule's Wharfe—
quaere. Stephens, the clark, sayeth that he gave xx*s.* per
annum to the parish of St. Benet's, Paule's wharfe, for
ever : quaere.

** Sir Andrew Joyner of Bigods in Much Dunmow
parish in Essex hath two folios, stitcht, of manuscript letters
of state, wherin are two letters of Dr. William Aubrey's to
secretary Walsingham, and also lettres of queen Elizabeth's
owne handwriting to Cecill; also *Liber S[tæ] Mariae de
Reding*, a MS.; and other MSS.,—a long shelfe of them—
one of them writt tempore Henr. IV. This I had from
Mr. Andrew Paschal, rector of Chedzoy, Somerset.

⟨*Letter by Dr. W. Aubrey: supra, p.* 59.⟩

*** MY GOOD COOSEN,

I HAVE sente unto you again my yonge coosen[a]
inclosede in a bagge, as my wyffe cariethe yet one of
myne ; trustinge in God, that shortly both, in theyr severall
kyndes, shall come to lyght and live long, and your's
having *genium*, for ever. I knowe not, for lack of suffici-
encie of witte and learninge, how to judge of it at all. But
in that shadowe of judgemente that I have, truste me
beinge vearie farre from meanynge to yelde any thyng,
to your owne eares, of yourselfe. The matter dothe so
strive with the manner of the handlinge that I am in
dowpte whyther I shall preferre the matter for the sub-

---

* MS. Aubr. 8, fol. 19[v].   [a] i.e. John Dee's book, the 'child
** MS. Aubr. 8, fol. 1[v].   of his invention.'
*** MS. Aubr. 6, fol. 23.

stance, weyght, and pythines of the multitude of argumentes
and reasones, or the manner for the methode, order, per-
spicuitie, and elocution, in that height and loftynesse that
I did nott beleve our tonge (I meane the Englyshe) to be
capable of. Marie, our Brittishe, for the riches of the
tonge, in my affectionate opinion, is more copious and more
advawntageable to utter any thinge by a skillfull artificer.
This navie which you aptlie, accordinge to the nature and
meaninge of your platt, call pettie, is so sette furthe by
you, thos principall and royall navies of the Grecianes and
Trojanes described by Homer and Vergill are no more
bownde to them, then it is to you.

You argue or rather thoondre so thicke and so strong
for the necessitie and commoditie of your navie, that you
leade or rather drawe me *obtorto collo* to be of opinion with
you, the benefitte therofe to be suche as it wilbe a brydle
and restreynte for conspiracies of foreyne nationes, and of
owre owne a salfegarde to merchants from infestationes
of pyrates; a readie meane to breed and augmente
noombers of skillfull marryners and sowldiers for the
sea, a mayntynawnce in proces of tyme for multitudes
of woorthie men that otherwise wolde be ydle. Who
can denie, as you handle the matter, and as it is in trothe,
but that it will be a terror to all princes for attemptinge
of any soodeyne invasions,* and hable readilie to with-
stande any attempte foreyne or domesticall by sea? And
where this noble realme hath ben long defamede for
suffringe of pyrates disturbers of the common traffyke
upon these seas, yt will, as you trulye prove, utterlie
extingwishe the incorrigible, and occupie the reformed
in that honourable service.

The indignitie that this realme hath long borne in the
fyshinge rownde aboute yt, with the intolerable injuries that
owre nation hath indurede and doe still, at strangers
handes, besides the greatnes of the commoditie that they
take owte of our mowthes, hath ben, and is suche, that the
same almoste alone were cause sufficiente to furnishe your

* MS. Aubr. 6, fol. 23ᵛ.

navie if it may have that successe and consideration that it
deserveth, it will be a better wache for the securitie of the
state than all the intelligencers or becones that may be
devisede: and a stronger wall and bulwarke than either
Calleys was, or a brase of such townes placed in the most
convenient parte of any continente of France, or the Lowe-
countrey. As her majestie of right is *totius orbis Britannici
domina, et lex maris,* whiche is given in the reste of the
worlde by Labro in our learning to Antoninus the Emperor,
so she showlde have the execution and effect therof in
our worlde, yf your navie were as well setled as you have
plottede it. But what doe I by this bare recitall deface
your reasones so eloquentlie garnishede by you with the
furniture of so much and so sundrie lernynge? I will of
purpose omitt howe fully and howe substantially you
confute the stronge objectiones and argumentes that you
inforce and presse againste your selfe. I wolde God all
men wolde as willinglie beare the light burdynes that you
lay upon them for the supportation of the chardges as you
have wiselie and reasonablie devisede the same. And so
the dearthe and scarsitie that curiouse or covetouse men
may pretende to * feare, you so sowndlie satisfie, that it is
harde with any probabilitie to replie. As for the sincere
handlinge and govermente it is not to be disperede yf the
charge shall be with good ordinawnces and instructiones
placede carefullie in chosen persones of good credite and
integritie. See howe boldlie upon one soodeyne readinge
I powre my opinion to your bosome of this your notable
and strange discowrse. And yet I will make bold to
censure it also as he dyd in the poore slipper when he was
nott able to fynd any faulte in any one parte of the
workemanship of the noble picture of that goddes. I
pray you, Sir, seyinge you meane that your navie shall
contynewe in time of peace furnishede with your noombre
of men, what provision or ordre make you, howe they shall
occupie and exercise themselves all the while? Assure
your selfe those whelpes of yours neyther can nor will be

* MS. Aubr. 6, fol. 24.

ydle, and excepte it may please you to prescribe unto
them some good occupation and exercise, they will occupie
themselves in occupationes of their owne choice, wherof
few shall be to your lykinge or meanynge. Peradventure
you meane of purpose to reserve that to the consideration
of the state. And where you in vearie good proportion,
lawierlike, share goodes taken by pyrates amonge sundrie
persones of your navie, and some portion to itselfe, reserv-
inge the moytie to the prince, you are to remembre that
the same are challenged holly to belong to her highnesse
by prerogative. Let me be also bold to offer to your
consideration whether it be expedient for you so freely
to deale with the carryinge of ordinawnces out of the
realme beinge a matter lately pecuted [a] by the knowledge
et convenientia of, etc. You doe, to veary great purpose
inserte the two orationes of Georgius Gemistus Plethon,
the one to Emanuel by fragments, and the other to his
sonne Theodore *ad verbum,* for the worthynes and varietye
of many wise and sownd advises given by him to those
princes in a hard tyme, when they were in feare of that
Turkish conquest, that did after followe to the ruine of
that empire of Constantinople. However well doeth he
handle the differences and rates of customes and tributes,
the moderate and sober use of apparell *in ipsis principibus!*
How wisely doethe [*] he condemne the takeinge up of all
the newe attires and apparell of strange nations, as though
he had written to us at this tyme, who doe offende as
deepely therein as the Greekes then dyd! How franke
is he to his prince in useinge the comparisone between
the Eagle that hath no varietie of colours of feathers,
and yet of a princelie nature and estimation, and the
Peocock, a bird of no regall propertie nor credit yet
glisteringe angelically with varietie of feathers of all
lively colours. There is one sentence in the later oration
which I have thought to note because in apparence it
dothe oppugne in a maner your treatise. The wordes

---

[a] Anthony Wood has put dots under this word, and noted in the margin ' sic.'
[*] MS. Aubr. 6, fol. 24ᵛ.

are these, *Prestat longè terrestribus copiis ac militum et ducum virtute, quàm nautarum et similium hominum vilium arte, fiduciam ponere.*

Good coosen, pardon my boldnes. I doe this bicause you may understande that I have roone over it. And yet was I abrode all the fowle day yesterday. I pray you pardon me agayne for nott sendinge of it to you accordinge to promisse. And for that your man is come, and for that I have spente all my paper, I will no longer trowble you at this tyme, savinge with my right heartie commendations to your selfe and to my coosen your good mother from me and from my woman. From Kewe this Soonday in the morninge, the 28 of July.

Yours assuredlie at commawndement,

W. AUBREY.

To his verie lovinge coosen and assured
freende Mr. John Dee, at Mortelake.

Notes.

[1] Aubrey gives in trick the coat :—' in the 1 and 6, gules[a], a chevron between 3 eagles heads erased or [Aubrey]; in the 2, ..., a lion rampant ...; in the 3, ..., a chevron between 3 (lions' ?) paws ...; in the 4, ..., three cocks gules; and in the 5, parted per pale ... and ..., 3 fleur-de-lys counter-changed.' The crest is ' an eagle's head erased or [Aubrey].'

[2] In MS. Aubr. 8, fol. 7, is the memorandum :—' Insert ♀ to Liber B.'— ' Liber B.' was a volume of antiquarian notes, collected by Aubrey, now lost (Macray's *Annals of the Bodleian*, p. 367). Aubrey wanted to copy into it something from this MS. ♀. Two other memoranda in the same place are : — (*a*) 'William Aubrey, LL.D. : extract out of *De jure feciali*, and *De legati deli- quentis judice competente*, by Dr. Zouch,' as is done *supra*, p. 58 ; (*b*) ' Memor- andum the xx *s.* per annum bread at St. Benet's, Paul's wharf'; see *supra*, p. 61.

Aubrey, in MS. Ballard 14, fol. 119, writing to Anthony Wood on Aug. 29, 1676, says :—' This day accidentally Mr. St. George shewed me my grandfather, Dr. William Aubrey's, life in their office' (i. e. the College of Arms), ' written, I suppose, by Sir Daniel Dun, his son-in-lawe. He came to Oxon at 14, and was LL. Dr. at 25.'

[3] Aubrey was very enthusiastic about these notices of his grandfather. Writing to Anthony Wood, on May 19, 1668 (MS. Wood F. 39, fol. 118), he says :—' My grandfather Dr. William Aubrey—Thuanus in his *Annales* makes an honourable mention of him, and also it is set downe in the life of Mary, queen of Scotts (he being one of the commissioners) that he was very jealous of her being putt to death—which the chroniclers mention too I'me sure, and Stow. If you would be pleased to turne to Thuanus and the life aforesaid you (would) very much oblige me, and you shall have a payre of gloves, for his sake.'

[a] It should be 'azure.'

' Edward Seymour, created earl of Hertford in 1559, had in 1553 married secretly Katherine, daughter of Henry Grey, duke of Suffolk. In 1561 Elizabeth sent them prisoners to the Tower, and the marriage was disputed in the law-courts. William Seymour, his grandson, who succeeded as 2nd earl in 1621, married in 1610 Arabella Stuart. She was sent prisoner to the Tower by James I: but Dr. W. Aubrey had died in 1595.

⁵ Aubrey, in MS. Aubr. 8, fol. 6ᵛ, has a note :—' Meredith Lloyd respondet that Telesinus (Teliessen) was a British priest to whom Gildas writes.'

Francis Bacon (1561–1626).

⟨*His coat of arms.*⟩

* Quarterly, on the 1 and 4, gules on a chief argent two mullets sable [Bacon], on the 2 and 3, barry of six or and azure, over all a bend gules [. . .], a crescent on the fesse point for difference; impaling, sable, a cross engrailed between 4 crescents argent, a crescent sable on the fesse point [Barnham].

⟨*Miscellaneous Notes.*⟩

** Chancellor Bacon :—The learned and great cardinal Richelieu was a great admirer of the lord Bacon.

So was Monsieur Balzac : e.g. *les Oeuvres diverses*, dissertation sur un tragedie, à Monsieur Huygens de Zuylichen, p. 158—' Croyons, pour l'amour du chancilier Bacon, que toutes les folies des anciens sont sages et tous leur songes mysteries.'

Quaere if I have inserted* his irrigation in the spring showres.

Vide *Court of King James* by Sir Anthony Welden, where is an account of his being viceroy here when the king was in Scotland, and gave audience to ambassadors in the banquetting-house.

*** Lord Chancellor Bacon :—Memorandum, this Oct. 1681, it rang over all St. Albans that Sir Harbottle Grimston, Master of the Rolles, had removed the coffin of this most renowned Lord Chancellour to make roome for his owne to lye-in in the vault there at St. Michael's church.

**** Sir Francis Bacon, knight, baron of Verulam and

* MS. Aubr. 6, fol. 67. see *infra*, p. 84.
** MS. Aubr. 8, fol. 15ᵛ. *** MS. Aubr. 8, fol. 16ᵛ.
* i. e. in the life in MS. Aubr. 6; **** MS. Aubr. 6, fol. 67.

viscount of St. Albans, and Lord High Chancellor of England :—vide his life writt by Dr. William Rawley before *Baconi Resuscitatio*, in folio.

⟨ *His admirers and acquaintances.* ⟩

It appeares by this following inscription that Mr. Jeremiah Betenham of Graye's Inne was his lordship's intimate and dearely beloved friend. This inscription is on the freeze of the summer house on the mount in the upper garden of Grayes Inne, built by the Lord Chancellor Bacon. The north side of the inscription is now perished[a]. The fane was a Cupid drawing his bowe.

Franciscus Bacon, Regis Solicitator Generalis, executor testamenti Jeremie Betenham nuper lectoris hujus hospitii, viri innocentis et abstinentis et contemplativi, hanc sedem in memoriam ejusdem Jeremie extruxit, anno Domini, 1609.

In his lordship's prosperity Sir Fulke Grevil, lord Brookes, was his great friend and acquaintance ; but when he was in disgrace and want, he was so unworthy as to forbid his butler to let him have any more small beer, which he had often sent for, his stomach being nice, and the small beere of Grayes Inne not liking his pallet. This has donne his memorie more dishonour then Sir Philip Sydney's friendship engraven on his monument hath donne him honour. Vide . . . History, and (I thinke) Sir Anthony Weldon.

. . . . Faucet, of Marybon in the county of Middlesex, esqr., was his friend and acquaintance, as appeares by this letter which I copied from his owne handwriting (an elegant Roman hand). 'Tis in the hands of Walter Charlton, M.D., who begged it not long since of Mr. Faucet's grandsonne.

. . . . [b]

* Richard[c], earle of Dorset, was a great admirer and friend of the lord chancellor Bacon, and was wont to have Sir Thomas Billingsley[d] along with him to remember and to putt-down in writing my lord's sayings at table.

---

[a] Dupl. with 'lost.'
[b] Part of the page left blank for insertion of the letter.
* MS. Aubr. 6, fol. 67ᵛ.

[c] Richard Sackville, 3rd earl, ob. 1624.
[d] See *infra*, sub nomine.

Edward, lord Herbert of Cherbery.

John Dun[a], dean of Paul's.

George Herbert.

Mr. Ben: Johnson was one of his friends and acquaintance, as doeth appeare by his excellent verses on his lordship's birth-day in his second volume, and in his *Underwoods*, where he gives him a character and concludes that 'about his time, and within his view were borne all the witts that could honour a nation or help studie.'

* Lord Bacon's birth-day: *Underwoods*, p. 222.

> Haile, happy genius of this ancient pile,
> How comes it all things so about thee smile?
> The fire, the wine, the men! and in the midst
> Thou stand'st as if some mysterie thou didst!
> Pardon, I read it in thy face, the day,
> For whose returnes, and many, all these pray:
> And so doe I. This is the sixtieth yeare
> Since Bacon, and my lord, was borne, and here,
> Sonne to the grave wise Keeper of the Seale,
> Fame and foundation of the English weale.
> What then his father was, that since is he,
> Now with a title more to the degree,
> England's High Chancellour, the destin'd heir
> In his soft cradle of his father's chaire,
> Whose even thred the Fates spinne round and full
> Out of their choysest and their whitest wooll.
>   'Tis a brave cause of joy; let it be knowne,
> For 'twere a narrow gladnesse, kept thine owne.
> Give me a deep-crown'd bowle, that I may sing
> In raysing him the wisdome of my king.

Discoveries, p. 101.

Yet there happened in my time one noble speaker † who was full of gravity in his speaking. His language (where he could spare or passe-by a jest) was nobly censorious. No man ever** spake more neatly, more pres⟨ent⟩ly, more weightily, or suffered lesse emptinesse, lesse idlenesse, in what he utter'd. No member of his speech but consisted of the owne graces: his hearers could not cough, or looke aside from him, without losse. He commanded where he spoke; and had his judges angry, and pleased, at his devotion. No

† Dominus Verulanus.

---

[a] Donne.   * MS. Aubr. 6, fol. 69.   ** MS. Aubr. 6, fol. 69ᵛ.

man had their affections more in his power. The feare of every man that heard him was lest he should make an end.

Cicero is sayd to be the only wit that the people of Rome had, equall'd to their empire, *ingenium par imperio*. We had many, and in their severall ages (to take in but the former *seculum*) Sir Thomas Moore, the elder Wiat, Henry, earle of Surrey, Chaloner, Smith, Eliot, bishop Gardiner, were for their times admirable ; Sir Nicholas Bacon was singular and almost alone in the beginning of queen Elizabeth's times ; Sir Philip Sydney and Mr. Hooker (in different matter) grew great masters of wit and language and in whom all vigour of invention and strength of judgment met ; the earle of Essex, noble and high ; and Sir Walter Rawleigh, not to be contemn'd either for judgement or stile ; Sir Henry Savile, grave and truly letter'd ; Sir Edwin Sandys, excellent in both ; lord Egerton, the Chancellour, a grave and great orator, and best when he was provoked ; but his learned and able (though unfortunate) successor is he who hath fill'd up all numbers, and performed that in our tongue which may be compar'd or preferr'd either to insolent Greece or haughty Rome. In short, within his view, and about his times, were all the wits borne that could honour a language or helpe study. Now things dayly fall, wits grow downeward and eloquence growes backward, so that he may be nam'd and stand as the marke and ἀκμή of our language.

I have ever observ'd it to have been the office of a wise patriot among the greatest affaires of the state to take care of the commonwealth of learning *, for schooles they are the seminaries of state and nothing is worthier the study of a statesman then that part of the republick which wee call the advancement of letters. Witnesse the care of Julius Caesar, who in the heate of the civill warre writ his bookes of analogie and dedicated them to Tully. This made the lord St. Albans entitle his worke *Novum Organum*, which though by the most of superficiall men who cannot gett beyond the title of nominalls, it is not penetrated nor understood, it really openeth all defects of learning whatsoever, and is a booke

> Qui longum noto scriptori porriget aevum [a].

My conceit of his person was never increased towards him by his place or honour, but I have and doe reverence him for the greatnesse that was only proper to himselfe in that he seem'd to me ever by his worke one of the greatest men and most worthy of admiration that have been in many ages. In his adversity I ever prayed that God would give him strength ; for greatnes he could not want. Neither could I condole in a word or syllable for him, as knowing no accident could doe harme to vertue but rather helpe to make it manifest.

* MS. Aubr. 6, fol. 70.   [a] HORAT., *Ars Poet.* 346.

* He came often to Sir John Danvers at Chelsey.
Sir John told me that when his lordship had wrote the
History of Henry 7, he sent the manuscript copie to him
to desire his opinion of it before 'twas printed. Qd. Sir
John 'Your lordship knowes that I am no scholar.' ' 'Tis
no matter,' said my lord, 'I know what a schollar can say ;
I would know what *you* can ª say.' Sir John read it, and
gave his opinion what he misliked which Tacitus did not
omitt (which I am sorry I have forgott) which my lord
acknowledged to be true, and mended it : 'Why,' said he,
' a scholar would never have told me this.'

Mr. Thomas Hobbes (Malmesburiensis) was beloved by
his lordship, who was wont to have him walke with him
in his delicate groves where he did meditate : and when
a notion darted into his mind, Mr. Hobbs was presently
to write it downe, and his lordship was wont to say that
he did it better then any one els about him ; for that
many times, when he read their notes he scarce understood what they writt, because they understood it not
clearly themselves.

In short, all that were *great and good* loved and honoured
him.

Sir Edward Coke, Lord Chiefe Justice, alwayes envyed
him, and would be undervalueing his lawe, as you may
find in my lord's lettres, and I knew old lawyers that
remembred it.

〈*Personal characteristics.*〉

He was Lord Protector during King James's progresse
into Scotland, and gave audience in great state to ambassadors in the banquetting-house at Whitehall.

His lordship would many times have musique in the
next roome where he meditated.

The aviary at Yorke-house was built by his lordship ;
it did cost 300 *li*.

At every meale, according to the season of the yeare,

---

he had his table strewed with sweet herbes and flowers, which he sayd did refresh his spirits and memorie.

When his lordship was at his country house at Gorhambery, St. Albans seemed as if the court were[a] there, so nobly did he live. His servants had liveries with his crest (a boare . . .); his watermen were more imployed by gentlemen then any other, even the king's.

King James sent a buck to him, and he gave the keeper fifty pounds.

He was wont to say to his servant Hunt, (who was a notable thrifty man, and loved this world, and the only servant he had that he could never gett to become bound for him) 'The world was made for man, Hunt; and not man for the world.' Hunt left an estate of 1000*li.* per annum in Somerset.

None of his servants durst appeare before him without Spanish leather bootes: for he would smell the neatesleather, which offended him.

The East India merchants presented his lordship with a cabinet of jewells, which his page, Mr. Cockaine, recieved, and decieved his lord.

Three of his lordship's servants[†] kept their coaches, and some kept race-horses—vide Sir Anthony Welden's *Court of King James.*

Sir Thomas Meautys, Mr. (Thomas) Bushell, Mr. . . . Idney.

* He was[b] a παιδεραστής. His Ganimeds and favourites tooke bribes; but his lordship always gave judgement *secundum aequum et bonum.* His decrees in Chancery stand firme, i.e. there are fewer of his decrees reverst then of any other Chancellor.

His dowager[c] maried her gentleman-usher, Sir (Thomas, I thinke) Underhill, whom she made deafe and blind with too much of Venus. ☞ She was living since the beheading of the late King.—Quaere where and when she died.

---

[a] Subst. for 'had been.'

* MS. Aubr. 6, fol. 68.

[b] His brother-in-law, Mervyn Touchet, second earl of Castlehaven, was executed on this charge, May 14, 1631.

[c] Alice, daughter and co-heir of Bennet Barnham.

He had a delicate [a], lively hazel eie ; Dr. Harvey told me it was like the eie of a viper.

I have now forgott what Mr. Bushell sayd, whether his lordship enjoyed his Muse best at night, or in the morning.

⟨*His poems*⟩.

His lordship was a good poet, but conceal'd, as appeares by his letters. See excellent verses of his lordship's which Mr. Farnaby translated into Greeke, and printed both[b] in his Ἀνθολογία, scil.

> The world's a bubble, and the life of man
> Less then a span, etc.

* Ἀνθολογία : Florilegium epigrammatum selectorum ; Thomas Farnaby, London, 1629, pag. 8.—'Huc elegantem viri clarissimi domini Verulamii *παρῳδίαν adjicere adlubuit'—opposit to it on the other page—'quam παρῳδίαν e nostrati bona nos Graecam qualemcunque sic fecimus, et rhythmice.'

> The world's a bubble, and the life of man
>   Lesse then a span ;
> In his conception wretched, from the wombe
>   So to the tombe ;
> Curst from his cradle, and brought up to yeares
>   With cares and feares.
> Who then to fraile mortality shall trust
> But limmes in water or but writes in dust.
>
> Yet since with sorrow here we live opprest,
>   What life is best ?
> Courts are but onely superficiall scholes
>   To dandle fooles ;
> The rurall parts are turn'd into a den
>   Of savage men ;
> And wher's a city from all vice so free,
> But may be term'd the worst of all the three ?

---

[a] Over 'delicate,' Aubrey has written 'T. Hobbes,' either as his authority for the statement, or comparing Bacon's eyes with Hobbes', which were ' hazell ' and ' ful of life.'

[b] i. e. the original, and the Greek version.

* MS. Aubr. 6, fol. 71[v].

Domestick cares afflict the husband's bed
    Or paines his hed;
Those that live single take it for a curse,
    Or doe things * worse;
Some would have children; those that have them mone,
    Or wish them gone.
What is it then to have, or have no wife,
But single thraldome or a double strife?

Our owne affections still at home to please
    Is a disease;
To crosse the sea to any foreine soyle,
    Perills and toyle;
Warres with their noise affright us; when they cease
    W'are worse in peace.
What then remaines? but that we still should cry
Not to be borne, or, being borne, to dye.

⟨*His writings.*⟩

* His reading of Treason.
His reading of Usurie.
Decrees in Chancery.
Cogitata et Visa: printed in Holland by Sir William Boswell, Resident there: who also there printed Dr. Gilbert's Magnetique Philosophie.
Speech in Parliament of naturalization of the Scottish nation: printed 1641.
His apothegmes, 8vo.

Essaies { . . . . .
        . . . . .
        . . . . .

Advancement of learning.
History of King Henry the 7th.
Novum Organon.—At the end of his *Novum Organon* Hugh Holland wrote these verses :—

    Hic liber est qualis potuit non scribere Stultus,
      Nec voluit Sapiens: sic *cogitavit* Hugo.

* 'doe things' subst. for 'live much.'   * MS. Aubr. 6, fol. 74.

Naturall Historie.

Of ambassadors: published by Francis Thynne out of Sir Robert Cotton's library, 1650.

Speech touching duells, in the Starre-chamber: in the Bodleian library at Oxford.   Reprint it.

All the rest of his lordship's workes you will find in Dr. William Rawley's *Resuscitatio.*

A piece of philosophy halfe as thick as the grammar set forth by Dr. Rawley, 1660.

.   .   .   .   .

.   .   .   .   , 167–.

* *Apothegmata.*

His lordship being in Yorke-house garden lookeing on fishers as they were throwing their nett, asked them what they would take for their draught ; they answered *so much* : his lordship would offer them no more but *so much.*   They drew-up their nett, and ⟨in⟩ it were only 2 or 3 little fishes : his lordship then told them it had been better for them to have taken his offer. - They replied, they hoped to have had a better draught ; '*but*,' sayd his lordship, '*Hope is a good breakfast, but an ill supper.*'

When his lordship was in dis-favour, his neighbours hearing how much he was indebted, came to him with a motion to buy Oake-wood of him.   His lordship told them, '*He would not sell his feathers.*'

The earle of Manchester being removed from his place of Lord Chiefe Justice of the Common Pleas[a] to be Lord President of the Councell, told my lord (upon his fall) that he was sorry to see him made such an example. Lord Bacon replied 'It did not trouble him since *he* was made *a President.*'

The bishop of London did cutt-downe a noble clowd of trees at Fulham.   The Lord Chancellor told him that he was *a good expounder of darke places.*

Upon his being in dis-favour his servants suddenly went

---

* MS. Aubr. 6, fol. 68.   [a] *Rectius,* of the King's Bench.

away; he compared them to the flying of the vermin when the howse was falling.

One told his Lordship it was now time to looke about him. He replyed, 'I doe not looke *about* me, I looke *above* me.'

Sir Julius Cæsar (Master of the Rolles) sent to his lordship in his necessity a hundred pounds for a present †; quaere + de hoc of Michael Malet.

† Most of these enformations I have from Sir John Danvers.

His Lordship would often drinke a good draught of strong beer (March beer) to-bedwards, to lay his working fancy asleep: which otherwise would keepe him from sleeping great part of the night.

I remember Sir John Danvers told me, that his lordship much delighted in his curious * garden at Chelsey, and as he was walking there one time, he fell downe in a dead-sowne. My lady Danvers rubbed his face, temples, etc. and gave him cordiall water: as soon as he came to himselfe, sayd he, 'Madam, I am no good *footman*.'

⟨*His death and burial.*⟩

* Mr. Hobbs told me that the cause of his lordship's death was trying an experiment: viz., as he was taking the aire in a coach with Dr. Witherborne (a Scotchman, Physitian to the King) towards High-gate, snow lay on the ground, and it came into my lord's thoughts, why flesh might not be preserved in snow, as in salt. They were resolved they would try the experiment presently. They ** alighted out of the coach, and went into a poore woman's howse at the bottome of Highgate hill, and bought a hen, and made the woman exenterate it, and then stuffed the bodie with snow, and my lord did help to doe it himselfe. The snow so chilled him, that he immediately fell so extremely ill, that he could not returne to his lodgings (I suppose then at Graye's Inne), but went to the earle of Arundell's house at High-gate, where they putt him into a good bed warmed with a panne, but

* Dupl. with 'pretty.'   * MS. Aubr. 6, fol. 68.
        ** MS. Aubr. 6, fol. 68ᵛ.

it was a damp bed that had not been layn-in in about a yeare before, which gave him such a cold that in 2 or 3 dayes, as I remember he * told me, he dyed of suffocation.

Mr. George Herbert, Orator of the University of Cambridge, haz made excellent verses on this great man. So haz Mr. Abraham Cowley in his Pindariques. Mr. Thomas Randolph of Trin. Coll. in Cambr. haz in his poems verses on him.

* In the north side of the chancell of St. Michael's church (which, as I remember, is within the walles of Verulam) is the Lord Chancellor Bacon's monument in white marble in a niech, as big as the life, sitting in his chaire in his gowne and hatt cock't, leaning his head on his right hand. Underneath is this inscription which they say was made by his friend Sir Henry Wotton.

Franciscus Bacon, Baro de Verulam,
Sti Albani Vicecomes, seu, notioribus titulis,
Scientiarum Lumen, Facundiae Lex,
sic sedebat.
Qui postquam omnia Naturalis sapientiae
et Civilis arcana evolvisset,
Naturae decretum explevit
' Composita solvantur,'
Anno Domini MDCXXVI
aetatis LXVI.
Tanti viri
mem.

† His lordship's secretarie, who maried a kinswoman ((Anne) Bacon), who is now the wife of Sir Harbottle Grimston, Master of the Rolles.
‡ His mother was (Anne) Cooke, sister of . . . Cooke of Giddy-hall in Essex, 2nd wife to Sir Nicholas Bacon.

Thomas Meautys †
superstitis cultor,
defuncti admirator,
H. P.

⟨*His relatives.*⟩

** He had a uterine ‡ brother ANTHONY BACON, who was a very great statesman and much beyond his brother Francis for the politiques, a lame man, he was a pensioner to, and lived with . . . earle of Essex. And to him he dedicates the first edition of his Essayes, a little booke no bigger then a primer, which I have seen in the Bodlyan Library.

His sisters were ingeniose and well-bred; they well understood the use of the globes, as you may find in the preface of Mr. Blundevill of the Sphaere : see if it is not dedicated to them. One of them was maried to Sir John Cunstable of Yorkshire. To this brother in lawe he dedicates his second edition of his Essayes, in 8vo; his last, in 4to, to the duke of Bucks.

* Blundevill's *Exercises*, preface :—'I began this arithmetique more then seven yeares since for that vertuous gentlewoman Mris Elizabeth Bacon, the daughter of Sir Nicholas Bacon, knight (a man of most excellent witt and of a most deep judgement and sometimes Lord Keeper of the great seale of England), and lately the loving and faithfull wife of my worshipfull friend Mr. Justice Windham, who for his integrity of life and for his wisdome and justice dayly shewed in government and also for his good hospitalitie deserved great commendation; and though at her request I had made this arithmetique so plaine and easie as was possible (as to my seeming) yet her continuall sicknesse would not suffer her to exercise herself therin.'

⟨*His residences.*⟩

** I will write something of Verulam, and his house at Gorhambery.

At Verulam is to be seen, in some few places, some remaines of the wall of this citie †; which
† Verolamium, Virolamium, Cassivelani oppidum.
was in compass about . . . miles. This magnanimous Lord Chancellor had a great mind to have made it a citie again : and he had designed it, to be built with great uniformity: but Fortune denyed it him, though she proved kinder ⟨to⟩ the great Cardinal Richelieu, who lived both to designe and finish that specious towne of Richelieu, where he was borne; before, an obscure and small vilage. (The ichnographie, etc., of this towne and palais is nobly engraved).

Within the bounds of the walls of this old citie of Verulam (his lordship's Baronry) was Verulam howse,

* MS. Aubr. 6, fol. 70ᵛ.   ** MS. Aubr. 6, fol. 68ᵛ.

about ½ a mile from St. Albans; which his Lordship built, the most ingeniosely contrived little pile †,

that ever I sawe. No question but his lordship was the chiefest architect; but he had for his assistant a favourite of his (a St. Albans man) Mr. . . . Dobson (who was his lordship's right hand) a very ingeniose person (Master of the Alienation Office); but he spending his estate upon woemen ᵃ, necessity forced his son William Dobson to be the most excellent painter that England hath yet bred, qui obiit Oct. 1648; sepult. S. Martin's in the fields *.

** The view of this howse from the entrance into the gate by the high-way is thus. The parallel ᵇ sides answer one another. I doe not well remember if on the east side were bay windowes, which his lordship much affected, as may be seen in his essay *Of Building*. Quaere whether the number of windowes on the east side were 5 or 7: to my best remembrance but 5. This model I drew by memorie, 1656.

VERULAM HOWSE ᶜ.

This howse did cost nine or ten thousand the building, and was sold about 1665 or 1666 by Sir Harbottle Grimston, baronet, (now Master of the Rolles) to two carpenters for fower hundred poundes; of which they made eight hundred poundes. Memorandum :—there were good chimney-pieces; the roomes very loftie, and all were very well wainscotted. Memorandum :—there were two bathing-roomes or stuffes, whither his Lordship retired afternoons as he sawe cause. All the tunnells of the chimneys were carried into the middle of the howse, as in this draught; and round about them were seates. The top of the howse was well leaded. From the leads was a lovely prospect to the ponds, which were opposite to the

---

ᵃ Dupl. with 'luxuriously.'

* Explicit MS. Aubr. 6, fol. 68ᵛ.

** MS. Aubr. 6, fol. 72.

ᵇ Dupl. with 'respective.'

ᶜ Aubrey's drawing will be found among the facsimiles at the end of this volume.

east side of the howse, and were on the other side of the
stately walke of trees that leades to Gorhambery-howse :
and also over that long walke of trees, whose topps afford
a most pleasant * variegated verdure, resembling the
workes in Irish-stitch. The kitchin, larder, cellars, &c.,
are under ground. In the middle of this howse was
a delicate staire-case of wood, which was curiously carved,
and on the posts of every interstice was some prettie
figure, as of a grave divine with his booke and spectacles,
a mendicant friar, &c.—(not one thing twice). Memorandum :—on the dores of the upper storie on the outside
(which were painted darke umber) were the figures of the
gods of the Gentiles (viz. on the south dore, 2d storie,
was Apollo ; on another, Jupiter with his thunderbolt,
etc.) bigger then the life, and donne by an excellent hand ;
the heightnings were of hatchings of gold, which when the
sun shone on them made a most glorious shew.

Memorandum :—the upper part of the uppermost dore,
on the east side, had inserted into it a large looking-glasse,
with which the stranger was very gratefully decieved, for
(after he had been entertained a pretty while, with the
prospects of the ponds, walks, and countrey, which this
dore faced) when you were about to returne into the
roome ᵃ, one would have sworn *primo intuitu*, that he had
beheld another prospect through the howse : for, as soon
as the stranger was landed on the balconie, the conserge ᵇ
that shewed the howse would shutt the dore to putt this
fallacy on him with the looking-glasse. This was his
lordship's summer-howse : for he sayes (in his essay) one
should have seates for summer and winter as well as
cloathes.

From hence to Gorhambery is about a little mile, the
way easily ascending, hardly so acclive as a deske.

From hence to Gorambury in a straite line leade three
parallell walkes : in the middlemost three coaches may
passe abreast : in the wing-walkes two may. They consist

---

* MS. Aubr. 6, fol. 72ᵛ.

ᵃ Here followed 'the servant would

shutt the dore' : scored out.

ᵇ French 'concierge.'

of severall stately trees of the like groweth and heighth,
viz. elme, chesnut, beach, hornebeame, Spanish-ash, cervice-
tree, &c., whose topps (as aforesaid) doe afford from the
walke on the howse the finest shew that I have seen, and
I sawe it about Michaelmas, at which time of the yeare
the colour of leaves are most varied. The manner of the
walke is thus :—

u	u	u	u
t	t	t	t
s	s	s	s
r	r	r	r
o	o	o	o
n	n	n	n
m	m	m	m
x	x	x	x
u	u	u	u
t	t	t	t
s	s	s	s
r	r	r	r
o	o	o	o
n	n	n	n
m	m	m	m
x	x	x	x
u	u	u	u
t	t	t	t
s	s	s	s
r	r	r	r
o	o	o	o
n	n	n	n
m	m	m	m

* The figures of the ponds were thus: they were
pitched at the bottomes with pebbles of severall colours,
which were work't in to severall figures, as of fishes, &c.
which in his lordship's time were plainly to be seen
through the cleare water, now over-grown with flagges
and rushe

If a poor bodie had brought his lordship halfe a dozen
pebbles of a curious colour, he would give them a shilling,
so curious was he in perfecting his fish-ponds, which
I guesse doe containe four acres. In the middle of the

* MS. Aubr. 6, fol. 73.

middlemost pond, in the island, is a curious banquetting-house of Roman architecture, paved with black and white marble; covered with Cornish slatt, and neatly wainscotted.

(*a*)=cutt hedge about the island.

(*b*)=walke between the hedge and banquetting-howse.

Memorandum :—about the mid-way from Verolam-house to Gorambery, on the right hand, on the side of a hill which faces the passer-by, are sett in artificiall manner the afore-named trees, whose diversity of greens on the side of the hill are exceeding pleasant. These delicate walkes and prospects entertaine the eie to Gorambery-howse, which is a large, well-built Gothique howse, built (I thinke) by Sir Nicholas Bacon, Lord Keeper, father to this Lord Chancellor, to whom it descended by the death of Anthony Bacon, his middle brother, who died sans issue. *The Lord Chancellor made an addition of

* MS. Aubr. 6, fol. 73ʳ.

a noble portico, which fronts the garden to the south : opposite to every arch of this portico, and as big as the arch, are drawen, by an excellent hand (but the mischief of it is, in water-colours), curious pictures, all emble-maticall, with mottos under each : for example, one I remember is a ship tossed in a storme, the motto, *Alter erit tum Tiphys.* Enquire for the rest.

Over this portico is a stately gallerie, whose glasse-windowes are all painted ; and every pane with severall figures of beast, bird, or flower : perhaps his lordship might use them as topiques for locall memory. The windowes looke into the garden, the side opposite to them no window, but that side is hung all with pictures at length, as of King James, his lordship, and severall illustrious persons of his time. At the end you enter is no windowe, but there is a very large picture, thus :—in the middle on a rock in the sea stands King James in armour, with his regall ornaments ; on his right hand stands (but whither or no on a rock I have forgott), King Henry 4 of France, in armour ; and on his left hand, the King of Spaine, in like manner. These figures are (at least) as big as the life, they are donne only with umbre and shell gold : all the heightning and illuminated part being burnisht gold, and the shadowed umbre, as in the pictures of the gods on the dores of Verolam-house. The roofe of this gallerie is semi-cylindrique, and painted by the same hand and same manner, with heads and busts of Greek and Roman emperours and heroes.

In the hall (which is of the auncient building) is a large storie very well painted of the feastes of the gods, where Mars is caught in a nett by Vulcan. On the wall, over the chimney, is painted an oake with akornes falling from it ; the word, *Nisi quid potius.* And on the wall, over the table, is painted Ceres teaching the soweing of corne ; the word, *Moniti meliora.*

The garden is large, which was (no doubt) rarely planted and kept in his lordship's time : vide vitam Peireskii de domino Bacon. Here is a handsome dore, which opens into Oake-wood; over this dore in golden letters on blew are these six verses [a].

* The oakes of this wood are very great and shadie. His lordship much delighted himselfe here: under every tree he planted some fine flower, or flowers, some wherof are there still (1656), viz. paeonies, tulips, . . .

From this wood a dore opens into . . . , a place as big as an ordinary parke, the west part wherof is coppice-wood, where are walkes cutt-out as straight as a line, and broade enoug for a coach, a quarter of a mile long or better.—Here his lordship much [b] meditated, his servant Mr. Bushell attending him with his pen and inke horne to sett downe his present notions.—Mr. Thomas Hobbes told me, that his lordship would employ him often in this service whilest he was there, and was better pleased with his *minutes*, or notes sett downe by him, then by others who did not well understand his lordship. He told me that he was employed in translating part of the Essayes, viz. three of them, one wherof was that of the Greatnesse of Cities, the other two I have now forgott.

The east of this parquet (which extends to Veralam-howse) was heretofore, in his lordship's prosperitie, a paradise; now is a large ploughed field. This eastern division consisted of severall parts; some thicketts of plumme-trees with delicate walkes; some of rasberies. Here was all manner of fruit-trees that would grow in England; and a great number of choice forest-trees; as the whitti-tree, sorbe-, cervice-, etc., eugh [c]. The walke⟨s⟩, both in the coppices and other boscages, were most ingeniosely designed: at severall good viewes [d], were erected elegant sommer-howses well built of Roman architecture, well wainscotted and cieled; yet standing, but defaced, so that one would have thought the Barbarians had made a conquest here. This place in his lordship's time was

[a] A blank space is left in the MS. for their insertion.

* MS. Aubr. 6, fol. 74.

[b] Subst. for 'was wont' (to meditate).

[c] i. e. yew.

[d] 'Belvideri' is written over 'good viewes,' as an alternative.

a sanctuary for phesants, partridges, etc. birds of severall kinds and countries, as white, speckled etc., partridges.   In April, and the springtime, his lordship would, when it rayned, take his coach (open) to recieve the benefit of irrigation, which he was wont to say was very wholsome because of the nitre in the aire and the *universall spirit of the world.*

His lordship was wont to say, *I will lay my mannor of Gorambery on't,* to which Judge .... made a spightfull reply, saying he would not hold a wager against that, but against *any other* mannour of his lordship's he would. Now this illustrious Lord Chancellor had only this mannor of Gorambery.

Roger Bacon (1214–1294).

* Roger Bacon, friar ordinis ⟨S. Francisci⟩ :—Memorandum, in Mr. Selden's learned verses before Hopton's *Concordance of yeares,* he speakes of friar Bacon, and sayes that he was a Dorsetshire gentleman.   There are yet of that name in that countie, and some of pretty good estate. I find by . . . (which booke I have) that he understood the making of optique glasses ; where he also gives a perfect account of the making of gunpowder, vide pag. . . . ejusdem libri.

** Friar Roger Bacon :—Dr. Gerard Langbain had a Catalogue[1] of all his workes, which Catalogue Dr. ⟨Thomas⟩ Gale, schoolmaster of Paule's, haz now.

Note.

[1] The reference is probably to a list of pieces by Roger Bacon which were found among Thomas Allen's MSS.   Langbaine's draft of it is found in MS. Langbaine 7, p. 393 : see Clark's Wood's *Life and Times,* iv. 253.

Thomas Badd (1607–1683).

*** The . . . happinesse a shoemaker haz in drawing on a fair lady's shoe. . . . I know one that it was the hight of his ambition to be prentice to his mris⟨'s⟩ shoemaker upon that condicion.

* MS. Aubr. 6, fol. 6ᵛ.   ** MS. Aubr. 8, fol. 9ᵛ.
*** MS. Aubr. 21, p. 11.

Sir Thomas Bad's [a] father, a shoemaker, married the brewer's widow of Portsmouth, worth 20,000 *li.*

Edward Bagshaw (1629–1671).

* Edward Bagshaw was borne at Broughton in Northamptonshire ; 42 when he dyed—from his widowe [1].

** My old acquaintance, Mr. Edward Bagshawe, B.D., 3rd son of Edward Bagshawe, esq., a bencher of the Middle Temple, was borne (the day nor moneth certaine to be knowne) November or December at Broughton in Northamptonshire, where Mr. Boldon [h], quondam Coll. Aeneinas., was parson.

He was a king's scholar at Westminster schole, then student of Christ Church. Scripsit severall treatises.

Obiit on St. Innocents day, 28 Dec., 1671, in Tuttle street, Westminster, a prisoner to Newgate 22 weekes for running into a praemunire for refusing to take the oath of allegiance (he boggled at the word 'willingly' in the oath): aetatis 42. Sepult., Newyeares day, in the fanatique burying-place by the Artillery-ground in Moorfields, where his sorrowfull widdowe will place his epitaph.

1500 or 2000 people were at his funerall.

*** 'Here [e] lyes interred | the body of | Mr. Edward Bagshaw | minister of the Gospell | who recieved from God | faith to embrace it | courage to defend it | and patience to suffer for it | when by most despised and by many persecuted | esteeming the advantages of birth, education, and learning | as things of worth to be accounted losse for the knowledge | of Christ. | From the reproaches of pretended friends | and persecutions of professed adversaries | he | took sanctuary | by the will of God | in eternall rest.'

---

[a] Sir Thomas Badd, of Cames Oysells, created a baronet in 1642.

* Aubrey, in MS. Wood, F. 39, fol. 319[v].

** Idem, ibid., fol. 163[v]: Jan. 27, 167½.

[b] Robert Bolton, obiit 1631.

*** Cited by Aubrey, in MS. Wood, F. 39, fol. 175[v].

[e] Anthony Wood notes 'made, they say, by Dr. ⟨John⟩ Owen,' Puritan dean of Christ Church, Oxford.

Note.
[1] MS. Aubr. 27 :—'A review and conclusion of the Antidote against Mr. Baxter's palliated cure of Church Divisions,' by Edward Bagshaw, Lond. 1671, has the note 'donum Margaretae, viduae autoris : Jan. 27, 1671 (i.e. ½), Jo. Awbrey.'

Jean Louis Guez de Balzac (1594–1655).

* Monsieur de Balzac ended his dayes in a Cappucine's cell, and was munificent to them : vide *Entretiens de monsieur de Balzac*, printed above 20 yeares since.

Richard Bancroft (1544–1610).

In MS. Aubr. 6, fol. 119ᵛ, is this jotting :—
'Dr. Mat. Skinner. *Resp*. 'tis archbishop Bancroft's picture—quod N.B., and inscribe.'
This is probably to be interpreted as meaning—' Enquire whether the portrait,' in a certain place, 'is that of Dr. Matthew Skinner.' Finding that it is the portrait of Richard Bancroft, 'see that the name is inscribed on it,' for future identification.

John Barclay (1582–1621).
Robert Barclay (1648–1690).

** Johannes Barclaius, Scoto-Britannus:—from Sam. Butler—was in England some time tempore regis Jacobi. He was then an old man, white beard ; and wore a hatt and a feather, which gave some severe people offence.

Dr. John Pell tells me, that his last employment was Library-Keeper of the Vatican, and that he was there poysoned.

Memorandum :—this John Barclay haz a sonne*, now (1688) an old man, and a learned quaker, who wrote a Systeme of the Quakers' Doctrine in Latineᵇ, dedicated to King Charles II, now (to) King James II ; now translated by him into English, in . . . . . The Quakers mightily value him. The booke is common.

* MS. Aubr. 6, fol. 2.
** MS. Aubr. 8, fol. 53ᵛ.
* Robert Barclay was *not* son of John Barclay ; see the dates *supra*.

ᵇ Theologiae verae Christianae apologia, Amstel. 1676   The English version appeared in 1678.

Isaac Barrow (1630–1677).

* Isaac Barrow, D.D.—from his father, (who was borne Aprill 22, 1600, ½ a yeare older then King Charles 1st), May 17, 1682.

His father, Thomas Barrow, was the second son of Isaac Barrow of Spinney Abbey in the countie of Cambridge, esq., who was a Justice of the Peace there above fourtie yeares. The father of Thomas never designed him for a tradesman, but he was so severe to him ⟨that⟩ he could not endure to live with him and so came to London and was apprentice to a linnen-draper. He kept shop at the signe of the White-horse in Forster lane near St. Forster's church in St. Leonard's parish; and ⟨his son[a]⟩ was christened at St. John Zacharie's in Forster lane, for at that time St. Leonard's church was pulled downe to be re-edified. He was borne anno Dni 1630 in October[b] after King Charles IInd. Dr. Isaac Barrow had the exact day and hower of his father, which may be found amongst his papers. His father sett it downe in his English bible, a faire one, which they used at the king's chapell when he was in France and he could not get it again. His father travelled with the King, Charles 2nd, where ever he went; he was sealer to the Lord Chancellor beyond sea, and so when he came into England. Amongst Dr. Barrowe's papers it may be found. Dr. Tillotson has all his papers— quaere for it, and for the names of all writings both in print and MSS.

He went to schoole, first to Mr. Brookes at Charterhouse two yeares. His father gave to Mr. Brookes 4 *li.* per annum, wheras his pay was but 2 *li.*, to be carefull of him; but Mr. Brokes was negligent of him, which the captain of the school acquainted his father (his kinsman) and sayd that he would not have him stay there any longer than he[c] did, for that he[c] instructed him.

Afterwards to one Mr. Holbitch, about fower years, at

Felton[a] in Essex; from whence he was admitted of Peter-house College in Cambridge first, and went to schoole a yeare after. Then he was admitted of Trinity College in Cambridge at 13 yeares old.

Quaere whose daughter his mother was.

His mother was Anne, daughter of William Buggin of North Cray in Kent, esq. She died when her sonne Isaac was about fower yeares old.

Anno Domini . . . he travelled, and returned, anno Domini . . .

He wrote . . . . . What MSS.?—quaere Dr. Tillotson, and quaere Mr. Brabazon Aylmer, bookseller, nere Exchange Alley.

His humour when a boy and after :—merry and cheerfull and beloved where ever he came. His grandfather kept him till he was 7 years old: his father was faine to force him away, for there he would have been good for nothing there.

A good poet, English and Latin. He spake 8 severall languages.

* His father dealt in his trade to Ireland where he had a great losse, neer 1000 *li.*; upon which he wrote to Mr. Holbitch, a Puritan, to be pleased to take a little paines more than ordinary with him, because the times growing so bad, and such a losse then received, that he did not knowe how he might be able to provide for him, and so Mr. Holbitch tooke him away from the howse where he was boarded to his owne howse, and made him tutor to my lord viscount Fairfax, ward to the lord viscount Say and Seale, where he continued so long as my lord continued.

This viscount Fairfax[b] died a young man. This viscount Fairfax, being a schooleboy, maried a gentleman's daughter

in the towne there, who had but a thousand pounds. So
leaving the schoole, would needs have Mr. Isaac Barrow
with him, and told him he would maintaine him. But
the lord Say was so cruel to him that he would not allow
anything that 'tis thought he dyed for want. The 1000 *li*.
could not serve him long.

During this time old Mr. Thomas Barrow was shutt-up
at Oxford and could not heare of his sonne. But young
Isaac's master, Holbitch, found him out in London and
courted him to come to his schoole and that he would make
him his heire. But he did not care to goe to schoole again.

When my lord Fairfax faild and that he sawe he grew
heavy upon him, he went to see one of his schoolfellowes,
one Mr. Walpole, a Norfolke gent., who asked him ' What
he would doe ? ' He replyed he ' knew not what to doe :
he could not goe to his father at Oxford.' Mr. Walpole
then told him ' I am goeing to Cambridge to Trinity College
and I will maintaine you there '; and so he did for halfe
a yeare till the surrender of Oxford ; and then his father
enquired after him and found him at Cambridge. And
the very next day after old Mr. Barrow came to Cambridge,
Mr. Walpole was leaving the University and (hearing
nothing of Isaac's father) resolved to take Isaac along with
him to his howse. His father then asked him what profession he would be of, a merchant or etc.? He begd
of his father to lett him continue in the University. His
father then asked what would maintain him. He told
him 20 *li*. per annum : ' I warrant you,' sayd he, ' I will
maintaine myselfe with it.' His father replyed ' I'le make
a shift to allow you that.' So his father then went to his
tutor and acquainted him of, etc. His tutor, Dr. Duport,
told him that he would take nothing for his reading to
him, for that he was likely to make a brave scholar, and
he would helpe him to halfe a chamber for nothing. And
the next newes his father heard of him was that he was
chosen in to the howse. * Dr. Hill * was then master of

* MS. Aubr. 8, fol. 100.
* Thomas Hill, intruded Master by the Parliamentary Visitors, 1645-1653.

the college. He mett Isaac[a] one day and layd his hand upon his head and sayd ' thou art a good boy; 'tis pitty that thou art a cavalier.'

He was a strong and a stowt man and feared not any man. He would fight with the butchers' boyes in St. Nicholas' shambles, and be hard enough for any of them.

He went to travell 3 or 4 yeares after the king was beheaded, upon the colledge account[b]. He was a candidate for the Greeke professor's place, and had the consent of the University but Oliver Cromwell putt in Dr. Widrington[c]; and then he travelled.

He was abroad 5 yeares[d], viz. in Italie, France, Germany, Constantinople.

As he went to Constantinople, two men of warre (Turkish shippes) attacqued the vessell wherin he was. In which engagement he shewed much valour in defending the vessell; which the men that were in that engagement often testifye, for he never told his father of it himselfe.

Upon his returne, he came in ⟨a⟩ ship to Venice, which was stowed with cotton-wooll, and as soon as ever they came on shore the ship fell on fire, and was utterly consumed, and not a man lost, but not any goods saved— a wonderfull preservation.

His personall valour—At Constantinople, being in company with the English merchants, there was a Rhadamontade that would fight with any man and bragged of his valour, and dared any man there to try him. So no man accepting his challenge, said Isaac (not then a divine), ' Why, if none els will try you I will '; and fell upon him and chastised him handsomely that he vaunted no more amongst them.

After he had been 3 years beyond sea, his correspondent dyed, so that he had no more supply; yet he was so well beloved that he never wanted.

At Constantinople he wayted on the consul Sir Thomas Bendish, who made him stay with him and kept him there a yeare and a halfe, whether he would or no.

<hr/>

[a] Dupl. with ' the boy.'
[b] ? i. e. receiving his fellowship.
[c] Ralph Widdrington, Reg. Prof. Greek, 1654–1660.
[d] 1655–59.

At Constantinople, Mr. Dawes (afterwards Sir Jonathan Dawes, who dyed sherif of London), a Turkey merchant, desired Mr. Barrow to stay but such a time and he would returne with him, but when that time came he could not goe, some businesse stayd him. Mr. Barrow could stay no longer; so Mr. Dawes would have had Mr. Barrow have C[a] pistolles. 'No,' said Mr. Barrow, 'I know not whether I shall be able to pay you.' ''Tis no matter,' said Mr. Dawes. To be' short, forced him to take fifty pistolls, which at his returne he payd him again.

* Memorandum, his pill (an opiate, possibly Matthews his pil), which he was wont to take in Turkey, which was wont to doe him good, but he tooke it preposterously at Mr. Wilson's, the sadler's, neer Suffolke-house, where he was wont to lye and where he dyed, and 'twas the cause of his death—quaere + de hoc there.

As he lay expiring[b] in the agonie of death, the standers-by could heare him say softly 'I have seen the glories of the world'—⟨from⟩ Mr. Wilson.

I have heard Mr. Wilson say that when he was at study, was so intent at it that when the bed was made, or so, he heeded it not nor perceived it, was so *totus in hoc*; and would sometimes be goeing out without his hatt on.

He was by no meanes a spruce man[c], but most negligent in his dresse. As he was walking one day in St. James's parke, looking . . . , his hatt up, his cloake halfe on and halfe off, a gent. came behind him and clapt him on the shoulder and sayd 'Well, goe thy wayes for the veriest scholar that ever I[d] mett with.'

He was a strong man but pale as the candle he studied by.

His stature was . . .

The first booke he printed was Euclid's Elements in Latin, printed at Cambridge, impensis Gulielmi Nealand, bibliopolae, Anno Domini MDCLV.

[a] i. e. 100.
* MS. Aubr. 8, fol. 100ᵛ.
[b] Dupl. with 'unravelling.'
[c] Dupl. with 'he was not a Dr. Smirke '—in Andrew Marvell's satire.
[d] Subst. for 'I sawe.'

Euclidis data succincte demonstrata, printed at Cambridge ex officina Joannis Field, impensis Gulielmi Nealand, bibliopolae, anno Domini 1657.

Euclid's Elements in English.

Euclid's Elements in Latin—in the last impressions of this is an appendix about the sphaere itselfe, it's segments and their surfaces, most admirably derived and demonstrated by the doctrine of infinite arithmetique and indivisibles.

* Lectiones XVIII Cantabrigiae in scholis publicis habitae in quibus opticorum phaenomenωn genuinae rationes investigantur ac exponuntur. Annexae sunt lectiones aliquot geometricae. Londini, prostant venales apud Johannem Dunmore et Octavianum Pulleyn. MDCLXIX.

Archimedes.

Apollonius.

Theodosius.

Now printing, 22 initiating lectures about mathematics ᵃ, to which will be subjoined some lectures that he read about Archimedes, proving that he was an algebraist, and giving his owne thoughts by what method Archimedes came to fall on his theoremes.

Bookes writ by the learned Dr. Isaac Barrow and printed for Brabazon Aylmer at the Three Pidgeons over against the Royall Exchange in Cornhill :—

12 Sermons preached upon severall occasions; in 8vo, being the first volume.

10 Sermons against evil speaking; in 8vo, being the second volume.

8 Sermons of the love of God and our neighbour; in 8vo, being the third volume.

The duty and reward of bounty to the poor, in a sermon, much enlarged, preached at the Spittall upon Wednesday in Easter weeke anno Domini 1671, in 8vo.

A sermon upon the Passion of our blessed Saviour preached at Guildhall chapell on Good Fryday the 13th day of April 1677, in 8vo.

---

* MS. Aubr. 8, fol. 101.

ᵃ ' In geometrie' is written over 'about mathematics' in explanation.

A learned treatise of the Pope's supremacy, to which is added a discourse concerning the unity of the church ; in 4to.

The sayd discourse concerning the Unity of the Church is also printed alone in 8vo.

An exposition of the Lord's Prayer, of the Ten Commandments, of the doctrine of the Sacraments ; in 8vo.

All the sayd books of the learned Dr. Isaac Barrow (except the sermon of bounty to the poor) are since the author's death published by Dr. Tillotson, deane of Canterbury.

'The true and lively effigies of Dr. Isaac Barrow' in a large print, ingraven from the life by the excellent artist D. Loggan ; price, without frame, 6d.

* Thomas Barrow, (father of Isaac, S.T.D.) was brother to Isaac Barrow late lord bishop of St. Asaph, and sonne of Isaac Barrow of Spiney Abbey, who was sonne of Philip Barrow ª, who hath in print a method of Physick, and he had a brother Isaac Barrow, a Dr. of Physick, who was a benefactor to Trinity Colledge in Cambridge, and was there tutor to Robert Cecill that was earle of Salisbury and Lord Treasurer.

** Isaac Barrow, D.D., (⟨a⟩ Cambridge ⟨man⟩, borne in Essex), is buried in the south crosse aisle of Westminster Abbey with this inscription ᵇ :—

Isaacus Barrow

S.T.P. Regi Carolo II° a sacris

Vir prope divinus et vere magnus si quid magna habent
Pietas, probitas, fides, summa eruditio, par modestia,
Mores sanctissimi undiquaque et suavissimi.
Geometriae professor Londini Greshamensis,
Graecae linguae et Matheseos apud Cantabrigienses suos,
Cathedras omnes, ecclesiam, gentem ornavit.
Collegium SS. Trinitatis praeses illustravit,
Jactis bibliothecae vere regiae fundamentis auxit.

---

* MS. Aubr. 8, fol. 101ᵛ.

ª See Cooper's *Athenae Cant.* ii. 96.

** MS. Aubr. 6. fol. 51. Aubrey gives in trick the coat :—'sable, two swords in saltire between four fleur-de-lys . . .'

ᵇ Anthony Wood notes :—' This was made for Dr. Barrow, Vicechancellor of Cambridge, vide part iii,' i. e. MS. Aubr. 8, *ut supra.*

Opes, honores, et universum vitae ambitum,
Ad majora natus, non contempsit sed reliquit seculo.
Deum quem a teneris coluit cum primis imitatus est,
Paucissimis egendo, beneficiendo quam plurimis,
Etiam posteris quibus vel mortuus concionari non desinit.
Caetera et poene majora ex scriptis peti possunt.
Abi lector et aemulare.
Obiit IVto die Maii anno Domini MDCLXXVII
aetatis suae XLVII.
Monumentum hoc Amici posuere.

This epitaph was contrived by Dr. John Mapletoft and perfected by Dr. ⟨Thomas⟩ Gale.

He was the . . . son of . . . Barrow, ⟨who⟩ was a brewer at Lambith; a King's Scholar at Westminster.

Anno 1655 he printed at Cambridge Euclidis Elementorum libri XV breviter demonstrati.

Anno . . . , he travelled; was at Constantinople; sawe part of Graece, Italie, France.

He was a good poet, of great modestie and humanity, careles of his dresse.

. . . Barrow (16..–168.).

* Dr. . . . Barrow, M.D., secretary to the lord generall Monke in Scotland, and who wrote the life or history of the generall, was cosen-german to Thomas (father of Isaac, D.D.). He was a very good-humoured man. He much resembled and spake like Dr. Ezerel Tong. Obiit 2 yeares since: quaere ubi.

Thomas Batchcroft (15..–1670).

** Memorandum: in Sir Charles Scarborough's time (he was of Caius College) Dr. . . . (the head of that house) would visit the boyes' chambers, and see what they were studying; and Charles Scarborough's genius let him to the mathematics, and he was wont to be reading of Clavius upon Euclid. The old Dr. had found in the title '. . . . . . , *e Societate Jesu,*' and was much scandalized

* MS. Aubr. 8, fol. 100ᵛ.
** MS. Aubr. 8, fol. 60ᵛ. Thomas

Batchcroft was Master of Gonville and Caius College, 1625–49, 1660–1670.

at it. Sayd he, 'By all meanes leave-off this author, and-
read Protestant mathematicall bookes.'

One sent this Doctor a pidgeon-pye from New-market or
thereabout, and he askt the bearer whither 'twas hott,
or cold? He did out-doe Dr. Kettle.

George Bate (1608–1668).

* Kingston super Thames; north aisle chap⟨el⟩.

> Spe resurrectionis felicis
> heic juxta sita est
> Elizabetha
> conjux lectissima
> Georgii Bate, M.D.,
> Car. 2 medici primarii,
> Qui cineres suos adjacere curavit
> ut qui unanimes convixerant
> quasi unicorpores condormientes
> una resurgant.
> Mortem obiit 17 Apr., 1667, aet. 46
> ex hydro-pulmon.,
> funesta Londini conflagratione
> acceleratam.
> Obiit ille 19 Apr., 1668
> aetatis suae 60.

Francis Beaumont (1584–1616).

** Mr. Francis Beaumont was the son of Judge Beau-
mont [a]. There was a wonderfull consimility
of phansey † between him and Mr. John
Fletcher, which caused that dearnesse of
frendship between them.

† Utrumque nostrum [b]
incredibili modo
Consentit astrum.
HORACE, lib. 2,
ode 17.

I thinke they were both of Queen's College in Cambridge.
I have heard Dr. John Earles (since bishop of Sarum),

---

* Note in pencil (partly inked
over) by Aubrey at end of MS. Rawl.
766. The slip is addressed (not by
Aubrey) 'To Mr. Thomas Awbrey at
Broad Chalke—, to be left at the
Lambe in Katherine Streete in Salisbury.' The seal is 'party per chevron,
. . . and or (?), in chief 2 eagles (or
falcons) rising, a mullet for difference,'
a coat for Stephens. Aubrey gives in
trick, as on the monument, 'sable, a
fesse engrailed argent, between 3 dexter
hands couped bendways or.'

** MS. Aubr. 6, fol. 116ᵛ.

[a] Francis Beaumont, Justice of the
Common Pleas, 1593.

[b] Subst. for 'illorum.'

who knew them, say that his maine businesse was to correct the overflowings[a] of Mr. Fletcher's witt.

They lived together on the Banke side, not far from the Play-house, both batchelors; lay together—from Sir James Hales, etc.; had one wench in the house between them, which they did so admire; the same cloathes and cloake, &c., betweene them.

He writt (amongst many other) an admirable elegie on the countesse of Rutland, which is printed with verses before Sir Thomas Overburie's *Characters*. John Earles, in his verses on him, speaking of them,

> 'A monument that will then lasting bee,
> When all her marble is more dust then shee.'

Ex registro:—he was buryed at the entrance of St. Benedict's chapell where ⟨is⟩ the earl of Middlesex' monument, in Westminster Abbey, March 9, 161⅝†.

† Memorandum:—Isaac Casaubon was buryed at the entrance of the same chapell. He dyed July 8, 1614.

I searched, severall yeares since, in the Register-booke of St. Mary Overies, for the obiit of Mr. John Fletcher, which I sent to Mr. Anthony à Wood.

He hath a very good prefatory letter before Mr. Speght's edition of Sir Geofrey Chaucer's *Workes* printed by Adam Islip, 1602, London, where he haz judicious observations of his writing.

William Bedwell (15..–1632).

[*] . . . Bedwell, professor of . . . at Gresham College, translated into English Pitisci *Trigonometria*. Published *The turnament of Totnam*. He was an Essex man—from his grand-niece.

William Beeston (16..–1682).

[**] Did I tell you that I have mett with old Mr. . . .[b] who knew all the old English poets, whose lives I am

---

[a] 'Super' is written above 'over.'
[*] MS. Aubr. 7, fol. 6.
[**] Aubrey, in MS. Wood F. 39,

fol. 357: written Sept. 1, 1681.
[b] Blank in MS., Aubrey forgetting the name at the moment.

taking from him : his father was master of the . . . play-house.

* The more to be admired, quaere—he was not a company keeper; lived in Shorditch; would not be debauched; and if invited to court, was in paine.

W. Shakespeare—quaere Mr. Beeston, who knowes most of him from Mr. Lacy. He lives in Shoreditch at Hoglane within 6 dores north of Folgate. Quaere etiam for *Ben Jonson.*

** Old Mr. Beeston, whom Mr. ⟨John⟩ Dreyden calles 'the chronicle of the stage,' died at his house in Bishopsgate street without, about Bartholomew-tyde, 1682. Mr. Shipey in Somerset-house hath his papers.

Richard Benese (14..–1546).

*** I did see, many yeares since, in a countrey-man's house, a little booke in 8vo in English, called

Arsmetrie, or the Art of numbring:

printed in an old black letter about Henry VIII. The author's name I doe not remember—quaere in Duck lane.

The next old mathematicall booke in English that I have seen hath this title, viz :—

This booke sheweth the manner of measuring of all manner of land, as well of woodland as of lande in the felde, and comptinge the true nombre of acres of the same.

✠

Newlye invented and compiled by Syr Rycharde Benese, chanon of Marton Abbay besyde London.

❡ Printed in Southwarke in Saint Thomas hospital by me James Nicolson.

'Tis a quarto.

---

* MS. Aubr. 8, fol. 45ᵛ. The first part of the note seems to be a char-acter of Beeston ; the second part is a note of questions to be put to him.
** MS. Aubr. 7, fol. 6.
*** MS. Aubr. 8, fol. 71.

* This Sir Richard Benese was also author of a little booke, in 8vo, called . . . .
: quaere Absolom Leech for it—'tis about physick.

Berkeley.

** Mris . . . Barckley, sister of the late lord Fitz-Harding[a], was cosen german to Mr. Sydney Godolphin, and also his mistresse. He loved her exceedingly. After Mr. Godolphin's death she maried one Mr. Davys who I thinke is now [b] dead, and she lives at Twicknam—from Philip Packer, esq.

Willoughby Bertie, 3rd earl of Abingdon (1692–1760).

*** ⟨Willoughby⟩ Bertie, filius primus Jacobi Bertie, 2ⁿᵈⁱ filii Jacobi, comitis de Abington, natus Westmonast. 28 die Novembris, 2ʰ. P.M. 1692.—The child is yet living, notwithstanding the 8ᵗʰ house[c]: mend the figure, but the time is right.

**** I know not how to retreive the fashion or shape of the old engine of *the battering-ramme*, but from the coate of the Bertyes, which is ' or, 3 battering rammes barrewise,' as in the margent, the timber is proper, the head azure, the hornes and ironworke gilded.

***** Memorandum :—the battering ramme, the armes of Bertie, hung in equilibrio in an engine they call the

---

* MS. Aubr. 8, fol. 70ᵛ.

** MS. Aubr. 7, fol. 6.

ᵃ Charles Berkeley, created viscount Fitz-hardinge 1663, killed in the sea-fight, June 3, 1665.

ᵇ MS. Aubr. 7 (fol. 5) is dated

' January 168⅘.'

*** MS. Aubr. 23, fol. 90.

ᶜ i. e. in the scheme of the nativity, which portended immediate death.

**** MS. Aubr. 6, fol. 11.

***** MS. Aubr. 8, fol. 5.

triangles—from Mr. Nicolas Mercator: vide Bertie's coate in primo volumine[a]. See[b] the old glasse windowes in Aldersgate street—from Mr. ⟨Edward⟩ Bagshawe.

Henry Billingsley (15..–1606).

* Sir Henry Billingsley[1], knight.—On the north side of the chancell of St. Katharine Coleman church London at the upper end is this inscription, viz :—

Here lieth buried the body of Elizabeth, late the wife of Henry Billingsley, one of the Queene's majestie's customers of her port of London, who dyed the 29th day of July in the yeare of our Lord God 1577.

In obitum ejus.

Stat sua cuique dies atque ultima funeris hora
   Cum Deus hinc et mors invidiosa vocant ;
Nec tibi nec pietas tua vel forma, Elizabetha,
   Praesidium leto[c] ne trahereris erat.
Occidis exactis ternis cum conjuge lustris,
   At septem vitae lustra fuere tuae.
Fecerat et proles jam te numerosa parentem,
   Filiolae trinae, caetera turba mares.
Undecimo partu cum mors accessit et una
   Matrem te et partum sustulit undecimum—
Scilicet ex mundo, terrena ex fece, malisque,
   Sustulit ; at superis reddidit atque Deo.
Est testis sincera fides, testis tua virtus,
   Grata viro virtus, grata fidesque Deo.

Quem posuit tumulum tibi conjux charus, eodem
   In tumulo condi mortuus ipse petit.

⟨Vide⟩ the Register book ⟨of the church⟩.

Memorandum :—Billingsley (a village) is in the countie of Salop. 'Tis a Shropshire familie ; but the village now is one Mr. Norton's.

This Sir Henry Billingsley was one of the learnedst

---

[a] i.e. in MS. Aubr. 6, *ut supra.*
[b] This sentence possibly refers to some other topic than the preceding.
* MS. Aubr. 6, fol. 35ᵛ.   [c] MS. ' laeto.'

citizens that London has bred. This was he that putt forth
all Euclid's Elements in English with learned notes and
preface of Mr. John Dee, and learned men say 'tis the best
Euclid. He had been sheriff and Lord Mayor of the
city of London. His howse was the faire howse in Fen-
church street where now Jacob Luce lives, a merchant, of
of whom quaere +. Vide in Fuller's Worthies and Stowe's
Survey. His Euclid was printed at London by John
Day, 1570.

'The Translator to the Reader—Wherfore considering
the want and lack of such good authors hitherto in our
English tongue, lamenting also the negligence and lacke
of zeale to their countrey in those of our nation to whom
God hath given both knowledge and also abilitie to translate
into our tongue and to publish abroad such good authors
and bookes : Seeing moreover that many good witts, both
of gentlemen and others of all degrees, much desirous and
studious of these artes,—I have for their sakes with some
chardge and great travaile faithfully translated into our
vulgar tounge and set abroad in print this booke of Euclid
wherunto I have added plaine declarations and examples,
manifold additions, scholies, annotations, and inventions
which I have gathered.'—He promises (here) some more
translations and sayes that in religion he hath alreadie
don, quaere.

Memorandum P. Ramus in his Scholia's sayes that the
reason why mathematiques did most flourish in Germanie
was that the best authors were rendred into their mother
tongue, and that publique lectures of it were also read in
their owne tongue—quod nota bene.

Memorandum when I was a boy, one Sir . . . Billingsley
had a very pleasant seate with a faire[a] oake-wood adjoyning to it, about a mile ½[b] east of Bristoll—quaere if[c], etc.

Vide de Sir Thomas Billingsley, pag. ⟨44 b⟩[d]; who was
gentleman of the horse to Richard, earl of Dorset. He

---

[a] 'faire' is scored out.
[b] i. e. 1½ mile.
[c] i. e. if descended from Alderman Henry Billingsley.
[d] i. e. MS. Aubr. 6, fol. 67ᵛ— in Francis Bacon's life.

managed the great horse best of any man in England. He taught the Prince Elector and brothers to ride. Quaere if descended hence.

In those dayes[a] merchants travelled much abroad into Italie, Spaine, etc. Quaere Mr. Abraham Hill of what company he was. Probably good memorialls may be there found of his generous and publique spirit. *Respondet*:— He was of the Goldsmiths' Company, where is a good picture of him.

R. B., i.e. Robert[b] Billingsley, teaches Arithmetique and Mathematiques at . . . in . . . . He hath printed a very pretty little booke of arithmetique and algebra, London (scilicet, ⟨*The*⟩ *Idea of Arithmetic*): was Sir Henry's great grandson—from Mr. Abraham Hill, Regiae Societatis Socius.

* In the table of benefactors in the church of St. Catherine Colman, viz.—

'1603 { Dame Elizabeth } Billingsley did will to the
       { Sir Henry   }
poor 1s. per weeke for ever and 200 *li.* which their heires etc. have not payd '—

The minister here, Mr. Dodson, sayes that it was not payd because the parish did not find-out in due time land to make a purchase of.

Many yeares since Mr. Abraham Hill, Regiae Societatis Socius, citizen, told me that Sir Henry Billingsley was of the Goldsmiths' Company, and that his picture was in Goldsmiths' Hall, which I went lately to see. No picture of him, and besides the clarke of the Company told me that he is sure *he* was never of that Company. But Mr. Hill tells me since that in Stowe's Survey you may see of what Company all the Lord Mayers were, which see[c] and tell me.

** Sir H. Billingsley—Mr. Leeke, mathematician, saith that he was of the company of goldsmiths, quaere. Quaere

---

[a] i.e. Henry Billingsley's, to whom in this paragraph Aubrey harks back.

[b] 'Richard,' *infra*, p. 103.

* MS. Aubr. 7, fol. 9.

[c] This injunction was addressed to Anthony Wood.

** MS. Aubr. 8, fol. 18.

the clarke of the company : vide register booke. Vide
Heralds' Office (Salop, and neer Bristowe). Vide Fuller's
Worthyes where he mentions the Lord Mayers.

* *Ex registro* ⟨of St. Catherine Coleman⟩ :—Sir Henry
Billingsley, knight, buried in the vault under his pewe in
the church of St. Catherine Coleman, London, December
the 18th, 1606. I find by the register that he had two
more wives besides Elizabeth mentioned in the inscription ;
his second was the lady Trapps ; third, . . .

Memorandum his house (which is a very faire one),
which is neer the church, is still remayning untoucht by
the fire. In the parlour windowe are scutchions of his
family, which gett. There now lives Mr. Lucy ᵃ, a great
merchant.

He was sheriff of the citie of London anno Domini
⟨1584⟩, reginae Elizabethae 26 ; he was Lord Mayor of
the city of London anno Domini ⟨1596⟩, reginae Elizabethae 38—Sir Thomas Skinner served one part and
Sir Henry Billingsley the other :—Baker's Chronicle,
reigne queen Elizabeth.

** Out of the visitation in the great booke ᵇ of Wilts,
Dorset, and Somerset :—

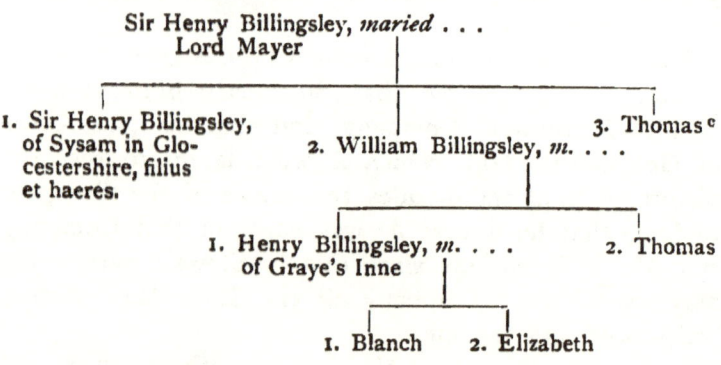

* MS. Aubr. 8, fol. 90.

ᵃ Anthony Wood notes ' Luce, in
vol. i, p. . . .' i.e. MS. Aubr. 6, fol.
35ᵛ, *ut supra*, p. 100.

** MS. Aubr. 8, fol. 89ᵛ.

ᵇ In the library of the College
of Arms.

ᶜ Aubrey notes here :—' Quaere if
this Thomas was not Sir Thomas
Billingsley, the famous horseman ?' :
see *supra*, p. 100.

* Sir Henry Billingsley⟨'s life is⟩ already donne[a]. Friar Whitehead [2], of Austin Friars (now Wadham College), did instruct him. He kept him at his house and there I thinke he dyed.

Notes.

[1] Aubrey gives in colour this very elaborate coat :—'quarterly in the 1 and 4, gules, a fleur-de-lys or, a canton of the second ; in the 2, . . ., on a cross between four lions rampant 5 mullets . . .; in the 3, per saltire or and azure two birds (? martlets) ; *impaling*, quarterly, in the 1 and 4, azure 2 lions passant in pale or; in the 2, or, a fess sable, 2 mullets in chief gules ; in the 3, barry of six argent and gules a bend sable and a canton gules.'

[2] See Clark's Wood's *City of Oxford*, ii. 454, 471. It is suggested that Billingsley in his Euclid published Whitehead's papers as his own.

Martin Billingsley.

** Mr. Martin Billingsley (captain ⟨Edward⟩ Shirburne knew him) was a writing master in London. He printed an excellent copie-booke (quaere if he descended from this[b]) : vide his scutcheon[c] above his picture before his booke.

*** Martin Billingsley, who made the copie booke, 1623, port.[d] ut in margine, '. . . , a cross between 4 lions rampant . . . , 5 mullets . . . on the cross.'

Richard Billingsley.

**** Richard Billingsley[e] scripsit :—

'An Idea of Arithmetick, at first designed for the use of the free-schoole at Thurlow in Suffolk, by R. B. school-master there': stitch't 8vo, 3 sheetes, London, 'printed by J. Flesher, and are to be sold by W. Morden booke-seller in Cambridge, 1655.'

Thomas Billingsley (obiit 167..).

***** Sir Thomas Billingsley was the best horseman in England, and out of England no man exceeded him.

* MS Aubr. 8 (Aubrey's volume of *Lives of the English Mathematicians*), fol. 76.

[a] i. e. written ; viz. in MS. Aubr. 6, *ut supra.*

** MS. Aubr. 6, fol. 35[v].

[b] i.e. from Sir Henry Billingsley.

[c] As given in next paragraph.

*** MS. Aubr. 8, fol. 18.

[d] 'Portavit,' bore to his arms.

**** MS. Aubr. 8, fol. 18.

[e] Called 'Robert,' *supra*, p. 101.

***** MS. Aubr. 6, fol. 67[v].

He taught this[a] earle ⟨of Dorset⟩ and his 30 gentlemen to ride the great horse. He taught this[b] Prince Elector Palatine of the Rhine and his brothers.

He ended his dayes at the countesse of Thanet's (daughter and co-heire of Richard, earl of Dorset) . . . 167-; dyed praying on his knees.

John Birkenhead (1615–1679).

* Sir John Birkenhead, knight, was borne at Nantwych[c] in Cheshire. His father was a sadler there, and he had a brother a sadler, a trooper in Sir Thomas Ashton's regiment, who was quartered at my father's, who told me so.

He went to Oxford university at . . . old, and was first a servitor of Oriall colledge: vide *Antiq. Oxon.*[d] Mr. Gwin[e], minister of Wilton, was his contemporary there, who told me he wrote an excellent hand, and, in 163[7 or 8] when William Laud, archbishop of Canterbury, was last there, he had occasion to have some things well transcribed, and this Birkenhead was recommended to him, who performed[f] his businesse so well, that the archbishop recommended him to All Soules' college to be a fellow, and he was accordingly elected[g]. He was scholar enough, and a poet.

After Edgehill fight, when King Charles I first had his court at Oxford, he was pitched upon as one fitt to write the Newes, which Oxford Newes was called *Mercurius Aulicus*, which he writt wittily enough, till the surrender of the towne (which was June 24, 1646). He left a collection of all his *Mercurius Aulicus's* and all his other pamphletts, which his executors (Sir Richard Mason and Sir Muddiford Bramston) were ordered by the king to give to the Archbishop of Canterbury's library.

[a] i.e. Richard Sackville, 5th earl; obiit 1677.

[b] i.e. Charles Louis, Elector Palatine 1648–80; his brothers were Prince Rupert and Prince Maurice.

* MS. Aubr. 6, fol. 85.

[c] Anthony Wood corrects this to 'Northwich.'

[d] i.e. Anthony Wood's *Hist. et Antiq. Univ. Oxon.*, 1674. Birkenhead became servitor at Oriel in 1632, aged 15.

[e] Philip Gwyn, matr. at Oriel in 1634.

[f] Subst. for 'dischardged.'

[g] In 1639.

After the surrender of Oxford, he was putt out of his fellowship by the Visitors, and was faine to shift for himselfe as well as he could. Most part of his time he spent at London, where he mett with severall persons of quality that loved his company, and made much of him.

He went over into France, where he stayed some time, I thinke not long. He received grace there from the dutches of Newcastle, I remember he tolde me.

He gott many a fourty shillings (I beleeve) by pamphletts, such as that of 'Col. Pride,' and 'The Last Will and Testament of Philip earle of Pembroke,' &c.

At the restauration of his majestie he was made Master of the Facultees, and afterwards one of the Masters of Requests. He was exceedingly confident ᵃ, witty, not very gratefull to his benefactors, would lye damnably. He was of midling stature, great goggli eies, not of a sweet aspect.

He was chosen a burghes of Parliament at Wilton in Wiltshire, anno Domini 166⟨1⟩, i.e. of the King's long parliament. Anno 167⟨9⟩ upon the choosing of *this* Parliament ᵇ, he went downe to be elected, and at Salisbury heard * how he was scorned and mocked at Wilton (whither he was goeing) and called *Pensioner*, etc.—

[Vendidit hic auro patriam, dominumque potentem
Imposuit; leges fixit pretio atque refixit.

VIRG. *Aeneid*, lib. vi. 621.

—This was Curio: vide Servium de hoc]—he went not to the borough where he intended to stand; but returned to London, and tooke it so to heart that he insensibly decayed and pined away; and so, December . . . †, 1679, dyed at his lodgeings in Whitehall, and was buried Saturday, December 6, in St. Martyn's churchyard ‡ in-the-Fields, neer the church, according to his will and testament. His executors intend to sett up an inscription for him against the church wall.

† quaere Anthony Wood to whom I writt the day of his death, which as I remember was the same day that Mr. Hobbes died.
‡ His reason ᵉ was because he sayd they removed the bodies out of the church.

ᵃ Subst. for 'bold': Aubrey writes here κυνώπης, in explanation.

ᵇ MS. Aubr. 6 was written in

Feb. 16⁷⁸/₇₉.

* MS. Aubr. 6, fol. 85ᵛ.

ᵉ For choosing a grave in the

He had the art of locall memory; and his topiques were the chambers, &c., in All Soules colledge (about 100), so that for 100 errands, &c., he would easily remember.

* He was created Dr. of LL. ; had been with the king [a].

His library was sold to Sir Robert Atkins for 200 *li*. His MSS. (chiefly copies of records) for 900 *li*.

Henry Birkhead (1617–1696).

** My old acquaintance, Dr. Henry Birkhed, formerly fellow of your college [b] (but first was commoner of Trinity College Oxon) was an universally ⟨belove⟩d man.

He had his schoole education under Mr. Farnary [c] and ⟨was his⟩ beloved disciple.

He died at the Bird-cage (at his sister's, Mris Knight, the famous singer) in St. James's parke, ⟨on⟩ Michaelmas-eve 1696, aged about 80.

He was borne in London ⟨at the⟩ Paul-head tavern (which his father kept) in Paule's chaine ⟨in⟩ St. Paul's church-yard anno 1617, baptized the 25 of September. John Gadbury haz his nativity from him.

I will aske his sister (Mris Knight) for a very ingeniose diatribe that he wrote on Martialis epigram. lib. ⟨xi. 94. 8⟩,

> jura, verpe, per Anchialum,

which he haz cleared beyond his master Farnaby, Scaliger, or any other. 'Scaliger,' he sayd, 'speakes the truth, but not the whole truth.' 'Tis pity it should be lost, and I would reposit it in the Museum.

I gave my Holyoke's dictionary to the Museum. Pray looke on the blank leaves at the end of it, and you will find a thundering copie of verses that he gave me, in the praise of this king [d] of France. Now he is dead, it may be look't-upon.

---

churchyard, and not, as was usual with persons of substance, in the church.

* MS. Aubr. 6, fol. 85.

[a] These words, added (? by Wood) in pencil, probably give the reason assigned in the royal mandate recommending him for D.C.L.

** Aubrey in MS. Tanner 24, fol. 159: Nov. 21, 1696.

[b] i. e. All Souls: the letter is written to Thomas Tanner.

[c] Thomas Farnaby, *ut infra*.

[d] Louis XIV.

Richard Blackbourne (1652–17..?).

* Richard Blackburne, Londinensis, was of Trinity College, Cambridge, M.A. Tooke his M.D. degree at Leyden about 5 or 6 yeares since. He practises but little; studies much. A generall scholar, prodigious memorie, sound judgment; but 30 yeares old now.

John Blagrave (1550–1611).

In MS. Aubr. 8 (Aubrey's *Lives of English Mathematic:ans*), fol. 76, ' Mr. John Blagrave of Reding ' is noted as a life to be written, and the coat is given in trick ' or, on a bend sable, 3 greaves argent.' In the Index (fol. 8) at the beginning of the same volume he is noted :— John Blagrave of Reding, vide his will, quaere Mr. Morden.'

Robert Blake (1599–1657).

** . . . Blake, admirall, was borne at . . . . in com. Somerset ; was ª of Albon-hall, in Oxford. He was there a young man of strong body, and good parts. He was an early riser and studyed well, but also tooke his robust pleasures of fishing, fowling, &c. He would steale swannes—from H. Norborne, B.D., his contemporary there ᵇ.

He served in the House of Commons for . . . .ᶜ Anno Domini ⟨1649⟩ he was made admirall. He did the greatest actions at sea that ever were done, viz., . . .

. . . Blake obiit anno Domini ⟨1657⟩ and was buried in King Henry 7th's chapell ; but upon the returne of the king, his body was taken up again and removed by Mr. Wells' occasion, and where it is now, I know not. Quaere Mr. Wells of Bridgewater.

Vide Diurnalls, and Rushworth's History ; vide Anthony Wood's *Hist.* ⟨*et Antiq. Oxon.*⟩.

---

* Aubrey in MS. Wood, F. 39, fol. 354ᵛ : June 21, 1681.

** MS. Aubr. 8, fol. 33.

ª Matric. at St. Alban Hall Jan. 26, 161⅘, aged 17; took B.A. from Wadham Feb. 10, 161⅘.

ᵇ At St. Alban Hall. Norborne matric. in Oct. 1620; and took B.D. in 163⅞.

ᶜ Bridgewater, 1640.

Sir Henry Blount (1602–1682).

* Sir Henry Blount, Tittinghanger, natus Dec. 15, 1602, 9[h] P.M.

** Sir Henry Blount obiit 9th Oct. last [a] in the morning.

*** Sir Henry Blount[1], knight :—he was borne (I presume) at Tittinghanger in the countie of Hertford. It was heretofore the summer seate of the Lord Abbot of St. Alban's.

He was of Trinity College in Oxford[b], where was a great acquaintance[c] between him and Mr. Francis Potter. He stayed there about ⟨four⟩ yeares. From thence he went to Grayes Inne, where he stayd . . . . and then sold his chamber there to Mr. Thomas Bonham[2] (the poet) and travelled—voyage into the Levant. May 7, 1634, he embarqued at Venice for Constantinople : vide his *Voyage into the Levant*, printed London 16—, in 4to. He returned . . .

He was pretty wild when young, especially addicted to common wenches. He was a 2d brother.

He was a gentleman pensioner to King Charles I, on whom he wayted (as it was his turne) to Yorke (when the King deserted the Parliament); was with him at Edge-hill fight; came with him to Oxford; and so returned to London ; walkt[d] into Westminster hall with his sword by his side; the Parliamentarians all stared upon him as a *Cavaleer*, knowing that he had been with the King: was called before the House of Commons, where he remonstrated to them he did but his duty, and so they acquitted him.

In these dayes he dined most commonly at the Heycock's[e] ordinary, neer the Pallzgrave-head taverne, in the Strand, which was much frequented by Parliament-men and gallants. One time colonel Betridge being there

* MS. Aubr. 23, fol. 121.

** MS. Aubr. 23, a slip at fol. 103[v].

[a] i.e. Oct. 1682.

*** MS. Aubr. 6, fol. 102.

[b] Matric. June 30, 1615 ; B.A. June 18, 1618.

[c] Subst. for ' friendship.'

[d] Dupl. with ' came.'

[e] Dupl. with ' combe-makers.'

(one* of the handsomest men about the towne) and bragged much how the woemen loved him; Sir H. Blount did lay a wager of . . . . with him that let them two goe together to a bordello; he only (without money) with his handsome person, and Sir Henry with a xx*s.* piece on his bald crowne, that the wenches should choose Sir Henry before Betridge; and Sir H. won the wager. E⟨dmund⟩ W⟨yld⟩, esq., was one of the witnesses.

Memorandum :—there was about 164.. a pamphlet (writt by Henry Nevill, esq., ἀνονύμως) called *The Parliament of Ladies*, 3 or 4 sheets in 4to, wherin Sir Henry Blount was first to be called to the barre for spreading abroad that abominable and dangerous doctrine that it was far cheaper and safer to lye with common wenches[b] then with ladies of quality[c].

☞ His estate left him by his father was 500 *li.* per annum, which he sold to . . . . (quaere) for an annuitie of 1000 *li.* per annum in anno Domini 16..; and since his elder brother dyed.

Anno Domini 165⟨½⟩ he was made one of the comittee for regulating the lawes. He was severe against tythes, and for the abolishing them, and that every minister should have 100 *li.* per annum and no more.

Since he was . . . year old he dranke nothing but water or coffee. 1647 or therabout, he maryed to Mris [Hester[d]] Wase, [daughter of Christopher Wase[d]], who dyed 1679; by whom he haz two sonnes, ingeniose young gentlemen. Charles Blount (his second son) hath writt *Anima Mundi*, 8vo, 167⟨9⟩ (burnt by order of the bishop of London) and of *Sacrifices*, 8vo.

I remember twenty yeares since he inveighed much against sending youths to the universities—quaere if his sons there—because they learnt there to be debaucht; and that the learning that they learned there* they were to

---

* Dupl. with 'who was an extra-ordinary handsome man.'
  b Subst. for 'whores.'
  c Dupl. with 'honour.'

d The words in square brackets are insertions by Anthony Wood.
  * MS. Aubr. 6, fol. 102ᵛ.

unlearne againe, as a man that is buttond or laced too hard, must unbutton before he can be at his ease. Drunkennesse he much exclaimed against, but he allowed wenching. When coffee first came-in he was a great upholder of it, and hath ever since been a constant frequenter of coffee houses, especially Mr. . . . Farre at the Rainbowe by Inner Temple Gate, and lately John's coffee house in Fuller's rents.

☞ The first coffee house in London †
† And the next was Mr. Farr's a barber, which was set up in anno . . . was in St. Michael's Alley in Cornehill, opposite to the Church; which was sett up by one . . . Bowman (coachman to Mr. Hodges, a Turkey merchant, who putt him upon it) in or about the yeare 1652. 'Twas about 4 yeares before any other was sett up, and that was by Mr. Far. Jonathan Paynter, opposite to St. Michael's Church, was the first apprentice to the trade, viz. to Bowman. Memorandum :—the Bagneo, in Newgate Street, was built and first opened in Decemb. 1679 : built by . . . . (Turkish merchants).

He is a gentleman of a very clear judgement, great experience, much contemplation, not of very much reading, of great foresight into government. His conversation is admirable. When he was young, he was a great collector of bookes, as his sonne is now.

He was heretofore a great *shammer*, i.e. one that tells falsities not to doe any body any injury, but to impose on their understanding :—e. g. at Mr. Farre's ; that at an inne (nameing the signe) in St. Alban's, the inkeeper had made a hogs-trough of a free-stone coffin ; but the pigges, after that, grew leane, dancing and skipping, and would run up on the topps of the houses like goates. Two young gentlemen that heard Sir H. tell this *sham* so gravely, rode the next day to St. Alban's to enquire : comeing there, nobody had heard of any such thing, 'twas altogether false. The next night as soon as the⟨y⟩ allighted, they came to the Rainbowe and found Sir H., looked louringly on him, and told him they wonderd he was not ashamed to tell such storys as, &c., 'Why, gentlemen,' (sayd Sir H.) 'have you been there to make enquiry?' 'Yea,' sayd they. 'Why truly, gentlemen,' sayd Sir H. 'I heard you tell strange things that I knew to be false. I would not have gonne over the threshold of the dore to have found you in a lye:' at which all the company laught at the two young gentlemen.

He was wont to say that he did not care to have his servants goe to church, for there servants infected one another to goe to the alehouse and learne debauchery; but he did bid them goe to see the executions at Tyburne, which worke more upon them then all the oratory in the sermons.

His motto over his printed picture is that which I have many yeares ago heard him speake of, viz.:—*Loquendum est cum vulgo, sentiendum cum sapientibus.*

He is now (1680) neer or altogether 80 yeares, his intellectualls good still, and body pretty strong.

This last weeke[a] of Sept. 1682, he was taken very ill at London, and his feet swelled; and removed to Titting-hanger.

Notes.

[1] Aubrey gives in colours the coats:—'or, 2 bars nebulé sable [Blount]'; and 'or, 2 bars nebulé sable [Blount]; impaling, barry of six or and gules [Wase].' Also the references (a) 'vide Anthony Wood's ⟨*Hist. et*⟩ *Antiq. Oxon.*'; (b) 'vide Heralds' Office.' Aubrey, in MS. Wood F. 39, writing on April 7, 1673, says of Blount, 'His father was Sir Thomas Pope Blount, and his grandmother (as I remember I have heard Dr. Hannibal Potter say) was our founder's daughter.'

[2] Aubrey, in MS. Wood F. 39, fol. 199, speaks of him as 'Tom Bonham, of Essex, that haz made many a good song and epitaph—

When the shrill scirocco blowes.'

Edmund Bonner (1495–1569).

[a] Mr. Steevens[b], . . . whom I mett lately accidentally, informed me thus:—that bishop Bonner was of Broadgates hall; that he came thither a poor boy, and was at first a skullion boy in the kitchin, afterwards became a servitor, and so by his industry raysed to what he was.

[a] A note added after the preceding life had been written.

[a] Aubrey in MS. Wood, F. 39, fol.

273[v]: May 30, 1674.

[b] See *sub nomine*, Thomas Stephens.

When he came to his greatnes, in acknowledgement from whence he had his rise, he gave [a] to the kitchin there a great brasse-pott, called Bonner's pott, which was taken away in the parliament time. He has shewed the pott to me, I remember. It was the biggest, perhaps, in Oxford : quaere the old cooke how much it contayned.

John Booker (160½–1667).

* John Booker, astrologer, natus Manchester, March 23, 1601, 20[h] 10′ P. M.

James Bovey (1622–16..).

** James Bovey[1] borne at London May 7th, 1622, 6 a clock in the morning [b].

James Bovey, esq., was the youngest son of Andrew Bovey, merchant, cash-keeper to Sir Peter Vanore, in London.

He was borne in the middle of Mincing Lane, in the parish of Saint Dunstan's in the East, London, anno 1622, May 7th, at six a clock in the morning. Went to schoole at Mercers Chapell, under Mr. Augur. At 9 sent into the Lowe Countreys ; then returned, and perfected himselfe in the Latin and Greeke. ⟨At⟩ 14, travelled into France and Italie, Switzerland, Germany, and the Lowe Countreys. Returned into England at 19 ; then lived with one Hoste, a banquier, 8 yeares, was his cashier 8 or 9 yeares. Then traded for himselfe (27) till he was 31 ; then maried the only daughter of William de Vischer, a merchant ; lived 18 yeares with her, then continued single. Left off trade at 32, and retired to a countrey life, by reason of his indisposition, the ayre of the citie not agreing with him. Then in these retirements he wrote *Active* [c] *Philosophy*, (a thing not donne before) wherin are enumerated all the Arts and Tricks practised in Negotiation. and how they were to be ballanced by counter-prudentiall rules.

---

[a] Anthony Wood notes here, 'false'; i.e. having inquired at Pembroke (in 1674), he found no trace of this tradition.

* MS. Aubr. 23, fol. 121.
** MS. Aubr. 7, fol. 12.
[b] The horoscope is 1 ft blank.
[c] Dupl. with '*Negotiative*.'

Whilest he lived with Mr. Hoste, he kept the cash of the ambassadors of Spaine that were here; and of the farmers, called by them *Assentistes*, that did furnish the Spanish and Imperiall armies of the Low-Countreys and Germany; and also many other great cashes, as of Sir Theodore Mayern, etc.; his dealing being altogether in money-matters: by which meanes he became acquainted with the ministers of state both here and abroad.

When he was abroad, his chiefe employment was to observe the affaires of state and their judicatures, and to take the politique surveys in the countreys he travelled thorough, more especially in relation to trade. He speakes [a] the Low-Dutch, High-Dutch, French, Italian, Spanish and Lingua Franco, and Latin, besides his owne.

When he retired from businesse he studied the Lawe-Merchant, and admitted himselfe of the Inner Temple, London, about 1660. His judgment haz been taken in most of the great causes of his time in points concerning the Lawe-Merchant. As to his person he is about 5 foot high, slender [b], strait, haire exceeding black and curling at the end, a dark hazell [c] eie, of a midling size, but the most sprightly that I have beheld. Browes and beard of the colour as his haire. A person of great temperance, and deepe thoughts, and a working head, never idle. From [d] 14 he had a candle burning by him all night, with pen, inke, and paper, to write downe thoughts as they came into his head; that so he might not loose a thought. Was ever a great lover of Naturall Philosophie. His whole life has been perplex't in lawe-suites, (which haz made him expert in humane affaires), in which he alwaies over-came. He had many lawe-suites with powerfull adversaries; one lasted 18 yeares. Red-haired men never had any kindnesse for him. He used to say :—

In rufa pelle non est animus sine felle.

In all his travells he was never robbed.

---

[a] Subst. for ' understands.'
[b] Subst. for ' spare body.'
[c] Subst. for ' a very black eie.'
[d] Dupl. with ' From his youth he.'

He has one son, and one daughter who resembles him.

From 14 he began to take notice of all prudentiall rules as came in his way, and wrote them downe, and so continued till this day, Sept. 28, 1680, being now in his 59th yeare.

For his health he never had it very well, but indifferently, alwaies a weake stomach, which proceeded from the agitation of the braine.   His dyet was always fine diet: much chicken ª.

He wrote a Table of all the Exchanges in Europe.

* He hath writt (which is in his custodie, and which I have seen, and many of them read) these treatises, viz.

1. The Characters, or Index Rerum ⟨etc.ᵇ⟩

** A Catalogue of the treatises written of Active Philosophy by James Bovey, of the Inner Temple, esquire, 1677.

1. The Characters, or Index Rerum : in 4 tomes.
2. The Introduction to Active Philosophy.
3. The Art of Building a Man : or Education.
4. The Art of Conversation.
5. The Art of Complyance.
6. The Art of Governing the Tongue.
7. The Art of Governing the Penn.
8. The Government of Action.
9. The Government of Resolution.
10. The Government of Reputation.
11. The Government of Power : in 2 tomes.
12. The Government of Servients.
13. The Government of Subserviency.
14. The Government of Friendshipp.
15. The Government of Enmities.
16. The Government of Law-suites.
17. The Art of Gaining Wealth.

ª Dupl. with 'fowle.'
* MS. Aubr. 7, fol. 12ᵛ.
ᵇ Aubrey, on fol. 12ᵛ, gives the full list of 32 titles copied (with some slight changes of spelling, etc.) from Bovey's own list, given *infra*.
** MS. Aubr. 7, fol. 13ᵛ, Bovey's autograph.

18. The Art of Buying and Selling ᵃ.

19. The Art of Preserving Wealth.

20. The Art of Expending Wealth.

21. The Government of Secresy.

22. The Government of Amor Conjugalis : in 2 tomes.

23. Of Amor Concupiscentiae.

24. The Government of Felicity.

25. The Lives of Atticus, Sejanus, Augustus.

26. The Causes of the Diseases of the Mind.

27. The Cures of the Mind, vizᵗ. Passions, Diseases, Vices, Errours, Defects.

28. The Art of Discerning of Men.

29. The Art of Discerning a Man's selfe.

30. Religion from Reason : in 3 tomes.

31. The Life of Cum-fu-zu, soe farr wrote by J. B.

32. The Life of Mahomett, wrot by Sir Walter Raleigh's papers, with some small addition for methodizing the same.

* I have desired him to give these MSS. to the library of the Royal Society.

He made it his businesse ᵇ to advance the trade of England, and many men have printed his conceptions.

Note.

[1] Aubrey gives in trick the coat :—' ermine, on a bend sable cottised gules, five besants, between 2 eagles proper;' and an impression of Bovey's seal with the same coat.

Richard Boyle, earl of Cork (1566–1643).

** Earl of Corke :—vide countesse of Warwick's funerall sermon, 2 or 3 shops ᶜ within Paul's churchyard.

*** Earl of Corke [1]—Thomas, earl of Strafford made him disgorge 1500 *li.* per annum, which he restored to the church—⟨from⟩ Mr. . . . Anderson.

Earl of Corke bought of captaine Horsey *fourtie plough-*

ᵃ No. 18 is no. 19 in Aubrey's copy; no. 19 is no. 18 in Aubrey's copy.

ᵃ MS. Aubr. 7, fol. 12ᵛ.

ᵇ 'From a child' followed : scored out.

** MS. Aubr. 8, fol. 11ᵛ.

ᶜ i.e. Aubrey remembered seeing the sermon in a shop there. He went and found it, and has excerpts *infra*, p. 116.

*** MS. Aubr. 8 fol. 12.

lands in Ireland for fourtie pounds. (A. Ettrick assures me, ' I say againe fourtie ploughlands.')

The queen gave Lismore to Sir Walter Raleigh, and . . . to Sir John Anderson, etc. to etc., eâ intentione to plant them, which they did not ; and were not planted till since the last rebellion—quaere Mr. Anderson, who sayes that Ireland could not be secure till it was enough peopled with English.

My lady Petty sayes he had a wife or two before, and that he maried Mris. Fenton[2] without her father's consent— (quaere Secretary Fenton's Christian name[3]).

* . . . Boyle, the first earle of Corke :—the countesse of Thanet, his great-grand-daughter, daughter to this earle of Corke and Burlington, haz told me that her father has a booke in folio—thick—of her grandfather's writing, ⟨giving⟩ the place, day, and hour of birth, and by what steps, wayes, and degrees he came to his greatnes. Which she will doe her endeavour to gett me an extract of it, but it is in Ireland and (I thinke) must be kept there, and is an heir-loome to the family.

⟨*Excerpts from Anthony Walker's Sermon.*⟩

** Of Richard Boyle, first earl of Corke, and his seventh daughter, Mary, countess of Warwick.

'THE VIRTUOUS WOMAN FOUND : Being a Sermon preached at Felsted, in Essex, at the Funerall of the most excellent and religious lady, the Right honourable MARY Countesse Dowager of Warwick. By Anthony Walker, D.D. rector of Fyfield, in the sayd countie. The 2d Edition corrected. Printed at London, for Nath. Ranew, at the King's Arms, in St. Paul's Church-yard, 1680.' (The Epistle dedicatory is dated May 27, 1678.)

Pag. 44.—' She was truly excellent and great in all respects: great in the honour of her birth, being born a lady and a virtuosa both ; seventh daughter of that eminently honourable, Richard, the first earle of Cork ; who being born a private gentleman, and younger brother of a younger brother, to no other heritage than is expressed in the device and motto, which his humble gratitude inscribed on all the palaces he built,

God's Providence, mine Inheritance ;

by that Providence, and his diligent and wise industry, raised such an honour and estate, and left such a familie, as never any subject of these three kingdomes did, and that with so unspotted a reputation of integrity that the most invidious scrutiny could find no blott, though it winnowed all the methods of his rising most severely, which our good lady hath often told me with great content and satisfaction.

This noble lord, by his prudent and pious consort, no lesse an ornament and honour to their descendants than himself, was blessed with five sonnes, (of which he lived to see four lords and peeres of the kingdome of Ireland, * and a fifth, more than these titles speak, a soveraigne and peerlesse in a larger province,—that of universall nature, subdued and made obsequious to his inquisitive mind), and eight daughters. And that you may remark how all things were extraordinary in this great personage, it will, I hope, be neither unpleasant, nor impertinent, to add a short story I had from our lady's own mouth :—Master Boyl, after earle of Cork (who was then a widdower), came one morning to waite on Sir Jeofry Fenton, at that time a great officer † of state in that kingdome of Ireland, who being ingaged in business, and not knowing who it was who desired to speake with him, a while delayed him access ; which time he spent pleasantly with his young daughter in her nurse's arms. But when Sir Jeoffry came, and saw whom he had made stay somewhat too long, he civilly excused it. But master Boyl replied, he had been very well entertayned; and spent his time much to his satisfaction, in courting his daughter, if he might obtaine the honour to be accepted for his son-in-lawe. At which Sir Jeoffry, smiling (to hear one who had been formerly married, move for a wife carried in arms, and under two years old,) asked him if he would stay for her? To which he frankly answered him he would, and Sir Jeoffry as generously promised him he should then have his consent. And they both kept their words honourably. And by this virtuous lady he had thirteen children, ten of which he lived to see honourably married, and died a grandfather by the youngest of them.

† Secretary of Estate.

Nor did she derive less honour from the collateral, than the descending line, being sister by soul and genius, as well as bloud, to these great personages, whose illustrious, unspotted, and resplendent honour and virtue, and whose usefull learning and accurate pens, may attone and ** expiate, as well as shame, the scandalous blemishes of a debauched, and the many impertinencies of a scribling, age :—

* MS. Aubr. 7, fol. 10ᵛ.   ** MS. Aubr. 7, fol. 11.

(1), Richard, the truly right honourable, loyal, wise, and virtuous, earl of Burlington and Cork, whose life is his fairest and most laudable character ;

(2), the right honourable Roger earle of Orery, that great poet, great statesman, great soldier, and great every-thing which merits the name of great or good ;

(3), Francis lord Shannon, whose *Pocket Pistol*, as he stiles his book, may make as wide breaches in the walls of the Capitol, as many canons ;

(4), and that honourable and well known name Robert Boyl, esquier, that profound philosopher, accomplished humanist, and excellent divine, I had almost sayd lay-bishop, as one hath stiled Sir Henry Savil; whose works alone may make a librarie †.

† Why does he not mention ... lord Killimeke⁴; who was slain at the great battell of Liskarrill, in Ireland ?

The female branches also (if it be lawfull so to call them whose virtues were so masculine, souls knowing no difference of sex) by their honours and graces (by mutuall reflections) gave, and received lustre, to, and from, her :—

the eldest of which, the lady Alice, was married to the lord Baramore ;

the second, the lady Sarah, to the lord Digby, of Ireland ;

the third, the lady Laetitia, to the eldest son of the lord Goring, who died earle of Norwich ;

the fourth, the lady Joan, to the earle of Kildare, not only primier earle of Ireland, but the *ancientest house* in Christendome of that degree, the present earle being the six and twentieth, or the seaven and twentieth, of lineal descent : and, as I have heard, it was that great antiquary King Charles the First his observation, that the three ancientest families of Europe for nobility, were the *Veres* in England, earls of Oxford, and the *Fitz-Geralds* in Ireland, earls of Kildare, and *Momorancy* in France : 'tis observable * that the present earle of Kildare is a mixture of blood of Fitz-Geralds and Veres ;

the fifth, the lady Katharine, who was married to the lord viscount Ranelaugh ‡, and mother to the present generous earle of Ranelaugh, of which family I could have added an eminent remark, I meet with in Fuller's "Worthies ;"

‡ (Arthur) Jones.

this lady's character is so signalized by her known merit among all persons of honour, that as I need not, so I dare not, attempt beyond this one word—she was our lady's *Friend-Sister* ;

the sixth, the lady Dorothy Loftus ;

the seaventh, (the number of perfection) which shutt-up and crown'd this noble train (for the eighth, the lady Margaret, died unmaried), was our excellent lady Mary, married to Charles, earle of Warwick ; of whom, if I should use the language of my text, I should neither

* MS. Aubr. 7, fol. 11ᵛ.

despair their pardon, nor fear the reproach of rudeness—*Many daughters*, all his daughters, *did virtuously but thou*—PROV. xxxi. 29, 30, 31.

——————— But shee † needed neither borrowed shades, nor reflexive lights, to set her off, being personally great in all naturall endowments and accomplishments of soul and body, wisdome, beautie, favour, and virtue ;

† Mary, countess of Warwick.

great by her tongue, for never woman used one better, speaking so gracefully, promptly, discreetly, pertinently, holily, that I have often admired the edifying words that proceeded from her mouth ;

great by her pen, as you may (*ex pede Herculem*) discover by that little ‡ tast of it the world hath been happy in, the hasty fruit of one or two interrupted houres after supper, which she professed to me, with a little regret, when she was surprised with it's sliding into the world without her knowledge, or allowance, and wholly beside her expectation ;

‡ Her ladyship's *Pious Meditations.*

great by being the greatest mistresse and promotress, not to say the foundress and inventress, of a new science—the art of obliging ; in which she attain'd that sovereign perfection, that she reigned over all their hearts with whom she did converse ;

great in her nobleness of living and hospitality ;

great in the unparallelld sincerity of constant, faithfull, condescending friendship, and for that law of kindness which dwelt in her lips and heart ;

great in her dexterity of management ;

great in her quick apprehension of the difficulties of her affaires, and where the stress and pinch lay, to untie the knot, and loose and ease them ;

great in the conquest of herselfe ;

great in a thousand things beside, which the world admires as such : but she despised them all, and counted them but loss and dung in comparison of the feare of God, and the excellency of the knowledge of Christ Jesus.'

Notes.

[1] Aubrey gives in trick the coat :—' per bend crenellée argent and gules [Boyle]; impaling, . . ., a cross vert between 4 fleur de lys . . . [Fenton],' surmounted by an earl's coronet.

A leaf containing an earlier draft of this life (as shown by the coat tricked in the inner margin) has been cut out between fol. 14 and fol. 15 of MS. Aubr. 6. The excision was made by Aubrey himself, a line being drawn by him across the excision from fol. 14ᵛ to fol. 15, to mark the transposition of a passage. The reason for the cutting out of this leaf is suggested in a letter of Aubrey to Anthony Wood (MS. Wood F. 39, fol. 360, July 14, 1681), where he says his 'Lives' contain 'severe touches on the earl of Corke, Dr. Wallis, etc.' In the margin of the excised leaf a note, given on the authority of 'Mr. A. E.' i. e. Anthony Ettrick, seems to speak of amours and bastards of the earl.

² Catherine Fenton, daughter of Sir Geoffrey Fenton, Secretary of State for Ireland 1581–1603.

³ Anthony Wood, in answer to this query, suggests :—' Jeffrey, quaere.'

⁴ Lewis Boyle, second son of Richard, first earl of Cork, created viscount Boyle of Kynalmeaky, 162⁵⁄₆.

Robert Boyle (162⁶⁄₇–1691).

* Mr. Robert Boyle ;—vide Oliver Hill's . . . , where he is accused of grosse plagiarisme. Dr. ⟨Robert⟩ Wood went to schoole with him at Eaton Colledge.

** Mr. R. Boyle, when a boy at Eaton ⟨was⟩ verie sickly and pale—from Dr. ⟨Robert⟩ Wood, who was his schoole-fellow.

*** The honourable Robert Boyle¹ esq., the ⟨fifth⟩ son of Richard Boyle, the first earle of Corke, was borne at Lismor† in the county of Corke, the ⟨25⟩ day of ⟨January⟩ anno ⟨162⁶⁄₇⟩.

† It was anciently an University, and a great towne or city. It had twenty churches. 'Twas the seate of king John.— From Elizabeth, countesse of Thanet.

He was nursed by an Irish nurse, after the Irish manner, wher they putt the child into a pendulous satchell (insted of a cradle), with a slitt for the child's head to peepe out.

He learn't his Latin . . . . . Went to the university of Leyden. Travelled France, Italy, Switzerland. I have oftentimes heard him say that after he had seen the antiquities and architecture of Rome, he esteemed none ᵃ any where els.

He speakes Latin very well, and very readily, as most men I have mett with. I have heard him say that when he was young, he read over Cowper's dictionary : wherin I thinke he did very well, and I beleeve he is much beholding to him for his mastership of that language.

His father in his will, when he comes to the settlement and provision for his son Robert, thus,—

Item, to my son Robert, whom I beseech God to blesse with a particular blessing, I bequeath, &c.

Mr. R. H.ᵇ, who has seen the rentall, sayes it was 3000 *li.*

* MS. Aubr. 8, fol. 12ᵛ.
** MS. Aubr. 8, fol. 6ᵛ.
*** MS. Aubr. 6, fol. 16ᵛ.

ᵃ Subst. for ' cared not for.'
ᵇ Probably Robert Hooke.

per annum : the greatst part is in Ireland. His father left him the mannor of Stalbridge in com. Dorset, where is a great freestone house ; it was forfeited by the earle of Castlehaven.

He is very tall (about six foot high) and streight, very temperate, and vertuouse, and frugall : a batcheler ; keepes a coach ; sojournes with his sister, the lady Ranulagh. His greatest delight is chymistrey. He haz at his sister's a noble laboratory, and severall servants (prentices to him) to looke to it. He is charitable to ingeniose men that are in want, and foreigne chymists have had large proofe of his bountie, for he will not spare for cost to gett any rare secret. At his owne costs and chardges he gott translated and printed the New Testament in Arabique [2], to send into the Mahometan countreys. He has not only a high renowne in England, but abroad ; and when foreigners come to hither, 'tis one of their curiosities to make him a visit.

Notes.

[1] Aubrey gives in colours the Boyle coat (*supra*, p. 119), with a mullet gules for difference. Anthony Wood adds the reference :—'see in the first sheet of the second part,' i. e. of MS. Aubr. 7, viz. the excerpts *supra* from Anthony Walker's sermon.

[2] The Gospels and Acts in Malay (in Arabic character), Oxford, 1677.

William Brereton, 3rd baron, (1631–1680).

* William, lord Brereton, obiit March 17, 1680 [a] ; buried at St. Martin's-in-the-fields : scripsit *Origines Moriens* in Latin verse.

** William, lord Brereton [1] of ⟨Leighlin⟩ :—this vertuous and learned lord (who was my most honoured and obligeing friend) was educated at Breda, by John Pell, D.D., then Math. Professor there of the Prince of Orange's 'ilustrious schoole.' Sir George Goring, earl of Norwich (who was my lord's grandfather), did send for him over, where the ⟨Doctor⟩ (then Mr. John Pell) tooke great care of him, and made him a very good Algebrist.

* MS. Aubr. 7, fol. 5.   [a] 16⅞, in this case.

** MS. Aubr. 8, fol. 33.

He hath wrote a poem called *Origines Moriens*, a MS.

Obiit March 17, 16$\frac{79}{80}$, London, and is buried at St Martin's church in the fields.

He was an excellent musitian, and also a good composer.

Note.

[1] Anthony Wood adds the reference 'quaere in Coll. Exon.' Wood seems to have thought that Sir William Brereton of Honford in Cheshire (an officer in the Parliamentary army, mentioned in the *Athenae*) might be found among the Exeter College matriculations and might be connected with this peer's family.

Edward Brerewood (1565–1613).

* Mr. Edward Brerewood [1] was borne . . .

He was of Brasen-nose College in Oxon. My old cosen Whitney [2], fellow there long since, told me, as I remember, that his father was a citizen of W⟨est⟩ Chester; that (I have now forgot on what occasion, whether he had outrun the exhibition from his father, or what), but he was for some time in straightes in the College; that he went not out of the College gates in a good while, nor (I thinke) out of his chamber, but was in slip-shoes, and wore out his gowne and cloathes on the bord and benches of his chamber, but profited in knowledge wonderfully.

He writ his *Logica*, and . . ., *de meteoris, de ponderibus et nummis* (which he dedicates to his countryman, Lord Chancellor Egerton, who was no doubt his patron).

He was astronomie professor at Gresham College, London, where he died anno 1613, and was buried in Great Saint Helen's chancell: so *Hist. and Antiq. of Oxon.,* lib. 2. pag. 219 b.

'Tis pity I can pick-up no more of him.

Notes.

[1] Anthony Wood added the reference ' vide A. W.'s ⟨*Hist. et*⟩ *Antiq.* '; but scored it out, finding himself anticipated in the text of the notice.

[2] James Whitney, matric. April 19, 1611 at St. Mary Hall, but took his degrees from Brasenose (Clark's *Reg. Univ. Oxon.* II. iii. 334).

* MS. Aubr. 6, fol. 33^v.

Arthur Brett (16.. –1677).

⟨In MS. Aubr. 22 (Aubrey's Collection of Grammars) is a tract of 6 pp.

'A demonstration how the Latine tonge may be learn't'; Lond. 1669; 'by Arthur Bret, M.A. of Ch. Ch. in Oxford and of Westminster Schoole.'⟩

Henry Briggs (1556–163$\frac{0}{1}$).

* Henry Briggs was borne at . . . (vide Anthony Wood's *Oxon. Antiquit.*: quaere his nephew who is beadle to Stationers' Hall; quaere *Vaticinium Carolinum*, an English poem).

He was first of St. John's College in Cambridge. Sir Henry Savill sent for him and made him his geometrie professor. He lived at Merton College in Oxon, where he made the dialls at the buttresses of the east end of the chapell with a bullet for the axis.

He travelled into Scotland to comune with the honourable . . . lord Nepier[1] of Marcheston about making the logarithmicall tables.

☞ Looking one time on the mappe of England he observed that the[a] two rivers, the Thames and that Avon which runnes to Bathe and so to Bristowe, were not far distant, scilicet, about 3 miles—vide the mappe. He sees 'twas but about 25 miles from Oxford; getts a horse and viewes it and found it to be a levell ground and[b] easie to be digged. Then he considered the chardge of cutting between them and the convenience of making a mariage between those rivers which would be of great consequence for cheape and safe carrying of goods between London and Bristow, and though the boates[c] goe slowly and with meanders, yet considering they goe day and night they would be at their journey's end almost as soon as the waggons, which often are overthrowne and liquours spilt and other goods broken. Not long after this he dyed and

---

* MS. Aubr. 6, fol. 47^{v}.
[a] Subst. for 'that the beginnings of the Thames and Avon.'

[b] Dupl. with 'and sappable.'
[c] Dupl. with 'the Bylanders.'

the civill warres brake-out. It happened by good luck that one Mr. Matthewes of Dorset had some acquaintance with this Mr. * Briggs and had heard him discourse of it. He was an honest simple man, and had runne out of his estate and this project did much run in his head. He would revive it (or els it had been lost and forgott) and went into the country to make an ill survey of it (which he printed) about anno . . ., but with no great encouragement of the countrey or others. Upon the resfauration of King Charles II he renewed his designe and applyed himselfe to the king and counsell. His majestie espoused it more (he told me) then any one els. In short, for want of management and his non-ability, it came to nothing, and he is now dead of old age. But Sir Jonas Moore (☞ an expert mathematician and a practicall man), being sent to survey the mannor of Dantesey in Wilts (which was forfeited to the crowne by Sir John Danvers his foolery), went to see these streames and distances. He told me the streames were too small unlesse in winter; but if some prince or the Parliament would rayse money to cutt through the hill by Wotton-Basset which is not very high, then there would be water enough and streames big enough. He computed the chardge, which I have forgott, but I thinke it was about 200,000 *li.*

Insert his letter to Dr. John Pell *de logarithmis* written anno Dni 1628.

Mr. William Oughtred calls him the English Archimedes in . . . .

An epitaph on H. Briggs among H. Burched's poems [2].

** Mr. Briggs—vide and quaere Dr. Whitchcot, behind St. Lawrence Church; he knew him.———Respondet quod non.

*** Mr. Norwood to the reader, before his Trigonometrie:—'of the construction and divers applications of Logarithmes Mr. Brigs hath written a booke called *Arithmetica Logarithmica*, and since again began another excellent worke of like nature entituled *Trigonometria Britannica*. I have onely seen (in the hands of a friend of his) a printed copie of so much as he had done, namely the tables: but whilest he was in hand with the rest, he departed this life. It was writ in Latin.'

Notes.

[1] John Napier, of Merchiston, born 1550, died 1617. His son Alexander was created baron Napier in 1627.

[2] MS. Aubr. 6, fol. 48 is two leaves, pp. 49–52, sign. I, of a printed book, a miscellany of Greek and Latin verses. The first piece on p. 49 is six Greek lines ' Epitaphium D. Henrici Briggi ob mathesin et pietatem famigerati, denati 1631. Januar. ult.' The second piece is 32 Latin verses ' in bibliothecam Oxoniensem tertio amplificatam MDCXXXVI.'

Thomas Brightman (1562–1607).

⟨*A Letter from Edward Gibson about Thomas Brightman*[1].⟩

Sir,   * Hawnes, Dec. 21, ⟨16⟩81.

Since you have desired and have been put into an expectation of receiving some information concerning Mr. Brightman, tho I have litle or nothing to serve you and your freind with, I send this to let you know that I find nothing of his arms; that upon the stone is engraven

'Here lyeth the body of Thomas Brightman, deceased, minister of this parish, who dyed Aug. 24, 1607.'

Over his head are these sad rimes (I hope they are Oxford, tho not much for the honour of it).—

> Christ cals his churches candlestiks of old,
> Altho the candlesticks but the candles hold.
> The lights on them hee calleth angels pure,
> Not barely candles, for those must endure.
> Candles when burn't out are soon forgott,
> But ministers, as angels, must not rot.

* MS. Aubr. 8, fol. 49.

Sith God doth ministers so eternize,
Let not us mortals give them lower prize.
And specially to Brightman's recommendacion
And bee entomed a light to th' revelation
Wee must, wee ought, to make such saints last
In whom wee know the times to come and past.

> I am, Sir, Yours to serve you,
> Edw. Gibson.

Dr. Fuller, amongst his *Worthies*, hath something of Mr. Brightman.

* For Mr. John Aubrey: leave this at Mr. Hooke's lodging in Gresham College.

Note.

[1] In MS. Aubr. 8, fol. 3, Anthony Wood has jotted down 'quaere Mr. Aubrey of Thomas Brightman, Dr. ⟨William⟩ Butler, Henry Billingsley, Sir George Wharton'—Aubrey's notes, so far, about these four having been scanty.

In MS. Aubr. 8, fol. 48ᵛ, opposite Gibson's letter Wood notes an odd omission in it:—'Quaere *in what church* Mr. Thomas Brightman was buried ʔ'

Alexander Brome (1620–1666).

** H. Brome assured me that his brother Alexander was in his accedence at 4 yeares old and a quarter[1].

Note.

[1] This is a marginal note opposite the life of Katherine Philips, and is intended to be a parallel instance of precocious reading, the boy being taken, first, through the Psalter, and then through the Bible, before beginning his 'accidence' (i.e. Latin Grammar): cp. the course of Anthony Wood's education, Clark's Wood's *Life and Times*, i. 46, 47, 48. Henry Brome was a London bookseller.

Christopher Brookes (16 . . –1665).

*** Christopher Brookes, of Oxford, a mathematical instrument maker. He was sometime manciple of Wadham College: his widowe lived over against the Theatre.

This C. B. printed ͣ 1649 an 8vo of about 2 sheetes,

---

* MS. Aubr. 8, fol. 48.   ͣ Clark's Wood's *Life and Times*,
** MS. Aubr. 8, fol. 38ᵛ.   ii. 237.
*** MS. Aubr. 7, a slip at fol. 8ᵛ.

scil. 'A new quadrant of more natural easie and manifold performance than any other heretofore extant': but it was his father-in-lawe's[a] invention. I had it from his widow about 1665.

Elizabeth Broughton.

* In the Heralds' Office—Heref⟨ordshire⟩—

Edward Broughton, *m.* Isabell, daughter of
of Kington, eldest | Rafe Beeston, of
son, 1634 | Warwickshire.
Elizabeth.

⟨Arms [b]:—⟩ 'argent, 2 bars gules, on a canton of the second a cross of the field, a martlet or for difference.'

Mris. Elizabeth Broughton was daughter of . . . Broughton of . . . in Herefordshire, an ancient family. Her father lived at the mannour-house at Canon-Peon. Whether she was borne there or no, I know not: but there she lost her mayden-head to a poor young fellow, then I beleeve handsome, but, in 1660, a pittifull poor old weaver, clarke of the parish. He had fine curled haire, but gray. Her father at length discoverd her inclinations and locked her up in the turret of the house, but she (like a . . .) getts downe by a rope; and away she gott to London, and did sett-up for her selfe.

She was a most exquisite beautie, as finely shaped as nature could frame; and had a delicate witt. She was soon taken notice of at London, and her price was very deare—a second Thais. Richard, earle of Dorset, kept her (whether before or after Venetia[c], I know not, but I guesse before). At last she grew common and infamous and gott[d] the pox, of which she died.

I remember thus much of an old song of those dayes,

---

[a] William Onghtred.
* MS. Aubr. 6, fol. 101[v].
[c] Venetia Stanley.

[b] Given by Aubrey in colours in a lozenge.
[d] Dupl. with ' had.'

which I have seen in a collection—'twas by way of litanie
—viz. :—

> From the watch at twelve a clock,
> And from Bess Broughton's buttond * smock,
>   *Libera nos, Domine.*

In Ben Johnson's execrations against Vulcan, he concludes thus :—

> Pox take thee, Vulcan ! May Pandora's pox
> And all the ills that flew out of her box
> Light on thee. And if those plagues will not doe
> Thy wive's pox take thee, and *Bess Broughton's* too.

—In the first edition in 8vo her name is thus at
length.

I see that there have been famous woemen before our
times.

>   Vixêre fortes ante Agamemnona
>   Multi, etc.
>   HORACE, lib. 4, ode 9.

I doe remember her father (1646), neer 80, the handsomest shaped man that ever my eies beheld, a very wise
man and of an admirable elocution. He was a com-
mittee-man in Herefordshire and Glocestershire. He was
commissary to colonel Massey. He was of the Puritan
party heretofore ; had a great guift in praying, etc. His
wife (I have heard my grandmother say, who was her
neighbor) had as great parts as he. He was the first that
used the improvement of land by soape-ashes when he
lived at Bristowe, where they then threw it away.

William Brouncker, 2nd viscount (1620–1684).

* William, lord viscount Brouncker of Lions in Ireland :
he lived in Oxford when 'twas a garrison for the King :
but he was of no university, he told me. He addicted

---

* Aubrey notes in the margin :   sempstresse helped to worke it.'
—' Barbara C.C. ⟨i.e. countess of   * MS. Aubr. 7, fol. 18.
Castlemaine⟩ had such a one : nay

himselfe only to the study of the mathematicks, and was a very great artist in that learning.

His mother was an extraordinary great gamester, and playd all, gold play; she kept the box herselfe. Mr. . . . Arundall (brother of the lord Wardour) made a song in characters of the nobility. Among others, I remember this,

> Here's a health to my lady Brouncker and the best
> card in her hand,
> And a health to my lord her husband, with ne're a foot
> of land.

He was president of the Royall Society about 15 yeares [1].

He was . . . . of the Navy office [2].

He dyed April the 5th, 1684; buried the 14th following in the vault which he caused to be made (8 foot long, 4 foot broad, and about 4 foot high) in the middle of the quire of Saint Katharine's, neer the Tower, of which convent he was governour. He gave a fine organ to this church a little before his death; and whereas it was a noble and large choire, he divided ⟨it⟩ in the middle with a good skreen (at his owne chardge), which haz spoiled ⟨it⟩.

⟨*A note written by him* [3].⟩

* Sir,

These are to give notice that on Friday next the thirtieth day of this instant November, 1677, being St. Andrew's day, the council and officers of the Royal Society are to be elected for the year ensuing. At which election your presence is expected in Gresham Colledge at nine of the clock in the forenoon precisely.

(For John Aubrey, esq.)   Brouncker, P. R. S.

Notes.

[1] He was President, 1663, from the incorporation of the Royal Society, to 1677.

[2] He was a Lord of the Admiralty in 1680, and again in 1682. .

[3] The signature is in long sloping letters, like the children's puzzles of thirty years' back, which could be read only when the paper was held edgeways. It has beaten Anthony Wood, who notes at the side:—' What this name is I know not.'

* MS. Aubr. 23, fol. 26.

William Browne (1591–1645).

* The earle of Carnarvon does not remember Mr. Brown[1],
and I ask't his lordship lately again if any of his servants
doe : he assures me *no*.

Note.

[1] The inquiry was made of Charles Dormer, second earl of Carnarvon.
William Browne, author of *Britannia's Pastorals*, had been tutor in 1624 to
Robert Dormer (created earl of Carnarvon in 1628) in Exeter College.

Robert Burton (157⁴⁄₇–16³⁸⁄₄₀).

** Memorandum. Mr. Robert Hooke of Gresham College
told me that he lay in the chamber in Christ Church that
was Mr. Burton's, of whom 'tis whispered that, *non obstante*
all his astrologie and his booke of Melancholie, he ended
his dayes in that chamber by hanging him selfe.

Thomas Bushell (1594–1674).

*** Mr. Thomas Bushell was an . . . shire man, borne
. . . : quaere Thomas Mariet, esq. [He• was borne at
Marston in . . . shire, neer him.]

He was one of the gentlemen that wayted on the Lord
Chancellour Bacon. 'Twas the fashion in those dayes for
gentlemen to have their suites of clothes garnished with
buttons. My Lord Bacon was then in disgrace, and his
man Bushell having more buttons then usuall on his
cloake, etc., they sayd that his lord's breech made buttons
and Bushell wore them—from whence he was called
buttond Bushell.

He was only an English scholar, but had a good witt
and a working and contemplative head. His lord much
loved him.

* MS. Aubr. 7, fol. 9.

** MS. Aubr. 23, fol. 29, a note
appended to 'the scheme of the
nativity of *Democritus junior* on his
monument at Christ Church in Oxon :
he writt the *Melancholy*.'

*** MS. Aubr. 6, fol. 97ᵛ.

• The words in square brackets
are the answer to the inquiry, added
later.

His genius lay most towards naturall philosophy, and particularly towards the discovery, drayning, and improvement of the silver mines in Cardiganshire ^a, etc.

He had the strangest bewitching way to drawe-in people (yea, discreet and wary men) into his projects that ever I heard of. His tongue was a chaine and drewe in so many to be bound for him and to be ingaged in his designes that he ruined a number. Mr. Goodyere of . . . in Oxfordshire was undon by him among others; see ^b part iii. pag. 6 b.

He was master of the art of running in debt, and lived so long that his depts were forgott, so that they were the great-grandchildren of the creditors.

He wrote a stich't treatise of mines and improving of the adits to them and bellowes to drive-in wind, which Sir John Danvers, his acquaintance, had, and nayled it[1] to his parlor-wall at Chelsey, with some scheme, and I beleeve is there yet: I sawe it there about 10 yeares since.

During the time of the civill warres, he lived in Lundy island.

Anno 1647 or 8, he came over into England; and when he landed at Chester, and had but one Spanish threepence (this I had then from . . . . of Great Tew, to whom he told it), and, sayd he, 'I^c could have been contented to have begged a penny, like a poor man.' At that time he sayd he owed, I forgett whether it was 50 or sixty thousand pounds: but he was like Sir Kenelm Digby, if he had not 4d., wherever he came he would find respect and credit.

☞ Memorandum, after his master the lord chancellor dyed, he maried . . . , and lived at Enston, Oxon; where having some land lyeing on the hanging of a hill faceing the south, at the foot wherof runnes a fine cleare stream which petrifies, and where is a pleasant solitude, he spake to his servant

---

^a Dupl. with 'Wales.'
^b The reference is to MS. Aubr. 8, (*Lives*, part iii.): see *infra*, p. 134.

^c Dupl. with 'I could have contentedly begged, like a poor man.'

Jack † Sydenham to gett a labourer to cleare some boscage
which grew on the side of the hill, and also
to dig [a] a cavity in the hill to sitt, and read or
contemplate. The workman had not workt an
hower before he discovers not only a rock, but
a rock of an unusuall figure with pendants
like icecles as at Wokey hole (Somerset), which
was the occasion of making that delicate grotto
and those fine walkes.

(Jack
Sydenham)lived
before with Sir
Charles Snell at
Kington St.
Michaell. He
was wont to
carry me in his
armes : a grace-
full servant. He
gave me this
account.

Here in fine weather he would walke all night. Jack
Sydenham sang rarely : so did his other servant, Mr. Batty.
They went very gent. in cloathes, and he loved them as
his children.

He did not encumber him selfe with his wife, but here
enjoyed himselfe thus in this paradise till the war brake
out, and then retired to Lundy isle.

He had donne something (I have forgott what) that made
him obnoxious to the Parliament or Oliver Cromwell, about
1650 ; would have been hangd if taken ; printed severall
letters to the Parliament, etc., dated from beyond sea, and
all that time lay privately in his howse in Lambeth marsh
where the [b] pointed pyramis is. In the garret there, is
a long gallery, which he hung all with [c] black, and had
some death's heads and bones painted. At the end where
his couch was, was in an old Gothique nich (like an old
monument) painted a skeleton incumbent [d] on a matt. At
the other end where was his pallet-bed was an emaciated
dead man stretched out. Here he had severall mortifying
and divine motto's (he imitated his lord [e] as much as he
could), and out of his windowes a very pleasant prospect.
At night he walkt in the garden and orchard. Only Mr.
Sydenham, and an old trusty woman, was privy to his
being in England.

He dyed about 1676 or 1677—quaere where—he was
80 yeares of age. [He [f] dyed in Scotland yard neer

[a] Dupl. with 'make.'
[b] Dupl. with 'the turret.'
[c] Subst. for 'painted with.'
[d] Subst. for 'stretched.'
[e] Bacon.
[f] Added later.

Whitehall about 1675 or 1677; Mr. Beach the quaker can tell me exactly.]

His entertainment to Queen Henrietta Marie at Enston was in anno 163⟨6, 23 August⟩. Insert, i. e. sowe [a] my book (which J. S.[b] gave my grandfather Isaac Lyte) in this place. . . . Goodall[2], of Ch. Ch. Oxon, composed[c] the musique; I remember the student of Ch. Ch. which sang the songs (⟨I⟩ now forgett his name).

* Mr. Bushell had a daughter maried to a merchant . . . in Bristowe.

He was a handsome proper gentleman when I sawe him at his house aforesayd at Lambith. He was about 70 but I should have not guessed him hardly 60. He had a perfect healthy constitution; fresh, ruddy face; hawke-nosed, and was temperate.

As he had the art of running in dept, so sometimes he was attacqued and throwen into prison; but he would extricate him selfe again straingely.

He[d] died about 3 yeares since (⟨from⟩ Sir William Dugdale), i. e. about 1677; and was buried at . . .

Memorandum :—in the time of the civill warres his [e] hermitage over the rocks at Enston were hung with black-bayes; his bed had black curtaines, etc., but it had no bed-postes but hung by 4 cordes (covered with black-bayes) instead of bed postes. When the queen-mother came to Oxon to the king, she either brought (as I thinke) or somebody gave her an entire mummie from Egypt, a great raritie, which her majestie gave to Mr. Bushell, but I beleeve long ere this time the dampnesse of the place haz spoyled it with mouldinesse.

Memorandum :—the grotto [f] belowe lookes just south; so that when it artificially raineth, upon the turning of a cock, you are enterteined with a rainebowe. In a very

[a] i.e. sew in.
[b] Jack Sydenham, *supra*, p. 132.
[c] Dupl. with 'did sett.'
* MS. Aubr. 6, fol. 98.
[d] Subst. for 'whether he lived to see the king's restauration I cannot now perfectly remember; but he did, or neer it: and (I thinke) dyed in London. Quaere Mr. Watts the taylor.'
[e] Dupl. with 'his pretty house at the.'
[f] Subst. for 'rock.'

little pond (no bigger then a basin) opposite to the rock, and hard by, stood (1643, Aug. 8) a Neptune, neatly cutt in wood, holding his trident in his hand, and ayming with it at a duck which perpetually turned round with him, and a spanniel swimming after her—which was very pretty, but long since spoyled. I heare that . . . earl of Rochester, in whose possession it now is, doeth keepe it very well in order.

* Mr. Bushell was the greatest arts-master to runne in dept (perhaps) in the world. He died one hundred and twenty thousand pounds in dept. He had so delicate a way of making his projects alluring and feazible, profitable, that he drewe to his baites not only rich men of no designe, but also the craftiest knaves in the countrey, such who had cosened and undon others: e. g. Mr. Goodyeere, who undid Mr. Nicholas Mees's father, etc.

Vide *Plea for Irish cattle.*

Vide * φ p. 148, Bushell's rocks.

Quaere his servant John Sydenham for the collection of remarques of severall partes of England, by the said Mr. Bushell.

** Memorandum:—his ingeniose invention of *aditus* with bellowes to bring fresh aire into the mines: quaere Mr. Beech (quaker) if he hath his printed booke or where it may be had. He gave one to Sir John Danvers, which was nayled in the parlour to the wainscot: 'twas but about 8 sheetes.

Quaere Dr. Plott (⟨author of⟩ Antiquities of Oxonshire) of the booke I gave him some yeares since of the songs and entertainment of Mr. Bushell to queen Henrietta Marie at his rocks. If he had it not, perhaps Anthony Wood had it. Mr. E⟨dmund⟩ W⟨yld⟩ sayes that he tap't the mountaine of Snowdon in . . . in Wales, which was like to have drowned all the countrey; and they were like to knock him and his men in the head.

Mr. Thomas Bushell lay some time (perhaps yeares) at Capt. Norton's, in the gate at Scotland-yard, where he dyed seven yeares since (now, 1684), about 80 aetat.

† Now, 1687, gon: all new paved.

Buried in the little cloysters at Westminster Abbey: vide the Register. Somebody putt [a] B. B. upon the stone † .—From Mr. Beech the quaker.

Notes.

[1] 'Nailed,' I suppose, after the fashion of nailing counterfeit coins to the counter, or vermin to the stable door. Sir John Danvers had probably lost money in the 'scheme.'

[2] Stephen Goodall, chaplain of Ch. Ch., died in Oxford, in Sept. 1637.— Griffiths' *Index to Wills . . . at Oxford*, p. 24.

Anthony Wood says the music was composed by Samuel Ives. Aubrey's copy of these poems is now among Anthony Wood's books in the Bodleian.

Samuel Butler (161⅔–1680).

*Mr. Samuel Butler was [b] borne ‡ at Pershore in Worcestershire, as we suppose: his brother lives there.

‡ He was born in Worcestershire, hard by Barbon-bridge, ⅓ a mile from Worcester, in the parish of St. John, Mr. Hill thinkes, who went to schoole with him.

He went to schoole at Worcester—from Mr. Hill.

His father ⟨was⟩ a man but of slender fortune, and to breed him at schoole was as much education as he was able to reach to. When [c] but a boy he would make observations and reflections on every thing one sayd or did, and censure it to be either well or ill. He never was at the university, for the reason alledged.

He came when a young man to be a servant to the countesse of Kent, whom he served severall yeares. Here, besides his study, he employed his time much in painting and drawing, and also in musique. He was thinking once to have made painting his profession—from Dr. Duke. His love to and skill in painting made a great friendship

[a] *Sic* in MS.: either a slip of the stone-cutter for T. B., or a heartless recalling of his nick-name (*supra*, p. 130).

* MS. Aubr. 6, fol. 114ᵛ.

[b] Subst. for 'was borne at Powyk, neer Worcester (where he went to schoole).'

[c] Subst. for 'when he was a boy.'

between him and Mr. Samuel Cowper (the prince of limners of this age).

He then studyed the Common Lawes of England, but did not practise. He maried a good jointuresse, the relict of . . . . Morgan, by which meanes he lives comfortably.

After the restauration of his majestie when the court at Ludlowe was againe sett-up, he was then the king's steward at the castle there.

He printed a witty Poeme called *Hudibras*, the first part anno 166.. which tooke extremely[a]; so that the king and Lord Chancellor Hyde † would have him sent for, and accordingly he was sent for. They both promised him great matters, but to this day he haz got *no* employment, only the king gave him . . . *li.*

† The Lord Chancellor Hyde haz his picture in his library over the chimney.

He is of a middle stature, strong sett, high coloured, a head of sorrell haire, a severe and sound judgement: a good fellowe. He haz often sayd that way (e.g. Mr. Edmund Waller's) of quibling with sence will hereafter growe as much out of fashion and be as ridicule as quibling with words—quod N.B. He haz been much troubled with the gowt, and particularly 1679, he stirred not out of his chamber from October till Easter.

Obiit Anno $\begin{cases} \text{Domini 1680} \\ \text{circiter 70.} \end{cases}$.

He dyed of a consumption September 25; and buried 27, according to his appointment[b], in the churchyard of Convent Garden; scil. in the north part next the church at the east end. His feet touch the wall. His grave, 2 yards distant from the pillaster of the dore, (by his desire) 6 foot deepe.

About 25 of his old acquaintance at his funerall. I myself being one [of[c] the eldest, helped to carry[d] the pall with Tom Shadwell, at the foot, Sir Robert Thomas

[a] Subst. for 'which tooke, nothing so much!'

[b] Subst. for 'desire.' Persons of position were usually buried in church.

[c] The words in square brackets are struck out, apparently only because Aubrey thought they went too much into detail.

[d] Subst. for 'beare.'

and Mr. Saunders, esq., at the head ; Dr. Cole and Dr. Davenant, middle].   His coffin covered with black bayes ;

S. B. 1680ᵃ.

* Insert in vita Sam. Butler his verses of the Jesuites, not printed, which I gave to you ᵇ about 12 or 14.

** *Hudibras unprinted.*

No Jesuite ever took in hand,
To plant a church in barren land ;
Or ever thought it worth his while
A Swede or Russe to reconcile ;
For where there is not store of wealth,
Souls are not worth the charge of health ᶜ.
Spaine and ᵈ America had two designes
To sell their ᵈ Ghospell for their mines ;
For had the Mexicans been poore,
No Spaniard twice had landed on their shore.
'Twas gold the Catholick Religion planted,
Which, had they wanted gold, they still had wanted.

He had made very sharp reflexions upon the court in his last part ᵉ :—

Did not the learned Glynne and Maynard
To prove true subjects traytors straine hard?

*** Mr. Saunders (the countesse of Kent's kinsman) sayd that Mr. John Selden much esteemed him for his partes, and would sometimes employ him to write letters for him beyond sea, and to translate for him.   He was secretarie to the duke of Bucks, when he was Chancellor of Cambridge. He might have had preferments at first ; but he would not accept any but very good ones, so at last he had none at all, and dyed in want.

ᵃ The inscription on the coffin.
* MS. Aubr. 7, fol. 5ᵛ.
ᵇ Anthony Wood, in obedience to this injunction, inserted the leaf which is now fol. 115 of MS. Aubr. 6.
** MS. Aubr. 6, fol. 115.

ᶜ Subst. for 'the charges of their health.'
ᵈ Read, perhaps, ' on,' ' her.'
ᵉ See Clark's Wood's *Life and Times*, i. 186, note 2.
*** MS. Aubr. 6, fol. 114ᵛ.

He painted well and made it (sometime) his profession.

He wayted some yeares on the countess of Kent : she gave her gentlemen 20 *li.* per annum a-piece. Mr. John Selden tooke notice of his partes and would many times make him write or translate for him.

Obiit sine prole.

* Samuel Butler writt my lord [John ᵃ] Rosse's Answer to [Robert ᵇ] the marquesse of Dorchester.

Memorandum :—satyricall witts disoblige whom they converse with, etc. ; and consequently make to themselves many enemies and few friends ; and this was his manner and case. He was of a leonine-coloured haire, sanguino-cholerique, middle sized, strong.

William Butler (1535–161⅛).

** . . . ᶜ Butler, physitian ; he was of Clare-hall in Cambridge, never tooke the degree of Doctor, though he was the greatest physitian of his time.

The occasion of his being first taken notice of was thus † :—About the comeing-in of ᵈ king
† From Edmund Waller, esqre. James, there was a minister of . . . (a few miles from Cambridge), that was to preach before his majestie at New-market. The parson heard that the king was a great scholar, and studyed so excessively that he could not sleep, so somebody gave him some opium, which had made him sleep his last, had not Dr. Butler ᵉ used this following remedy. He was sent for by the parson's wife. When he came and sawe the parson, and asked what they had donne, he told her that she was in danger to be hanged for killing her husband, and so in great choler left her. It was at that time when the cowes came into the backside to be

---

* MS. Aubr. 8, fol. 7.

ᵃ Inserted by Anthony Wood.

ᵇ Inserted by Wood, who wrote 'Henry' and then changed it to 'Robert.'

** MS. Aubr. 6, fol. 26ᵛ.

ᶜ Anthony Wood inserts the Christian name ' William.'

ᵈ Subst. for 'Upon the first of King James.'

ᵉ Dupl. with ' this physitian.'

milk't. He turnes back, and asked whose cowes those were. She sayd ⟨her⟩ husband's[a]. Sayd he, 'will you give one of these cowes to fetch your husband to life again?' That she would, with all her heart. He then causes one presently to be killed and opened, and the parson † to be taken out of his bed and putt

into the cowes warme belly, which after some time brought him to life, or els he had infallibly dyed.

Memorandum :—there is a parallell storie to this in Machiavell's Florentiac History, where 'tis sayd that one of the Cosmo's being poysoned was putt into a mule's belly, sowed up, with a place only for his head to come out.

He was a humorist[c]. One time king James sent for him to New-market, and when he was gon halfe way ⟨he⟩ left the messenger and turned back; so then the messenger made him ride before him.

I thinke he was never maried. He lived in an apothecary's shop, in Cambridge, ⟨John⟩ Crane, to whom he left his estate; and he in gratitude erected the monument[d] for him, at his owne chardge, in the fashion[e] he used. He was not greedy of money, except choice pieces of gold or rarities.

He would many times (I have heard say) sitt among the boyes at St. Maries church in Cambridge (☞ and just so would the famous attorney-generall Noy, in Lincoln's Inne, who had many such froliques and humours).

I remember Mr. Wodenoth, of King's College, told me, that being sent for to . . . . . . he told him that his disease was not to be found in Galen or Hippocrates, but in Tullie's Epistles, *Cum non sis ubi fueris, non est cur velis vivere.*

I thinke he left his estate to the apothecarie. He gave to the chapell of Clare-hall, a bowle[f], for the communion, of gold (cost, I thinke, 2 or 300 *li.*), on which is engraved

---

[a] 'Husband's' subst. for 'hers.'
[b] No doubt Edmund Waller, *supra*; and Thomas Gale, *infra.*
[c] Dupl. with 'a man of great moodes.'
[d] *infra*, p. 142.
[e] Subst. for 'habit.'
[f] Subst. for 'plate.'

a pelican feeding her young with the bloud from her breast (an embleme of the passion of Christ), no motto, for the embleme explained it selfe.

He lies buried in the south side of St. Marie's chancell, in Cambridge, wher is a decent monument, with his body halfe way, and an inscription, which gett.

He was much addicted to his humours, and would suffer persons of quality to wayte sometimes some houres at his dore, with coaches, before he would recieve them. Once, on the rode from Cambridge to London, he tooke a fancy to a chamberlayn or tapster in his inne, and tooke him with him, and made him his favourite, by whom only accession was to be had to him, and thus enriched him. Dr. Gale[1], of Paul's schoole, assures me that a French man came one time from London to Cambridge, purposely to see him, whom he made stay two howres for him in his gallery, and then he came out to him in an old blew gowne; the French gentleman makes him 2 or 3 very lowe bowes downe to the ground; Dr. Butler whippes his legge over his head, and away goes into his chamber, and did not speake with him.

He kept an old mayd whose name was Nell. Dr. Butler would many times goe to the taverne, but drinke by him-selfe. About 9 or 10 at night old Nell comes for him with a candle and lanthorne, and sayes 'Come you home, you drunken beast.' By and by Nell would stumble; then her master calls her 'drunken beast'; and so they did *drunken beast* one another all the way till they came home.

* A serving man brought his master's water to doctor Butler, being then in his studie (with turn'd barres) but would not bee spoken with. After much fruitlesse impor-tunity, the man told the doctor he was resolved he should see his master's water; he would not be turned away— threw it on the Dr's. head. This humour pleased the Dr. and he went to the gent. and cured him—(from) Mr. R. Hooke.

* MS. Aubr. 8, fol. 22.

A gent. lying a-dyeing, sent his servant with a horse for the doctor. The horse being exceeding dry, ducks downe his head strongly into the water, and plucks downe the Dr. over his head, who was plunged in the water over head and eares. The Dr. was madded, and would returne home. The man swore he should not; drew his sword, and gave him ever and anon (when he would returne) a little prick, and so drove him before him—⟨from⟩ Mr. . . . Godfrey.

* Some instances of Dr. Butler's cures :—from Mr. James Bovey.—The Dr. lyeing at the Savoy in London, next the water side, where was a balcony look't into the Thames, a patient came to him that was grievously tormented with an ague. The Dr. orders a boate to be in readinesse under his windowe, and discoursed with the patient (a gentleman) in the balcony, when on a signall given, 2 or 3 lusty fellowes came behind the gentleman and threw him a matter of 20 feete into the Thames. This surprize absolutely cured him.

A gentleman with a red, ugly, pumpled face came to him for a cure. Said the Dr., '*I must hang you.*' So presently he had a device made ready to hang him from a beame in the roome ; and when he was e'en almost dead, he cutts the veines that fed these pumples, and lett-out the black ugly bloud, and cured him.

Another time one came to him for the cure of a cancer (or ulcer) in the bowells. Said the Dr., 'can ye ——?' 'Yes,' said the patient. So the Dr. ordered a bason for him to ——, and when he had so donne the Dr. commanded him to eate it up. This did the cure.

** *Inscription on his monument*ᵃ.

This inscription was sent to me by my learned and honoured friend, Dr. Henry More, of Cambridge.

---

* MS. Aubr. 8, fol. 24.
** MS. Aubr. 8, fol. 23. The inscription is Henry More's autograph.

ᵃ Anthony Wood queries 'Where is this monument?' having forgotten MS. Aubr. 6: *supra*, p. 140.

Nunc positis novus exuviis

Gulielmus Butlerus, Clarensis Aulae
quondam Socius, Medicorum omnium
quos praesens aetas vidit facile princeps,
hoc sub marmore secundum Christi adventum expectat, et monumentum hoc
privata pietas statuit, quod debuit
publica. Abi, viator, et ad tuos reversus,
narra te vidisse locum in quo salus
jacet.

LABOR

Nil proh! marmor agis, Butlerum dum tegis, ullum
  Si splendore tuo nomen habere putas.
Ille tibi monumentum est, tu diceris ab illo :
  Butleri vivis munere, marmor iners.
Sic homines vivus, mira sic mortuus arte,
  Phoebo chare senex, vivere saxa facis.

QUIES

Butlero Herôum hoc posuere dolorque fidesque.
Hei! quid agam, exclamas et palles, Lector?   At unum
Quod miseris superesse potest, locus hic monet : ora.
      Obiit CIƆIƆCXVII. Janua. XXIX.
      Aeta. suae LXXXIII.

* A scholar made this drolling epitaph :—
Here lies Mr. Butler who never was Doctor,
Who dyed in the yeare that the Devill was Proctor[2].
Memorandum :—There is now in use[a] in London a sort
of ale called *Dr. Butler's ale.*
** Dr. Butler :—This inscription I recieved from Dr.
Henry Moore of . . . Cambridge.   Quaere if his coat of
arms is not there, and what?   Quaere his coat of arms[b].
From Dr. H. More :—More's father was a very strong
bodyed man. 'Twas forty stooles he gave his father ; he

---

* MS. Aubr. 6, fol. 26ᵛ.   ^b For the answer to this query,
^a Dupl. with 'fashion.'   see *infra.*
** MS. Aubr. 8, fol. 25.

had almost killed him.   Told him he would be the better for't as long as he lived.

That he was chymical I know by this token that his mayd came running-in to him one time, like a slutt and a furie, with her haire about her eares, and cries[a], 'Butler ! come and looke to your Devills yourselfe, and you will : the stills are all blowne up !'   She tended them, and it seemes gave too great a heate.   Old Dr. Ridgely[3] knew him, and I thinke was at that time [b] with him.—From this Dr. Ridgely his sonne.

* Dr. Butler of Cambridge :—⟨*Arms* :—⟩ 'azure, three lozenges in fess between 3 covered cups or.—This is the coate of armes on his monument.   By reason of time and the ill colours I cannot *positively* say whether the field is azure or vert, but I beleeve 'tis the former.'—This information I had from Mr. Vere Philips, fellow of King's College, Cambridge.
Notes.

[1] Thomas Gale, Head Master of St. Paul's School 1672–1697, D.D. Trin. Coll. Cambr. 1675.

[2] Aubrey does not explain this ' drollery.'   I can see nothing Satanic in the names of the Cambridge proctors for 1617–18, John Smithson and Alexander Read.

[3] Thomas Ridgley (Rugeley), M.D., St. John's, Cambr. 1608 ; his son Luke Ridgely, M.D., Christ's, Cambr.

Cecil Calvert, 2nd baron Baltimore (1606–1675).

** Cecil Calvert, lord Baltemore, absolute lord and proprietary of Maryland and Avalon in America, son to ⟨George⟩ Calvert (secretary of estate to king James), was gentleman-commoner of Trinity College, Oxon, contemporary with Mr. Francis Potter, B.D.

*** Now if I would be rich, I could be a prince.   I could goe into Maryland, which is one of the finest countrys of the world ; same climate with France ; between Virginia and New England.   I can have all the favour of my lord

[a] Dupl. with 'said.'
[b] Dupl. with ' then.'
* MS. Aubr. 8, fol. 22.

** Aubrey in MS. Wood F. 39, fol. 138 : Sept. 2, 1671.
*** Ibid., fol. 141[v] : Oct. 27, 1671.

Baltemore I could wish.—His brother is his lieutenant there ; and a very good natured gentleman.—Plenty of all things : ground there is 2000 miles westwards.

I could be able I believe to carry a colony of rogues ; another, of ingeniose artificers ; and I doubt not one might make a shift to have 5 or 6 ingeniose companions, which is enough.

William Camden (1551–1623).

* Mr. William Camden, Clarencieux—vide Fuller's *Holy State* where is something of his life and birth, etc.: vide *England's Worthies*: quaere at the Heralds' Office when he was made Clarencieux.

Mr. Edward Bagshawe (who had been second schoole-master of Westminster schoole) haz told me that Mr. Camden had first his place and his lodgeings (which is the gate-house by the Queen's Scholars' chamber in Deanes-yard), and was after made the head schoole-master of that schoole, where he writt and taught *Institutio Græcae Grammatices Compendiaria: in usum Regiae Scholae Westmonasteriensis*, which is now the common Greeke grammar of England, but his name is not sett to it. Before, they learned the prolix Greeke Grammar of Cleonard.

He writt his *Britannia* first in a large 8°.

Annales reg. Elizabethae.

There is a little booke in 16mo. of his printed, viz.: A Collection of all the Inscriptions then on the Tombes in Westminster Abbey.

'Tis reported, that he had bad eies ᵃ (I guesse lippitude) which was a great inconvenience to an antiquary.

Mr. Nicholas Mercator has Stadius's *Ephemerides*, which had been one of Mr. Camden's ; his name is there (I knowe his hand) and there are some notes by which I find he was astrologically given.

. * MS. Aubr. 6, fol. 119. Aubrey gives in trick the coat :—' or, a fess engrailed between 6 cross crosslets fitchée sable.'

ᵃ Subst. for ' was short-(sighted).'

In his *Britannia* he haz a remarkable astrologicall observation, that when Saturn is in Capricornus a great plague is certainly in London. He had observed it all his time, and setts downe the like made by others before his time. Saturn was so posited in the great plague 1625, and also in the last great plague 1665. He likewise delivers that when an eclipse happens in . . . . . . that 'tis fatall to the towne of Shrewsbury, for . . .

He was basted by a courtier of the queene's in the cloysters at Westminster for . . . queen Elizabeth in his history—from Dr. John Earle, dean of Westminster.

My honoured and learned friend, Thomas Fludd, esq., a Kentish gentleman, (⟨aged⟩ 75, 1680) was neighbour and an acquaintance to Sir Robert Filmore, in Kent, who was very intimately acquainted with Mr. Camden, who told Sir Robert that he was not suffered to print many things in his *Elizabetha*, which he sent over to his acquaintance and correspondent Thuanus, who printed it all faithfully in his *Annalls* without altering a word— quod N. B.

He lies buried in the South cross-aisle of Westminster Abbey, his effigies ½ on an altar, with this inscription :—

Qui fide antiqua et opera assidua
Britannicam antiquitatem indagavit
Simplicitatem innatam
honestis studiis excoluit
Animi solertiam candore illustravit
Gulielmus Camdenius
ab Elizabetha regina ad regis armorum
(Clarentii titulo) dignitatem evocatus
Hic
Spe certa resurgendi in Christo
S.E.
Qui obiit anno Domini 1623, 9 Novembris,
Aetatis suae 74:

in his hand a booke, on the leaves wherof is writt BRITANNIA.

Mr. Camden much studied the Welsh language, and

kept a Welsh servant to improve him ⟨in⟩ that language, for the better understanding of our antiquities.—From Mr. Samuel Butler.

* Sir William Dugdale tells me that he haz minutes of King James's life to a moneth and a day, written by Mr. William Camden; as also his owne life, according to yeares and . daye, which is very briefe, but 2 sheetes, Mr. Camden's owne hand writing. Sir William Dugdale had it from ⟨John⟩ Hacket †, bishop of Coventry and Lichfield, who did filch it from Mr. Camden as he lay a dyeing.

† ⚭ Quaere Sir William Dugdale. Vide how bishop Hacket came by it. ‡ He (Dr. Th.) told Sir Wiliam Dugdale so, who told me of it.

** Quaere Mr. Ashmole to retrive and looke out Mr. Camden's minutes (memorandums) of King James I from his entrance into England, which Dr. Thorndyke ‡ filched from him as he lay a dyeing. 'Tis not above 6 or 8 sheetes of paper, as I remember. Those memoires were continued within a fortnight of his death.

*** Quaere Dr. Buzby if Mr. Camden ever resigned the schoolmaster's place ᵃ? And if he did not dye at Westminster at the schoole house—vide bishop Hackett's life, which is printed before his sermons.

**** Memorandum :—Mr. Camden's nativity is in his Memoires of King James, which gett.

***** William Camden : quaere Sir William Dugdale who haz his papers ?

Anthony Wood's lettre sayth that some of them are in Sir Henry St. George's hands ᵇ, 'written and tricked with Mr. Camden's owne hand' : ergo quaere ibidem.

****** When my grandfather ᶜ went to schoole at Yatton-Keynell (neer Easton-Piers) Mr. Camden came to see the

---

* MS. Aubr. 6, fol. 119ᵛ.

** MS. Aubr. 6, a slip pasted on to fol. 119.

*** MS. Aubr. 6, fol. 119ᵛ.

ᵃ 'Non' is added by Anthony Wood in red ink, in answer to this inquiry.

**** MS. Aubr. 6, fol. 119.

***** MS. Aubr. 8, fol. 18.

ᵇ See Clark's Wood's *Life and Times*, ii. 268.

****** MS. Ballard 14, fol. 133; a letter from Aubrey to Anthony Wood, dated July 15, 1681.

ᶜ Isaac Lyte.

church, and particularly tooke notice of a little painted-glasse-windowe in the chancell, which (ever since my re-membrance) haz been walled-up, to save the parson the chardge of glazing it.

William Canynges (1399–1474).

* The antiquities of the city of Bristowe doe very well deserve some antiquarie's paines (and the like for Gloucester). Here were a great many religious houses. The collegiate church (priorie of Augustines) is very good build-ing, especially the gate-house. The best built churches of any city in England, before these new ones at London since the conflagration. Severall monuments and in-scriptions.

Ratliff church (which was intended ª for a chapel) is an admirable piece of architecture of about Henry VII's time. It was built by alderman . . . Canning, who had fifteen shippes of his owne (or 16). He gott his estate chiefly by carrying of pilgrims to St. Jago of Compostella. He had a fair house in Ratliff Street that lookes towards the water side, ancient Gothique building, a large house that, 1656, was converted to a glasse-house. See the anno-tations on Norton's Ordinall in *Theatrum Chemicum*, where 'tis sayd that Thomas Norton of Bristow got the secret of the philosopher's stone from alderman Canning's widow.

This alderman Canning did also build and well endow the religious house at Westbury or Henbury (vide Speede's mappe and chronicle); 'tis about two or three miles from Bristowe in the rode to Aust-passage.

In his old age he retired to this house and entred into that order. He built his owne monument at his church at Ratcliff where is an inscription, which gett [1]; ☞ but he was not interred there but at Westbury.

Note.

[1] See J. Britton's Historical and Architectural essay relating to Redcliffe Church, Bristol, with plans, views, account of its monuments, &c. 1813.

* MS. Aubr. 8, fol. 105.   ª Subst. for 'built.'

William Cartwright (1611–1643).

* William Cartwright, M.A., Aedis Christi, Oxon., natus juxta Teuxbury in com. Glocestriae, September, 1611; baptizatus [a] 26 Sept.

** Glocestershire is famous for the birth of William Cartwright at a place called Northway neer Tewksbury. Were he alive now he would be sixty-one.

He writt a treatise of metaphysique—quaere Dr. ⟨Thomas⟩ Barlowe, etc., de hoc: as also of his sermons, particularly the sermon that by the king's command he preached at his returne from Edge-hill fight.

'Tis not to be forgott that king Charles 1st dropt a teare at the newes of his death.

William Cartwright was buried in the south aisle in Christ Church, Oxon. Pitty 'tis so famous a bard should lye without an inscription.

*** William Cartwright was borne at Northway neer Tewksbury, Gloucestershire—this I have from his brother, who lives not far from me [b], and from his sisters whom I called upon in Glocestershire at Leckhamton. His sister Howes was 57 yeares old the 10 March last: her brother William was 4 yeares older.

His father was a gentleman of 300 *li.* per annum. He kept his inne at Cirencester, but a year or therabout, where he declined and lost by it too. He had by his wife 100 *li.* per annum, in Wiltshire, an impropriation, which his son has now (but having many children, lives not handsomely and haz lost his learning: he was by the second wife, whose estate this was). Old Mr. Cartwright lived sometime at Leckhampton, Gloc., wher his daughters now live.

* MS. Aubr. 8, fol. 4ᵛ.

[a] 'At Northway': so his baptismal certificate in MS. Wood F. 49, fol. 25.

** Aubrey, in MS. Wood F. 39, fol. 138ᵛ: Sept. 2, 1671.

*** Aubrey in MS. Wood F. 39, fol. 141: Oct. 27, 1671.

[b] Aubrey, at this date, was in hiding at Broad Chalk.

Lucius Cary, viscount Falkland (1610–1643).

* Lucius Carey[1], second lord Falkland, was the eldest son of Sir Henry Carey, Lord Lievetenant of Ireland, the first viscount Falkland.

His mother was daughter and heir of Sir ⟨Laurence⟩ Tanfield, Lord Chief Baron of the Exchequer, by whom he had Great Tue, in Oxfordshire (formerly the Rainesfords), and the Priory of Burford, in Oxfordshire, which he sold to ⟨William⟩ Lenthall, the Speaker of the Long Parliament.

He was borne . . . (quaere) ; had his University education at the University of Dublin, in Ireland. He travelled, and had one Mr. . . . (a very discreet gentleman) to be his governor[2], whom he respected to his dyeing day.

He maried Letice, the daughter of Sir ⟨Richard⟩ Morison, by whom he had two sonnes : the eldest lived to be a man, died *sine prole* ; the second was father to this lord Falkland now living.

This lady Letice was a good and pious lady, as you may see by her life writt about 1649, or 50, by . . . Duncomb, D.D. But I will tell you a pretty story from William Hawes, of Trin. Coll., who was well acquainted with the governor aforesaid, who told him that my lady was (after the manner of woemen) much governed by, and indulgent to, the nursery ; when she had a mind to beg any thing of my lord for one of her woemen[a] (nurses, or &c.) ; she would not doe it by herselfe (if she could helpe it), but putt this gentleman upon it, to move it to my lord. My lord had but a small estate for his title ; and the old gentleman would say, 'Madam, this is so unreasonable a motion to propose to my lord, that I am certaine he will never graunt it ';—e. g. one time to lett a farme[b] twenty pound per annum under value. At length, when she could not prevaile on him, she would say that, 'I warrant you, for all this, I will obtaine it of

my lord ; *it will cost me but the expence of a few teares.'*
Now she would make her words good ; and this great
witt, the greatest master of reason and judgement of his
time, at the long runne, being storm'd by her *teares* (I presume there were kisses and secret embraces that were also
ingredients), would this pious lady obtain her unreasonable
desires of her poor lord.

> Haec verba, me hercule, una falsa lacrumula,
> Quam, oculos terendo misere, vix vi expresserit,
> Restinguet.
>
> TERENT. *Eunuch.* Act 1, Scene 1.

N.B.:—my lord in his youth was very wild, and also
mischievous, as being apt to stabbe and doe bloudy mis-
chiefs ; but 'twas not long before he tooke-up to be
serious, and then grew to be an extraordinary hard
student. I have heard Dr. Ralph Bathurst †
say that, when he was a boy, my lord lived
at Coventrey (where he had then a house),
and that he would sett up very late at nights
at his study, and many times came to the
library at the schoole ‡ there.

† A mayd that lived with my lord lived with his father⁵.
‡ There is Euclid's Harmoniques written with Philemon Holland's owne hand, in a curious Greeke character ; he was school-master here.

The studies in fashion in those dayes (in
England) were poetry, and controversie with
the church of Rome. My lord's mother was a zealous
papist, who being very earnest to have her son of her
religion, and her son upon that occasion, labouring hard
to find the *trueth, was so far at last from setling
on the Romish church, that he setled and rested in
the Polish (I meane Socinianisme). He was the first
Socinian in England ; and Dr. ⟨Hugh⟩ Crescy, of Merton
Coll. (dean of ⟨Leighlin⟩ in Ireland, afterwards a Bene-
dictin monke), a great acquaintance of my lord's in those
dayes (anno . . .), told me, at Samuel Cowper's (1669),
that he himselfe was the first that brought Socinus's bookes
(anno . . .); shortly after, my lord comeing to him, and
casting his eie on them, would needs presently borrow.

* MS. Aubr. 6, fol. 93ᵛ.

them, to peruse; and was so extremely taken and satisfied
with them, that from that time was his conversion.

My lord much lived at Tue, which is a pleasant seat,
and about 12 miles from Oxford; his lordship was acquainted with the best witts of that University, and his
house was like a Colledge, full of learned men[a]. Mr.
William Chillingworth, of Trinity College in Oxford (afterwards D.D.), was his most intimate and beloved favourite,
and was most commonly with my lord; next I may reckon
(if not equall) Mr. John Earles, of Merton College (who
wrote the Characters); Dr. ⟨George⟩ Eglionby, of Ch. Ch.,
was also much in esteem with his lordship. His chaplaine,
Charles Gataker, (filius ⟨Thomae⟩ Gataker of Redriff, a
writer), was an ingeniose young gentleman, but no writer[b].
For learned gentlemen of the country, his acquaintance
was Sir H. Rainesford, of . . . neer Stratford-upon-Avon,
now . . . . (quaere Tom Mariet); Sir Francis Wenman[c],
of Caswell, in Witney parish; Mr. . . . Sandys, the traveller
and translator (who was uncle to my lady Wenman);
Ben. Johnson (vide Johnsonus Virbius, where he haz
verses, and 'twas his lordship, Charles Gattaker told
me, that gave the name to it); Edmund Waller, esq.;
Mr. Thomas Hobbes, and all the excellent[d] of that
peaceable time.

In the civill warres he adhered to King Charles I, who
after Edge-hill fight made him Principall Secretary of
Estate (with Sir Edward Nicholas), which he dischardged
with a great deale of witt and prudence, only his advice
was very unlucky to his Majestie, in perswading him
(after the victory[e] at Rowndway-downe, and the taking
of Bristowe), to sitt-downe before Glocester, which was
so bravely defended by that incomparably vigilant governor
coll. . . . Massey, and the diligent and careful soldiers
and citizens (men and woemen), that it so broke and

[a] Anthony Wood notes in the margin 'Jo⟨hn⟩ Triplett.'
[b] Charles Gataker was author of
several pamphlets.
[c] Subst. for 'Wayneman.'
[d] 'excellent' written over 'witts,' as
an alternative.
[e] Dupl. with 'victory by the Devizes.'

weakned the king's army, that 'twas the procatractique
cause of his ruine: vide Mr. Hobbes. After this, all
the King's matters went worse and worse. Anno domini
164⟨3⟩ at the . . . . fight (quaere which) at Newbery, my
lord Falkland being there, and having nothing to doe to
chardge; as the 2 armies were engageing, rode in like
a mad-man (as he was) between them, and was (as he
needs must be) shott. Some that* were your superfine
discoursing politicians and fine gentlemen, would needs
have the reason of this mad action of throwing away
his life so, to be his discontent for the unfortunate advice
given to his master as aforesaid; but, I have been
well enformed, by those that best knew him, and
* knew the intrigues behind the curtaine (as they say),
that it was the griefe of the death of Mris . . . Moray,
a handsome lady at court, who was his mistresse, and
whom he loved above all creatures, was the true cause
of his being so madly guilty of his own death, as afore
mentioned: (*nullum magnum ingenium sine mixtura de-
mentiae*).

The next day, when they went to bury the dead, they
could not find his lordship's body, it was stript, trod-upon,
and mangled; so there was one that had wayted on him
in his chamber would undertake to know it from all other
bodyes, by a certaine mole his lordship had in his neck,
and by that marke did find it. He lies interred in the
. . . . . at Great Tue aforesaid, but, I thinke, yet without
any monument; quaere if any inscription.

In the dining roome there is a picture of his at length,
and like him ('twas donne by Jacob de Valke, who taught
me to paint). He was but a little man, and of no great
strength of body; he had blackish haire, something flaggy,
and I thinke his eies black. Dr. Earles would not allow
him to be a good poet, though a great witt; he writt
not a smoth verse, but a greate deal of sense. He hath
writt . . . . .

He had an estate in Hertfordshire, at . . . . . , which came by Morrison (as I take it); sold not long before the late civill warres.

Notes.

¹ Aubrey gives in trick the coat 'argent, on a bend sable, 3 roses of the field [Cary],' surmounted with a viscount's coronet and wreathed with laurel for a poet.

² A pencil note in the margin says: 'quaere Baron Berty'; perhaps Vere Bertie, Puisne Baron of the Exchequer, 1675. The query would be for the name of the tutor on the foreign tour.

³ i.e. a maid, formerly in Lucius, lord Falkland's service, came into service with Dr. Bathurst's father, and told of his lordship's late studies.

Sir Charles Cavendish (16..–1652?).

* (From Mr. John Collins, mathematician:—) Sir Charles Cavendish¹ was borne at . . . , the younger brother to William, duke of Newcastle. He was a little, weake, crooked man, and nature having not adapted him for the court nor campe, he betooke himselfe to the study of the mathematiques, wherin he became a great master. His father left him a good estate, the revenue wherof he expended on bookes and on learned men.

He had collected in Italie, France, &c., with no small chardge, as many manuscript mathematicall bookes as filled a hoggeshead, which he intended to have printed; which if he had live⟨d⟩ to have donne, the growth of mathematicall learning had been 30 yeares or more forwarder then 'tis. But he died of the scurvey, contracted by hard study, about 1652 (quaere), and left one Mr. . . . . , an attorney of Clifford's Inne, his executor, who shortly after died, and left his wife executrix, who sold this incomparable collection aforesaid by weight to the past-board makers for wast paper. ☞ A good caution for those that have good MSS. to take care to see them printed in their life-times.

He dyed . . . . . and was buried in the vault of the family of the duke of Newcastle, at Bolsover, in the countie of ⟨Derby⟩.

* MS. Aubr. 6, fol. 29.

He is mentioned by Mersennus. Dr. John Pell (who knew him, and made him one of his XII jurymen contra Longomontanum) tells me that he writt severall things in mathematiques for his owne pleasure.

[1] Aubrey gives in trick the coat :—' sable, 3 bucks' heads caboshed argent [Cavendish]; quartering, argent, a fess between 3 crescents gules [Ogle], a crescent on the fess point for difference,' with the motto *Cavendo tutus.*

Charles Cavendish, Colonel, (1620–1643).

* Charles Cavendish, colonel, was second son to the right honourable ⟨William, 2nd⟩ earle of Devonshire, brother to this present earle, William.

He was borne at . . . . . anno . . . . He was well educated, and then travelled into France, Italie, &c.; but was so extremely delighted in travelling, that he went into Greece, all over; and that would not serve his turne but he would goe to Babylon, and then his governour would not adventure to goe any further with him; but to see Babylon he was to march in the Turks' armie. This account I had many yeares since, scilicet 1642, from my cosen Edmund Lyte, who was then gentleman usher to his mother the countesse dowager.

Mr. Thomas Hobbes told me that this Mr. Cavendish told him that the Greekes doe sing their Greeke.—In Herefordshire they have a touch of this singing; our old divines had. Our old vicar of Kington St. Michael, Mr. Hynd, did sing his sermons rather then reade them. You may find in Erasmus that the monkes used this fashion, who mocks them, that sometimes they would be very lowe, and by and by they would be mighty high, *quando nihil opus est.*—Anno 1660 comeing one morning to Mr. Hobbes, his Greeke Xenophon lay open on the board: sayd he, ' Had you come but a little sooner you had found a Greeke here that came to see me, who understands the old Greeke; I spake to him to read here in this booke, and he sang

* MS. Aubr. 6, fol. 29 : Aubrey repeats the coat given *supra.*

it; which putt me in mind of what Mr. Charles Cavendish told me' (as before); 'the first word is Ἔννοια, he pronounced it *ẽnnia*.' The better way to explaine it is by prick-song,

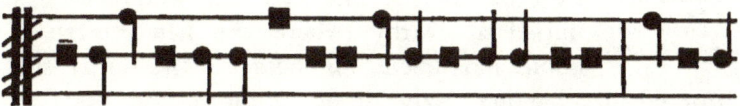

Μῆνιν ἄειδε θεὰ Πηληϊάδεω Ἀχιλῆος· ἄνθρωπος.

* Upon his returne into England the civill warres brake-out, and he tooke a comission of a colonel in his majestie's cause, wherin he did his majestie great service, and gave signall proofes of his valour;—e.g. out of *Mercurii Aulici*—

Grantham, in Lincolnshire, taken by col. Cavendish for the king, 23 March, 164⅔, and after demolished.—Young Hotham routed at Ancaster by col. Cavendish, 11 Apr. 1643.—Parliament forces routed or defeated at Dunnington by col. Cavendish, 13 June, 1643.

Mercurius Aulicus, Tuesday, Aug. 1, 1643; 'It was advertised from Newarke that his majestie's forces having planted themselves at the siege of Gainsborough in com. Linc., were sett upon by the united powers of Cromwell, Nottingham, and Lincolne, the garrisons of these townes being almost totally drawn-out to make-up this army, which consisted of 24 troupes of horse and dragoons. Against this force, col. Cavendish having the command of 30 troupes of horse and dragoons, drawes out 16 only, and leaving all the rest for a reserve, advanced towards them, and engaged himselfe with this small partie against all their strength. Which being observed by the rebells, they gott between him and his reserve, routed his 16 troupes, being forespent with often watches, killed lieevetenant-colonel Markam, most valiantly fighting in defence of his king and countrey. The most noble and gallant colonel himselfe, whilest he omitted no part of a brave commander, being cutt most dangerously in the head, was struck-off his horse, and so unfortunately shott with a brace of bullets after he was on the ground, whose life was most pretious to all noble and valiant gentlemen. Wherupon the reserve coming, routed and cutt downe the partie.'

This was donne either the 28 or 29 of July, 1643, for upon this terrible rout, the lord Willoughby of Parham forthwith yealded Gainsborough to the king's partie, July 30; the earle of Newcastle being then generall of that partie.

His body was first buried at . . . ,† but by order of his mother's will, when she was buried at Darby (where she has erected a noble monument for herselfe and lord) she ordered her sonne's body to be removed, and both to be layd in the vault there together, which was Feb. 18, 1674.

† Quaere if at Gainsborough or Newark ? as I remember 'twas Newarke.

Funerall Sermon, by William Naylour, her chaplain, preached at Darby, Feb. 18, 1674. Lond. for Henry Broome. Texte, 2 Sam. iii. 38th verse.—page 16:

'He was the souldiers' mignion, and his majestie's darling, designed by him generall of the northern horse (and his commission was given him), a great marke of honour for one of about five and twenty: "thus shall it be donne to the man whom the king delights to honour."

'Col. Cavendish was a princely person, and all his actions were agreable to that character: he had in an eminent degree that which the Greekes call εἶδος ἄξιον τυραννίδος, the semblance and appearance of a man made to governe. Methinkes he gave cleare this indication, the king's cause lived with him, the king's cause died with him—when Cromwell heard that he was slaine, he cried upon it *We have donne our businesse.*

'And yet two things (I must confess) this commander knew not, pardon his ignorance,—he knew not to flie away—he knew not how to aske quarter—though an older did, I meane . . . Henderson; for when this bold person entred Grantham on the one side, that wary gentleman, who should have attaqued it, fled away on the other. If Cato thought it usurpation in Caesar to give him his life, Cavendish thought it a greater for traytors and rebells of a common size to give him his. This brave hero might be opprest, (as he was at last by numbers) but he could not be conquered; the dying words of Epaminondas will fitt him, *Satis vixi, invictus etiam morior.*

* 'What wonders might have been expected from a commander so vigilant, so loyall, so constant, had he not dropt downe in his blooming age? But though he fell in his green yeares, heᵃ fell a prince, and a great one too, in this respect greater then Abner; for

* MS. Aubr. 8, fol. 39.
ᵃ Anthony Wood notes 'col. Charles Cavendish.'

Abner, that son of Mars, deserved his father's epithite, ἀλλοπρόσαλλος, *one of both sides,* first he setts-up Isbosheth, and then deserts him. Whereas Cavendish merited such a statue as the Roman senate decreed L. Vitellius, and the same inscription, *Pietatis immobilis erga Principem,* one whose loyaltie to his great master nothing could shake.

'Secondly, consider the noble Charles Cavendish in his extraction, and so he is a branch of that family, of which some descended that are kings of Scotland: this the word *Fuimus* joyned to his maternall † coate does plainly point at—not to urge at this time his descent by the father's side from one of the noblest families in England. An high extraction to some persons is like the dropsie, the greatnesse of the man is his disease, and renders him unweildie; but here is a person of great extract free from the swelling of greatness, as brisk and active as the lightest horseman that fought under him. In some parts of India, they tell us, that a nobleman accounts himselfe polluted if a plebeian touch him; but here is a person of that rank who used the same familiaritie ‡ and frankness amongst the meanest of his souldiers, the poorest miner, and amongst his equalls; and by stooping so low, he rose the higher in the common account, and was valued accordingly as a prince *, and a great one; thus Abner and Cavendish run parallell in their titles and appellations.

'Consider Abner in the manner of his fall, that was by a treacherous hand, and so fell Cavendish. II Sam. iii. 27, "And when Abner was returned to Hebron, Joab tooke him aside in the gate to speake with him quietly, and smote him there under the fifth rib, that he died, for the bloud of Asahel ᵃ his brother." Thus fell Abner; and thus Cavendish,—the colonell's horse being mired in a bog at the fight before Gainsborough, 1643, the rebels surround him, and take him prisoner· and after he was so, a base raskall comes behind him, and runs him through. Thus fell two great men by treacherous handes.

'Thirdly and lastly, the place of his fall, that was in Israel ... Here Abner fell in his, and Cavendish fell in our Israel—the Church of England. . . . In this Church brave Cavendish fell, and what is more then that, in this Churches quarrel. . . .

'Thus I have compared colonel Cavendish with Abner, a fighting and a famous man in Israel; you see how he does equal, how he does exceed him.'

Margin notes:

† His mother was daughter to the lord Bruce, whose ancestors had been kings of Scotland.

‡ Sir Robert Harley (son), an ingeniose grnt. and expert soldier, haz often sayd, that (generally) the commanders of the king's army would never be acquainted with their soldiers, which was an extraordinary prejudice to the king's cause. A captaine's good look, or good word (some times), does infinitely winne them, and oblige them; and he would say 'twa· to admiration how souldiers will venture their lives for an obligeing officer.—quod N. B.

---

* MS. Aubr. 8, fol. 39ᵛ.   ᵃ 'Abner' in MS. by a slip.

John Cecil, 4th earl of Exeter (1628–1678).

* . . . Cecil, earl of Exeter (quaere my lord chief baron Montagu [a] de nomine Christiano [b]), earle of Exeter, translated monsieur Balsac's letters, as appeares by his epistle to my lord in the first volumne, lib. V, lettre V, and Vol. 2[d], lib. V, lettre VI—'et je suis sans doute beaucoup plus honneste homme en Angleterre qu'en France, puisque j'y parle par vostre bouche.'

William Cecil, lord Burghley (1520–1598).

** Cecil, lord Burleigh :—Memorandum, the true name is *Sitsilt*, and is an ancient Monmouthshire family, but now come to be about the size [c] of yeomanry. In the church at Monmouth, I remember in a south windowe an ancient squtcheon of the family, the same that this family beares. 'Tis strange that they should ~~be so~~ vaine to leave off an old British name for a Romancy one, which ~~I beleeve Mr. Verstegan did putt into~~ their heads, telling his lordship, in his booke, that they were derived from the ancient Roman *Cecilii*.

The first lord Burley (who was Secretary of Estate) was at first but ⟨a⟩ country-schoole-master, and (I thinke Dr. Thomas Fuller sayes, vide *Holy State*) borne in Wales.

I remember (when I was a schooleboy at Blandford) Mr. Basket, a reverend divine, who was wont to beg us play-dayes, would alwayes be [d] uncovered, and sayd that ''twas the lord Burleigh's custome, *for* (said he) *here is my Lord Chanceller, my Lord Treasurer, my Lord Chief Justice, &c., predestinated.*'

'He made Cicero's Epistles his glasse, his rule, his oracle, and ordinarie pocket-booke' (Dr. J. Web in preface of his translation of Cicero's *Familiar Epistles*).

---

* MS. Aubr. 8, fol. 59[v].

[a] Sir William Montagu, Chief Baron of the Exchequer 1676–1686.

[b] John Cecil, succeeded as fourth earl in 1643.

** MS. Aubr. 8, fol. 60.

[c] Dupl. with 'degree.'

[d] Subst. for 'keepe.'

Thomas Chaloner (1595–1661).

* Thomas Chaloner [1], esq., [bred ª up in Oxon], was the ⟨third⟩ son of Dr ⟨Thomas⟩ Chaloner, who was tutor (i. e. *informator* ᵇ) to prince Henry (or prince Charles—vide bishop Hall's Letters de hoc).

He was a well-bred gentleman, and of very good naturall parts, and of an agreable humour. He had the accomplishments of studies at home, and travells in France, Italie, and Germanie.

About anno . . . (quaere John Collins) riding a hunting in Yorkeshire (where the allum workes now are), on a common, he [2] tooke notice of the soyle and herbage, and tasted the water, and found it to be like that where he had seen the allum workes in Germanie. Wherupon he gott a patent of the king (Charles I) for an allum worke (which was the first that ever was in England), which was worth to him two thousand pounds per annum, or better : but tempore Caroli Iᵐⁱ some courtiers did thinke the profitt too much for him, and prevailed so with the king, that, notwithstanding the patent aforesayd, he graunted a moeitie, or more, to another (a courtier), which was the reason that made Mr. Chaloner so interest himselfe for the Parliament-cause, and, in revenge, to be one of the king's judges.

He was as far from a puritan as the East from the West. He was of the naturall religion, and of Henry Martyn's gang, and one who loved to enjoy the pleasures of this life. He was (they say) a good scholar, but he wrote nothing that I heare of, onely an anonymous pamphlett, 8vo, scil. *An account of the Discovery of Moyses's Tombe*; which was written very wittily. It was about 1652. It did sett the witts of all the Rabbis of the

---

* MS. Aubr. 7, fol. 19.

ª The words in square brackets are added by Anthony Wood. Chaloner matriculated at Exeter College,

June 7, 1611.

ᵇ i. e. 'tutor,' in the sense of instructor (not, of comptroller of the household).

Assembly then to worke, and 'twas a pretty while before the shamme was detected, which was by ——

He had a trick sometimes to goe into Westminster hall in a morning in Terme time, and tell some strange story^a (sham), and would come thither again about 11 or 12 to have the pleasure to heare how it spred; and sometimes it would be altered, with additions, he could scarce knowe it to be his owne. He was neither proud nor covetous, nor a hypocrite: not apt to doe injustice, but apt to revenge.

After the restauration of King Charles the Second, he [3] kept the castle at the Isle of Man †, where he had a prettie wench that was his concubine; * where when newes was brought him that there were some come to the castle to demaund it for his majestie, he spake to his girle to make him a posset, into which he putt, out of a paper he had, some poyson, which did, in a very short time, make him fall a vomiting exceedingly; and after some time vomited nothing but bloud. His retchings were so violent that the standers by were much grieved to behold it. Within three howres he dyed. The demandants of the castle came and sawe him dead; he was swoln so extremely that they could not see any eie he had, and no more of his nose then the tip of it, which shewed like a wart, and his coddes were swoln as big as one's head. This account I had from George Estcourt, D.D., whose brother-in-lawe, . . . Hotham, was one of those that sawe him.

† This is a mistake. E(dmund) W(yld) esq. assures me that 'twas JAMES CHALONER that dyed in the Isle of Man: and that THOMAS CHALONER dyed or went beyond the sea; but which of them was the eldest brother he knowes not, but he ghesses JAMES to be the elder, because he had 1500 *li.* per annum (circiter), which THOMAS had not.

Notes.

[1] Aubrey gives in trick the coat 'azure, 3 cherubs' heads or.' In MS. Aubr. 8, fol. 6ᵛ, is a note:—'Is Chaloner's shield cum vel sine chevron. Resp.—cum chevron, prout per seale.'

[2] Anthony Wood assigns the discovery, and first working, of the alum-mine to Thomas Chaloner the father, towards the end of Elizabeth's reign.

[3] Anthony Wood says that James Chaloner, brother of Thomas, poisoned himself in 1660 at Peel Castle. Thomas died in 1661 at Middleburg in Zeeland.

^a Dupl. with 'false,' i.e. falsehood.   * MS. Aubr. 7, fol. 19ᵛ.

George Chapman (1557–1634).

* On the south side of St. Giles church in the church-yard by the wall, one entire Portland stone[1], a yard and ½ high *fere*, thickness half a yard.

D. O. M.
Georgius Chapmannus
Poeta Homericus Philosophus
. . . . . . o (etsi Christianus
. . . . . . otus) per quam celeriter
. . . V : LXXVII fatis concessit
. . . die Maii anno Salutis
Humanae M D C XXXIV
H. S. E.
Ignatius Jones architectus
regius ob honorem bonarum
literarum familiari suo
hoc monumentum
D. S. P. F. C.

Note.

[1] In MS. Aubr. 8, fol. 61[v], Aubrey gives a rough drawing of the monument. The lower part is an oblong block, 'thicknes ½ yard: one entire Portland stone' with the inscription on the front. Above is a laurel wreath carved in stone. Behind is what seems to be a mural tablet.

In MS. Aubr. 8, fol. 6[v], Aubrey asks, 'quaere if . . . Chapman is in the first part?' i.e. in MS. Aubr. 6 (Lives, Part i.); but no life of Chapman is found in that volume.

Walter Charleton (16$\frac{19}{20}$–1707).

** Walter Charleton, M.D., borne at Shepton-Malet[a] in com. Somerset, Feb. 2[d], 1619, about 6 h. P.M., his mother being then at supper.

*** 'Dom. G. Charleton, D. M.: nascitur die Mercurii[b] $\frac{2}{12}$ Febr., aerae Christi 16$\frac{19}{20}$, hor. 12, mom. 18 P. M.'—this[o] is my lord William Brounckar's doeing and is his owne hand-writing.

* MS. Aubr. 8, fol. 61. Aubrey has been unable to make out the whole inscription.

** MS. Aubr. 23, fol. 53[v], and a slip at fol. 100[v].

[a] 'His father was minister there':

Aubrey in MS. Wood F. 39, fol. 144.

*** MS. Aubr. 23, fol. 54.

[b] Wednesday.

[o] i.e. the horoscope which Aubrey has there.

Thomas Charnock (1526–1581).

* Mr. ⟨Andrew⟩ Paschal, rector of Chedzoy, hath the originall scroll of Mr. Charnock, scilicet, of the philosopher's stone.

** Mr. Charnock, the chymist, mentioned in ⟨Ashmole's⟩ *Theatrum Chymicum*, was buryed in Otterhampton neer Bridgewater, anno 1581 ᵃ, April 21, aged 55 yeares— ⟨from⟩ Mr. Paschal: vide Mr. Paschal's lettre, here inserted ᵇ before ⟨the life of⟩ Nicholas Mercator, p. 32.

*** *Concerning Mr. Charnocke.*

Sir,

Mr. Wells of Bridgewater performed his promise. He writes that the house was lately pulled down, and is new built from the ground, all except the wall at the east end. He could make nothing of what was only left over the chimney; but he found the little dore that led out of the lodging-chamber into the little *Athanor* roome. Of that you have an account in the enclosed draught.

The two roses I take to be the white and red, termes common with Charnocke for the two magisteries. The two animals over them I suppose are wolves, denoting the ᶜ ☿ abounding with a volatile ᵈ ☉ and used for preparing and purifying one of the principal ingredients into the worke. Out of it growes (if those authors may be credited) most precious fruits.

I obliged a painter to goe over soon after I had been there and take all he could find exactly. He was there, but I could never get anything from him: an ingeniose man, but egregiously carelesse.

Looking back I find this noted by me—June 22, 1681; the place in the *Athanor* roome in which he kept his

---

* MS. Aubr. 21, fol. 77.

** MS. Aubr. 8, fol. 9ᵛ.

ᵃ Anthony Wood noted here 'rather 1680; if you meane Stephen Charnock, the divine': but saw his error and erased the note.

ᵇ i. e. as fol. 56–58 of MS. Aubr. 8.

*** MS. Aubr. 8, fol. 58ᵛ; the heading is by Aubrey; the letter is the original.

ᶜ Earth.

ᵈ Salt.

lampe was stone-work about 15 inches deep and so much
square in the clear from side to side. Over it a wooden
collar with a rabit* as to lett-in a cover close. No place
to come into the square but by the collar, contrived probably
after the accident of burning his tabernacle mentioned in
his printed pieces.

I find this added :—'Twas painted about the chimney
thus :—on the left side of the chimney proceeded from
a red stalk streaked with white, first, a paire of red branches,
then a paire of white, then of red, then one of white to
the top ; something like a rabbit's head painted looking
from the chimney to the foot of the sayd stalk.—The next
picture separated as by a pillar on the chimney :—from
one stalke, two white branches, of either side one ; then
two red, above; then two white; then at the top this

, the balls of a dusky yellow.—The next picture is
also distinguished by a pillar on the chimney to the
right side : this ⟨is⟩ quite obscured by smoake.

In the left corner of the roome another picture described,
with double branches, white, then red, then white, then one
on the top red.

This is all I can say of that place, of which I wish I were
capable of sending a better account.

The other side of Mr. Wells's paper gives you one of
the schemes in the middle of the roll, which is now by me.

The transcription of the thing, said to be Ripley's,
should cost Mr. Ashmole nothing, were I not under an
obligation not to impart it to any. It may be greatly to
his losse who did communicate it to me, if the owner
should know I have it. If I can contrive a way to send
it with leave I shall be ambitious to gratify that worthy
person.

your etc.
And. Paschall.

* Rabbet = 'a groove cut along the edge of another board, required to fit
edge of a board . . . to receive a it.'—*Century Dictionary*.
corresponding projection cut on the

. * To his much honoured friend John Aubrey, esqre.,
these present, at Mr. Hooke's lodgeings in Gresham College,
London.

** Sir,
    I received and returne thankes for yours.
Since my last I got leave to transcribe what Mr. Charnocke wrote on the backside of the rolle, which I heer
send you. I kept as neare as I could to the very errours
of his pen, by which it may in part be seen that he was,
as he professes, an *unlettered* scholar. The inside of the rolle
(which is all in Latine, and perhaps the same with the
scrowle mentioned in *Theatrum Chemicum*, p. 375) was
composed by a great master in the Hermetic philosophy
and written by a master of his pen. Some notes written
in void spaces of it by Mr. Charnocke's hand shew he did
not (at least throughly) understand it. But it seemes to
me that this rolle was a kind of *Vade mecum* or manuall
that the students in that wisdome carryed about with
them. I presume 'twas drawn out of Raymund Lully, of
which I shall be able to gaine fuller satisfaction when
I have his workes come down.
    I was also, since my last, at Mr. Charnocke's house in
Comag, where the rolle was found; and saw the place
where 'twas hid. I saw the litle roome and contrivance
he had for keeping his worke, and found it ingeniosely
ordered so as to prevent a like accident to that which
befell him New Yeare's day, 1555; and this pretty place
joining as a closet to his chamber was to make a servant
needlesse and the worke of giving attendance more easy
to himselfe. I have also a litle iron instrument found
there which he made use of about his fire. I sawe on the
doore of his little *Athanor*-room, if I may so call it, drawn
by his own hand, with course colours and work, but ingeniously, an embleme of his worke, at which I gave some
guesses, and so about the walls of his chamber. I thinke

---

* Address, on MS. Aubr. 8, fol. 53.   ** MS. Aubr. 8, fol. 57. The letter
Postage is marked as '6d.'   is the original.

there was in all 5 panes of this worke, all somewhat differing from each other, some very obscure and almost worne out. They told me that people had been unwilling to dwell in that house, because reputed troublesome,—I presume from some traditionall storyes of this person, who was looked on by his neighbours as no better than a conjurer.

As I was taking horse to come home from this pleasant entertainment, I see a pretty ancient man come forth of the next doore. I asked him how long he had lived there. Finding that it was the place of his birth, I inquired if he had ever heard anything of that Mr. Charnocke. He told me he had heard his mother (who dyed about 12 or 14 yeares since and was 80 yeares of age at her decease) often speake of him ; that he kept a fire in, divers yeares ; that his daughter lived with him ; that once he was gone forth, and by her neglect (whome he trusted it with in his absence) the fire went out and so all his worke was lost ; the brazen head was very neare comeing to speake, but so was he disappointed.

I suppose the pleasant-humoured man—for that he was so appeares by his breviary—alludeing to Frier Bacon's story, did so put off the inquisitivenes of his simple neighbours, and thence it is come down there by tradition till now.

Indeed it appeares by the inclosed lines that when he wrote the rolle he had attained but to the white stone, which is perhaps not half the way to the red,

(' Put me to my sister Mercury, I congeale into silver ') ; and, if the old woman's tale were true, he might afterwards be going on and be come neare to the red and then that vexing accident might befall him ; and this might be, notwithstanding what is sayd in the fragment, referred to the yeare 1574, for (being so neare the red as the traditionall story sayes he was) he might see in that 50th yeare of his age that the white was ferment to the red.

You may observe my calculation differs in one thing from Mr. Ashmole's in his notes upon *Theatrum Chemicum,*

p. 478 : for he makes 'the presse' to have been (out of Stowe) 1558, but I (out of Dr. Burnet's History) 1557 ; and consequently he supposes the presse to have been after the finishing of the Breviary, but I presume he set on the Breviary after he was pressed. So indeed he him-selfe plainly averres in the 4 last lines of chapter 4 of his Breviary (*Theatrum Chemicum*, p. 296). I mention this to give a reason for my dissenting from your worthy friend, to whome I must intreat you to communicate these in-formations that I have had opportunity to gather, and also present my humble service.

Sir,

I thought when I set pen to paper to have given you an account of some conversation I have had with a person who is a zealous friend and admirer of this sort of know-ledge, but I see I have already gone beyound bounds. I shal onely say he hath almost convinced me that it is not so hidden and obscure, so difficult and unaccountable, as men commonly seeme to beleeve. I am in hopes to receive, by Mr. Hooke's and Mr. Lodwick's favour, the lamp for which he was pleased to give directions some time since.

I have not yet seen my miller and his invention, though he promised to bring it to me ; I presume 'tis not yet ready. I expect him dayly.

Pray give my humble service to our worthy friend, and to Mr. Pigott.

I am sure I now need the[a] . . . .

* I shall be glad to heare of a new edition of the *Theatrum*[b] and that you will speed the printing of your MS. of Raymund Lullye's. If it doe not goe soon to the presse, how joyfull should I be to have the perusall of it ! 'Tis the onely grievous thing I suffer in this solitude that I may not see good bookes and good men, but I must be content.

[a] Line frayed off.
* MS. Aubr. 8, fol. 56ᵛ.

[b] Elias Ashmole's *Theatrum Chemi-cum Britannicum*, 1652.

* The first thing written on the back side [a] is as followes :—

At Stockeland, Bristowe, iiii myles from Brigewater, 1566.

The principall rules of naturall philosophy figuratively set fourth to the obtayning of the philosopher's stone, collectyd out of xl auctors by the unletteryd scholer Thomas Charnocke, student in the sciencis off astronomie, physick, and naturall philosophie, the same year that he dedicatyd a booke off the science to queene Elizabeth of Englande which was Anno Domini 1566, and the viii yere off her raigne.

⟨MS. Aubr. 8, fol. 56ᵛ, gives the rest of the writing on the back of the roll; but the outer edge of the leaf is torn off, and the writing consequently imperfect⟩

<pre>
**. . . . . his pose
   . . . . . on the white and red rose
   . . . . black appere sartayne
   . . . xx or it wax bright
   . . . lx after to black againe
   . . . xx or it be perfet ᵇ white
   . . . it or all quick things be dedd
   . . . . . or this rose be redd
        Thomas Charnocke [in ᶜ red letters]
              1572.
</pre>

This is the philosopher's dragon which eateth upp his one tayle
Beinge famisshed in a doungen of glas and all for my prevayle
⟨Ma⟩ny yeres I keapt this dragon in pryson strounge.
⟨Bef⟩ore I coulde mortiffy him I thought it lounge
⟨But⟩ at the lenght by God's grace yff ye beleve my worde
⟨I⟩ vanquished him wythe a fyrie sword.

[Then ᵈ followes the picture of a dragon with a black stone under his foot, with a white stone neare his breast, with a red stone over his head: his tayle is turned to his gapeing mouth.]

The dragon speketh :—

<pre>
. . . . . souldiers in armoure bright
. . . ⟨n⟩ot have kylled me in fyelde in fighte
. . . ⟨Cha⟩rnock nother for all his philosophie
. . . ⟨pr⟩yson and famyne he had not famysshed me
</pre>

---

* MS. Aubr. 8, fol. 56.
[a] i. e. of the roll mentioned, *supra*, p. 164.
** MS. Aubr. 8, fol. 56ᵛ.
ᵇ ' Perfet ' is scored through.

ᶜ A note added in the text by Paschall.
ᵈ A description by Paschall of a drawing on the roll, after the above verses.

⟨Guy of W⟩arwicke nor Bevys of Southehampton

. . . . such a venomous dragon

. . . . fowght with Hidra the serpent

. . . . . . e cowlde not have his intent

. . . . n the wyse inclose too in a toonne off brasse

. . . . d shutt up in a doungeon of glasse

. . . . lyffe was so quick and my poyson so strounge

. . . . e cowlde kyll me it was full lounge

. . . . he hyld me in prison day and nyght

. . ⟨k⟩eapt me from sustenance to mynishe me myght

. . . When I saw none other remedye

. . . very hunger I eate myne one bodye

. . . . . by corruption I became black and dedd

⟨Th⟩at precious stone which is in my hedd

. . . be worth a M^{li} to him that hath skyll

⟨F⟩or that stone's sake he wysely dyd me kyll

⟨In d⟩eath I dyd hym forgyve even at the very hower

⟨Se⟩inge that he wylbe beneficiall unto the poore

When I was alyve I was but stronge poyson

Profittable for few things in conclusion

⟨Now th⟩at I ame now dying in myne owne blood

⟨N⟩ow I do excell all other wordeley good

⟨A⟩ new name is given me of those that be wysse

⟨No⟩w I ame named the elixer off great price

⟨If y⟩ou wyll make prouff, put to me my sister mercury

⟨I will co⟩ngoyle hir into sylver in the twinkling off an eye

. . . . . . qualites I have many mo

. . . ⟨foo⟩lyshe and ingenorant shall never kno

Few prelates and Masters of art within this reame

Do knowe aryght what I do meane

My great grawnt-father was killyd by Ravnde Lulli, knight of Spayne

And my g⟨r⟩awnt-father by Syr Gorge Rippley, a chanon of
       Yenglande sartayne

And my father by a chanon of Lechefelde was kylled truly

Who gave hym to his man Thomas Davton when he dyd dye

And my mother by Mr. Thomas Norton off Bristow slayn was

And each of these were able to make *⊙ or ☽ in a glasse

And now I ame made the great and riche elixer allso

That my master shall never lack whether he ryde or go

But he and all other must have great feare and aye

As secrettely as they can to exchaunge my increase awaye.

Here Charnock changeth to a better cheere

For the sorrow that he hath sufferyd many a yere

    * The symbols for sun and moon = gold and silver.

Or that he could accomplish the regiment of his fyre
. . . . ᵃor he saw his desier
Wherefore in thy hartt now prease God allway
And do good deeds with it whatsoever thou may
Therefore thy god gave this science unto thee
To be his stuarde and refresh the poore and needie.

Anno D. 1526—Thomas Charnocke borne at Feversham in Kent.

He travailed all England over to gain his knowledge.

1554—He attained the secret from his master of Salisbury close, who dying left his worke with him.

He lost it by fireing his tabernacle on a New Yeare's day.

About this time being 28 yeares of age, he learned the secret againe of the prior of Bathe.

He began anew with a servant, and againe by himselfe alone without a servant.

He continued it nine monthes; was within a month of his reckoning; the crowe's head began to appear black.

1557—He, pressed on a warre proclaimed against the French (Burnet's History, part 2, p. 355), broke and cast all away. January 1, he began; July 20, he ended, his Breviary.

1562—He marryed Agnes Norden at Stockland, Bristoll.

1563—He buryed Absolon his son.

1566—He dedicated a booke to Queen Elizabeth 9 yeares after the Breviary was penned.

He dated the rolle at Stockland.

1572—He wrote the posy on the rolle.

He wrote his aenigma ad Alchimiam ᵇ and de Alchimia ᶜ.

1573—the fragment ᵈ of ' knocke the child on the head.'

1574—that he never saw the white ferment to the red till that 5cth yeare of his age.

ᵃ Half a line which Paschall could not read.
ᵇ Printed in Ashmole's *Theatrum Chemicum.*
ᶜ Printed ibid. ᵈ Printed ibid.

1576—the difficulty of the philosophick number in the roll.
1581—Buryed at Otterhampton neare Stockland out of
    his house at Comage where he kept his worke.
1587—Bridget Charnock (probably his daughter that kept
    his house when his fire was sayd to go out),
    marryed to one . . . Thatcher in Stockland.

Collected out of the Roll, the register, and *Theatrum Chemicum*.

Geoffrey Chaucer (1328–1400).

* Sir Geffrey Chaucer: memorandum—Sir Hamond
L'Estrange, of . . . , in . . . had his Workes in MS.,
a most curious piece, most rarely writt and illumined,
which he valued at 100 *li*. His grandson and heire still
haz it.—From Mr. Roger L'Estrange.

He taught his sonne the use of ⟨the⟩ astrolabe at 10;
prout per his treatise of the Astrolabe.

Dunnington Castle, neer Newbury, was his; a noble
seate and strong castle, which was held by the King
(Charles I[st]) (who governour?) but since dismanteled.

Memorandum:—neer this castle was an oake, under
which Sir Jeofrey was wont to sitt, called *Chaucer's-oake*,
which was cutt downe by . . . . . . tempore Caroli I[mi]; and
so it was, that . . . . . . was called into the starre chamber,
and was fined for it. . . . Judge Richardson[a] harangued
against him long, and like an orator, had topiques from
the Druides, etc. This information I had from . . . an
able attorney that was at the hearing.

His picture is at his old howse at Woodstock (neer the
parke-gate), a foot high, halfe way: has passed from
proprietor to proprietor.

** One Mr. Goresuch of Woodstock dined with us at
Rumney marsh, who told me that at the old Gothique-
built howse neer the parke-gate at Woodstock, which was
the howse of Sir Jeffrey Chaucer, that there is his picture,

* MS. Aubr. 8, fol. 27.   ** Aubrey, in MS. Wood F. 39,
[a] Sir Thomas Richardson, Chief   fol. 200: April 7, 1673.
Justice of the King's Bench, 1631.

which goes with the howse from one to another—which see.

William Chillingworth (1602–164¾).

* William Chillingworth[1], D. D.,—vide Anthony Wood's *Antiq. Oxon.* in Trinity College—was borne in Oxford. His father was a brewer.

About anno . . . he was acquainted with one . . . who drew him and some other scholars over to Doway, where he was not so well entertained as he thought he merited for his great disputative witt. They made him the porter (which was to trye his temper, and exercise his obedience): so he stole over and came to Trinity College againe, where he was fellowe.

William Laud, A. B. C.[a], was his godfather and great friend. He sent his grace weekly intelligence of what passed in the university[2]. Sir William Davenant (poet laureat) told me that notwithstanding this doctor's great reason, he was guiltie of the detestable crime of treachery. Dr. Gill[3], filius D[ris] Gill (schoolmaster of Paules schoole), and Chillingworth held weekely intelligence one with another for some yeares, wherein they used to nibble at states-matters. Dr. Gill in one of his letters calles King James and his sonne, the old foole and the young one, which letter Chillingworth communicates to W. Laud, A. B. Cant. The poore young Dr. Gill was seised, and a terrible storme pointed towards him, which, by the eloquent intercession and advocation of Edward, earle of Dorset, together with the teares of the poore old Doctor his father, and supplication on his knees to his majestie, were blowne-over. I am sorry so great a witt should have such a naeve.

> Absentem qui rodit amicum,
> Qui non defendit alio culpante, solutos
> Qui captat risus hominum famamque dicacis,
> Fingere qui non visa potest, commissa tacere
> Qui nequit : hic niger est; hunc tu, Romane, caveto.
>
> HORAT. lib. I, sat. iv.

---

* MS. Aubr. 6, fol. 121[v].   [a] i. e. Arch Bishop of Canterbury.

He was a little man, blackish haire, of a saturnine complexion.

The lord Falkland (vide ⟨life of⟩ lord Falkland) and he had such extraordinary clear reasons, that they were wont to say at Oxon that if the great Turke were to be converted by naturall reason, these two were the persons to convert him.

He lies buried in the south side of the cloysters at Chichester, where he dyed of the *morbus castrensis* after the taking of Arundel castle by the parliament : wherin he was very much blamed by the king's soldiers for his advice in military affaires there, and they curst *that little priest* and imputed the losse of the castle to his advice. In his sicknesse he was inhumanely treated by Dr. Cheynell[4], who, when he was to be buryed, threw his booke into the grave with him, saying, 'Rott with the rotten ; let the dead bury the dead.' Vide a pamphlet of about 6 sheets writt by Dr. Cheynell (maliciously enough) where he gives an account of his life.

This following inscription was made and set-up by Mr. Oliver Whitby[5], his fellowe-collegiate at Trinity College and now one of the prebendarys of this church :

† This is a mistake ; he was not Chantor of the Church, but Chancellor of the Church of Sarum, whose office was antiently to read a lecture in Latin, quarterly, in the pulpit in the library, either in Theologie or the Canon Lawe. Since the Reformation 'twas commuted into preaching on the Holy-dayes. He never swore to all the points of the Church of England.

‡ Minister of Petworth.

Virtuti sacrum.
Spe certissimae resurrectionis
Hic reducem expectat animam
GULIELMVS CHILLINGWORTH,
S. T. P.
Oxonii natus et educatus,
Collegii S^{tae} Trinitatis olim
Socius, Decus et Gloria.
Omni Literarum genere celeberrimus,
Ecclesiae Anglicanae adversus Romano-Catholicam
Propugnator invictissimus,
Ecclesiae Sarisburiensis Praecentor † dignissimus ;
Sine Exequiis,
Furentis cujusdam Theologastri,
Doctoris Cheynell ‡,
Diris et maledictione sepultus :
Honoris et Amicitiae ergò,
Ab OLIVERO WHITBY,

Brevi hoc monimento,
Posterorum memoriae consecratus,
Anno Salutis,
1672.[a]

My tutor, W. Browne[6], haz told me, that Dr. Chilling-worth studied not much, but when he did, he did much in a little time. He much delighted in Sextus Empeiricus. He did walke much in the College grove, and there contemplate, and meet with some *cod's-head* or other, and dispute with him and baffle him. He thus prepared himselfe before-hand. He would alwayes be disputing; so would my tutor. I thinke it was an epidemick evill of that time, which I thinke now is growne out of fashion, as unmannerly and boyish. He was the readiest and nimblest disputant of his time in the university, perhaps none haz equalled him since.

I have heard Mr. Thomas Hobbes, Malmesb. (who knew him), say, *that he was like a lusty fighting fellow that did drive his enimies before him, but would often give his owne party smart* [b] *back-blowes.*

When Doctor Kettle, (the president of Trin. Coll. Oxon.) dyed[7], which was in anno ⟨1643⟩ Dr. Chillingworth was competitor for the presidentship, with Dr. Hannibal Potter and Dr. Roberts. Dr. Han. Potter had been formerly chaplain to the bishop of Winton, who was so much Dr. Potter's friend, that though (as Will Hawes haz told me) Dr. Potter was not lawfully elected, upon referring themselves to their visitor (bishop of Winton), the bishop (Curle) ordered Dr. Potter possession; and let the fellowes gett him out if they could. This was shortly after the lord Falkland was slaine, who had he lived, Dr. Chillingworth assured Will Hawes, no man should have carried it against him : and that he was so extremely discomposed and wept bitterly for the losse of his deare friend, yet notwithstanding he doubted not to have an astergance[8] for it.

---

[a] 1642, in MS.   [b] Dupl. with 'terrible.'

Notes.

[1] William Chillingworth was elected Scholar of Trinity June 2, 1618 (then of St. Martin's parish, Oxon, aged 19), and Fellow, June 10, 1628.

[2] For another instance of reports sent to Laud (who was Chancellor of Oxford 1630–41) about Oxford matters, see Clark's Wood's *Life and Times*, ii. 238.

[3] Alexander Gill matr. at Trinity College, June 26, 1612, was Clerk at Wadham College, April 20, 1613, but rejoined Trinity and from thence took his D.D., March 9, 163$\frac{4}{5}$. He was usher to his father in St. Paul's School 1621–28, being removed for the offence here related.

[4] Francis Cheynell, a native of Oxford (like Chillingworth), Fellow of Merton 1629, D.D. July 24, 1649.

[5] Oliver Whitby, matr. at Trinity, Oct. 15, 1619; Archdeacon of Chichester, Dec. 23, 1672.

[6] William Browne, of Blandford St. Mary, Dorset, aged 16, elected Scholar of Trinity May 28, 1635, M.A. March 18, 164$\frac{1}{2}$.

[7] Anthony Wood, in a marginal note, objects—'This cannot be: Dr. Kettle died after Chillingworth.' But Wood is wrong. Kettell died in July 1643; Chillingworth in January, 164$\frac{2}{3}$; Potter was admitted President August 8, 1643.

[8] 'Astergance,' apparently an Aubrey form for 'abstergence,' i. e. consolation. The meaning perhaps is:—although Chillingworth was grieved for Falkland's (or Kettell's) death, he had looked for the consolation of being promoted to the Presidentship of his College.

John Clavell (1601–1642).

* John Clavell, the famous thiefe, borne May 11, 1601, 11^h 30′ P.M.

John Cleveland (1613–1658).

** John Cleveland was borne at . . . (quaere Mr. Nayler) in Warwickshire. He was a fellow of St. John's Colledge in Cambridge, where he was more taken notice of for his being an eminent disputant, then a good poet. Being turned out of his fellowship for a malignant he came to Oxford, where the king's army was, and was much caressed by them. He went thence to the garrison at Newark upon Trent, where upon some occasion of drawing of articles, or some writing, he would needs add a short conclusion, viz. 'and hereunto we annex our lives, as a labell to our trust.' After the king was beaten out of the field, he came to London, and retired in Grayes

* MS. Aubr. 23, fol. 121ᵛ.   ** MS. Aubr. 6, fol. 6ᵛ.

Inne. He, and Sam. Butler, &c. of Grayes Inne, had [a]
a clubb every night. He was a comely plump man,
good curled haire, darke browne. Dyed of the scurvy,
and lies buried in St. Andrew's church, in Holborne,
anno Domini 165.. (quaere Mr. Nayler [b], of . . .).

George Clifford, earl of Cumberland (1558–1605).

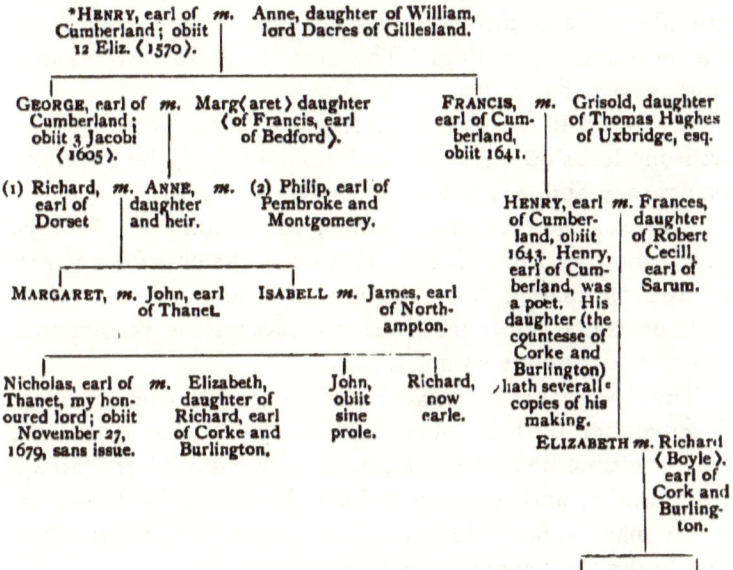

| *HENRY, earl of Cumberland; obiit 12 Eliz. (1570).* | m. | Anne, daughter of William, lord Dacres of Gillesland. |

| GEORGE, earl of Cumberland; obiit 3 Jacobi (1605). | m. | Marg⟨aret⟩ daughter ⟨of Francis, earl of Bedford⟩. | | FRANCIS, earl of Cumberland, obiit 1641. | m. | Grisold, daughter of Thomas Hughes of Uxbridge, esq. |

(1) Richard, earl of Dorset — m. ANNE, daughter and heir. — m. (2) Philip, earl of Pembroke and Montgomery.

HENRY, earl of Cumberland, obiit 1643. Henry, earl of Cumberland, was a poet. His daughter (the countesse of Corke and Burlington) /hath severall [c] copies of his making. — m. Frances, daughter of Robert Cecill, earl of Sarum.

MARGARET, m. John, earl of Thanet.

ISABELL m. James, earl of Northampton.

ELIZABETH m. Richard ⟨Boyle⟩. earl of Cork and Burlington.

Nicholas, earl of Thanet, my honoured lord; obiit November 27, 1679, sans issue. — m. Elizabeth, daughter of Richard, earl of Corke and Burlington.

John, obiit sine prole.

Richard, now earle.

† This George, earl of Cumberland, built the
greatest fleet of shipping that ever any subject
did. He had a vast estate, and could then ride
in his owne lands from Yorkeshire to West-
morland. He had . . . castles.

† From Elizabeth, countesse of Thanet.

The best account of his expedition with his fleet to
America is to be found in Purchas's *Pilgrim*. He tooke
from the Spaniards to the value of seaven or 8 hundred
thousand poundes. When he returned with this riche

[a] MS. has 'did had,' i.e., Aubrey
at first thought of writing 'did have.'
[b] Perhaps John Nayler, fellow of
St. John's College, Cambridge.

* Aubrey, in MS. Rawl. D. 727,
fol. 96ᵛ.
[c] Subst. for 'a great many.'

cargo (the richest without doubt that ever subject brought), the queene's councell (where he had some that envyed him—

Virtutis comes Invidia)

layed their heads together and concluded 'twas too much for a subject to have, and confiscated it all to the queen, even shippes and all, and to make restauration to the Spaniard, that he was forced to sell fifteene thousand pounds per annum. My lady Thanet told me she sawe the accounts in writing. The armada of the Argonautes was but a trifle to this.

As I take it, Sir Walter Ralegh went this brave voyage with his lordship ; and Mr. Edmund Wright, the excellent navigator ; and, not unlikely, Mr. Harriot too.

This was the breaking of that ancient and noble family ; but Robert, earl of Salisbury (who was the chiefest enemie) afterwards maried his daughter, as above, as he might well be touch't in conscience, to make some recompence after he had donne so much mischiefe.

That he was an acquaintance of Sir Walter Raleigh, I remember by this token, that Sir James Long told me that one time he came to Draycot with Sir Walter Raleigh from Bathe, and, hunting a buck in the parke there, his horse made a false step in a conie-borough and threw him and brake the kennell-bone of his shoulder.

Henry Clifford, earl of Cumberland (1591–1643).

* From the pedigree of the earles of Cumberland[1] in the hands of Elizabeth, countesse of Thanet, daughter of the earle of Burlington and Corke.

George, ⟨third⟩ earl of Cumberland, had seaven † castles in the north. He was buryed with his ances-

† Quaere quot castella[a]. tors at Skippon Castle. Obiit about the beginning of King James's raigne.

Vide epistle to George, earl of Cumberland, before the *History of the Massacre.*

---

* MS. Aubr. 8, fol. 28.   [a] The number was doubtful, see *supra*, p. 175.

Henry, ⟨fifth⟩ earl of Cumberland, was a poet; the countesse of Corke and Burlington haz still his verses. He was of Christ Church, Oxon[2]. Nicholas, earl of Thanet, was wont to say that the mare of Fountaines-abbey did dash, meaning that since they gott that estate (given to the church) they did never thrive but still declined.

Henry, lord Clifford, first earl of Cumberland, obiit 34 Henry VIII (1542); sepult. in ecclesia Skippon. Knight of the Garter.

| Henry, lord Clifford, second earle of Cumberland, obiit 12 Eliz., 8 Januarii 1570 (i.e. ♅). He was knight of the most noble order of the Garter, and lord of Westmorland and Vesse. Buried in Skippon Church. | *m.* Anne, daughter of William, lord Dacres of Gillesland, his second wife. She died in Skipton Castle in July 1581, and was buryed in the vault of that Church. |

| 1. George, third earl of Cumberland, knight of the Garter, that made the famous expedition to America. Obiit 1605 in the Savoy at London. Sepult. in Skippon Church. | *m.* Margaret, daughter of Francis, earl of Bedford. | 2. Francis, erearl of Cumberland. | *m.* Mris Grizell Hughes of Uxbridge, widow to Thomas[a] Nevill, lord Abergavenny. |

| Richard, earle of Dorset. Obiit at Dorset house, 28 March, 1624. | *m.* Lady Anne Clifford (quaere obiit). | *m.* Philip, earl of Pembroke, etc. | Henry, lord Clifford; last earl of Cumberland of that line. Obiit in Yorke, 1643. | *m.* Frances Cecill, only daughter of Robert, earl of Salisbury, Lord High Treasurer. Obiit 14 Feb. 1643. |

had issue only two daughters.

Elizabeth Clifford, *maried* (1635) Richard borne in Skipton Castle, 1613. Boyle, earle of Corke and Burlington.

* Henry, the last earle of Cumberland, was an ingeniose gentleman for those times and a great acquaintance of the Lord Chancellor Bacon's; and often writt to one another, which lettres the countesse of Corke and Burlington, my lady Thanet's mother, daughter and heir of that family, keepes as reliques; and a poeme in English that her father wrott upon the Psalmes and many other subjects, and very well, but the language being now something out of fashion, like Sir Philip Sydney's, they will not print it.

Notes.

[1] Aubrey gives in trick the coat:—'checquy or and azure, a fess gules [Clifford],' surmounted by an earl's coronet. Anthony Wood has a note here:—'George, earl of Cumberland, A.M. 1592 : A.B. Aed. Christi, 1608, quaere'—this latter degree belongs to Henry, fifth earl.

[2] Matric. Jan. 30, 160⅘ : took B.A. Feb. 16, 160⅞.

[a] 'Thomas,' is in error for Edward.

* Aubrey, in MS. Wood F. 39, fol. 208 : May 17, 1673.

Sir Edward Coke (155½–1633).

* Vide his life by . . .: quaere his nephew or sonne [a] Roger Coke. Sir Edward Coke [1], knight, Lord Chiefe Justice of the King's Bench, was borne at . . . in Norfolke. I heard an old lawyer (. . . Dunstable) of the Middle Temple, 1646, who was his country-man, say that he was borne to 300 *li*. land per annum [2], and I have heard some of his country say again that he was borne but to 40 *li*. per annum. What shall one beleeve?

Quaere Roger Coke of what house he was in Cambridge, or if ever at the University.

Old John Tussell (that was my attorney) haz told me that he gott a hundred thousand pounds in one yeare, viz. 1° Jacobi, being then attorney-generall. His advice was that every man of estate (right or wrong) should sue-out his pardon, which cost 5 *li*. which [b] was his fee.

He left an estate of eleaven thousand pounds per annum. Sir John Danvers [3], who knew him, told me that when one told him his sonnes would spend the estate faster then he gott it, he replyed 'they cannot take more delight in spending of it then I did in the getting of it.'

He was chamber-fellow to the Lord Chiefe Baron Wyld's father (Serjeant Wyld [4]). He built the black buildings at the Inner Temple (now burn't) which were above the walke toward the west end, called then 'Coke's buildings.'

After he was putt out of his place of Lord Chief Justice of the King's Bench [c], to spite him, they made him sheriff of Buckinghamshire, anno Dni . . . ; at which time he caused the sheriff's oath to be altered, which till that time was, amongst other things, to enquire after and apprehend all Lollards. He was also chosen, after he was displaced, a burghesse to sitt in Parliament.

† From Roger Coke.   † He was of wonderfull painstaking, as appeares by his writings. He was short-sighted but never used spectacles to his dyeing day, being then 83

---

* MS. Aubr. 6, fol. 28.
[a] 'Or sonne' is scored out.
[b] Dupl. with 'which belonged to him.'   [c] Nov. 15, 1616.

yeares of age. He was a very handsome proper man and
of a curious complexion, as appeares by his picture at
the Inner Temple, which his grandson gave them about
1668, at length, in his atturney-generall's fusted gowne,
which the house haz turned into judge's robes.

He maried, his second wife, . . ., the relickt of Sir . . .
Hatton, who was with child when he maried her [a].—⟨from⟩
⟨Elizabeth⟩ lady Purbec ; vide B. Johnson's masque of
the Gipsies.

He dyed at Stoke-poges in com. Bucks . . . 1638 [b]
(quaere), but is buryed at . . . in Norfolk.

For his moralls, see *Sir W. Raleigh's Tryall.*

He shewed himselfe too clownish and bitter in his
carriage to Sir Walter Ralegh at his triall, where he sayes
' Thou traytor,' at every word, and ' thou lyest like a traytor.'
See it in Sir Walter Ralegh's life, Lond. 1678, 8vo.

His rule :—

> Sex horas somno, totidem des legibus aequis,
>   Quatuor orabis, des epulisque duas,
>   Quod reliquum est tempus sacris largire Camenis.

He playes [c] with his case as a cat would with a mouse,
and be so fulsomely pedantique that a school boy would
nauseate it. But when he comes to matter of lawe, all
acknowledge him to be admirable. When Mr. Cuff [d],
secretary to the earle of Essex, was arraigned, he would
dispute with him in syllogismes, till at last one of his
brethern said, ' Prithee, brother, leave off : thou doest
dispute scurvily.' Cuff was a smart man and a great
scholar and baffeld him. Said Cooke

' Dominum cognoscite vestrum ' ;

Cuff replied, ' My lord, you leave out the former part of the
verse [e], which you should have repeated,

Acteon ego sum '—

reflecting on his being a cuckold.

---

[a] Three lines of the text are suppressed here.
[b] Sept. 3, 1633.
[c] Subst. for 'will play.'

[d] Henry Cuff: Clark's Wood's *Life
and Times*, i. 424.
[e] OVID, *Metam.* iii. 230

N 2

* The world expected from him a commentary on Littleton's Tenures; and he left them his Common-place book, which is now so much made use of.

Sir Edward Coke did envie[a] Sir Francis Bacon, and was wont to undervalue his lawe : vide de hoc in the lord Bacon's lettres, where he expostulates this thing with Sir Edward Coke, and tells him that he may grow when that others doe stand at a stay.

Memorandum :—he was of Clifford's Inne before he was of the Inner Temple, as the fashion then was first to be of an Inne of Chancery.

Memorandum :—when the play called *Ignoramus* (made by one Ruggle of Clare-hall) was acted with great applause before King James, they dressed Sir Ignoramus like Chief Justice Coke and cutt his beard like him and feigned his voyce. Mr. Peyton, our vicar of Chalke, was then a scholar at Kings College and sawe it. This drollery did ducere in seria mala : it sett all the lawyers against the clergie, and shortly upon this Mr. Selden wrote of Tythes not jure divino.

Notes.

[1] Aubrey gives in trick the coat :—'. . ., 3 eagles displayed . . .'

[2] In MS. Aubr. 8, fol. 97[v], Aubrey has this note :—' Sir Edward Coke, Lord Chief Justice—when I was first of the Middle Temple, I heard an old (80 (years old)) Norfolke gentleman of the (name of) Dunstable affirme that Sir Edward Coke was borne but to 300 *li.* a yeare land.'

[3] This story is repeated at the foot of the leaf :—' Sir John Danvers told me that he had heard one say to him, reflecting on his great scraping of wealth, that his sonnes would spend his estate faster then he gott it. He replied, they cannot take more delight in the spending of it then I did in the getting of it.'

[4] George Wilde, Serjeant at Law, 1614 ; father of Sir John Wilde, Chief Baron of the Exchequer, 1648.

Jean Baptiste Colbert (1619–1683).

** Monsieur . . . Colbert was a merchant and an excellent accomptant, i. e. for Debtor and Creditor. He is of Scotish extraction and that obscure enough, his grandfather being a Scotish bag-piper to the Scotch regiment.

* MS. Aubr. 6, fol. 27[v].
[a] Subst. for 'envyed.'
** MS. Aubr. 6, fol. 5. Aubrey

gives in trick the coat ' . . ., a serpent in pale vert.'

Cardinal Mezarin found that his stables were very chardge-able to him, and was imposed upon in accompts. He hearing of this merchant Colbert to be a great master in this art, sends for him and desires him to make inspection into his accounts and putt him into a better method to avoyd being abused. Which he did, and that so well that he imployed him in ordering the accounts of all his estate and found him so usefull that he also made use of him to methodize and settle the accompts of the king. This was his rise.—From Dr. John Pell.

John Colet (1466–1519).

* John Colet, D.D., deane of St. Paule's, London—vide Sir William Dugdale's Historie of Paule's church. After the conflagration his monument being broken, his coffin, which was lead, was full of a liquour which conserved the body. Mr. Wyld and Ralph Greatorex tasted it and 'twas of a kind of insipid tast, something of an ironish tast. The body felt, to the probe of a stick which they thrust into a chinke, like brawne. The coffin was of lead and layd in the wall about 2 foot ½ above the surface of the floore.

Henry Coley (1633–1695 ?).

** My friend Mr. Henry Coley was borne in Magdalen parish in the city of Oxon, Octob. 18, 1633. His father was a joyner over against the Theater.

He is a tayler in Graies Inne lane.

He hath published an ingeniose discourse called *Clavis Astrologiae*, in English, 1669.

He is a man of admirable parts, and more to be expected from him every day: and as good a natured man as can be. And comes by his learning meerly by the strong impulse of his genius. He understands Latin and French: yet never learned out his grammar.

*** Henry Coley[1] natus Oxon, neer Kettle-hall, Octob. 18, horâ 2. 15′ 4″ P.M.—his father a joyner.

* MS. Aubr. 8, fol. 60ᵛ.   fol. 131: June 14, 1671.
** Aubrey in MS. Wood F. 39,   *** MS. Aubr. 8, fol. 86.

He was a woman's tayler : tooke to the love of astrologie, in which he grew in a short time a good proficient ; and in Mr. W. Lilly's later time, when his sight grew dimme, was his amanuensis.

He hath great practise in astrologie, and teacheth mathematiques. He hath published *Clavis Astrologiae*, 1675, a thick octavo, the second edition, wherein he has compiled clearly the whole science out of the best authors.

Note.

[1] Aubrey gives 'ab Astronomiâ Britannicâ,' Coley's nativity and the 'latitudo planetarum' at his birth, on the scheme

'Henry Coley, astrologer, born at Oxon, 1633, October 18, 2ʰ 15′ 4″ P.M., latit. 51° 42′.'

John Collins (162⅔–1683).

* John Collins, accomptant, was borne at Wood-eaton neer Oxford, March the 5th, 162⅔, about half an houre after 5 at night (Saturday night): this I had from himselfe.

** John Collins obiit London, November 10, 1683.

*** John Collins :—adde his sheet *Of interest*, and *Plea for Irish cattle* : all the rest are set downe, but not when printed. And also his *Historie of salt and fisherie* [a], 1682, printed by A. Godbid, 4to.

**** John Collins, a learned mathematician, fellow of the Royal Society: scripsit plurima : he was not an University man, but was first prentice to ⟨Thomas⟩ Allam the bookebinder.

Anthony Cooper, earl of Shaftesbury (1621–168⅔).

***** Anthony, earl of Shaftesbury :—Mcmoires relating the principall passages of his life, in folio, stitcht, printed by Samuel Lee, 1681.

Samuel Cooper (1609–1672).

****** Samuel Cowper, his majestie's alluminer and my honord friend, obiit May . . ., 1672 : sepultus in Pancrace

* MS. Aubr. 23, fol. 28.
** MS. Aubr. 7, fol. 5.
*** MS. Aubr. 8, fol. 25.
[a] See Clark's Wood's *Life and Times*, iii. 24.

**** Aubrey in MS. Wood F. 39, fol. 316: April 9, 1679.
***** MS. Aubr. 8, fol. 16ᵛ.
****** MS. Aubr. 6, fol. 2.

chancell, next grave to father . . . Symonds, e societate
Jesu—their coffins touch.   Aetat. circiter 6—.

Thomas Cooper (1517 ?–1594).

* Thomas Cooper, Magdalenensis — vide Anthony Wood's
Antiq. Oxon.: quaere if he was not schoolmaster at
Winchester Colledge ?

Dr. Edward Davenant told me that this learned man had
a shrew to his wife, who was irreconcileably angrie with him
for sitting-up late at night so, compileing ᵃ his Dictionarie,
(*Thesaurus linguae Romanae et Britannicae*, Londini, 1584 ;
dedicated to Robert Dudley, earl of Leicester, and Chancellor
of Oxford).   When he had halfe-donne it, she had the
opportunity to gett into his studie, tooke all his paines out
in her lap, and threw it into the fire, and burnt it.   Well,
for all that, that good man had so great a zeale for the
advancement of learning, that he began it again, and went
through with it to that perfection that he hath left it to us,
a most usefull worke.   He was afterwards made bishop of
Winton.

He dyed ⟨29 Apr. 1594⟩.

*In Thesaurum Thomae Cooper, Magdalenensis, hexasticon Richardi
Stephani.*

Vilescat rutila dives Pactolus arena,
  Hermus, et auriferi nobilis unda Tagi,
Vilescant Croesi gemmae Midaeque talenta,

† Verstegan deservedly blames him for that expression.   Major apud Britones † eruta gaza patet :

Hoc, Wainflete, tuo gens Anglica debet alumno,
  Qui vigili nobis tanta labore dedit.

** Mr. Pulleyn ᵇ tells me that Cowper who wrot the
Dictionary was not bishop of Winton but of Lincoln : vide
and mend it ᶜ.

Richard Corbet (1583–1635).

*** Epitaph on master Vincent Corbet, gardiner, father
of the bishop : B. J⟨onson's⟩ *Underwoods*, p. 177.

---

* MS. Aubr. 6, fol. 91ᵛ.
ᵃ Subst. for 'about.'
** MS. Aubr. 8, a slip at fol. 4.
ᵇ Josias Pullen, Vice-Principal of

Magdalen Hall.
  ᶜ Anthony Wood notes :—' afterwards of Winton.'
  *** MS. Aubr. 6, fol. 69.

* Richard Corbet, episcopus (ex last edition of his poemes, in preface sc.p. 16) was made deane of Christ Church, 1620; bishop of Oxon, 1628; bishop of Norwich, 1632. Vide Anthony Wood's *Antiq. Oxon.*

** Richard Corbet[1], D.D., was the son of Vincent Corbet—vide his poem—

> ' better * known
> By Poynter's name then by his owne
> Here lies engaged till the day
> Of raysing bones and quickning clay :
> No wonder, reader, that he hath
> Two sirnames in one epitaph,
> For this one doth comprehend
> All that both families could lend—

who was a gardner at Twicknam, as I have heard my old cosen Whitney say. Vide in B. Johnson's *Underwoods* an epitaph on this Vincent Corbet, where he speakes of his nurseries etc., p. 177.

He was a Westminster scholar; old parson Bussey, of Alscott in Warwickshire, went to schoole with him—he would say that he was a very handsome man, but something apt to abuse, and a coward.

He was a student (vide Anthony Wood's *Antiq. Oxon.*) of Christ-church in Oxford. He was very facetious, and a good fellowe. One time he and some of his acquaintance being merry at Fryar Bacon's study (where was good liquor sold), they were drinking on the leads of the house, and one of the scholars was asleepe, and had a paire of good silke stockings on. Dr. Corbet (then M.A., if not B.D.) gott a paire of cizers and cutt them full of little holes, but when the other awaked, and percieved how and by whom he was abused, he did chastise him, and made him pay for them.

After he was D. of Divinity, he sang ballads at the Crosse at Abingdon on a market-day. He and some of

---

* MS. Aubr. 8, fol. 15ᵛ.   ** MS. Aubr. 6, fol. 106.
* Subst. for ' farther.'

his camerades were at the taverne by the crosse,† (which by the way was then the finest of England ; ❲ I remember it when I was a freshman : it was admirable curious Gothique architecture, and fine figures in the niches : 'twas one of those built by king ... for his queen : vide Chronicle).

† 'Twas after the fashion of the crosse in High-street in Bristowe, but more curious worke. Quaere if not marble?

The ballad singer complaynd, he had no custome, he could not putt-off his ballades. The jolly Doctor putts-off his gowne, and putts-on the ballad singer's leathern jacket, and being a handsome man, and had a rare full voice, he presently vended a great many, and had a great audience.

After the death of Dr. ⟨William Goodwyn⟩, he was made deane of Christ-church (quaere if ever canon); vide[a] part iii, pag. 7 b.

He had a good interest with great men, as you may find in his poems, and with the then great favourite, the duke of Bucks ; his excellent witt was lettres of recommendation to him. I have forgott the story, but at the same time that Dr. ⟨Samuel⟩ Fell thought to have carried it, Dr. Corbet putt a pretty trick on ⟨him⟩ to lett him take a journey on purpose to London for it, when he had already the graunt of it.

He preacht a sermon before the king at Woodstock (I suppose king James, quaere) and no doubt with a very good grace ; but it happened that he was out, on which occasion there were made these verses :—

> A reverend deane,
> With his band[b] starch't cleane,
>   Did preach before the King ;
> In his band string was spied
> A ring that was tied [2],
>   Was not that a pretty thing ?
> If then without doubt,
> In his text he was out
>   . . . . . . next,

[a] i. e. MS. Aubr. 8, fol. 15ᵛ, *ut supra.* He was never Canon of Ch. Ch.
[b] Dupl. with 'ruffe.'

The ring without doubt
Was the thing putt him out,
For all that were there,
On my conscience, dare sweare,
That he handled it more than his text :—

vide the verses.

* His conversation^a was extreme pleasant.   Dr. Stubbins[3]
was one of his cronies ; he was a jolly fatt Dr. and a very
good house-keeper; parson of ⟨Ambrosden⟩ in Oxfordshire.
As Dr. Corbet and he were riding in Lob-lane, in wett
weather, ('tis an extraordinary deepe dirty lane) the
coach fell ; and Dr. Corbet sayd that Dr. Stubbins was
up to the elbowes in mud, he was up to the elbowes in
Stubbins.

Anno Domini ⟨1628⟩ he was made bishop of Oxford, and
I have heard that he had an admirable, grave, and venerable
aspect.

One time, as he was confirming, the country people
pressing in to see^b the ceremonie, sayd he, *'Beare-off there,
or I'le confirme yee with my staffe.'*   Another time being to
lay his hand on the head of a man very bald, he turns to
his chaplaine (Lushington) and sayd,*'Some dust, Lushington,'*
(to keepe his hand from slipping).   There was a man with
a great venerable beard ; sayd the bishop, ' *You, behind the
beard.'*

His chaplain, Dr. Lushington[4], was a very learned and
ingeniose man, and they loved one another.   The bishop
sometimes would take the key of the wine-cellar, and he and
his chaplaine would goe and lock themselves in and be merry.
Then first he layes downe his episcopall hat,—'*There lyes
the Dr.'*   Then he putts of his gowne,—'*There lyes the
Bishop.'*   Then 'twas,—'*Here's to thee, Corbet,'* and ' *Here's
to thee, Lushington.'*—From Josias Howe, B.D., Trin.
Coll. Oxon.

* MS. Aubr. 6, fol. 106^v.
^a Subst. for ' company.'
^b Subst. for 'pressing upon the.'

He built a pretty house (quaere) neer the cawsey beyond Friar Bacon's studie.

He married [5] . . . , whom 'twas sayd he begott. She was a very beautifull woman, and so was her mother. He had a son (I think Vincent) that went to schoole at Westminster, with Ned Bagshawe; a very handsome youth, but he is run out of all, and goes begging up and downe to gentlemen.

He was made bishop of Norwich, Anno Domini ⟨1632⟩. He dyed ⟨28 July, 1635⟩. The last words he sayd were, '*Good night, Lushington.*' He lyes buried in the upper end of the choire at Norwich, [on the south side of the monument of bishop Herbert, the founder, under a faire gravestone of free-stone, from whence the inscription [6] and scutcheon of brasse are stollen [a]].

His poems are pure naturall witt, delightfull and easie.

Quaere what he hath writt besides his poems: vide part iii, p. [b] 7 b.

It appeares by his verses to Master Ailesbury [7], Dec. 9, 1618, that he had knowledge of analyticall learning, being so well acquainted with him and the learned Mr. Thomas Harriot.

* I have not seen the date of his *Iter Boreale*; but it ends thus :—

> We return'd, but just with so much ore,
> As Rauleigh from his voyage, and no more.

** Memorandum :—his antagonist Dr. ⟨Daniel⟩ Price, the anniversarist, was made deane of the church at Hereford. Dr. ⟨William⟩ Watts, canon of that church, told me, 1656, that this deane was a mighty pontificall proud man, and that one time when they went in procession about the cathedrall church, he would not doe it the usually way in his surplice, hood, etc., on foot, but rode on a mare, thus habited, with the Common-Prayer booke in his hand,

[a] The words in square brackets are substituted for 'with this inscription . . . (vide).'
[b] i.e. MS. Aubr. 8, fol. 15ᵛ, *ut*

infra.
* MS. Aubr. 6, fol. 106.
** MS. Aubr. 6, fol. 106ᵛ.

reading. A stone-horse happend to breake loose * . . . he would never ride in procession afterwards.

* In the cathedral church of Norwich, upper end of the choeur, towards the steppes to the altar, in the middle is a little altar-tombe of bishop Herbert the founder; south of which tombe is a faire freestone gravestone of bishop Corbet, the inscription and shield of brasse are stollen. Vide A. Wood's *Antiq. Oxon.* ⟨His⟩ son ⟨is a⟩ fainiant.

Notes.

¹ Aubrey gives in colours the coat, 'or, a raven sable [Corbet],' wreathed with laurel.

² An alternative reading is given :—

'A ring he espyed
In his band-string tyed.'

³ John Stubbinge, D.D., Ch. Ch., 1630: vicar of Ambrosden, co. Oxon., 1635.

⁴ Thomas Lushington, D.D., Pembr., June 22, 1632, obiit Dec. 22, 1661. Notes of his life are found in Wood MS. F. 39, fol. 203ᵛ, 204, 259.

⁵ Alice, daughter of Leonard Hutton, sometime Student of Christ Church, Canon of St. Paul's 1609–1632.

⁶ In MS. Aubr. 8, fol. 9, Aubrey has a note, 'bishop Richard Corbet: vide memorandum 1671 in libro B pro reliquiis inscriptionis.' A copy of what was still legible of the inscription is found in a letter from Aubrey to Wood in Wood MS. F. 39.

⁷ Sir Thomas Aylesbury, 1576–1657, Master of the Requests. He had been of Christ Church, Oxford.

Tom Coryat (1577–1617).

** Old major Cosh was quartered (Sept. 18, 1642) at his mother's house at Shirburne in Dorsetshire; her name was Gertrude.

This was when Sherburne castle was besieged, and when the fight was at Babell hills, between Sherburn and Yeovill: the first fight in the civill warres that was considerable. But the first *brush* was between the earle of Northampton (father to Henry, the lord bishop of London) and the lord Brooke, neer Banbury: which was the later end of July, or the beginning of August, 1642. Iᵇ was sent for into the

* Three lines of the text are here suppressed.
* MS. Aubr. 8, fol. 15ᵛ.

** MS. Aubr. 7, fol. 6ᵛ.
ᵇ Subst. for 'I left Oxford': see *supra*, p. 37.

countrey to my great griefe, and departed the 9th of Aug. 'Twas before I went away, I beleeve in Aug. Quaere de hoc.

But to returne to T. Coryat: had he lived to returne into England, his travells had been most estimable, for though he was not a wise man, he wrote faithfully matter of fact.

Abraham Cowley (1618–1667).

* Mr. Abraham Cowley[1]: he was borne in Fleet-street, London, neer Chancery-lane; his father a grocer, at the signe of . . .

He was secretarie to the earle of St. Alban's (then lord Jermyn) at Paris. When his majestie returned, the duke of Buckingham hearing that at Chertsey was a good farme of about . . . *li.* per annum, belonging to the quecne-mother, goes to the earl of St. Alban's and the commissioners to[a] take a lease of it. They answered that 'twas beneath his grace to take a lease of them. That was all one, he would have it, payd for it, and had it, and freely and generously gave it to his deare and ingeniose friend, Mr. Abraham Cowley, for whom purposely he bought it.

He lies interred at Westminster Abbey, next to Sir Jeffrey Chaucer, N., where the duke of Bucks has putt a neate monument of white marble, viz. a faire pedestall, wheron the inscription :—

> Abrahamus Couleius,
> Anglorum Pindarus, Flaccus, Maro,
> Deliciae, Decus, Desiderium aevi sui,
> Hic juxta situs est.

> Aurea dum volitant latè tua scripta per orbem,
> Et famâ aeternùm vivis, divine Poeta,
> Hic placidâ jaceas requie; custodiat urnam
> Cana Fides, vigilentque perenni lampade Musae;
> Sit sacer iste locus. Nec quis temerarius ausit
> Sacrilegâ turbare manu venerabile bustum.
> Intacti maneant, maneant per secula, dulcis
> Coulei cineres serventque immobile saxum.

---

* MS. Aubr. 6, fol. 113ᵛ.   [a] Subst. for ' to buy it.'

Sic vovet,

Votumque suum apud posteros sacratum esse voluit, qui viro in-comparabili posuit sepulcrale marmor, GEORGIUS dux BUCKING-HAMIAE.

† His grace the   Abraham Cowley excessit e vitâ anno aetatis suae 49 ;
duke of Bucks
held a tassell of   et, honorificâ pompâ elatus ex Aedibus Bucking-
the pall.   hamianis, viris † illustribus omnium ordinum exequias
celebrantibus, sepultus est die 3 mensis Augusti anno Domini 1667.

Above that a very faire urne, with a kind of ghirland of ivy about it.

The inscription was made by Dr. ⟨Thomas⟩ Spratt, his grace's chapellane : the Latin verses were made, or mended, by Dr. ⟨Thomas⟩ Gale.

On his very noble gravestone, his scutcheon, and

Abrahamus Couleius
H. S. E.
1667.

Memorandum :—this George, duke of Bucks, came to the earl of St. Albans and told him he would buy such a lease in Chertsey belonging to the queen mother. Said the earle to him, ' that is beneath your grace, to take a lease.' ' That is all one,' qd. he, ' I desire to have the favour to buy it for my money.' He bought it, and then freely bestowed it on his beloved Cowley : which ought not to be forgotten.

By Sir J. Denham :—

Had Cowley ne're spoke, nor Th.ᵃ Killigrew writt,
They'd both have made a ⟨very⟩ good witt.

—A. C. discoursed very ill and with hesitation.

He writ when a boy at Westminster . . . poems and a comedy called *Love's Riddle*, dedicated to Sir Kenelme Digby ; printed, London, . . ., 8vo.

*Abraham Cowley :—vide his will, scilicet, for his true and lasting charity, that is, he settles his estate in such a manner that every yeare so much is to be payd for the enlarging of poor prisoners cast into gaole by cruel credi-tors for some debt. This I had from Mr. Dunning of London, a scrivener, who is an acquaintance of Dr. Cowley's

ᵃ i. e. Tom.   * MS. Aubr. 6, a slip at fol. 113ᵛ.

brother. I doe thinke this memorable benefaction is not
mentioned in his life in print before his workes ; and it is
certainly the best method of charity.

Note.

¹ Aubrey notes that he was of 'Cambridge,' and gives in trick the coat :—
'. . ., a lion rampant . . ., within a bordure engrailed . . .,' wreathed in
laurel.

... Cradock.

* Memorandum:—Mris Smyth• told me of one . . .
Cradock in the west (where Mris Smyth's relations or
birth) from a cratch dyed worth 10,000 *li.*—Quaere de hoc,
e.g. ⟨at⟩ Taunton or Warminster.

William Croone (1633–1684).

** . . . Croun, M. D., obiit Sunday Oct. 12, 1684,
London; buried at St. Mildred's in the Poultry. His
funerall sermon is printed. He was fellow of the Physitians'
College and also Regiae Societatis Socius.

... Curtin.

*** Madam Curtin, a good fortune of 3000 *li.*, daughter
to Sir William Curtin, the great merchant, lately married
her footman, who, not long after marriage, beates her, getts
her money, and ran away.

Robert Dalzell, earl of Carnwarth (15..–1654).

**** 'Twas the lord Kenwurth that sayd to the earl of
Salisbury *Ken you an ape, sir,*—from Elizabeth, countesse of
Thanet.

Note.

The Rev. H. E. D. Blakiston, of Trinity College, suggested to me the
transliteration of 'Kenwurth' to 'Carnwath.' Robert Dalzell succeeded as
second earl of Carnwath in 1639, died 1654. He might be in conflict about
Scotch matters with William Cecil, second earl of Salisbury, commissioner to
treat with the Scots at Ripon, in 1640.

* MS. Aubr. 23, fol. 36.   *** MS. Aubr. 21, p. 11.
• Jane Smyth, see *sub nomine.*   **** MS. Aubr. 8, fol. 6ᵛ.
** MS. Aubr. 7, fol. 5ᵛ.

Sir Charles Danvers (1568–160⁰/₁).

* Sir Charles Danvers was beheaded on Tower-hill with Robert, earle of Essex, February the 6th, 1600 ª. I find in the register of the Tower chapell only the sepulture of Robert, earl of Essex, that yeare; wherfore I am induced to beleeve that his body was carryed to Dantesey [1] in Wilts to lye with his ancestors. Vide Stowe's Chronicle, where is a full account of his and the earle's deportment at their death on the scaffold.

With all their faylings, Wilts cannot shew two such ᵇ brothers.

His familiar acquaintance were . . . ᶜ, earl of Oxon; Sir Francis and Sir Horace Vere; Sir Walter Ralegh, etc.— the heroes of those times.

Quaere my lady viscountesse Purbec and also the lord Norris for an account of the behaviour and advice of Sir Charles Danvers in the businesse of the earl of Essex, which advice had the earle followed he had saved his life.

** Of Sir Charles Danvers, from my lady viscountesse Purbec:—Sir Charles Danvers advised the earle of Essex, either to treat with the queen—hostages . . . , whom Sir Ferdinando Gorges did let goe; or to make his way through the gate at Essex house, and then to hast away to Highgate, and so to Northumberland (the earl of Northumberland maried his mother's sister), and from thence to the king of Scots, and there they might make their peace; if not, the queen was old and could not live long. But the earle followed not his advice, and so they both lost their heads on Tower-hill.

Note.

[1] In MS. Aubr. 3, fol. 46, Aubrey writes, in reference to burials at Dantesey, 'quaere, if Sir Charles Danvers that was beheaded?—He was buryed in the Tower chapell.' Aubrey's description of the burial-place of the Danvers family (MS. Aubr. 3, fol. 46), with the inscriptions, is printed in J. E. Jackson's Aubrey's *Wiltshire Collections*, pp. 223–225; the pedigree of Danvers is there given at p. 216.

* MS. Aubr. 8, fol. 25ᵛ.

ª i. e. 160¹/.

ᵇ Dupl. with 'shew the like two brothers,' scil. as Sir Charles Danvers

and his brother Henry, earl of Danby.

ᶜ Edward Vere, seventeenth earl of Oxford.

** MS. Aubr. 8, fol. 26ᵛ.

Elizabeth Danvers.

* His[1] mother, an Italian, prodigious parts for a woman. I have heard my father's mother say that she had Chaucer at her fingers' ends.

A great politician; great witt and spirit, but revengefull[a].

Knew how to manage her estate as well as any man; understood jewells as well as any jeweller.

Very beautifull, but only short-sighted. To obtain pardons for her sonnes[b] she maryed Sir Edmund Carey, cosen-german to queen Elizabeth, but kept him to hard meate.

Smyth of Smythcotes—Naboth's vineyard—digitus Dei[2].

The *arcanum*—'traditio lampadis' in the family of Latimer[3] of poysoning king Henry 8—from my lady Purbec.

Notes.

[1] i. e. Henry, earl of Danby's. She was Elizabeth, daughter of John Nevill, the last lord Latimer. 'An Italian' may mean that she knew that language, among her other accomplishments. I can make nothing of a note added by Aubrey here, which seems to read '. . . Cowley, crop-ear'd.'

[2] I do not know to what circumstance, in the history of the Danvers family, Aubrey here applies 1 Kings xxi. 19.

[3] Catherine Parr, last consort of Henry VIII, was widow of John, 3rd lord Latimer; and step-mother of John, 4th lord Latimer, the father of this Elizabeth Danvers, whose grand-daughter ('viscountess Purbeck') was Aubrey's informant.

Henry Danvers, earl of Danby (1573–1644).

** Henry Danvers[1], earl of Danby; vide his christning and epitaph in libro[2] A. in Dantesey church: vide ⟨David⟩ Lloyd's *State-worthies*, 8vo, 1679.

Quaere my brother William, and J. Stokes, for the examination order of the murther[3] at Cosham in North Wilts. Old L. Shippon, Oxon,

'From Turke and Pope,' etc.

R. Wisdome was then lecturer and preacht that day, and Henry Long expired[c] in his armes. My great-grandfather,

* MS. Aubr. 8, fol. 25.

[a] Aubrey, in the margin, notes 'Anne Bulleyn.'

[b] For the murder of Henry Long.

** MS. Aubr. 8, fol. 25.

[c] Dupl. with 'dyed.'

I.

O

R. Danvers, was in some trouble about it, his horses and men being in that action. His servants were hanged and so . . . Long of Linets. Vide Degory Wheare's Epistles and John Owen's Epigrams.

Physick Garden ⟨at Oxford⟩ : inscriptions there ; inscription at Dantesey.

⟨He⟩ gave to Sir Thomas Overbury *cloath*.

⟨He⟩ perfected his Latin when a man by parson Oldham of Dodmerton. ⟨He was a⟩ perfect master of the French ; a historian ; tall and spare ; temperate ; sedate and solid ; a very great favorite of prince Henry ; lived most at Cornbury ; a great improver of his estate, to 11000 *li.* per annum at the least ; sold the 7 Downes, and turned the ᵃ ⓐ into lease ; afterwards bought fee-simple neer Cirencester.

* Henry, earl of Danby, ⟨was a⟩ great oeconomist. All his servants ⟨were⟩ sober and wise ᵇ in their respective places. ⟨He⟩ kept . . . gentlemen : ⟨among them⟩ colonel Legge ᶜ (governor of Portsmouth); and his brother ; Mr. Arthur Drake (brother of Sir . . . Drake, baronet).

** Earl of Danby—he was page to Sir Philip Sydney— from my cozen Elizabeth Villers : quaere +.

*** Memorandum :—anno Domini, 16—, regno regis Caroli primi, Henry, earle of Danby, built an almeshowse in this parish ⟨Dantesey, co. Wilts⟩ for ⟨six⟩ poore people and ᵈ a schoole—quaere the salary ⁴ of both.

Notes.

¹ Aubrey gives in trick the coat :—'⟨gules⟩, a chevron between 3 mullets ⟨or⟩ [Danby] ; quartering, ⟨gules⟩, a saltire engrailed ⟨argent⟩, an annulet for difference [Nevill, lord Latimer],' surmounted by an earl's coronet.

² i. e. in MS. Aubr. 3, fol. 46 : see *supra*, p. 192. The epitaph contains English verses by George Herbert.

³ Henry, brother of Sir Robert, Long was killed, possibly in fair fight, by Sir Charles, brother of this Henry, Danvers : see the *Archaeological Magazine*, i. 306. In consequence, the Danvers brothers had to seek safety in France. In MS. Aubr. 3, fol. 44ᵛ, Aubrey notes 'Sommerford magna—the assassination of

ᵃ This symbol I cannot explain. lord Dartmouth.
* MS. Aubr. 8, fol. 25ᵛ.   ** MS. Aubr. 3, fol. 46.
ᵇ Dupl. with 'discreet.'   *** MS. Aubr. 3, fol. 44ᵛ.
ᶜ George Legge, created (1682) ᵈ Over the almshouse : ibid. fol. 45.

Harry Long was contrived in the parlour of the parsonage here. Mr. Atwood was then parson ; he was drown'd comeing home.'

Richard Atwood, M.A. Oxon, 1576: another instance of ' Digitus Dei.'

⁴ See Jackson's Aubrey's. *Wiltshire Collections*, p. 228.

Sir John Danvers (15..–1594).

* Sir John Danvers, the father, ⟨was⟩ a most beautifull and good and even-tempered person. His picture ⟨is⟩ yet extant—my cosen John Danvers (his son ª) haz it at . . . . Memorandum, George Herbert's verses on the curtaine.

He was of a mild and peaceable nature, and his sonnes' sad accident ᵇ brake his heart.

** By the same ᶜ (orator of the University of Cambridge), pinned on the curtaine of the picture of old Sir John Danvers, who was both a handsome and a good man :—

> Passe not by : search and you may
> Find a treasure worth your stay.
> What makes a Danvers would you find ?
> In a faire bodie, a faire mind.
> Sir John Danvers' earthly part
> Here is copyed out by art :
> But his heavenly and divine
> In his progenie doth shine.
> Had he only brought them forth,
> Know that much had been his worth.
> Ther's no monument to a sonne :
> Reade him there ᵈ, and I have donne.

Sir John Danvers (1588 ?–1655).

*** Sir John Danvers :—His first wife was the lady ⟨ Magdalen⟩ Herbert, a widowe, mother of the lord Edward

* MS. Aubr. 8, fol. 25ᵛ.

ª Grandson.

ᵇ Their flight, after the murder of Henry Long.

** MS. Aubr. 3, fol. 46.

ᶜ George Herbert. This note follows

Herbert's verses on the gravestone of Henry Danvers.

ᵈ i. e. in his son, Henry, earl of Danby.

*** MS. Aubr. 8, fol. 18ᵛ.

Herbert of Cherbery and George Herbert, orator.   By her
he had no issue ; she was old enough to have been his
mother.   He maried her for love of her witt.   The earl
of Danby[a] was greatly displeased with him for this dis-
agreable match.

   * Sir John, his sonne, was then[b] a child about six.   An
ingeniose person, e. g. Chelsey house and garden, and
Lavington garden[c].   A great friend of the king's partie
and a patron to distressed and cashiered cavaliers, e. g.
captain Gunter, he served ; Christopher Gibbons (organist);
captain Peters, etc.—Lord Bacon's friend.   But to revenge
himselfe of his sister, the l⟨ady⟩ Garg⟨rave⟩ to[d] ingra-
tiate himself more with the P⟨rotector⟩ to null his brother,
earl of Danby's, will, he, contrary to his owne naturall
inclination, did sitt in the high court of justice at the
king's triall.

   Dantesey (2500 *li*. per annum), not entailed, ⟨was⟩
forfeited and given to the duke of Yorke.

   His son, John, by his last wife (⟨Grace⟩ Hughes), has
500 *li*. per annum (old land) in Oxonshire, which was part
of judge[e] Danvers' estate tempore Edwardi IV, one of the
judges with Litleton.

   Henry, the eldest son of Sir John Danvers, dyed before
his father, and left his two sisters co-heires, viz. Elizabeth[f]
⟨who⟩ married Robert Viliers (only son of viscount Purbec),
and Anne, married to Sir ⟨Henry⟩ Lee of Ditchley.

The Danvers-Villiers family.

⟨MS. Aubr. 21, fol. 97, gives 'eight coelestiall schemes', being the
nativities of Robert Danvers, esq. (that is, Robert Villers, son of
the viscount Purbec[2]), the lady Elizabeth his wife, and their six
children, vid[t]. foure daughters and two sonnes, diligently calculated

---

[a] His elder brother.

* MS. Aubr. 8, fol. 25[v].

[b] i. e. at the time of his father's
death, *supra*, p. 195.

[c] i. e. the arrangement of these
gardens proved his good taste.

[d] Dupl. with 'to collogue with the P.'

[e] Sir Robert Danvers, justice of the
Common Pleas, 1450 ; Sir Thomas
Littelton (the jurist), justice of the
Common Pleas, 1466.

[f] This is the 'Elizabeth, viscountess
Purbeck,' who so frequently appears
in these biographies as an informant
of Aubrey.

according to art by the Tables of Regiomontanus by W. C.' This paper supplies the following dates :—⟩

* Robert Danvers [3], esq., *m.* the lady Danvers [a], born	
born 19 Oct., 1624,	Tuesday, 7 Aprill, 1629,
11[h] 48' P.M.	5[h] 26' P.M.

Mris Frances Danvers, born Friday 12 July 1650, 0[h] 16' P.M.

Mris Elizabeth Danvers, born Monday 10 November 1651, 10[h] 21' P.M.

Mris Ann Danvers, born Sunday 23 October 1653, 5[h] 10' A.M.

Mris Mary Danvers, born Saturday 10 November 1655, 7[h] 28' A.M.

Mr. Robert Danvers, born Saturday 14 Martii 165$\frac{9}{?}$, 5[h] 30' A.M.

Mr. Edward Danvers, born Thursday 28 Martii 1661, 4[h] 9' A.M.

** Memorandum, 1676, July 19, P.M., about 6[h], my lord viscount (Robert) Purbec, filius, was hurt in the neck by Mr. Fielding [4] in Fleet Street.

⟨Ask Elizabeth, viscountess Purbec⟩ the year and day when her son, the lord Purbec, was killed in a duel at Liege? Respondet: he was killed in a duell at Liege about a year before the death of King Charles II [d]—I thinke in the month of Aprill.

Notes.

[1] In MS. Aubr. 21, fol. 97[v], is a note :—' These,' I suppose the schemes given on the recto of the leaf, ' were done when he,' Robert Danvers, ' was in Caersbrooke Castle, prisoner, in the Isle of Wight.'

[2] In MS. Aubr. 23, on a slip at fol. 121[v], is the note :—' Lord . . . Purbec,' i. e. John Villiers, created viscount Purbeck in 1619, ' natus at Godbee, Sept. 6, 12[h] P.M., 1591 : melancholy. His mother saith he was borne Sept. 6, Monday, 12[h] P.M., 1591. Mris Toman writeth that it was 2[h] 30' P.M.'

[3] Robert Wright (took the name of Danvers), son of Frances (daughter of Sir Edward Coke; wife of John Villiers, of note 2) who eloped in 1621 with Sir Robert Howard. He styled himself ' viscount Purbeck '; died 1675.

[4] Robert Fielding (' Beau' Fielding) afterwards married his widow, Margaret, daughter of Ulick Burke, marquis of Clanricarde.

* MS. Aubr. 21, fol. 97.   [a] Elizabeth, daughter of Henry Danvers, *ut supra.*
** MS. Aubr. 21, fol. 97[v].

Michael Dary (16..–1679).

* Michaell Dary, mathematician, and a gunner of the Tower (by profession, a tobacco-cutter), an admirable algebrician, was buryed in the churchyard neer Bethlem on May-day 1679. With writing in the frostie weather[a] his fingers rotted and gangraened. He was an old man ; I guesse about 66 +.

Edward Davenant, merchant (15..–16..).

** Edward Davenant, merchant : he lies buried behind the bishop's stall at Sarum with this inscription[b] :—

Literas, lyceo, rerumque usus, emporio, etc.

*** Memorandum:—Mr. ⟨Edward⟩ Davenant, merchant in London, eldest brother of John Davenant, bishop of Sarum, broke (the seas being crosse to him); but being a person of great estimation with the merchants, they favoured him, and he went into Ireland. He did set up the trade of pilchard fishing at Wythy Island[c] there, where he was a Justice of Peace, and in 20 yeares he gott there about ten thousand pounds, payd his debts, and left his family well. This account I had from my worthy and intimate friend, Mr. John Davenant, grandsonne to him.

Edward Davenant, D.D. (16..–16⁷⁹⁄₈₀).

**** Edward Davenant[1], S. Theol. Dr., was the eldest son of ⟨Edward⟩ Davenant, merchant of London, who was elder brother to the right reverend father in God, the learned John Davenant, bishop of Sarum.

I will first speake of the father, for he was a rare[d] man in his time, and deserves to be remembred. He was of a healthy complexion[e], rose at 4 or 5 in the morning, so

---

* MS. Aubr. 6, fol. 1ᵛ.

[a] The winter of 1678–79 was a severe one : Clark's Wood's *Life and Times*, ii. 426, 432, 439.

** MS. Aubr. 6, fol. 45.

[b] Omitted here, because given, *infra*, p. 199, from fol. 43.

*** MS. Aubr. 26, p. 16.

[c] Whiddy Island, in Bantry Bay.

**** MS. Aubr. 6, fol. 43.

[d] Subst. for ' an incomparable.'

[e] There followed '(except the gout),' scored out.

that he followed his studies till 6 or 7, the time that other
merchants goe about their businesse; so that, stealing so
much and so quiet time in the morning, he studied as
much as most men. He understood Greeke and Latin
perfectly, and was a better Grecian then the bishop. He
writt a rare Greeke character as ever I sawe. He was
a great mathematician, and understood as much of it as
was knowen in his time. Dr. Davenant, his son, hath
excellent notes of his father's, in mathematiques, as also
in Greeke, and 'twas no small advantage ⟨to⟩ him to have
such a learned father to imbue arithmeticall knowledge
into him when a boy, night times when he came from
schoole (Merchant Taylors'). He understood trade very
well, was a sober and good menager, but the winds and
seas cross'd him. He had so great losses that he broke,
but his creditors knowing it was no fault of his, and also
that he was a person of great vertue and justice, used not
extremity towards him; but I thinke gave him more
credit, so that he went into Ireland, and did sett up
a fishery for pilchards at Wythy Island, in Ireland, where
in . . . yeares he gott 10000 *li.* ; satisfied and payd his
creditors; and over and above left a good estate to his
son. His picture bespeakes him to be a man of judgement,
and parts, and gravity extraordinary. There is written
Expecto. He slipt comeing downe the stone stayres at
the palace at Sarum, which bruise caused his death. He
lyes buried in the south aissle of the choire in Sarum
Cathedral behind the bishop's stall. His son, Dr. Davenant,
sett up and made this inscription for him, which I will
remember as well as I can :—

> Literas, lyceo, rerumque usus, emporio,
> Nostris edoctus, ingentis hinc prudentiae
> Extulit merces insulas ad Hibernicas ;
> Ubi annos viginti custos pacis publicae
> Populum ditavit inopem, emollivit ferum,
> Gratus et charus Anglis et Hibernicis.
> Musis dilectus Latiis, nec minus Atticis,
> Studiisque fratrem, hujus ecclesiae praesulem,

Sequebatur aemulus. Omnes in illius pectore
Fulserunt Gratiae, sed praenituit Pietas,
Quae in egenos tantum non fuit prodiga.
Post varios casus, in vitae actu ultimo
Cum luctu [a] bonorum, plausu omnium, exiit.
Quid multis? Scias hoc, lector: vivus memoria
Pollebat mirâ, mortuus redolet suavi.

                 Aetatis suae . . .
Obiit anno
                 Aerae Christianae . . .

* Dr. Edward Davenant was borne at his father's howse at Croydon in Surrey (the farthest handsome great howse on the left hand as you ride to Bansted Downes) anno Domini . . . (vide register). I have heard him say, hē thankt God his father did not know the houre of his birth; for that it would have tempted him to have studyed astrologie, for which he had no esteeme at all.

He went to school at Merchant Taylors' school, from thence to Queen's Colledge in Cambridge, of which house his uncle, John Davenant, (afterwards bishop of Sarum), was head, where [b] he was fellowe.

When his uncle was preferred to the church of Sarum, he made his nephew treasurer of the church, which is the best dignity, and gave him the vicaridge of Gillingham in com. Dorset, and then Paulsholt parsonage, neer the Devises, which last in the late troubles he resigned to his wive's brother ⟨William⟩ Grove.

He was to his dyeing day of great diligence in study, well versed in all kinds of learning, but his genius did most strongly encline him to the mathematiques, wherin he has written (in a hand as legible as print) MSS. in 4to a foot high at least. I have often heard him say (jestingly) that he would have a man knockt in the head that should write any thing in mathematiques that had been written of before. I have heard Sir Christopher Wren say that he does beleeve he was the best mathematician in the world about 30 or 35 + yeares agoe. But being a divine he was

---

unwilling to print, because the world should not know how he had spent the greatest part of his time.

He very rarely went any farther then the church, which is hard by his house. His wife was a very discreet and excellent huswife, that he troubled himselfe about no mundane affaires, and 'tis a private place, that he was but little diverted with visitts.

I have writt to his executor, that we may have the honour and favour to conserve his MSS. in the Library of the Royal Societie, and to print what is fitt. I hope I shall obtaine my desire. And the bishop of Exon (⟨Thomas⟩ Lamplugh) maried the Dr's second daughter Katherine, and he was tutor to Sir Joseph Williamson, our President. He had a noble library, which was the aggregate of his father's, the bishop's, and his owne.

He was of middling stature, something spare; and weake, feeble leggs; he had sometimes the goute; was of great temperance, he alwayes dranke his beer at meales with a toast, winter and summer, and sayd it made the beer the better.

He was not only a man of vast learning, but of great goodnes and charity; the parish and all his friends will have a great losse in him. He tooke no use for money upon bond. He was my singular good friend, and to whom I have been more beholding then to any one beside; for I borrowed five hundred pounds of him for a yeare and a halfe, and I could not fasten any interest on him.

He was very ready to teach and instruct. He did*me the favour to informe me first in Algebra. His daughters were Algebrists.

His most familiar learned acquaintance was Lancelot Morehouse, parson of Pertwood. I remember when I was a young Oxford scholar, that he could not endure to heare of the *New* (Cartesian, or &c.) *Philosophy*; 'for,' sayd he, 'if a new philosophy is brought-in, a new divinity will shortly follow' (or 'come next'); and he was right.

He dyed at his house at Gillingham aforesaid, where he

* MS. Aubr. 6, fol. 44.

202 of the same month.

and his predecessor, Dr. ⟨John⟩ Jessop, had been vicars one hundred and . . . yeares, and lyes buryed in the chancell there. Obiit March 9th, 16$\frac{19}{80}$, and was buried the 31 of the same month.

He was heire to his uncle, John Davenant, bishop of Sarum. Memorandum:—when bishop Coldwell[2] came to this bishoprick, he did lett long leases, which were but newly expired when bishop Davenant came to this sea; so that there tumbled into his coffers vast summes. His predecessor, Dr. Tounson, maried his sister, continued in the see but a little while, and left severall children un-provided for, so the king or rather duke of Bucks gave bishop Davenant the bishoprick out of pure charity[3]. Sir Anthony Weldon sayes (in his *Court of King James*), 'twas the only bishoprick that he disposed of without symony, all others being made merchandise of for the advancement of his kindred. Bishop Davenant being invested, maried all his nieces to clergie-men, so he was at no expence for their preferment. He granted to his nephew (this Dr.) the lease of the great mannour of Poterne, worth about 1000 *li.* per annum; made him threasurer of the church of Sarum, of which the corps is the parsonage of Calne, which was esteemed to be of the like value. He made severall purchases, all which he left him; insomuch as the churchmen of Sarum say, that he gained more by this church then ever any man did by the church since the Reformation, and take it very unkindly that, at his death, he left nothing (or but 50 *li.*) to that church which was the source of his estate. How it happened I know not, or how he might be workt-on in his old age, but I have heard severall yeares since, he had sett downe 500 *li.* in will for the Cathedral Church of Sarum.

He had 6 sonnes and 4 daughters. There was a good schoole at Gillingham: at winter nights he taught his sonnes Arithmetic and Geometrie; his 2 eldest daughters, especially Mris Ettrick, was a notable Algebrist.

☞ *Memoria.* He had an excellent way of improving

his children's memories, which was thus : he would make one of them read a chapter or &c., and then they were (*sur le champ*) to repeate what they remembred, which did exceedingly profitt them ; and so for sermons, he did not let them write notes (which jaded their memorie), but gave an account *vivâ voce.* When his eldest son, John, came to Winton-schoole (where the boyes were enjoyned to write sermon notes) he had not wrote ; the master askt him for his notes—he had none, but sayd, ' If I doe not give you as good an account of it as they that doe, I am much mistaken.'

* Edward Davenant, D.D., obiit 12 of March 16$\frac{79}{80}$, and is seated in the north side of the east end of the chancell at Gillingham, Dorset.—From Anthony Ettrick, esq.

** By Dr. Edward Davenant, S.T.P., *Versus mne-monici ad computationes cossicas.* Memorandum :—Dr. Davenant hath excellent explanations of these verses, which transcribe : his son James[4], at Oriel College Oxon, hath them.

Notes.

[1] Aubrey gives in trick the coat :—'gules, between 9 cross-crosslets fitchée or, 3 escallops ermine [Davenant].'

[2] John Coldwell was consecrated Dec. 26, 1591, and died Oct. 14, 1596.

[3] Robert Tounson, consecrated July 9, 1620, died May 15, 1621, leaving a widow and fifteen children. The congé d'élire on behalf of Davenant was issued May 29, 1621.

[4] James Davenant, matric. at Oriel, July 23, 1656.

John Davenant (1576–1641).

*** John Davenant, episcopus Sarum : his epitaph made by bishop Pierson[a].

He bought the advowson of Newton-tony, Wilts, which he gave to Queene's College[b], Cambridge—quaere if not others.

He hung the choire of Sarum with purple velvet, which was plundered in the sacrilegious times.

* MS. Aubr. 8, fol. 8ᵛ.
** MS. Aubr. 10, fol. 31.
*** MS. Aubr. 6, fol. 44ᵛ.

[a] John Pearson, bishop of Chester 1672-86.
[b] Of which he had been President.

Sir William Davenant (160⅝–1668).

* Sir William Davenant [1], knight, Poet Laureate, was borne [about[a] the end of February — vide A. Wood's *Antiq. Oxon.*—baptized 3 of March A.D. 160⅝], in . . . street in the city of Oxford at the Crowne taverne.

† Robert[b] was a fellow of St. John's College in Oxon; then preferred to the parsonage of West Kington by bishop Davenant, whose chaplaine he was.

His father was John Davenant, a vintner there, a very grave and discreet citizen: his mother was a very beautifull woman, and of a very good witt, and of conversation extremely agreable. They had three sons, viz. 1, Robert †, 2, William[c]; and 3, Nicholas (an attorney): and two handsome daughters, one married to Gabriel Bridges (B.D., fellow of C. C. Coll., beneficed in the Vale of White Horse), another to Dr. ⟨William⟩ Sherburne (minister of Pembridge in Hereford, and a canon of that church).

Mr. William Shakespeare was wont to goe into Warwickshire once a yeare, and did commonly in his journey lye at this house in Oxon. where he was exceedingly respected. [I[d] have heard parson Robert ⟨Davenant⟩ say that Mr. W. Shakespeare haz given him a hundred kisses.] Now Sir William would sometimes, when he was pleasant over a glasse of wine with his most intimate friends—e. g. Sam. Butler (author of Hudibras), &c.—say, that it seemed to him that he writt with the very spirit that Shakespeare, and seemd[e] contented[f] enough to be thought his son. [He[g] would tell them the story as above, in which way his mother had a very light report[h].]

He went to schoole at Oxon to Mr. Sylvester (Charles Whear, filius Degorii W., was his schoolefellowe), but I feare he was drawne from schoole before he was ripe enough.

* MS. Aubr. 6, fol. 46.

[a] The words here put in square brackets are a later insertion: the first clause is scored out.

[b] Subst. for 'Robert was vicar of West Kington, chaplain to bishop Davenant.'

[c] Aubrey adds 'vide p. 79 (Suckling)'; i.e.fol. 110 of this MS. Aubr. 6,

in the life of Sir John Suckling *infra*.

[d] The words in square brackets are scored out.

[e] Dupl. with 'was.'

[f] 'Contentended' in MS.

[g] The words in square brackets are scored out.

[h] Dupl. with 'whereby she was called a whore': also scored out.

He was preferred to the first dutches of Richmond to wayte on her as a page. I remember he told me, she sent him to a famous apothecary for some Unicornes-horne, which he was resolved to try with a spider which he incircled[a] in it, but without the expected successe; the spider would goe over, and thorough and thorough, unconcerned.

He was next a servant (as I remember, a page also) to Sir Fulke Grevil[b] lord Brookes, with whom he lived to his death, which was that a servant of his (that had long wayted on him and his lordship had often told him that he would doe something for him, but did not but still putt him off with delayes) as he was trussing up his lord's pointes comeinge from stoole (for then their breeches were fastned to the doubletts with points—then came in hookes and eies—which not to have fastened was in my boy-hood a great crime) stabbed him. This was at the same time that the duke of Buckingham was stabbed by Felton, and the great noise and report of the duke's, Sir William told me, quite drowned this of his lord's, that 'twas scarce taken notice of. This Sir Fulke G. was a good witt, and had been a good poet[c] in his youth. He wrote a poeme in folio which he printed not till he was old, and then, (as Sir W. said) with too much judgment and refining, spoyld it, which was at first a delicate thing.

He writt a play or playes, and verses, which he did with so much sweetnesse and grace, that by it he got the love and friendship of his two Mecaenasses, Mr. Endymion Porter, and Mr. Henry Jermyn (since earl of St. Albans), to whom he has dedicated his poem called *Madegascar*. Sir John Suckling also was his great and intimate friend.

After the death of Ben Johnson he was made in his place Poet Laureat.

He gott a terrible clap of a black handsome wench that lay in Axe-yard, Westminster, whom he thought on when

---

[a] Dupl. with 'empaled.'
[b] Anthony Wood notes in the margin 'Grevill, lord Brookes.'
[c] Wood notes in the margin, 'Sir Fulk Grevill, poet.'

he speakes of *Dalga* in *Gondibert*, which cost him his nose, with which unlucky mischance many witts were to⟨o⟩ cruelly bold : e. g. Sir John Menis, Sir John Denham, &c.

* In 1641, when the troubles began, he was faine to fly into France, and at Canterbury he was seised on by the mayor—vide Sir John Menis' verses—

> 'For Will had in his face the flawes
> And markes recieved in countrey's cause :
> They flew on him like lyons passant,
> And tore his nose as much as was on't,
> And call'd him superstitious groome,
> And Popish Dog, and Cur of Rome.
> . . . . . 'Twas surely the first time
> That Will's religion was a crime.'

In the civill warres in England he was in the army of William, marquess of Newcastle (since duke), where he was generall of the ordinance. I have heard his brother Robert say, for that service there was owing to him by King Charles the First 10000*li*. During that warre, 'twas his hap to have two aldermen of Yorke his prisoners, who were something stubborne, and would not give the ransome ordered by the councell of warr. Sir William used them civilly, and treated them in his tent, and sate them at the upper end of his table à la mode de France, and having donne so a good while to his chardge, told them (privately and friendly) that he was not able to keepe so chargeable guests, and bad them take an opportunity to escape, which they did ; but having been gon a little way they considered with themselves that in gratitude they ought to goe back and give Sir William their thankes ; which they did, but it was like to have been to their great danger of being taken by the soldiers ; but they happened to gett safe to Yorke.

The King's party being overcome, Sir William Davenant (who received the honour of knighthood from the duke of Newcastle by commision) went into France ; resided chiefly in Paris where the Prince of Wales then was. He then began to write his romance in verse, called *Gondibert*, and had not writt above the first booke, but being very fond of it, prints it (before a quarter finished), with an epistle of his to Mr. Thomas Hobbes and Mr. Hobbes' excellent epistle to him printed before it. The courtiers with the Prince of Wales could never be at quiet about this piece, which was the occasion of a very witty but satericall little booke of verses in 8vo. about 4 sheetes, writt by George, duke of Buckes, Sir John Denham, etc.—

'That thou forsak'st thy sleepe, thy diet,
And which is more then that, *our quiet*.'

This last word Mr. Hobs told me was the occasion of their writing.

Here he layd an ingeniose designe to carry a considerable number of artificers (chiefly weavers) from hence to Virginia ; and by Mary the queen-mother's meanes, he got favour from the king of France to goe into the prisons and pick and choose. So when the poor dammed wretches understood what the designe was, the⟨y⟩ cryed *uno ore*— '*Tout tisseran !*' i. e. *We are all weavers !* Will. ⟨took⟩ 36, as I remember, if not *more, and shipped them ; and ᵃ as he was in his voyage towards Virginia, he and his *tisseran* were all taken by the shippes then belonging to the Parliament of England. The slaves I suppose they sold, but Sir William was brought prisoner to England. Whither he was first a prisoner at Caresbroke-castle in the Isle of Wight, or at the Tower of London, I have forgott : he was a prisoner at both. His *Gondibert*, 4to, was finished at Caresbroke-castle. He expected no mercy from the Parliament, and had no hopes of escaping ⟨with⟩ his life. It pleased God that the two aldermen of Yorke aforesayd hearing that he was taken and brought to London to be tryed for his life, which they understood was in extreme danger, they were touch⟨ed⟩ with so much generosity and goodnes, as,

* MS. Aubr. 6, fol. 47.   ᵃ Subst. for 'and went with them.'

upon their owne accounts and meer motion, to try what they could to save Sir William's life who had been so civill to them and a meanes to save theirs, to come to London : and acquainting the Parliament with it, upon their petition, etc., Sir William's life was saved†.

Being freed from imprisonment, (because playes, scil. Tragedies and Comoedies, were in those Presbyterian times scandalous) he contrives to set-up an Opera *stylo recitativo,* wherein serjeant Maynard and severall citizens were engagers. It began at Rutland-house, in Charter-house-yard; next, (scil. anno . . .) at the Cock-pitt in Drury-lane, where were acted very well *stylo recitativo, Sir Francis Drake's*
. . ., and *the Siege of Rhodes* (1st and 2d part). It did affect the eie and eare extremely. This first brought scenes in fashion in England ; before, at playes, was only a hanging.

Anno Domini 1660 was the happy restauration of his majestie Charles II. Then was Sir Wm. made . . . .
. . . . ; and the Tennis court in Little Lincolnes-Inne fielde was turn'd into a play-house for the duke of Yorke's players, where Sir William had lodgeings, and where he dyed, April the ⟨7th⟩ 166⟨8⟩‡.

‡ It is now a Tennis court again, upon the building of the duke's house in Dorset garden.

I was at his funerall. He had a coffin of walnutt-tree ; Sir[b] John Denham say'd 'twas the finest coffin that ever he sawe. * His body was carried in a herse from the play-house to Westminster-Abbey, where, at the great west dore, he was

§ Which is neer to the monument of Dr. Isaac Barrow.— Memorandum : —my honoured friend Sir Robert Moray lies by him ; but *sans* inscription.

recieved by the sing⟨ing⟩ men and choristers, who sang the service of the church ('I am the Resurrection, &c.') to his § grave, which is in the south crosse aisle, on which, on a paving stone of marble, is writt, in imitation of that on Ben Johnson, '*O rare Sir Will. Davenant.*'

His first lady was Dr. . . . 's daughter, physitian,

. . . . by whom he had a very beautifull and ingeniose son that dyed above 20 yeares since. His 2d lady was the daughter of . . . by whom he had severall children: I sawe some very young ones at the funerall. His eldest is Charles Davenant, LL.Dr., who inherits his father's beauty and phancy[a]. He practises at Doctors Commons. He writt a play called *Circe*, which haz taken very well.

Sir William hath writt about 25 (quaere) playes; the romance called *Gondibert*; and a little poeme called *Madagascar*.

His private opinion was that Religion at last,—e.g. a hundred yeares hence,—would come to settlement, and that in a kind of ingeniose Quakerisme.

* That sweet swan of Isis, Sir William Davenant, dyed the seaventh day of April last, and lyes buried amongst the poets in Westminster abbey[b], by his antagonist, Mr. Thomas May, whose inscription of whose marble was taken away by order since the king came in.

Sir William was Poet Laureat; and Mr. John Dryden hath his place. But me thought it had been proper that a laurell should have been sett on his coffin—which was not donne.

He hath writt above 20 playes; besides his *Gondibert* and *Madagascar*.

. *Note.*

[1] Aubrey gives in trick the Davenant coat, *ut supra*, p. 203, but wreathed in laurel: see the facsimile at the end of vol. iv. of Clark's Wood's *Life and Times*.

John Davenport (1597–16$\frac{6}{7}\frac{9}{0}$).

** Sir John Dugdale told me that he would enquire about Mr. John Davenport, and send to you.—This was halfe a yeare since, at least.

*** Sir John Dugdale saith that John Davenport was a nonconformist; and he hath enquired of his relations,

[a] Subst. for 'spirit.'

* Letter from Aubrey to Anthony Wood, of date May 19, 1668; MS. Wood F. 39, fol. 118.

[b] Wood queries:—'in S. Bennet chapel, quaere.'

** MS. Aubr. 7, fol. 9ᵛ: a memo. intended for Anthony Wood.

*** Aubrey in MS. Wood F. 39, fol. 390: July 15, 1689.

I.   P

who know nothing of him, if dead or alive, but they believe
he is dead.   He went over sea—he thinkes to the Bar-
badoes, or some of these plantations ª, or to Holland.

John Davys (1550–1605).

* Memorandum :—Mr. Browne, the mathematicall instrument maker of the Minories, told me that the sea-
quadrant was invented by Captaine Davy . . . yeares
since,—he that found out the streights called Davys's
Streights.

Arthur Dee (1579–1651).

** 'Arthur Dee,' (sonne of John Dee), a physitian at
Norwych, 'was born 13 Julii 1579, manè, horâ 4. 30' fere
(vel potius, 25 min.) in ipso ortu solis, ut existimo'—Thus
I find it in his father's *Ephemerides*.

Obiit Norwychi about 1650.

*** ⟨Arthur Dee told Dr. Bathurst and Dr. Wharton⟩
† Mrs. Dee, 'that (being but a boy) he used† to play at
wife to his son
Mr. Rowland quoits with the plates of gold made by pro-
Dee, told me the
other day that jection in the garret of Dr. Dee's lodgings in
Dr. Arthur Dee
hath often told Prague. . . . When he was 9 yeares of age and
her the same. at Trebona in Germany with his father, he was
design'd to succede Kelly as his father's speculator.'

**** ⟨Arthur Dee⟩ 'has often told Mr. Whitefoot, of
Norwich, who buried him, that he had more than once seen
the philosopher's stone, and he thinks that he has written
some peice on that subject.   He was a man of a very
pleasant conversation and had good practice in Norwich :
a great acquaintance of Dr. ⟨Thomas⟩ Browne's.'

John Dee (1527–1608).

***** John Dee:—Mr. Ashmole hath his nativitie.
Resp.—'tis in his *Theatrum Chemicum*.   Hee had a very

ª Davenport was pastor at New-
haven in New England.
  * MS. Aubr. 7, fol. 18ᵛ.
  ** MS. Aubr. 6, fol. 37: also *verbatim* from the *Ephemerides Stadii*,
in MS. Aubr. 23, fol. 77.

*** In a letter from Elias Ashmole to
Anthony Wood: MS. Ballard 14, fol. 13.
  **** In a letter from Dr. John
Conant to Anthony Wood, 1683 : MS.
Wood F. 49, fol. 101.
  ***** MS. Aubr. 8, fol. 6ᵛ.

faire cleare rosie complexion : so had the earl of Rochester, exceeding.

* 'Johannes Dee, natus Londini, 1527, Julii 13, 4ʰ 2' P.M.'—this nativity[1] I copied out of the learned John Dee's papers in the hands of Elias Ashmole, esq.

** From Elias Ashmole—the father of this John Dee was a vintner in . . . London.

*** John Dee—from Meredith Lloyd :—Talbot, marying an inheritresse of the prince of South Wales (who was descended from Howel Da, i. e. Howelus bonus : the same family from whom John Dee was descended).—Dr. Troutbec hath Raymund Lully's . . . (a chymical tract) with John Dee's marginall notes.

**** I left about 1674, with Mr. Elias Ashmole, 3 pages in folio concerning him[2].

Memorandum :—Mr. Meredith Lloyd tells me that his

† J. Dee's father was a vintner in London at the signe of . . . in . . . : from Elias Ashmole, esqre, who had it from his grandsonne (sonne of Arthur).

father was Roland Dee[3], a Radnorshire gentleman †, and that he hath his pedigree, which he hath promised to lend to me. He was descended from Rees, prince of South Wales.

My great-grandfather, William Aubrey (LL.Dr.), and he were cosins, and intimate acquaintance. Mr. Ashmole hath letters between them, under their owne hands, viz. one of Dr. W. A. to him[a] (ingeniosely and learnedly written) touching the *Sovraignty of the Sea*, of which J. D. writt a booke which he dedicated to queen Elizabeth and desired my great grandfather's advice upon it. Dr. A.'s countrey-house was at Kew, and J. Dee lived at Mortlack, not a mile distant. I have heard my grandmother say they were often together.

Arthur Dee, M.D., his son, lived and practised at Norwich, an intimate friend of Sir Thomas Browne, M.D., who told me that Sir William Boswell, the Dutch ambassador, had all John Dee's MSS.: quaere his executors for his papers. He[b] lived then somewhere in Kent.

---

* MS. Aubr. 23, fol. 78.
** MS. Aubr. 23, fol. 77ᵛ.
*** MS. Aubr. 8, fol. 9ᵛ.

**** MS. Aubr. 6, fol. 37.
[a] See *supra*, pp. 61–65.
[b] Sir William Boswell.

Memorandum:—Sir William Boswell's widowe lives at Bradburne, neer Swynoke, in Kent. Memorandum:—Mr. Hake, of the Physitians' Colledge, hath a MS. of Mr. John Dee's, which see or gett.

Quaere A. Wood for the MSS. in the Bodlean library of Doctor Gwyn, wherein[a] are severall letters between him and John Dee, and Doctor Davies, of chymistrey and of magicall secrets, which my worthy friend Mr. Meredith Lloyd hath seen and read: and he tells me that he haz been told that Dr. Barlowe gave it to the Prince of Tuscany[b].

Meredith Lloyd sayes that John Dee's printed booke of Spirits, is not above the third part of what was writt, which were in Sir Robert Cotton's library; many whereof were much perished by being buryed, and Sir Robert Cotton bought the field to digge after it.

Memorandum:—he told me of John Dee, etc., conjuring † Vide Almanac, at a poole† in Brecknockshire, and that they about the poole in Brecon. found a wedge of gold; and that they were troubled and indicted as conjurers at the assizes; that a mighty storme and tempest was raysed in harvest time, the countrey people had not knowen the like.

His picture in a wooden cutt is at the end of Billingsley's Euclid, but Mr. Elias Ashmole hath a very good painted copie of him from his sonne Arthur. He had a very fair, clear[c] complexione (as Sir Henry Savile); a long beard as white as milke. A very handsome man.

Investigatio cinerum △

Old goodwife Faldo[4] (a natif of Mortlak in Surrey), 80+aetatis (1672[d]), did know Dr. Dee, and told me he dyed at his howse in Mortlack, next to the howse where the tapistry hangings are made, viz. west of that howse; and that he dyed about 60+, 8 or 9 yeares since (January, 1672), and lies buried in the chancell, and had a stone

---

Anthony Wood notes, 'false.'
See Clark's Wood's *Life and Times*, ii. 158.
[c] Dupl. with 'sanguine.'
[d] '1672' is added in pencil.

(marble) upon him. Her mother tended him in his sick-

† A Brief History
of Muscovia, by
Mr. John Milton,
Lond. 1682,
pag. 100, scil.
1588. 'Dr. Giles
Fletcher went
ambassador
from the Queen
to Pheodor then
emperour;
whose relations,
being judicious
and exact, are
best read
entirely by
themselves. This
emperour. upon
report of the
great learning
(of) the
mathematician,
invited him to
Mosco, with
offer of two
thousand pound
a-yeare, and
from Prince
Boris one
thousand
markes; to
have his
provision from
the emperor's
table, to be
honourably
recieved, and
accounted as
one of the chief
men in the land.
All which Dee
accepted not.'

nesse. She told me that he did entertain the Polonian ambassador at his howse in Mortlak, and dyed not long after; and that he shewed the eclipse with a darke roome to the said ambassador †. She beleeves that he was eightie years old when he dyed. She sayd, he kept a great many stilles goeing. That he layd the storme Sir Everard Digby. That the children dreaded him because he was accounted a conjurer. He recovered the basket of cloathes stollen, when she and his daughter (both girles) were negligent : she knew this.

He is buried (upon the matter) in the middest of the chancell, a little towards the south side. She sayd, he lies buried in the chancell between Mr. Holt and Mr. Miles, both servants to queen Elizabeth, and both have brasse inscriptions on their marble, and that there was on him a marble, but without any inscription, which marble is removed ; on which old marble is signe of two or three brasse pinnes. A daughter of his (I thinke, Sarah) maried to a flax-dresser, in Southwarke: quaere nomen.

He dyed within a yeare, if not shortly, after the king of Denmark was here: vide Sir Richard Baker's *Chronicle* and Capt. Wharton's *Almanac*.

* He built the gallery in the church at Mortlak. Goody Faldo's father was the carpenter that work't it.

A stone was on his grave, which is since removed. At the upper end of the chancell then were steppes, which in Oliver's dayes were layd plaine by the minister, and then 'twas removed. The children when they played in the church would runne to Dr. Dee's grave-stone. She told me that he forewarned Q. Elizabeth of Dr. Lopez attempt against her (the Dr. bewrayed, —— himselfe).

He used to distill egge-shells, and 'twas from hence

* MS. Aubr. 6, fol. 38.

that Ben Johnson had his hint of the alkimist, whom he meant.

He was a great peace-maker ; if any of the neighbours fell out, he would never lett them alone till he had made them friends.

He was tall and slender. He wore a gowne like an artist's gowne, with hanging sleeves, and a slitt.

A mighty good man he was.

He was sent ambassador for Queen Elizabeth (shee thinkes) into Poland.

Memorandum :—his regayning of the plate for . . . . 's butler, who comeing from London by water with a basket of plate, mistooke another basket that was like his. Mr. J. Dee bid them goe by water such a day, and looke about, and he should see the man that had his basket, and he did so ; but he would not gett the lost horses, though he was offered severall angells. He told a woman (his neighbour) that she laboured under the evill tongue of an ill neighbour (another woman), which came to her howse, who he sayd was a witch.

In J. David Rhesus' *British Grammar*, p. 60 :—' Juxta Crucis amnem (*Nant y groes*), in agro *Maessyuetiano*, apud Cambro-brytannos, erat olim illustris quaedam *Nigrorum* familia, unde *Joan Du*, id est, *Johannes* ille cognomento *Niger*, Londinensis, sui generis ortum traxit : vir certe ornatissimus et doctissimus, et omnium hac nostra aetate tum Philosophorum tum Mathematicorum facile princeps : monadis illius Hieroglyphicae et Propaedeumatum aphoristicorum de praestantioribus quibusdam Naturae virtutibus, aliorumque non paucorum operum insignium autor eximius. Vir praeterea ob tam multam experientiam frequenti sua in tot transmarinas regiones peregrinatione comparatam, rerum quamplurimarum et abditarum peritissimus.'

Notes.

[1] In MS. Aubr. 6, fol. 36, Aubrey gives the horoscope, with astrological notes, e. g. that there is 'a reception between Saturn and Luna,' that ' Jupiter is in his exaltation and lord of the ascendant,' etc.

[2] In MS. Aubr. 7, fol. 6, Aubrey notes :—' vide the new additions in John Dee's life.' This perhaps refers to MS. Aubr. 6, foll. 36-38, as being additional to the paper which he here says he left with Ashmole.

[3] In MS. Aubr. 6, fol. 37, Aubrey gives in colours the coat, ' gules, a lion rampant within a bordure indented or,' adding the note :—' Memorandum in

the scutcheon at the beginning of his preface the bordure is engrailed : I believe that is the truest, for 'twas donne with care —sed quaere.'

In MS. Aubr. 6, fol. 36ᵛ, he gives in trick the coat for Dee's match '1578, Febr. 5,' with Jane Fromundz, viz. :—'in the 1 and 6, gules, a lion rampant within a bordure engrailed or [Dee]; in the 2, or, a lion rampant gules [. . .]; in the 3, . . . , a lion rampant crowned sable [. . .]; in the 4, azure, a lion rampant . . . [Dun]; in the 5, argent, on 2 bends gules 6 cross crosslets or [. . .],' as the coat of John Dee; impaling ' per chevron ermines and gules, a chevron between 3 fleur de lys or' [Fromundz], for Jane Fromundz. The motto is 'A Domino factum est istud.'

  ¹ Aubrey's conversation with 'goodwife Faldo,' written down at the time (Oct. 22, 1672), is found in a letter to Anthony Wood, in MS. Wood F. 39, fol. 192.

Thomas Deere ($16\frac{3}{4}\frac{8}{0}$–16– . .).

*Thomas Deere, natus March 15°, 1639, 15ʰ 7′ P.M., at New Sarum—John Gadbury's advice, 1 April, 1676.

** Thomas Deare's letter :—

'From Stackton in parochia de Fordingbridge, die Jovisᵃ, 9 Martii, 167⅝, 2ʰ 30′ P.M.

The Accydents of the native, etc.

In November 1655, aged 15 yeare 8 moneths, went to London, to a master, a clerke in the Kinge's Bench.

In November followinge, aged 16 yeare 8 moneths, had the small pox.

In February and March 1658, an ague and feavor.

At the same tyme an uncle (the mother's brother) dyed, which gave the native a good legacy.

In 1661, purchased an estate.

In August 1662, hee marryed, which was one of the worst acts that etc.

In July 1663, hee had a sonn born, etc.

In June 1667, another sone.

In the same yeare in September, his father dyed etc., aged 70 etc.

In 1666, a very great feavor; in ⟨16⟩67, another ; in '68, a surfeite which caused another ⟨fever⟩, etc.

In May '71, another sunn which lived but a fortnight, etc.

Many other accidents there are and remarkeable, but

---

* MS. Aubr. 21, fol. 96.   ** MS. Aubr. 23, fol. 7.
ᵃ i. e. Thursday.

I suppose 3 or 4 or but 2 of these may doe well enough [a] etc. Yet as to preferrment, etc.—In Aug. 1667, I was courted by the old earle of Pembrook [b] to be his chiefe steward; but, hee always vexed with false informations against me, I left his ymployment.'

* Memorandum :—Mr. Th. Deer is now (Jan. 167$\frac{7}{8}$) in prison at Fisherton-Anger.

Gideon de Laune (1565?–1659).

** . . . De Laune:—he was apothecary to Mary the queen mother: came into England . . .

He was a very wise man, and as a signe [c] of it left an estate of 80,000 *li*.

Sir William Davenant was his great acquaintance and told me of him, and that after his returne into England he went to visit him, being then octogenary, and very decrepit with the gowt, but had his sight and understanding. He had a place made for him in the kitchen chimney; and, *non obstante* he was master of such an estate, Sir William sawe him slighted not only by his daughter-in-lawe, but by the cooke-mayd, which much affected him—misery of old age.

He wrote a booke of prudentiall advice, in quadrans, 8vo, in English verse, which I have seen, and there are good things in it.

Sir John Denham (1615–166$\frac{8}{9}$). ·

*** Sir John Denham was unpolished with the small-pox : otherwise a fine complexion.

**** From Anthony Wood :—in the Matriculation booke he finds it thus written—'Johannes Denham, Essex, filius Johannis Denham de Horseley parva in com. praed., militis, aetat. 16, 1631.'

***** Sir John Denham [1], Knight of the Bath, was borne at Dublin in Ireland, anno Domini . . .

[a] For purposes of testing the astro-logical scheme.
[b] Philip Herbert, fifth earl, succeeded 1655, died 1669.
* MS. Aubr. 23, fol. 7ᵛ.

** MS. Aubr. 8, fol. 7ᵛ.
[c] Subst. for ' proofe.'
*** MS. Aubr. 8, fol 6ᵛ.
**** MS. Aubr. 23, fol. 84.
***** MS. Aubr. 6, fol. 105.

Quaere Dr. Buzby if he was a Westminster schollar—I have forgot. Anno . . . he was admitted of Trinity Colledge in Oxford, where he stayed . . . His tutor there was . . . . . I have heard Mr. Josias Howe say that he was the dreamingst young fellow ; he never expected such things from him as he haz left the world. When he was there he would game extremely ; when he had played away all his money he would play away his father's wrought rich gold cappes.

His father was Sir John Denham, one of the Barons of the Exchequer. He had been one of the Lords Justices in Ireland : he maried Ellenor †, one of the daughters of Sir Garret Moore, knight, lord baron of Mellifont, in the kingdome of Ireland, whom he maried during his service in Ireland in the place of Chief Justice there.

† She was a beautifull woman, as appeares by her monument at Egham. Sir John, they say, did much resemble his father.

From Trinity Colledge he went to Lincolnes-Inne, where (as judge Wadham Windham[a], who was his contemporary, told me) he was as good a student as any in the house. Was not suspected to be a witt.

At last, viz. 1640, his play of *The Sophy* came out, which did take extremely: Mr. Edmund Waller sayd then of him, that he *broke-out like the Irish Rebellion ‡—threescore thousand strong*, before any body was aware[b].

‡ His play came out at that time.

He was much rooked by gamesters, and fell acquainted with that unsanctified crew, to his ruine. His father had some suspition of it, and chid him severely, wherupon his son John (only child) wrot a little essay in 8vo, printed . . . , *Against § gameing and to shew the vanities and inconveniences of it*, which he presented to his father to let him know his detestation of it[2]. But shortly after his father's death ¶ (who left 2,000 or

§ Vide Justus Turcaeus[c] *de lusu aleae*, where he proves 'tis a disease and that it proceeds from pride, and that the Spaniards (the proudest nation) are most[d] addicted to it.
¶ January 6, 1638[e], sepult. at Egham in Surrey.

---

[a] Judge of the King's Bench, 1660.
[b] Dupl. with 'when noboby suspected it.'
[c] Subst. for 'Paschalius.'
[d] Subst. for 'most guilty of it.'
[e] i. e. 163⅞.

1,500 *li.* in ready money, 2 houses well furnished, and much plate) the money was played away first, and next the plate was sold. I remember about 1646 he lost 200 *li.* one night at New-cutt. Anno . . . (I ghesse 1642) he was high-sheriff of the countie of Surrey.

At the beginning of the civill warre he was made governor of Farnham-castle for the king, but he was but a young soldier, and did not keepe it. In 164⅔, after Edghill fight, his poeme called *Cowper's Hill* was printed at Oxford, in a sort of browne paper, for then they could gett no better.

164⁰⁹ (quaere) he conveyed, or stole away, the two dukes of Yorke and Glocester from St. James's (from the tuition of the earle of Northumberland), and conveyed them into France to the Prince of Wales and Queen-mother. King Charles II sent him and the lord Culpepper envoyes to the king of Poland, . . .

Anno 1652, he returned into England, and being in some straights was kindly entertayned by the earle of Pembroke at Wilton, where I had the honour to contract an acquaintance with him. Here he translated the . . . booke of Vergil's *Æneis*, and also burlesqu't it † : quaere Mr. Christopher Wase who was then there, tutor to William [a], lord Herbert. He was, as I remember, a yeare with my lord of Pembroke at Wilton and London; he had then sold all the lands his father had left him.

† He burlesqued Virgil, and burnt it, sayeing that 'twas not fitt that the best poet should be so abused.— From Mr. Christopher Wase.

His first wife was the daughter and heire of . . . Cotton, of . . . in Glocestershire, by whom he had 500 *li.* per annum, one son and two daughters. *His son did not *patrem sapere.* He was of Wadham College [b] in Dr. Wilkins's time: he dyed *sine prole*, I thinke, there.—One of his daughters is maried to . . . Morley, of Sussex, esq.; the other . . .

He was much beloved by King Charles the First, who much valued him for his ingenuity. He graunted him the reversion of the surveyor of his majestie's buildings, after

---

[a] 'William, lord,' subst. for 'the lord.' * MS. Aubr. 6, fol. 105ʳ.
[b] John Denham, fellow-commoner of Wadham, in July 1654.

the decease of Mr. Inigo Jones; which place, after the restauration of King Charles II he enjoyed to his death, and gott seaven thousand pounds, as Sir Christopher Wren told me of, to his owne knowledge. Sir Christopher Wren was his deputie.

Anno Domini 166.. he maried his 2d wife, ⟨Margaret⟩ Brookes, a very beautifull young lady; Sir John was ancient and limping. The duke of Yorke fell deepely in love with her, though (I have been morally assured) he never had carnall knowledge of her. This occasioned Sir John's distemper of madnesse in 166.., which first appeared when he went from London to see the famous free-stone quarries at Portland in Dorset, and when he came within a mile of it, turned back to London again, and did[a] not see it. He went to Hownslowe, and demanded rents of lands he had sold many yeares before; went to the king, and told him he was the Holy Ghost. But it pleased God that he was cured of this distemper, and writt excellent verses (particularly on the death of Mr. Abraham Cowley) afterwards. His 2d lady had no child; was poysoned by the hands of Co. of Roc.[b] with chocolatte.

At the coronation of King Charles II he was made Knight of the Bath.

He dyed (vide A. Wood's *Antiq. Oxon.*) at the house of his office (which he built, as also the brick-buildings next the street in Scotland-yard), and was buried, anno Domini 166⅞, March the 23, in the south crosse aisle of Westminster Abbey, neer Sir Jeffrey Chaucer's monument, but hitherto (1680) without any memoriall for him.

Memorandum:—the parsonage-house at Egham (vulgarly called *The Place*) was built by baron Denham; a house very convenient, not great, but pretty, and pleasantly scituated, and in which his son, Sir John, (though he had better seates), did take most delight in. He sold it to John Thynne, esq. In this parish is a place called Cammomill-hill, from the cammomill that growes there

---

[a] Subst. for 'and then would not.'
[b] Elizabeth Mallet, wife of John Wilmot, second earl of Rochester.

naturally; as also west of it is Prune-well-hill (formerly part of Sir John's possessions), where was a fine tuft of trees, a clear spring, and a pleasant prospect to the east, over the levell of Middlesex and Surrey. Sir John tooke great delight in this place, and was wont to say (before the troubles) that he would build there a retiring-place to entertaine his muses; but the warres forced him to sell that as well as the rest. He sold it to Mr. . . . Anstey. In this parish W. and by N. (above *Runney Meade*) is *Cowper's Hill*, from whence is a noble prospect, which is incomparably well described by that sweet swan, Sir John Denham; printed first at Oxon shortly after Edghill fight, 164$\frac{2}{3}$.

Memorandum :—he delighted much in bowles, and did bowle very well.

He was of the tallest, but a little incurvetting at his shoulders, not very robust. His haire was but thin and flaxen, with a moist curle. His gate was slow, and was rather a stalking (he had long legges), which was wont to putt me in mind of Horace, *De Arte Poetica* :—

> ' Hic, dum sublimes versus ructatur, et errat
> Si veluti merulis intentus decidit auceps
> In puteum foveamve : '——

His eie was a kind of light goose-gray, not big; but it had a strange piercingness, not as to shining and glory, but (like a Momus) when he conversed with you he look't into your very thoughts.

He was generally temperate as to drinking; but one time when he was a student of Lincolne's-Inne, having been merry at the taverne with his camerades, late at night, a frolick came into his head, to gett a playsterer's brush and a pott of inke, and blott out all the signes between Temple-barre and Charing-crosse, which made a strange confusion the next day, and 'twas in Terme time. But it happened that they were discovered, and it cost him and them some moneys. This I had from R. Estcott [a], esq., that carried the inke-pott.

---

[a] Richard Escott matr. at Exeter, July 3, 1612 ; afterwards of Lincoln's Inn.

In the time of the civill warres, George Withers, the poet, begged Sir John Denham's estate at Egham of the Parliament, in whose cause he was a captaine of horse. It ⟨happened⟩ that G. W. was taken prisoner, and was in danger of his life, having written severely against the king, &c. Sir John Denham went to the king, and desired his majestie not to hang him, for that whilest G. W. lived he should not be the worst poet in England.

Scripsit *the Sophy* : *Cowper's Hill* : *Essay against Gameing* : Poems, 8vo, printed anno Domini . . . ; Cato Major sive De Ṣenectute, translated into English verse, London, printed by H. Heringman, in the New Exchange, 1669.

Memorandum :—in the verses against Gondibert, most of them are Sir John's. He was satyricall when he had a mind to it.

Notes.

[1] Aubrey gives in colours the coat : 'gules, 3 lozenges ermine [Denham],' surrounded by laurels. He adds the note:—'this coate is in stone and thus coloured, on the roofe or vaulting of the cathedral church at Winchester: Sir John told me his family was originally westerne.' He adds the reference 'vide A. Wood's Hist. Oxon.'

[2] Aubrey, in MS. Wood F. 39, fol. 193, writing Oct. 22, 1672, says:—'Sir John Denham wrott an essay against gameing, to shew his detestation of it to his father, printed by N. Brookes, at the Angel in Cornhill. I have it, about 3 or 4 sheetes, 8vo. His name is not to it, but I know 'twas his; and a kinsman of his, that was one of his father's clarkes, gave the copy to Brookes: and Sir John Denham owned it to me.'

René Descartes (1596–165⁰⁄₁).

* Monsieur Renatus Des Cartes,

'nobilis Gallus, Perroni dominus, summus mathematicus et philosophus ; natus Hagae Turonum pridie Calendas Apriles, 1596 ; denatus Holmiae Calendis Februarii, 1650' —this inscription I find under his picture graved by C. V. Dalen.

How he spent his time in his youth, and by what method he became so knowing, he tells the world in his treatise entituled Of Method. The Societie of Jesus glorie in that theyr order had the educating of him. He lived severall

* MS. Aubr. 6, fol. 33ᵛ.

yeares at Egmont (neer the Hague), from whence he dated
severall of his bookes.   He was too wise a man to encomber
himselfe with a wife; but as he was a man, he had the
desires and appetites of a man; he therefore kept a good
conditioned hansome woman that he liked, and by whom
he had some children (I thinke 2 or 3). 'Tis pity but
comeing from the braine[a] of such a father, they should be
well cultivated. He was so eminently learned that all
learned men made visits to him, and many of them would
desire him to shew them his . . . of instruments (in those
dayes mathematicall learning lay much in the knowledge of
instruments, and, as Sir H. S.[b] sayd, in doeing of tricks),
he would drawe out a little drawer under his table, and
shew them a paire of compasses with one of the legges
broken; and then, for his ruler, he used a sheet of paper
folded double. This from Alexander Cowper (brother of
Samuel), limner to Christina, queen of Sweden, who was
familiarly acquainted there with Des Cartes.

   * Mr. Hobbes was wont to say that had Des Cartes kept
himselfe wholy to geometrie that he had been the best
geometer in the world. He did very much admire him,
but sayd that he could not pardon him for writing in the
defence of transubstantiation which he knew to bee absolutely
against his judgment[c]—quod N. B.

Robert Devereux, earl of Essex (1567–160⁰⁄₁).

   ** Ex registro capellae Turris London, scil. 1600[d], 'Robert,
earle of Essex, beheaded, Febr. 6th.'
   From my lady Elizabeth, viscountesse Purbec, repeated
by her :—

1. There is none, oh none but you,
      Who from me estrange your sight,
      Whom mine eyes affect to view
      And chained eares heare with delight.

---

[a] Dupl. with 'loines.'   [b] Sir Henry Savile.   * MS. Aubr. 9, fol. 8ᵛ.
            [c] Dupl. with ' opinion,' or ' conscience.'
         ** MS. Aubr. 8, fol. 31.   [d] i.e. 160⅟.

2. Others' beauties others move,
   In you I all graces find:
   Such are the effects of love
   To make them happy that are kind.

3. Woemen in fraile beauty trust,
   Only seeme you kind to me,
   Still be truly kind and just
   For that can't dissembled bee.

4. Deare, afford me then your sight,
   That surveighing all your lookes
   Endlesse volumnes I may write
   And fill the world with envyed bookes.

5. Which when after ages view
   All shall wonder and despayre,
   Women, to find a man so true,
   And men, a woeman halfe so faire—

made by Robert, earl of Essex, that was behcaded.

* The tradition is that the bell of Lincoln's-Inne was
brought from Cales (Cadiz), tempore reginae Elizabethae,
plundered in the expedition ● under ⟨Robert Devereux⟩,
earl of Essex.

Sir Everard Digby (1578–160⅝).

** Sir Everard Digby (father of Sir Kenelme) scripsit
libellum Latinè cui titulus :—

Everardi Dygbei de duplici methodo—

in 8vo, in dialogues.

I have heard Mr. John Digby say (his grandsonne) that
he was the handsomest man (accounted) in England.

*** Sir Everard Digby was a most gallant gentleman and
one of the handsomest men of his time. He writt something in Latin *de methodo*, which I did light upon 23 yeares
ago at a country man's howse in Herefordshire; and
Mr. Francis Potter told me he writt *de arte natandi*.

'Twas his ill fate to suffer in the powder-plott. When

* MS. Aubr. 6, fol. 1ᵛ.   ● In 1596.   ** MS. Aubr. 8, fol. 10.
*** Aubrey, in MS. Wood F. 39, fol. 178: July 6, 1672.

his heart was pluct out by the executioner (who, *secundum formam*, cryed 'Here is the heart of a traytor!'), it is credibly reported, he replied, 'Thou liest!' This my lord Bacon speakes of, but not mentioning his name, in his *Historia vitae et mortis*.

Sir Kenelm Digby (1603–1665).

* Sir Kenelm Digby[1], knight: he was borne at ⟨Gotehurst, Bucks⟩ on the eleventh of June[2]: see Ben: Johnson, 2d volumne :—

> 'Witnesse thy actions done at Scanderoon
> Upon *thy* birthday, the eleaventh of June.'

[Memorandum :—in the first impression in 8vo it is thus; but in the folio 'tis *my*, instead of *thy*.]

Mr. Elias Ashmole assures me, from two or three nativities by Dr. ⟨Richard⟩ Nepier, that Ben: Johnson was mistaken and did it for the ryme-sake.—In Dr. Napier's papers of nativities, with Mr. Ashmole, I find :—'Sir Kenelme Digby natus July 11, 5^h 40' A.M. 1603, 14 Leo ascending,' and another scheme gives it at '4^h A.M., 26 Cancer ascending'; and there are two others of Cancer and Leo.

He was the eldest son of Sir Everard Digby, who was accounted the handsomest gentleman in England. Sir Everard sufferd as a traytor in the gunpowder-treason ; but king James restored his estate to his son and heire. Mr. Francis Potter told me that Sir Everard wrote a booke *De Arte Natandi*. I have a Latin booke of his writing in 8vo :—Everardi[a] Dygbei *De duplici methodo libri duo*, in dialogues 'inter Aristotelicum et Ramistam,' in 8vo : the title page is torne out.—His second son was Sir John Digby, as valiant a gentleman and as good a swordman as was in England, who dyed (or was killed †) in the king's cause at Bridgewater, about 1644.

† I can easily learne, if you desire it[b].

It happened in 1647 that a grave was opened next to

---

* MS. Aubr. 6, fol. 99.
[a] This title is substituted in the margin. The text had 'de fallaciis,' scored out, and 'vide margent' written over.

[b] i.e. if Anthony Wood wants to know which of the suggestions is correct, Aubrey can find out.

Sir John Digby's (who was buried in summer time, it seemes), and the flowers on his coffin were found fresh, as I heard Mr. Harcourt (that was executed) attest that very yeare. Sir John died a batchelour.

Sir Kenelme Digby was held to be the most accomplished cavalier of his time. He went to Glocester hall in Oxon, anno ⟨1618⟩ (vide A. Wood's *Antiq. Oxon.*). The learned Mr. Thomas Allen (then of that house) was wont to say that he was the *Mirandula* of his age. He did not weare a gowne there [a], as I have heard my cosen Whitney say.

There was a great friendship between him and Mr. Thomas Allen; whether he was his scholar I know not. Mr. Allen was one of the learnedest men of this nation in his time, and a great collector of good bookes, which collection Sir Kenelme bought (Mr. Allen enjoyeing the use of them for his life) to give to the Bodlean Library, after Mr. Allen's decease, where they [b] now are.

He was a great traveller, and understood 10 or 12 languages. He was not only master of a good and gracefull judicious stile, but he also wrote a delicate hand, both fast-hand and Roman. I have seen lettres of his writing to the father [c] of this earle of Pembroke, who much respected [d] him.

He was such a goodly handsome person, gigantique and great voice, and had so gracefull elocution and noble addresse, etc., that had he been drop't out of the clowdes * in any part of the world, he would have made himselfe respected. But the Jesuites spake spitefully, and sayd 'twas true, but then he must not stay there above six weekes. He was envoyé from Henrietta Maria (then Queen-mother) to Pope ⟨Innocent X⟩ where at first he was mightily admired; but after some time he grew high, and

---

[a] i.e. although in Glocester Hall, he did not matriculate in the University. This was by no means infrequent all through the seventeenth century, and was especially common with students of Roman Catholic families.

[b] Subst. for 'they remain.'

[c] i.e. to Philip Herbert, fifth earl of Pembroke, obiit 1669; father of William, sixth earl, obiit 1674, and Philip, seventh earl, obiit 1683. MS. Aubr. 6 was written in 1680.

[d] Subst. for 'loved.'

* MS. Aubr. 6, fol. 99ᵛ.

hectored with his holinesse, and gave him the lye. The pope sayd he was mad.

He was well versed in all kinds of learning. And he had also this vertue[a], that no man *knew better how to abound, and to be abased*, and either was indifferent to him. No man became grandeur better[b]; sometimes again he would live only with a lackey, and horse with a foote-cloath.

He was very generous, and liberall to deserving persons. When Abraham Cowley was but 13 yeares old, he dedicated to him a comedy[c], called *Love's Riddle*, and concludes in his epistle[d]—'The Birch that whip't him then would prove a Bay.' Sir K. was very kind to him.

When he was at Rome one time, (I thinke he was envoyé from Mary the Queen-mother to Pope ⟨Innocent X⟩) he contrasted[e] with his holinesse.

Anno . . . (quaere the countesse of Thanet) much against his mother's, etc., consent, he maried that celebrated beautie and courtezane, Mrs. Venetia Stanley, whom Richard earle of Dorset kept as his concubine, had children by her, and setled on her an annuity of 500 *li.* per annum; which after Sir K. D. maried was unpayd by the earle; and for which annuity Sir Kenelme sued the earle, after mariage, and recovered it. He would say that a handsome lusty man that was discreet might make a vertuose wife out of a brothell-house. This lady carried herselfe blamelessly, yet (they say) he was jealous of her†. She dyed suddenly, and hard-hearted woemen[f] would censure him severely.

† Richard earle of Dorset invited her and her husband once a yeare, when, with much desire and passion he beheld her, and only kissed her hand; Sir Kenelme being still by.

After her death, to avoyd envy and scandall, he retired in to Gresham Colledge at London, where he diverted himselfe with his chymistry, and the professors' good conversation. He wore there a long mourning cloake, a high crowned hatt, his beard unshorne, look't like a hermite, as signes of

---

[a] Dupl. with 'excellency.'
[b] Subst. for 'more.'
[c] Dupl. with 'play.'
[d] Subst. for 'dedication.'

[e] A pen-slip for 'contested': see *supra.*
[f] Dupl. with 'people.'

sorrowe for his beloved wife, to whose memory he erected a sumptuouse monument, now quite destroyed by the great conflagration. He stayed at the colledge [a] two or 3 yeares.

The faire howses in Holbourne, between King's street and Southampton street, (which brake-off the continuance of them) were, about 1633, built by Sir Kenelme; where he lived before the civill warres. Since the restauration of Charles II he lived in the last faire house westward in the north portico of Convent garden, where my lord Denzill Hollis lived since. He had a laboratory there. I thinke he dyed in this house—sed quaere.

He was, 164.., prisoner for the king (Charles I) at Winchester-house, where he practised chymistry [b], and wrote his booke of [c] Bodies and Soule, which he dedicated to his eldest son, Kenelme, who was slaine (as I take it) in the earle of Holland's riseing [d].

Anno 163 ... tempore Caroli I^{mi} he received the sacrament in the chapell at Whitehall, and professed the Protestant religion, which gave great scandal to the Roman Catholiques; but afterwards he *looked back.*

He was a person of very extraordinary strength. I remember one at * Shirburne (relating to the earl of Bristoll) protested to us, that as he, being a midling man, being sett in ⟨a⟩ chaire, Sir Kenelme took up him, chaire and all, with one arme.

He was of an undaunted courage, yet not apt in the least to give offence. His conversation was both ingeniose and innocent.

Mr. Thomas White, who wrote *de Mundo*, 1641 [e], and Mr. . . . Hall of Leige, e societate Jesu, were two of his great friends.

As for that great action of his at Scanderoon, see the

---

[a] Dupl. with 'he was here two.'

[b] Subst. for 'studied chymistry': 'made artificiall stones' is written over as an alternative.

[c] Subst. for 'de Corpore.'

[d] July 1648.

[*] MS. Aubr. 6, fol. 100.

[e] '2' is written over the '1,' perhaps as a correction.

Turkish Historie. Sir ⟨Edward⟩ Stradling, of Glamorganshire, was then his vice-admirall, at whose house is an
excellent picture of his, as he was at that time: by him
is drawn an armillary sphaere broken, and undernethe is
writt IMPAVIDUM FERIENT (Horace). See excellent
verses of Ben: Johnson (to whome he was a great patrone)
in his 2d volumne.

There is in print in French, and also in English (translated by Mr. James Howell), a speech that he made at
a philosophicall assembly at Montpelier, 165.. *Of the
sympathetique powder*—see it [a]. He made a speech at the
beginning of the meeting of the Royall Society *Of the
vegetation of plants.*

He was borne to three thousand pounds per annum.
His ancient seat (I thinke) is Gote-herst in Buckinghamshire. He had a fair estate also in Rutlandshire. What
by reason of the civil warres, and his generous mind, he
contracted great debts, and I know not how (there being
a great falling out between him and his *then* only son,

† He married
. . . sister to this
present Henry,
duke of
Norfolke, no
child living by
her. His 2d
wife . . .
Fortescue, by
whom he has . . .
Quaere the
issue ?

John †) he settled his estate upon . . . Cornwalleys, a subtile sollicitor [b], and also a member
of the House of Commons, who did putt
Mr. John Digby to much charge in lawe:
quaere what became of it ?

Mr. J. D. had a good estate of his owne,
and lived handsomely then at what time I
went to him two or 3 times in order to your *Oxon.
Antiqu.*; and he then brought me a great book, as
big as the biggest Church Bible that ever I sawe, and
the richliest bound, bossed with silver, engraven with
scutchions and crest (an ostrich); it was a curious
velame [c]. It was the history of the family of the Digbyes,
which Sir Kenelme either did, or ordered to be donne.
There was inserted all that was to be found any where
relating to them, out of records of the Tower, rolles,
&c. All ancient church monuments were most exquisitely

---

[a] Afterwards Aubrey added ' I have seen.'

[b] Subst. for ' a lawyer.'   [c] i. e. vellum.

limmed by some rare artist. He told me that the compileing of it did cost his father a thousand pound. Sir
Jo. Fortescue sayd he did beleeve 'twas more. When Mr.
John Digby did me the favour to shew me this rare MS.,
'This booke,' sayd he, 'is all that I have left me of all the
estate that was my father's!' He was almost as tall and
as big as his father: he had something [a] of the sweetnesse
of his mother's face. He was bred by the Jesuites, and
was a good scholar. He dyed at . . .

Vide in . . . Lives when Sir Kenelme dyed.

Sir John Hoskyns enformes me that Sir Kenelme Digby
did translate Petronius Arbiter into English.

Notes.

[1] Aubrey gives in trick the coat:—'azure, a fleur de lys argent [Digby];
impaling, argent on a bend azure 3 bucks' heads caboshed or [Stanley]'; and
adds the reference 'vide his life in . . .' some book, presumably, whose title
he had forgot.

[2] 'June' was written; but Aubrey noted in the margin 'Quaere Mr. Ashmole
pro nativitate by Dr. ⟨Richard⟩ Nepier.' The answer to this query is found in
MS. Aubr. 23, a slip at fol. 121[v], 'Sir Kenelm Digby natus July 11, 5[h] 40' A.M.
1603; another scheme gives it at 4[h] A.M.' Having got this information,
Aubrey then struck out 'June' in the text, and substituted 'July'; and added
the paragraph which follows.

Venetia Digby (1600–1633).

[*] Venetia Stanley [1] was daughter of Sir . . . Stanley.

She was a most beautifull desireable creature; and being
matura viro was left by her father to live with a tenant and
servants at Enston-abbey † (his land, or the earl
of Derby's) in Oxfordshire; but as private as
that place was, it seemes her beautie could
not lye hid. The young eagles had espied
her, and she was sanguine and tractable, and
of much suavity (which to abuse was greate
pittie).

† At the west
end of the
church here [2]
were two towers
as at Welles or
Westminster
Abbey, which
were standing
till about 1656.
The romes of
the abbey were
richly wains-
cotted, both
sides and roofe.

In those dayes Richard, earle of Dorset
(eldest son [b] and heire to the Lord Treasurer, vide pedegree)

[a] Subst. for 'much.'
[*] MS. Aubr. 6, fol. 101[v].
[b] Grandson; his father Robert,

second earl, died in 1609, a year
after his father, Thomas Sackville,
first earl.

lived in the greatest splendor of any nobleman of England.
Among other pleasures that he enjoyed, Venus was not the
least. † This pretty creature's fame quickly
came to his Lordship's eares, who made no
delay to catch at such an opportunity.

† Sam. Daniel:
—Cheekes of
Roses, locks of
amber | To b'-
emprisond in a
chamber | etc.

I have now forgott who first brought her to
towne, but I have heard my uncle Danvers [a] say (who was
her contemporary) that she was so commonly courted, and
that by grandees, that 'twas written over her lodging one
night *in literis uncialibus,*

PRAY COME NOT NEER,
FOR DAME VENETIA STANLEY LODGETH HERE.

The earle of Dorset, aforesayd, was her greatest gallant,
who was extremely enamoured of her, and had [b] one if not
more children by her. He setled on her an annuity of
500 *li.* per annum.

Among other young sparkes of that time, Sir Kenelme
Digby grew acquainted with her, and fell so much in love
with her that he married her, much against the good will
of his mother ; but he would say that ' a wise man, and
lusty, could make an honest woman out of a brothell-house.'

‡ Venetia
Stanley :—her
picture is at the
earl of
Rutland's at
Belvoir.—From
my cosen
Montague.—
MS. Aubr. 8,
fol. 25.

Sir Edmund Wyld had her picture‡ (and you
may imagine was very familiar with her), which
picture is now (vide) at Droitwytch, in Worcestershire, at an inne, where now the towne
keepe their meetings. Also at Mr. Rose's, a
jeweller in Henrietta-street in Convent garden,
is an excellent piece of hers, drawne after she was newly
dead.

She had a most lovely and sweet-turn'd face, delicate
darke-browne haire. She had a perfect healthy constitution;
strong ; good skin ; well proportioned ; much enclining to
a *Bona Roba* (near altogether). Her face, a short ovall;
darke-browne eie-browe, about which much sweetness, as
also in the opening of her eie-lidds. The colour of her

---

[a] John Danvers, p. 196, *supra.*   [b] Subst. for 'had some children.'

cheekes was just that of the damaske rose, which is
neither too hott nor too pale. She was of a
just [a] stature, not very tall.

† Her picture by Vandyke is now at Abermarleys, in Carmarthenshire, at Mr. Cornwalleys' sonne's widowe's (the lady Cornwalleys's) howse, who was the daughter and heire of . . . Jones, of Abermarles.

Sir Kenelme had severall pictures of her
by Vandyke, &c. † He had her hands cast in
playster, and her feet, and her face. See Ben:
Johnson's 2d volumne, where he hath made her
live in poetrey, in his drawing of her both
body and mind :—

‘ Sitting, and ready to be drawne,
What makes these tiffany, silkes, and lawne,
Embroideries, feathers, fringes, lace,
When every limbe takes like a face !’—&c.

* When these verses were made she had three children
by Sir Kenelme, who are there mentioned, viz. Kenelme,
George, and John.

She dyed in her bed suddenly. Some suspected that
she was poysoned. When her head [b] was opened there was
found but little braine, which her husband imputed to her
drinking of viper-wine; but spitefull woemen would say
'twas a viper-husband who was jealous of her that she
would steale a leape. I have heard some say,—e. g. my
cosen Elizabeth Falkner,—that after her mariage she
redeemed her honour by her strick't living. Once a yeare
the earle of Dorset invited her and Sir Kenelme to
dinner, where the earle would
behold her with much passion,
and only kisse her hand.

Sir Kenelme erected to her
memorie a sumptuouse and
stately monument [c] at . . . Fryars [d]
(neer Newgate-street) in the east
end of the south aisle, where
her bodie lyes in a vault of brick-worke, over which are

[a] Dupl. with ‘ good.’
* MS. Aubr. 6, fol. 101.
[b] Subst. for ‘ braine.’
[c] Aubrey gives (MS. Aubr. 6, fol.

101) a drawing of this monument here given in facsimile.
[d] ‘ . . . Fryars’ is written over ‘ Christ Church,’ as an alternative.

three steps[a] of black marble, on which was a stately altar of black marble with 4 inscriptions in copper gilt affixed to it: upon this altar her bust of copper gilt, all which (unlesse the vault, which was onely opened a little by the fall) is utterly destroyed by the great conflagration. Among the monuments in the booke mentioned in Sir Kenelm Digby's life, is to be seen a curious draught of this monument, with copies of the severall inscriptions.

About 1676 or 5, as I was walking through Newgate-street, I sawe Dame Venetia's bust standing at a stall at the Golden Crosse, a brasier's shop. I perfectly remembred it, but the fire had gott-off the guilding: but taking notice of it to one that was with me, I could never see it afterwards exposed to the street. They melted it downe. How these curiosities would be quite forgott, did not such idle fellowes as I am putt them downe!

Memorandum:—at Goathurst, in Bucks[b], is a rare originall picture of Sir Kenelme Digby and his lady Venetia, in one piece, by the hand of Sir Anthony van Dyke. In Ben. Johnson's 2d volumne is a poeme called 'Eupheme[3], left to posteritie, of the noble lady, the ladie Venetia Digby, late wife of Sir Kenelme Digby, knight, a gentleman absolute in all numbers: consisting of these ten pieces, viz. Dedication of her Cradle; Song of her Descent; Picture of her Bodie; Picture of her Mind; Her being chose a Muse; Her faire Offices; Her happy Match; Her hopefull Issue; Her 'ΑΠΟΘΕΩΣΙΣ, or Relation to the Saints; Her Inscription, or Crowne.'

Her picture drawn by Sir Anthony Vandyke hangs in the queene's draweing-roome, at Windsor-castle, over the chimney.

Venetia Stanley was (first) a miss to Sir Edmund Wyld; who had her picture, which after his death, serjeant Wyld (his executor) had; and since the serjeant's death hangs now in an entertayning-roome at Droitwich in Worcester-shire. The serjeant lived at Droitwich.

[a] Dupl. with 'degrees.'
[b] 'Or Bedfordshire' followed, scored out.

Notes.

[1] Aubrey gives in trick the coat :—'argent on a bend azure 3 bucks' heads caboshed or [Stanley, earl of Derby].' Another hand has enlarged this first sentence to 'daughter of Sir Edward Stanley of Eynstonn in com. Oxon, son of Sir Thomas Stanley, knight, younger son to Edward, earl of Derby.' A note by ' E. M.' (? Edmund Malone) says, ' This is Anthony Wood's handwriting.' It is certainly not ; but it very probably is Sir William Dugdale's, which is sometimes mistaken for Wood's.

[2] Einsham abbey is the place meant. See the facsimile in Clark's Wood's *Life and Times,* i. 228.

[3] In MS. Aubr. 6, fol. 70ᵛ also, this is quoted, but there scored out, as ' Eupheme, being a poem left to posterity,' &c. There, for 'a Muse,' Aubrey reads ' his Muse.'

Leonard Digges (15..–1571 ?).

*Jacobus Digges [1], de Berham, armig. — **m.** Philippa, filia Johannis Engeham de Chart, uxor 2ᵈᵃ.

Leonard Diggs, de Wotton. — **m.** Sara, filia ⟨Thomae⟩ Wilford, de Hartridge in parochia de Cranbroke.

Maria, uxor ... Barber. | Thomas Digges, filius et haeres Leonardi. — **m.** Anna, filia Warhami St. Leger, militis. | Anna, uxor Willelmi Digges de Newington. | Sara, uxor ... Martyn.

Jacobus [a] Digges, de Bech, Armiger. | Leonardus Digges, filius secundus. | Dudlius Digges, de Chilham, miles : modo (1619) superstes, legatus ad Imperatorem Russiae. — **m.** Maria, minima filia et cohaeres Thomae Kemp de Olney, militis.

Thomas Diggs, primus filius, armiger. | Johannes, filius 2dus. | Dudlius, filius 3tius. | Anna. | Elizabetha.

** Memorandum this visitation [b] was in anno 1619 by John Philpot.

They [c] were, for severall generations, of Barham in Kent. John, the sonne of Roger Digges of Mildenhall (which Roger is the first in this genealogie), vixit tempore Henrici III ; and writt then Dig.—Memorandum here are 14 generations or descents to the last line : quod N. B.

Mr. Leonard Digges translated Claudian *de raptu Proserpinae* into English, 4to, 1617 and 1628.

* MS. Aubr. 8, fol. 73.
[a] This entry is scored out.
** MS. Aubr. 8, fol. 73ᵛ.
[b] i. e. from which Aubrey excerpted

the genealogy above : probably a MS. in the Heralds' Office.
[c] The family of Digges.

* Leonard Digges, esquire, of Wotton [2] in Kent—he wrote a thin folio called *Pantometria*, printed 15.. At the end he discourses of regular solids, and I have heard the learned Dr. John Pell say it is donne admirably well. In the preface he speakes of cutting glasses in such a particular manner that he could discerne pieces of money a mile off; and this he saies he setts downe the rather because severall are yet living that have seen him doe it.

. . . Prognostication [3] everlasting, 4to, ⟨Lond.⟩ 15⟨64⟩.

(A 4to) ' *Tectonicon*, briefly shewing the exact measuring and speedy reckoning all manner of land, squares, timber, stone, steeples, pillars, globes, etc., for declaring the perfect making and large use of the carpenter's ruler, containing a quadrant geometricall, comprehending also the rare use of the square, and in the end a little treatise opening the composition and appliancie of an instrument called The Profitable Staffe, with other things pleasant and necessarie, most condusible for surveyors, landmeaters, joyners, carpenters, and masons: published by Leonard Digges, gentleman, 1556.'

'L. D. to the Reader—Although many have put forth sufficient and certain rules to measure all manner of superficies, etc., yet in that the art of numbring hath been required, yea, chiefly those rules hid and as it were locked up in strange tongues, they doe profit or have furthered very little, for the most part, yea, nothing at all, the landmeater, carpenter, mason, wanting the aforesayd. For their sakes I am here provoked not to hide but to open the talent I have recieved, yea, to publish in this our tongue very shortly if God give life a volumne containing the flowers of the sciences mathematicall largely applied to our outward practise profitably pleasant to all manner men. Here mine advice shall be to those artificers, that will profit in this or any of my bookes ☞ now published, or that hereafter shall be, first confusedly to read them through, then with more judgement, read at the third reading wittily to practise. So, few things shall be

* MS. Aubr. 8, fol. 72ᵛ.

unknowne. Note, oft diligent reading joyned with ingenious practise causeth profitable labour. Thus most
hartely farewell, loving reader, to whom I wish myselfe
present to further thy desire and practise in these.'

The method that carpenters etc. used before this booke
was published was very erronious, as he declares.

* ☞ See in the beginning of ⟨Thomas⟩ Digges'
Stratio⟨ti⟩cos, and also towards the later end, concerning
him and his father. I remember the sonne sayes there that
he was muster-master to the States of Holland : and see
more concerning his father (who was an esquire of Chilham
Castle in Kent) in the preface to his *Pantometria.*—It
is an ancient family in Kent. Vide his *Ala seu scala
Mathematices* etc.

** A prognostication everlasting, once again published
by Leonard Digges, gentleman, in the yeare of our Lord
1564 ;—

in 4to, dedicated to Sir Edward Fines, knight of the
garter, lord Clinton and Saye, etc. His first impression
was in 1553—' not onely your lordship's tasck move⟨d⟩ of
a prognostication seemed then to make that argument
fittest, but also the manifest imperfections and manifold
errors yearly committed did crave the ayd of some that
were both willing and able to performe the truthe in like
matters.'

Notes.

[1] In MS. Aubr. 8, fol. 73ᵛ, Aubrey gives in trick the coat :—' gules, on a cross
argent five eagles displayed sable [Digges] '; on fol. 72ᵛ, 75ᵛ, he gives the same
coat, with the motto   IN ARDUA VIRTUS ;
on fol. 11, he gives the coat and motto, but adds that there is a crescent ' in
medio scuti.'

[2] ' Wotton ' is substituted for ' . . . Castle,' to which a marginal note was
added, ' I think 'tis Chilham Castle.' In MS. Aubr. 8, fol. 11, Aubrey wrote :—
' . . . Digges, esq., of Chilham Castle, Kent—vide prefaces of his *Pantometrie*
and *Ala seu Scala Mathematices*, etc. His son makes mention of his life in his
Stratioticos.'

[3] A pencil note on fol. 73 gives the title, with the press mark in the 1674
Catal. libr. impress. Bibl. Bodl., viz.—'A perpetual prognostication for weather :
C. 2. 13. Art.'

* MS. Aubr. 6, fol. 51ᵛ.   ** MS. Aubr. 8, fol. 75.

Thomas Digges (15 . . -1595).

* Mr. Thomas Digges :—he wrote a booke in 4to, entituled—

'*Stratioticos*, compendiously teaching the science of nombres as well in fractions as integers, and so much of the rules and aequations algebraicall and art of nombers cossicall as are requisite for the profession of a soldier; together with the modern militarie discipline, offices, lawes and orders in every well-governed camp and armie inviolably to be observed.'

First published by him, 1579, and dedicated 'unto the right honourable Robert, earle of Leicester.' The second edition, 1590.

He was muster-master generall of all her majestie's forces in the Low Countries, as appeares in page 237.

At the end of this booke (the last paragraph) speaking of 'engins and inventions not usual to be thought on and had in readinesse.'—

'Of these and many mo important mattars militare, I shall have occasion at large to dilate in my treatise of great artillerie and pyrotechnie, ☞ whose publication I have for divers due respects hitherto differred.'

He was the onely sonne of the learned Leonard Digges, esqr, of whom he speakes in the preface to his *Stratioticos*.

Pliny, Nat. Hist. lib. vii. cap. 51 ;—' Una familia Curionum in qua tres continua serie Oratores extiterunt.' In *this* family have been four learned men in an uninterrupted descent—scilicet, two eminent mathematicians (Leonard and Thomas), Sir Dudley Digges, Master of the Rolles, and his sonne Dudley, fellow of Allsoules College, Oxon.

** Alae seu scalae mathematicae, quibus visibilium remotissima coelorum theatra conscendi et planetarum omnium itinera novis et inauditis methodis explorari, tum hujus portentosi syderis (in Cassiopea) in mundi boreali plaga insolito fulgore coruscantis distantia et magnitudo immensa situsque protinus tremendus indagari Deique stupendum ostentum terricolis expositum cognosci liquidissime possit.

Thoma Diggesio, Cantiensi, stemmatis generosi, autore, Lond. 1573.

Dedicated

'Ad Guliel. Cecilium, praeclariss. ordinis equitem auratum, baronem Burghleium, summumque Angliae Thesaurarium,' etc.

—luce clarius deprehendi longè supra lunam ipsam esse. Tum demum antiquorum et recentiorum omnium astronomorum modos cometarum et corporum coelestium distantias et magnitudines metiendi quos unquam legeram in animum sevocare coeperam, nec quenquam reperire poteram qui viam huic subtilissimae parallaxi examinandae convenientem demonstravit. Solus igitur, omnium astronomorum antiquorum et recentiorum ope orbatus, (in fluctuanti dubitationum plurimarum pelago jactatus) ad meipsum redii: brevissimoque spatio (foelicibus mathematicis spirantibus auris) portum optatum assequendi varios cursus expeditissimos hactenus a nemine exploratos atque ab omni erroris scopulo tutissimos inveni. Quos in exigui libelli formam redactos honori tuo exhibere decrevi, mei officii testimonium (nisi me fallit Philautia) haud vulgari genio conscriptum, neque brevi temporum curriculo periturum—

* Praefatio Authoris.

Sed plura de hujus stellae historia scribere non decrevi quia eximius vir Johannes Dee (quum in reliqua philosophia admirandus, tum harum scientiarum peritissimus, quem tanquam mihi parentem alterum mathematicum veneror, quippe qui in tenerrimâ meâ aetate plurima harum suavissimarum scientiarum semina menti meae inseruerit, alia a patre meo prius sata amicissime fidelissimeque

nutriverit atque auxerit) hanc sibi tractandam assumpserit
materiam quam . . . Conatus igitur sum et assequutus
variis problematibus demonstrative et practice exactissime
parallaxin hujus phaenomeni et cujusvis etiam alterius
concludere, licet Saturni Jovis et Martis parallaxeis adeo
sint exiguae ut sensuum imbecillitate vix discerni possint.
Si tamen ulla arte vere animadverti queant (hoc ausim
dicere) aut his nostris sequentibus problematibus aut
nullis penitus praeceptis geometricis inveniri posse—Si
aequi bonique consuleris, majora (annuenti potentissimo)
in posterum promitto, quibus (non probabilibus solummodo
argumentis sed firmissimis apodixibus) demonstrabitur
verissimam esse Copernici hactenus explosum de terrae
motu paradoxum—1573.

To these *Alae seu Scalae* Mr. Digges hath annexed

Parallaticae commentationis praxeos nucleus quidam,
Jo. Day—

writ by John Dee, a small treatise, Lond. 1573; and
hath writ thus

Lectori Benevolo.

—Me autem isti meo opusculo annectere et in lucem
simul emittere variae impulere causae—1ma ne charis-
simus mihi illius author debita suae inventionis privaretur
laude: cum nonnulli fortassis si postea ederetur suspicari
possint a meis methodis derivatum fuisse. Fateor equidem
adeo late mea sese extendere fundamina ut tum istiusmodi
tum plurimi etiam alii nuclei inde excerpi possint, etc.

* *Pantometria*, containing longimetria, planimetria,
stereometria—was writ by Leonard Digges, esq., but
published by his sonne Thomas Digges esqr. and dedicated to Sir Nicholas Bacon, knight, Lord Keeper, lately
reviewed and augmented by the author, printed at
London, 1591.

In the preface, thus :—

'But to leave things doone of antiquity long ago, my
father, by his continuall painfull practises, assisted with

* MS. Aubr. 8, fol. 75.

demonstrations mathematicall, was able, and sundry times hath, by proportionall glasses duely situate in convenient angles, not onely discovered things farre off, read letters, numbred peeces of money with the very coyne and super-scription thereof cast by some of his freends on purpose upon downes in open fields but also seven miles off declared what hath been doone at that instant in private places ; he hath also at sundry times by the sunne fired powder and discharged ordinance halfe a mile and more distant—which things I am the bolder to report for that there are yet living diverse of these his doeings *oculati testes*, and many other matters far more strange and rare which I omit as impertinent to this place. But for invention of these con-clusions I have heard him say nothing ever helped him so much as the exquisite knowledge he had, by continuall practise, attained in geometricall mensurations.'

Michael Drayton (1563–1631).

* Michael Drayton, esq., natus in Warwickshire at Ather-ston upon Stower (quaere Thomas Mariett).

He was a butcher's sonne. Was a squire ; viz. one of the esquires to Sir Walter Aston, Knight of the Bath, to whom he dedicated his Poeme. Sir J. Brawne of . . . was a great patron of his.

He lived at the bay-windowe house next the east end of St. Dunstan's Church in Fleet-street. Sepult. in north + of Westminster Abbey. The countesse of Dorset ª (Clifford) gave his monument : this Mr. Marshall (the stone-cutter), who made it, told me so.

Sir Edward Bissh, Clarencieux, told me he asked Mr. Selden once (jestingly) whether he wrote the com-mentary to his ' Polyolbion ' and ' Epistles,' or Mr. Drayton made those verses to his notes.

Vide his inscription given by the countess of Dorset.

* MS. Aubr. 8, fol. 8ᵛ.

ª ' The countesse of Dorset, that was governes to prince Charles, now our King, was at the cost of erecting his monument' : Aubrey, in MS. Wood F. 39, fol. 208 : May 17, 1673.

In Westminster Abbey, neer Spencer.

MICHAEL DRAYTON, ESQUIER,

A memorable Poet of this age, exchanged his Laurel for
a Crowne of Glorie, Anno 1631.

> Doe, pious marble, let thy readers knowe
> What they, and what their children owe
> To DRAYTON'S name, whose sacred dust
> We recommend unto thy trust.
> Protecte his mem'ry, and preserve his storie,
> Remaine a lasting monument of his glorye.
> And when thy ruines shall disclame
> To be the treas'rer of his name,
> His name, that cannot fade, shall bee
> An everlasting monument to thee.

A MERCU-
RIE'S CAP IN
THE SUN [a].

A
PEGA-
SUS [a].

Here is his bust in alablaster. The inscription is on
black marble.

Mr. Marshall, the stone-cutter, of Fetter-lane, also told
me, that these verses were made by Mr. Francis Quarles,
who was his great friend, and whose head he wrought
curiously in playster, and valued for his sake. 'Tis pitty
it should be lost. Mr. Quarles was a very good man.

Sir Erasmus Dryden (1553–1632).

*Sir Erasmus Dryden, of ⟨Canons Ashby⟩ in North-
amptonshire :—John Dreyden, esq., Poet Laureat, tells me
that there was a great friendship between his great grandfather's father [b] and Erasmus Roterodamus, and Erasmus
was god-father to one of his sonnes, and the Christian name

---

[a] i.e. at the side of the inscription this
is carved; Aubrey gives a rough sketch
of the figures, a sun in his glory charged
with a mercury's cap, on a wreath ; a
shield gouttée, with a Pegasus.
* MS. Aubr. 8, fol. 102[v].

[b] Erasmus was in England 1497 and 1510. The Dryden pedigree is :—

David Dryden
|
John Dryden, obiit 1584
|
Sir Erasmus, obiit 1632
|
┌──────────────┴──────────────┐
John   Erasmus (3rd son)
|
John (the poet)

of Erasmus hath been kept in the family ever since. The poet's second sonne is Erasmus.

And at . . . , the seate of the family, is a chamber called 'Erasmus's chamber.'

I ghesse that this coate[a]—'azure, a lion rampant and in chief a sphere between 2 estoiles or'—was graunted in Henry 8th's time by the odnesse of the charge.

John Dryden (1631-1700).

[*] John Dreyden, esq., Poet Laureate. He will write it[b] for me himselfe.

[**] John Dryden, poeta, ⟨born⟩ 19 Aug. 1631, 5^h 33' 16'' P.M.

[***] 'Natus insignis poeta
1631
Aug. 9°, 5^h 53' P.M.
Latit. 52° North.'

This is the nativity of Mr. John Dreyden, poet laureat, by Mr. John Gadbury, from whom I had it.

Sir William Dugdale (1605-168⅝).

[****] Sir William Dugdale, Garter, ⟨born⟩ 12 Sept. 1605, 3^h 15' P.M.

[*****] 'Sir[1] William Dugdale avow'd to mee ⟨that⟩ at the time of his birth (10 September, as I thinke, which was the birth day of Francis the first) a swarme of bees came and settled under the window where hee was borne, September 18. Johan. Gybbon.'

Memorandum that Sir William Dugdale did not tell his son or Mr. Gibbons de Edward the Confessor and he laught at it—quod N.B.

'Sir[2] William Dugdale was borne September 12, 1605' —from Mr. Gibbons, Blewmantle. That afternoon a swarme

---

[a] Given in trick by Aubrey.
[*] MS. Aubr. 6, fol. 108ᵛ.
[b] i.e. his life. The page has been left blank for the fulfilment of this promise: cf. Milton, *infra*.
[**] MS. Aubr. 23, fol. 121: out of

Dr. Richard Napier's papers.
[***] MS. Aubr. 23, fol. 87.
[****] MS. Aubr. 23, fol. 121: out of Dr. Richard Napier's papers.
[*****] MS. Aubr. 7, a slip at fol. 8ᵛ.

I.   R

of bees pitch't under his mother's chamber window, as it were an omen of his laborious collections.

Notes.

[1] This is a note in the handwriting of John Gibbon ('Blue Mantle' pursuivant, 1668); followed by a memorandum by Aubrey.

[2] A note by Gibbon, correcting the previous one: followed by a memorandum by Aubrey.

Sir John Dunstable.

* Sir John Dunstable :—the cellar he calls his library.— Parliament men prepare themselves for the businesse of the nation with ale in the morning. Some justices doe sleepe on the bench every assizes.

** At Chippenham the Deputye Lieutenants mett to see the order of the militia, but quales D : Lieutenants tales officiarii. After a taedious setting (at dinner, and drinking after dinner) the drummes beate and the soldiers to march before the windowe to be seen by the Deputy Lieutenants. Justice Wagstaffe [1] (colonell) had not marcht before 'em many yardes but downe a falls all along in the dirt. His myrmidons, multâ vi, heav'd him up, and then a cryd out 'Some drinke, ho!' and so there was an end of that businesse.

Note.

[1] The hero of the anecdote is no doubt Sir John Dunstable. In the *Dramatis personae* for Aubrey's projected comedy, one of the characters is 'Justice Wagstaffe' (MS. Aubr. 21, p. 2), over which name Aubrey has written 'Sir J. Dunstable,' apparently as the name of the person he meant to copy.

Saint Dunstan (925–988).

*** I find in Mr. Selden's verses before Hopton's 'Concordance of Yeares,' that he was a Somersetshire gentleman. He was a great chymist.

The storie of his pulling the devill by the nose with his tongues as he was in his laboratorie [a], was [b] famous in church-windowes. Vide . . . Gazaei *Pia Hilaria,* ⟨where it is⟩ delicately described.

* MS. Aubr. 21, p. 19.

** MS. Aubr. 21, p. 2.

*** MS. Aubr. 8, fol. 31ᵛ.

[a] Dupl. with 'his *athanor* roome.'

[b] Dupl. with 'is famous in picture and poetrie.'

He was a Benedictine monke at Glastonbury, where he was afterwards abbot, and after that was made arch-bishop of Canterbury. He preached the coronation sermon at Kingston, and crowned king ⟨Edwy⟩. In his sermon he prophesyed, which the Chronicle mentions.

Mr. Meredith Lloyd tells me that there is a booke in print of his de lapide philosophorum ; quaere nomen.

Edwardus Generosus gives a good account of him in a manuscript which Mr. Ashmole haz.

Meredith Lloyd had, about the beginning of the civill warres, a MS. of this Saint's concerning chymistrey, and sayes that there are severall MSS. of his up and downe in England : quaere Mr. Ashmole.

Edwardus Generosus mentions that he could make a fire out of gold, with which he could sett any combustible matter on fire at a great distance. Memorandum :—in Westminster library is an old printed booke, in folio, of the lives of the old English Saints : vide.

Meredith Lloyd tells me that, three or 400 yeares ago, chymistry was in a greater perfection, much, then now ; their proces was then more seraphique and universall : now they looke only after medicines.

Severall churches are dedicated to him : two at London : quaere if one at Glastonbury.

Sir Edward Dyer (15..–1607).

* Sir Edward Dyer, of Somersetshire (Sharpham Parke, etc.), was a great witt, poet, and acquaintance of Mary, countesse of Pembroke, and Sir Philip Sydney. He is mentioned in the preface of the ' Arcadia.' He had four thousand pounds per annum, and was left fourscore thousand pounds in money ; he wasted it almost all. This I had from captaine Dyer, his great grandsonne, or brother's great grandson. I thought he had been the sonne of the Lord Chiefe Justice Dyer, as I have inserted in one of these papers, but that was a mistake. The judge was of the same family, the captain tells me.

* MS. Aubr. 8, fol. 1ᵛ.

R 2

St. Edmund (1170?–1240).

* Seth, lord bishop of Sarum, tells me that he finds Saint Edmund was borne at Abington. He was archbishop of Canterbury. He built the college at Sarum, by St. Edmund's Church: it is now Judge Wyndham's sonne's howse. He resigned his archbishoprick, and came and retired hither. In St. Edmund's church here[a], were windowes of great value. Gundamore[b] offered a good summe for them; I have forgott ⟨what⟩. In one of them was the picture of God the Father, like an old man (as the fashion was), which much offended Mr. Shervill, the recorder, who in zeale (but without knowledge) clambered up on the pewes[c] to breake the windowe, and fell downe and brake his legg (about 1629); but that did not excuse him for being question'd in the Starre-chamber for it. Mr. Attorney Noy was his great friend, and shewed his friendship there. But what Mr. Shervill left undonne, the soldiers since have gonne through with, that there is not a piece of glass-painting left.

'Edmundus, Cant.[d] A.B., primus legit Elementa Euclidis, Oxoniæ, 1290[e]; Mr. Hugo perlegit librum Aristotelis Analytic. Oxon.; Rogerus Bacon vixit A.D. 1292.'—This out of an old booke in the library of University College, Oxon.

Thomas Egerton, lord Ellesmere (1540–161⁴⁄₇).

** Sir Thomas Egerton[1], Lord Chancellor, was the naturall sonne of Sir Richard Egerton of ⟨Ridley⟩ in Cheshire.—This information I had 30 yeares since from Sir John Egerton of Egerton in Cheshire, baronet, the chiefe of that family.

He was of Lincoln's-Inne, and I have heard Sir John

---

* MS. Aubr. 8, fol. 32.
[a] At Salisbury.
[b] Gondomar, ambassador of Spain to James I, 1617–23.
[c] Subst. for 'seates.'
[d] i.e. 'Cantuar. archiepiscopus,'

Aubrey using his contraction for arch-bishop (A. B.) instead of the Latin.
[e] *Sic*, in Aubrey's MS., but in error: perhaps 1210 was intended.
** MS. Aubr. 6, fol. 83ᵛ.

Danvers say that he was so hard a student, that in three
or 4 yeares time he was not out of the howse. He had
good parts, and early came into good practise.

My old father, Colonel Sharington Talbot †, told me
that (Gilbert, I thinke), earle of Shrewesbury,
desired him to buy that noble mannour of
Ellesmer for him, and delivered him the money.

† He had, I
believe, 200
adopted sonnes.

Egerton liked the bargain and the seate so well, that truly
he e'en kept it for himselfe, and afterwards made it his
baronry, but the money he restored to the earl of Shrewsbury again *.

Dyed . . . , and was buried . . ..

He was a great patron to Ben Johnson, as appeares
by severall epistles to him.

His son and heire, since earle of Bridgewater, was an
indefatigable ringer—vide the ballad.

* Chancellor Egerton haz a monument in the south
wall of St. Martin's-in-the-fields chancell ; but the upper
part (greatest) is covered with a pue or gallerie.

> Tuta ^b frequensque via est, per amici fallere nomen ;
> Tuta frequensque licet sit. via, crimen habet.
> OVID ⟨Ars Amat. i. 585⟩.

Translated by Theophilus Wodinoth :—

A safe and common way it is by friendship to decieve,
But safe and common though it be, 'tis knavery, by your leave.

Note.

¹ Aubrey gives in colours the coat :—' argent, a lion rampant gules between
3 pheons sable [Egerton].'

George Ent (16 . . –1679).

** G. Ent ᶜ obiit Septemb. 2, 1679. Buried in the north
of the rotundo at the Temple Church. Motto of his
ring :—
    Quam totus homuncio nil est ᵈ.

ᵃ Here followed, scored out as being
in error, 'he was created earle of
Bridgewater.'

* MS. Aubr. 8, fol. 9.

ᵇ A quotation jotted down as applic-

able to the Shrewsbury story, *supra*.

** MS. Aubr. 8, fol. 29.

ᶜ Eldest son of Sir George : see in
the life of Thomas Triplett.

ᵈ Petron. Satir. cap. 34 (Bücheler).

Note.

In August, 1674, this George Ent came to Oxford, to live there. He brought with him a letter of introduction from Aubrey to Anthony Wood, which is now in MS. Ballard 14. Wood and he did not get on, and Aubrey several times makes excuses for his friend; e. g. Aug. 26, 1674 (MS. Ballard 14, fol. 110), ' he is a very honest gentleman and his rhodomontades you will easily pardon.' The quarrels, however, became fiercer. Aubrey to Wood, March 9, 167⅘, (MS. Ballard 14, fol. 115):—' I am exceeding sorry for Mr. Ent's strange-nesse to you; but 'tis confess't his friends must beare with him. I did not shew him your letter; but, expostulating with him, and he being cholerique, etc., I read only that paragraph where he "introduced into your company two boy-bachelors and upbrayded you with dotage "—.'

Desiderius Erasmus (1467–1536).

* 'Nascitur Erasmus Roterodamus anno 1467, Octob. die 27, horâ 16, 30'': poli elevatio 54° 0''—⟨from⟩ David Origanus, p. 603.

'Mercurius, Venus, Luna et Leo conjuncti, praesertim in ascendente, faciunt oratores doctissimos. Talis ex parte fuit constitutio Erasmi Roterodami, cujus judicium gravis-simum, ingenium acutissimum, et oratio copiosissima, ex scriptis editis eruditissimis, omnibus nota est. Habuit enim Mercurium cum Venere in horoscopo, in signo aereo Libram, et Jovem trigono radio Mercurium et Venerem intuentem '—⟨from ibid.⟩ pag. 601.

Obiit anno Domini MDXXXVI, mense Julii—vide praefationem de obitu Erasmi ante Epistolas, impressas Antverpiae MDXLV.

** Erasmus Roterodamus was like to have been a bishop—vide Epistolas.

*** Desiderius Erasmus, Roterodamus :—

His name was 'Gerard Gerard,' which he translated into 'Desiderius Erasmus.'

He was *begot* (as they say) *behind dores*—vide an Italian booke in 8vo. *de famosi Bastardi* : vide Anton. Possevini *Apparatus*. His father (as he says in his life, writt by himselfe) was the tenth and youngest son of his grand-father : who was therfore designed to be dedicated to

---

* MS. Aubr. 6, fol. 5ᵛ.   ** MS. Aubr. 8, fol. 7.
*** MS. Aubr. 6, fol. 5ᵛ.

God.—' Pater Gerardus cum Margareta (medici cujusdam Petri filia), spe conjugii (et sunt qui intercessisse verba dicunt), vixit.'

His father tooke great care to send him to an excellent schoole, which was at Dusseldorf, in Cleveland. He was a tender chitt, and his mother would not entruste him at board[a], but tooke a house there, and made him cordialls, etc.—from John Pell, D.D.

He loved not fish, though borne in a fish towne—from Sir George Ent, M.D.

⟨From⟩ Dr. John Pell:—he was of the order of . . . , whose habit was the same ₁that the pest-house master at . . . (I thinke, Pisa: quaere Dr. John Pell) in Italie wore; and walking in that towne, people beckoned him to goe out of the way, taking him to be the master of the pest-house; and he not understanding the meaning, and keeping on his way, was there by one well basted. He made his complaint when he came to Rome, and had a dispensation for his habit.

He studied sometime in Queens Colledge in Cambridge: his chamber was over the water. Quaere Mr. Paschal more particularly; and if a fellowe: 'he[b] had his study when a young scholar here.

'The staires which rise up to his studie at Queens Colledge in Cambridge doe bring first into two of the fairest chambers in the ancient building; in one of them, which lookes into the hall and chiefe court, the Vice-President kept in my time; in that adjoyning, it was my fortune to be, when fellow. The chambers over are good lodgeing roomes; and to one of them is a square turret adjoyning, in the upper part of which is that study of Erasmus; and over it leades. To that belongs the best prospect about the colledge, viz. upon the river, into the corne-fields, and countrey adjoyning, etc.; ☞ so that it might very well consist with the civility of the House to

---

[a] Subst. for 'would not adventure him at the boarding schoole.'

[b] i.e. Andrew Paschal (B.D. 1661)

had lived in the rooms formerly occupied by Erasmus.

that great man (who was no fellow, and I think stayed not long there) to let him have that study. His keeping roome might be either the Vice-President's, or, to be neer to him, the next; the room for his servitor that above, over it, and through it he might goe to that studie, which for the height, and neatnesse, and prospect, might easily take his phancy.' This from Mr. Andrew Paschal, Rector of Chedzoy in Somerset, June 15, 1680.

He mentions his being there in one of his Epistles, and blames the beere there. One, long since, wrote, in the margent of the booke in ⟨the⟩ College library in which that is sayd, ' *Sicut erat in principio*, etc.' ; and all Mr. Paschall's time they found fault with the brewer.

He had the parsonage (quaere value) of Aldington in Kent, which is about 3 degrees perhaps a healthier place then Dr. Pell's parsonage in Essex. I wonder they could not find for him[a] better preferment ; but I see that the Sun and Aries being in the second house[b], he was not borne to be a rich man.

He built a schoole at Roterdam, and endowed it, and ordered the institution[c]. Sir George Ent was educated there. A statue in brasse is erected to his memory on the bridge in Roterdam.

'The last five bookes of Livy nowe extant, found by Symon Grinaeus in the library of a monastery over against the citie of Wormbs, are dedicated by Erasmus Roterodamus unto Charles the son of William lord Montjoy in the reigne of Henry the eight of famous memory, king of England, etc.'—Philemon Holland's translation.

Sir Charles Blount, of Maple-Durham, in com. Oxon. (neer Reding), was his scholar (in his Epistles there are some to him), and desired Erasmus to doe him the favour[*] to sitt for his picture, and he did so, and it is an excellent piece : which picture my cosen John Danvers, of Baynton (Wilts), haz : his wive's grandmother was Sir Charles Blount's daughter or grand-daughter. 'Twas pitty such a

---

[a] Dupl. with ' find out.'
[b] In his horoscope.
[c] i. e. fixed the course of study.
[*] MS. Aubr. 6, fol. 6.

rarity should have been aliend from the family, but the issue male is lately extinct. I will sometime or other endeavour to gett it for Oxford Library.

They were wont to say that Erasmus was interpendent between Heaven and Hell, till, about the year 1655 (quaere Dr. Pell), the Conclave at Rome damned him for a heretique, after he had been dead . . . . yeares.

Vita Erasmi, Erasmo autore, is before his Colloquia, printed at Amstelodam. MDCXLIV. But there is a good account of his life, and also of his death, scil. at Basil, and where buried, before his Colloquies printed at London.

His deepest divinity is where a man would least expect it : viz. in his Colloquies in a Dialogue between a Butcher and a Fishmonger, Ἰχθυοφαγία.

Scripsit.

Colloquia : dedicated 'optimae spei puero Johanni Erasmio Frobenio.'

Liber utilissimus de conscribendis epistolis : dedicated 'ad Nicolaum Beraldum.'

Liber Adagiorum.

Verborum Copia.

Epistolae.

Exhortatio ad pacem ecclesiasticam.

Paraphrasis in quatuor Evangelistas.

Matth.—dedicated Carolo, Imperatori.

Joan.—dedicated Ferdinando, Catholico.

Lucas—to Henr. 8, Rex Angl.

Marcus—to Francisc. I, Gall. Rex.

Novum Testamentum transtulit : memorandum—Henry Standish, bishop of St. Asaph, wrote a booke against his Translation on the New Testament ; vide Sir Richard Baker's *Chronicle* (Henry VIII).

If my memorie failes me not, I have read in the first edition of Sir Richard Baker's *Chronicle* (quaere) that the Syntaxis in our English Grammar was writt by Erasmus.

Memorandum :—Julius Scaliger contested with Erasmus, but gott nothing by it, for, as Fuller sayth, he was like a badger, that never bitt but he made his teeth meet. He was the Πρόδρομος of our knowledge, and the man that made the rough and untrodden wayes smooth and passable [a].

Anthony Ettrick (1622–1703).

* Anthony Ettrick, esq., borne at Berford in the parish of Wimburne-Minster com. Dorset, November the 15th (viz. the same day that Queen Katherine), A.D. 1622—quaere horam—on a Sunday. His mother would say he was a Sundaye's bird.

His eldest son, Mr. William Ettrick, was borne also on the 15 of November, A.D. 1651.

Maried Aug. 1651.

Reader at the Middle Temple 167–.

John Evelyn (1620–1706).

** John Evelyn, esq., Regiae Societatis Socius. drew his first breath at Wotton in the county of Surrey [1], A.D. 1620, 31 October, 1 [ma] hora mane.

Note.

[1] In MS. Wood F. 49, fol. 39, is the cover of Aubrey's *Surrey Collections* :—
'An essay towards the description of the county of Surrey, by Mr. John Aubrey, Fellow of the Royall Societie.' On the back of this, fol. 39', Aubrey has the note :—'Note that the annotations marked J. E. are of John Evelyn, esq., R.S.S.' These Surrey collections are now MS. Aubr. 4.

Thomas Fairfax, 3rd baron (1611–1671).

*** Thomas, lord Fairfax of Cameron, Lord Generall of the Parliament armie :—Memorandum, when Oxford was surrendred [b] (24° Junii 1646), the first thing generall Fairfax did was to sett a good guard of soldiers to preserve the Bodleian Library. 'Tis said there was more hurt donne by the cavaliers (during their garrison) by way of embezilling and cutting-off chaines of bookes, then there

[a] Dupl. with 'easie.'
* MS. Aubr. 23, fol. 37'.
** MS. Aubr. 23, fol. 94.
*** MS. Aubr. 8, fol. 60.

[b] Wood 514, no. 19*, is a pass granted at the time of the siege, with Sir Thomas Fairfax's signature and seal.

was since. He was a lover of learning, and had he not taken this speciall care, that noble library had been utterly destroyed—quod N. B.; for there were ignorant senators enough who would have been contented to have had it so. This I doe assure you from an ocular witnesse, E. W. esq.[a]

He haz a copie of verses before . . . . . in folio.

George Feriby (1573–16..).

* In tempore Jacobi one Mr. George Ferraby was parson of Bishops Cannings in Wilts : an excellent musitian, and no ill poet. When queen Anne came to Bathe, her way lay to traverse the famous Wensdyke, which runnes through his parish. He made severall of his neighbours good musitians, to play with him in consort, and to sing. Against her majestie's comeing, he made a pleasant pastorall, and gave her an entertaynment with his fellow songsters in shepherds' weeds and bagpipes, he himself like an old bard. After that wind musique was over, they sang their pastorall eglogues (which I have, to insert in to liber B.).

He was one of the king's chaplaines. 'Twas he caused the 8 bells to be cast there, being a very good ringer.

He hath only one sermon in print that I know of, at the funerall of Mr. ⟨John⟩ Drew of the Devises, called *Life's Farwell*.

He was demy, if not fellow, of Magdalen College, Oxon.

** Thomas[b] Ferraby, formerly a demy or fellow of Magdalen College, Oxon, minister of Bishops Cannings, Wilts, was an ingeniose man and a good musitian and composer.

He treated queen Anne at Wednsdytch in his parish with a pastorall of his owne writing and composing and sung by his neighbours clad in shepherds' weeds, whom he brought-up to musique.

He gave another entertayment in Cote-field to king

[a] Edmund Wyld (?).
* Aubrey in MS. Wood F. 39, fol. 136: Aug. 9, 1671.

** Aubrey in MS. Wood F. 39, fol. 369: Aug. 15, 1682.
[b] In error for ' George.'

James, with carters singing, with whipps in their hands;
and afterwards, a footeball play.

This parish would have challenged all England for
musique, ringing, and footeball play.

He was one of his Majestie's chaplaines. One sermón
is among my grandfather Lyte's old bookes in the country,
at the funerall of ⟨John⟩ Drew, esquire, called *Life's
farewell*, printed . . .

Nicholas Fiske (15.. –166..).

* Dr. . . . Fisk ᵃ, a physitian, practised physick and
astrologie, and had good practise in both, in Convent
Garden, London. Mr. Gadbury acknowledges in print
to have had his greatest helpes in astrologicall knowledge
from him, and sayes that he was an able artist.

He wrote ᵇ and printed a treatise of the conjunction of
Saturne and Jupiter.

Obiit about 20 yeares since and buryed in Convent
Garden.

Thomas Flatman (16.. –1688).

** Mr. Thomas Flatman, quondam Novi Collegii socius,
then a barrister of the Inner Temple, an excellent painter
and poet. The next terme his poems will be in print.

*** Mr. Thomas Flatman [1] died at his house in Fleet
street on Thursday December ⟨6th⟩, buried the 9th of
that moneth, at St. Bride's, neer the railes of the communion table, in the grave with his sonne, on whom he
layd a fair marble gravestone with an inscription and
verses. His father is living yet, at least 80, a clarke of
the Chancery.

**** Thomas Flatman, filius, natus 1673, Oct. 4, hora
18 P.M. This native dyed of the small pox about
Christmas (December) 1682.

* MS. Aubr. 8, fol. 10.

ᵃ 'Fisk, M.D., or so called':
Aubrey's note in MS. Aubr. 8, fol. 5.

ᵇ 'An astrological discourse' by
N. F., 1650, 12mo, is in the Brit.

Mus. Libr.

** Aubrey, in MS. Wood F. 39, fol.
135ᵛ: Aug. 9, 1671.

*** MS. Aubr. 7, fol. 8ᵛ.

**** MS. Aubr. 23, fol. 58.

Sir William Fleetwood (1535–1594).

* Sir Miles [a] Fleetwood, Recorder of London, was of the Middle Temple; was Recorder of London, when King James came into England; made his harangue to the City of London (ἀντανάκλασις), 'When I consider your wealth I doe admire your wisdome, and when I consider your wisdome I doe admire your wealth.' It was a two-handed rhetorication, but the citizens tooke ⟨it⟩ in the best sense.

He was a very severe [b] hanger of highwaymen, so that the fraternity were resolved to make an example of him [c]: which they executed in this manner: They lay in wayte for him not far from Tyburne, as he was to come from his house at . . . in Bucks; had a halter in readinesse; brought him under the gallowes, fastned the rope about his neck and on the tree, his hands tied behind him (and servants bound), and then left him to the mercy of his horse, which he called *Ball*. So he cryed 'Ho, Ball! Ho, Ball!' and it pleased God that his horse stood still, till somebody came along, which was halfe a quarter of an hour or +. He ordered that this horse should be kept as long as he would live, and it was so—he lived till 1646 :—from Mr. Thomas Bigge, of Wicham [d].

One day goeing on foote to Yield-hall, with his clarke behind him, he was surprised in Cheapside with a sudden and violent looseness neer the Standard. He [e] . . . bade his man hide his face [e] . . .

His seate was at Missenden in the county of Bucks, where his descendents still remaine.

He is buried at . . . in com. Bucks.

John Fletcher (1579–1625).

* John Fletcher, invited to goe with a knight into Norfolke or Suffolke in the plague-time 1625, stayd but to make himselfe a suite of cloathes; fell sick of the plague, and dyed.

** Mr. John Fletcher, poet: in the great plague, 1625, a knight of Norfolk (or Suffolke) invited him into the countrey. He stayed but to make himselfe a suite of cloathes, and while it was makeing, fell sick of the plague and dyed ᵃ. This I had (1668) from his tayler, who is now a very old man, and clarke of St. Mary Overy's.

John Florio (1545?–1625).

*** John Florio was borne in London in the beginning of king Edward VI, his father and mother flying from the Valtolin ('tis about Piedmont or Savoy) to London for religion: Waldenses.——The family is originally of Siena, where the name is to this day.

King Edward dying, upon the persecution of queen Mary, they fled back again into their owne countrey, where he was educated.

Afterwards he came into England, and was by king James made 'informator' to prince Henry for the Italian and French tongues, and clarke to the closet to queen Anne.

Scripsit:—

First and second fruits, being two books of the instruction to learne the Italian tongue:

Dictionary;

and translated Montagne's Essayes.

He dyed of the great plague at Fulham anno 1625.

---

* MS. Aubr. 8, fol. 45ᵛ.
** MS. Aubr. 8, fol. 54.
ᵃ 'And was buryed August 29th, 1625': Aubrey, in MS. Wood F. 39, fol. 253: Jan. 31, 167¾.

*** Aubrey, in MS. Wood F. 39, fol. 133: June 10, 1671. Ibid., fol. 131, Aubrey says the information was from Florio's grandson, 'Mr. Molins.'

Sir Edward Ford (1605–1670).

* Edward Ford [a], esquire, printed 5 or 6 sheetes in 4to— Mr. Edmund Wyld haz it—

'A designe for bringing a river from Rickmansworth in Hartfordshire to St. Gyles in the fields, the benefits of it declared and the objections against it answered, by Edward Ford of Harting in Sussex, esq., London, printed for John Clarke, 1641.' Memorandum that now (168½) London is growne so populous and big that the new river of Middleton can serve the pipes to private houses but twice a weeke, quod N. B.

I beleeve this was afterwards Sir Edward Ford, quondam a gentleman commoner of Trinity College, Oxon : de quo vide in prima parte A. W.

Vide in my trunke of papers a printed sheet of his of . . .

['Twas [b] he built the high water-house over against Somerset howse, pulled downe since the restauration because a nusance.]

** 'Experimental proposalls how the king may have money to pay and maintaine his fleetes with ease to the people, London may be re-built and all proprietors satisfied, money be lent at 6 *li.* per cent on pawnes, and the fishing trade sett-up; and all without strayning or thwarting any of our lawes or customes,' by Sir Edward Forde, London, printed by W. Godbid, 1666—a 4to pamphlet.

*** Sir Edward Ford's body was brought over into England, and buried at Harting Church in Sussex with his ancestors—obiit Sept. 3.

---

* MS. Aubr. 8, fol. 6ᴏᵛ. Aubrey gives in trick the coat :—'azure, a chevron wavy between 3 griffins segreant or.'

[a] An erased note, ibid., says : 'He proposed to a parliament, tempore regis Jacobi, a way of bringing water to London from Richmondsworth, and printed a little booke of it, which Mr. Edmund Wyld has, and is exceeding scarce : see it, and take the title.'

[b] This sentence is scored out.

** Aubrey, in MS. Wood F. 39, fol. 273 : May 30, 1674.

*** Aubrey, in MS. Wood F. 39, fol. 135ᵛ : Aug. 9, 1671.

His brother tells me that this August he is 65 years old and that Sir Edward was borne in Aprill and one yeare and a half older then he.

Sir Edward Ford first proposed his invention, the way of farthings for this nation, and was opposed. He could not gett a patent here: prince Rupert would have it, if he could. So then he went into Ireland and dyed fortnight before he had effected the getting of his patent.

* Sir Edward Ford writt no books, but two or three pamphletts of a sheet or so, which I have some where, and have informed you of. One was an ingeniose proposall of a publique banke, as I remember, for the easy raysing of money and to avoyd the griping usurers and to promote trade.

Samuel Foster (15 . . –1652).

** From Mr. Bayes, the watchmaker, his nephew :—
Mr. Samuel Foster was borne at Coventry (as I take it); he was sometime usher of the schoole there. Was professor of . . . at Gresham Colledge, London, . . . yeares; where, in his lodgeing, on the wall in his chamber, is, of his owne hand draweing, the best diall I doe verily beleeve in the whole world. Inter etc. it shewes you what a clock 'tis at Jerusalem, Gran Cairo, etc. It is drawen very artificially. He dyed . . . July 1652, buryed at St. Peter's the Poor, in Broad-street, London. A neighbour of Mr. Paschall's, neer Bridgewater, in Somerset, hath all his MSS.: which I have seen, I thinke ½ foot thick in 4to.

John Foxe (1517–1587).

*** Adjoyning[a] is this inscription[b] of John Fox.

Christo S. S.

Johanni Foxo, ecclesiae Anglicanae martyrologo fidelissimo, antiquitatis historicae indagatori sagacissimo, Evangelicae veritatis propugnatori acerrimo, thaumaturgo admirabili qui martyres Marianos

---

* Aubrey, in MS. Wood F. 39, fol. 192ᵛ: Jan. 18, 167¾.
** MS. Aubr. 8, fol. 14ᵛ.
*** MS. Aubr. 7, fol. 17.

[a] To the monument of John Speed in the chancel of St. Giles Cripplegate.
[b] 'Printed also in Stowe's Survey': Anthony Wood's note.

tanquam Phoenices ex cineribus redivivos praestitit, patri suo omni
pietatis officio in primis colendo, Samuel Foxus, illius primogenitus,
hoc monumentum posuit, non sine lachrymis.

Obiit die xviii mensis April.

Anno Salutis 1587, jam

Septuagenarius.

Vita vitae mortalis est spes

vitae immortalis.

Nicholas Fuller (1557–162¾).

* The 13th of February, 1623, Mr. Nicholas Fuller[a],
rector of Allington, was buried—ex registro.

Thomas Fuller (1608–1661).

** Thomas Fuller, D.D., borne at Orwincle † in North-
amptonshire. His father was minister there,
and maried . . . one of the sisters of John
Davenant, bishop of Sarum.—From Dr. Edward Davenant.

† J. Dreyden, poete, was borne here.

He was a boy of a pregnant witt, and when the bishop
and his father were discoursing, he would be by and
hearken, and now and then putt in, and sometimes beyond
expectation, or his yeares.

He was of a middle stature; strong sett [b]; curled haire;
a very working head, in so much that, walking and
meditating before dinner, he would eate-up a penny loafe,
not knowing that he did it. His naturall memorie was
very great, to which he had added the *art of memorie*:
he would repeate to you forwards and backwards all the
signes from Ludgate to Charing-crosse.

He was fellow of Sydney College in Cambridge, where
he wrote his *Divine Poemes*. He was first minister of
Broad Windsor in Dorset, and prebendary of the church
of Sarum. He was sequestred, being a royalist, and was
afterwards minister of Waltham Abbey, and preacher of
the Savoy, where he died, and is buryed.

* Aubrey in Wood MS. F. 39, fol.
171 : May 10, 1672.

[a] *Supra*, p. 31.

** MS. Aubr. 8, fol. 18ᵛ.

[b] Dupl. with ' strong made.'

I.   S

He was a pleasant facetious person, and a *bonus socius*.

Scripsit ' Holy Warre '; ' Holy State '; ' Pisgah Sight ';
' England's Worthies '; severall Sermons, among others,
a funerall sermon on Henry Danvers, esq., the eldest son
of Sir John Danvers, (and only ⟨son⟩ by his second wife.
Dantesey), brother to Henry earl of Danby, preached at
Lavington in Wilts 1654: obiit 19° Novembr.

He was minister of Waltham Crosse in Essex, and also
of the Savoy in the Strand, where he dyed (and lies
buryed) not long after the restauracion of his majestie.

Simon Furbisher (1585–16. .).

* Symon Furbisher, the famous jugler, natus 30 May.
1585, 9ʰ 30′ A.M.

John Gadbury (1627–1704).

** Mr. Gadbury the astrologer's father, a taylor, takes
the measure of a young lady for a gowne and clappes up
a match.

Note.

Anthony Wood in the *Ath. Oxon.* gives a more correct version of this
story. William Gadbury, a farmer, of Wheatley, co. Oxon, made a stolen
marriage with a daughter of Sir John Curson of Waterperry. Their son, John
Gadbury, was apprentice to an Oxford tailor, before he set up as an astrologer.
The correspondence between Aubrey and Wood in MS. Wood F. 51, shows
that the publication of this story in Wood's *Athenae* was, very naturally,
resented by Gadbury. Aubrey to Wood, Aug. 20, 1692, Gadbury is ' extremely
incens't against you : . . . he sayes that you have printed lyes concerning him.'
Aubrey to Wood, Oct. 21, 1693, ' I shewed your letter to Mr. Gadbury, wherin
you tell him that what he desires should be amended as to himselfe shall be
donne in the Appendix,' i. e. the third volume of the *Athenae*, on which Wood
was then at work, ' to be printed : but he huft and pish't, saying that your
copies are flown abroad and the scandalls are irrevocable and that he will have
a fling at you in print to vindicate himselfe.' Wood was blind to the indiscretion
he had committed : Wood to Aubrey, Nov. 1692, MS. Ballard 14, fol. 153 :—
' I wonder at nothing more then that Mr. Gadbury should take it amiss of
those things that I say of him : for whereas the generality of scholars did
formerly take him to have been bred an academian, because he was borne at
Oxon, and so, consequently, not to be much admird, now their eyes being
opend and knowing that his education hath been mechanical they esteem him
a prodigie of parts and therfore are much desirous that his picture may hang in
the public gallery at the schooles.'

* MS. Aubr. 23, fol. 121.　　　　　　　** MS. Aubr. 21, p. 11.

Thomas Gale (1636–1702).

⟨MS. Aubr. 6, foll. 3, 4. This catalogue is not in Aubrey's hand: perhaps it is Gale's autograph, sent to Aubrey in answer to a request for a list of his books.⟩

Libri editi curâ et operâ Tho. Gale.

Psalterium juxta exemplar Alexandrinum bibliothecae regiae: Graecè, 8vo.

Scriptores mythologici; Palaephatus, Cornutus, etc.: Graecè, 8vo.

Historiae poeticae scriptores; Apollodorus, Eratosthenes, etc.; Graecè, 8vo.

Rhetores antiqui; Demetrius, Phalereus, Tiberius, etc.: Graecè, 8vo.

Iamblichus Chalcidensis de mysteriis Aegyptiorum, etc.: Graecè, folio.

Johannes Eriugenan, cum notis: Lat., fol.

S. Maximi expositiones in S. Gregorium Nazianzenum: Graecè, fol.

Historiae Britannicae, Anglo-Saxonicae, Anglo-Danicae, etc., scriptores XX nunquam prius editi, 2^bus voluminibus, ffol.

Libri Graeci et Latini praelo parati.

Pentateuchus juxta exemplar Alexandrinum bibliothecae regiae, cum notis, etc.: Graecè, fol.

Liber prophetae Isaiae juxta exemplar Alexandrinum: Graecè, cum commentario, folio.

Basilii, Chrysostomi, Andreae Cretensis, aliorumque Graecorum patrum Homiliae, nondum editae magno numero, Graecè, fol.

Iamblichus de vita Pythagorae et ejusdem ad philosophiam protreptici, ex codicibus MSS. emendatus et nova versione donatus: 8vo.

Iamblichus de mathematica secundum Pythagoricos nunc primum ex MSS. Codd. editus, cum versione Latina: 8vo.

Leonis imperatoris et Basilii cubicularii de re navali Graecorum opuscula, nunc primum ex codd. Graecis eruta cum versione Latina : accedit his Appendix eorum omnium locorum quae apud Graecos et Latinos scriptores extant de re navali : 8vo.

Tertium et ultimum volumen Historicorum gentis Angliae ab Henrico III° usque ad Henricum VII^{um} nunquam hactenus editorum : fol.

Antonini Itinerarium per Britanniam, cum commentario in quo multa ad chorographiam Britanniae explicandam adducuntur : 8vo.

Venerabilis Bedae Historia ecclesiastica, ad antiquissimos codices emaculata et multis locis restituta : fol.

Matthaei Paris Historia, ad codices antiquos emendata et multis repurgata erroribus, una cum copiosis notis et monumentis coaevis : fol.

Codex legum antiquarum gentis Anglicanae ab Ethelberto rege Cantii ad Edvardum primum : in hac collectione continentur quam plurimae leges Saxonicae et aliae nondum editae praeter eas quas Lambertus edidit : fol.

The History of Edward the 2d and of the troubles which happen'd in his reigne, extracted out of the rolls of the Tower, together with those rolls and other authentick evidences at large : ffol.

The Baronage of England in III parts : 1st, of its original; 2^d, of its continuance and alteration; 3^d, of its rights and privilidges.

William Gascoigne (1612?–1644).

* There was a most gallant gentleman and excellent mathematician that dyed ^a in the late warres, one Mr. Gascoigne, of good estate in Yorkshire; to whom Sir Jonas Moore acknowledged to have received most of his knowledge. He was bred up by the Jesuites. I thought to have taken memoires of him; but deferring it, death

---

* MS. Ballard 14, fol. 129 : a letter from Aubrey to Anthony Wood, of date March 19, 168⅞.   ^a Dupl. with 'killed.'

took away Sir Jonas. But I will sett downe what I remember.

* . . . Gascoigne, esq., of Middleton, neer Leeds, York-shire, was killed at the battaile of Marston-moore, about the age of 24 or 25 at most.

Mr. ⟨Richard⟩ Towneley, of Towneley, in Lancashire, esq., haz his papers.—From Mr. Edmund Flamsted, who sayes he found out the way of improveing telescopes before Des Cartes.

Mr. Edmund Flamsted tells me, Sept. 1682, that 'twas at Yorke fight he was slaine.

Henry Gellibrand (1597–1637).

** Henry Gellibrand was borne in London. He was of Trinity Colledge in Oxon (vide Anthony Wood's *Antiq. Oxon.*). Dr. Potter and Dr. ⟨William⟩ Hobbes knew him. Dr. Hannibal Potter was his tutor, and preached his funeral sermon in London. They told me that he was good for little a great while, till at last it happened accidentally, that he heard a Geometrie[a] lecture. He was so taken with it, that immediately he fell to studying it, and quickly made great progresse in it. The fine diall over the Colledge Library is of his owne doeing. Con-struxit Logarithmos Henrici Briggs, jussu Autoris τοῦ μακαρίτου, 1631. He was Astronomy Professor in Collegio Greshamensi, Lond. Scripsit Trigonometriam. He being one time in the country, shewed the tricks of drawing[b] what card you touched, which was by combination with his confederate, who had a string that was tyed to his leg, and the leg of the other, by which his confederate gave him notice by the touch; but by this trick, he was reported to be a conjuror.

Vide *Canterbury's Doome*[c] about Protestant martyrs, ⟨inserted in⟩ the Almanac; ⟨and⟩ that he kept conventicles in Gresham College.

* MS. Aubr. 8, fol. 31.
** MS. Aubr. 6, fol. 49.
[a] Subst. for 'mathematicall.'
[b] Dupl. with 'telling.'
[c] By William Prynne.

. . . Gerard.

* One Mr. Gerard, of Castle Carey in Somerset, collected the antiquities of that county, Dorset, and that of Devon : which I cannot for my life retrive. His executor had them, whose estate was seized for debt; and ⟨they⟩ utterly lost.

Adrian Gilbert (— - —).

** . . . Ralegh *m.* Katherine Champernon *m.* . . . Gilbert

Sir Walter Ralegh　　　　　　Adrian Gilbert,
　　　　　　　　　　　　　　chymist ; sine prole.

This Adrian Gilbert was an excellent chymist, and a great favourite of Mary, countesse of Pembroke, with whom he lived and was her operator. He was a man of great parts, but the greatest buffoon in England ; cared not what he said to man or woman of what quality soever. Some curious ladies of our country have rare receipts of his. 'Twas he that made the curious wall about Rollington parke at Wilton.

*** Mr. Elias Ashmole sayes that amongst his papers of John Dee or Dr. ⟨Richard⟩ Napier he finds that one of them held great correspondence with Adrian Gilbert. Quaere of him de hoc.

Alexander Gill (1567–1635).
Alexander Gill (1597–1642).

**** Dr. Gill, the father, was a very ingeniose person, as may appear by his writings. Notwithstanding he had moodes and humours, as particularly his whipping-fitts :—

> As Paedants out of the schoole-boies breeches
> doe clawe and curry their owne itches

　　　　　　　　Hudibras, part . . . canto . . . .

* MS. Wood F. 39, fol. 128, a
letter from Aubrey to Anthony Wood,
of date Nov. 17, 1670. ⸱

** MS. Aubr. 6, fol. 74ᵛ.
*** MS. Aubr. 6, fol. 79ᵛ.
**** MS. Aubr. 8, fol. 51ᵛ.

This Dr. Gill whipped . . . Duncomb, who was not long after a colonel of dragoons at Edgehill-fight, taken pissing against the wall. He had his sword by his side, but the boyes surprized him : somebody had throwen a stone in at the windowe ; and they seised on the first man they lighted on. * I thinke his name was *Sir John D.* (Sir John Denham told me the storie), and he would have cutt the doctor, but he never went abroad but to church, and then his army went with him. He complained to the councill, but it became ridicule, and so his revenge sank.

Dr. Triplet came to give his master a visit, and he whip't him. The Dr. gott . . . Pitcher, of Oxford, who had a strong * and a sweet base, to sing this song under the schoole windowes, and gott a good guard to secure him with swords, etc., and he was preserved from the *examen* of the little myrmidons which issued-out to attach him ; but he was so frighted that he bes . . . . him selfe most fearfully.

> In Paul's church-yard in London
> There dwells a noble firker ;
> Take heed you that pass
> Lest you tast of his lash
>   .   .   .   .   .   .
>   Still doth he cry
>   Take him up, take him up, Sir,
>   Untrusse with expedition.
>   Oh the birchen tool
>   That he winds i' th' school
>   Frights worse than an inquisition.
>
> If that you chance to passe there,
> As doth the man of blacking ;
> He insults like a puttock
> O're the prey of the buttock
> With a whip't a . . . sends him packing.
>   Still doth he cry, etc.

For when this well truss't trounser
Into the school doth enter
With his napkin at his nose
And his orange stuft with cloves
On any . . . . he'l venter.
    Still doth, etc.

A French-man voyd of English
Enquiring for Paul's steeple
His *Pardonnez-moy*
He counted a toy,
For he whip't him before all people.
    Still doth he cry, etc.

A Welsh-man once was whip't there
Untill he did bes . . . . him
His *Cuds-pluttera-nail*
Could not prevail
For he whip't the Cambro-Britan.
    Still doth he cry, etc.

* A captain of the train'd-band
Yclept * Cornelius Wallis
He whip't him so sore
Both behind and before
He notch't his . . . . like tallyes.
    Still doth he cry, etc.

For a piece of beef and turnip,
Neglected, with a cabbage,
He took up the pillion
Of his bouncing mayd Jillian
And sowc't her like a baggage.
    Still doth he cry, etc.

A porter came in rudely
And disturb'd the humming concord,
He took-up his frock
And he payd his nock
And sawc't him with his owne cord.
    Still doth he cry, etc.

---

* MS. Aubr. 8, fol. 52ᵛ.   * Dupl. with 'sirnam'd.'

Gill upon Gill[a], or
Gill's . . . . uncas'd, unstript, unbound.

'Sir,
Did *you* me this epistle send,
Which is so vile and lewdly pen'd,
In which no line I can espie
Of sense or true orthographie?
So slovenly it goes,
In verse and prose,
For which I must pull down your hose.'
'O good sir!' then cry'd he,
'In private let it be,
And doe not sawce me openly.'
'Yes, sir, I'le sawce you openly
Before Sound[b] and the company;
And that none of thee may take heart
Though thou art a batchelour of Art,
Though thou hast payd thy fees
For thy degrees:
Yet I will make thy . . . . to sneeze.
And now I doe begin
To thresh it on thy skin
For now my hand is in, is in.
First, for the themes which thou me sent
Wherin much nonsense thou didst vent,
And for that barbarous piece of Greek
For which in Gartheus[c] thou didst seeke.
And for thy faults not few,
In tongue Hebrew,
For which a grove of birch is due.
Therfore me not beseech
To pardon now thy breech
For I will be thy . . . .-leech, ...-leech.
Next for the offense that thou didst give
When as in Trinity thou didst live,

---

[a] Dialogue-wise between Alexander
Gill, father, and Alexander Gill, son.

[b] Interlinear note :—' The usher.'
[c] Interlinear note :—' Rowland.'

And hadst thy . . . . in Wadham College mult
For bidding sing *Quicunque vult*^a
And for thy blanketting^b
And many such a thing
For which thy name in towne doth ring
And none deserves so ill
To heare as bad as Gill—
Thy name it is a proverb still,
Thou vented^c hast such rascall geer.
Next thou a preacher were
For which the French-men all cry Fie!
To heare such pulpitt-ribauldrie^d.
And sorry were to see
So worthy a degree
So ill bestowed on thee.
But glad am I to say
The Masters made the⟨e⟩ stay
Till thou in quarto^e didst them pray.
But now remaines the vilest thing,
The alehouse barking 'gainst the king
And all his brave and noble peeres;
For which thou ventredst for thy eares.
And if thou hadst thy right,
Cutt off they had been quite
And thou hadst been a rogue in sight.
　But though thou mercy find
Yet I'le not be so kind
But I'le jerke thee behind, behind.'

Joseph Glanville (1636–1680).

* Joseph Glanville, D.D.:—vide his funerall sermon^f in
St. Paul's church-yard at the signe of . . . .

^a Marginal note:—'When he was clark of Wadham College and being by his place to begin a Psalme, he flung out of church, bidding the people sing to the praise and glory of God *quicunque vult*.'

^b Marginal note:—'he was tossed in a blanket.'

^c MS. has 'ventest.'

^d Marginal note:—'A knave's tongue and a whore's tayle who can rule ?'

^e Marginal note:—'He did sitt 4 times for his degree.'

* MS. Aubr. 8, fol. 9^v.

^f i.e. Aubrey remembered having seen the sermon in a bookseller's

* Dr. Joseph Glanville, minister of Bathe, was taken ill at Bridgewater, and returned home and dyed, Tuesday, November 9, 1680, and lies interred in . . . at Bath abbey.

He was author of *The zealous and impartiall Protestant*, 4to, stitch't, printed by Henry Brome, London, 16⟨81⟩: his name is not to it. Had he lived the Parliament would have questioned him for it.

Owen Glendower (1359 (?)–1415).

** Quaere if you can find of what howse the famous Owen Glendower was. He was of Lincolns Inne, and dyed obscurely (I know where) in this county ⟨Herefordshire⟩, keeping of sheepe.

. . . Skydmore of Kenchurch married his sister, and . . . Vaughan of Hergest was his kinsman; and these two mayntayned him secretly in the ebbe of his fortune.

Robert Glover (1544–1588).

*** The learned herald, Mr. . . . Glover, was borne at . . . , ... in Somersetshire; vide Fuller's 'Worthies' de hoc.

I have heard Sir Wm. Dugdale say, that though Mr. Camden had the name, yet Mr. Glover was the best herald that did ever belong to the office. He tooke a great deale of paines in searching the antiquities of severall counties. He wrote a most delicate hand, and pourtrayed finely.

There is (or late was) at a coffee-house at the upper end of Bell-yard (or Shier-lane), under his owne hand, a Visitation of Cheshire, a most curious piece, which Sir Wm. Dugdale wish't me to see; and he told me that at York, at some ordinary house (I thinke a house of entertainment) he sawe such an elaborate piece of Yorkshire. But severall counties he surveyd, and that with

---

shop; cf. *supra*, p. 115. The sermon was by Joseph Pleydell.

* MS. Aubr. 6, fol. 2.

** Aubrey, in MS. Wood F. 39, fol. 138ᵛ: Sept. 2, 1671.

*** MS. Aubr. 8, fol. 98.

great exactnes, but after his death they were all scattered abroad, and fell into ignorant hands.

He lies interred neer Mr. Foxe's monument (who wrote the *Martyrologie*) in St. Giles' Cripplegate Chancell, but I could not find any inscription concerning him. ☞ Quaere the register when he was buried. 'Twas Mr. John Gibbons[a], Blewmantle, told me he was buried here. I thinke Mr. Glover was Blewmantle.

Jonathan Goddard (1617–167⅔).

* Jonathan Godard, M.D., borne at Greenwich (or Rochester, where his father commonly lived ; but, to my best remembrance, he told me at the former). His father was a ship-carpenter.

He was of Magdalen hall, Oxon. He was one of the College of Physitians, in London; Warden of Merton College, Oxon, *durante perduellione*; physitian to Oliver Cromwell, Protector; went with him into Ireland. Quaere if not also sent to him into Scotland, when he was so dangerously ill there of a kind of calenture or high fever, which made him mad that he pistolled one or two of his commanders that came to visit him in his delirious rage.

Collegii Greshamensis Praelector[b] medicinae ; where he lived, and had his laboratory[c] for Chymistrie. He was an admirable Chymist.

He had three or fower medicines wherwith he did all his cures: a great ingredient was *Radix Serpentaria.*— From Mr. Mich. Weekes, who looked to his stills.

He intended to have left his library and papers to the Royall Societie, had he made his will, and had not dyed so suddainly[d]. So that his bookes (a good collection) are fallen into the hands of[e] a sister's son, a scholar in Caius Coll. Camb. But his papers are in the hands of

---

[a] Aubrey in MS. Tanner 25, fol. 50, says '*Day-Fatality* was writt by Mr. . . . Gibbons, Blewmantle, but I have added severall notes to it.'

* MS. Aubr. 8, fol. 21ᵛ.

[b] MS. has 'praelectoris,' by a slip.

[c] Subst. for 'stills.'

[d] Dupl. with 'untimely.'

[e] Subst. for 'of a niece of his who maried a tradesman.'

Sir John Bankes, Reg. Soc. Socius. There were his lectures at Chirurgions' hall ; and two manuscripts in 4to, thicke volumnes, readie for the presse, one was a kind of Pharmacopœia (his nephew has this). 'Tis possible his rare universall medicines aforesayd might be retrived amongst his papers. My Lord Brounker has the recipe but will not impart it.

He was fellowe of the Royall Societie, and a zealous member for the improvement of naturall knowledge amongst them. They made him their drudge, for when any curious experiment was to be donne they would lay[a] the taske on him.

He loved wine and was most curious in his wines, was hospitable, but dranke not to excesse, but it happened that comeing from his club at the Crowne taverne in Bloomesbery, a foote, 11 at night, he fell downe dead of an apoplexie in Cheapside, at Wood-street end, March 24, Anno Domini 167$\frac{3}{4}$, aetat. 56. Sepult. in the church of Great St. Helen, Londini.

Sir Edmund Bury Godfrey (1621–1678).

* Sir Edmund-Bury Godfrey was of Christ's Church in Oxon, and chamber-fellowe to my cosen W⟨illiam⟩ Morgan of Wells, in Peckwater, in north-east angle.

He was afterwards of Grayes Inne, and chamber-fellow to my counsell, Thomas Corbet, esq. I thinke Mr. Corbet told me he was called to the barre. But by match, or &c. he concieved he should gaine more by turning *wood-monger*.

The rest of his life and death is *lippis et tonsoribus notum*.

[Knighted[b] for his great service done in London fire, 1666.]

Thomas Goodwyn.

** . . . Goodwyn: he was borne in Norfolke: of the University of, I beleeve, Cambridge.

---

[a] Subst. for ' impose.'	[b] Note added by Anthony Wood.
* MS. Aubr. 8, fol. 59ᵛ.	** MS. Aubr. 8, fol. 15ᵛ.

He was . . . of the court of Ludlowe (in which place Jack Butts was his successor).

He maried first Barbara . . . . . daughter of Sir W. Long, of Draycot-Cerne, in Wilts : 2d, . . . Brabazon, of . . . Hereffordshire ; obiit sine prole.

He was a generall scolar, and had a delicate witt ; was a great historian, and an excellent poet. He wrote, among other things, . . . , a Pastorall, acted at Ludlowe about 1637, an exquisite piece. *The Journey into France*, crept in bishop Corbet's poems, was made by him, by the same token it made him misse of the preferment of . . . at court, Mary the queen-mother remembring how he had abused her brother, the king of France ; which made him to accept of the place at Ludlowe, out of the view of the world.

When he sat in court there, he was wont to have Thuanus, or Tacitus, or etc. before him. He was as fine a gentleman as any in England, though now forgott. Obiit, at or about Ludlowe, circiter . . . (quaere Sir J. H. and Sir James Long).

The Journey into France was made by Mr. Thomas Goodwyn, of Ludlowe, . . . ; certaine.

Thomas Gore (163½–1684).

* Genesis Thomae Gore armigeri by Charles Snell, esq. :—

'Tuesday, 20ᵐᵒ Martii 163½, 11ʰ 00′ P. M. tempus aestimatum geneseos Thomae Gore, de Alderton 〈Wilts〉, armigeri.'

Note.

This Thomas Gore, a writer on heraldry, was a correspondent of Anthony Wood : see Clark's *Wood's Life and Times*, ii. 140, iv. 229. Aubrey habitually, in his letters to Wood, refers contemptuously to him as ' the cuckold of Alderton.'

Sir Arthur Gorges (15..–1625).

** ' Sir Arthur Gorges ᵃ was buried August the 22ᵗʰ 1661 '—*ex registro Chelsey.*

---

* MS. Aubr. 23, fol. 51 : also in MS. Aubr. 8, a slip at fol. 102.
** MS. Aubr. 7, fol. 16ᵛ.   ᵃ Eldest son of the translator.

In obitum illustrissimi viri D[i]. Arthuri
Gorges, equitis aurati, epicedium.

Te deflent nati, natae, celeberrima conjux ;
Te dolet argutae magna caterva scholae.

† transtulit
Lucanum.

At Lucanus † ait se vivo non moriturum
Arthurum Gorges : transtulit ipse decus.
Aethereas cupiens Arthurus adire per auras
Et nonus ex ejus nomine natus adest.

In the aisle of the Gorges, viz. south side of the church
of Chelsey on an altar monument made for his father or
grandfather—'D[s]. Arthur Gorge, eq. aur., filius ejus natu
maximus.'

John Gower (1327 ?–1408).

* John Gower, esq., poet, has a very worshipfull monument in the north side of the church of St. Saviour's
Southwarke ; an incumbent figure : about his head is
a chaplet of gold—

meriti, etc.—

and a silver collar of SSS about his neck.

Vide iterum, and also his booke.

John Graunt (1620–1674).

** Captaine John Graunt (afterwards, major) was borne
(ex MS[to] patris sui) 24° die Aprilis, ½ an houre before eight
a clock on a Munday morning, the signe being in the
9 degree of Gemini that day at 12 a clock, Anno Domini
1620.

He was the sonne of Henry Graunt, who was borne
18 January 1592[a], being Tuesday, at night ; et obiit
21 March, 166½, being Fryday, between one and two in
the morning ; buryed in the vault in the new vestrie in
St. Michaels church in Cornhill. He was borne in . . . ,
Hantshire.

His son John was borne at the 7 Starres in Burchin
Lane, London, in the parish of St. Michael's Cornhill.

---

* MS. Aubr. 8, fol. 53[v].   gives in trick the coat :—'ermine, on a
** MS. Aubr. 6, fol. 97. Aubrey   chevron gules 5 besants.'   [a] 1592½.

He wrote *Observations on the bills of mortality* very ingeniosely (but I beleeve, and partly know, that he had his hint from his intimate and familiar friend Sir William Petty), to which he made some *Additions*, since printed. And he intended, had he lived, to have writt more on the subject.

He writt also some *Observations on the advance of excise*, not printed : quaere his widowe for them.

To give him his due prayse, he was a very ingeniose and studious person, and generally beloved, and rose early in the morning to his study before shop-time. He understood Latin and French. He was a pleasant facetious companion, and very hospitable.

He was bred-up (as the fashion then was) in the Puritan way; wrote short-hand dextrously; and after many yeares constant hearing and writing sermon-notes, he fell to buying and reading of the best Socinian bookes, and for severall yeares continued of that opinion. At last, about . . . , he turned a Roman Catholique, of which religion he dyed a great zealot.

He was free of the drapers' company, and by profession was a haberdasher of small-wares. He had gone through all the offices [a] of the city so far as common-councell-man. Captain of the trayned-bands severall yeares; major, 2 or 3 yeares.—He was a common councell man 2 yeares, and then putt out (as also of his military employment in the trayned band) for his religion.

He was admitted a fellowe of the Royall Societie, anno 16 . . (about 1663).

He broke [b] . . . . He dyed on Easter eve [c] 1674; buryed on the Wednesday in Easter-weeke in St. Dunstan's church in Fleet Strete under the gallery about the middle (or more west) north side, anno aetatis suae 54.

He had one son, a man, who dyed in Persia; one daughter, a nunne at . . . (I thinke, Gaunt). His widowe yet alive.

---

[a] Subst. for ' degrees.'
[b] i. e. became bankrupt.

[c] Died April 18, buried April 22, 1674.

* Major John Graunt dyed on Easter-eve 1674, and was buryed the Wednesday followeing in St. Dunstan's church in Fleet street in the body of the said church under the piewes towards the gallery on the north side, i.e., under the piewes (*alias* hoggsties) of the north side of the middle aisle (what pitty 'tis so great an ornament of the citty should be buryed so obscurely!), aetatis anno 54°.

Was borne in Burchin lane, at the 7 Starres, in St. Michael's Cornhill parish, at which place he continued his trade till about 2 yeares since.

His 'Observations on the bills of mortality $\begin{cases} 1. \text{ Political} \\ 2. \ldots \ldots \\ 3. \ldots \ldots \end{cases}$,

hath been printed more then once; and now very scarce.

He wrott some 'Observations on the advance of the excise,' not printed; and intended to have writt more of the bills of mortality; and also intended to have written something of religion.

He was by trade a haberdasher of small wares, but was free of the drapers' company. A man generally beloved; a faythfull friend. Often chosen for his prudence and justnes to be an arbitrator; and he was a great peace-maker. He had an excellent working head, and was very facetious and fluent in his conversation.

** He had gonne thorough all the offices of the city so far as common councill man. He was common councill man two yeares. Captaine of the trayned band, severall yeares: major of it, two or three yeares, and then layd downe trade and all other publique employment for his religion, being a Roman Catholique.

Ex MSS. patris ejus :—' My son, John Graunt, was borne 24th day of April halfe an howre before 8 a clock on a Monday morning anno Domini 1620.'

He was my honoured and worthy friend—cujus animae propitietur Deus, Amen.

His death is lamented by all good men that had the

* Aubrey, in MS. Wood F. 39, fol. 270: May 26, 1674.
** Ibid., fol. 270ᵛ.

I.   T

happinesse to knowe him ; and a great number of ingeniose persons attended him to his grave. Among others, with teares, was that ingeniose great virtuoso, Sir William Petty, his old and intimate acquaintance, who was sometime a student at Brase-nose College.

Edward Greaves (1608–1680).

* Sir Edward Greaves, M.D., obiit Thursday November 11, 1680 in Convent Garden ; buried in the church there.

Scripsit *Morbus epidemicus, or the new desease,* 4to, stitch't, printed at Oxford about 1643.

Port⟨avit⟩ 'gules, an eagle displayed or, crowned argent.'

. . . Gregory.

** . . . Gregorie, famous peruq-maker, buryed at St. Clement Danes church dore west. Quaere inscription in rythme from baron [a] Gregory, baron of the exchequer.

Vide Cotgrave's french dictionary ubi peruqes are called Gregorians.

*** Peruques not commonly worne till 1660. Memorandum there was one Gregorie in the Strand that was the first famous periwig-maker ; and they were then called Gregorians (mentioned in Cotgrave's Dictionarie *in verbo* perruque). He lies buried by the west church-dore of St. Clements Danes, where he had an inscription which mentioned it. 'Twas in verse and Sir William Gregorie (one of the Barons of the Exchequer) read and told it me. Quaere of him + de hoc.

Sir Thomas Gresham (1519–1579).

**** Memorandum [1] :—Mr. Shirman, the attorney, at Inneholders-hall, hath a copie of Sir Thomas Gresham's will [2], which procure.

Notes.

[1] Aubrey in MS. Aubr. 8, fol. 8, gives in trick the coats :—(*a*), 'argent, a chevron ermine between 3 mullets pierced sable : crest, a grasshopper : motto,

* MS. Aubr. 6, fol. 2.　　　　*** MS. Aubr. 8, fol. 28.
** MS. Aubr. 8, fol. 7.　　　　**** MS. Aubr. 6, fol. 2.
[a] Subst. for 'the judge.'

Fortun amy [Sir Thomas Gresham, 1601]': and (*b*), 'or, on a bend vert 3 bucks' heads caboshed argent.'

² Twice alluded to in MS. Aubr. 8, viz., (fol. 8) 'Copie out Sir Thomas Gresham's will from Mr. Shirman'; (fol. 12) 'Sir Thomas Gresham, knight : quaere copie of his will from Mr. Shirman, attornie.'

Fulke Greville, lord Brooke (1554–1628).
Robert Greville, lord Brooke (1607–164⅔).

* Sir Fulke Greville, lord Brokes, adopted a parke-keeper's sonne his heire, who (I thinke) had but one eie : vide de hoc in Dr. Heylen's Historie of the church of England . . . . Vide Sir William Davenant's life ᵃ in part 1ˢᵗ ⟨i. e. in MS. Aubr. 6⟩.

Poems, in folio, London, printed . . .

'The life ᵇ of the renowned Sir Philip Sidney, with the true Interest of England, as it then stood in relation to all Forrain Princes : And particularly for suppressing the power of Spain, stated by him. Written by Sir Fulke Grevil, knight, lord Brook, a servant to Queen Elisabeth, and his companion and friend. London, printed for H. Seile, over against St. Dunstan's church, in Fleet-street, M.DC.LII.'

Vide in Sir William Dugdale's *Warwickshire* his noble castle ᶜ, and monument with this inscription : 'Here lies the body of Sir Fulke Grevile knight servant to Q. Eliz., counsellor to King James, and friend to Sir Philip Sidney.'

⟨Robert Greville, second⟩ lord Brookes, was maried to ⟨Catherine Russell⟩ daughter of the earle of Bedford. He was killed at the siege of Lichfield, March the 2d (St. Chad's day, to whom the Church is dedicated) ⟨164⅔⟩ by a minister's sonne, borne deafe and dumbe, out of the church. He was armed *cap à pied*; only his bever was open. I was then at Trinity College in Oxon. and doe perfectly remember the story.

The lord Brookes, that was killed at Lichfield, printed a booke about Religion, a little before the civill warres, by

---

* MS. Aubr. 8, fol. 4ᵛ.   ᵃ *Supra*, p. 205.
ᵇ Aubrey notes of this book 'I have it.'
ᶜ Dupl. with 'seat.'

the same token that in[a] ⟨a⟩ song on the Lords then, his ⟨character⟩ was :—'*Brook is a foole in print.*'

Peter Gunning (1614–1684).

* . . . Gunning. episcopus Eliensis ;—his father was a minister in the Wild of Kent ; and 'tis thought he was borne there, scil. at Brenchley.

Edmund Gunter (1581–1626).

** Mr. Edmund Gunter[1] :—for his birth, etc, see in *Antiq. Oxon.* ⟨by⟩ A. Wood.

Captain Ralph Gretorex, mathematical instrument maker in London, sayd that he was the first that brought mathematicall instruments to perfection. His booke of the quadrant, sector, and crosse-staffe did open men's understandings and made young men in love with that studie. Before, the mathematical sciences were lock't up in the Greeke and Latin tongues and so [b] lay untoucht, kept safe in some libraries. After Mr. Gunter published his booke, these sciences sprang up amain, more and more to that height it is at now (1690).

When he was a student at Christ Church, it fell to his lott to preach the Passion sermon, which some old divines that I knew did heare, but they sayd that 'twas sayd of him then in the University that our Saviour never suffered so much since his passion as in that sermon, it was such a lamentable one—

Non omnia possumus omnes.

The world is much beholding to him for what he hath donne well.

Gunter is originally a Brecknockshire family, of Tregunter. They came thither under the conduct of Sir Bernard Newmarch when he made the conquest of that county (Camden).—' Aubrey, Gunter, Waldbeof, Havard, Pichard ' (which is falsely express'd in all Mr. Camden's bookes, scil. Prichard, which is non-sense).

---

[a] Dupl. with ' that in libelling characters of the Lords then, his was.'
* MS. Aubr. 8, fol. 14ᵛ.   ** MS. Aubr. 8, fol. 78ᵛ.   [b] Dupl. with ' there.'

Note.

[1] Aubrey gives in trick the coat:—'sable, 3 gauntletts argent'; and adds 'quaere if these gauntletts are dextre or sinistre?'

John Guy (15.. –1628).

* Memorandum :— . . . Guy, alderman of Bristoll, was the wisest man of his time in that city. He was as their oracle and they chose him for one of their representatives to sitt in Parliament.

'Twas he that brought in the ⟨bill⟩ for lowering of interest from ten in the hundred to eight per centum.

. . . Gwyn.

** Surlinesse and inurbanitie too common in England : chastise these very severely[n].

A better instance of a squeamish and disobligeing, slighting, insolent, proud, fellow[b], perhaps cant be found then in . . . Gwin, the earl of Oxford's[c] secretary. No reason satisfies him, but he overweenes, and cutts some sower faces that would turne the milke in a faire ladie's breast.

William Habington (1605-1645).

*** William Habington, of Hindlip in Worcestershire, esq., maried Luce, daughter of William ⟨Herbert⟩, lord Powes, 1634, as by the Worcestershire Visitation it appeares.

He was a very learned gentleman, author of a poem called Castara. He wrote a live of one of the kings of England. *Note.*

Aubrey gives in trick the coat:—' argent, on a bend gules 3 eagles displayed, or; impaling, party per pale argent and gules 3 lions rampant counterchanged, within a bordure gobony, or and . . . , a crescent for difference.'

* MS. Aubr. 6, fol. 2.

** MS. Aubr. 21, p. 11; and repeated almost *verbatim*, ibid. fol. 24ᵛ. Aubrey's character *Sir Fastidious Overween* in his projected comedy *The Country Revel* was to be copied from this Gwyn.

[a] In his projected comedy.

[b] 'Coxcome' on fol. 24ᵛ.

[c] Aubrey de Vere, succeeded as 20th earl in 1632, died 1702, the last of that house.

*** MS. Aubr. 7, fol. 7.

Sir Matthew Hale (1609–1676).

* *Judge Hale's accidents.*

1609, natus, November 1ˢᵗ, in the evening, his father then being at his prayers.

1612, death of his mother, April 23.

1614, his father dyed, moneth not known.

1625, went to Oxon to Magdalen Hall; vide A. Wood's *History of Oxon* when matriculated.

1628, admitted of the society of Lincolne's Inne, November 8.

1636, this yeare called to the barre, quaere in what terme.

1640, maried the first time. He was a great cuckold.

1656, his second mariage to his servant mayd, Mary.

1660, made Lord Chief Baron.

1671, Lord Chiefe Justice of England, 18 May.

1676, Christmas day, he dyed.

** Sir Matthew Hales, Lord Chief Justice of the King's Bench, was borne at Alderley in com. Glouc., November 1ˢᵗ, 1609; christned the 5ᵗʰ. Quaere Mr. Edward Stephens horam, for he has it exactly. When his mother fell in labour, his father was offering up his evening sacrifice.

*** That incomparable man for goodnes and universality of learning, Sir Matthew Hales, Lord Chief Justice of England, hath writt the description of Gloucestershire, an elaborate piece, and ready for the presse. The transcripts of the Tower for it cost him 40 *li*.

John Hales (1584–1656).

**** Mr. John Hales, . . . ᵃ, was borne at Wells, I thinke I have heard Mr. John Sloper say (vicar of Chalke; his mother was Mr. Hales's sister, and he bred him at Eaton).

* MS. Aubr. 23, fol. 3.
** MS. Aubr. 23, fol. 20ᵛ.
*** Aubrey, in MS. Wood F. 39, fol. 144: Oct. 27, 1671.

**** MS. Aubr. 6, fol. 119ᵛ.
ᵃ Space left for his degree: M.A. (Merton, 20 June, 1609).

His father was a steward to the family of the Horners :—
>   Hopton, Horner, Smyth, and Thynne,
>   When abbots went out, they came in [a].

Went to school, at Bath (as I take it). Fellow of Merton Colledge. Assisted Sir Henry Savill in his edition of Chrysostome (*cum aliis*). Afterwards fellow of Eaton College.

Went chaplain to Sir Dudley Carlton (ambassador to . . .). I thinke was at the Synod of Dort.

When the Court was at Windsor, the learned courtiers much delighted ⟨in⟩ his company, and were wont to grace him with their company.

I have heard his nephew, Mr. Sloper, say, that he much loved to read . . . Stephanus, who was a *familist*, I thinke that first wrote of that sect of the Familie of Love : he was mightily taken with it, and was wont to say that sometime or other those fine notions would take in the world. He was one of the first Socinians in England, I thinke the first.

He was a generall scolar, and I beleeve a good poet : for Sir John Suckling brings him into the Session of the Poets :
>   'Little Hales all the time did nothing but smile,
>   To see them, about nothing, keepe such a coile.'

He had a noble librarie of bookes, and those judicially chosen, which cost him . . . *li.* (quaere Mr. Sloper); and which he sold to Cornelius Bee, bookeseller, in Little Britaine, (as I take it, for 1000 *li.*) which was his maintenance after he was ejected out of his fellowship at Eaton College. He had then only reserved some few for his private use, to wind-up his last dayes withall.

The ladie Salter (neer Eaton) was very kind to him after the sequestration; he was very welcome to her ladyship, and spent much of his time there. At Eaton he lodged (after his sequestration) at the next house ⟨to⟩ the Christopher (inne), where I sawe him, a prettie little man,

---

[a] Substituted for :—
>   'Hopton, Homer, Knocknaile and Thynne,
>   When abbots went downe, then they came in.'

sanguine, of a cheerfull countenance, very gentile, and courteous; I was recieved by him with much humanity: he was in a kind of violet-colourd cloath gowne, with buttons and loopes (he wore not a black gowne), and was reading Thomas à Kempis; it was within a yeare before he deceased. He loved Canarie; but moderately, to refresh his spirits.

He had a bountifull mind. I remember in 1647, a little after the Visitation [a], when Thomas Mariett, esq., Mr. William Radford, and Mr. Edward Wood (all of Trinity College) had a frolique from Oxon to London, on foot, having never been there before, they happened to take Windsore in their way, made their addresse to this good gentleman, being then fellow. Mr. Edward Wood was the spookes-man, remonstrated that they were Oxon scholars: he treated them well, and putt into Mr. Wood's hands ten shillings.

He lies buried in the church yard at Eaton, under an altar monument of black marble, erected at the sole chardge of Mr. . . . Curwyn, with a too long epitaph. He was no kiff or kin to him.

* Mr. John Hales dyed at Mris Powney's house, a widow-woman, in Eaton, opposite to the churchyard, adjoyning to the Christopher Inne southwards. 'Tis the howse where I sawe him.

She is a very good woman and of a gratefull spirit. She told me that when she was maried, Mr. Hales was very bountifull to them in helping them [b] to live in the world. She was very gratefull to him and respectfull to him.

She told me that Mr. Hales was the common godfather there, and 'twas pretty to see, as he walked to Windsor, how his godchildren asked him blessing [c]. When he was bursar, he still gave away all his groates for the acquittances to his godchildren; and by that time he came to Windsor bridge, he would have never a groate left.

This Mris Powney assures me that the poor were more

[a] Scil. of Oxford University by the Parliamentary Commission.

* Aubrey, in MS. Wood F. 39, fol. 368: 'St. Anne's day,' July 26, 1682.

[b] Dupl. with 'in setting them up to.'

[c] Dupl. with 'fell on their knees.'

relieveable, that is to say, that he recieved more kindnesse from them than from the rich. That that I putt downe of my lady Salter (sister to Brian Duppa, bishop of Sarum), from his nephew ⟨John⟩ Sloper, vicar of Chalke, is false ᵃ. She had him to her house indeed, but 'twas to teach her sonne, who was such a blockhead he could not read well.

Cornelius Bee bought his library for 700 *li.*, which cost him not lesse then 2,500 *li.* Mris Powney told me that she was much against the sale of 'em, because she knew it was his life and joy.

He might have been restored to his fellowship again, but he would not accept the offer. He was not at all covetous, and desired only to leave x *li.* to bury him.

He bred-up our vicar, [Sloper ᵇ], who, she told me, never sent him a token ; and he is angry with her, thinks he left her too much.

She is a woman primitively good, and deserves to be remembred. I wish I had her Christian name. Her husband has an inscription on a gravestone in Eaton College chapel towards the south wall.

She has a handsome darke old-fashioned howse. The hall, after the old fashion, above the wainscot, painted cloath, with godly sentences out of the Psalmes, etc., according to the pious custome of old times ; a convenient garden and orchard. She has been handsome : a good understanding, and cleanlie.

Joseph Hall (1574–1656).

* Joseph Hall, bishop of Exon, etc. : he was a keeper's son in Norfolke (I thinke, neer Norwich).—From old Mr. Theophilus Woodenoth.

He wrote most of his fine discourses at Worcester, when he was deane there.—From Mr. Francis Potter, who went to schole there.

ᵃ Dupl. with ' a mistake.'   ᵇ Inserted by Anthony Wood.

* MS. Aubr. 8, fol. 60.

Monsieur Balzac exceedingly admired him and often quotes him : vide Balzac's *Apologie*.

Edmund Halley (1656–174½).

* Mr. Edmund Hally, astronomer, born October 29, 1656, London—this nativity I had from Mr. Hally himself.

** Mr. Edmund Halley[a], Artium Magister, the eldest son of ⟨Edmund⟩ Halley, a soape-boyler, a wealthy citizen of the city of London ; of the Halleys, of Derbyshire, a good family.

He was born in Shoreditch parish, at a place called Haggerston, the backside of Hogsdon.

At 9 yeares old, his father's apprentice taught him to write, and arithmetique. He went to Paule's schoole to Dr. Gale : while he was there he was very perfect in the Caelestiall Globes insomuch that I heard Mr. Moxon (the globe-maker) say that if a star were misplaced in the globe, he would presently find it.

At . . . he studyed Geometry, and at 16 could make a dyall, and then, he said, thought himselfe a brave fellow.

At ⟨16⟩ went to Queen's Colledge in Oxon, well versed in Latin, Greeke, and Hebrew : where, at the age of nineteen, he solved this useful probleme in astronomie, never donne before, ☞ viz. 'from 3 distances given from the sun, and angles between, to find the orbe' (mentioned in the Philosophicall Transactions, Aug. or Sept. 1676, No. 115), for which his name will be ever famous.

Anno Domini . . . tooke his degree of Bacc. Art.; Anno Domini . . . tooke his degree of Master of Arts[b].

Anno . . . left Oxon, and lived at London with his father till ⟨1676⟩; at which time he gott leave, and a viaticum of his father, to goe to the Island of *Sancta*

---

* MS. Aubr. 23, fol. 28[v].

** MS. Aubr. 6, fol. 50.

[a] Aubrey gives in colours the coat : 'sable, a fret and a canton argent ';

also Halley's horoscope.

[b] Halley did not graduate in the ordinary course, but was made M.A. by diploma in 1678.

Hellena, purely upon the account of advancement in Astronomy, to make the globe of the Southerne Hemisphere right, which before was very erroneous, as being donne only after the observations of ignorant seamen. There he stayed . . . moneths. There went over with him (amongst others) a woman . . . yeares old, and her husband . . . old, who had no child in . . . yeares : before he came from the island, she was brought to bed of a child. At his returne, he presented his Planisphere, with a short description, to his majesty who was very well pleased with it ; but received nothing but prayse.

I have often heard him say that if his majestie would be but only at the chardge of sending out a ship, he would take the longitude and latitude, right ascensions and declinations of . . . southern fixed starres.

Anno 1678, he added a spectacle-glasse to the shadowe-vane of the lesser arch of the sea-quadrant (or back-staffe) ; which is of great use, for that that spott of light will be manifest when you cannot see any shadowe.

He went to Dantzick to visit Hevelius, Anno 167–.

December 1ˢᵗ, 1680, went to Paris.

* Edmund Haley :—cardinall d'Estrée caressed him and sent him to his brother the admirall with a lettre of recommendation.—He hath contracted an acquaintance and friendship with all the eminentst mathematicians of France and Italie, and holds a correspondence with them.

He returned into England, Januarii 24°, 168½.

Quaere Mr. Partridge of his *Directio mortis*, scilicet about 35 aetatis.

** ⟨Quaere⟩ Edmund Halley who cutts his schemes in wood ? they are well.

⟨David⟩ Loggan informes me that one . . . Edwards, the manciple of . . . College Oxon, doth cut in wood very well.

Note.

In the earl of Macclesfield's library at Shirburne Castle, Oxon., are several MSS. by Halley ; among them a common-place book.

* MS. Aubr. 8, fol. 10.   ** Aubrey, in MS. Wood F. 49, fol. 39ᵛ.

Baldwin Hamey (1600-1676).

* In the midd aisle (or nave) of Chelsey church, a faire
flat marble grave-stone :—

The return of Baldwin Hamey, Dr. of Physick, on the 14 of May
being Whitsunday in the yeare of our Lord 1676 and in the 76th yeare
of his age.   Psalm 146, vers. 4.

His breath goeth, etc.

William Harcourt (1610-1679).

** Father Harcourt—he told me that he was of the
familie of Stanton Harcourt, A.D. 1650. He was confessor, and afterwards co-executor, to the lady Inglefield.

*** *Petrification of a kidney*. When father Harcourt
suffered ᵃ at Tyburne, and his bowells, etc. throwne into
the fire, a butcher's boy standing by was resolved to have
a piece of his kidney which was broyling in the fire. He
burn't his fingers much, but he got it; and one . . .
Roydon, a brewer in Southwark, bought it, a kind of
Presbyterian. The wonder is, 'tis now absolutely petrified :
I have seen it. He much values it.

**** Mr. Roydon, brewer in Southwarke (opposite the
Temple), haz the piece of Father Harcourt's kidney which
was snatcht out of the fire, and now petrified and very
hard. But 'twas not so hard when he first had it. It
being alwayes carried in the pocket hardened by degrees
better then by the fire—like an agate polished.

Thomas Hariot (1560-1621).

***** Mr. Thomas Hariot¹—from Dr. John Pell, March
31, 1680. Dr. Pell knowes not what countreyman ᵇ he was
(but an Englishman he was)—[There ᶜ is a place in Kent

---

* MS. Aubr. 7, fol. 16ᵛ. Hamey
was M.D., Leyden ; incorporated at
Oxford, Feb. 4, 16⅜⅜.

** MS. Aubr. 8, fol. 5ᵛ.

*** MS. Aubr. 6, fol. 10ᵛ.

ᵃ In June, 1679 : Clark's Wood's
Life and Times, ii. 453.

**** MS. Aubr. 8, fol. 63ᵛ.

***** MS. Aubr. 6, fol. 35.

ᵇ 'Country,' with Aubrey, = county.

ᶜ Added as a suggestion that Hariot's
family may be looked for in those
counties.

called Harriot's-ham, now my lord Wotton's [2]; and in Wostershire in the parish of Droytwich is a fine seat called Harriots, late the seate of Chiefe Baron Wyld]

He thinkes he dyed about the time he (Dr. Pell) went to Cambridge. He sayes my lord John Vaughan can enforme me, and haz a copie of his will: which vide.

* Mr. Thomas Hariot—Mr. Elias Ashmole thinkes he was a Lancashire man: Mr. ⟨John⟩ Flamsted promised me to enquire of Mr. Townley.

** ☞ I very much desire to find his buriall: he was not buryed in the Tower chapelle.

*** Mr. Thomas Harriot[a]:—Memorandum:—Sir Robert Moray (from Francis Stuart[b]), declared at the Royal Society—'twas when the comet[c] appeared before the Dutch warre—that Sir Francis had heard Mr. Harriot say that he had seen nine cometes, and had predicted seaven of them, but did not tell them how. 'Tis very strange: excogitent astronomi.

**** Mr. Hariot went with Sir Walter Ralegh into Virginia, and haz writt the Description of Virginia, which is printed.

Dr. Pell tells me that he finds amongst his papers (which are now, 1684, in Dr. Busby's hands), an alphabet that he had contrived for the American language, like Devills[d].

He wrote a Description of Virginia, which is since printed in Mr. Purchas's Pilgrims.

Vide Mr. Glanvill's Moderne Improvement of Usefull Knowledge, where he makes mention of Mr. Thomas Harriot, pag. 33.

When ⟨Henry Percy, ninth⟩ earle of Northumberland, and Sir Walter Ralegh were both prisoners in the Tower, they grew acquainted, and Sir Walter Raleigh recommended

* MS. Aubr. 8, fol. 12.
** MS. Aubr. 8, fol. 91.
*** MS. Aubr. 8, fol. 12.
[a] Aubrey writes in the margin the reference 'vide pag. 40,' i. e. fol. 9', *ut infra*.
[b] Subst. for 'Steward.'
[c] See Clark's Wood's *Life and Times*, ii. 24, 25, 33, 53.
**** MS. Aubr. 6, fol. 35.
[d] Perhaps because the letters ended in tridents; see Clark's Wood's *Life and Times*, i. 498, and the facsimile.

Mr. Hariot to him, and the earle setled an annuity of two hundred pounds a yeare on him for his life, which he enjoyed. But to[a] Hues † (who wrote *De Usu Globorum*) and to Mr. Warner he gave an annuity but of sixty pounds per annum. These 3 were usually called *the earle of Northumberland's three Magi*. They had a table at the earle's chardge, and the earle himselfe had them to converse with, singly or together.

† Robert Hues was buried in Xt. Ch. Oxon.

He was a great acquaintance of Master . . . Ailesbury, to whom Dr. Corbet sent a letter in verse, Dec. 9, 1618, when the great blazing starre appeared,—

> 'Now for the peace of God⟨s⟩ and men advise,
> (Thou that hast wherwithall to make us wise),
> Thine owne rich studies and deepe Harriot's mine,
> In which there is no drosse but all refine.'

⟨Vide⟩ Dr. Corbet's poems.

The bishop of Sarum (Seth Ward) told me that one Mr. Haggar (a countryman of his), a gentleman and good mathematician, was well acquainted with Mr. Thomas Hariot, and was wont to say, that he did not like (or valued not) the old storie of the Creation of the World. He could not beleeve the old position ; he would say *ex nihilo nihil fit*. But sayd Mr. Haggar, a *nihilum* killed him at last : for in the top of his nose came a little red speck (exceeding small), which grew bigger and bigger, and at last killed him. I suppose it was that which the chirurgians call a *noli me tangere*.

* Mr. Hariot dyed of an ulcer in his lippe or tongue— vide Dr. Read's Chirurgery, where he mentions him as his patient, in the treatise of ulcers (or cancers).

The Workes of Dr. Alexander Reade, printed, London, 1650 ; in the treatise of Ulcers, p. 248. 'Cancrous ulcers (*ozana*) also seise on this part. This griefe hastened the end of that famous mathematician Mr. Hariot with whom I was acquainted but short time before his death ; whom at one time, together with Mr. Hughes (who wrote of the globes), Mr. Warner, and Mr. Torporley, the noble earle of Northumberland, the favourer of all good learning and Maecenas of learned men, maintained while he was in the Tower, for their worth and various literature.'

He made a philosophicall theologie, wherin he cast-off the Old Testament, and then the New one would (consequently) have no foundation. He was a Deist. His doctrine he taught to Sir Walter Raleigh, Henry, earle of Northumberland, and some others. The divines of those times look't on his manner of death as a judgement upon him for nullifying the Scripture.

Ex Catalogo librorum impressorum bibl. Bodleianae in Academia Oxoniensi, Oxon., MDCLXXIV :—

Thomas Hariot:—Historia Virginiae, cum iconibus, Lat. per C. C. A. edita per Th. de Bry, *Franc.* 1590 (A. 8. 7. *Art*).

—Same in English, *Lond.* 1588 (E. 1. 25. *Art. Seld.*).

Thomas Hariotus:—Artis analyticae praxis ad aequationes Algebraicas resolvendas, *Lond.* 1631 (F. 2. 12. *Art. Seld.*).

Notes.

¹ Aubrey gives the coat :—' per pale, ermine and ermines, 3 crescents counter-changed [Hariot].'

² Charles Henry Kirckhoven, created baron Wotton, Aug. 31, 1650; created earl of Bellomont, Feb. 11, 16⁴⁸/₄₉.

Sir Edward Harley (1624–1700).

* Sir Edward Harley, knight of the Bath, was borne at his castle of Brampton Bryan in Herefordshire. He was of Magdalen Hall, Oxon ; was governor of Dunkirke for his majestie king Charles 2ᵈ, where he then sounded that sea from Graveling to Newport—which notes he haz by him—of great use to seamen because of the shelves.

Sir Robert Harley (1580–1656).

** Old Sir Robert Harley translated all the Psalmes very well. He was of Oriell College.

* Aubrey, in MS. Wood F. 39, fol. 138 : Sept. 2, 1671. ** Aubrey, in MS. Wood F. 39, fol. 141 : Oct. 27, 1671.

Sir Robert Harley (1626–1673).

* Sir Robert Harley[a], second sonne of Sir Robert Harley of Brampton-Bryan, told me that he was borne the morning that my Lord Chancellour Bacon dyed (9° Aprilis) ; sed quaere, et vide his picture if 'twas not the 6th.

He maried . . .

He dyed at Brampton-Brian 16 Nov. Sunday, 6[h] A.M., anno Domini 1673.

James Harrington (161½–1677).

** James Harrington, esq.—he was borne the first Fryday[b] in January Anno Domini 1611, near Northampton. Quaere Mr Marvell's epitaph on him.

*** James Harrington[1], esq., borne the first Fryday in January 1611, neer Northampton; the son of [Sir[c] Sapcote] Harrington of . . . in the countie of . . . , by . . . , daughter of Sir . . . Samuel[d], was borne at [Upton[e]] (Sir . . . Samuel's house in Northamptonshire) anno . . .

He was a ⟨gentleman⟩ commoner of Trinity Colledge in Oxford. He travelled France, Italie, and the Netherlands. His genius lay chiefly towards the politiques and democraticall goverment.

He was much respected by the queen of Bohemia[2], who was bred up by the lord Harrington's lady, and she owned the kindnes of the family.

Anno 1647, if not 6, he was by order of Parliament made one of his Majestie's Bedchamber, at Holmeby, &c. The king loved his company; only he would not endure to heare of a Commonwealth: and Mr. Harington passionately loved his majestie. Mr. Harrington and the king often disputed about goverment. He was on the scaffold

---

* MS. Aubr. 23, fol. 72.
[a] See *supra*, p. 157.
** MS. Aubr. 8, fol. 11.
[b] i e. Friday, Jan. 3, 161½. The date is noted also in MS. Aubr. 21, fol. 103.
*** MS. Aubr. 6, fol. 98.

[c] Written in pencil only, being a later insertion.
[d] Jane, daughter of Sir William Samwell of Upton, co. Northts.
[e] Written in pencil only, being a later addition.

with the king when he was beheaded; and I have at these meetings[a] oftentimes heard him speake of king Charles I with the greatest zeale and passion imaginable, and that his death gave him so great griefe that he contracted a disease by it; that never any thing did goe so neer to him. Memorandum :—Mr. ⟨Thomas⟩ Herbert, the traveller, was th' other of his Bedchamber by order of Parliament, and was also on the scaffold. He gave them both there some watches: vide Speech.

He made severall essayes in Poetry, viz. love-verses, &c., and translated . . . . booke of Virgill's Æn.; but his muse was rough, and Mr Henry Nevill, an ingeniose and well-bred gentleman, a member of the House of Commons, and an excellent (but concealed) poet, was his great familiar and confident friend, and disswaded him from tampering in poetrie which he did *invitâ Minervâ*, and to improve his proper talent, viz. Politicall Reflections.

Whereupon he writ his *Oceana*, printed London ⟨1656⟩. Mr. T. Hobbes was wont to say that Henry Nevill had a finger in that pye; and 'tis like enough. That ingeniose tractat, together with his and H. Nevill's smart discourses and inculcations, dayly at coffee-houses, made many proselytes.

In so much that, anno 1659, the beginning of Michaelmasterme, he had every night a meeting at the (then) Turke's head, in the New Pallace-yard, where they take water, the next house to the staires, at one Miles's, where was made purposely a large ovall-table, with a passage in the middle for Miles to deliver his Coffee. About it sate his disciples, and the virtuosi. The discourses in this kind were the most ingeniose, and smart, that ever I heard, or expect to heare, and band⟨i⟩ed with great eagernesse: the arguments in the Parliament howse were but flatt to it.

He now printed a little pamphlet (4to) called *Divers modells of Popular Government*, printed by Daniel Jakeman; and then his partie desired him to print another little pamphlet called *The Rota*, 4to.

[a] Scil. of the *Rota* club, described *infra*.

I.   U

Here[a] we had (very formally) a *ballotting-box*, and balloted how things should be caried, by way of tentamens. The room was every evening[b] full as it could be cramm'd. I cannot now recount the whole number :—

Mr. Cyriack Skinner, an ingeniose young gentleman, scholar to John Milton, was chaire-man. There was Mr. Henry Nevill ; major John Wildman ; Mr. ⟨Charles⟩ Woo⟨l⟩seley, of . . . , Staffordshire ; Mr. ⟨Roger⟩ Coke, grandson of Sir Edward ; Sir[c] William Poultney (chairman); [Sir[c] John Hoskins ; J⟨ames⟩ Arderne[d] ;] Mr. Maximilian Petty, a very able man in these matters, and who had more then once turn'd the councill-board of Oliver Cromwell, his kinsman ; Mr. Michael Malett ; Mr. ⟨Philip⟩ Carteret, of Garnesey ; ⟨Francis⟩ Cradoc, a merchant ; Mr. Henry Ford ; major . . . Venner ; Mr. Edward Bagshaw ; [Thomas Mariet, esq.[e] ;] ⟨William⟩ Croon, M.D. ; *cum multis aliis* now slipt out of my memorie †.

† Dr. Robert Wood· was of the *Rota*.—MS. Aubr. 8, fol. 11.

⟨Besides⟩ which[f] were, as auditors[g], severall, e. g. the earle[h] Tirconnel ; Sir John Penruddock ; etc. ; Mr. John Birkenhead ; as myselfe.

. . . Stafford, esq., as antagonists[i].

Several officers[k].

We many times adjourned to the Rhenish-wine howse. One time Mr. Stafford and his gang came in, in drink, from the taverne[l], and affronted the Junto (Mr. Stafford tore their orders and minutes). The soldiers offerd to kick them downe stayres, but Mr. Harrington's moderation and persuasion hindred it.

The doctrine was very taking, and the more because, as to human foresight, there was no possibility of the king's

---

[a] i. e. at the meetings at Miles's.
[b] Subst. for ' night.'
[c] Dupl. with ' Mr.'
[d] These two names are struck out, as is Mariet *infra.*
[e] Struck out.
[f] Subst. for ' Also, as.'
[g] i. e. as listeners only. Those above were of Harrington's ' party.' The ' antagonists,' who wished to break up the meetings, follow.
[h] Dupl. with ' lord.'
[i] Dupl with ' opponents.'
[k] ' Officers ' dupl. with ' soldiers.' These, like Aubrey, were ' auditors ' only.
[l] Subst. for ' came in drunke.'

returne. But the greatest part of the Parliament-men perfectly hated this designe of *rotation by ballotting*; for they were cursed tyrants, and in love with their power, and 'twas death to them, except 8 or 10, to admitt of this way, for H. Nevill proposed it in the Howse, and made it out to them, that except they embraced that modell of goverment they would be ruind—*sed quos perdere vult Jupiter* etc., *hos, &c.*

Pride of senators for life is insufferable; and they were able to grind any one they owed ill will to. to powder; they were hated by the armie and their countrey they re-presented, and their name and memorie stinkes—'twas worse then tyranny. Now this modell upon rotation was :— that the third part of the Senate[a] should rote out by ballot every yeare, so that every ninth yeare the Howse would be wholly alterd; no magistrate to continue above 3 yeares, and all to be chosen by ballot, then which manner of choice, nothing can be invented more faire and impartiall.

Well: this meeting continued Novemb., Dec., Jan., till Febr. 20 or 21; and then, upon the unexpected turne upon generall Monke's comeing-in, all these aierie modells vanished. Then 'twas not fitt, nay treason, to have donne such; but I well remember, he[b] severall times (at the breaking-up) sayd, 'Well, the king will come in. Let him come-in, and call a Parliament of the greatest Cavaliers in England, so they be men of estates, and let them sett but 7 yeares, and they will all turn Common-wealthe's men.'

He was wont to find fault with the constitution of our goverment, that 'twas *by jumps*, and told a story of a cavaliero he sawe at the Carnival in Italie, who rode on an excellent managed horse that with a touch of his toe would jumpe quite round. One side of his habit was Spanish, the other French; which sudden alteration of the same person pleasantly surprized the spectators. 'Just so,' said he, "'tis with us. When no Parliament, then absolute monarchie; when a Parliament, then it runnes to Commonwealth.'

[a] Dupl. with 'Howse.'   [b] Harrington.

* Anno Domini 1660, he was committed[a] prisoner to the Tower, where he was kept . . . . ; then to Portsey castle. His durance in these prisons (he being a gentleman of a high spirit and hot head) was the procatractique cause of his deliration or madnesse ; which was not outragious, for he would discourse rationally enough and be very facetious company, but he grew to have a phancy that[b] his perspiration turned to flies, and sometimes to bees —— *ad cætera sobrius* ; and he had a timber *versatile* built[c] in Mr. Hart's garden (opposite to St. James's parke) to try the experiment. He would turne it to the sun, and sitt towards it ; then he had his fox-tayles there to chase away and massacre all the flies and bees that were to be found there, and then shutt his chassees[d]. Now this experiment was only to be tryed in warme weather, and some flies would lye so close in the cranies and the cloath (with which it was hung) that they would not presently shew themselves. A quarter of an hower after perhaps, a fly or two, or more, might be drawen-out of the lurking holes by the warmeth ; and then he would crye out, ' Doe not you see it apparently that these come from me ? ' 'Twas the strangest sort of madnes that ever I found in any one : talke of any thing els, his discourse would be very ingeniose and pleasant.

Anno . . . he married to his old sweet-heart Mris . . . Dayrell †, of . . . , a comely and discreete ladie. The motto to his seale, which was party per pale baron et femme Harrington and Dayrell was . . . It happening so, from some private reasons, that he could not enjoy his deare in the flower and heate of his youth, he would never lye with her, but loved and admired her dearly : for she was *vergentibus annis* when he maried her, and had lost her sweetenesse.

† His wife was . . . Dayrell. Round about his seale, which was party per pale baron and femme[e], were these words, sc.H. *In longum colere faas*.

---

* MS. Aubr. 6, a slip at fol. 98ᵛ.
[a] Subst. for ' sent.'
[b] Dupl. with ' grew conceited that.'
[c] Subst. for ' a versatile timber house built.'

[d] i.e. window frames ; French ' châsse.'
[e] i.e. the coat given in note 1 from MS. Aubr. 8, fol. 29ᵛ.

He was of a middling stature, well-trussed man, strong
and thick, well-sett, sanguine, quick-hott-fiery hazell eie,
thick moyst curled haire, as you may see by his picture.
In his conversation very friendly, and facetious, and
hospitable.

For above twenty yeares before he died (except his
imprisonment) he lived in the Little-Ambry (a faire house
on the left hand), which lookes into the Deane's-yard in
Westminster. In the upper story he had a pretty gallery,
which looked into the yard (over . . . court) where he.
commonly dined, and meditated, and tooke his tobacco.

His *amici* were :—Henry Nevill, esq., who never forsooke
him to his dyeing day. Though[a] a whole yeare before
he died, his memorie and discourse were taken away by a
disease (' twas a *sad sight to see such a sample of mortality,
in one whom I lately knew, a brisque, lively cavaliero),
this gentleman, whom I must never forget for his constant
friendship, payd his visits as duly and respectfully as when
his friend (J. H.) was in the prime of his understanding—
a true friend.

† Mr. Andrew Marvell made a good epitaph for him, but ⟨it⟩ would have given offence. ——† Mr. Andrew Marvell, who made an
epitaph for him, which quaere.

—His uncle, ... Samuel, esq. ;

—his son, Mr. . . . Samuel, an excellent
architect, that has built severall delicate howses (Sir Robert
Henley's, Sir Thomas Grosvenor's in Cheshire);

—Sir Thomas Dolman ;

—Mr. Roger L'Estrange ;

—Dr. John Pell ;

—J. A.[b]

He was wont to say that ' Right reason in contemplation
is vertue in action, *et vice versa. Vivere secundum naturam*
is to live vertuously, the Divines will not have it so'; and
that ' when the Divines would have us be an inch above
vertue, we fall an ell belowe it.'

---

[a] Subst. for 'though neer ⟨i.e. near⟩ a.'

[*] Verso of the slip at fol. 98ᵛ of MS. Aubr. 6.

[b] i. e. John Aubrey.

These verses he made, about anno . . . , . . .

* [*Upon*[a] *the state of nature.*

The state of nature never was so raw,
But oakes bore acornes and ther was a law
By which the spider and the silkeworme span;
Each creature had her birthright, and must man
Be illegitimate! have no child's parte!
If reason had no wit, how came in arte?
                    ingenium i. e. quoddam ingenitum.]

By Mr. James Harrington, esq., autor *Oceanae*, whose handwriting this is.

** Hic jacet | Jacobus Harrington, armiger | filius maximus natu | Sapcotis Harrington de Rand | in comitatu Lincolniae, equitis aurati | et Janae (matris ejus) filiae | Gulielmi Samuel de Upton in | comitatu Northampton, militis | qui | obiit septimo die Septembris | aetatis suae sexagesimo sexto | anno Domini 1677. | Nec virtutis nec animi dotes | arrha licet aeterni in animam amoris Dei | corruptione eximere queant corpus | Gen. iii. 19 | Pulveris enim es et reverteris | in pulverem | :—

author of the *Oceana*—he lyes buried in the chancell of St. Margarite's Church at Westminster, the next grave to the illustrious Sir Walter Raleigh, under the south side of the altar where the priest stands.

*** ☞ Pray remember to looke upon Mr. James Harrington's life: upon my alterations there. It was a philosophicall or politicall club, where gentlemen came at night to divert themselves with political discourse, and to see the way of balloting. It began at Miles's coffee-house about the middle of Michaelmas-terme, and was given over upon general Monke's comeing-in.

Sir John Hoskyns, etc., deane Arderne[b], etc., would not like to have their names seen.

Notes.

[1] In MS. Aubr. 6, fol. 98[v], Aubrey gives the reference ' vide Anthony Wood's

* MS. Aubr. 21, fol. 3.

[a] The passage in square brackets is Harrington's autograph.

** Aubrey, in MS. Wood F. 39, fol. 308: June 6, 1678.

*** A slip pasted to a slip inserted at fol. 98[v] of MS. Aubr. 6, a direction to Anthony Wood.

[b] *supra*, p. 290.

Hist. et Antiq. Oxon.,' and the coat ' . . . , a fret . . . '. In MS. Aubr. 8, fol. 29ᵛ, he gives the coat for Harrington's marriage, viz. :—' . . . , a fret . . . [Harrington]; impaling, . . . , a lion rampant crown'd . . . [D'ayrell].'

² The princess Elizabeth, daughter of James I. Sir John Harington, her tutor, was created (July 21, 1603) baron Harington of Exton. He married Anne Kelway, and was grand-uncle to the author of *Oceana.*

³ Robert Wood, M.A. (Mert.) 1649, appointed Fellow of Linc. Coll. by the Parliamentary Visitors, Sept. 19, and admitted Oct. 23, 1650; ejected by the King's Commissioners, Aug. 18, 1660.

Samuel Hartlib (16..-1670).

In MS. Aubr. 22 (Aubrey's collection of Grammars) is a tract :—
'The true and ready way to learne the Latine tongue,' by Samuel Hartlib, esq., Lond. 1654, with the inscription 'Jo. Aubrey, dedit S. Hartlib, 1654.'

William Harvey (1578-1657).

* William Harvey [1], M.D., natus at Folkestone in Kent: ** borne at the house which is now the post-house, a faire stone-built house, which he gave to Caius College in Cambridge, with some lands there : vide his will. His brother Eliab would have given any money or exchange for it, because 'twas his father's, and they all borne there; but the Doctor (truly) thought his memory would better be preserved this way, for his brother has left noble scates, and about 3000 *li.* per annum, at least.

*** Hemsted in Essex towards Audeley End : ibi sepultus Dr. Harvey.

**** Quaere Mr. ⟨William⟩ Marshall, the stone-cutter, for the inscription in the church there.

***** Quaere Mr. Marshall in Fetterlane for the copie of the inscription on his monument in Essex.

****** Dr. W. Harvey: ⟨ask his⟩ epitaph ⟨from⟩ Mr. Marshall.—Quaere Anthony Wood if there is a MS. in bibl. Bodleiana that speakes of the circulation of the bloud : Dr. ⟨Luke⟩ Ridgeley and Dr. Trowtbec can enforme me from Meredith Lloyd. —— Memorandum,

* MS. Aubr. 23, fol. 121ᵛ.
** MS. Aubr. 6, fol. 64.
*** MS. Aubr. 23, fol. 108ᵛ.
**** MS. Aubr. 6, fol. 64.
***** MS. Aubr. 6, fol. 66ᵛ.
****** MS. Aubr. 8, fol. 18.

Mr. Parker tells me that Mr. ⟨John⟩ Oliver, the City surveyor, had his father Marshall's inscriptions and papers; ergo vide there for the Doctor's inscription and also for the inscription of Inigo Jones.

* Dr. William Harvey—ex libro[2] meo B.

Over Dr. Harvey's picture in the great parlour under the library at the Physitians' College at Amen-corner (burnt) :—

Gul. Harveus, an. aetat. 10, in Schola Cantuar. primis doctrinae rudimentis imbutus ; 14, Col. Gonvil. et Caii alumnus ; 19, peragravit Galliam et Italiam ; 23, Patavii praeceptores habuit Eust. Rudium, Tho. Minad , H. Fab. ab Aquapend., Consul Anglor. 16 fit ; 24, Doctor † . . . Smyth. Med. et Chirurg. Reversus Lond. praxin exercuit, et uxorem † duxit ; 25, Coll. Med. Socius ; 37, Anatom. et Chirurg. Professor ; 54, Medicus Regius factus. Scripsit de Motu Sanguinis, et de Gen. Animal. Obiit 30 Jun. MDCLVII. Aetat. 80.

—(But I well remember that Dr. Alsop, at his funerall, sayd that he was 80, wanting one ; and that he was the eldest of 9 brethren.)

He lies buried in a vault at Hempsted in Essex, which his brother Eliab Harvey built ; he is lapt in lead, and on his brest in great letters

DR. WILLIAM HARVEY.

I was at his funerall, and helpt to carry him into the vault.

In the library at the Physitians' Colledge was the following inscription above his statue (which was in his doctorall robes) :—

GUL. HARVEUS, natus A.D. 1578, Apr. 2. Folkston, in Com. Cantii, primogenitus Thomae Harvei et Joannae Halk : fratres germani, Tho. Jo. Dan. Eliab. Mich. Mat. : sorores, Sarah, Amey.

Under his white marble statue, on the pedestall, thus,

GULIELMO HARVEO,
Viro
Monumentis suis immortali,
Hoc insuper
Coll. Med. Lond.
Posuit.

* MS. Aubr. 6, fol. 64.

Qui enim Sanguin. Motum
(ut et Animal. Ortum) dedit
meruit esse
Stator Perpetuus.

* Dr. Harvey added (or was very bountifull in contributing to) a noble building of Roman architecture (of rustique worke, with Corinthian pillasters) at the Physitians' College aforesaid, viz. a great parlour a for the Fellowes to meet in, belowe ; and a library, above. On the outside on the freeze, in letters 3 inches long, is this inscription :—

Suasu et Cura Fran. Prujeani, Præsidis, et Edmundi Smith, Elect., inchoata et perfecta est hæc fabrica. An. MIƆCLIII.

All these remembrances and building was destroyed by the generall fire.

He was alwayes very contemplative, and the first that I heare of that was curious in anatomie in England. He had made dissections of frogges, toades, and a number of other animals, and had curious observations on them, which papers, together with his goods, in his lodgings at Whitehall, were plundered at the beginning of the Rebellion, he being for the king, and with him at Oxon ; but he often sayd, that of all the losses he sustained, no greife was so crucifying to him as the losse of these papers, which for love or money he could never retrive or obtaine. When Charles I b by reason of the tumults left London, he attended him, and was at the fight of Edge-hill with him ; and during the fight, the Prince and duke of Yorke were committed to his care : he told me that he withdrew with them under a hedge, and tooke out of his pockett a booke and read ; but he had not read very long before a bullet of a great gun grazed on the ground neare him, which made him remove his station. He told me that Sir Adrian Scrope c was dangerously wounded there, and left for

---

dead amongst the dead· men, stript; which happened to
be the saving of his life. It was cold, cleer weather, and
a frost that night; which staunched his bleeding, and
about midnight, or some houres after his hurt, he awaked,
and was faine to drawe a dead body upon him for warmeth-
sake.

After Oxford was surrendred, which was 24 July[a] 1646,
he came to London, and lived with his brother Eliab
a rich[b] merchant in London, on . . . hill, opposite to
St. Lawrence (Poultry) church[c], where was then a high
leaden steeple (there were but two, viz.. this and St.
Dunstan's in the East), and at his brother's country house
at Roe-hampton.

His brother Eliab bought, about 1654, Cockaine-house,
now *(1680) the Excise-Office, a noble house, where the
Doctor was wont to contemplate on the leads of the house,
and had his severall stations, in regard of the sun, or
wind.

He did delight to be in the darke, and told me he could
then best contemplate. He had a house heretofore at
Combe, in Surrey, a good aire and prospect, where he had
caves made in the earth, in which in summer time he
delighted to meditate.—He was pretty well versed in
the Mathematiques, and had made himselfe master of
Mr. Oughtred's Clavis Math. in his old age; and I have
seen him perusing it, and working problems, not long
before he dyed, and that booke was alwayes in his meditating
apartment.

His chamber was that roome that is now the office of
Elias Ashmole, esq.; where he dyed, being taken with the
dead palsye, which tooke away his speech. As soone as
he sawe he was attaqued, he presently sent for his brother,
and nephews, and gave one a watch, another another thing,
etc., as remembrances of him. He dyed worth 20,0co *li.*
which he left to his brother Eliab. In his will he left

---

[a] *Rectius* June: Clark's Wood's *Life and Times*, i. 128.
[b] Subst. for 'great.'

[c] Subst. for 'St. Dunstan's church in the . . . .'
* MS. Aubr. 6, fol. 65.

his old friend Mr. Thomas Hobbes 10 *li.* as a token of his love.

His sayings.—He was wont to say that man was but a great mischievous baboon.

He would say, that we Europaeans knew not how to order or governe our woemen, and that the Turkes were the only people used them wisely.

He was far from bigotry.

He had been physitian to the Lord Chancellor Bacon, whom he esteemed much for his witt and style, but would not allow him to be a great philosopher. 'He writes philosophy like a Lord Chancelor,' said he to me, speaking in derision; 'I have cured him.'

About 1649 he travelled again into Italy, Dr. George (now Sir George) Ent, then accompanying him.

At Oxford, he grew acquainted with Dr. Charles Scarborough, then a young physitian (since by king Charles II knighted), in whose conversation he much delighted; and wheras before, he * marched up and downe with the army, he tooke him to him and made him ly in his chamber, and said to him, 'Prithee leave off thy gunning, and stay here; I will bring thee into practice.'

I remember he kept a pretty young wench to wayte on him, which I guesse he made use of for warmeth-sake as king David did, and tooke care of her in his will, as also of his man servant.

For 20 yeares before he dyed he tooke no manner of care about his worldly concernes, but his brother Eliab, who was a very wise and prudent menager, ordered all not only faithfully, but better then he could have donne himselfe.

He was, as all the rest of the brothers, very cholerique; and in his young days wore a dagger (as the fashion then was, nay I remember my old schoolemaster, old Mr. Latimer, at 70, wore a dudgeon, with a knife, and bodkin, as also my old grandfather Lyte, and alderman Whitson of Bristowe, which I suppose was the common fashion in

* MS. Aubr. 6, fol. 65ᵛ.

their young dayes), but this Dr. would be to⟨o⟩ apt to draw-out his dagger upon every slight occasion ⁿ.

He was not tall ; but of the lowest stature, round faced, olivaster ᵇ complexion ; little eie, round, very black, full of spirit ; his haire was black as a raven, but quite white 20 yeares before he dyed.

I first sawe him at Oxford, 1642, after Edgehill fight, but was then too young to be acquainted with so great a Doctor. I remember he came severall times to Trin.ᶜ Coll. to George Bathurst, B. D., who had a hen to hatch egges in his chamber, which they dayly opened to discerne ᵈ the progres and way of generation. I had not the honour to be acquainted ⟨with⟩ him ᵉ till 1651, being my she cosen Montague's physitian and friend. I was at that time bound for Italy (but to my great griefe disswaded by my mother's importunity). He was very communicative, and willing to instruct any that were modest and respectfull to him. And in order to my journey, gave me, i. e. dictated to me, what to see, what company to keepe, what bookes to read ³, how to manage my studies : in short, he bid me goe to the fountain head, and read Aristotle, Cicero, Avicenna, and did ᶠ call the neoteriques shitt-breeches. He wrote a very bad hand ⁴, which (with use) I could pretty well read.

I have heard him say, that after his booke of the Circulation of the Blood * came-out, that he fell mightily in his practize, and that 'twas beleeved by the vulgar that he was crack-brained ; and all the physitians were against his opinion, and envyed him ; many wrote against him, as Dr. Primige, Paracisanus, etc. (vide Sir George Ent's booke). With much adoe at last, in about 20 or 30 yeares time, it was recieved in all the Universities in the world ;

ⁿ The records of the Steward's court of the University of Oxford show several cases of homicide, in the sixteenth and seventeenth centuries, from the hasty drawing of daggers worn as part of the ordinary dress. See also *supra*, p. 150.

ᵇ Dupl. with ' complexion like wainscott.'

ᶜ Dupl. with ' our.'

ᵈ Dupl. with ' see.'

ᵉ Subst. for ' to know him.'

ᶠ Subst. for ' would.'

* MS. Aubr. 6, fol. 66.

and, as Mr. Hobbes sayes in his book 'De Corpore,' *he is the only man, perhaps, that ever lived to see his owne doctrine established in his life time.*

He understood Greek and Latin pretty well, but was no critique, and he wrote very bad Latin. The *Circuitus Sanguinis* was. as I take it, donne into Latin by Sir George Ent (quaere), as also his booke *de Generatione Animalium*, but a little book in 12ᵐᵒ against Riolani (I thinke), wherein he makes-out his doctrine clearer, was writt by himselfe, and that, as I take it, at Oxford.

His majestie king Charles I gave him the Wardenship of Merton Colledge in Oxford, as a reward for his service, but the times suffered him not to recieve or injoy any benefitt by it.

He was physitian, and a great favorite of the Lord High Marshall of England, Thomas* Howard, earle of Arundel and Surrey, with whom he travelled as his physitian in his ambassade to the Emperor . . . at Vienna, Anno Domini 163–. Mr. W. Hollar (who was then one of his excellencie's gentlemen) told me that, in his voyage, he would still be making of excursions into the woods, makeing observations of strange trees, and plants, earths, etc., naturalls, and sometimes like to be lost, so that my Lord Ambassador would be really angry with him, for there was not only danger of thieves, but also of wild beasts.

He was much and often troubled with the gowte, and his way of cure was thus; he would then sitt with his legges bare, if it were frost, on the leads of Cockaine house, putt them into a payle of water, till he was almost dead with cold, and betake himselfe to his stove, and so 'twas gonne.

He was hott-headed, and his thoughts working would many times keepe him from sleepinge; he told me that then his way was to rise out of his bed and walke about his chamber in his shirt till he was pretty coole, i. e. till he began to have a horror, and then returne to bed, and sleepe very comfortably.

I remember he was wont to drinke coffee; which he and

* Subst. for 'William.'

his brother Eliab did, before Coffee-houses were in fashion in London.

* All his profession would allowe him to be an excellent anatomist, but I never heard of any that admired his therapeutique way.   I knew severall practisers in London • that would not have given 3*d*. for one of his bills; and that a man could hardly tell by one of his bills [b] what he did aime at.

He did not care for chymistrey, and was wont to speake against them with an undervalue.

It is now fitt, and but just, that I should endeavour to undecieve the world in a scandall that I find strongly runnes of him, which I have mett amongst some learned young men : viz. that he made himselfe a way to putt himselfe out of his paine, by opium ; not but that, had he laboured under great paines, he had been readie enough to have donne it ; I doe not deny that it was not according to his principles upon certain occasions to . . . . : but the manner of his dyeing was really, and *bonâ fide*, thus, viz. the morning of his death about 10 a clock, he went to speake, and found he had the dead palsey in his tongue ; then he sawe what was to become of him, he knew there was then no hopes of his recovery, so presently sends for his young nephewes to come-up to him, to whom he gives one his watch ('twas a minute watch with which he made his experiments) ; to another, another remembrance, etc.; made signe to . . . Sambroke, his apothecary (in Black-Fryars), to lett him blood in the tongue, which did little or no good ; and so he ended his dayes.   His practise was not very great towards his later end ; he declined it, unlesse to a speciall friend,—e. g. my lady Howland, who had a cancer in her breast, which he did cutt-off and seared, but at last she dyed of it.

† I have seen him ride in 1654 or 5.   He rode on horseback with a foot-cloath to visitt his patients †, his man following on foote, as the fashion then was, which was very decent, now

* MS. Aubr. 6, fol. 66ᵛ.   • Dupl with ' this towne.'
                        ᵇ i. e. prescriptions.

quite discontinued   The judges rode also with their foote-cloathes to Westminster-hall, which ended at the death of Sir Robert Hyde, Lord Chief Justice.   Anthony earl of Shafton [a], would have revived, but severall of the judges being old and ill horsemen would not agree to it.

Lettres on naturalls: ⟨quaere⟩ Mr. Samb⟨roke⟩.

The scandall aforesaid is from Sir Charles Scarborough's saying that he had, towards his latter end, a preparation of opium and I know not what, which he kept in his study to take, if occasion should serve, to putt him out of his paine, and which Sir Charles promised to give him; this I beleeve to be true ; but doe not at all beleeve that he really did give it him.   The palsey did give him an easie passe-port.

I remember I have heard him say he wrote a booke *De insectis,* which he had been many yeares about, and had made curious researches and anatomicall observations on them.   This booke was lost when his lodgings at White-hall were plundered in the time of the rebellion.   He could never for love nor money retrive them or heare what became of them and sayd *'twas the greatest crucifying to him that ever he had in all his life.*

* Dr. Harvy [5] told me, and any one if he examines himself will find it to be true, that a man could not fancy —truthfully—that he is imperfect in any part that he has, verbi gratiâ, teeth, eie, tongue, spina dorsi, etc.   Natura tends to perfection, and in matters of generation we ought to consult more with our sense and instinct, then our reason, and prudence, fashion of the country, and interest. We see what contemptible [b] products are of the prudent politiques [c], weake, fooles, and ricketty children, scandalls to nature and their country.   The heralds are fooles [d]— *tota errant via.*   A blessing goes with a marriage for love upon a strong impulse.

[a] i. e. Shaftesbury; Lord High Chancellor, 1672.

* MS. Aubr. 21, fol. 12.

[b] Dupl. with ‘despicable.’

[c] i. e. of those who have married for policy.

[d] i. e. in inducing gentlemen to marry into noble families in order to impale a distinguished coat.

* *Sowgelder.* To see, Sir John, how much you are mistaken; he that marries a widdowe makes himself cuckold.
Exempli gratia, to speake experimentally and in my trade,
if a good bitch is first warded with a curre, let her ever
after be warded with a dog of a good straine and yet she
will bring curres as at first, her wombe being first infected
with a curre. So, the children will be like the first husband
(like raysing up children to your brother). So, the adulterer,
though a crime in law, the children are like the husband.

Sir John. Thou dost talke, me thinks, more under-
standingly of these matters then any one I have mett with.

Sowgelder. Ah! my old friend Dr. Harvey—I knew
him right well—he made me sitt by him 2 or 3 hours
together discoursing. Why! had he been stiffe, starcht *,
and retired, as other formall doctors are, he had known
no more then they. From the meanest person, in some
way, or other, the learnedst man may learn something.
Pride has been one of the greatest stoppers b of the advancement of learning.

Notes.

[1] Aubrey gives (MS. Aubr. 6, fol. 64) in trick the coat:—' or, on a chief
indented sable 3 crescents argent [Harvey]; quartering . . . , 2 bars wavy
. . . , on a chief . . . a lozenge charged with a Maltese cross . . . .'

[2] i.e. the inscriptions given here are extracted from the lost volume B. of
Aubrey's antiquarian collections. July 2, 1674, Aubrey to Wood, in MS.
Ballard 14, fol. 103 :—' My brother William hath my liber B, wherin is the
epitaph etc. of Dr. William Harvey's life.'

[3] On MS. Aubr. 6, fol. 61, the blank address-side of Francis Potter's letter
(of date Dec. 7, 1652) to Aubrey are found Aubrey's jottings of this conversation :—

' Vesalius
Bantinus
Anthocologia
J. Riolani.

_____

de oculo

Julius Placentinus : *de oculo et*
auditu
de oculo et visione
Fabricius Aquapendente.

Ad legendos hosce bonos autores cohortatus sum a doctore Gulielmo Harveo.'

* MS. Aubr. 21, fol. 15. The marrying a widow.
sowgelder, in Aubrey's comedy, is   a Dupl. with ' proud.'
dissuading Sir John Fitz-ale from   b Dupl. with ' retarders.'

⁴ Aubrey has preserved two specimens of this bad hand. MS. Aubr. 21, fol. 77, he marks as 'Dr. Harvey's bill for my purge, Nov. 19, 1655,' and notes 'The recipe is Dr. Harvey's own handwriting.' MS. Aubr. 21, fol. 107, is a prescription addressed for 'Mr. Aubrey, Apr. 23, 1653,' on which Aubrey notes 'This is Dr. William Harvey's owne writing.'

⁵ This passage, and the next, are taken from Aubrey's projected comedy, *The Country Revel*. In all likelihood they are a reminiscence of Harvey's familiar conversation : see p. 300, *supra*.

John Hawles (1645–1716).

* 'Remarks upon the Tryalls of Edward Fitzharris, Stephen Colledge, count Coningsmark, the lord Russell, col. Sydney, Henry Cornish, and Charles Bateman ; as also of Shaftsbury's Grand Jury, Wilmore's *Homine replegiando*, and the award of execution against Sir Thomas Armstrong' : by John Hawles, barrister, of Lincoln's Inne : London, 1689.

He was the sonne of Thomas Hawles, esq., and borne at his father's house in the close in Salisbury. He went to school at Winton College, and was a gentleman commoner of Queen's College, Oxon. He is an exceeding ingeniose young gentleman.

Richard Head (1637?–1686?).

** From Mr. Bovey :— . . . Meriton—his true name was Head (Mr. Bovey knew him). Borne . . . ; was a bookeseller in Little Britaine.

He had been amongst the gipsies. He looked like a knave with his gogling eies. He could transforme ª himselfe into ⟨any⟩ shape. Brake 2 or 3 times. Was at last a bookeseller, or towards his later end. He maintained himselfe by scribling. He ⟨got⟩ 20s. per sheet. He wrote severall pieces, viz. *The English Rogue*¹, *The Art of Wheadling*, etc.

He was drowned goeing to Plymouth by long sea about 1676, being about 50 yeares of age.

Note.

¹ In MS. Aubr. 6, fol. 1ᵛ, Anthony Wood notes 'Meriton Latrone in "the

---

* MS. Aubr. 7, fol. 9.   ** MS. Aubr. 7, fol. 15'.
                    ª Subst. for 'transmographie.'

I.   X

English Rogue"; I have it (i. e. the book) in my other study.'—' The English Rogue described in the life of Meriton Latrone,' Lond. 1666.

James Heath (1629–1664).

* Quaere of Sir . . . Heath in Pumpe Court; quaere capt. Sherburne and J. Davys de hoc.

Ex registro St. Bartholomew the lesse, London, Anno Dom. 1664. ' James Heath, gent., dyed the 16th, and was buryed the 19th of August, consumption and dropsey, in the church neere the skreene dore.'

The clarke here told me that once he had a pretty good estate, but in his later time maintained him selfe much by writing bookes[1]. He was hardly 40 yeares old when he dyed. He left 4 or 5 children on the parish, now all or most maried. Two were bound apprentices to weavers.

Note.

[1] James Heath, ejected by the Parliamentary Visitors (1648) from his Studentship in Christ Church, wrote histories of portions of the Civil War.

Elize Hele (15.. –1635).

** Lady Hele[a] in Devon, 800 *li.* per annum—Sir John Maynard.

The lady Hele of Devon gave by her will 800 *li.* per annum to be layd out for charitable uses and by the advice and prudence of serjeant Maynard[b]. He did order it[c] according to the best of his understanding, and yet he sayd that he haz lived to see every one of these benefactions abused—quod N. B.

*** Sir Robert Henley (16.. –1680?).

Sir Robert Henley, of Bramswell, Hants, baronet, decubuit[d], Thursday, about 3[h] P.M., Feb. 14, Valentine's

* MS. Aubr. 8, fol. 21.

** MS. Aubr. 6, a jotting on a slip at fol. 86, explained by the next paragraph, which is found on the back of the slip.

[a] ' Mr. Elize Hele ': see the details of the endowment in Lysons' Britannia (Devonshire), pp. 405, 609.

[b] John Maynard (1602–1690): Serjeant at Law 1654.

[c] 'did ordered' in MS., by a slip for ' did order it.'

*** MS. Aubr. 23, fol. 96[v].

[d] i.e. took to his bed. The astrologer

day. He was taken ill a hunting about noon, I think the Tuesday before. The yeare when, quaere? 1673.

Edward Herbert, baron Herbert of Chirbury (1583-1648).

* Edward [1], lord Herbert of Cherbery — vide memorandum [a], 1672. Vide 8vo booke by . . . , ubi his life, and description of a noble monument designed by him. Vide [b] lib. B, Montgomery, p. 126.—Severall whispering places in Wales, one here at Montgomery :—⟨so I am told by⟩ Meredith Lloyd.—Prophetick [c], America—vide lib. B, Montgomery.

⟨James⟩ Usher, Lord Primate of Ireland, was sent for by him, when in his death-bed, and he would have received the sacrament. He sayd indifferently of it that 'if there was good in any-thing 'twas in that,' or 'if it did no good 'twould doe no hurt.' The primate refused it, for which many blamed him. He dyed at his house in Queen street, very serenely ; asked what was a clock, answer so . . . : ' then,' sayd he, ' an houre hence I shall depart.' He then turned his head to the other side and expired. In his will he gave speciall order to have his white stone-horse (which he loved) to be well fed and carefully looked after as long as he lived. He had two libraries, one at London, the other at Montgomery ; one [2] wherof he gave to Jesus College, Oxon.

Vide his mother's, the [d] . . . , funerall sermon, preached at Chelsey by Dr. Donne, wherunto are annexed Latin and Greeke verses by her sonne, George Herbert.

Verses. Poemes.

Vide more of this lord in Lloyd's State-Worthies, 8vo. 1679.

Amici :—John Donne, D.D.; Sir John Danvers, etc.

then took his ' decumbiture,' i. e. position of the stars at the time of his being laid up.

* MS. Aubr. 8, fol. 28.

[a] i. e., I suppose, in Aubrey's pocket Almanac for 1672: see pp. 39, 51.

[b] ' lib. B' is a lost volume of Aubrey's own antiquarian notes.

[c] See, for the explanation of this jotting, in George Herbert's life, *infra*, p. 310.

[d] The blank is perhaps for ' wife of Sir John Danvers.'

* (August, 1648)—St. Giles-in-the-fields: 'August 5th, buried Edward, lord Herbert, baron of Cherbery.'

Mr. ⟨Thomas⟩ Fludd tells me he had constantly prayers twice a day in his howse, and Sundayes would have his chaplayne read one of Smyth's sermons.   Vide Mr. Davys, attorney.

** Sir Edward Herbert, afterward lord Cherbery, etc., dyed at his house, in Queen street, in the parish of St. Giles in the fields, London, and lies interred in the chancell, under the lord Stanhope's inscription.

On a black marble grave-stone thus:

> Heic inhumatur corpus
> Edvardi Herbert, Equitis
> Balnei, Baronis de Cherbury
> et Castle-Island. Auctoris Libri
> cui titulus est *De Veritate.*
> Reddor ut herbae,
> Vicessimo die Augusti,
> Anno Domini 1648.

I have seem him severall times with Sir John Danvers: he was a black man.

Memorandum:—the castle of Montgomery was a most romancy seate. It stood upon a high promontory, the north side 30 + feete high. From hence is a most delightsome prospect, 4 severall wayes. Southwards, without the castle, is *Prim-rose hill*: vide Donne's Poems, p. 53.

† In the parke.   *** Upon this Prim-rose hill †,
> Where, if Heaven would distill
> A showre of raine, each severall drop might goe
> To his owne prim-rose, and grow manna so ;
> And where their forme and their infinitie
> Make a terrestriall galaxie,
> As the small starres doe in the skie ;
> I walke to find a true-love, and I see
> That 'tis not a meer woman that is shee,
> But most, or more, or lesse than woman be, etc.

* MS. Aubr. 8, a slip at fol. 95.   ** MS. Aubr. 8, fol. 95.
*** MS. Aubr. 8, fol. 95ᵛ.

In this pleasant solitude did this noble lord enjoy his muse. Here he wrote his *De Veritate.* Dr. Coote (a Cambridge scholar and a learned) was one of his chaplains. Mr. Thomas Masters, of New College, Oxon, lived with him till 1642.

This stately castle was demolished since the late warres at the chardge of the countrey.

Notes.

¹ In MS. Aubr. 8, fol. 95, Aubrey gives in trick the coat :—' Party per pale, azure and gules, 3 lions rampant argent' [Herbert of Chirbury] : surmounted by a baron's coronet.

² It was his London library that he gave to Jesus College : so Aubrey, 2 Sept. 1671, in MS. Wood F. 39, fol. 138.

George Herbert (1593-1633).

* Mr. George Herbert was kinsman (remote) and chapelaine to Philip, earl of Pembroke and Montgomery, and Lord Chamberlayn. His lordship gave him a beneficeᵃ at Bemmarton † (between Wilton and Salisbury), a pittifull little chappell of ease to Foughelston. The old house was very ruinous. Here he built a very handsome howse for the minister, of brick, and made a good garden and walkes. He lyes in the chancell, under no large, nor yet very good, marble grave-stone, without any inscription.

† In the records of the Tower it is writt Bymerton.

Scripsit :—Sacred Poems, called *The Church*, printed, Cambridge, 1633 ; a booke entituled *The Country Parson*, not printed till about 1650, 8vo. He also writt a folio in Latin, which because the parson ‡ of Hineham could not read, his widowe (then wife to Sir Robert Cooke) condemned to the uses of good houswifry.

‡ This account I had from Mr. Arnold Cooke, one of Sir Robert Cooke's sonnes, whom I desired to aske his mother-in-laweᵇ for Mr. G. Herbert's MSS.

He was buryed (according to his owne desire) with the singing service for the buriall of dead, by the singing men of Sarum. Fr⟨ancis⟩ Sambroke (attorney) then assisted as a chorister boy ; my uncle, Thomas

* MS. Aubr. 8, fol. 96.   ᵃ Subst. for ' the parsonage of Bemmarton.'
ᵇ i.e. step-mother.

Danvers, was at the funerall. Vide in the Register booke at the office when he dyed, for the parish register is lost.

Memorandum :—in the chancell are many apt sentences of the Scripture. At his wive's seate, *My life is hid with Christ in God*, Coloss. iii. 3 (he hath verses on this text in his poëms). Above, in a little windowe blinded, within a veile (ill painted), *Thou art my hideing place*, Psalm xxxii. 7.

He maried Jane, the third daughter of Charles Danvers, of Bayntun, in com. Wilts, esq. but had no issue by her. He was a very fine complexion and consumptive. His mariage, I suppose, hastened his death. My kinswoman was a handsome *bona roba* and ingeniose.

When he was first maried he lived a yeare or better at Dantesey house. H. Allen, of Dantesey, was well acquainted with him, who has told me that he had a very good hand on the lute, and that he sett his own lyricks or sacred poems. 'Tis an honour to the place, to have had the heavenly and ingeniose contemplation of this good man, who was pious even to prophesie ;—e. g.

> ' Religion now on tip-toe stands,
> Ready to goe to the American strands.'

* George Herbert :—⟨ask⟩ cozen Nan Garnet pro ⟨his⟩ picture ; if not, her aunt . . . Cooke.

Mary Herbert, countess of Pembroke (1555–1621).

** Mary [1], countesse of Pembroke, was sister to Sir Philip Sydney ; maried to Henry, the eldest son of William, earle of Pembroke aforesayd ; but this subtile old earle did foresee that his faire and witty daughter-in-lawe would horne his sonne and told him so and advised him to keepe her in the countrey and not to let her frequent the court.

She was a beautifull ladie and had an excellent witt, and had the best breeding that that age could afford. Shee

* MS. Aubr. 8, fol. 5ᵛ.   ** MS. Aubr. 6, fol. 18.

had a pritty sharpe-ovall face. Her haire was of a reddish yellowe.

She was very salacious, and she had a contrivance that in the spring of the yeare[a] . . . the stallions . . . were to be brought before such a part of the house, where she had a *vidette* to look on them. . . . One of her great gallants was crooke-back't Cecill, earl of Salisbury.

In her time Wilton house was like a College, there were so many learned and ingeniose persons. She was the greatest patronesse of witt and learning of any lady in her time. She was a great chymist and spent yearly a great deale in that study. She kept for her laborator[b] in the house Adrian Gilbert (vulgarly called Dr. Gilbert), halfe brother to Sir Walter Ralegh, who was a great chymist in those dayes. 'Twas he that made the curious wall about Rowlington-parke, which is the parke that adjoyns to the house at Wilton. Mr. Henry Sanford was the earle's secretary, a good scholar and poet, and who did penne part of the *Arcadia* dedicated to her (as appeares by the preface). He haz a preface before it with the two letters of his name. 'Tis he that haz verses before Bond's Horace. She also gave an honourable yearly pension to Dr. ⟨Thomas⟩ Mouffett, * who hath writt a booke *De insectis*. Also one . . . Boston, a good chymist, a Salisbury man borne, who[c] did undoe himselfe by studying the philosopher's stone, and she would have kept him but he would have all the gold to him selfe and so dyed I thinke in a goale.

At Wilton is a good library which Mr. Christopher Wase can give you the best account of of any one; which was collected in this learned ladie's time. There is a manuscript very elegantly written, viz. all the Psalmes of David translated by Sir Philip Sydney, curiously bound in crimson velvet. There is a MS. writt by Dame Marian[d] of hunting

---

[a] Some portions of the text, three lines in all, are suppressed here.

[b] Subst. for 'elaborator.'

* MS. Aubr. 6, fol. 81ᵛ.

[c] Subst. for 'but he.'

[d] Anthony Wood corrects this to 'Juliana,' i. e. Berners.

and hawking, in English verse, written in King Henry the 8th's time (quaere Mr. Christopher Wase farther). There is the legier book of Wilton, one page Saxon and the other Latin, which Mr. Dugdale perused.

This curious seate of Wilton and the adjacent countrey is an Arcadian place and a paradise. Sir Philip Sydney was much here, and there was* . . . great love between him and his faire sister . . . I have heard old gentlemen (old Sir Walter Long of Dracot and old Mr. Tyndale) say . . . The first Philip, earle of Pembroke, . . . inherited not the witt of either the brother or sister.

† Jack Markham saies they were not ⟨married⟩.

‡ He dyed 1644 or 1645.

This countesse, after her lord's death, maried † to Sir Matthew Lister ‡, knight, one of the Colledge of Physitians, London. He was (they say) a learned and a handsome gentleman. She built then a curious house in Bedfordshire called Houghton Lodge neer Ampthill. The architects were sent for from Italie. It is built according to the description of Basilius's house in the first booke of the *Arcadia* (which is dedicated to her). It is most pleasantly situated and hath fower visto's, each prospect 25 or 30 miles. This was sold to the earle of Elgin for . . . *li.* The house did cost 10,000 *li.* the building.

I thinke she was buryed in the vault in the choire at Salisbury, by Henry, earl of Pembroke, her first husband : but there is no memoriall of her, nor of any of the rest, except some penons and scutcheons.

* An epitaph on the lady Mary, countesse of Pembroke (in print somewhere), by William Browne, who wrote the *Pastoralls*, whom William, earle of Pembroke, preferr'd to be tutor to the first earle of Carnarvon (⟨Robert⟩ Dormer), which was worth to him 5 or 6000*li.*, i. e. he bought 300 *li.* per annum land—from old Jack Markham—

> Underneath this sable hearse
> Lies the subject of all verse:

ᵃ Some expressions in the text, two lines in all, are suppressed here.

* MS. Aubr. 6, a slip at fol. 81.

Sydney's sister, Pembroke's mother.
Death! er'st thou shalt kill [a] such another
Fair and good and learn'd as shee,
Time will throw a [b] dart at thee.

Note.

[1] Aubrey gives in trick the coat :—' parted per pale azure and gules, 3 lions rampant argent [Herbert] ; impaling, ⟨or⟩, a pheon ⟨azure⟩ [Sydney].'

Richard Herbert (15..–1596).

* (Ex libro B, p. 126) :—In a buriall-place in the church at Montgomery (belonging to the castle) is a great freestone monument of Richard Herbert, esq. (father to the learned lord Herbert of Cherbery, and Mr. George Herbert, who wrote the sacred poëms), where are the effigies of him and Magdalene his wife, who afterwards was maried to Sir John Danvers of Wilts, and lies interred at Chelsey church but without any monument. Dr. Donne, dean of St. Paul's, preached her funerall sermon, to which are annexed severall verses, Latin and Greeke, by Mr. George Herbert, in memorie of her. She was buryed, as appeares by the sermon, July 1, 1627.

In Sepulchrum Richardi Herberti, armigeri, et Magdalenae uxoris ejus, hendecasyllaba.

> Quid virtus, pietas, amorve recti,
> Tunc cum vita fugit, juvare possunt?
> In coelo relevent perenne nomen,
> Hoc saxum doceat, duos recludens
> Quos uno thalamo fideque junctos
> Heic unus tumulus lapisve signat.
> Jam longum sape, Lector, et valeto,
> Aeternum venerans ubique nomen.

** In Brecknockshire, about 3 miles from Brecknock, is a village called Penkelly (Anglicè *Hasel-wood*), where is a little castle. It is an ancient seate of the Herberts. Mr. Herbert, of this place, came, by the mother's side, of Ŵgan. The lord Cherbery's ancestor came by the second

---

[a] Subst. for 'kill'st.'
[b] Dupl. with ' his.'

* MS. Aubr. 8, fol. 95.
** MS. Aubr. 8, fol. 95ᵛ.

venter, who was a miller's daughter. The greatest part of
the estate was settled on the issue by the 2d venter,
viz. Montgomery castle, and Aberystwith. Upon this
match with the miller's daughter are to this day recited, or
sung, by the Welsh, these verses: viz. :—

> Ô gway vinney (dhyw) râg wilidh
> Vôd vinhad yn velinidh
> A' vôd vy mam yn velinidhes
> A' môd inney yn arglwydhes.

To this sence[1] :—

> O God! Woe is me miserable, my father was a
> miller, and my mother a milleresse, and I am now
> a ladie.

Note.

[1] A more exact rendering is :—

> 'O woe is me (God) for shame,
> That my father is a miller
> And that my mother is a miller's wife,
> And that *I* am a peeress.'

William Herbert, 1st earl of Pembroke (1507–1570).

* William[1], earle of Pembroke, the first earle of that
family, was borne (I thinke I have heard my cosen Whitney
say) in . . . in Monmouthshire. Herbert, of Colbrooke in
Monmouthshire, is of that family.

He was (as I take it) a younger brother, a mad fighting
young fellow. 'Tis certaine he was a servant to the house
of Worcester, and wore their blew-coate and badge. My
cosen Whitney's great aunt gave him a golden angell[a] when
he went to London. One time being at Bristowe, he was
arrested, and killed one of the sheriffes of the city. He
made his escape through Back-street, through the (then
great) gate, into the Marsh, and gott into France.

Memorandum :—upon this action of killing the sheriffe,
the city ordered the gate to be walled-up, and only a little
posterne gate or dore, with a turnestile for a foot-passenger,
which continued so till Bristowe was a garrison for the king,

---

* MS. Aubr. 6, fol. 80.   [a] 'one time' followed, scored out.

and the great gate was then opened, in 1644, or 1645. When I was a boy there, living with my father's mother, who was maried to alderman John Whitson †

† He was the greatest benefactor to the city that haz been since the Reformacion. He gave 500 *li.* per annum at least to the city to maintain ... blew-coates, boies and maydes. He dyed about 1629 : vide register.

(who was my god-father), the story was as fresh as but of yesterday. He was called *black Will Herbert.*

In France he betooke himself into the army, where he shewd so much courage, and readinesse of witt in conduct, that in short time he became eminent, and was favoured by ⟨Francis I⟩ the king, who afterwards recommended him to Henry the VIII of England, who much valued him, and heaped favours and honours upon him.

Upon the dissolution of the abbeys, he gave him the abbey of Wilton, and a *country* of lands and mannours thereabout belonging to it. He gave him also the abbey of Remesbury in Wilts, with much lands belonging to it. He gave him Cardiff-Castle in Glamorganshire, with the ancient crowne-lands belonging to it.

Almost all the country held of this castle. It was built by Sir Robert Fitzhamond the Norman, who lies buried at Tewkesbury abbey with a memorial : and he built the abbey of Glocester. It afterwards came to Jasper, duke of Bedford, etc. ; so to the crowne. I have seen severall writings of Sir John Aubrey's at Llantrithid in Glamorganshire, which beginne ᵃ thus :—
'Ego Jaspar, frater regum et patruus, dux Bedfordiae, comes Pembrochiae, et dominus de Glamorgan et Morgannog, omnibus ad quos hoc presens scriptum pervenerit, salutem, etc.'

He maried ⟨Anne⟩ Par, sister of queen Katharine Par, daughter and co-heire of ⟨Thomas⟩ Par (I thinke ², marquisse of Northampton), by whom he had 2 sonnes, Henry, earle of Pembroke, and ⟨Edward⟩ the ancestor of the lord Powys.

He was made Privy Councellor and conservator of King Henry the Eight's * will. He could neither write nor

---

ᵃ Dupl. with ' runne.'   * MS. Aubr. 6, fol. 8oᵛ.

read, but had a stamp for his name. He was of good naturall parts; but very cholerique. He was strong sett but bony, reddish-favoured, of a sharp eie [a], sterne looke.

In queen Mary's time, upon the returne of the Catholique religion, the nunnes came again to Wilton abbey, and this William, earl of Pembroke, came to the gate (which lookes towards the court by the street, but now is walled-up) with his cappe in hand, and fell upon his knee to the lady abbesse † and the nunnes, crying peccavi. Upon queen Mary's death, the earle came to Wilton (like a tygre) and turnd them out, crying, 'Out ye whores, to worke, to worke, ye whores, goe spinne.'

† The last lady abbesse here was....Gawen, of Norrington, belonging to Chalke, where that family haz been 400 yeares (sold about 1665 to Judge Wadham Windham).

He being a stranger in our country, and an upstart, was much envyed. And in those dayes (of sword and buckler), noblemen (and also great knights, as the *Longs*), when they went to the assizes or sessions at Salisbury, etc., had a great number of retainers following them; and there were (you have heard), in those dayes, feudes (i. e. quarrells and animosities) between great neighbours. Particularly this new earle was much envyed by the then lord Sturton of Sturton [3], who would, when he went or returned from Sarum (by Wilton was his rode), sound his trumpetts, and give reproachfull challenging words; 'twas a relique of knighthood errantry.

From my great-uncles, the Brownes of Broad Chalke :— in queen Elizabeth's time, some bishop (I have forgot who) that had been his chaplain, was sent to him from the queen and council, to take interrogatories of him. So he takes out his pen ·and inke, examines and writes. When he had writt a good deale, sayd the earle, 'Now lett me see it.' 'Why,' q[d] the bishop, 'your lordship cannot read it?' 'That's all one : I'le see it,' q[d] he, and takes it and teares it to pieces : 'Zounds, you rascall,' q[d] he, 'd'ee thinke I will have my throate cutt with a penknife?' It seemes they had a mind to have pick't a hole in his coate, and to have gott his estate.

[a] Dupl. with 'face.'

'Tis reported that he caused himself to be lett bloud, and bled so much that it was his death, and that he should say as he was expiring, ' They would have Wilton—they would have Wilton,' and so gave up the ghost.

Memorandum :—this William (the founder of this family) had a little cur-dog which loved him, and the earl loved the dog. When the earle dyed the dog would not goe from his master's dead body, but pined away, and dyed under the hearse; the picture of which dog is under his picture, in the Gallery at Wilton. Which putts me in * mind of a parallell storie in Appian (Syrian Warr) :—Lysimachus being slaine, a dog that loved him stayed a long time by the body and defended it from birds and beasts till such time as Thorax, king of Pharsalia, finding it out gave it buriall. And I thinke there is such another story in Pliny : vide.

He was buried in . . . of St. Paule's, London, where he had a magnificent monument, which is described, with the epitaph, by Sir William Dugdale, which vide.

** This present earl of Pembroke (1680) has at Wilton 52 mastives and 30 grey-hounds, some beares, and a lyon, and a matter of 60 fellowes more bestiall than they.

Notes.

[1] Aubrey gives in trick the coat :—' party per pale azure and gules, 3 lions rampant argent [Herbert]; impaling, argent, 2 bars azure within a bordure engrailed sable [Parre],' surmounted by an earl's coronet.

[2] In error. It was Sir Thomas Parre's son William (brother of this Anne, countess of Pembroke) who was created marquess of Northampton in 154⅞.

[3] Charles Stourton, succeeded as 7th baron in 1548 ; executed for murder in 1557.

William Herbert, 3rd earl of Pembroke (1580–1630).

*** William, earl of Pembroke, Chancellor of the University of Oxford, natus anno MDLXXX, viii Apr. ; obiit anno MDCXXX, x Calend. Apr.[a]—His death fell out according to prediction. He dyed a bed of an apoplexie.

**** Wilhelmus, comes Pembrochiae, Cancellarius Univ.

Oxon., natus anno MDLXXX, viii Apr.; obiit anno
MDCXXX, x Calend. Apr.—His nativity was calculated
by old Mr. Thomas Allen: his death was foretold, which
happened true at the time foretold.   Being well in health,
he made a feast; ate and dranke plentifully; went to bed;
and found dead in the morning.

* William, earle of Pembroke, Lord Chamberlain, and
Chancellor of the University of Oxford :—

'Natus Anno MDLXXX, viii Apr.
Obiit Anno MDCXXX, x Calend. Apr.'—

I find this under his engraved picture.

He dyed of an apoplexy, and it fell-out right according
to prediction, because of which he made a great supper,
and went to his bed well, but dyed in his sleep.

He was a most magnificent and brave peer, and loved
learned men.   He was a poet.   There is a little booke in
12mo or 16mo which containes his wife's and Sir Benjamin
Rudyer's who was his friend and contemporary.

John Heydon (1629–166..).

** From Elias Ashmole, esq[re], scilicet that he[a] had the
booke called *The way to blisse* from his adoptive father
Backhowse[b] at Swallowfield in com. Berks., a MSS. writt
in queen Elizabeth's time, hand and stile ἀνονυμῶς.

Mr. . . . Heyden maried Nicholas Culpepper's widdowe,
and lights there[c] on the aforesayd MSS., and prints a booke
with a great deale of *The way to blisse* word for word and
verses that are printed in the commendation of other
bookes; and instead of such and such old philosophers[d]
putts downe John Bowker and William Lilly which they
never heard of: and is so impudent in one of his bookes
since as to say Mr. Ashmole borrowed of him.

---

* MS. Aubr. 6, a slip at fol. 81.   ' Sir William Backhouse, quaere.'
** MS. Aubr. 8, fol. 4ᵛ.   ᶜ i. e. among N. Culpepper's papers.
ᵃ i. e. Ashmole.   ᵈ i. e. cited in the MS. he was ex-
ᵇ Anthony Wood notes here :—   ploiting.

Peter Heylyn (1599-1662).

* Dr. Heylin was buried in the choire neer his own [sub-dean's [a]] stall, May the 10th 1662 [b], but his inscription is on the wall of the north aisle.

** ⟨Aubrey gives a copy of the inscription, noting, on the line 'posuit hoc illi moestissima conjux':—⟩ who, about a year after, fell in love with a lifeguardman that I know, whom she had maried (aetat. 23), had not cruel death quench't that amorous flame.

Il port 'sable, 3 horse-heads erased argent.'

Nicholas Hill (1570?-1610).

*** Mr. Nicholas Hill:—This Nicholas Hill was one of the most learned men of his time: a great mathematician and philosopher and traveller, and a poet [c]. His writings had the usuall fate of those not printed in the author's life-time. He was so eminent for knowledge, that he was the favourite of . . . † the great earle of Oxford, who had him to accompanie him in his travells (he was his steward), which were so splendid and sumptuous, that he kept at Florence a greater court then the Great Duke. This earle spent in that . . . . of travelling, the inheritance of ten or twelve thousand pounds per annum.

† 'Twas that earle of Oxford that lett the f— before queen Elizabeth: wherupon he travelled. Vide Stowe de hoc, in Elizabeth about the end.

Old Serjeant Hoskins (the poet, grandfather to this Sir John Hoskins, baronet, my hon[d] friend) knew him (was [d] well acquainted with him), by which meanes I have this tradicion which otherwise had been lost; as also his very name, but only for these verses [1] in Ben Johnson's 2d volumine, viz. :—

. . . .

. . . .

---

* Aubrey in Wood MS. F. 39, fol. 160[v]: 16 Jan. 167½.

[a] Inserted by Anthony Wood.

[b] Wrongly changed by Wood to 1663.

** Ibid., fol. 156: 30 Dec. 1671.

*** MS. Aubr. 6, fol. 38[v].

[c] The words follow, scored out, 'but no writer that ever I heard of, or if he was,' [his writings].

[d] Subst. for 'or remembered him.

I fancy that his picture, i. e. head, is at the end of the Long Gallery of Pictures at Wilton †, which is the most philosophicall aspect that I have seen, very much of Mr. T. Hobbes of Malmesbury, but rather *more antique.* 'Tis pitty that in noblemen's galleries, the names are not writt on, or behind, the pictures.

He writt ' Philosophia Epicureo-Democritiana, simpliciter proposita, non edocta ': printed at Colen, in 8vo or 12mo: Sir John Hoskins hath it.

Thomas Henshawe, of Kensington, esq., R. Soc. Soc., hath a treatise of his in manuscript, which he will not print, viz. 'Of the Essence of God, &c. Light.' It is mighty paradoxicall :—*That there is a God;* What he is, in 10 or 12 articles : *Of the Immortality of the Soule,* which he does demonstrate παντουσία and ὀντουσία.

[Fabian Philips, the cursiter, remembers him ᵃ.]

He was, as appears by A. Wood's *Historie,* of St. John's Colledge in Oxford, where he mentions him to be a great Lullianist.

In his travells with his lord, (I forget whither Italy or Germany, but I thinke the former) a poor man begged him to give him *a penny.* 'A penny!' said Mr. Hill, 'what dost say to ten pound?' 'Ah! ten pound!' (said the beggar) 'that would make a man happy.' N. Hill gave him immediately 10*li.* and putt it downe upon account,—' Item, to a beggar ten pounds, to make him happy.'

* He printed 'Philosophia Epicurea Democritiana,' dedicated 'filiolo Laurentio.'—There was one Laurence Hill that did belong to the queen's court, that was hangd with ᵇ Green and Berry about Sir Edmund-Berry Godfrey. According to age, it might be this man, but we cannot be certain.

** Mr. Thomas Henshaw bought of Nicholas Hill's

ᵃ The statement in square brackets is scored out, and the comment added 'negat.' Aubrey had enquired of Philips.

* Aubrey in MS. Wood F. 39, fol. 389 : 15 July 1689.
ᵇ Wood notes 'false.'
** Ibid., fol. 389ᵛ.

widow, in Bow lane, some of his bookes; among which
is a manuscript *de infinitate et aeternitate mundi.* He finds
by his writings that he was (or leaning) a Roman Catholique. Mr. Henshaw believes he dyed about 1610: he
dyed an old man. He flourished in queen Elizabeth's
time. I will search the register of Bowe.

 * I have searched the register of Bow, ubi non inventus
Nicolas Hill.

 ** Vide tom. 1 of Ben: Johnson's workes, pag. 48, epigram
CXXXIV, title 'The famous voyage' . . .

> Here sev'rall ghosts did flitt,
> About the shore, of . . . . , but late departed ;
> White, black, blew, greene ; and in more formes out-
>   started
> Than all those *Atomi* ridiculous
> Wherof old Democrite and Hill Nicholas,
> One sayd, the other swore, the world consists.

Note.

[1] Aubrey was most anxious to have these verses inserted, three times directing
Anthony Wood to do so. MS. Aubr. 8, a slip at fol. 4 :—'Past on Nicholas
Hill, in his proper place in part 1st' (i.e. MS. Aubr. 6), but no copy of the
verses is there given. MS. Aubr. 8, fol. 7 :—'Insert B. Johnson's verses
of Nicholas Hill.' MS. Wood F. 39, fol. 351ᵛ: 13 Jan. 168¾:—'B. Johnson
speakes of N. Hill in his "Voyage to Holbourne from Puddle-dock in a ferry
boate.

> A dock there is . . . . called *Avernus*
> . . . . concern us."'

Thomas Hobbes (1588–1679).

⟨This, the most elaborate of these 'Brief Lives,' occupies by itself
MS. Aubr. 9. For the letters introductory to it, see *supra*, pp. 17–20.

The various papers of which the MS. is composed are bound up
confusedly, and the separate notes are in some cases entered on a page,
or a page and its opposite, in no order. Considerable re-arrangement
has therefore been necessary; but the exact MS. references have
been given throughout. Some few notes relating to Hobbes, found
in other Aubrey MSS., have here been brought into their natural
place.⟩

 * Aubrey in MS. Wood F. 39, fol. 389.
 ** Ibid., fol. 354 : 21 June 1681.

I.   Y

* The Life of Mr. Thomas Hobbes, of Malmesburie[a].

⟨*Introduction.*⟩

The writers[b] of the lives of the ancient philosophers used to, in the first place, to speake of their lineage[c]; and they tell us that in processe of time severall great[d] families accounted it their glory to be branched[e] from such or such a *Sapiens*.

Why now should that method be omitted in this *Historiola* of our Malmesbury philosopher? Who though but[f] of plebeian descent[g], his renowne haz and will give brightnesse to his name and familie, which hereafter may arise glorious and flourish in riches and may justly take it an honour to be of kin to this worthy person, so famous, for his learning[h], both at home and abroad.

⟨*Pedigree.*⟩

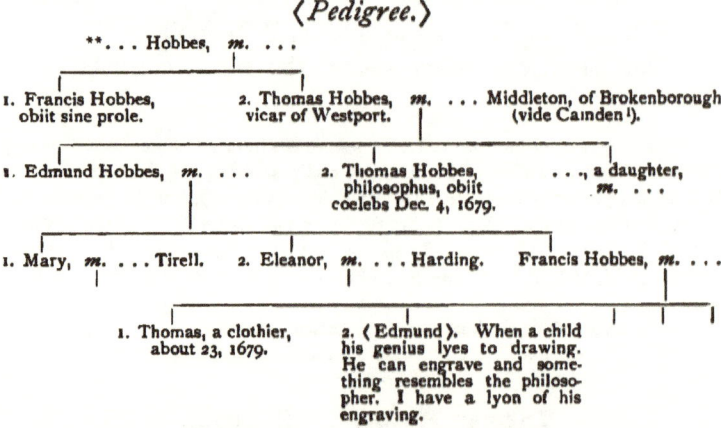

**... Hobbes, *m.* ...

1. Francis Hobbes, obiit sine prole.
2. Thomas Hobbes, vicar of Westport. *m.* ... Middleton, of Brokenborough (vide Camden[i]).

1. Edmund Hobbes, *m.* ...
2. Thomas Hobbes, philosophus, obiit coelebs Dec. 4, 1679.
..., a daughter, *m.* ...

1. Mary, *m.* ... Tirell.
2. Eleanor, *m.* ... Harding.
Francis Hobbes, *m.* ...

1. Thomas, a clothier, about 23, 1679.
2. ⟨Edmund⟩. When a child his genius lyes to drawing. He can engrave and something resembles the philosopher. I have a lyon of his engraving.

This heraldique way of expressing a genealogie is most intelligible and makes the best impresse in the memory or

* MS. Aubr. 9, fol. 30.

[a] This title is subst. for 'Supplementum vitae Thomae Hobbes, Malmsburiensis': see p. 17.

[b] There are two other drafts of the opening sentence :—'The ancients, when they writt the lives'; 'It was usuall with the writers of the lives of the ancient philosophers, in the'.

[c] Dupl. with 'stock.'

[d] Dupl. with 'rich' or 'illustrious.'

[e] Dupl. with 'derived.'

[f] Dupl. with 'though of no illustrious family.'

[g] Dupl. with 'extraction.'

[h] Dupl. with 'great parts.'

** MS. Aubr. 9, fol. 29ᵛ.

[i] i.e. for the etymology; *infra*, p. 324.

fancy; but ᵃ will it not be thought here to⟨o⟩ pompous and affected by his enemies and the nation of critiques? *Prescribe Trebate.*

My brother ᵇ W. A. will set all this right ¹.

⟨ *His father.* ⟩

* Thomas Hobbes ², then, whose life I write, was second son of Mr. Thomas Hobbes, vicar of Westport juxta Malmesbury, who maried . . . Middleton of Brokinborough (a yeomanly family). ** He was also vicar of Charlton (a mile hence): they are annexed, and are both worth 60 or 80*li.* per annum.—*** Memorandum, Brokenborough also is appendant to Charlton vicaridge—160*li.* per annum —from Philip Laurence, whose father-in-law was vicar. [**** The vicaridge of Malmesbury is but xx nobles per annum = 6*li.* 13*s.* 4*d.*; but Coston and Radbourne belongs to it, which addition is equal to 50 or 60*li.* per annum.]

***** Thomas, the father ᶜ, was one of the ignorant ' Sir Johns ᵈ' of queen Elizabeth's time ; could ᵉ only read the prayers of the church and the homilies ; and disesteemed ᶠ learning (his son Edmund told me so), as not knowing the sweetnes of it.

****** As to his father's ignorance and clownery, 'twas as good metall in the oare which wants excoriating and refineing. A witt requires much cultivation, much paines, and art and good conversation to perfect a man.

⟨ *His father's brother.* ⟩

******* He ᵍ had an elder brother ³ whose name was

ᵃ Aubrey's MS. is only a rough draft for Anthony Wood's perusal. Hence these queries.

ᵇ For the pedigree supplied by William Aubrey, see *infra*, p. 388.

* MS. Aubr. 9, fol. 30.

** MS. Aubr. 9, fol. 29ᵛ.

*** MS. Aubr. 9, fol. 7ᵛ.

**** MS. Aubr. 9, fol. 29ᵛ.

***** MS. Aubr. 9, fol. 30.

ᶜ Dupl. with ' vicar.' Anthony

Wood wrote in the margin 'vicar of Malmsbury,' but scored it out, as in error.

ᵈ Wood wished to add ' or Sir Rogers.'

ᵉ Dupl. with ' did.'

ᶠ Dupl. with ' valued not.'

****** MS. Aubr. 9, fol. 29ᵛ.

******* MS. Aubr. 9, fol. 30.

ᵍ i. e. Thomas, the father.

Francis, a wealthy man, and had been alderman † of the borough; by profession a glover ‡, which is a great trade here ‖, and in times past much greater. Having no * child, he contributed much to, or rather altogether maintained, his nephew Thomas at Magdalen hall in Oxon; and when he dyed gave him an *agellum* (a moweing-ground^a) called the Gasten-ground, lyeing neer to the horse-faire, worth 16 or 18 poundes per annum; the rest of his landes he gave to his nephew Edmund.

† 'Alderman' is the title of the chiefe magistrate here. Alderman and . . .; vide; quaere Sir J(ames) Long.
‡ Shall I expresse or conceale this (*glover*)? The philosopher would acknowledge it.—MS. Aubr. 9, fol. 29ᵛ.
‖ Malmesbury famous for good gloves.

** At Sherston about 3 miles hence (vide map) are groundes likewise called the Gasten-grounds—perhaps 'tis Garston grounds. At Sherston was heretofore a castle, and perhaps (and quaere) if these grounds are not where the *vallum* or bulwarkes might be drawne. *Gaer*, Britannicè, signifies some such thing, vide Dr. Davys' British Dictionary.

In Hexham's Dutch dictionary *Gast* signifies 'a guest'; so that *Gasten-ground* will be 'the ground for the guests'; probably to putt the horses of the guests (that came to lye at the abbey) to grasse. They speake broad in our countrey, and do pronounce guest, *gast*, etc. Monasterys had their guest-halls; and it should seeme they had likewise their guest-grounds for the strangers' horses: as here.

⟨*His brother and sister.*⟩

*** Thomas, the vicar of Westport, maried . . . Middleton⁴ of Brokenborough † (of a yeomanly family), by whom he had two sonnes and one daughter (quaere my brother William Aubrey)—Edmund, his eldest (was bred-up to ᵇ his uncle's profession of a glover); and Thomas (philosopher), second son, whose

† Brokenbrig: vide Camden.—MS. Aubr. 9, fol. 30ᵛ.

---

* MS. Aubr. 9, fol. 31.
ᵃ Dupl. with 'pasture.' In MS. Aubr. 3, fol. 28, Aubrey calls it 'a good moweing ground, called Gaston, not far from the house he ⟨T. H.⟩ was borne in.'
** MS. Aubr. 9, fol. 30ᵛ.
*** MS. Aubr. 9, fol. 31.
ᵇ Dupl. with 'with,' i.e. with his uncle, as well as to his trade.

life I now write. Edmund was neer[a] two yeares elder then his brother Thomas, and something resembled him in aspect[b], not so tall, but fell much short of him in his intellect, though he was a good plain understanding countrey-man[c]. He had been bred at schoole with his brother; could have made theme, and verse, and understood a little Greek to his dyeing day. He dyed (quaere William Aubrey) about 13 yeares since, aetat. circiter 80.

⟨ *His nephews and nieces.* ⟩

This Edmund had only one son named Francis, and two daughters maried to countreymen (renters) in the neighborhood. This Francis pretty well resembled his uncle Thomas, especially about the eie; and probably had he had good education might have been ingeniose; but he drowned his witt[d] in ale †. He was left by his father and uncle Thomas, 80 *li.* (quaere W. A.) or better per annum, but he was an ill husband. He dyed about two yeares after his father, and left five children.—His eldest son is Thomas, a clothier, now about 23, living at ‡ . . . (quaere W. A.[e]). The second, ⟨Edmund⟩, lives at . . . ‖, and has some lines of Thomas the philosopher. When he was a child[f], his genius inclined him to (* quaere W. A.) draweing[g] and engraving in copper. He is now about 21.

† This part much given to drunkennes.

‡ He did live at Tedbury.

‖ Did live at Chippenham.

⟨ *Description of Malmsbury.* ⟩

⟨As may be seen from his intended preface (*supra*, p. 19) Aubrey thought of beginning the life of Hobbes with an account of Malmsbury. For this purpose in MS. Aubr. 9 he has drawn three plans[h] :—

(a) plan of environs of Malmsbury (a slip at fol. 31ᵛ).

[a] Dupl. with ' about.'
[b] Dupl. with ' face.'
[c] In MS. Aubr. 3, fol. 28, Aubrey says, ' He ⟨T. H.⟩ had an elder brother, named Edmund Hobbes, more then once alderman of Malmesbury ': but this is probably an error, from confusing him with the uncle.

[d] Dupl. with ' parts.'
[e] i. e. William Aubrey.
[f] Dupl. with ' boy '
[*] MS. Aubr. 9, fol. 32.
[g] Dupl. with ' pourtraying.'
[h] Other drawings of Malmsbury by Aubrey are in MS. Aubr. 3, fol. 35 and 39.

(b) plan of Malmsbury (fol. 31ᵛ).

(c) a drawing of the house in which Hobbes was born (fol. 31ᵛ). These are reproduced in facsimile at the end of this edition.

He gives there (fol. 31ᵛ) these dimensions of the town :—'From St. John's Bridge ⟨south limit of the town⟩ to the abbey ⟨north⟩ is about a quarter of a mile; and from the same bridge to Westport church ⟨west limit⟩ is neer about a mile. Height of the borough from the levill belowe is about 100 foot high.'

The references on the plan of Malmsbury (see the facsimile) are:—

' *a*=the house of his birth.

ω = Westport church.

W =the West port (*olim*).

β=the smyth's shop.

δ=the private house where Mr. Latimer taught him.

ξ=Three Tunnes (as I take it), opposite to the smyth's shop.

✚ =the religious ⟨house⟩ dedicated to Our Lady: the chapell is yet standing.

H =⟨Hobbes's⟩ house at the upper ⟨end⟩ faces the Horse fayre.

⊗ =quaere if not a chapell here?'

On fol. 31ᵛ of MS. Aubr. 9, Aubrey has these remarks about these plans, etc. :—

'If these notes are not now inserted, probably they will be lost : or should it not be a marginall commentary?'

'I have drawne this rude sketch meerly for your clearer under-standing, not that I think it worth while to grave it for 'tis at randome. I intended if it had pleased God that I had prospered in the world to have had taken an exact map * of Malmesbury.'

'Whitechurch, about a mile ferè off:—quaere ubi stat?' 'Vide Speed's mappe in Wiltshire.'

'Burnevall, quasi Bournevall.')

⟨Description of Westport.⟩

* Westport [5] is the parish without the west-gate (which is now demolished), which gate stood on the neck of land that joines Malmesbury (vide verses [6]) to Westport. Here [7] was, before the late warres, a very pretty church, consist-ing of 3 aisles, or rather a nave and two aisles (which tooke up the whole area [b]), dedicated to St. Mary; and

---

* On this Anthony Wood comments: —'I think 'tis fit it should be drawne and represented, for the abbey sake.

'Tis cheap to have cut in box.'

* MS. Aubr. 9, fol. 32.

[b] scil. of the 'neck of land.'

a fair spire-steeple, with five tuneable bells, which, when the towne was taken (about 1644; quaere William Aubrey) by Sir W. Waller, were converted [a] into ordinance, and the church pulled-downe to the ground, that the enemie might not shelter themselves against the garrison. The steeple was higher then that now standing in the borough, which much added to [b] the prospect. The windowes were well painted, and in them were inscriptions that declared much antiquitie; now is here rebuilt a church like a stable.

⟨*Place and date of his birth.*⟩

Thomas Hobbes, Malmesburiensis, Philosophus, was borne at his father's house in Westport, being that extreme howse that pointes into, or [c] faces, the Horse-fayre; the farthest howse on the left hand as you goe to Tedbury, leaving the church on your right. To prevent mistakes, and that hereafter may rise no doubt [d] what house was famous for this famous man's birth; I doe here testifie that in April, 1659, his brother Edmond went with me into this house, and into the chamber where he was borne. Now things begin to be antiquated, and I have heard some guesse it might be at the howse where his brother Edmund lived and dyed. But this is so, as I here [e] deliver it. This house was given

† Quaere William Aubrey if … Potluck [f]. by Thomas, the vicar, to his daughter † . . . . . whose daughter or granddaughter possessed [g] it, when I was there. * It is a firme house, stone-built and tiled, of one roome (besides [h] a buttery, or the like, within) below, and two chambers above. 'Twas in the innermost where he first drew breath.

The day of his birth was April the fifth, Anno Domini ⊥ 1588, on a Fryday morning, which that yeare was Good Fryday. His mother fell in labour with him upon the fright of the invasion of the Spaniards—

[a] Dupl. with 'melted.'
[b] Dupl. with 'adorned.'
[c] Dupl. with 'and.'
[d] Anthony Wood notes here 'as it was concerning Homer.'
[e] Dupl. with 'as I say.'
[f] See *infra*, p. 388.
[g] Dupl. with 'enjoyed.'
[*] MS. Aubr. 9, fol. 33.
[h] Dupl. with 'with.'

[* Fama[a] ferebat enim, sparsitque per oppida nostra
　　　Extremum genti classe venire diem ;
Atque metum tantum concepit tunc mea mater
　　　Ut pareret geminos meque metumque simul.]

—** he told me himself between the houres of four and
six: but by rectification his nativity is found to be
at . . .†.

† See my
collection of
genitures[a],
where I have it
more exact
from his owne
mouth, viz.
5 h. 2′ mane.

His horoscope[9] is Taurus, having in it a
satellitium of 5 of the 7 planets. It is a maxime
in astrologie—vide Ptol. Centil.—that a native
that hath a *satellitium* in his ascendent becomes[b]
more eminent in his life then ordinary[c], e. g. divers which
see in Origanus, etc., and Oliver Cromwell had so, etc.

⟨*His school and college life.*⟩

At four yeares old [10] he went to schoole in Westport
church, till eight ; by that time [d] he could read well, and
number four figures. Afterwards he went to schoole to
Malmesbury, to Mr. Evans, the minister of the towne ;
and afterwards to Mr. Robert Latimer, a young man of
about nineteen or twenty, newly come from the University,
who then kept a private schoole in Westport, where the
broad place (quaere nomen) is, next dore north from the
smyth's shop, opposite to the Three Cuppes[e] (as I take it).
He was a batchelour and delighted in his scholar, T. H.'s
company, and used to instruct him, and two or three
ingeniose youths more, in the evening till nine a clock.
Here T. H. so well profited in his learning, that at fourteen
yeares of age, he went away a good schoole-scholar to
Magdalen-hall, in Oxford. It is not to be forgotten, that
before he went to the University, he had turned Euripidis

* MS. Aubr. 9, fol. 32[v].
[a] Quoted from Hobbes' metrical life of himself.
** MS. Aubr. 9, fol. 33.
[b] Dupl. with 'proves.'
[c] Aubrey notes opposite this sentence :—'This is good.'

[d] Dupl. with 'and then.' Subst. for 'at eight yeares of age he could.'
[e] Written at first 'Three Tunnes (quaere William Aubrey)': and then changed when W. A. answered the query.

Medea * out of Greeke into Latin Iambiques, which he
presented to his master. Mr. H. told me that he would faine
have had them, to have seen how he did grow in . . . . .
Twenty odde ᵃ yeares agoe I searcht all old Mr. Latimer's
papers, but could not find them; the ᵇ good huswives
had sacrificed them.

I have heard his brother Edmund and Mr. Wayte (his
schoolefellowe) say that when he was a boy he was
playsome enough, but withall he had even then a contemplative melancholinesse; he would gett him into a
corner, and learne his lesson by heart presently. His
haire was black, and his schoolfellows ᶜ were wont to call
him 'Crowe.'

This Mr. Latimer was a good Graecian, and the first
that came into our parts hereabout since the Reformation.
He was afterwards minister of Malmesbury, and from
thence preferred to a better living of 100 *li.* per annum,
or +, at Leigh-de-la-mere within this hundred.

At Oxford Mr. T. H. used, in the summer time especially,
to rise very early in the morning, and would tye the leaden-
counters (which they used in those dayes at Christmas,
at post and payre) with pacthreds ᵈ, which he did besmere
with ᵉ birdlime, and bayte them with parings of cheese, and
the jack-dawes would spye them a vast distance up in the
aire †, and as far as Osney-abbey, and strike at
the bayte, and so be harled in the string,
which the wayte of the counter would make
cling about ther wings. He did not much
care for logick, yet he learnd it, and thought himselfe a
good disputant. He tooke great delight there to goe to
the ᶠ booke-binders' shops, and lye gaping on mappes, of
which he takes notice in his life written by himselfe in
verse :

† This story he
happened to tell
me, discoursing
of the Optiques,
to instance such
sharpnes of sight
in so little an eie.

---

* MS. Aubr. 9, fol. 34.
ᵃ Dupl. with '25 +.'
ᵇ Dupl. with 'the oven' ⟨dupl. with
'pies'⟩ 'had devoured them.'
ᶜ Dupl. with 'the boyes.'

ᵈ Dupl. with 'strings.'
ᵉ Dupl. with 'draw through.'
ᶠ Anthony Wood corrects to 'the
stationers' shops.'

Ergo ad amoena magis me verto, librosque revolvo,
  Quos prius edoctus, non bene doctus eram.
* Pascebamque animum chartis imitantibus orbem,
  Telluris faciem, et sydera picta videns,
Gaudebam soli comes ire, et cernere cunctis
  Terricolis justos qua facit arte dies ; etc.

** Quaere A⟨nthony⟩ W⟨ood⟩ what moneth and day he was matriculated ?

[He^a came^b to Magdalen hall in the beginning of an. 1603, at what time, Dr. James Hussee, LL.D., was principall. This James Hussee was afterwards knighted by king James and was made Chancellour of Sarum. This Dr. Hussee was a great encourager of towardly youths. But he resigning his principallity about 1605, Mr. John Wilkinson succeeded him: so that Mr. Hobs was under the government of two principalls.¹¹—Thomas Hobs was admitted to the reading of any book of logic ('ad^c lectionem cujuslibet libri logices '), that is, he was admitted to the degree of Bachelaur of Arts, 5 Feb., 1607^d, and in the Lent that then began did determine^e, that is, did his exercise for the completion of that degree. Vide *Hist. ⟨et Antiq. Univ.⟩ Oxon.*, lib. 2, pag. 376 a.]

⟨Enters the earl of Devonshire's service.⟩

*** After he had taken his batchelor of Arts degree (quaere A. Wood de hoc), the than principall of Magdalen-hall (Sir James Hussey^f) recommended him to his yong lord when he left Oxon, who had a conceit^g that he should profitt more in his learning if he had a scholar of his owne age to wayte on him then if he had the information of a grave doctor. He was his lordship's page, and rode a hunting and hawking with him, and kept his privy-purse.

By this way of life he had almost forgott his Latin; vide Latin verses. He therefore * bought him bookes of an Amsterdam print that he might carry in his pocket (particularly Caesar's Commentarys), which he did read in the lobbey, or ante-chamber, whilest his lord was making his visits.

⟨*Is servant to Francis Bacon.*⟩

The Lord Chancellour Bacon loved to converse † with him.

† This, I beleeve, was after his first lord's death ᵇ.

He assisted his lordship in translating severall of his Essayes into Latin, one, I well remember, is ᶜ that *Of the Greatnes of Cities*: the rest I have forgott. His lordship was a very contemplative person, and was wont to contemplate in his delicious walkes at Gorambery ¹², and dictate to Mr. Thomas Bushell, or some other of his gentlemen, that attended him with inke and paper ready to sett downe presently his thoughts. His lordship would often say that he better liked Mr. Hobbes's taking his thoughts ᵈ, then any of the other, because he understood what he wrote, which the others not understanding, my Lord * would many times have a hard taske to make sense of what they writt.

It is to be remembred that about these times, Mr. T. H. was much addicted to musique, and practised on the base-violl.

⟨*Visits his native county, Wiltshire.*⟩

1634: this summer—I remember 'twas in venison season ᵉ (July or August)—Mr. T. H. came into his native country ᶠ to visitt his friends, and amongst others he came

---

ᵃ Dupl. with 'then.'

ᵇ The chronology is here difficult. William Cavendish, second earl of Devonshire, died 20 June, 1628; and it is he whom Hobbes regarded as his 'first' lord (see his inscription, *infra*, p. 386), not his father William, first earl, who died 3 March, 162⅘. Bacon died 9 Apr. 1626.

ᶜ Dupl. with 'was.'

ᵈ Dupl. with 'notions.'

* MS. Aubr. 9, fol. 36.

ᵉ Subst. for 'time'

ᶠ In the first attempt at this paragraph Aubrey wrote, 'T. H. came into his native country. I was then a little youth and went to schoole to Mr. Robert Latimer at Leigh-de-la-mere in the church about a mile from my father's house (Easton Pierse).'

then to see his old school-master, Mr. Robert Latimer †,

at Leigh-de-la-mer, where I was then at
schoole ‡ in the church ª, newly entred into my
grammar by him. Here was the first place and
time that ever I had the honour to see this
worthy, learned man, who was then pleased to
take notice of me, and the next day visited ᵇ my
relations ᶜ. He was then a proper man, briske,
and in very good habit ᵈ. His hayre was then
quite black ᵉ. He stayed at Malmsbury and
in the neighborhood a weeke or better. 'Twas
the last time that ever he was in Wiltshire.

‡ I had then a fine little horse and commonly rode —(but this is impertinent)— i.e. I was not a vulgar boy and carried not a satchell at my back.—Sed hoc inter nos.— MS. Aubr. 9, fol. 31.

* His conversation about those times was much about
Ben: Jonson, Mr. Ayton, etc.

⟨*His mathematical studies.*⟩

** He was (vide his life) 40 yeares ᶠ old before he looked
on geometry ; which happened accidentally. Being in a
gentleman's library in . . . , Euclid's Elements lay open,
and 'twas the 47 El. ᵍ libri I. He read the proposition.

† He would now and then sweare, by way of emphasis ᵇ. 'By † G—,' sayd he, 'this is impossible !' So
he reads the demonstration of it, which referred
him back to such a proposition ; which proposition he read. That referred him back to another, which
he also read. Et sic deinceps, that at last he was demon-
stratively convinced of that trueth. This made him in
love with geometry.

I have heard Sir Jonas Moore (and others ¹³) say
that 'twas a great pity he had not began the study of

ª In a second attempt it stood '. . . at Leigh-de-la-mere. I was then a little youth newly entred into my grammar by him, and we went to schoole in the church.'

ᵇ Dupl. with 'came to.'

ᶜ Dupl. with 'friends.'

ᵈ Dupl. with 'equipage'

ᵉ Here followed 'and moist-curled,' dupl. with 'and with moist curles';

but both struck out.

* MS. Aubr. 9, fol. 35ᵛ.

** MS. Aubr. 9, fol. 36.

ᶠ Anthony Wood writes here 'do not you mean 40 ?' Aubrey had written ' 4 ' by a pen-slip ; afterwards he corrected it.

ᵍ ' Element ' used for 'proposition.'

ᵇ Subst. for 'He would now and then use an emphaticall oath.'

the mathematics sooner, for such a working head [a] would have made great advancement in it. So had he donne [b], he would not have layn so open to his learned mathematicall antagonists [c]. But one may say of him, as one (quaere who) sayes of Jos. Scaliger, that where he erres, he erres so ingeniosely, that one had rather erre with him then hitt the mark [d] with Clavius. I have heard Mr. Hobbes say * that he was wont to draw lines [e] on his thigh and on the sheetes, abed, and [f] also multiply and divide. He

acuteness of intellect

[†] Vide de hoc in his *De corpore*, and also in his 5 Dialogue. Quaere Dr. Blackburne :— MS. Aubr. 9, fol. 36 .

would often complain that algebra † (though of great use) was too much admired, and so followed after, that it made men not contemplate and consider so much the nature and power of lines, which was a great hinderance to the groweth of geometrie; for that though algebra did rarely well and quickly, and easily in right lines, yet 'twould not *bite* in *solid* (I thinke) geometrie. Quod N.B.

** Memorandum—After he began to reflect on [g] the interest of the king of England as touching his affaires between him and the parliament, for ten yeares together his thoughts were much, or almost altogether, unhinged from the mathematiques; but chiefly intent on his *De Cive*, and after that on his *Leviathan*: which was a great putt-back to his mathematicall improvement [h]—quod N.B.—for in ten yeares' (or better) discontinuance of that study (especially) one's mathematiques will become very rusty [i].

⟨*Champions the king's cause against the parliament.*⟩

*** Vide *Mr. Hobbes considered*, p. 4: printed London 1662 (since reprinted, 1680, by William Crooke):—

1640: 'when the parliament sate that began in April 1640 and was dissolved in May following, and in which

---

[a] Dupl. with 'curious witt.'
[b] 'Began it early' is written over, in explanation.
[c] Dupl. with 'to the witts.'
[d] Dupl. with 'then doe well.'
* MS. Aubr. 9, fol. 37
[e] 'In his bed' followed, scored out.

[f] Dupl. with 'as.'
** MS. Aubr. 9, fol. 36ᵛ.
[g] Dupl. with 'study.'
[h] Dupl. with 'knowledge.'
[i] Dupl. with 'rubiginous.'
*** MS. Aubr. 9, fol. 37.

many pointes of the regall power, which were necessary for the peace of the kingdome and safety of his majestye's person, were disputed * and denyed, Mr. Hobbes wrote a little treatise in English, wherin he did sett-forth and demonstrate, that the sayd power and rights were inseperably annexed to the soveraignty, which soveraignty they did not then deny to be in the king; but it seemes understood not, or would not understand, that inseperability. Of this treatise, though not printed, many gentlemen had copies, which occasioned much talke of the author; and had not his majestie dissolved the parliament, it had brought him in danger of his life.'

* Vide *Mr. Hobbes considered*, if more may not be inserted, scilicet as to the politiques. Sed cave—

<blockquote>
Incedis per ignes
Suppositos cineri doloso.
HORATIUS *ad Asin. Pollionem*, ode 1, lib. 2.
</blockquote>

Memorandum the parliament was then sitting and runne violently against the king's prerogative.

** Memorandum he told me that bp. Manwaring [b] (of St. David's) preach'd *his doctrine*; for which, among others, he was sent prisoner to the Tower. Then thought Mr. Hobbes, 'tis time now for me to shift for my selfe, and so withdrew [c] into France, and resided [d] at Paris. As I remember, there were others [e] likewise did preach his doctrine. This little MS. treatise grew to be [f] his book *De Cive* [g], and at last grew there to be the so formidable and . . . LEVIATHAN; the manner of writing of which booke (he told me) was thus. He walked much and contemplated, and he had in the head of his staffe [h] a pen and inke-horne, carried alwayes a note-booke in his pocket,

---

[a] Subst. for 'discussed.'
* MS. Aubr. 9, fol. 38ᵛ.
** MS. Aubr. 9, fol. 37.
[b] Anthony Wood notes 'Roger Manneringe.'
[c] Dupl. with 'went.'

[d] 'Mostly' followed: scored out.
[e] Anthony Wood notes 'Robert Sibthorpe, vicar of Brackley.'
[f] Dupl. with 'became.'
[g] 'At Paris' followed: scored out.
[h] Dupl. with 'cane.'

and as soon as a thought [a] darted, he presently entred it into his booke, or otherwise he might [b] perhaps have lost it. He had drawne the designe of the booke into chapters, etc. so he knew whereabout it would come in. Thus that booke was made.

'He wrote and published the Leviathan far from the intention either of disadvantage to his majestie, or to flatter Oliver (who was not made Protector till three or four yeares after) on purpose to facilitate his returne ; for there is scarce a page in it that he does not upbraid him.'— *Mr. Hobbes considered*, p. 8.

* ''Twas written in the behalfe of the faithfull subjects of his majestie, that had taken his part in the war, or otherwise donne their utmost endeavour to defend his majestie's right and person against the rebells : wherby, having no other meanes of protection, nor (for the most part) of subsistence, were forced to compound with your masters, and to promise obedience for the saving of their lives and fortunes, which, in his booke he hath affirmed, they might lawfully doe, and consequently not bear arms against the victors. They had done their utmost endeavour to performe their obligation to the king, had done all they could be obliged unto ; and were consequently at liberty to seeke the safety of their lives and livelihood wheresoever, and without treachery.'—⟨ibid.⟩ p. 20.

'His majestie was displeased with him' (at Paris) 'for a while, but not very long, by means of some's complayning of and misconstruing his writing. But his majestie had a good opinion of him, and sayd openly that he thought Mr. Hobbes never meant him hurt.'—p. 28.

'Before his booke *De Homine* came forth, nothing of the optiques writt intelligibly. As for the Optiques of Vitellio [c], and several others, he accounts them rather geometry than optiques.'—p. 54. [Will not this p. 54 more aptly come in in another place ?]

'So also of all other arts ; not every one that brings

[a] Dupl. with 'notion.'
[b] Dupl. with ' or els he should.'
* MS. Aubr. 9, fol. 38.
[c] Subst. for 'of Euclid and Vitellio.'

from beyond seas a new gin, or other janty devise, is
therfore a philosopher. For if you reckon that way, not
only apothecaries and gardiners, but many other sorts of
workmen will put-in for, and get the prize—

'Then, * when I see the gentlemen of Gresham Colledge
apply themselves to the doctrine of motion (as Mr. Hobbes
has done, and will be ready to helpe them in it, if they
please, and so long as they use him civilly), I will looke
to know some causes of naturall events from them, and
their register, and not before; for nature does nothing but
by motion.

'The reason given by him, why the drop of glasse so much
wondred at shivers into so many pieces by breaking only
one small part of it, is approved for probable by the Royall
Societie and registred in their colledge : † but
he has no reason to take it for a favour, because
hereafter the invention may be taken, by that
means, not for his, but theirs.'—p. 55.

'As for his selfe-prayse ‡, they can have very
little skill in morality, that cannot see the justice
of commending a man's selfe, as well as of any
thing else, in his own defence.'—p. 57.

† This clause I
leave to your
judgment, if not
fitt to be left out.
—MS. Aubr. 9,
fol. 38ᵛ.
‡ Should these
excerpts of his
moralls come in
here, or rather
be cast-after to
another place ?
—MS. Aubr. 9,
fol. 38ᵛ.

'Then for his morosity and peevishnesse, with which
some asperse him, all that know him familiarly, know the
contrary. 'Tis true that when vain and ignorant young
scholars, unknowne to him before, come to him on purpose
to argue with him, and fall into undiscreet and uncivill
expressions, and he then appeare not well contented, 'twas
not his morosity, but their vanity, which should be blamed.'—
⟨*Mr. Hobbes considered*⟩ p. 59.

⟨*Residence in Paris.*⟩

** During his stay at Paris he went through a course
of chymistry with Dr. . . . Davison; and he there
also studied Vesalius's Anatomie. This I am sure was
before 1648; for that Sir William Petty (then Dr. Petty,

physitian) studied and dissected with him. Vide pag. 18 b. A. W. [a]

⟨Return to England.⟩

† Quaere de hoc: vide his life.—'Twas 1650 or 1651.— MS. Aubr. 9, fol. 38ᵛ. ‡ Quaere etiam de hoc. I thinke true as I remember.— MS. Aubr. 9, fol. 38ᵛ.

* Anno 165–†, he returned into England, and lived most part ‡ in London, in Fetter lane, where he writt, or finished, his booke *De Corpore*, . . . [b], in Latin and then in English; and writt his lessons against the two Savillian professors at Oxon °, etc.; vide the anno Domini when printed. (Puto 1655 or 56.)

⟨Kindness to his nephew.⟩

§ Or brother: I have now forgott. But surely 'twas to his nephewe ᵈ.— MS. Aubr. 9, fol. 39ᵛ. ‖ I doe not insert this to be published, but only my familiar way of writing to you and to give to you the greater testimonie.— MS. Aubr. 9, fol. 39ᵛ.

** 1655 or 1656: about this time he setled the piece of land (aforesayd), given to him by his uncle, upon his nephew Francis § for life, the remaynder to his nephew's eldest son, Thomas Hobbes. He also not long after ° dischardged a mortgage (to my knowledge ‖, to Richard Thorne, an attorney) of two hundred pounds, besides the interest thereof, with which his nephew Francis (a careles ᶠ husband) had incumbred his estate.

⟨Residence in London.⟩

He was much in London till the restauration of his majesty, having here convenience not only of bookes, but of learned conversation, as Mr. John Selden, Dr. William Harvey, John Vaughan, etc., wherof anon in the catalogue of his acquaintance.

I have heard him say, that at his lord's house in the

[a] i. e. fol. 50ᵛ of the MS., where is a note by Anthony Wood, as given *infra*, p. 367.

* MS. Aubr. 9, fol. 39.

[b] Subst. for 'which came out anno . . .' Anthony Wood notes, 'Vide catalogue of ⟨Hobbes's⟩ books in *Hist.* ⟨*et Antiq. Univ.*⟩ *Oxon.*, and vide transcript thence.'—MS. Aubr. 9, fol. 38ᵛ.

[c] 'his *Dialogi*' followed: scored out.

** MS. Aubr. 9, fol. 40.

[d] In MS. Aubr. 3, fol. 28, Aubrey says that Thomas Hobbes gave it to 'his elder brother, named Edmund Hobbes.'

[e] 'a yeare +' followed: scored out.

[f] Dupl. with 'an ill.'

countrey[a] there was a good library, and bookes enough for him, and that his lordship stored the library with what

† Methinkes in the country, in long time, for want of good conversation, one's under-standing (witt, invention) growes mouldy.—MS. Aubr. 9, fol. 39ᵛ.

bookes he thought fitt to be bought; but he sayd, the want of learned [b] conversation † was a very great inconvenience[c], and that though he conceived[d] he could order his thinking as well perhaps as another man, yet he found a great defect[e].

〈*Acquaintance and studies.*〉

Amongst other of his acquaintance I must not forget our common friend, Mr. Samuel Cowper, the prince of limners of this last age, who drew his picture † as like

‡ This picture I intend ' to be borrowed of his majesty, for Mr. 〈David〉 Loggan to engrave an accurate piece by, which will sell well both at home and abroad. Mr. Loggan is well acquainted.—MS. Aubr. 9, fol. 39ᵛ.

as art could afford, and one of the best pieces that ever he did: which his majesty, at his returne, bought of him, and conserves as one of his great rarities in his closet at Whitehall.

* 1659. In 1659 his lord was—and some yeares before—at Little Salisbury-house (now turned to the Middle-Exchange), where he wrot, among other things, a poeme, in Latin hexameter and pentameter, of the encroachment of the clergie (both Roman and reformed) on the civil power [14]. I remember I saw then 500 + verses, for he numbred every tenth as he wrote. I remember he did read Cluverius's *Historia Universalis*, and made-up his poeme from thence. His amanuensis remembers this poeme, for he wrote them out, but knows 〈not what became of it〉.

His place of meditation was then in the portico in the garden.

His manner [g] *of thinking:*—he sayd that he sometimes

---

[a] Dupl. with ' in Derbyshire.'
[b] Dupl. with 'good.'
[c] Dupl. with 'want.'
[d] Subst. for 'thought.'
[e] Aubrey notes opposite this: ' better this expression.'
[f] Dupl. with 'designe.'
* MS. Aubr. 9, fol. 42. On fol.

41ᵛ Aubrey makes this apology for its coming there out of due order of time :—' Give notice how things are to be right placed, for all things comes not into my memory chronologically and this seemes almost necessary to be forced.'
[g] Dupl. with 'way.'

would sett his thoughts upon researching[a] and contemplating, always with this rule[b] that he very much and deeply considered one thing at a time (scilicet, a weeke or sometimes a fortnight). ∨

There was a report ‡ (and surely true) that in parliament, not long after the king was setled, some of the bishops made a motion to have the good old gentleman burn't for a heretique. Which he hearing, feared that his papers might be search't by their order, and he told me he had burn't part of them.—I have received word[d] from his amanuensis and executor that he 'remembers there were such verses[e] for he wrote them out, but knowes not what became of them, unlesse he presented them to Judge Vaughan[f], or burned them as I did seeme to intimate.' ☞ But I understand since by W. Crooke, that he can retrive a good[g] many of them.

† Quaere[c] the bishop of Sarum de hoc, i.e. pro tempore.—MS. Aubr. 9, fol. 41ᵛ.

⟨Secures the protection of Charles II.⟩

* 1660. The[h] winter-time of 1659 he spent in Derbyshire. In ¹⁵March following was the dawning of the coming in of our gracious soveraigne, and in April the Aurora.

** I then sent a letter to him in the countrey to advertise him of the Advent[i] of his master the king and desired him by all meanes to be in London before his arrivall; and knowing[k] his majestie was a great lover of good painting I must needs presume he could not but suddenly see

---

[a] Subst. for 'researching and contemplating one thing, then of another; but he had a method for it.'

[b] Dupl. with 'proviso' or 'observation.'

[c] MS. Aubr. 9, fol. 7—'quaere bishop Sarum when he was motioned to be burnt.' *Ibid.*, fol. 7ᵛ, 'Quaere bp. Sarum ⟨Seth Ward⟩ who and when (annum) the motion in parliament was to have Mr. Hobbes burnt.'

[d] *Infra*, p. 382.

[e] Dupl. with 'such a poeme.'

[f] Sir John Vaughan, Chief Justice of the Common Pleas, 1668–1674.

[g] Dupl. with 'great.'

* MS. Aubr. 9, fol. 40.

[h] Subst. for '1660. The winter before (of 1659) he spent his time in Derbyshire.'

** MS. Aubr. 9, fol. 39ᵛ.

[i] Dupl. with 'good newes.'

[k] Dupl. with 'hearing.'

Mr. Cowper's curious pieces, of whose fame he had so much heard abroad and seene some of his worke, and likewise that he would sitt to him for his picture, at which place and time he would have the best convenience^a of renewing his majestie's graces to him. *He returned me thankes for my friendly intimation and came to London in May following.

It happened, about two or three dayes after his majestie's happy returne, that, as he was passing in his coach through the Strand, Mr. Hobbes was standing at Little Salisbury-house gate (where his lord then lived). The king espied him, putt of his hatt very kindly to him, and asked him how he did. About a weeke after he had^b orall conference with his majesty at^c Mr. S. Cowper's, where, as he sate for his picture, he was diverted^d by Mr. Hobbes's pleasant discourse^e. Here his majestie's favours were redintegrated to him, and order was given that he should have free accesse to his majesty, who was always much delighted in his witt and smart repartees.

The witts at Court were wont to bayte him. But he

† This is too low witt to be published.—MS. Aubr. 9, fol. 40ᵛ.

feared none of them ^f, and would make his part good. The king would call him *the beare* † : ' Here comes the beare to be bayted! '

Repartees. He was marvellous happy and ready in his replies, and that without rancor (except provoked)—but now^g I speake of his readinesse in replies as to witt and drollery. He would say that he did not care to give, neither was he adroit ^h at, a present answer to a serious quaere : he had as lieve they should have expected an ⁱ extemporary solution to an arithmeticall probleme, for he turned and winded and compounded in philosophy, politiques, etc., as if he had

---

^a Dupl. with ' opportunity.'
* MS. Aubr. 9, fol. 41.
^b Aubrey writes opposite on fol. 40ᵛ:—' *embouche*, such word in English ?'
^c MS. has 'and,' by a slip for 'at.'
^d Dupl. with ' enterteyned.'
^e Dupl. with ' facetiae.'

^f Dupl. with ' the witts.'
^g Aubrey wishes to limit the readiness in reply to cases of light badinage: in serious subjects Hobbes was slow and deliberate.
^h Dupl. with ' good.'
ⁱ Dupl. with ' a present answer.'

been at analyticall[a] worke. He alwayes avoided, as much
as he could, to conclude hastily (*Humane Nature*, p. 2).
Vide[b] p. 15 b.

⟨*Re-enters the household of the earl of Devonshire.*⟩

† Quaere when.
Quaere W.
Crooke de hoc.
[You[d] say
somewhere[e]
that he went
into Derbyshire,
1675. Here,
while he was at
London, he was
much sought
after and
courted : taught
and directed
those that sought
after him.]—MS.
Aubr. 9, fol. 41[v].

* Memorandum—from 1660 till the time †
he[c] last went into Derbyshire, he spent most of
his time in London at his lord's (viz. at Little
Salisbury-howse; then, Queen Street; lastly,
Newport-house), following his contemplation
and study. ☞ He contemplated and
invented (set downe a hint with a pencill
or so) in the morning, but compiled[f] in the
afternoon.

⟨*His treatise De Legibus.*⟩

1664. In[g] 1664 I sayd to him ' Me thinkes 'tis pitty that
you that have such a cleare reason and working[h] head did
never take into consideration the learning of the lawes';
and I endeavoured to perswade him to it. But he answered
that[i] he was not like to have life enough left to goe through
with such a long and difficult taske. I then presented him
the lord chancellor Bacon's Elements of the Lawe (a thin
quarto), in order therunto and to drawe him on; which he
was pleased to accept, and perused; and the next time I
came to him he shewed me therin two cleare paralogismes in
the 2nd page (*one*, I well remember, was in page 2), which
I am heartily sory are now out of my remembrance.
** I desponded, for his reasons, that he should make any
tentamen[k] towards this designe; but afterwards, it seemes, in
the countrey he writt his treatise *De Legibus* [16] (unprinted)

[a] Dupl. with ' mathematicall.'
[b] i. e. see further about this on fol.
45[v] of the MS., the note found *infra*,
p. 356.
* MS. Aubr. 9, fol. 42.
[e] Subst. for ' he last left London,
he was often in London at his lord's.'
[d] The two sentences in square
brackets are added by Anthony Wood.

[e] *Infra*, p. 346.
[f] Dupl. with ' penned': see *infra*,
p. 351.
[g] Subst. for ' about.'
[h] Dupl. with ' inventive.'
[i] Subst. for ' that 'twas a long,
taedious, and difficult taske.'
** MS. Aubr. 9, fol. 43.
[k] Dupl. with ' attempt.'

of which Sir John Vaughan, Lord Chiefe Justice of the Common Pleas, had a transcript, and I doe affirme that he much admired it.

* Insert here part of his lettre to me about it.

'Tis thus, viz., in a letter to me[a], dated Aug. 18, 1679, among severall other things, he writes[b] :—

' I have been told that my booke of the Civill Warr is come abroad and am heartily sorry for it, especially because I could not get his majestie to license it, not because it is ill printed or hath a foolish title set to it, for I beleeve that any ingeniose man may understand the wickednes of

† Quaere is it best to let the letter stand whole[c] or to let that part, of the Civill Warr, be referred to the catalogue of bookes?

that time, notwithstanding the errors of the presse †.

' The treatise *De Legibus* (at the end of it) is imperfect. I desire Mr. Horne[d] to pardon me that I cannot consent to his motion ; nor shall Mr. Crooke himselfe get my consent to print it.

' I pray you present my humble thankes to Mr. Sam. Butler.

'The privilege of stationers is, in my opinion, a very great hinderance to the advancement of all humane learning[e].

' I am, sir, your very humble servant,

' Th. Hobbes.'

⟨*Proposed foundation at Malmsbury.*⟩

** 1665. This yeare he told me that he was willing to doe some good to the towne where he was borne ; that his majestie loved him well, and if I could find out something in our countrey that was in his guift, he did beleeve he could

‡ The burghesses give a school-master X *li.* per annum out of their . . . .

beg it of his majestie, and seeing[f] he was bred a scholar, he thought it most proper to endowe[g] a free-schoole there ; which is wanting *now* ‡ (for, before the reformation, all monasteries had great

---

* MS. Aubr. 9, fol. 42ᵛ.
[a] Dupl. with ' I. A.'
[b] Subst. for ' sayes.'
[c] Dupl. with ' together.'
[d] A London bookseller, who had offered to publish an authorized copy.

[e] Subst. for ' knowledge.'
** MS. Aubr. 9, fol. 43.
[f] Dupl. with ' since.'
[g] Dupl. with ' found': and subst. for ' erect.'

schooles appendant to them; e. g. Magdalen schoole and
New College schoole). After ᵃ enquiry I found out a piece
of land in Bradon-forest (of about 25 *li.* per annum value)
that was in his majesties guift ᵇ, which he designed ᶜ to
have obtained of his majestie for a salary for
a schoolmaster; but † the queen's priests ᵈ
smelling-out the designe and being ᵉ his
enemies, hindred ᶠ this publique and charitable
intention.

† Aubrey queries—'Will not this give offence?'— Anthony Wood replies—'Perhaps no.'—MS. Aubr. 9, fol. 42ᵛ.

⟨ Controversy with Dr. John Fell ⟩

[1674 ᵍ. Anno ʰ Domini 1674 Mr. Anthony à Wood sett
forth an elaborate worke of eleven ⁱ yeares study,
intituled *the History and Antiquities of the
University of Oxford*, wherin, in every respective
Colledge and Hall, he mentions the writers
there educated and what bookes they wrote.
The deane of Christ Church having plenipoten-
tiary ᵏ power of the presse there], perused
every sheet before 'twas to be sent to the
presse ˡ; and maugre the author and to his ᵐ sore
displeasure did expunge and inserted what he
pleased. Among other authors ‡, he made
divers alterations in Mr. Wood's copie in the
account he gives of Mr. T. Hobbes of Malmesbury's life,
in pag. 444, 445 ⁿ, Lib. II—

‡ Memorandum —bishop John Fell did not only expunge and insert what he pleased in Mr. Hobbes' life; but also in the lives of other very learned men, to their disparagement, particularly of Dr. John Prideaux, afterwards bishop of Worcester, and in the life of Dr. ⟨William⟩ Twiss.—MS. Aubr. 9, fol. 48ᵛ.

ᵃ Subst. for 'Upon.'
ᵇ Dupl. with 'power' or 'possession.'
ᶜ Dupl. with 'hoped.'
ᵈ Dupl. with 'but queen Katharine.'
ᵉ Dupl. with 'hating him.'
ᶠ Dupl. with 'prevented.'
ᵍ '1674' is struck out and 1 ⁴⁴⁸ substituted for it—this latter being the date of Wood's altercations with Dr. Fell. 1674 was the date of publication: see *infra.*
ʰ Anthony Wood struck out the passage enclosed in square brackets, and sent Aubrey a more elaborate account (now fol. 48, 48ᵛ of MS. Aubr. 9) to take its place. This is printed

in Clark's Wood's *Life and Times,* ii. 291, 292; and is perhaps the paper which Wood blames Aubrey for having kept, *ibid.* ii. 475, 476.
ⁱ Aubrey added, in the margin, the correction 'A. W. sayes but ten.'
ᵏ Dupl. with 'the absolute.'
ˡ Wood adds 'and after.'
ᵐ Dupl. with 'his great griefe, expunged and inserted what he thought fitt.'
ⁿ Corrected by Wood to '376, 377.' The mistake is made in Hobbes's printed epistle, and Aubrey copied it thence.

'Vir sane de quo (inter tot prosperae et adversae famae
qui de eo sparguntur hominum sermones) hoc verissime
pronuntiare fas est, animum ipsi obtigisse, uti omnis scientiae
capacissimum et infertum, ita divitiarum, saeculi, et invidiae
negligentissimum ; erga cognatos et alios pium et beneficum ;
inter eos quibuscum vixit, hilarem et apertum, et sermone
libero ; apud exteros in summa semper veneratione habitum,'
&c. ; this and much more was quite dashed out of the
author's copie by the sayd deane.

† Me thinkes ᵃ
page 15 might
be something
extracted and
abridged; but
doe you consider
of it.
* These † additions and expunctions being
made by the sayd deane of Christ Church,
without ᵇ the knowledge or advice of the authour
and quite contrary to his mind, he told him
it was fitt Mr. Hobbes should know it ᶜ, because that
his name being set to the booke and all people knowing
it to be his, he should be liable to an answer, and so consequently be in perpetuall controversie.   To this the deane
replied, 'Yea, in God's name ; and great reason it was
that he should know what he had done, and what he had
donne he would answer for,' etc.

1674. Hereupon ᵈ, the author acquaints ᵉ J. A., Mr.
Hobbes's correspondent, with all that had passed ; J. A.
acquaints Mr. Hobbes.   Mr. Hobbes takeing it ill, was
resolved to vindicate himselfe in an Epistle to the Author.
Accordingly an epistle, dated Apr. 20, 1674, was sent to
the author in MS., with an intention to publish it when the
History of Oxford was to be published.   Upon the reciept
of Mr. Hobbes's Epistle by Anthony à Wood, he forthwith
repaired, very honestly and without any guile, to the dean
of Christ Church to communicate it to him ᶠ.   The deane
read it over carelesly, and not without scorne, and when

ᵃ Note on fol. 43ᵛ of MS. Aubr. 9.
'Page 15' in Aubrey's numbering is
now fol. 45 of the MS.
  * MS. Aubr. 9, fol. 45.
  ᵇ Corrected by Wood to 'without
the advice and quite contrary to the
mind of the author.'
  ᶜ Corrected by Wood to 'know

what he had done.'
  ᵈ Wood adds 'in the beginning of
1674.'
  ᵉ i. e. John Aubrey.
  ᶠ Wood adds 'and to let him see
that he would do nothing underhand
against him.'

he had donne, bid Mr. Wood tell Mr. Hobbes, 'that he was an old man, had one foote in the grave, that he should mind his latter end, and not trouble the world any more with his papers,' etc., or to that effect.

In the meane time Mr. Hobbes meetes with the king in the Pall-mall, in St. James's parke; tells him how he had been served by the deane of Christ Church, in a booke then in the presse (scilicet the 'History' aforesayd), intituled the History and Antiquities of the Universitie of Oxon, and withall desires his majestie to be pleased to give him leave to vindicate himselfe. The king seeming to be troubled at the dealing of the deane, gave Mr. Hobbes leave, conditionally that he touch no-body but him who had abused him, neither that he should reflect upon the Universitie.

Mr. Hobbes understanding that this History would be published at the common Act at Oxon, about 11 July, the said yeare 1674, prints his Epistle[a] at London, and sends downe divers copies to Oxon, which being dispersed at coffee-houses and stationers' shops, a copie forthwith came to the deane's hands, who upon the reading of it fretted and fumed[b], sent[c] for the author of the History and chid him, telling withall that he had corresponded with his enemie (Hobbes). The author replied that surely he had forgot what he had donne, for he had communicated to him before what Mr. Hobbes had sayd and written; wherupon the deane recollecting himselfe, told him that Hobbes should suddenly heare more of him[d]; so that the last sheete[e] of paper being then in the presse and one leafe thereof being left vacant, the deane supplied it

[a] Wood adds 'that he had sent to Mr. Wood.' See Clark's Wood's *Life and Times*, ii. 288.

[b] Wood adds 'at it as a most famous libell.'

[c] Corrected by Wood to 'and, soon after, meeting with the author.'

[d] Wood adds ' and that he would have the printer called to account for printing such a notorious libell.'

[e] The advance-copies of Wood's *Hist. et Antiq. Univ. Oxon.* were issued July 17, 1674 (Wood's *Life and Times*, ii. 289); the ordinary issue took place on July 27 (*ibid.*, 290), being perhaps delayed for the insertion of the rejoinder to Hobbes; Hobbes's epistle had been circulated on July 11 (*ibid.*, p. 288).

with this answer. Both the epistle and answer I here exhibite.

* Here insert the Epistle [a] and Answer [b].

To this angry [c] answer the old gentleman never [d] made any reply, but slighted [e] the Dr's passion and forgave it. But 'tis supposed it might be the cause why Mr. Hobbes was not afterwards so indulgent, or spared the lesse to speake his opinion, concerning the Universities and how much their doctrine and method had contributed to the late troubles [e. g. in his History of the Civill Warre].

⟨ *Withdraws to Derbyshire.* ⟩

1675, mense . . . , he left London *cum animo nunquam revertendi*, and spent the remaynder of his dayes in Derbyshire with the earl of Devonshire at Chatsworth and Hardwyck, in contemplation and study. He wrote there [f] . . . (vide vitam).

⟨ *His death and burial.* ⟩

** Then [g], ⟨insert an account of⟩ his sicknesse, death, buriall and place, and epitaph, *which send for* [h].

*** Extracted out of the executor's lettre (January 16, 1679) to me :—

'To his highly honoured friend, Jo. Aubrey, esq., these.'—

(His sicknesse) 'Worthy sir—he fell sick about the middle of October last,' etc. [i]—

**** ☞ He dyed worth neer 1000 *li.*, which (considering his charity) was more then I expected: vide his verses [k] in the last page.—From W. Crooke, from Mr. Jackson who had 500 *li.* of his in his hands.—

---

* MS. Aubr. 9, fol. 46.

[a] Aubrey inserts a copy as fol. 44 of MS. Aubr. 9.

[b] See it in Wood's *Hist. et Antiq.* at the end.

[c] Dupl. with 'scurrilous.'

[d] Subst. for 'never replied.'

[e] Dupl. with 'neglected.'

[f] See *infra*, p. 363.

** MS. Aubr. 9, fol. 53[v].

[g] Aubrey proposed bringing this in after the Catalogue of his writings: but it is better here.

[h] See the answers to these enquiries in the letters appended to this life.

*** MS. Aubr. 9, fol. 22[v].

[i] As in the letter *infra*, p. 382.

**** MS. Aubr. 9, fol. 53[v].

[k] i. e. the metrical autobiography, *infra*, p. 363.

⟨*Personal characteristics.*⟩

* Describe face, eyes, forehead, nose, mouth, eyebrows, figure of the face, complexion; stature of body; shape (slender, large, neat, or otherwise); figure of head and magnitude of head; shoulders (large, round, etc.); arms, legs, how ?—

** Mr. Hobbes's person, etc. :—hazel, quick eie, which continued to his last. He was a tall man, higher then I am by about halfe a head (scil. . . . feet), i. e. I could putt my hand between my head and his hatt.—When young he loved musique and practised on the lute. In his old age he used to sing prick-song every night (when all were gonne and sure nobody could heare him) for his health, which he did beleeve would make him live two or three yeares longer.

*** In his youth unhealthy; of an ill yellowish complexion: wett in his feet, and trod both his shoes the same way.

**** *His complexion.* In his youth he was unhealthy, and of an ill complexion (yellowish).

† This only *inter nos.*—MS. Aubr. 9, fol. 45ᵛ. His † lord, who was a waster, sent him up and downe to borrow money, and to gett gentlemen to be bound for him, being ashamed to speake him selfe: he tooke colds, being wett in his feet (then were no hackney coaches to stand in the streetes), and trod both his shoes aside the same way. Notwithstanding he was well-beloved: they lov'd his company for his pleasant facetiousnes and good-nature ᵃ.

From forty, or better, he grew healthier, and then he had a fresh, ruddy, complexion. He was *sanguineo-melancholicus*; which the physiologers say is the most ingeniose complexion. He would say that 'there might be good witts of all complexions; but good-natured, impossible.'

Head. In his old age he was very bald ᵇ (which claymed a veneration); yet within dore, he used to study, and sitt,

---

* MS. Aubr. 9, fol. 7.
** MS. Aubr. 3, fol. 27ᵛ.
*** MS. Aubr. 3, fol. 28.

**** MS. Aubr. 9, fol. 46.
ᵃ Dupl. with 'suavitas.'
ᵇ Dupl. with 'recalvus.'

bare-headed, and sayd he never tooke cold in his head, but that the greatest trouble was to keepe-off the flies from pitching on the baldnes. His head was . . . inches in compasse (I have the measure), and of a mallet-forme (approved by the physiologers).

* *Skin.* His skin was soft and of that kind which my Lord Chancellor Bacon in his *History of Life and Death* calles a goose-skin, i. e. of a wide texture :—

　　Crassa cutis, crassum cerebrum, crassum ingenium.

Face not very great ; ample forehead ; whiskers yellowish-redish, which naturally turned up—which is a signe of a brisque witt, e.g. James Howell, Henry Jacob of Merton College.

⟨*Beard.*⟩ Belowe he was shaved close, except a little tip under his lip. Not but that nature [a] could have afforded a venerable beard (Sapientem pascere barbam—Horat. Satyr. lib. 2), but being naturally of a cheerfull and pleasant humour [b], he affected not at all austerity and gravity and to looke severe. [Vide [c] page 47 of *Mr. Hobbes considered* —‘Gravity and heavinesse of countenance are not so good marks of assurance of God's favour, as a chearfull, charitable, and upright behaviour, which are better signes of religion than the zealous maintaining of controverted doctrines.’] He desired not [d] the reputation of his wisdome to be taken [e] from the cutt of his beard, but from his reason—

　　Barba non facit philosophum. ‘Il consiste tout en la pointe de sa barbe et en ses deux moustaches ; et, par consequence, pour le diffaire il ne faut que trois coups de ciseau.’—Balzac, *Lettres*, tom. 2, p. 242.

**Eie.* He had a good eie, and that of a hazell colour, which was full of life and spirit, even to the last. When he was earnest in discourse, there shone (as it were)

---

* MS. Aubr. 9, fol. 45ᵛ.

[a] Dupl. with ‘ he.’

[b] Subst. for ‘ nature.’

[c] This quotation is subst. for ‘ He would say that cheerfulnes of counten-ance was a signe of God's grace.’

[d] Dupl. with ‘ depended not on.’

[e] Dupl. with ‘ esteemed ’ or ‘ mea-sured.’

** MS. Aubr. 9, fol. 46.

a bright live-coale within it. * He had two kind of looks :—when he laugh't, was witty, and in a merry humour, one could scarce see his eies; by and by, when he was serious and positive ᵃ, he open'd his eies round (i. e. his eie-lids). He had midling eies, not very big, nor very little (from Sir W⟨illiam⟩ P⟨etty⟩).

** *Stature.* He was six foote high, and something better (quaere James Wh⟨eldon⟩), and went indifferently erect, or rather, considering his great age, very erect.

Sight; witt. His sight and witt continued to the last. He had a curious sharp sight, as he had a sharpe witt, which was also so sure and steady (and contrary to that men call *bro⟨a⟩dwittednes*) that I have heard him often-times say that in *** multiplying and dividing he ᵇ never mistooke a figure : and so in other things.

⟨*Habits of body and mind.*⟩

He thought much and with excellent method and stedi-nesse, which made him seldome make a false step.

His bookes, vide page ° 22. **** ☞ He had very few bookes. I never sawe (nor Sir William Petty) above halfe a dozen about him in his chamber. Homer and Virgil were commonly on his table; sometimes Xenophon, or some probable historie, and Greek Testament, or so.

***** *Reading.* He had read much, if one considers his long life; but ᵈ his contemplation was much more then his reading. He was wont to say that if he had read as much as other men, he ᵉ should have knowne no more then other men.

****** *His physique.* He seldome used any physique (quaere Sir W⟨illiam⟩ P⟨etty⟩). What 'twas I have forgot,

* MS. Aubr. 9, fol. 45ᵛ.
ᵃ Dupl. with ' earnest.'
** MS. Aubr. 9, fol. 46.
*** MS. Aubr. 9, fol. 47.
ᵇ Dupl. with ' he was never out.'
° i. e. fol. 54, as given here. Oppo-site it, on fol. 53ᵛ, is the direction ' Let this be brought in to it's proper place: referre this to p. 17 ' (i.e. fol. 47).

**** MS. Aubr. 9, fol. 54.
***** MS. Aubr. 9, fol. 47.
ᵈ Subst. for ' but 'twas but little in respect of his contemplation (think-ing).'
ᵉ Subst. for ' he should have con-tinued still as ignorant as other men.'
****** MS. Aubr. 9, fol. 46ᵛ.

but will enquire of Mr. Shelbrooke his apothecary at the Black Spread-eagle in the Strand.

Memorandum—Mr. Hobbes was very sick and like to dye at Bristoll-house in Queen Street, about 1668.

* He had a sicknes, anno . . .

He was wont to say that he had rather have the advice, or take physique from an experienced old woman, that had been at many sick people's bed-sides, then from the learnedst but unexperienced physitian.

** 'Tis[a] not consistent with an harmonicall soule to be a woman-hater, neither had he an abhorrescence to good wine but . . .—this only *inter nos*.

*** *Temperance and diet.* He was, even in his youth, (generally) temperate, both as to wine and women, (et tamen haec omnia mediocriter)—

Homo sum, humani nihil a me alienum puto.

I have heard him say that he did beleeve he had been in excesse[b] in his life, a hundred times; which, considering his great[c] age, did not amount to above once a yeare. When he did drinke, he would drinke to excesse to have the benefitt of vomiting, which he did easily; by which benefit neither his witt was disturbt longer then he was spuing nor his stomach oppressed; but he never was, nor could not endure to be, habitually a good fellow, i.e. to drinke every day wine with company, which, though not to drunkennesse, spoiles the braine.

For his last 30+yeares, his dyet, etc., was very moderate and regular. After sixty he dranke no wine, his stomach grew weak, and he did eate most fish, especially whitings, for he sayd he digested fish better then flesh. He rose about seaven, had[d] his breakefast of bread and butter; and

---

tooke his walke, meditating till ten; then he did putt
downe the minutes of his thoughts, which he penned in
the afternoon.

* He had an inch thick board about 16 inches square,
whereon paper was pasted. On this board he drew his
lines (schemes). When a line came into his head, he
would, as he was walking, take a rude memorandum of
it, to preserve it in his memory till he came to his
chamber. ☞ He was never idle; his thoughts were
always working.

** His dinner was provided for him exactly by eleaven,
for he could not now stay till his lord's howre—scil. about
two: that his stomach could not beare.

After dinner he tooke a pipe of tobacco, and then threw
himselfe immediately on his bed, with his band off, and
slept (tooke a nap of about halfe an howre).

In the afternoon he penned his morning thoughts.

Exercises. Besides his dayly walking, he did twice or
thrice a yeare play at tennis † (at about 75 he
did it); then went to bed there and was well
rubbed ‡. This he did believe would make him
live two or three yeares the longer.

*** In the countrey, for want of a tennis-
court, he would walke up-hill and downe-hill in
the parke, till he was in a great sweat, and then
give the servant some money to rubbe him.

**** *Prudence.* He gave to his amanuensis, James Wheldon (the earle of Devon's baker; who writes a delicate
hand), his pention at Leicester, yearly, to wayte on him,
and take a care of him, which he did performe to him living
and dying, with great respect and diligence: for which
consideration he made him his executor.

Habit. In cold weather he commonly wore a black
velvet coate, lined with furre; if not, some other coate so
lined. But all the yeare he wore a kind of bootes ° of

† Quaere James
Wheldon *de hoc*
—how often, and
to what age?—
MS. Aubr. 9,
fol. 46ᵛ.
‡ Memorandum
there was no
bagnio in his
time. That in
Newgate Street
was built about
the time of his
death.—MS.
Aubr. 9, fol. 46ᵛ.

* MS. Aubr. 9, fol. 45ᵛ.
** MS. Aubr. 9, fol. 47.
*** MS. Aubr. 9, fol. 46ᵛ.

**** MS. Aubr. 9, fol. 47.
° Dupl. with 'buskins.'

Spanish leather, laced or tyed along the sides with black
ribons.

Singing.   He had alwayes bookes of prick-song lyeing
on his table:—e.g. of H. Lawes' etc. *Songs*—which at
night, when he was abed, and the dores made fast, and
was sure nobody heard him, he sang aloud (not that he
had a very good voice) but [a] for his health's sake: he did
beleeve it did his lunges good, and conduced much to
prolong his life.

   * *Shaking palsey.*   He had the shaking palsey in his
handes; which began in France before the yeare 1650,
and haz growne upon him by degrees, ever since, so that
he haz not been able to write very legibly since 1665 or
1666, as I find by some of his letters [b] to me.

   ⟨*His readiness to help with advice and money.*⟩

   ** His goodnes of nature and willingnes to instruct any
one that was willing to be informed and modestly desired
it, which I am a witnesse of as to my owne part and also
to others.

   *** *Charity.*   His brotherly love to his kinred hath
already been spoken of.   He was very charitable (pro
suo modulo) to those that were true objects of his bounty [c].
One time, I remember, goeing in the Strand, a poor and
infirme old man craved [d] his almes.   He, beholding him
with eies of pitty and compassion, putt his hand in his
pocket, and gave him 6*d.*   Sayd [e] a divine (scil. Dr. Jaspar
Mayne) that stood by—'Would you have donne this, if
it had not been Christ's command?'—'Yea,' sayd he.—
'Why?' quoth the other.—'Because,' sayd he, 'I was in
paine to consider [f] the miserable condition of the old man;
and now my almes, giving him some reliefe, doth also
ease me.'

---

[a] Dupl. with 'but to cleare his
pipes.'
   * MS. Aubr. 9, fol. 50.
   [b] Subst. for 'letters he hath honoured me withall.'
   ** MS. Aubr. 9, fol. 46ᵛ.

*** MS. Aubr. 9, fol. 50.
   [c] Dupl. with 'charity.'
   [d] Dupl. with 'begged.'
   [e] Subst. for 'sayd one that stood
by.'
   [f] Dupl. with 'apprehend.'

⟨*Slanders concerning him.*⟩

Aspersions and envy. His work was attended with envy, which threw severall aspersions and false reports on him. For instance, one (common) was that he was afrayd to lye alone at night in his chamber, [I have often heard him say that he was not afrayd of *sprights*, but afrayd of being knockt on the head[a] for five or ten pounds, which rogues might thinke he had[b] in his chamber]; and severall other tales, as untrue.

I have heard some positively affirme that he had a yearly pension from the king of France,—possibly for having asserted such a monarchie as the king of France exercises, but for what other grounds I know not, unles it be for that the present[c] king of France is reputed an encourager of choice and able men in all faculties who can contribute to his greatnes. I never heard him speake of any such thing; and, since his death, I have inquired of his most intimate friends in Derbyshire, who write to me they never heard of any such thing. Had it been so, he, nor they, ought to have been ashamed of it, and it had been becoming the munificence of so great a prince to have donne it.

Atheisme[d]. Testimonie[e]. For his being branded with atheisme, his writings and vertuous life testifie[f] against it. No man hath written better of . . . , perhaps not so well. To prevent such false and malicious reports, I thought fit to insert and affirme as abovesayd. * And that he was a Christian 'tis cleare, for he recieved the sacrament of Dr. ⟨John⟩ Pierson, and in his confession to Dr. John Cosins, at . . . , on his (as he thought) death-bed, declared that he liked the religion of the church of England best of all other.

---

[a] ' by rogues' followed, scored out.
[b] Dupl. with ' had about him.'
[c] Louis XIV.
[d] Anthony Wood notes, on fol. 47ᵛ, ' he used to take the sacrament, and acknowledge a supreeme being.'

[e] Here Aubrey intended (see *infra*) to cite evidence as to Hobbes's religious opinions.
[f] Dupl. with ' give it the lye.'
* MS. Aubr. 9, fol. 47ᵛ.

He would have the worship of God performed with musique (*ad me* [a]).

⟨*Addenda.*⟩

* Though he left his native countrey [b] at 14, and lived so long, yet sometimes one might find a little touch of our pronunciation.—Old Sir Thomas Malette [c], one of the judges of the King's Bench, knew Sir Walter Ralegh, and sayd that, notwithstanding his great travells, conversation, learning, etc., yet he spake broade Devonshire to his dyeing day.

** Memorandum—'twas he (as he him selfe haz told me) that ⟨invented⟩ the method of the oeconomie of the earle of Devon's family and way of stating or keeping of the accounts.

⟨*Portraits of Hobbes.*⟩

⟨i.⟩ *** Desire Sir Christopher Wren or Mr. Thomas Henshawe to speake to the king for his picture [d] of Mr. Hobbes for Mr. ⟨David⟩ Loggan to engrave it.

⟨ii.⟩ **** He did, anno 16 . . (vide the date [e], which is on the backside) doe me the honour to sitt for his picture to Jo. Baptist Caspars, an excellent painter, and 'tis a good piece, which I presented to the ⟨Royall⟩ Societie 12 yeares since (but will it not be improper for me to mention my owne guift?).

***** Hanc
Thomae Hobbes
Malmesburiensis effigiem
ad vivum depictam (1663)
Regiae Societati
Londinensi

---

[a] i.e. it was to Aubrey himself that Hobbes expressed this opinion.

* MS. Aubr. 9, fol. 45[v].

[b] Dupl. with 'Though he went from Malmesbury.'

[c] Puisne Judge of the King's Bench, 1641–45 and 1660–63.

** MS. Aubr. 9, fol. 41[v].

*** MS. Aubr. 9, fol. 28.

[d] By Samuel Cowper, *supra*, p. 338.

**** MS. Aubr. 9, fol. 54[v].

[e] Dr. Philip Bliss has written a note here, ' 1663: see loose paper— Aubrey's inscription,' referring to MS. Aubr. 9, fol. 7[v], as given below.

***** MS. Aubr. 9, fol. 7[v].

D.D.D.
Johannes Aubrey
de Easton-Piers
ejusdem Soc.
S.
1670.

~~Gett a brasse wyer to hang it * by.~~

⟨iii.⟩ * Mr. Hobbes's motto upon his owne picture at Sir Charles Scarborough's :—

> Si quaeris de me Mores inquire : sed Ille
> Qui quaerit de me, forsitan alter erit.

(Sir Charles Scarborough confessed to me that he made this distich.)

⟨iv.⟩ ** Memorandum—there was a good painter at the earl of Devonshire's in Derbyshire not long before Mr. Hobbes dyed, who drew him with the great decayes of old age. Mr. William Ball hath a good copie of it.

⟨v.⟩ *** His motto about his picture :—

> En quam modicè habitat philosophia.

⟨*His seal.*⟩

**** This—

. . . , a bend engrailed between 6 martletts . . . ,

was the seale [17] he commonly sealed his letters with, but 'twas not his coate.

Quare whose coate it may be—if *Hobbes*?

Quaere James Wheldon the executor if this be *his* coate of armes—for 'tis some seale—and what the colours are.—Respondet that the heralds did offer him a coat of armes but he refused it.

⟨*He was 'plebeius homo.'*⟩

***** Sir William Dugdale (Clarenceux), and Sir Edward Bisshe, the heralds, had an esteeme and respect for him,

---

* i. e. either to attach this inscription to the picture, or to hang the picture by.
* MS. Aubr. 9, fol. 49.
** MS. Aubr. 9, fol. 55.

*** MS. Aubr. 9, fol. 42ᵛ.
**** MS. Aubr. 9, fol. 28. Aubrey gives the coat in trick.
***** MS. Aubr. 9, fol. 53ᵛ.

in so much that they would have graunted him a coate of armes; but he refused it—which methinkes he neede[a] not have donne.

Vide Alexander Broome's poemes :—

> He that weares a brave soule and dares honestly doe
> Is a herault to himselfe and a godfather too.

* Vide Ben Jonson's *Underwoods*—that ' the most worthy men have been rock't in meane cradles.'

⟨His sayings.⟩

** 'Tis of custome in the lives of wise men to putt downe their sayings. Now if trueth (uncommon) delivered clearly and wittily may goe[b] for a saying, his common discourse was full of them, and which for the most part were sharpe and significant.

Here insert the two printed papers of his sayings.

*** Quaere Mr. Ben. Tuke at the Ship in Paule's Church-yard for the paper of his sayings, which Dr. Francis Bernard and his brother Charles, etc.—a club—made.

**** The sheet[c] of old Mr. Hobbes sayings was not published by his executor, as is there printed. 'Twas (indeed) donne by Mr. . . . Blunt, Sir Henry Blunt's sonne, and 'tis well donne.

***** I sayd, somewhere before, that (though he was ready and happy in repartying *in drollery*) he did not care[d] to give a present answer *to a question*, unless he had thoroughly considered it before : for he was against ' too hasty concluding,' which he did endeavour as much as he could to avoid.—This is in p. 12[e].

---

[a] Dupl. with ' might.'

* MS. Aubr. 9, fol. 29. In MS. Aubr. 6, fol. 1ᵛ, Aubrey cites the same passages from Brome and Jonson, and also :—
' J. Gadbury : " the heavens are the best heraulds." '

** MS. Aubr. 9, fol. 46.

[b] Dupl. with ' goes.'

*** MS. Aubr. 9, fol. 55.

**** MS. Aubr. 9, fol. 50.

[e] Anthony Wood has a note (MS. Aubr. 9, fol. 47ᵛ) about these :—' If you think that those sayings are true, pray publish them : for they being printed in one sheet, will be quickly lost.'

***** MS. Aubr. 9, fol. 45ᵛ.

[d] Dupl. with ' love.'

[e] i.e. fol. 41 of MS. Aubr. 9; *supra*, p. 340.

* Thomas Hobbs ⟨said⟩ that if it were not for the gallowes, some men are of so cruell a nature as to take a delight[a] in killing men [18] more than I should to kill a bird.—Entred[b] in idea.

** When Spinoza's *Tractatus Theologico-Politicus* first came out ⟨1670⟩, Mr. Edmund Waller sent it to my lord of Devonshire and desired him to send him word what Mr. Hobbes said of it. Mr. H. told his lordship :—

> Ne judicate ne judicemini[c].

He told me he had cut thorough him a barre's length, for he durst not write so boldly.

*** I have heard him inveigh much against the crueltie of Moyses for putting so many thousands to the sword for bowing to[d] .... vide text.

I have heard him say that Aristotle was the worst teacher that ever was, the worst polititian and ethick— a countrey-fellow that could live in the world ⟨would be⟩ as good: but his rhetorique and discourse of animals was rare.

**** T. H.'s saying:—rather use an old woman[e] that had many yeares been at sick people's bedsides, then the learnedst young unpractised physitian.

***** ☞ I remember he was wont to say that 'old men were drowned inwardly, by their owne moysture; e.g. first, the feet swell; then, the legges; then, the belly; etc.' —This saying may be brought in, perhaps, as to the paragraph of his sicknesse and death.

⟨From⟩ Elizabeth, viscountesse Purbec. When Mr. T. ^not Aubrey Hobbes was sick in France, the divines came to him, and tormented him (both Roman Catholic, Church of England, and Geneva). Sayd he to them 'Let me alone,

---

* MS. Aubr. 9, a slip at fol. 3.

[a] Dupl. with 'sport.'

[b] i. e. elsewhere in this life.

** MS. Aubr. 9, fol. 7.

[c] St. Matt. vii. 1.

*** MS. Aubr. 9, fol. 47[v].

[d] The golden calf: Exod. xxxii.

26–28.

**** MS. Aubr. 9, a slip pasted to fol. 5.

[e] Dupl. with 'an old tender,' i. e. attendant.

***** MS. Aubr. 9, fol. 54[v].

or els I will detect all your cheates from Aaron to your-
selves.' I thinke I have heard him speake something to this
purpose.

Mr. Edmund Waller sayd to me, when I desired him
to write some verses in praise of him, that he was afrayd
of the churchmen: he quoted Horace—

Incedo per ignes
Suppositos cineri doloso:

that, what was chiefly to be taken notice of in his elogie
was that he, being but *one*, and a private person, pulled-
downe all the churches, dispelled the mists of ignorance,
and layd-open their priest-craft.

⟨*His writings.*⟩

⟨Aubrey several times notes his intention of drawing up a list of
Hobbes' writings. In MS. Aubr. 9, fol. 53ᵛ, is a memorandum 'An
exact Catalogue of all the bookes he wrote,' with a mark showing
that it was to be brought in before the notice of Hobbes's death,
supra, p. 346. MS. Aubr. 9, fol. 22, is headed 'Catalogus librorum ab
autore scriptorum,' and is left blank for their insertion.

In MS. Aubr. 9, fol. 18ᵛ, is James Wheldon's answer to the inquiry
suggested (*ut supra*) on fol. 53ᵛ :—viz.⟩

* *A Catalogue of his bookes.*

His Latine poem *of the wonders of the Peake.*
His translation of *Thucidides* out of Greek into English.
His *Humane nature*, and *De corpore politico* in English.
His *Leviathan* in English.

His philosophy in three parts { *De corpore* / *De homine* / *De cive* } in Latine.

His dialogue *of the Civill Warr*, in English, printed
lately against his will.

Of his disputations with Dr. Wallis and what he has
written in philosophy and mathematicks Mr. ⟨William⟩
Crook can best give you the titles with the order and times
of their edition, some Latine, some English; as also of
His translation of *the Odysses and Iliads of Homer.*

There is also a small peece in English called *A Breefe of Aristotle's Rhetorick* printed by Andrew Crooke, which was his, though his name be not to it.

There is a little booke called *Mr. Hobbes considered*, wherein there is some passages relating to his life.

⟨In MS. Aubr. 9, fol. 54ᵛ, Aubrey notes the omission of a list of Hobbes's writings, and on fol. 55 he adds a transcript (with some notes of his own) of a list by William Crooke, Hobbes' publisher, supplementary to that given in Anthony Wood's *Hist. et Antiq. Univ. Oxon.* ii. 377.⟩

* I have no time now (in this transcript) to write the catalogue of his bookes, and I thought to have sent your paper ᵃ (which I keepe safe) but Dr. Blackburne desires the perusall of it.—This catalogue here I received last night from William Crooke.

** A supplement to Mr. A.ᵇ Wood's catalogue (in his 'History') of Mr. Hobbes his workes: viz.—

The travells of Ulysses, being the translation of the 9, 10, and 11 bookes of Homer's Odysses into English; London, printed 1674.

Epistola ad D. Ant. à Wood, Latin, 1675ᶜ.

A translation of the 24 bookes of Homer's Iliads and the 24 bookes of his Odysses.

Also, his preface about the vertues of heroique poesie, in English, printed 1675, and 1677.

A letter to the duke of Newcastle about liberty and necessity, printed 1676, and 1677. [I have this somewhere among my bookes, printed about 30 yeares since. It was edited first by John Davys of Kidwelly; and there is a preface to it with S. W., i. e. Seth Ward, who then had a high esteeme of him.]

* MS. Aubr. 9, fol. 54ᵛ.

ᵃ Possibly a paper by Anthony Wood containing an account of Hobbes, in preparation for the *Athenae*: cp. Clark's Wood's *Life and Times*, ii. 480.

** MS. Aubr. 9, fol. 55.

ᵇ Wood changes this to 'A. à:'

see Clark's Wood's *Life and Times*, i. 22.

ᶜ Corrected to '1674': with a marginal note:—[1675] 'I believe a mistake for 1674.' For this letter, see Clark's Wood's *Life and Times*, ii. 288.

De Mirabilibus Pecci [a]—English and Latin, 1678—a New-year's guift to his lord, who gave him 5 *li.*, about 1627.

Decameron Physiologicum, or ten dialogues of naturall philosophy, to which is added the proportion of straight line to halfe the arc of quadrant, English, 1678 [b].

Considerations upon the reputation, loyalty, manners, and religion of Thomas Hobbes, written by himselfe, printed 1680, with part of severall of his letters to W. Crooke —[This [c] was first printed by Andrew Crooke 1662, ἀνονύμως.]

Vita Thomae Hobbes, 4to, printed 1680 ; in Latin verse ; quarto.

Idem, in English, translated by . . . ; 1680, folio.

An historicall narration concerning heresie and the punishment thereof, English, 1680.

[Where [d] is the book against Dr. Wallis in 4to that came out in Jan. 16$\frac{78}{80}$?].

* He haz omitted here Aristotel's Rhetorique, printed long since by Andrew Crooke, but without his name ; but Dr. Blackburne, W. Crooke, and I will lay our heads together and sett these things right.

☞ It ought not to be forgotten that there is before Sir William Davenant's heroique poem called Gondibert, a learned epistle of Mr. Hobbes's concerning poetrie, in answer to Sir William's.

And there is also a shorter letter of Mr. Hobbes's, which the Honourable . . . Howard has printed before his heroique poem, 8vo, called I thinke Bonduca, about 1668 or 9.

Mr. Hobbes wrote a letter to . . . (a colonell, as I remember) concerning Dr. Scargill's recantation sermon, preached at Cambridge, about 1670, which he putt into Sir John Birkenhead's hands to be licensed, which he

[a] Anthony Wood notes in margin: ' This is in Wood's Catalogue': i.e. Wood, *l. c.*, mentions the 1666 (second) edition of the piece (in Latin only).

[b] Marginal query :—' When was the first copie printed ? Vide Bibl. Bodlei.' The printed edition is not in the 1674 *Catal. impress. libb. Bibl. Bodl.*

[c] Added opposite, on fol. 54ʳ.

[d] This query is inserted by Anthony Wood.

* MS. Aubr. 9, fol. 54ʳ.

refused (to collogue and flatter the bishops), and would not returne it nor give a copie. Mr. Hobbes kept no copie, for which he was sorry. He told me he liked it well himselfe.—* Dr. ᵃ Birket, my old acquaintance, hath the ordering of Sir John Birkenhead's bookes and papers. He hath not found it yet but hath found a letter of Mr. Hobbes to him about it, and hath promised me if he finds it to let me have it. ☞ Memorandum—Sir Charles Scarborough told me that he haz a copie of it, but I could not obtaine it of him; but I will try again, if Dr. Birket cannot find it.

⟨*Notes about his writings.*⟩

⟨There are several scattered notes about Hobbes' writings dispersed throughout MS. Aubr. 9, which may be most conveniently brought together here.⟩

His Latin *Leviathan* is altered in many particulars, e. g. the doctrine of the Trinity, etc., and enlarged with many considerable particulars.—MS. Aubr. 9, fol. 42ᵛ.

The *Leviathan* is translated into Dutch.—MS. Aubr. 9, fol. 7ᵛ.

Quaere Ph. Laurence what volume the Dutch *Leviathan* printed and what volumine.—MS. Aubr. 9, fol. 7.

Humane Nature, London, by Thomas Newcombe, 1650, 12mo.—Anno 168⅘ is printed by Mr. Crooke *Humane Nature*, and *Libertie and Necessity*, in 8vo, which they call his 'Tripos.'—MS. Aubr. 9, fol. 7ᵛ.

Before Thucydides, he spent two yeares in reading romances and playes, which he haz often repented and sayd that these two yeares were lost of him—wherin perhaps he was mistaken too. For it might furnish him with copie of words.—MS. Aubr. 9, fol. 42ᵛ.

Thucydides, London, imprinted for Richard Mynne in Little Brittain at the signe of St. Paul, MDCXXXIV.—MS. Aubr. 9, fol. 7ᵛ.

---

* MS. Aubr. 9, fol. 55.
ᵃ Henry Birkhead is meant, 'Birket' representing the slurred pronunciation of the name. Anthony Wood has scored through the 'Dr.' and added a note :—'Birket is not a Dr.'

Mr. Henry Birchit of the Middle Temple promised to gett for me Mr. Hobbes' letter to . . . of Mr. Scargill's recantation, which he left with Sir John Birkenhead.—MS. Aubr. 9, fol. 54ᵛ.

T. Hobbes—quaere Mr. H. Birchet de letter of Scargill's recantation which Sir John Birkenhead would not licence.— MS. Aubr. 8, fol. 8.

⟨In MS. Aubr. 9 at the end are some of the printed tracts issued by Hobbes in his controversy with Dr. John Wallis, viz.:—

(1) A folio sheet ᵃ, headed

'To the right honorable and others the learned members of the Royal Society for the Advancement of the Sciences, presenteth to your consideration your most humble servant Thomas Hobbes (who hath spent much time upon the same subject) two propositions, whereof the one is lately published by Dr. Wallis, a member of your society. . . .

Dr. Wallis: *de motu*, cap. 5. prop. 1. | Thomas Hobbes, *Roset.* prop. 5.'

(2) A quarto sheet ᵇ, headed :

' To the right honourable and others the learned members of the Royal Society for the Advancement of the Sciences, presenteth to your consideration your most humble servant Thomas Hobbes a confutation of a theoreme which hath a long time passed for truth.'

(3) A quarto tract ᶜ (the ' Propositions' occupy 3 pages, the ' Considerations,' 4 pages), entitled :—

'Three papers presented to the Royal Society against Dr. Wallis, together with considerations on Dr. Wallis his answers to them, by Thomas Hobbes of Malmsbury; London, printed for the author and are to be had at the Green Dragon without Temple Bar: 1671.'⟩

With Mr. Hobbes's small tracts inscribed to the Royal Society came a letter offering that some of the small pieces of his might be published in the Transactions ; which was

---

ᵃ Marked MS. Aubr. 9, fol. 56.   ᵇ MS. Aubr. 9, fol. 57.
ᶜ MS. Aubr. 9, fol. 59.

not donne, through Mr. Oldenburgh's default.—MS. Aubr. 9, fol. 47ᵛ.

⟨At the end of MS. Aubr. 9 is a quarto tract of 14 pages, entitled :—

' Thomae Hobbesii Malmesburiensis vita, authore seipso ᵃ, Londini, typis, anno MDCLXXIX.'

The last two lines of it are :—

Octoginta annos complevi jam quatuorque
Et prope stans dictat Mors mihi, Ne metue.

On these Aubrey notes (MS. Aubr. 9, fol. 68ᵛ)—

' These two last verses Dr. Blackburne altered (because of quā in quatuor, long) in the copie printed with Mr. Hobbes's life in Latine, and some other alterations he made, but me thinkes the sense is not so brisque.'⟩

What did he write since he left London? Quaere ⟨his⟩ executor.—MS. Aubr. 9, fol. 22ᵛ.

His executor acquaints William Crooke (the author's printer ᵇ) and me, in a lettre ᶜ under his hand January 16, 1679, that neither Mr. Halleley (Mr. Hobbes's intimate friend and confident) nor him selfe have any thing in either of their hands of Mr. Hobbes's, the very little of that kind that he left behind him being disposed of 'according to his own order' before he removed from Chatsworth. Quaere what was that order?—MS. Aubr. 9, fol. 22ᵛ.

Mr. Thomas Hobbes ⟨has left⟩ in MSS.

——A dialogue concerning the common lawes.

——An epitome of the Civil Warres of England from 1640 to 1660.

——Answer to *The Catching of the Leviathan* by Dr. Bramhall.

——A historical narration concerning heresy and the punishment thereof.—MS. Aubr. 9, a slip at fol. 27ᵛ.

Translation of 1. 9, 10, 11 and 1⟨2⟩ bookes of Homer's Odysses in English verse.

ᵃ MS. Aubr. 3, fol. 28 :—' He writt his life last yeare (viz. 1673) in Latin verse.'

ᵇ Dupl. with ' bookeseller.'

ᶜ MS. Aubr. 9, fol. 16: see p. 381.

Ecclesiastica Historia in Latin verse, Amsterdam.—MS. Aubr. 9, a slip pasted on to fol. 27ᵛ.

Quaere Dr. Blackbourn and Mr. Crooke to know where lies or what is become of Mr. Hobbes' *Historia Ecclesiastica Romana?* Resp.—Dr. Blackbourne haz it; gett copie of it.—MS. Aubr. 7, a slip at fol. 8ᵛ.

In May 1688, his *Ecclesiastica Historia carmine elegiaco conscripta*, in Latin verse, was printed at Augusta Trino-bantum, scil. London. The preface was writt by Mr. Thomas Rymer, of Graie's Inne, but ἀνονυμῶς.—MS. Aubr. 9, fol. 54ᵛ.

Memorandum.—Mr. Hobbes told me he would write, in three columnes, his doctrine, the objections, and his answers, and deposit ᵃ it in the earle of Devon's library at . . . in Derbyshire. Dr. ⟨Thomas⟩ Bayly, principall of New-Inn-hall in Oxon, tells me he hath seen it there.—MS. Aubr. 9, fol. 2.

⟨MS. Aubr. 28 is a copy of the tract (63 pages).

'Mr. Hobbes considered in his loyalty, religion, reputation, and manners, by way of letter to Dr. Wallis'; London, printed for Andrew Crooke, 1662.

On the title-page Aubrey has the note :—

'This letter was writt (indeed) by Mr. Thomas Hobbes himselfe—Jo. Aubrey de Easton-Pierse':

and at the end

'The second impression ᵇ of this booke was from this very booke of mine.—'Twas not to be bought.'⟩

⟨ *Verses by him.* ⟩

* Insert the love verses he made not long before his death :—

** 1.

Tho' I am now past ninety, and too old
T' expect preferment in the court of Cupid,
And many winters made mee ev'n so cold
I am become almost all over stupid,

ᵃ Dupl. with 'leave.'
ᵇ Publ. in 1680; *supra*, p. 333.

* MS. Aubr. 9, fol. 42ᵛ.
** MS. Aubr. 9, fol. 49.

2.

Yet I can love and have a mistresse too,
As fair as can be and as wise as fair;
And yet not proud, nor anything will doe
To make me of her favour to despair.

3.

To tell you who she is were very bold;
But if i' th' character your selfe you find
Thinke not the man a fool thô he be old
Who loves in body fair a fairer mind.

---

* Catalogue [a] *of his learned familiar friends and acquaintances,* besides those already mentioned, that I remember him to have spoken of.

Mr. Benjamin Johnson, Poet-Laureat, was his loving and familiar friend and acquaintance.

⟨*Sir Robert*⟩ *Aiton,* Scoto-Britannus, a good poet and critique and good scholar. He was neerly related to his lord's lady (Bruce). And he desired Ben: Johnson, and this gentleman, to give their judgement on his style of his translation of Thucydides. ** He lyes buryd in Westminster Abbey, and hath there an elegant monument and inscription [b], which I will insert here or so much as may be pertinent.

Memorandum next after . . . Ayton should in order be named *Sydney Godolphin,* esq., who left him, in his will, a legacy of an hundred poundes: and Mr. Hobbes hath left him an eternall [c] monument in lib. . . . pag. . . . of his Leviathan.

Lucius Carey, lord Falkland was his great friend and admirer, and so was *Sir William Petty*; both which I have here enrolled amongst those friends I have heard him

---

* MS. Aubr. 9, fol. 50.

[a] Anthony Wood objects, on fol. 47ᵛ: 'You say p. 11' (i.e. fol. 40) 'that he was acquainted with Mr. Selden and Dr. Harvey. Why do you not set them downe here?' But, as Wood might have remembered, they

have been 'already mentioned.'

** MS. Aubr. 9, fol 47ᵛ.

[b] Aubrey has a memorandum, MS. Aubr. 9, fol. 7, 'take . . . Ayton's inscription.' See *supra,* p. 25.

[c] Dupl. with 'perpetuall' or 'lasting.'

speake of, but Dr. Blackburne left 'em both out[a] (to my admiration). I askt him why he had donne so? He answered because they were both ignote to foreigners.

Mr. Henry Gellibrand, Astronomy professor at Gresham Colledge.

* *James Harrington,* esq., who wrote against him in his *Oceana.*

Henry Stubbes[b].

Mr. Charles Cavendish[c], brother to the duke of Newcastle, a learned gentleman and great mathematician.

Mr. Laurence Rooke, Geometry and Astronomy professor.

Mr. . . . Hallely, his intimate friend, an old gent.

** When he was at Florence (16..; vide vitam) he contracted a friendship with the famous *Galileo Galileo, . . .*[d], whom he extremely venerated and magnified ; and not only as he was a prodigious witt, but for his sweetnes of nature and manners. They[e] pretty well resembled one another as to their countenances, as by their pictures doeth[f] appeare ; were both cheerfull and melancholique-sanguine ; and had both a consimilitie of fate, to be hated and persecuted by the ecclesiastiques.

† I have heard Mr. Edmund Waller say that (William) the lord marquisse of Newcastle was a great patron to Dr. Gassendi, and M. Des Cartes, as well as Mr. Hobbes, and that he hath dined with them all three at the marquiss's table at Paris.—MS. Aubr. 9, fol. 50ᵛ.

16..[g], *Petrus Gassendus*[h], S. Th. Doctor et Regius Professor Parisiis,—vide his titles— whom he never mentions but with great honour and respect †, 'doctissimus, humanissimus'; and they loved each other entirely.

As also the like love and friendship was betwixt him and

Marinus . . . Mersennus ;

Monsr. *Renatus Des Cartes*[i] ;

[a] In the *Auctarium Vitae Hobbianae,* 1681.

* MS. Aubr. 9, fol. 50ᵛ.

[b] See *infra,* p. 371.

[c] On fol. 52ᵛ, Aubrey repeats this name, 'Sir Charles Cavendish.'

** MS. Aubr. 9, fol. 51.

[d] Aubrey leaves a space for his title or profession, adding the reminder—'Expresse his quality.'

[e] Dupl. with 'They were not much unlike in their countenances.'

[f] Dupl. with 'may.'

[g] A memorandum for the date when they first met each other.

[h] See *infra.*

[i] See *infra,* p. 367.

as also—

⟨ *Johan. Franc.* ⟩ *Niceron* ;

Samuel Sorbier, M. D.—vide his epistle and Gassendus's before his *De Cive*.

… *Verdusius*, to whom he dedicates his … *Dialogi* (* vide my *Dialogi* for his Christian name—'tis dedicated to him).

** T. H. would say that *Gassendus* was the sweetest-natured man in the world.

Des Cartes and he were acquainted and mutually respected one another. He would say that had he kept himself to Geometry he had been the best geometer in the world but that his head did not lye for philosophy.

*** Mr. Hobbes was wont to say that had M[ieur] Des Cartes (for whom he had a high respect) kept himselfe to geometrie, he had been the best geometer in the world ; but he could not pardon him for his writing in defence of transubstantiation, which he knew was absolutely against his opinion[a] and donne meerly to putt a compliment[b] ⟨on⟩ the Jesuites.

**** I have heard Mr. Oates say that the Jesuites doe much glorie that he ⟨Des Cartes⟩ had his education under[c] them. 'Tis not unlikely that the Jesuites putt him upon that treatise.

Edmund Waller [d], esq., poet.

***** *Sir Kenelm Digby*, amicus T. H.

****** (1648 or 49 [e], at Paris.) *Sir William Petty* (of Ireland [f]), Regiae Societatis Socius, a person[g] of a stupendous invention [h] and of as great prudence and humanity, had an

---

* MS. Aubr. 9, fol. 50[v].

** MS. Aubr. 9, fol. 7.

*** MS. Aubr. 9, fol. 50[v].

[a] Dupl. with ' conscience.'

[b] Dupl. with ' flatter.'

**** MS. Aubr. 9, fol. 51.

[c] Dupl. with ' from.'

[d] Scored out here ; inserted *infra*, p. 369.

***** MS. Aubr. 9, fol. 7.

****** MS. Aubr. 9, fol. 51.

[e] Suggested by Aubrey as the date of the beginning of the intimacy between Hobbes and Petty. Anthony Wood objects in a note on fol. 50[v] :—
' Dr. Petty was resident in Oxford 1648–49, and left it (if I am not mistaken) 1652.' Aubrey notes :—
' Entred, vide p. 8[b] ' (i.e. fol. 37 [v] ; *supra*, p. 336).

[f] Aubrey notes :—' Quaere the name of his principall seate in Ireland.'

[g] Aubrey notes (fol. 50[v]) :—
' Quaere Sir John Hoskyns and Dr. Blackbonrne to word this well.'

[h] Dupl. with ' witt.'

high[a] esteeme of him. His acquaintance began at Paris, 1648 or 1649, at which time Mr. Hobbes studied Vesalius' Anatomy, and Sir William with him. He then assisted Mr. Hobbes in draweing his schemes *for his booke of optiques, for he had a very fine hand in those dayes for draweing[b], which draughts Mr. Hobbes did[c] much commend. His facultie[d] in this kind conciliated them the sooner to the familiarity[e] of our common friend,

Mr. S. Cowper aforesayd[f], at whose house they often mett.—He drew his picture twice: the first the king haz, the other is yet in the custody of his widowe; but he gave it, indeed, to me (and I promised I would give it to the archives at Oxon, ** with a short inscription on the back side, as a monument of his friendship to me and ours to Mr. Hobbes—sed haec omnia inter nos) *** but I, like a foole, did not take possession of it, for something of the garment was not quite finished, and he dyed, I being then in the countrey—sed hoc non ad rem.

**** ⟨*Sir William Petty.*⟩ I have a very fine letter from Mr. Hobbes to me where he gives him thanks and for his booke of Duplicate Proportion I sent him, which letter I will insert (so much as concerns it). Sir William Petty would keepe the originall *honoris ergo* and gave me a copie of it, which I have not leisure to looke out.

***** (At Paris.) *Mr. Abraham Cowley*, the poet, who hath bestowed on him an immortal pindarique ode, which is in his poems.

(1651 or 52.) *William Harvey*, Dr. of Physique and Chirurgery, inventor of the circulation of the bloud, who left him in his will ten poundes, as his brother told me at his funerall. Obiit anno 1657, aetat. 80, sepult. at Hempsted in Essex, in their[g] vault.

[a] Dupl. with 'particular.'
* MS. Aubr. 9, fol. 52.
[b] Dupl. with 'graphia.'
[c] Dupl. with 'liked.'
[d] Dupl. with 'excellency.'
[e] Dupl. with 'acquaintance.'

[f] *Supra*, p. 338.
** MS. Aubr. 9, fol. 51[v].
*** MS. Aubr. 9, fol. 52.
**** MS. Aubr. 9, fol. 50[v].
***** MS. Aubr. 9, fol. 52.
[g] i.e. the Harvey family.

Mr. Edmund Waller of Beconsfield was his great friend, and acquainted at Paris—I believe before.

When his Leviathan came out, he sent by his stationer's (Andrew Crooke) man a copie of it, well-bound, to *Mr. John Selden* in Aedibus Carmeliticis. Mr. Selden told the servant, he did not know Mr. Hobbes, but had heard much of his worth, and that he should be very glad to be acquainted with him. Wherupon Mr. Hobbes wayted on him. From which time there was a strict friendship between ⟨them⟩ to his dyeing day. He left by his will to Mr. Hobbes a legacy of ten poundes.

Sir John Vaughan, Lord Chiefe Justice of the Common Pleas, was his great acquaintance, to whom he made visitts three times or more in a weeke—out of terme in the morning ; in terme-time, in the afternoon.

Sir Charles Scarborough, M.D. (physitian to his royal highnesse the duke of Yorke), who hath a very good and † This was made like picture (drawne about 1655) *of him, by Sir Charles Scarborough, under which is this distich (they say of M.D. Mr. Hobbes's making †),

> Si quaeris de me, Mores inquire, sed Ille
> Qui quaerit de me, forsitan alter erit ;

and much loved his conversation.

Sir Jonas Moore, mathematicus, surveyor of his ‡ Does this majestie's ordinance, who had a great venera-
lamenting come
in aptest here, or tion for Mr. Hobbes, and was wont much to
pag.* 7?—MS.
Aubr. 9, fol. 52ᵛ. lament ‡ he fell to the study of the mathematiques so late.

Mr. Richard White, who writt Hemispherium Dissectum. **I have heard Mr. Thomas Hobbes commend Richard White for a solid mathematician and preferred him much before his brother *Thomas de Albiis* ᵇ for it.

---

* MS. Aubr. 9, fol. 53.

ᵃ 'Page 7,' i.e. fol. 36ᵛ ; *supra,* p. 333.

** MS. Aubr. 9, fol. 52ᵛ.

ᵇ Anthony Wood queries (fol. 53): 'Was not Thomas de Albiis of his acquaintance?' Aubrey answers: 'I beleeve he was.'

Sir Charles Cavendish [a].

Edward, lord Herbert of Cherbery and Castle Island.

Sir William Davenant, Poet Laureat after B. Johnson, and generall of the ordinance to the duke of Newcastle—at Paris [b] (e. g. epistle); perhaps before.

William Chillingworth, D.D.—he would commend this doctor for a very great witt; ' But by G——,' said he, ' he is like some lusty fighters that will give a damnable back-blow now and then on their owne party.'

George Eglionby, D.D. and deane of Canterbury, was also his great acquaintance. He died at Oxford [c], 1643, of the epidemique disease then rageing.

* *Jasper Mayne*, Doctor of Divinity (chaplain to William, marquesse of Newcastle), an old acquaintance of his.

Mr. Francis Osburne, author of ' Advice [d] to a son ' and severall other treatises, was his great acquaintance.

John Pell, Dr. of Divinity, mathematicus, quondam professor . . . [e] at Breda, who quotes him in his . . . contra Longomontanum *de Quadratura circuli*, for one of his jury (of 12).

Sir George Ent, M.D.—In a letter to Mr. J⟨ohn⟩ A⟨ubrey⟩ from Mr. Thomas Hobbes :—

' Worthy Sir,

I have receaved from Mr. Crooke the booke of Sir George Ent of the Use of Respiration. It is a very learned and ingeniose booke full of true and deepe philo-sophy. I pray you to present unto him my most humble service. Though I recieved it but three dayes since, yet, drawn-on by the easinesse of the style and elegancy of the language, I have read it all over, and I give you most

---

[a] See note, p. 366.

[b] i.e. their acquaintance began during Hobbes's abode there.

[c] Clark's Wood's *Life and Times*, i. 104.

* MS. Aubr. 9, fol. 53.

[d] Clark's Wood's *Life and Times*, i. 257.

[e] Aubrey notes in the margin, ' v. librum'; i.e. look up the title of the book Pell then published to discover the subject he was professor of.

humble thankes for sending it to me. I pray you present my service to Mr. Hooke[a].

I am,

Sir, your most obliged and humble servant,

THO: HOBBES.

Chatsworth,
  March 25,
    1679.'

Ralph Bathurst, S.T.D., now deane of Welles, who hath writt verses before his booke of Humane Nature[b].

Mr. Henry Stubbes, physitian, whom he much esteemed for his great learning and parts, but at latter end Mr. Hobbs differ'd with him for that he wrote against the lord chancellor Bacon, and the Royall Societie. He wrote in Mr. Hobbes' defence—vide librum[c].

Walter Charleton, M.D., physitian to his majestie, and one of the Colledge of Physitians in London, a high admirer of him.

Mr. Samuel Butler, the author of Hudibras.

In his . . . Dialogi (vide librum) he haz a noble elogie of *Sir Christopher Wren,* then a young scholar in Oxon, which quote ; but I thinke they were not acquainted.

Mr. ⟨Robert⟩ Hooke loved him, but was never but once in his company.

⟨*Sidney Godolphin*[d].⟩

* To conclude, he had a high esteeme for the Royall

---

[a] Aubrey notes : 'of Gresham Colledge.'

[b] This entry is scored out by Aubrey, in consequence of the following note by Anthony Wood on MS. Aubr. 9, fol. 52ᵛ :—'Dr. Bathurst was never acquainted with him. Those verses were written at the desire of Mr. Bowman, stationer of Oxford, as I have heard the Dr. say.'

[c] On fol. 52ᵛ Wood has the note :— 'Stubs wrot in his defence against Wallis in a book intituled "A severe enquirie into the late *Oneirocritica,*

or an exact account of the grammaticall part of the controversy between Mr. Thomas Hobbes and John Wallis, D.D." Lond. 1657, 4to.'

[d] Anthony Wood on fol. 52ᵛ has a note :—'Sydney Godolphin was his acquaintance. Why mention you not him ?' Aubrey answers :—'Mr. T. Hobbs told me he gave him an hundred pounds in his will, which he recieved : I thought I had entred him'; and later adds, ' 'Tis entred'; viz. *supra,* p. 365.

* MS. Aubr. 9, fol. 54.

Societie, having sayd (vide Behemoth pag. 242, part . . .)
that 'Naturall Philosophy was removed from the Universities
to Gresham Colledge,' meaning the Royall Societie that
meetes there ; and the Royall Societie (generally) had the

like for him : and he would long since have
been ascribed a member there, but for the
sake of one † or two persons, whom he tooke
to be his enemies. In their meeting at Gresham
Colledge is his picture, drawn by the life,
166– (quaere date [b]), by a good hand, which
they much esteeme, and severall copies have
been taken of it.

† Dr. Wallis (surely their Mercuries [a] are in opposition), and Mr. Boyle. I might add Sir Paul Neile, who disobliges everybody.— MS. Aubr. 9, fol. 53[v].

* Memorandum :—Dr. *Isaac Barrow* hath mentioned
Mr. T. Hobbes in his mathematicall lectures, printed and
unprinted.

** *Edmund Waller*, esq., of Beconsfield :—'but what he
was most to ⟨be⟩ commended for was that he being a
private person threw downe the strongholds (ὀχυρώματα) of
the Church, and lett in light.'

Robert Stevens, serjeant at Lawe, was wont to say of him,
and that truly, that 'no man had so much, so deeply,
seriously, and profoundly[c] considered humane nature as he.'

*** Mr. John Dreyden, Poet Laureat, is his great
admirer, and oftentimes makes use of his doctrine in his
playes—from Mr. Dreyden himselfe.

**** Memorandum he hath no countryman living hath
knowne him so long (1633[d]) as myselfe, or ⟨any⟩ of his
friends, &c. ⟨who⟩ doth know so much ⟨about him.⟩
When he had printed his translation of Thucydides ⟨1676:
edit. 2⟩, his life is writt by him selfe (at my request) in the
third person, a copie wherof I have by me, [to[e] publish after
his death if it please God I survive him.]

[a] Aubrey uses the astronomical symbol for the planet.
[b] 1663: see *supra*, p. 354.
* MS. Aubr. 9, fol. 54[v].
** MS. Aubr. 9, fol. 34[v].
[c] Dupl. with 'truly.'
*** MS. Aubr. 9, fol. 46[v].

**** MS. Aubr. 3, fol. 28.
[d] Changed by Aubrey, when revising, to 1634, *supra*, p. 331.
[e] Scored out. A marginal note, 'This Mr. Blackburn printed' (see *infra*, p. 395), is also scored out. As also is, 'all his works in . . . volumes.'

⟨*Opponents and critics.*⟩

* Now as he had these ingeniose and learned friends, and many more (no question) that I know not or now escape my memory; so he had many enemies (though undeserved; for he would not provoke, but if provoked, he was sharp and bitter): and as a prophet is not esteemed in his owne countrey, so he was more esteemed by foreigners then by his countreymen.

His chiefe antagonists were

—[*Dr.*ᵃ *John*] *Bramhall*, bishop of [Londonderry], aftcrwards [archbishop of Armagh and] primate of Ireland.

—*Seth Ward*, D.D., now bishop of Sarum, who wrote against him in his *Vindiciae Academiarum*ᵇ ἀνονυμῶς, and in . . . . . With whom though formerly he had some contest, for which he was sorry, yet Mr. Hobbes had a great veneration for hisᶜ worth, learning and goodnes.

—*John Wallis*, D.D., a great mathematician, and that hath deserved exceedingly of the commonwealth of learning for the great paines etc. . . ., was his great antagonist in the Mathematiques. 'Twas pitty, as is said before, that Mr. Hobbs began so late, els he would ⟨not⟩ have layn so open.

'Theophilus Pike' (⟨i. e.⟩ [*William*ᵈ] *Lucy*, bishop of St. David's) who wrote ['Observations, censures, and confutations of notorious errours' in his Leviathan, 1664; they are but weak ones.]

Mr. [*Richard*] *Baxter*, who wrote . . .

[*Edward*ᵉ *Hyde, earl of Clarendon*, who wrot against the politicall part of his Leviathan: I have mentioned this in some letter, but you have forgot it.]

* MS. Aubr. 9, fol. 54.
ᵃ The words in square brackets are insertions by Anthony Wood.
ᵇ See Clark's Wood's *Life and Times*, i. 296.
ᶜ Subst. for 'for this bishop's worth.'
ᵈ The words in square brackets are insertions by Anthony Wood.

ᵉ Added by Anthony Wood: who afterwards added the title of the treatise, opposite (on fol. 53ᵛ), viz. :—
[' Edward, earl of Clarendon: A survey of the dangerous and pernicious errours to church and state in Mr. Hobs book intit. Leviathan; Oxford, 1676, 4to.']

* Samuelis Siremesii ; Praxiologia apodictica, seu Philosophia moralis demonstrativa, pythanologiae Hobbianae opposita : Francofurti, 1677, 4to.

** (In 16mo)—Liberty and Necessity asserted by Thomas Hobbes and opposed by *Philip Tandy*, register-accomptant, formerly minister and now established so again, Lond. 1656.

⟨*Apologists and supporters.*⟩

⟨A few scattered notes in MS. Aubr. 9 may be conveniently brought together here.⟩

*** Meditationes Politicae iisdem continuandis et illustrandis addita Politica parallela xxv dissertationibus Academicis antehac exposuit Johannes Christopherus *Becmanus*, LL.D., editio 3ᵃ, Francofurti MDCLXXIX, vide pag. 417 ubi magnopere laudat T. Hobbium—which transcribe.

**** In 8vo :—Meditationes Politicae iisdemque continuandis et illustrandis addita Politica Parallela XXIV dissertationibus academicis antehac exposuit *Johannes Christopherus Becmanus*, D. et Hist. prof. publ. ord. in Acad. Francofurtanâ ; additae sunt dissertationes de lege regia et de quarta monarchia : editio tertia : Francofurti ad Oderam, anno MDCLXXIX :—pag. 417, 418 :—

'In Hobbesii libris eorum quae de cive et civitate agunt (nam reliqua nobis neutiquam curatio est) *scopus generalis* est e primis principiis naturae rationalis ac vitae socialis res politicas eruere (quo quidem nomine prae caeteris laudandus est cum nemo politicorum ante illum id ausus fuerit), *specialis* est dirigere principia sua ad monarchiam (qui si genium gentis spectes in qua vixit non minori laude dignus est, licebitque aliis eadem principia ad statum aristocraticum et democraticum applicare, modo sciat istos potius quam monarchiam reipublicae suae congruere).

In aliis scriptis quae publicavit itidem eo nomine laudandus est quod e primis principiis moralibus, licet haud perinde vulgò notis, res suas eruere conetur : sed rursus etiam culpandus quod sacra ad

* MS. Aubr. 9, fol. 52ᵛ.
** MS. Aubr. 9, fol. 53ᵛ.
*** MS. Aubr. 9, fol. 52ᵛ.
**** MS. Aubr. 9, fol. 5.

conceptus suos trahat cum hos ad sacra pertrahere indeque perficere debuisset. Profani tamen qui videntur apud eum occurrere loquendi modi non possunt plenum *atheismum* inferre, nunquam enim qui rebus moralibus mediocriter incumbit atheus esse potest, tanto minus Hobbesius qui ad prima usque principia moralium progredi conatur. Quod vero maxime sapere videtur, id vel *securitatem* dixeris vel *neutralismum* quendam, ut Deum quidem colat sed modum colendi a sacro codice derivandum esse non necessarium agnoscat ; esseque hunc animum ejus ex eo patet quod superius diximus, ipsum sacra ad conceptus suos morales trahere cum e contrario moralia quae habemus aut invenire etiam possumus e sacris peti debeant quippe quae clarius semper rem exprimunt quam sine eis exprimi potest. Acciditque hic ᵃ ipsi quod chymicorum multis aliisque rerum naturalium scrutatoribus qui, dum in causis secundis indagandis nimii sunt, eis ita alligantur ut ulterius eoque ad Deum usque pergere non opus esse judicent, unde similiter in *neutralismum* incidunt. Brevius—Hobbesius principia vitae socialis vere explicat sed male applicat ; unde omnis illa in doctrina ejus perversitas quam tamen Christiano vitandam esse merito cum piis probisque omnibus pronunciamus. Concludimus cum judicio autoris Gallici in *Itiner. Angl.* † pag. (edit. Germ.) 411, 412 :—

† This is in High-dutch, which I desire Mr. Th. Haack to render into English.

* Es [19] werden sehr wenig gefunden welche die Sachen genauer durchsehen denn Er und die der Natürlichen Wissen-schafft eine so lange Erfahrung beygebracht hätten. Ja Er ist ein überbliebenes von dem Bacon, unter welchem Er in seiner Jugend geschrieben und an allem was ich von Ihm gehöret und was ich in seiner Art zu sc⟨h⟩reiben mercke sehe ich wol, dasz Er viel davon behalten. Er hat durch das Studieren seine Weise die Dinge zu wenden und greiffet gerne in die Gleichnüssen. Aber Er hat natürlich viele von seiner schönen und guten Eigenschafft ja auch von seiner feinen Leibes Gestalt. Er hat der Priester-schafft seines Landes, den Mathematisten zu Oxfurt und ihren Anhänge⟨r⟩n eine Furcht eingejaget, darumb Ihre Majestät mir Ihn einem Bähren ᵇ ver⟨g⟩l⟨e⟩ichen, wider welche Er die doggen, umb sie zu üben anreitzet ; sonder Zweiffel hat Er die gekrönte Häupter in den Gründen seiner Welt Klugheit höchlich verbunden, und wenn Er die Lehren der Religionen nicht berühret, oder sich begnüget hätte d⟨i⟩e Presbyterianer und genannte Bischöffe seines Landes anzu-greiffen, find ich nichts darin zu tadeln.'

** Casparis Zeigleri de juribus majestatis tractatus Academicus ; Wittenbergae, 1681. Vide pag. 112 § IV

ᵃ *Sic* in MS. ᵇ *Supra*, p. 340.
* MS. Aubr. 9, fol. 4. ** MS. Aubr. 9. fol. 52ᵛ.

ubi honoris gratiâ citat Hobbium de differentiis inter pactum et legem ex element. philosoph. de Cive, cap. 14.

* (In 12mo)—Epistolica dissertatio de principiis justi et decori continens Apologiam pro tractatu clarissimi Hobbaei de Cive ἀνωνύμως, Amstelodami apud Ludovicum Elzevirium, MDCLI.

James Harrington, esquire: *Oceana*, vide.

** . . . Zeigler, a German jurisconsultus, quotes him with great respect, as also some other German civilians, of which enquire farther.

*** *Samuelis Pufendorf*: Elementa Jurisprudentiae Universalis ᵃ, 1672 : in praefatione—

'Nec parum debere nos profitemur Thomae Hobbes, cujus hypothesis in libro *de Cive*, etsi quid profani sapiat, pleraque tamen caetera satis arguta ac sana.

Quos heic velut in universum allegasse voluimus, in ipso autem opere quoties eorundem expressa fuit sententia ipsos numerare supersedimus, quia, praeter taedia crebrae citationis, rationes eorum potius quam autoritatem secuti sumus. Nam quando ab iisdem atque aliis veritatis studium dissentire nos subegit, nomina eorundem ideo dissimulavimus ne magnorum virorum naevos vellicando gloriolam captare velle videremur. Et stultum semper judicavimus, cum ipse te hominem noris ab erroribus haudquidquam immunem, aspera in alios censura reliquos ad paria tibi reponenda irritare.'

**** *Samuel Pufendorfius*, professor in jure naturae apud regem Sueciae: in praefatione sui libri De Jure Naturae et Gentium, Amstelodam. 1688 :

'Sic et Thomas Hobbius in operibus suis ad civilem scientiam spectantibus plurima habet quantivis pretii et nemo cui rerum ejusmodi est intellectus negaverit tam profunde ipsum societatis humanae et civilis compagem rimatum fuisse ut pauci priorum cum ipso heic comparari queant. Et qua a vero aberrat, occasionem tamen ad talia meditanda suggerit quae fortasse aliàs nemini in mentem venissent. Sed quod et hic in religione peculiaria sibi et horrida dogmata finxerit, hoc ipso apud multos non citra rationem sui

. * MS. Aubr. 9, fol. 53ᵛ.   in a partial citation in MS. Aubr. 9,
** MS. Aubr. 9, fol. 41ᵛ.   fol. 28.
*** MS. Aubr. 9, fol. 5ᵛ.   **** MS. Aubr. 9, fol. 6ᵛ.
ᵃ 'Elementorum Jur. Univ. lib. II,'

aversationem excitavit. Quanquam et illud non raro contingere videas ut ab illis maximo cum supercilio condemnetur abs quibus minime lectus fuit aut intellectus.'

⟨ *Conclusion.* ⟩

* I would have, just before FINIS,

> Pascitur in vivis Livor: post fata quiescit ;
> Tunc suus ex merito quemque tuetur honos.
>
> Ovid. *Eleg.* ᵃ

** Last of all insert the pindarique ode on Mr. Hobbes made by Mr. Abraham Cowley; and after that, in the next page, the verses made by Dr. Ralph Bathurst of Trinity College in Oxon, which are before Mr. Hobbes's *Humane Nature.*

⟨ *Copies of letters by, or about, Thomas Hobbes.* ⟩

i. *Thomas Hobbes to Josias Pullen.*

*** For my much honored freind Mr. Josias Pullen, Vice-principall of Magdalen Hall in Oxon.

Honour'd Sir,

I understand by a letter from Mr. Aubry that you desire to have the bookes I have published to put them into the library of Magdalen Hall. I have here sent them you, and very willingly, as being glad of the occasion, for I assure you that I owe so much honour and respect to that society that I would have sent them, and desired to have them accepted, long agoe, if I could have donne it as decently as now that you have assured me that your selfe and some others of your house have a good opinion of them so that though the house refuse them they are not lost. You know how much they have been decryed by Dr. Wallis and others of the greatest sway in the University, and therfore to offer them to any Colledge or Hall had been a greater signe of humility than I have yet attained to.

---

* MS. Aubr. 9, fol. 54.
ᵃ Ovid. *Amor.* i. 15. 39.
** MS. Aubr. 9, fol. 55.

*** MS. Aubr. 9, fol. 8; not the original, but a transcript by Aubrey.

For your owne civility in approving them, I give you many thanks; and remain

Sir,

Your most humble servant,

Tho. Hobbes.

1672 [a], London,
   Febr. 1st.

ii. *Thomas Hobbes to John Aubrey.*

* Noble Sir,

    I am very glad to hear you are well and continue your favours towards me.

'Tis a long time since I have been able to write my selfe, and am now so weake that it is a paine to me to dictate.

But yet I cannot choose but thanke you for this letter of Jan. 25th which I receaved not till the last of ffebruary. I was assured a good while since that Dr. Wallis his learning is no where esteemed but in the Universities by such as have engaged themselves in the defence of his geometry and are now ashamed to recant it. And I wonder not if Dr. Wallis, or any other, that have studyed mathematicks onely to gaine preferment, when his ignorance is discovered, convert his study to jugling and to the gaining of a reputation of conjuring, decyphering, and such arts [b] as are in the booke [c] you sent me.

As for the matter it selfe, I meane the teaching of a man borne deafe and dumbe to speake, I thinke it impossible. But I doe not count him deafe and indocible that can heare a word spoken as loud as is possible at the very entrance to his eare, for of this I am assured that a man borne absolutely deafe must of necessity be made to heare before he can be made to speake, much lesse to understand. And he that could make him heare (being a great and common good) would well deserve both to be honoured

---

[a] 167⅞.

* MS. Aubr. 9, fol. 9: the original, in James Wheldon's print-like writing.

[b] Subst. for 'jugleries.'

[c] Probably Dr. William Holder's ' *A Supplement to the Philosophical* *Transactions for July*, 1670,' London, 1678, accusing Dr. Wallis of robbing him of the credit of teaching a deaf-mute. See Clark's Wood's *Life and Times*, i. 309.

and to be enriched.   He that could make him speake
a few words onely deserved nothing.   But he that brags
of this and cannot doe it, deserves to be whipt.

Sir, I am most heartily
Your most faithfull and most humble servant,
THOMAS HOBBES.

Hardwick,
March the 5th, 1677 [a].

* To my most honored frend Mr. John Awbry, esqre,
to be left for him at Mr. Crooke's, a bookseller, at the
Green Dragon without Temple barre, London.

iii. *Thomas Hobbes to William Crooke*, with an enclosure
to John Aubrey.

⟨Hobbes' letter to Crooke is found as fol. 11 of MS. Aubr. 9 : the
enclosure to Aubrey, as foll. 12, 13.   Both are in James Wheldon's
handwriting.

It appears by the post-stamps on the backs of these letters that the
charge for a letter was 3*d.*, with 3*d.* for each enclosure.   Thus the
letters of Aug. 18, 1679, March 5, 16⅞⅞, Sept. 7, 1680, are all marked as
costing 3*d.* postage (MS. Aubr. 9, foll. 15ᵛ, 10ᵛ, 21ᵛ) ; while this letter
to Crooke, with its enclosure, cost 6*d.* (*ibid.*, fol. 11ᵛ) ; and the letter
of Jan. 16, 16⅞⅞, with its two enclosures, cost 9*d.* (*ibid.* fol. 17ᵛ).⟩

** Sir,
        I have receaved Sir George Ent's booke and Mr.
Aubrey's letter, to which I have written an answer, but I
cannot tell how to send it to him without your helpe, and
therefore I have sent it to you here inclosed, for I believe
he comes now and then to your shop, and I pray you
doe me the favour to deliver it to him.

I rest, your humble servant
THO. HOBBES.

Chatsworth,
March the 25th 1679.
*** For Mr. William Crooke,
Bookeseller,
At the Green Dragon without Temple barr
London.

---

[a] i. e. 167⅞.
* MS. Aubr. 9, fol. 10ᵛ.

** MS. Aubr. 9. fol. 11.
*** MS. Aubr. 9, fol. 11ᵛ.

* Worthy Sir,

I have receaved from Will: Crooke the booke of Sir George Ent of the use of respiration. It is a very learned and ingenious booke, full of true and deepe philosophy, and I pray you to present unto him my most humble service. Though I receaved it but three days since, yet drawn on by the easinesse of the style and elegance of the language I have read it all over. And I give you most hearty thankes for sending of it to me, and to Mr. Ent ᵃ who was pleased to bestow it upon me, and I am very glad to hear that Sir George him selfe is alive and in good health, though I believe he is very near as old as I am.

I knew not how to addresse my letter to you, but at all adventure I sent it inclosed in a letter to Mr. Crooke at whose shop I suppose you sometimes looke in as you passe the street.

I pray you present my service to Mr. Hooke and thanke him for the honour of his salutation.

I am, Sir, your most obliged and humble servant,
THOMAS HOBBES.

Chatsworth,
March the 25ᵗʰ, 1679.

** To my most honoured frend,
Mr. John Aubrey.

iv. *Thomas Hobbes to John Aubrey.*

*** Honored Sir,

I thanke you for your letter of Aug. 2ᵈ, and I pray you present my humble thanks to Sir George Ent that he accepteth of my judgment upon his booke. I fear it is rather his good nature then my merit. I am sorry for the news you write of his son.

I have been told that my booke of the Civill Warr is come abroad, and am sorry for it, especially because I could

---

* MS. Aubr. 9, fol. 12.
ᵃ Sir George Ent's son: *supra*, p. 245.
** The address: MS. Aubr. 9,

fol. 13ᵛ.
*** MS. Aubr. 9, fol. 14: the original, in James Wheldon's handwriting. .

not get his majestye to license it, not because it is ill printed
or has a foolish title set to it, for I believe that any
ingenious man may understand the wickednesse of that
time, notwithstanding the errors of the presse.

The treatise *De Legibus*, at the end of it, is imperfect.
I desire Mr. Horne to pardon me that I consent not to his
motion, nor shall Mr. Crooke himselfe get my consent to
print it.

I pray you present my humble service to Mr. Butler[a].

The priviledge of stationers is (in my opinion) a very great
hinderance to the advancement of all humane learning.

I am, Sir, your very humble servant,

THO. HOBBES.

Chatsworth,
Aug. the 18th, 1679.

* To my much honoured frend Mr. John Aubrey, at
Mr. Hooke's lodging in Gresham College, London.

v. *James Wheldon to William Crooke*, with enclosure to
John Aubrey, and a copy of Hobbes' will.

⟨Wheldon's letter to Crooke is found as foll. 16 and 17 of MS. Aubr.
9; the enclosure to Aubrey, as foll. 18, 19.⟩

** Hardwick, January the 16th, 1679[b].

Sir,

Three days since I receaved your letter of the 9th
instant together with one from Mr. Aubrey, and because
they contain both the same particulars I thinke it un-
necessary to repeat to you what I have written back to that
gentleman.

All that I can add is onely this, that neither Mr. Halleley
nor I have anything in either of our hands of Mr. Hobbes's
writing, the very little of that kind that he left behind him
being disposed of according to his own order before he
removed from Chatsworth.

According to Mr. Aubrey's direction I have here inclosed

---

[a] Author of *Hudibras*.
* MS. Aubr. 9, fol. 15[v].

** MS. Aubr. 9, fol. 16.
[b] 16⅞⅞.

my letter to him, which I pray you present to him with my
humble service as soon as you shall see him.

I am, Sir, your most humble servant,

JAMES WHELDON.

* To my much respected frend
   Mr. William Crooke
   at the Green Dragon without Templebarr
   In London ª.

** Hardwick, January the 16ᵗʰ, 1679 ᵇ.

Worthy Sir,

Having been abroad about businesse for some days,
I receaved, at my coming home, your letter of the third of
this month, which evidences the great esteeme you have for
Mr. Hobbes, for which I returne you my humble thanks,
and particularly for the paines you have been pleased
to take in the large account of what you your selfe,
Mr. Anthony a Wood, and Sir George Ent designe for
Mr. Hobbes his honour.

I am glad Mr. Crooke has receaved his Life in Prose,
which was the onely thing Mr. Halleley got possession of,
and sent it to him ᶜ by my hand. Mr. Halleley tells me now,
that Mr. Hobbes (in the time of his sicknesse) told him he
had promised it to Mr. Crooke, but said he was unwilling
it should ever be published as written by himselfe; and I
beleeve it was some such motive, which made him burne
those Latine verses Mr. Crooke sent him about that time.

For those Latine verses you mention about Ecclesiasticall
Power, I remember them, for I writ them out, but know
not what became of them, unlesse he presented them to
judge Vaughan, or burned them, as you seem to intimate.

He fell sick about the middle ᵈ of October last. His
disease was the strangury, and the physitians judged it

* MS. Aubr. 9, fol. 17ᵛ.

ª Readdressed in another (?William
Crooke's) hand :—'at Mr. Moore, in
Hammond Alley'; see p. 44.

** MS. Aubr. 9, fol. 18.

ᵇ 16⅞⅞.

ᶜ Subst. for 'Mr. Crooke.'

ᵈ Subst. for 'beginning.'

incurable by reason of his great age and naturall decay. About the 20th of November, my Lord being to remove from Chatsworth to Hardwick, Mr. Hobbes would not be left behind ; and therefore with a fether bed laid into the coach, upon which he lay warme clad, he was conveyed safely, and was in appearance as well after that little journey as before it. But seven or eight days after, his whole right side was taken with the dead palsy, and at the same time he was made speechlesse. He lived after this seven days, taking very little nourishment, slept well, and by intervalls endeavoured to speake, but could not. In the whole time of his sicknesse he was free from fever. He seemed therefore to dye rather for want of the fuell of life (which was spent in him) and meer weaknesse and decay, then by the power of his disease, which was thought to be onely an effect of his age and weaknesse. He was born the 5th of Aprill, in the year 1588, and died the 4th of December, 1679. He was put into a woollen shroud and coffin, which was covered with a white sheet, and upon that a black herse cloth, and so carryed upon men's shoulders, a little mile to[a] church. The company, consisting of the family and neighbours that came to his funerall, and attended him to his grave, were very handsomely entertained with wine, burned and raw, cake, biscuit, etc. He was buried in the parish church of Hault Hucknall, close adjoining to the raile of the monument of the grandmother of the present earle of Devonshire, with the service of the Church of England by the minister of the parish. It is intended to cover his grave with a stone of black marble as soon as it can be got ready, with a plain inscription of his name, the place of his birth, and the time of that and of his death.

As to his will, it is sent up to London to be proved there, and by the copy of it, which I here send you, I beleeve you will judge it fitt to make no mention of it in [*] what you designe to get written by way of Commentary on his life.

As for the palsey in his hands, it began in ffrance, before the year 1650, and has grown upon him by degrees ever

[a] Subst. for 'to the parish church.'   [*] MS. Aubr. 9, fol. 18ᵛ.

since ; but Mr. Halleley remembers not how long it has disabled him to write legibly.

Mr. Halleley never heard of a pension from the ffrench king and beleeves there was no such thing ever intended. He desires you to accept of his thanks for your favourable remembrance of him, and of the returne of his respects to you by me. And if hereafter you should want any thing which we know, that might contribute* to the honour of Mr. Hobbes's memory, upon the least notice, shall readily be imparted to you.

In the mean time, with much respect, I rest,

Sir, your much obliged and humble servant,

JAMES WHELDON.

* To my highly honoured frend, John Aubrey, esq., this humbly present.

** *A true copy of Mr. Hobbes's will.*

The 25th day of September in the 29th year of the raigne of our Soveraigne Lord, King Charles the Second, and in the yeare of our Lord God, 1677.

I, Thomas Hobbes, of Malmesbury, in the county of Wilts, gent. make this my last Will and Testament.

First, I bequeath to Mary Tirell, daughter of my deceased brother, Edmund Hobbes, forty pounds. Item, I bequeath to Elenor Harding, daughter also of my deceased brother, Edmund Hobbes, forty pounds. Item, I bequeath to Elizabeth Alaby, the daughter of Thomas Alaby, two hundred pounds, and because she is an orphan, and committed by me to the tuition of my executor, my will is, that she should be maintained decently by my executor, till she be 16 yeares of age, and that then the said two hundred pounds be delivered into her hands, being intended for her furtherance in marriage, but let her dispose of it as she please ; and if it happen that the said Elizabeth Alaby die before she come to the age of 16 yeares, then my will is, that the said 200 *li.*

---

* 'Anything' followed: scored out.

* MS. Aubr. 9, fol. 19ʳ.   ** MS. Aubr. 9, fol. 19.

be divided equally between the said Mary Tirell and Elenor Harding.

Item, whereas it hath pleased my good lord, the earle of Devonshire, to bid me oftentimes heretofore, and now at the making of this my last will, to dispose therein of one hundred pounds, to be paid by his lordship, for which I give him most humble thanks; I doe give and dispose of the same in this manner : There be five grand-children of my brother, Edmund Hobbes, to the eldest whereof, whose name is Thomas Hobbes, I have heretofore given a peece of land, which may and doth, I think, content him, and therefore to the other four that are younger, I dispose of the same 100 *li.* the gift of my lord of Devonshire, to be divided equally amongst them, as a furtherance to bind them apprentices.

And I make and ordaine James Wheldon, servant to the earle of Devonshire, my executor, to whom I give the residue of my money and goods whatsoever; and because I would have him in some sort contented for the great service he hath done me, I would pray his majestie to what I left him to add the arreare of my pension, or as much of it as it pleases his majestie.

(His name and seale.)

Sealed, signed and published
    in the presence of
        JOHN ASHTON,
        WILL^M BARKER.

Item I give unto Mary Dell the sum of ten pounds.

I pray* you keep his will private to your selfe and Mr. Hobbes's frends onely.

vi. *James Wheldon to John Aubrey.*

                * Chatsworth, Sept. the 7th, 1680.
Honoured Sir,
    Although for these three weekes, since I receaved your letter, I have made all the enquiry I can, yet all

---

   * Request added by Wheldon, at the end of the transcript of the will.
   * MS. Aubr. 9, fol. 20.

that I hear of the death and buriall of Sir Charles Cavendish
is that he was interred at Bolsover in the vault belonging
to the family of the duke of Newcastle about the year
1652 or 1653. I will continue to make further inquiry,
and if I can learne the day and the month of his death or
buriall will give you notice of it.

I have sent you underwritten Mr. Hobbes's epitaph
written by himselfe, which is but lately come to my hand
from a person that copyed it from the originall.

With much respect, I rest, Sir,

Your most humble and obliged servant,

JAMES WHELDON.

My lord of Devonshire has paid the hundred pounds to
Mr. Hobbes's kinred, which he bid Mr. Hobbes dispose of
in his will.

Condita hic sunt ossa
Thomae Hobbes
Qui per multos annos servivit
duobus comitibus Devoniae
(patri et filio).
Vir probus, et fama eruditionis.
Domi forisque bene cognitus
Obiit Anno Domini 1679, mensis Dec^{is} die 4°,
Aetatis suae 91.

* To my much honoured frend John Aubrey, esq.
To * be left at Mr. William Crooke's at the Green Dragon
without Temple barr, London.

vii. *William Aubrey to John Aubrey.*

** Kington, June 5th, 1680.

Deare brother,

I sopose I shall be here more then a week longer
as .... I know not whether Mr. John Stokes or Sir
John Knight have the key of the study.

* MS. Aubr. 9, fol. 21^v.

* This part of the address is scored
out, and there is substituted, ' for Dr.
Blackborn at Jonathan's Coffee.'

** MS. Aubr. 9, fol. 3. The letter

is sealed with the Aubrey coat :—'a
chevron between 3 eagles' heads
erased,' an annulet (?) for difference ;
and marked 'post payd 3d.' The
letter is mutilated.

Jo. Tay . . . buried 16 of July 1580.

Nicholas Fauckener, vicar, buried 20 July 1612.

Richard Hine[a] . . .

I shall e⟨n⟩devour to set the family of the Powers to rights. It was honest parson P⟨ower's⟩ grandmoth⟨er I⟩ think and Jonath. Deekes grandmother was Thomas Lyte's sisters. Alderman Lyte's grandm. was a P⟨ower⟩ of Stanton . . . . , which James Power, Mr. J. G. nephew might purchase againe with a wife, with 1500 *li.*, but which formerly was worth 360 *li.* per annum, but he's goeing to creep into one of Jon. Deeks' woolpacks, viz. his daughter.

I was at Malmesbury but did see ⟨neither⟩ the church nor register but desired Mr. Binnion the parson to doe against I come againe; but Francis Hobbes' widow's good memory did give me much satisfaction. The register at Westport is not 80 yeares old (not more): the paving [b] is all new .

The old vicar Hobs was a good fellow and had been at cards all Saturday night, and at church in his sleep he cries out 'Trafells is troumps [d] ' (viz. clubs). Then quoth the clark, ' Then, master, he tha⟨t⟩ have ace doe rub.'

He ⟨was⟩ a collirice [e] man, and a parson (which I thinke succeeded him at Westport) provoked him (a purpose) at the church doore , soe Hobs stroke him and was forcd to fly for it and . . . in obscurity beyound London ; died there, was about 80 yeares since.

Mr. William Hobs, a great clothier (old Graye's pre-disessor in the same house). He had at Cleverton 60 *li.* or 80 *li.* per annum, and was first or 2 cousin to the philo-sipher. But his line is extinct. He was parson Stump's god-father, and brake in his trade. He had 1000 *li.* left and was 1000 *li.* in debt ; and at London challenged one to throw with him one throw on the dye for 1000 *li.*, and wonn, payd his debt, and afterwards flourished in his trade, and if there

---

[a] Or Hynd : p. 154.

[b] Of the church at Westport.

[c] So that if there were any old gravestones in the church, they have

been destroyed.

[d] Broad Wiltshire for 'trumps'; see *supra*, p. 324.

[e] Choleric.

be any inscriptions of H⟨obbes⟩, it must be for him, in the abbye.

* Mr. William Gale of Chipnam was buried yesterday. I was at Dracot, Wensday last; Sir J. and his lady was writing to you. They are in mourning for the earl of Marleborow. He died to-morrow will be three week ᵃ. Sir J⟨ames⟩ L⟨ong⟩ is quartring his coat of arms.

　　To be left at Mr. Hooks lodgings
　　　　in Gresham Colledge
　　in Bishopsgate Street, London ᵇ.

⟨The lower part of this letter gave the following pedigree, but a piece has been torn off and is now MS. Aubr. 8, fol. 2.⟩

⟨*Pedigree of Hobbes.*⟩

... HOBBES

1. Francis Hobbes *m.* Katherine, daughter of (This Francis lived in Burnevall at Malmsbury, and died about 40 yeares since, sine prole). ... Phillips, a phisition at Malmsbury. She afterwards maried Mr. Potluck of Cirencester.

2. Thomas Hobbes, *m.* ... Mideton. vicar.

1. Edmund Hobbes *m.* Frances Ludlow, of Shipton, com. Glocester.

2. Thomas, 'of Malmsbury.'　Anne Hobs *m.* Thomas (see *infra*).　Laurence.

1. Mary Hobbes *m.* Roger Tirell, of Westport.　Elinor Hobbes *m.* John Harding, of Sadlewood in Glouster.　Francis Hobs *m.* Sarah (see *infra*).　Alexander.

1. Roger. 2. Isaac (25 years old).　1. Alce. 2. Sarah. 3. Mary.

1. Roger, aged 28, April last.　2. James, 23.　Mary.

Anne Hobs (*supra*: the philosopher's sister)　*m.*　Thomas Laurence.

1. Thomas, sine prole.　2. William.　Henry, sine prole.　John.

1. Frances, *m.* Richard Dicks, a souldier of the garison, and now not heard off.　2. Mary *maried* William Povey, of Malmsbury. (One daughter.)　3. Anne Laurence *maried* Richard Gay of Kington.

1. William. 2. Thomas. 3. Francis.　Thomas.

1. Thomas. 2. Robert, (R. Wiseman's godson).　3. Richard. 4. John.

* MS. Aubr. 9, fol. 3ᵛ.
ᵃ Admon. of William Ley, last earl of Marlborough of that family, was granted 9 June, 1680.
ᵇ A jotting on the back of the letter

is:—'Malmesbury:—where the steeple is was a church dedicated to St. Paul.'
ᶜ Then a common spelling for 'Alice.'

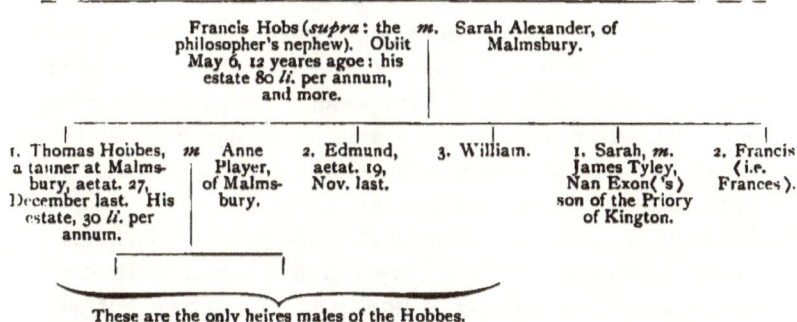

Francis Hobs (*supra*: the *m.* Sarah Alexander, of
philosopher's nephew). Obiit   Malmsbury.
May 6, 12 yeares agoe: his
estate 80 *li.* per annum,
and more.

1. Thomas Hobbes, *m* Anne   2. Edmund,   3. William.   1. Sarah, *m.*   2. Francis
a tanner at Malms- Player,   aetat. 19,   James Tyley,   (i.e.
bury, aetat. 27,   of Malms- Nov. last.   Nan Exon('s) Frances).
December last. His bury.   son of the Priory
estate, 30 *li.* per   of Kington.
annum.

These are the only heires males of the Hobbes.

It is uncertaine whether Anne Gay have any brother or
sister living, but it is pitty the poor woman should
have somthing if it be but 5 shillings. If you know the
executor speak for her.

I was saying to Francis Hobbes's widow (who remembers
her service to you) that her son should get one of Mr. Thomas
Hobbes's printed pictures.

In hast,

Your very affectionat brother,

WILLIAM AUBREY.

Keep a copie of Rogers' pedegree ᵃ.
* These to my honoured freind,
      Mr. John Awbrey
          present.

viii. *Hon. Charles Hatton to William Crooke.*

⟨MS. Aubr. 9, fol. 26. The letter is written by a secretary, the
signature C. Hatton being in a different hand. Crooke has endorsed
it (fol. 27ᵛ) 'Mr. Hatton's letter about Mr. Hobs': to which Aubrey
has added 'scil. the lord Hatton's son.' On fol. 27 is a note, probably
by Crooke, of the 'tracts' referred to, viz. 'Life ᵇ, Rheto⟨ric⟩ ᶜ, Considerations ᵈ, Natural Philosophy ᵉ.'

** Mr. Crooke,

    I thanke you for the perusall of Mr. Hobbs his tracts
which wase a civility I did not expect or desire, for

---

* This pedigree of Rogers in William
Aubrey's hand is found in MS. Aubr.
3, fol. 123.
  * The address on MS. Aubr. 8, fol. 2ᵛ.
  ᵇ Published 1681.

ᶜ Republished 1682.
ᵈ Republ. 1680.
ᵉ Publ. 1682.
  ** MS. Aubr. 9, fol. 26. The date
of the letter is circ. 1681–2.

I wou'd not have you at any time deliver any booke to any person who comes in my name unless he then payes you for it.   I did desire only to know exactly the particular price of each tract bound apart in marble'd leather, guilt on the backe and ribbed, which pray send me by the bearer by whom I returne you your booke.

I have cursorily looked over Mr. Hobbs his life in Latine which I beleeve will be a very vendible booke both here and beyond sea, for ther is noe lover of learning but will have the curiosity to be particularly informed of the life of soe eminent a person.   And truly the reading of it wase very satisfactory to me, for in my apprehension it is very well writ, but I cou'd have wish'd the author had more dilated upon some particulars; and because you intimate a designe to publish it in English I shall hint to you that the author of the life in Latine hath either not taken notice of at all, or too slightingly, some things very remarkeable relating to the temper of Mr. Hobbs his mind or to the infirmity of his body, as his extraordinary timorousnes which he himself in his Latine poem doth very ingeniously confess and attributes it to the influence of his mother's dread of the Spanish invasion in 88, she being then with child of him.   And I have been informed, I think by your self, that Mr. Hobbs wase for severall yeares before he died soe paralyticall that he wase scarce able to write his name, and that in the absence of his amanuensis not being able to write anything he made scrawls on a piece of paper to remind him of the conceptions of his mind he design'd to have committed to writing.   But the author * of his life in Latine only sa⟨i⟩th that about 60 yeares of age he wase taken with a trembling in his hands, the forerunner of the palsy ; which in my apprehension deserves to be enlarg'd upon, for it is very prodigious that neither the timorousness of his nature from his infancy, nor the decay of his vital heat in the extremity of old age, accompagnied with the palsy to that violence, shou'd not have chill'd the briske fervour and vigour of his mind, which did wonder-

* MS. Aubr. 9, fol. 26ᵛ.

fully continue to him to his last; which is a subject fit to be discours'd on by a genious equally philosophicall with Mr. Hobbs, wase that now to be hoped for. It is soe considerable to me that I cou'd not refrayne acquainting you that in my apprehension it wase convenient you tooke notice therof in his life you are setting forth in English.

I am, your assured freind,

C. HATTON.

* Mr. Crooke, at the Green Dragon,
   nere Temple-bar.

Notes.

[1] (P. 323.) On fol. 29ᵛ of MS. Aubr. 9, Anthony Wood notes:—'Send to Malmsburie to take out of the register the Christian name of Mr. Hobs' father, when Mr. Hobbs was borne, or when his said father was buried.' [On this Aubrey notes:—'As I remember he dyed at Thistleworth; vide the register booke at Thistleworth, where Mr. Hobbes his father lived in obscurity a reader, and there dyed about 1630.'] Wood goes on:—'I remember when I was there' (in 1676, Clark's Wood's *Life and Times*, ii. 410, 411) 'there were two inscriptions of the Hobs on brass plates; one dyed 1606, quaere. Take out the names of all the Hobs in the register.' Obedient to this advice, Aubrey sent his brother William to Malmesbury: *supra*, p. 387.

[2] (P. 323.) In MS. Aubr. 3, fol. 26, Aubrey puts the substance of this paragraph in a neater form:—

'Mr. Hobbes' father was minister of Westport, to which Brokenborongh and Charlton doe belong as chapells of ease, but all not worth above . . . . He was one of the clergie of Queen Elizabeth's time—a little learning went a great way with him and many other Sir Johns in those days—he read homilies.'

[3] (P. 323.) On fol. 30 of MS. Aubr. 9 is another draft of this paragraph:— 'He had an elder brother, Francis Hobbes, a wealthy man, and had been alderman of the borough' (dupl. with 'towne'); 'by profession a glover, which is a great trade here and was heretofore greater. He was *orbus*. He contributed much, or altogether maintained his nephew Thomas at Magdalen Hall in Oxon; and when he dyed gave him an *agellum* (vocat. "the Gasten"), which lyes neer the horse faire: valet per annum 16 *li.* vel 18 *li.*'

[4] (P. 324.) Anthony Wood notes:—'Quaere in the register of Brakenborough when they were maried and their you'l find her Christian name.'—MS. Aubr. 9, fol. 30ᵛ.

[5] (P. 326.) In MS. Aubr. 9, fol. 31ᵛ, Anthony Wood suggests the following paragraph for the transition from the account of Malmsbury to the life of Hobbes:—

'As Malmsbury was famous in this respect that it gave death and buriall to that famous philosopher of his time Johannes Scotus *alias* Erigina who was stabd to death with penknives by his scholars, where there was a statue set up in memory of him (ut in *Hist. et Antiq. Oxon.* lib. 1, pag. 16 *b*), so much more famous in later times for the birth of that great philosopher T. H.'

* The address: on MS. Aubr. 9, fol. 27ᵛ.

In MS. Aubr. 3, fol. 28, Aubrey begins his sketch of Hobbes' life thus :—
'Westport juxta Malmesbury:—This place is for nothing so famous as for the
birth of my honoured and learned friend and countryman, Mr. Thomas Hobbes,
author of *de Corpore, de Homine, de Cive*, etc.

He was borne the 5th day of Aprill 1588 at his father's howse, which is the
farthest on the left hand as you goe in the way or street called . . . , leaving
the church on the right hand.'

⁶ (P. 326.) The verses alluded to are in Hobbes's metrical life of himself
(MS. Aubr. 3, fol. 28—' he writt his life last yeare, viz. 1673, in Latin verse ').
Aubrey cites these lines, MS. Aubr. 9, fol. 31ᵛ :—

' T. H. *Vita* in verse

Oppidulum parvum est; habuit sed multa relatu
Digna, sed imprimis Coenobium celebre,
Et castrum (melius nisi sint dua castra vocanda)
Colle sita, et bino flumine cincta fere.

Vide mapp' ⟨perhaps Speed's map of Wiltshire : but on a slip at fol. 31ᵛ,
Aubrey gives a 'map' of Malmesbury: see *supra*, pp. 325, 326⟩.

On this Anthony Wood comments: 'See 1 vol. of *Monast. Anglican.* concerning
the monastery.'

⁷ (P. 326.) The matter of this paragraph is put a little more clearly in MS.
Aubr. 3, fol. 28 : 'Westport juxta Malmesbury:—The church was dedicated to
St. Mary. Here were three aisles ᵃ which tooke up the whole area. And ⟨the
church was⟩ reported to be more ancient then the abbey. In the windowes
(which were very good) were inscriptions which declared so much. Quaere, if
Madulph the Scottsman taught here—unde origo monasterii ⁄ Vide Camdenum
de hoc.

Before the late warres here was a prettie church, where were very good
windowes and a faire steeple, higher than the other, which much adorned the
towne of Malmesbury. In it were five tuneable bells, which Sir William
Waller or his army melted into ordinance, or rather sold. The church was
pulled downe that the enimie might not shelter themselves against the garrison
of Malmesbury.'

⁸ (P. 328.) Aubrey's *Collection of Genitures* is now MS. Aubr. 23. The
place Aubrey here refers to is fol. 52ᵛ in that MS., viz. :—

'Mr. Thomas Hobbes of Malmesbury borne at Westport juxta Malmesbury
1588, April 5, being Good Fryday, 5ʰ 2' mane, horâ solis' (i. e. at sunrise).
'I had the yeare, and day, and houre from his owne mouth.'

Aubrey in several places recurs to this point, e. g. in MS. Aubr. 3, fol. 28 :—

'Mr. Thomas Hobbes told me that he was borne Apr. 5ᵗʰ 1588 on Good
Fryday, in the morning between 4 and six.'

⁹ (P. 328.) Aubrey took great interest in this as an example in astrology,
in which 'art' he thoroughly believed. He alludes to Hobbes's horoscope
in several places, e. g. note on fol. 32ᵛ in MS. Aubr. 9 :—

'Dr. ⟨Francis⟩ Bernard, physitian, will write a discourse on his nativity.
Mr. John Gadbury hath calculated this nativity from my time given, and will
print it. Why should not I insert ' ⟨dupl. with 'print'⟩ ' the scheme and give
a summary of his judgement⁄ It would be gratefull to those that love that

---

ᵃ Or 'a nave and two aisles': *supra*, p. 326.

art.' Whereon Anthony Wood notes—'You should never ask these questions but do them out of hand forthwith—you have time enough, and if it be done by Easter terme 'tis well.'

MS. Aubr. 9, fol. 28 :—'⟨Send⟩ to Mr. J. Gadbury and Dr. Bernard ⟨T. H.'s⟩ accidents.'

MS. Aubr. 8, fol. 8 :—'T. Hobbes—Quaere Dr. Bernard pro his nativity : vide my Collection of Genitures ubi from his owne mouth more correct then formerly, viz. 5ʰ 2' mane.'

This horoscope is given in MS. Aubr. 8, fol. 82, and is reproduced in facsimile at the end of this edition.

Pasted on to fol. 1ᵛ of MS. Aubr. 9 is the scheme with this note :—' This scheme was erected according to the aestimate time by Mr. Henry Coley, astrologer.—Thomas Hobbes, Malmesburiensis, borne at Westport juxta Malmesbury, 1588, April 5, being Good Fryday, 5ʰ 2' mane, hora solis ᵃ. I had the yeare and day and houre from his owne mouth.'

¹⁰ (P. 328.) In MS. Aubr. 3, fol. 26, thus :—'At fower yeer old Mr. Thomas Hobbes went to schoole in Westport church till 8—then ᵇ the church was painted. At 8 he could read well and number a matter of four or five figures.

After, he went to Malmesbury to parson Evans.

† Who being a bachelor (not above 19) taught him and two or three more ingeniose laddes after supper till 9.

After him, he had for his schoolemaster, Mr. Robert Latimer †, a good Graecian ; by whom he so well profited that at 14 yeares old he went a good scholler to Magdalen Hall in Oxford.'

¹¹ (P. 330.) As seen in the next paragraph, there was some doubt as to which 'Principal of Magdalen Hall' recommended Hobbes to the earl of Devonshire's service. In MS. Aubr. 9, fol. 29, is the note :—

' Take notice of Dr. Blackburne's altering some times and dates,' ⟨in Hobbes' prose Latin life of himself, prefixed to the *Auctarium vitae Hobbianae*⟩ 'differing from this originall, e. g. of Mr. Hobbes being admitted at Magdalen Hall when Sir James Hussey was principall, which he would doe against my consent because he sayd it " would make a better picture," wheras by the matriculation-booke it appeares that Dr. Wilkinson was then the principall.'

¹² (P. 331.) On fol. 34ᵛ of MS. Aubr. 9, Aubrey has the following account of Gorhambury :—

' Memorandum in my Liber B ᶜ. I have sett downe an exact description of this delicious parquet ᵈ, now (1656) plowed up and spoil'd. The east part of it which extends towards Verulam-house (pulled downe, and the materialls sold by Sir H⟨arbottle⟩ Grimston, about ten yeares since) consisted of severall parts, viz. some thickets of plumme-trees, with fine walkes between ; some of rasberies. Here were planted most fruit-trees which would grow in our climate ; and also severall choice forest-trees. The walkes both of boscages and fruit-trees ; and in severall places where were the best prospects, were built elegant summer-houses ᵉ of Roman architecture, then standing (1656) well ᶠ wainscotted, but the paving gonne. One would have thought the most barbarous nation had made a conquest here. This place was, in his lordship's time, a sanctuary for phesants,

ᵃ i. e. at sunrise.
ᵇ i. e. at that time the old stained windows were still extant.
ᶜ Now lost : Clark's Wood's *Life*

and Times, iv. 192 : see *supra*, p. 65.
ᵈ Dupl. with ' parke.'
ᵉ Dupl. with ' banquetting-houses.'
ᶠ Dupl. with ' good.'

partridges, and those of severall kinds and nations, as Spanish, &c. speckled, white, etc. I have, in this lib. B., four leves in fol. close written of the two houses, gardens, woods, &c. and of his lordship's manner of living and grandarie, which perhaps would doe well in a description of Hartfordshire, or, perhaps [a], in his lordship's life.'

[13] (P. 332.) In MS. Aubr. 6, fol. 1ʳ, is this note :—'Dr. ⟨John⟩ Pell says that for a man to begin to study mathematics at 40 yeares old, 'tis as if one should at that age learne to play on the lute—applicable to Mr. Thomas Hobbes. Vide vitam Jonae Moore.'

[14] (P. 338.) In MS. Aubr. 3, fol. 26, thus :—

'Memorandum :—about the time of the King's returne †, he was makeing of a very good poëme in Latin hexameters. It was the history of the encroachment of the clergie (both Roman and Reformed) on the civill power. I sawe at least 300 verses (they were mark't). At what time there was a report the bishops would have him burn't for a heretique. So he then feared the search of his papers and burned the greatest part of these verses.'

† Quaere in what yeares his bookes were writ.

[15] (P. 339.) The first draft of this passage stood as follows, MS. Aubr. 9, foll. 40, 41 :—'In April following was the dawning of the coming in of our gracious soveraigne, who being a great lover of curious painting I knew could not but sett for his picture to my ever honoured friend Mr. S. Cowper, who [b] besides his art was an ingeniose person and of great humanity. In April I wrott a letter to Mr. Hobbes in Derbyshire, by all meanes desiring him to come-up and make use of the opportunity of renewing his majestie's graces to him at our friend's howse. He thanked me for '—etc.

[16] (P. 341.) Aubrey, writing to Wood, on Feb. 3, 167⅞, enlarges on this treatise : Wood MS. F. 39, fol. 196ᵛ :—

'The old gent. (T. Hobbes) is strangely vigorous, for his understanding, still ; and every morning walkes abroad to meditate.

'He haz writt a treatise concerning lawe, which 8 or 9 yeares since I much importuned him to doe, and, in order to it, gave him the Lord Chancellor Bacon's *Maximes of the Lawe*. Now every one will doe him the right to acknowledge he is rare for definitions, and the lawyers building on old-fashiond maximes (some right, some wrong) must need fall into severall paralogismes. Upon this consideration I was earnest with him to consider these things. To which he was unwilling, telling me he doubted he should not have dayes enough left to doe it.

'He drives on, in this, the king's prerogative high. Judge ⟨Sir Matthew⟩ Hales, who is no great courtier, has read it and much mislikes it, and is his enemy. Judge Vaughan has read it and much commends it.'

[17] (P. 355.) Note, however, that on some of the letters from Hobbes in MS. Aubr. 9, viz., those of date March 25, 1679 (fol. 11ᵛ, fol. 13ᵛ), and that of date Aug. 18, 1679 (fol. 15ᵛ), the seal shows a gate or portcullis, with an R turned backwards, i. e. Я, on the left side of it.

---

[a] Anthony Wood, in a note here, approves of this suggestion to add the account of Gorhambury to Aubrey's life of Bacon (*supra*, p. 77) :—''Tis fit you should speak of this, because not mentioned by Dr. ⟨William⟩ Rawley in his life.'

[b] Aubrey notes, fol. 40ᵛ, 'Bring this in elswhere.'

James Wheldon's letter of Jan. 16, 16⅔⅘ (fol. 17ᵛ), has a seal bearing a man's bust, with helmet and cuirass.

¹⁸ (P. 357.) In MS. Aubr. 21, p. 19, Aubrey, in his projected comedy, makes use of this verdict on the innate cruelty of some dispositions. He puts into the mouth of his country-justice this speech :—

"If ye talke of skinnes, the best judgment to be made of the fineness of skinnes is at the whipping-post by the stripes. Ah! 'tis the best lechery to see 'em suffer correction. Your London aldermen take great lechery to see the poor wretches whipt at the court at Bridewell.'

On which Aubrey goes on to comment : 'Old Justice Hooke gave . . . per lash to wenches; as also ~~my old friend~~ George Pott, esq. Vide Animadversions Philosophicall on that ugly kind of pleasure and of crueltie—were it not for the law there were no living; some would take delight in killing of men.'

¹⁹ (P. 375.) The substance is :—

'Hobbes brought to the investigation of facts an acute intellect and long experience, and carried on, into the next generation, the Baconian spirit.

'He had been Bacon's secretary, and owed much to his master, from whom, in particular, he borrowed his comparative, i.e. inductive, methods. But he had also fine natural gifts.

'He excited the fears, and therefore the hostility, of the clerical party in England, and of the Oxford mathematicians and their supporters. For this reason, Charles II compared him to a bear, worried by mastiffs.

'In his political system, he insisted on the necessity of wisdom in sovereigns. In not meddling with the Creeds of the Churches and in assailing the Presbyterians and the Bishops of England, he is not to be blamed.'

Note that, on fol. 42ᵛ of MS. Aubr. 9, is a note 'to the earl of Devon, then in Great Queen Street,' with a mark referring it to the opposite page. The then opposite page is, in the present foliation, fol. 48, but has now nothing to which the note can be attached. There are traces, however, which show that a slip has been torn off it.

Thomas Hobbes' life, by himself.

⟨ *Aubrey's preface.* ⟩

* This was the draught that Mr. Hobbs first did leave in my hands, which he sent for about two yeares before he died, and wrote that which is printed in his Life in Latin by Dr. Richard Blackburn which I lent to him and he was carelesse and not remaunded it from the printer and so 'twas made wast paper of.

⟨ *Hobbes' autobiography.* ⟩

** Thomas Hobbes, natus Apr. 5, 1588, Malmesburiae agri Wiltoniensis, literis Latinis et Graecis initiatus, annum agens decimum quartum missus est Oxonium : ubi per

* MS. Aubr. 9, fol. 25ᵛ.   ** MS. Aubr. 9, fol. 23.

quinquennium mansit, operam impendens studio Logicae et Physicae Aristotelicae.

Cum annum ageret vicesimum. commendatus ab amicis, Oxonio relicto, recepit se in domum domini Gulielmi Cavendish, baronis de Hardwick et (paulo post) comitis Devoniae: ubi filio ejus primogenito, adolescenti sibi fere coaetaneo, servivit, placuitque tum filio tum patri, temperans, sedulus, hilaris.

Anno sequente cum domino suo in urbe perpetuo fere degens, quod didicerat linguae Graecae et Latinae magna ex parte amiserat.

Deinde per Italiam et Galliam peregrinantem dominum sequutus, gentium illarum linguas eousque didicit ut intelligere eas mediocriter potuerit. Interea Graecam et Latinam paulatim perire sibi sentiens, Philosophiam autem Logicamque (in quibus praeclare profecisse se arbitrabatur) viris prudentibus derisui esse videns, abjecta Logica et Philosophia illa vana, quantum temporis habebat vacui impendere decrevit linguis Graecae et Latinae.

Itaque cum in Angliam reversus esset, Historias et Poetas (adhibitis grammaticorum celebrium commentariis) versavit diligenter, non ut floride sed ut Latine posset scribere, et vim verborum cogitatis congruentem invenire, itaque verba disponere ut lectio perspicua et facilis esset. Inter Historias Graecas, Thucididem prae caeteris dilexit et vacuis horis in sermonem Anglicum paulatim conversum cum nonnullâ laude circa annum Christi 1628 in publicum edidit, eo fine ut ineptiae democraticorum Atheniensium concivibus suis patefierent.

Eo anno comes Devoniae, cui jam servierat viginti annos, diem obiit, patre ejus biennio ante defuncto.

Anno sequente, qui erat Christi 1629, cum attigisset annum quadragesimum, rogatus a nobilissimo viro domino Gervasio Clinton ut vellet filium adolescentem suum comitari in Galliam, accepit conditionem. In peregrinatione illa inspicere coepit in elementa Euclidis; et delectatus methodo illius non tam ob theoremata illa quam ob artem rationandi diligentissime perlegit.

Anno Christi 1631 revocatus est in familiam comitissae Devoniae ut filium suum comitem Devoniae, natum annos 13, in literis instrueret; quem etiam circiter triennium post comitatus est in Galliam et Italiam, studiorum ejus et itinerum rector.

Dum moraretur Parisiis, principia scientiae naturalis investigare coepit. Quae cum in natura et varietate motuum contineri sciret, quaesivit inprimis qualis motus is esse posset qui efficit sensionem, intellectum, phantasmata, aliasque proprietates animalium, cogitatis suis cum reverendo patre Marino Mersenno, ordinis Minimorum, in omni genere philosophiae versatissimo viroque optimo, quotidie communicatis.

Anno Christi 1637 cum patrono suo in Angliam rediit et apud illum mansit; unde de rebus naturalibus commercia cum Mersenno per literas continuavit.

Interea Scoti, depulsis episcopis, sumpserunt arma contra regem, faventibus etiam ministris Anglis illis qui vocari solent Presbyteriani. Itaque convocatum est in Anglia Parlamentum illud notissimum quod inceptum est Nov. 3, 1640. Ex iis quae in illo Parlamento tribus quatuorve diebus primis consulta viderat, Bellum Civile ingruere et tantum non adesse sentiens, retulit se rursus in Galliam, scientiarum studio Parisiis tutius vacaturus cum Mersenno, Gassendo, aliisque viris propter eruditionem et vim in rationando celeberrimis—non enim dico philosophis, quia nomen illud, a plurimis nebulonibus jamdiu gestatum, tritum, inquinatum, nunc infame est.

Cum jam Parisiis ageret, libellum scripsit *De Cive*, quem edidit anno 1646, quo tempore, praevalentibus Parlamentariis, multi eorum qui partes regis sequuti erant, et in illis princeps Walliae (qui nunc est rex Angliae), Parisiis confluxerunt. Statuerat circa idem tempus, * hortatu amici cujusdam nobilis Languedociani, migrare in Languedociam, et praemiserat jam quae sibi necessaria erant, sed commendatus principi ut elementa Mathematicae illi praelegeret, substit⟨it⟩ Parisiis.

* MS. Aubr. 9, fol. 23ᵛ.

Quod ab hoc munere temporis habuit vacui consumpsit in scribendo librum qui nunc non solum in Anglia sed in vicinis gentibus notissimus est, nomine *Leviathan*; quem etiam in Anglia edendum curavit, ipse manens adhuc Parisiis, anno 1651, annum agens 63^m. In eo opere jus regium tum spirituale tum temporale ita demonstravit tum rationibus tum authoritate scripturae sacrae, ut perspicuum fecerit pacem in orbe Christiano nusquam diuturnam esse posse nisi vel doctrina illa sua recepta fuerit vel satis magnus exercitus cives ad concordiam compulerit: opus ut ille sperabat concivibus suis, praesertim vero illis qui ab episcopis steterant, non ingratum. Quanquam enim unicuique, illo tempore, scribere et edere theologica quae vellet liberum erat, quia regimen ecclesiae (potestate declarandi quae doctrinae essent haereses, ipsius regis authoritate sublata, episcopis exutis, rege ipso trucidato) tum nullum erat, diligenter tamen cavit ne quid scriberet non modo contra sensum scripturae sacrae sed etiam contra doctrinam ecclesiae Anglicanae qualis ante bellum ortum authoritate regia constituta fuerat. Nam et ipse regimen ecclesiae per episcopos prae caeteris formis omnibus semper approbaverat, atque hoc duobus signis manifestum fecit. Primo, cum in oppido Sti. Germani prope Parisios morbo gravissimo lecto affixus esset, venit ad eum Mersennus, rogatus a quodam amico communi ne amicum suum extra ecclesiam Romanam mori pateretur. Is lecto assidens (post exordium consolatorium) de potestate ecclesiae Romanae peccata remittendi aliquantisper disseruit, cui ille 'Mi pater,' inquit. 'haec omnia jamdudum mecum disputavi, eadem disputare nunc molestum erit: habes quod dicas amoeniora,—quando vidisti Gassendum?' Quibus auditis, Mersennus sermonem ad alia transtulit. Paucis post diebus accessit ad illum Dr. Johannes Cosenus, episcopus (post) Dunelmensis, obtulitque se illi comprecatorem ad Deum. Cui ille cum gratias reddidisset, 'Ita,' inquit, 'si precibus praeiveris juxta ritum ecclesiae nostrae.' Magnum hoc erga disciplinam episcopalem signum erat reverentiae.

Anno 1651 exemplaria aliquot illius libri, Londini recens

editi, in Galliam transmissa sunt, ubi theologi quidam Angli doctrinas quasdam in illo libro contentas, tum ut haereticas tum ut partibus regiis adversas, criminati sunt; et valuere quidem aliquamdiu calumniae illae in tantum ut domo regia prohibitus fuerit. Quo factum est ut, protectione regia destitutus, metuensque ne a clericis Romanis, quos praecipue laeserat, male tractaretur, in Angliam conatus sit refugere.

Rediens in Angliam concionantes quidem invenit in ecclesiis sed seditiosos; etiam preces extemporarias, et illas audaces et nonnunquam blasphemas; symbolum autem fidei nullum, decalogum nullum; adeo ut per tres primos menses non invenerit quibuscum in sacris communicare potuerit. Tandem ab amico ductus ad ecclesiam a suo hospitio * plusquam mille passus distantem ubi pastor erat vir bonus et doctus, qui et coenam Domini ritu ecclesiastico administravit, cum illo in sacris communicavit. Alterum hoc signum erat non modo hominis partium episcopalium sed etiam Christiani sinceri; nam illo tempore ad ecclesiam quamcunque legibus aut metu cogebatur nemo. Quae igitur episcopo cuiquam cum illo causa irae esse potuit, nisi ei qui neminem a se dissentire pati per superbiam posset?

Interea doctrinam ejus academici et ecclesiastici condemnabant fere omnes; laudabant nobiles, et viri docti, ex laicis. Refellebat nemo: conati refellere, confirmabant. Scripsit enim non ex auditione et lectione ut scholaris, sed ex judicio proprio cognita et pensitata omnia, sermone puro et perspicuo, non rhetorico. Stantem inter amicos et inimicos quasi in aequilibrio, fecerunt illi ne ob doctrinam opprimeretur, hi, ne augeretur. Itaque fortuna tenui, fama doctrinae ingenti, in patroni sui, comitis Devoniae, hospitio per caeterum vitae tempus perpetuo delituit, studio vacans geometriae et philosophiae naturalis; ediditque jam senex librum quendam quem inscripsit *De Corpore*, continentem Logicae, Geometriae, Physicae (tum sublunaris, tum coelestis) fundamenta, deducens Logicam quidem a significatione

* MS. Aubr. 9, fol. 24.

nominum, Geometriam autem et Physicam ex figurarum et effectuum naturalium generationibus.

Hominis ergo neque genere neque opibus neque negotiis belli aut pacis assueti vitam scribo et in publicum emitto, sed in omni genere scientiae excellentis et fere singularis. Cujus ingenium ut cognoscerent, partim etiam ut sua ostentarent, convenerunt ⟨ad⟩ eum viri innumeri tum nostrates tum exteri, et inter illos nonnulli legati principum aliique viri nobilissimi ; adeo ut conjectura inde facta de voluntate hominum eruditorum qui posthac erunt, non ingratum fore posteritati existimavi si quem vidisse voluerunt illius vitam literis posteritati tradiderim, praecipue quidem ut quae scientiis ille primus addidit, deinde etiam caetera vitae ejus quae a lectoribus desiderari posse videbuntur cognoscerent.

Quae scripsit de jure naturali, de constitutione civitatum, de jure eorum qui summam habent potestatem, et de officiis civium, in libris *Leviathan* et *De Cive* (quia domi forisque nota et maxime celebrata sunt) praetereunda censeo.

In Physicis causam sensuum, praecipue visus, una cum doctrina omni optica et natura lucis, refractionis reflectionisque causas naturales, ignotas ante, primus demonstravit, in libro *De Homine*. Item causas qualitatum sensibilium nimirum colorum, soni, caloris, et frigoris. Somnia autem et phantasmata quae antea pro spiritibus et mortuorum animis habebantur et rudi vulgo terriculamenta erant, omnia profligavit. Causam autem aestuum marinorum et descensionis gravium, a motu quodam telluris praecipue derivavit. Nam phaenomena illa omnia ad motum refert, non ad rerum ipsarum potentias intrinsecas neque ad qualitates occultas, ut ante illum omnes physici. De motu autem in libro *De Corpore* satis fuse scripsit et profundissime. In Ethicis ante illum nihil scriptum est praeter sententias vulgares. At ille mores hominum ab humana natura, virtutes et vitia a lege naturali, et bonitatem * maliciamque actionum a legibus civitatum, derivavit. In Mathematicis principia geometriae nonnulla correxit;

* MS. Aubr. 9, fol. 24ᵛ.

problemata aliquot difficillima, a summis geometris (ab ipsis geometriae incunabulis) summo studio frustra quaesita, invenit, nimirum haec—

1°. arcui circuli lineam rectam, areae circuli quadratum aequale, exhibere, idque variis methodis—in diversis libris.

2°. datum angulum dividere in data ratione ;

3°. cubi ad sphaeram rationem invenire— in *Problematibus Geometricis.*

4°. inter duas rectas datas medias continue proportionales invenire quotcunque—in *Problematibus Geometricis.*

5°. polygonum regulare describere quotcunque laterum— in *Roseto.*

6°. centrum gravitatis invenire quadrantis circuli et bilinei quod continetur arcu quadrantis et subtenta ejus— in *Roseto.*

7°. centra gravitatis invenire paraboli-formium omnium, in libro *De Corpore.*

Haec omnia primus construxit et demonstravit, et praeterea alia multa quae (quia legentibus occurrent et minoris sunt) praetereo.

Facient opinor haec ut vita ejus non indigna videatur quae tum ad exteros tum ad posteros scientiarum studiosos transmittatur, praesertim hoc tempore, cum scribuntur vulgo vitae obscurorum hominum nulla virtute insignium, desiderante nemine.

Scripsit praeterea, circa annum aetatis suae octagesimum, historiam belli civilis Anglicani inter regem Carolum primum et parlamentum ejus, anno . . .; item ortum et incrementa potestatis pontificiae, carmine Latino, versuum duûm millium, sed non sinebant tempora ut publicarentur.

Silentibus tandem adversariis, annum agens octagesimum, ⟨pri⟩mum, Homeri Odyssea edidit a se conversum in versus Anglicanos, . . .; deinde, proximo, etiam Iliada ; denique Cyclometriam, annum agens ⟨. . .⟩gessimum primum, integram nondum editam.

Quod ad formam attinet, vultu erat non specioso sed cum

I.   D d

loqueretur non ingrato.   Effigies ejus ad vivum a pictore
excellente descripta, qualis erat anno aetatis suae septuage-
simo, in conclavi regis Caroli secundi conservatur.   Extant
etiam ejusdem imagines ab aliis pictoribus diversis tempo-
ribus factae rogatu amicorum in Anglia non paucae et in
Gallia aliquot.

Natura sua et primis annis ferebatur ad lectionem histo-
riarum et poetarum ; et ipse quoque carmen tentavit, nec
(ut plurimi judicabant) infoeliciter.   Postea autem cum in
congressu quodam virorum doctorum, mentione facta de
causa sensionis, quaerentem unum quasi per contemptum
'quid esset sensus?' nec quemquam audivisset respondentem,
mirabatur quî fieri potuerit ut qui sapientiae titulo homines
caeteros tanto fastu despicerent suos ipsorum sensus quid
essent ignorarent.   Ex eo tempore de causa sentiendi saepe
cogitanti, forte fortunâ mentem subiit quod si res corporeae
et earum partes omnes conquiescerent aut motu simili semper moverentur * sublatum iri omnium rerum discrimen
et (per consequens) omnem sentionem, et propterea
causam omnium rerum quaerendam esse in diversitate
motuum : atque hoc principio usus est primo.   Deinde, ut
cognosceret varietates et rationes motuum, ad geometriam
cogebatur, et a principiis suis ingenio suo theoremata illa
quae supra commemoravi foeliciter demonstravit.   Tantum
interest inter illos qui proprio genio et illos qui in archivis
veterum aut ad quaestum docentium scientiarum veritatem
quaerunt.

In colloquiis familiaribus jucundus erat, praeterquam
illorum qui ad illum venerant disputandi causa contra
ea quae jam ediderat (nec revocari poterant) de jure
summarum potestatum civili aut ecclesiastico ; nam cum
his vehementius aliquando disputabat quam erat necessarium.

Naturaliter apertus erat, et inter adversarios qui multi
potentesque erant innocentia magis quam consilio tutus.

Justiciae erat cum scientissimus, tum tenacissimus.   Nec
mirum, cum esset pecuniae neglegentissimus, et pro tenui-

* MS. Aubr. 9, fol. 25.

tate fortunarum suarum ultra modum beneficus. Sed
beneficio patronorum suorum et regis optimi dulcissimique
Caroli secundi satis copiose senex vixit.

William Holder (1616–169⅞).

* William Holder [1], D.D., the . . . d son [a] of . . . Holder ;
his mother's mayden name was Brudenell. He was borne
the . . . in Nottinghamshire ; went to schoole at . . . ;
went to Pembroke-hall [b] in Cambridge, where he had
a Greeke-scholar's place. Anno ⟨163⅞⟩, Artium Bacca-
laureus ; anno ⟨1640⟩ Artium Magister.

About 1640, he maried . . . the . . . daughter of
⟨Christopher⟩ Wren, deane of Windsore and rector of
Knowyll in Wiltshire.

Anno Domini 1642, had his institution and induction for
the rectorie of Bletchington in com. Oxon.

In the troublesome times he was with his father-in-lawe
Wren at the garrison of Bristowe. After the surrender of
it to the Parliament, he lived . . . year at Knowyll
with him.

Anno about 1646 [c], he went to Bletchington to his
parsonage, where his hospitality and learning, mixt with
great courtesie, easily conciliated the love of all his
neighbours to him. The deane came with him thither,
and dyed and is buryed there.

He was very helpfull in the education of his brother-in-
law, Mr. Christopher Wren (now knighted), a youth of
a prodigious inventive witt, and of whom he was as tender
as if he had been his owne child, who [d] gave him his first
instructions in geometrie and arithmetique, and when he
was a young scholar at the University of Oxford, was
a very necessary and kind friend.

The parsonage-house at Bletchington was Mr. Christopher
Wren's home, and retiring-place ; here he contemplated,
and studied, and found-out a great many curious things

* MS. Aubr. 6, fol. 87ᵛ.

[a] i.e. 2nd (or 3rd) son.

[b] 'hall,' subst. for 'Colledge.'

[c] Subst. for '1647.'

[d] Subst. for 'whom he instructed first in.'

in mathematiques. About this house[a] he made severall
curious dialls, with his owne handes, which are still there
to be seen. ☞ Which see, as well worthy to be seen.

But to returne to this honest worthy gentleman—he is
a good poet. I have some very good verses (about 100)
in Latin on St. Vincent's-rocks and the hott-well, neere
Bristowe. [He is very musicall, both theorically and
practically, and he had a sweet voyce. He hath writt an
excellent treatise of musique, in English, which is writt
both *doctis et indoctis*, and readie for the presse. He is
extremely well qualified for his * place, of Sub-Deane of
the King's Chapell, to which he was preferred[b] anno
167⟨4⟩, as likewise of the Sub-Almoner, being a person
abhorring covetousnes, and full of pitty[c].

Anno 16– (vide his . . .) . . . Popham (the only son of
. . . Popham, admirall for the Parliament), being borne
deafe and dumbe[d], was sent to him to learne to speake,
which he taught him to doe : by what method, and how
soon, you may see in the Appendix concerning it to his
Elements of Speech, 8vo, London, printed ⟨1669⟩. It is
a most ingeniose and curious discourse, and untouched by
any other; he was beholding to no author; did only
consult with nature. This booke I sent to Mr. Anthony
Lucas, at Liege, who very much admires it and I have
desired him to translate it into French. Dr. John Wallis
unjustly arrogates the glory of teaching the sayd young
gentleman to speake, in the Philosophical Transactions,
and in Dr. Robert Plott's History of Oxfordshire; which
occasioned Dr. Holder to write a . . . against him, a
pamphlet in 4to, 167–.

He has good judgement in painting and drawing.

In anno ⟨1652⟩ he was made a prebendary of Ely.
Anno ⟨1663⟩ had the parsonage of ⟨Northwold⟩ in
Norfolk.

He is a handsome, gracefull person, and of a delicate

[a] Subst. for 'Here.'   'upon . . . Jones his death.'
* MS. Aubr. 6, fol. 88.   [c] Dupl. with 'bowells.'
[b] Anthony Wood notes here—   [d] See p. 378.

constitution, and of an even and smooth temper; so that, if one would goe about to describe a perfect good man, would drawe this Doctor's character. Of a just stature; grey eie; tall and well-sett; sanguine; thin skin; roundish face; gracefull elocution; his discourse so gent. and obligeing; cleer reason.

They say that *morum similitudo conci⟨li⟩at amicitiam*; then it will not be found strange that there should be such a conjunct friendship between this worthy gentleman and the right reverend father in God, Seth Ward, lord bishop of Sarum, his coetanean in Cambridge.

It ought not to be forgott the great and exemplary love between this Doctor and his vertuose wife, who is not lesse to be admired, in her sex and station, then her brother Sir Christopher; and (which is rare to be found in a woman) her excellences doe not inflate her. Amongst many other guifts she haz a strange sagacity as to curing of wounds, which she does not doe so much by presedents and reciept bookes, as by her owne excogitancy, considering the causes, effects, and circumstances. His majestie king Charles II, 167-, had hurt his . . . hand, which he intrusted his chirurgians to make well; but they ordered him so that they made it much worse, so that it swoll, and pained him up to his shoulder; and pained him so extremely that he could not sleep, and began to be feaverish. . . . told the king what a rare shee-surgeon he had in his house; she was presently sent for at eleven clock at night. She presently made ready a pultisse, and applyed it, and gave his majestie sudden ease, and he slept well; next day she dressed him, and in . . . perfectly cured him, to the great griefe of all the surgeons, who envy and hate her.

> Non Illo melior quisquam, nec amantior aequi
> Vir fuit: aut Illâ reverentior ulla Deorum.
> OVID. *Metam.* lib. i.

Note.

[1] Aubrey gives the coat, 'sable, a chevron between 3 anchors argent.' Anthony Wood adds the reference ' vide pag. 65 *a*,' i. e. fol. 95, of MS. Aubr. 6, in the life of John Wallis.

Hugh Holland (15— –1633).

* From Sir John Penrudock :—Hugh Holland, poeta :
he was descended of the family of the earles of Kent, etc.,
and was a Roman Catholique.   The lady Elizabeth Hatton
(mother to the lady Purb⟨ec⟩) was his great patronesse
(vide B. Jonson's masque of the Gipsies for these two
beauties).

Sir J⟨ohn⟩ P⟨enrudock⟩ asked him his advice as he
was dyeing, (or he then gave it) that, the best rule for him
to governe his life was to reade St. Hierome's Epistles.

He was buried in Westminster Abbey*, in the south
crosse aisle neer the dore of St. Benet's Chapell, i. e. where
the earl of Middlesex monument is, but there is no monument or inscription for him.   He was buryed July 23, 1633.

He was of a Lancashire family.

Tho. Holland, earl of Kent (his sonnes, dukes of Surrey),
tempore Rich. 2.

Philemon Holland (1551–1637).

** Philêmon Holland was schoole-master of the free-
schoole at Coventrey, and that for many yeares.   He made
a great many good scholars.   He translated T. Livius,
anno 15–, with one and the same pen, which the lady
. . . (vide at the end of his translation of Suetonius)
embellished with silver, and kept amongst her rare κειμήλια [b].
He wrote a good hand, but a rare Greeke character ;
witnesse the MS. of Euclid's Harmoniques in the library
belonging to the schoole.   He translated severall Latin
authors,—e. g. Tit. Livius, Plinii Hist. Natur., Suetonius
Tranquillus : quaere + .

One made this epigram on him :—

> ' Philêmon with 's translations doeth so fill us,
>   He will not let SUETONIUS be TRANQUILLUS.'

---

* MS. Aubr. 8, fol. 10.   Aubrey
gives the coat, ' azure, semée of fleur-
de-lys, a lion rampant argent [Hol-
land].'

* The words followed 'I thinke ;
quaere de hoc of A. Wood'; scored out.
** MS. Aubr. 8, fol. 20ᵛ.
[b] κειμελια in MS.

Wenceslaus Hollar (1607–1677).

* Winceslaus Hollar, natus Pragae 23 Julii, st⟨ilo⟩ v⟨etere⟩, 1607, about 8 A.M.

** Winceslaus Hollar, Bohemus, was borne at Prague.

His father was a Knight of the Empire: which is by lettres patent under the imperiall seale (as our baronets). I have seen it ᵃ: the seale is bigger then the broad seale of England: in the middle is the imperiall coate ; and round about it are the coates of the Princes Electors. His father was a Protestant, and either for keeping a conventicle, or being taken at one, forfeited his estate, and was ruined by the Roman Catholiques.

He told me that when he was a schoole-boy he tooke a delight in draweing of mapps; which draughts he kept, and they were pretty. He was designed by his father to have been a lawyer, and was putt to that profession ᵇ, when his father's troubles, together with the warres, forced him to leave his countrey. So that what he did for his delight and recreation only when a boy, proved to be his livelyhood when a man.

I thinke he stayd sometime in Lowe Germany, then he came into England, wher he was very kindly entertained by that great patron of painters and draughts-men ⟨Thomas Howard⟩ Lord High Marshall, earl of Arundell and Surrey, where he spent his time in draweing and copying rarities, which he did etch (i.e. eate with aqua fortis in copper plates). When the Lord Marshall went ambassador to the Emperor of Germany to Vienna, he travelld with much grandeur ; and among others, Mr. Hollar went with him (very well clad) to take viewes, landskapes, buildings, etc. remarqueable in their journey, which wee see now at the print shopps.

He hath donne the most in that way that ever any one did, insomuch that I have heard Mr. John Evelyn, R. S. S.,

---

* MS. Aubr. 23, fol. 121ᵛ.
** MS. Aubr. 6, fol. 26.

ᵃ i. e. Hollar's father's patent.
ᵇ Subst. for ' was bred up to it.'

say that at sixpence a print his labour would come to
. . . . . *li.* (quaere J⟨ohn E⟨velyn⟩⟩). He was very short-
sighted (μυοψ[a]), and did worke so curiously that the curiosity
of his worke is not to be judged without a magnifying-
glasse. When he tooke his landskaps, he, then, had a glasse
to helpe his sight.

At Arundel-house he maried with my ladie's wayting
woman, Mrs. . . . Tracy, by whom he haz a daughter,
that was one of the greatest beauties I have seen; his
son by her dyed in the plague, an ingeniose youth, drew
delicately.

When the civil warres brake-out, the Lord Marshall had
leave to goe beyond sea †. Mr. Hollar went
into the Lowe-Countries, where he stayed till
about 1649.

† Italie[b].

I remember he told me that when he first came into
England, (which was a serene time of peace) that the people,
both poore and rich, did looke cheerfully, but at his returne,
~~he found~~ the countenances of the people all changed,
melancholy, spightfull, as if bewitched.

I have sayd before that his father was ruined upon the
account of the Protestant religion. Winceslaus dyed a
Catholique, of which religion, I suppose, he might be ever
since he came to Arundel-howse.

He was a very friendly good-natured man as could be,
but shiftlesse as to the world, and dyed not rich[c]. He
maried a second wife, 1665, by whom he has severall
children. He dyed on our Ladie-day (25 Martii), 1677,
and is buried in St. Margaret's church-yard at Westminster
neer the north west corner of the tower. Had he lived till
the 13th of July following, he had been just 70 yeares old.

John Holywood (11— –1256).

* Jo. de Sacro Bosco :—Dr. ⟨John⟩ Pell is positive that
his name was Holybushe.

[a] for μύανψ.
[b] Thomas Howard, earl of Arundel, Surrey, and Norfolk, died at

Padua, 1646.
[c] Subst. for 'dyed but poor.'
* MS. Aubr. 7, fol. 5ᵛ.

Thomas Hoode.

* . . . Hood, M.D.—he practised Physick at Worcester, and printed a booke in 4to called *The Geodeticall Staffe*ᵃ.

Robert Hooke (1635–1703).

** Mr. Robert Hooke, curator of the Royall Societie at London, was borne at Freshwater in the Isle of Wight, A.D. ⟨1635⟩; his father was minister there, and of the family of the Hookes of Hooke in Hants.

*** July 19ᵗʰ, 1635, baptized Robert Hooke, the son of Mr. John Hooke.

**** Mr. Robert Hooke[1], M.A.:—his father, Mr. John Hooke, ***** had two or three brothers all ministers: quaere Dr. ⟨William⟩ Holder. He was of the family of Hooke of Hooke in Hampshire, in the road from London to Saram, a very ancient family and in that place for many (3 or more) hundred yeares.

****** His father was minister of Freshwater in the Isle of Wight. He maried . . . . . ., by whom he had two sonnes, viz. . . . of Newport, grocer (quaere capt. Lee) and had been mayer there, and Robert, second son, who was borne ᵇ at Freshwater aforesayd the nineteenth day of July, Anno Domini 1635—vide register, et obiit patris.

At . . . yeares old, John Hoskyns, the painter, being at Freshwater, to drawe pictures for . . . . esqre, Mr. Hooke observed what he did, and, thought he, 'why cannot I doe so too?' So he getts him chalke, and ruddle, and coale, and grinds them, and putts them on a trencher, gott a pencill, and to worke he went, and made a picture: then he copied ᶜ (as they hung up in the parlour) the pictures there, which he made like. Also, being a boy there, at

---

* MS. Aubr. 8, fol. 77ᵛ.

ᵃ *The use of the Jacob's Staffe.* Lond. 1590.

** MS. Aubr. 23, fol. 56ᵛ: as also in MS. Wood F. 39, fol. 270ᵛ.

*** MS. Aubr. 8, a slip at fol. 99.

**** MS. Aubr. 6, fol. 32.

***** MS. Aubr. 6, fol. 29ᵛ.

****** MS. Aubr. 6, fol. 32.

ᵇ Corrected by Anthony Wood to 'baptized.'

ᶜ Dupl. with 'drew.'

Freshwater, he made an . . . diall on a round trencher; never having had any instruction. His father was not mathematicall at all.

When his father dyed, his son Robert was but . . . old, to whom he left one hundred pounds, which was sent up to London with him, with an intention to have bound him apprentice to Mr. Lilly[a], the paynter, with whom he was a little while upon tryall; who liked him very well, but Mr. Hooke quickly perceived[b] what was to be donne, so, thought he, why cannot I doe this by my selfe and keepe my hundred pounds?' He also had some instruction in draweing from Mr. Samuel Cowper (prince of limners of this age); but whether from him before or after Mr. Lilly quaere?

☞ Quaere when he went to Mr. Busby's, the schoolemaster of Westminster, at whose howse he was; and he made very much of him. With him he lodged his c *li.*[c] There he learnd to[d] play 20 lessons on the organ. He there in one weeke's time made himselfe master of the first VI bookes of *Euclid,* to the admiration of Mr. Busby (now S.T.D.), who introduced him. At schoole here he was very mechanicall, and (amongst other things) he invented thirty severall wayes of flying, which I have not only heard him say, but Dr. Wilkins (at Wadham College at that time), who gave him his *Mathematicall Magique* which did him a great kindnes. He was never a King's Scholar, and I have heard Sir Richard Knight (who was his school-fellow) say that he seldome sawe him in the schoole.

Anno Domini ⟨1658⟩ (vide A. Wood's *Antiq. Oxon.*) he was sent to Christ Church in Oxford, where he had a chorister's place (in those dayes when the church musique was putt-downe[e]), which was a pretty good maintenance. He was there assistant to Dr. Thomas Willis in his chymistry; who afterwards recommended him to

---

a ? Sir Peter Lely.
b Subst. for ' learnd.'
c i. e. £100.
d Probably ' to play, ⟨in⟩ 20 les-

sons, on.'
e See Clark's Wood's *Life and Times,* i. 162, 163.

the hon^rle Robert Boyle, esqre, to be usefull to him in his chymicall operations. Mr. Hooke then read to him (R. B., esqre) Euclid's Elements, and made him under-stand ª Des Cartes' Philosophy. He was Master of Arts anno Domini . . . .

Anno Domini 166⟨2⟩ Mr. Robert Boyle recommended Mr. Robert Hooke to be Curator of the Experiments of the Royall Society, wherin he did an admirable good worke to the Common-wealth of Learning, in recommending the fittest person in the world to them. Anno ⟨1664⟩ he was chosen Geometry * Professour at Gresham College ². Anno Domini 166– Sir John Cutler, knight, gave a Mechanicall lecture, . . . pounds per annum, which he read.

Anno Domini 166⟨6⟩ the great conflagration of London happened, and then he was chosen one of the two surveyors † of the citie of London ; by which he hath gott a great estate. He built Bedlam, the Physitians' College, Montague-house, the Piller on Fish-street-hill, and Theatre there ; and he is much made use of in designing buildings.

† ⟨John⟩ Oliver, the glasse-painter, was the other.

He is but of midling stature, something crooked, pale faced, and his face but little belowe, but his head is lardge ; his eie full and popping, and not quick ; a grey eie. He haz a delicate head of haire, browne, and of an excellent moist curle. He is and ever was very temperate, and moderate in dyet, etc.

As he is of prodigious inventive head, so is a person of great vertue and goodnes. Now when I have sayd his inventive faculty is so great, you cannot imagine his memory to be excellent, for they are like two bucketts, as one goes up, the other goes downe. He is certainly the greatest mechanick this day in the world. His head lies much more to Geometry then to Arithmetique. He is (1680) a batchelour, and, I beleeve, will never marie. His elder brother left one faire daughter ³, which is his heire. In fine (which crownes all) he is a person of great suavity and goodnesse.

ª Dupl. with 'and taught him.'   * MS. Aubr. 6, fol. 32ᵛ.

Scripsit.

. . .

. . .

'Twas Mr. Robert Hooke that invented the Pendulum-Watches, so much more usefull than the other watches.

He hath invented an engine for the speedie working of division, etc., or for the speedie and immediate finding out the divisor.

An instrument for the Emperor of Germany, 169⅝.

* The first thing he published was—An attempt for the explication of the phaenomena observeable in the XXXV experiment of the honourable Robert Boyle, esq., touching the aire: printed for Sam. Thomson at the Bishop's head in Paule's churchyard, 1661, 8vo: not now to be bought, and, though no bigger then an almanack, is a most ingeniose piece.

The next moneth he published another little 4to pamphlet, —Discourse of a new instrument he haz invented to make more accurate observations in astronomy then ever was ** yet made, or could be made by any instruments hitherto invented, and this instrument (10 or 12 *li.* price) performes more, and more exact, then all the chargeable apparatus of the noble Tycho Brache or the present Hevelius of Dantzick.

⟨In MS. Aubr. 6, fol. 30, 31, is this letter from Aubrey to Anthony Wood, enclosing a communication from Hooke.⟩

Mr. Wood!   September 15, 1689.

Mr. Robert Hooke, R.S.S. did in anno 1670, write a discourse, called, 'An Attempt to prove the motion of the Earth,' which he then read to the Royal Society; but printed it in the beginning of the yeare 1674, a *strena* * to Sir John Cutler to whom it is dedicated, wherein he haz delivered the theorie of explaining the coelestial motions mechanically; his words are these, pag. 27, 28. viz. :—

* Aubrey, in MS. Wood F. 39, fol. 270ᵛ: May 26, 1674.
** Ibid., fol. 271.   ª i. e. New Year's gift.

[' In *the *Attempt to prove the motion of the earth*, etc., printed 1674, but read to the Royall Society, 1671 : pag. 27, line 31—

' I shall only for the present hint that I have in some of my foregoing observations discovered some new motions even in the Earth it self, which perhaps were not dreamt of before, which I shall hereafter more at large describe, when further tryalls have more fully confirmed and compleated these beginnings. At which time also I shall explaine a systeme of the world, differing in many particulars from any yet known, answering in all things to the common rules of mechanicall motions. This depends upon 3 suppositions; first, that all coelestiall bodys whatsoever have an attractive or gravitating power towards their own centers, whereby they attract not only their own parts, and keep them from flying from them, as we may observe the Earth to doe, but that they doe also attract all the other coelestial bodys that are within the sphere of their activity, and consequently that not only the Sun and the Moon have an influence upon the body and motion of the Earth, and the Earth upon them, but that Mercury also, Venus, Mars, Saturne, and Jupiter, by their attractive powers have a considerable influence upon its motion, as, in the same manner, the corresponding attractive power of the Earth hath a considerable influence upon every one of their motions also. The second supposition is this, that all bodys whatsoever, that are putt into direct and simple motion will soe continue to move forwards in a straight line, till they are by some other effectuall powers deflected and bent into a motion describing a circle, ellipsis, or some other uncompounded curve line. The third supposition is, that these attractive powers are soe much the more powerfull in operating, by how much nearer the body wrought upon is to their own centers. Now what these severall degrees are, I have not yet experimentally verified.'—*But these degrees and proportions of the power of attraction in the celestiall bodys and motions, were com-*

* The paragraph enclosed in square brackets is Hooke's autograph.

municated to Mr. Newton by R. Hooke, in the yeare 1678,
*by letters, as will plainely appear both by the coppys of the
said letters, and the letters of Mr. Newton in answer to
them, which are both in the custody of the said R. H., both
which also were read before the Royall Society at their
publique meeting, as appears by the Journall book of the
said Society.*—' But it is a notion which if fully prosecuted,
as it ought to be, will mightily assist the astronomer to reduce
all the coelestiall motions to a certaine rule, which I doubt
will never be done true without it. He that understands the
natures of the circular pendulum and circular motion, will
easily understand the whole ground of this principle, and
will know where to find direction in nature for the true stating
thereof. This I only hint at present to such as have ability
and opportunity of prosecuting this inquiry, and are not
wanting of industry for observing and calculating, wishing
heartily such may be found, having my self many other
things in hand, which I will first compleat, and therefore
cannot soe well attend ⟨to⟩ it. But this I durst promise
the undertaker; that he will find all the great motions of
the world to be influenced by this principle, and that the

† To · make a
demonstration
of it, telling him
the proportion
of the gravity to
the distance and
the curv'd line
that was thereby
made, to witt
that it was an
ellipsis in one of
the foci of which
was the sun and
that that gravi-
tation would
make the
aphelion and
perihelion
opposite to each
other in the same
diameter which
is the whole
celestiall theorie
of which Mr.
Newton has
made a
demonstration.

true understanding thereof will be the true
perfection of Astronomy.']

About 9 or 10 years ago, Mr. Hooke writt to
Mr. Isaac Newton, of Trinity College, Cambridge, to make † a demonstration of this
theory, not telling him, at first, the proportion
of the gravity to the distance, nor what was the
curv'd line that was thereby made. Mr. Newton,
in his answer to the letter, did expresse that
he had not known [b] of it; and in his first attempt
about it, he calculated the curve by supposing
the attraction to be the same at all distances:
upon which, Mr. Hooke sent, in his next letter,
the whole of his hypothesis, scil. that the
gravitation was reciprocall to the square of the distance,

---

[a] The text embodies Hooke's corrections of Aubrey's draft. The original draft is given in the margin.
[b] Dupl. with ' thought.'

['which* would make the motion in an ellipsis, in one of whose foci the sun being placed, the aphelion and perihelion of the planet would be opposite to each other in the same line, which is the whole coelestiall theory, concerning which Mr. Newton hath a demonstration,'] not at all owning he receiv'd the first intimation of it from Mr. Hooke. Likewise Mr. Newton haz in the same booke printed some other theories and experiments of Mr. Hooke's, as that about the oval figure of the earth and sea : without acknowledgeing from whom he had them, ['though* he had not sent it up with the other parts of his booke till near a month after the theory was read to the Society by Mr. Hooke, when it served to help to answer Dr. Wallis his arguments produced in the Royal Society against it.']

Mr. Wood! This is the greatest discovery in nature that ever was since the world's creation. It never was so much as hinted by any man before. I know you will doe him right. I hope you may read his hand. I wish he had writt plainer, and afforded a little more paper.

Tuus,
J. AUBREY.

Before I leave this towne, I will gett of him a catalogue of what he hath wrote ; and as much of his inventions as I can. But they are many hundreds ; he believes not fewer than a thousand. 'Tis such a hard matter to get people to doe themselves right.

Notes.

[1] Aubrey gives in trick the coat: 'quarterly, argent and sable a cross between 4 escallops all counterchanged [Hooke].'

[2] Aubrey used Hooke's rooms in Gresham College as the place to which he had his letters addressed. E. g. MS. Aubr. 8, fol. 55, is an envelope addressed :—

'To his much honoured friend John Awbrey, esqre, these present, at Mr. Hooke's lodgeings in Gresham College, London.'

MS. Aubr. 8, fol. 48, is an envelope addressed—

'For Mr. John Aubrey: leave these at Mr. Hooke's lodging in Gresham College.'

* The words in square brackets are Hooke's autograph, added at the time he made the corrections above.

[3] 'Mris. Grace Hooke, borne at Newport in the Isle of Wight 2do Maii, at 8h P.M.; she is 15 next May, scil. 1676. . . . Her father died by suspending him selfe, anno . . .': MS. Aubr. 23, fol. 56v.

Charles Hoskyns (1584–1609).

* Charles Hoskyns was brother to the Serjeant and the Doctor ; a very ingeniose man, who would not have been inferior to either but killed himself with hard study.

Note.

Charles Hoskins, of 'Lenwarne' parish, Hereford, was admitted probationer July 26, 1604, and fellow of New College in 1606; took B.A. April 13, 1608; and died in 1609.

John Hoskyns (1566–1638).

**John Hoskyns[1], serjeant-at-lawe, was borne at Mounckton in the parish of ⟨Llanwarne⟩ in the com. of Hereford, A° Dni ⟨1566⟩ [on [a] St. Mark's day].

Mounckton belonged to the priory of Llantony juxta Glocester, where his ancestors had the office of cupbearer (or 'pocillator') to the prior. I have heard there was a windowe given by one Hoskyns there, as by the inscription did appeare.

Whither the serjeant were the eldest brother[b] or no, I have forgott ; but he had a brother, John [2], D.D., a learned man, rector of Ledbury and canon of Hereford, who, I thinke, was eldest, who was designed to be a scholar, but this John (the serjeant) would not be quiet, but he must be a scholar too. In those dayes boyes were seldome taught to read that were not to be of some learned profession. So, upon his instant importunity, being then ten yeares of age, he learned to reade, and, at the yeare's end, entred into his Greeke grammar. This I have heard his sonne, Sir Benet Hoskyns, knight and baronett, severall times say.

He was of a strong constitution, and had a prodigious

* Aubrey in MS. Wood F. 39, fol. 142 : Oct. 27, 1671.

** Aubrey in MS. Rawl. D. 727, fol. 93.

[a] Added by Anthony Wood, from a letter of Aubrey's (MS. Wood F. 39, fol. 135v).

[b] 'He was the eldest,' is added by Anthony Wood.

memorie. At . . . yeares old, he went to Winton schole, where he was the flower of his time. I remember I have heard that one time he had not made his exercise (verse) and spake to one of his forme to shew him his, which he sawe. The schoolmaster presently calles for the exercises, and Hoskyns told him that he had writ it out but lost it, but he could repeate it, and repeated the other boye's exercise (I thinke 12 or 16 verses) only at once reading over. When the boy who really had made them shewed the master the same, and could not repeate them, he was whipped for stealing Hoskyns' exercise. I thinke John Owen [3] and he were schoole-fellowes. There were many pretty stories of him when a schooleboy, which I have forgott. I have heard his son say that he was a yeare at Westminster ; and not speeding there, he was sent to Winton.

The Latin verses in the quadrangle at Winton Colledge [4], at the cocks where the boyes wash their hands, were of his making, where there is the picture [a] of a good servant, with hind's feet, . . . head, a padlock on his lippes, . . . The Latin verses describe the properties of a good servant.

When he came to New College, he was *Terrae filius*; but he was so bitterly satyricall that he was expelled and putt to his shifts.

He went into Somersetshire and taught a schole for about a yeare at Ilchester. He compiled there a Greeke lexicon as far as M, which I have seen. He maried (neer there) a rich widowe, [of Mr. Bourne] ; she was a Moyle of Kent ; by whome he had only one sonne and one daughter.

[After [b] his mariage] he admitted himselfe at the Middle Temple, London. He wore good cloathes, and kept good company. His excellent witt gave him letters of commendacion to all ingeniose persons. At his [*] first comeing to London he gott acquainted with the under-secretaries at court, where he was often usefull to them in writing their Latin letters.

His great witt quickly made him be taken notice of.

[a] Dupl. with 'emblem.' [b] Scored out.

[*] MS. Rawl. D. 727, fol. 93[v].

Ben: Johnson called him *father*. Sir Benet (bishop Benet* of Hereford was his godfather) told me that one time desiring Mr. Johnson to adopt him for his sonne, 'No,' said he, 'I dare not ; 'tis honour enough for me to be your brother : I was your father's sonne, and 'twas he that polished me.' In shorte, his acquaintance were all the witts then about the towne ; e. g. Sir Walter Raleigh, who was his fellow-prisoner in the Tower, where he was Sir Walter's *Aristarchus* to reviewe and polish Sir Walter's stile ; John Donne, D.D. ; John Owen, (vide Epigr. 1—

Hic liber est mundus ; homines sunt, Hoskine, versus :
Invenies paucos hîc ut in orbe bonos ;)

⟨Richard⟩ Martyn, recorder of London ; Sir Benjamin Ruddyer, with whom it was once his fortune to have a quarrell and fought a duell with him and hurt him in the knee, but they were afterwards friends again ; Sir Henry Wotton, provost of Eaton College ; cum multis aliis.

His conversation was exceedingly pleasant, and on the roade he would make any one good company to him. He was a great master of the Latin and Greke languages ; a great divine. He understood the lawe well, but worst at that.

He was admitted at the Middle Temple anno . . . ; called to be a serjeant at lawe anno ⟨1623⟩ (vide ⟨Sir William Dugdale's⟩ *Origines Juridiciales*).

His verses on the fart in the Parliament house are printed in some of the *Drolleries*. He had a booke of poemes, neatly written by one of his clerkes, bigger then Dr. Donne's poemes, which his sonn Benet lent to he knowes not who, about 1653, and could never heare of it since. Mr. Thomas Henshawe haz an excellent Latin copie in rhythme in the prayse of ale of his.

He was a very strong man and active. He did the pomado in the saddle of the third horse in his armour (which Sir John Hoskins haz still) before William, earle of Pembroke. He was about my heighth.

* Robert Bennet, bishop of Hereford 1602–1617.

He had a very readie witt, and would make verses on the roade, where he was the best company in the world. In Sir H. Wotton's *Remaynes* are verses (dialogue) made on the roade by him and Sir Henry. He made an antheme (gett it) in English to be sung at Hereford Minster at the assizes ; but Sir Robert Harley (a great Puritan) was much offended at it. He made the epitaph on ⟨Peter⟩ Woodgate in New College cloysters. He made the best Latin epitaphs of his time ; amongst many others an excellent one on ⟨Sir Moyle⟩ Finch, this earl of Winchelsey's grandfather, who haz a noble monument at Eastwell in Kent.

I will now describe his seate at Morhampton (Hereff.), which he bought of . . .

* At the gate-house is the picture of the old fellowe that made the fires, with a block on his back, boytle and wedges and hatchet. By him, this distich :—

> Gratus ades quisquis descendis, amicus et hospes :
> Non decet hos humiles mensa superba Lares.

By the porch of the howse, on the wall, is the picture in the margent :—

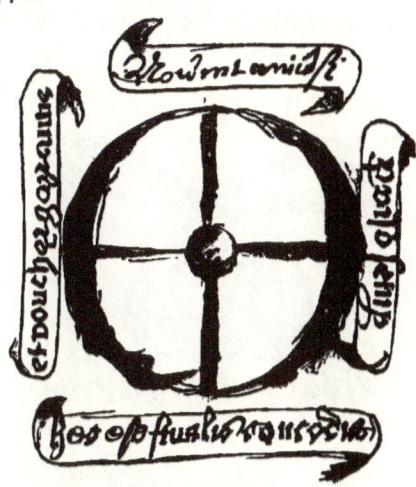

Above it are these verses :—

> Stat coelum, fateor, Copernice ; terra movetur ;
> Et mutant dominos tecta rotata suos.

* MS. Rawl. D. 727, fol. 94.

In the chapelle, over the altar, are these two Hebrewe words [a], viz. :—

וְשָׁמַעְתָּ וְסָלַחְתָּ

and underneath this distich (1 Reg. 8. 30) :—

> Hac quicunque orat supplex exoret in aede,
> Nec pereant servis irrita vota tuis.

Here is an organ that was queen Elizabeth's.

In the gallery ⟨is⟩ the picture of his brother (⟨the⟩ Doctor) in the pulpit, ⟨of the⟩ serjeant in his robes, the howse, parke, etc. ; and underneath are these verses :—

> Est casa, sunt colles, lateres [b], vivaria [c], lymphae,
> Pascua, sylva, Ceres [d] : si placet, adde preces [e].

In the garden, the picture of the gardiner, on the wall of the howse, with his rake, spade, and water-pott in his left hand.   By it, this distich :—

> Pascitur et pascit locus hic, ornatur et ornat :
> Istud opus nondum lapsus amaret Adam.

In the first leafe of his fee-booke he drew the picture of a purse as in the margent,

and wrote *καὶ δώμεν ὁσχίνδω.*

underneath, out of Theocritus.

---

[a] ' And when thou hearest, forgive.' 1 Kings viii. 30.
[b] Aubrey adds the interpretation :—' quarries.'
[c] ' Parke.'   [d] ' Harvest.'   [e] ' Chapelle.'

On his picture in the low gallery are writt on his deske these verses, viz. :—

Undecies senos exegi strenuus annos,
  Jam veniet nullo mors inopina die;
Quae dixi, scripsi, gessive negotia, lusus,
  Obruat aeterno pax taciturna sinu.
Si quid jure petunt homines, respondeat haeres,
  Dissipet ut cineres nulla querela meos.
* Quodque Deo, decoctor iniquus, debeo, solve,
  Quaeso, Fidejussor, { sanguine / nomine }, Christe, { tuo / meo }.

These verses with a little alteration are sett on his monument.

Under severall venerable and shady oakes in the parke, he had seates made; and where was a fine purling spring, he did curbe it with stone.

This putts me in mind of Fr. Petrarch's villa in Italie, which is not long since printed, where were such devises— vide Tomasini *Petrarcha redivivus*, Lat., Amsterdam, 12mo.

Besides his excellent naturall memorie, he acquired the artificiall way of memorie.

He wrote his owne life (which his grandsonne Sir John Hoskyns, knight and baronet, haz), which was to shew that wheras Plutarch, . . . , . . . , etc., had wrote the lives of many generalles, etc., grandees, that he, or an active man might, from a private fortune by his witt and industrie attained to the dignity of a serjeant-at-lawe—but he should have said that they must have parts like his too.—This life I cannot borrowe.

He wrote severall treatises. Amongst others :—
  a booke of style ;
  a method of the lawe (imperfect).
His familiar letters were admirable.

He was a close prisoner in the Tower, tempore regis Jacobi, for speaking too boldly in the Parliament house of the king's profuse liberality to the Scotts. He made a comparison of a conduit, whereinto water came, and

* MS. Rawl. D. 727, fol. 94ᵛ.

ran-out afarre-off. 'Now,' said he, 'this pipe reaches as
far as Edinborough.' He was kept a 'close prisoner'
there, i. e., his windowes were boarded up. Through a
small chinke he sawe once a crowe, and another time, a
kite; the sight whereof, he sayd, was a great pleasure to
him. He, with much adoe, obtained at length the favour
to have his little son Bennet to be with him; and he then
made this distich, viz.:—

> Parvule dum puer es, nec scis incommoda linguae,
> Vincula da linguae, vel tibi vincla dabit.

Thus Englished by him:—

> My little Ben, whil'st thou art young,
> And know'st not how to rule thy tongue,
> Make it thy slave whil'st thou art free,
> Least it, as mine, imprison thee.

   * I have heard that when he came out of the Tower, his
crest (before expressed) was graunted him, viz., 'a lyon's
head couped or, breathing fire.' The serjeant would say
jocosely that it was the only lyon's head in England that
tooke tobacco.

   Not many moneths before his death (being at the assises
or sessions at Hereford) a massive countrey fellowe trod on
his toe, which caused a gangrene which was the cause of
his death. One Mr. Dighton † of Glocester (an
experienced chirurgian who had formerly been
chirurgian in the warres in Ireland) was sent
for to cure him; but his skill and care could
not save him. His toes were first cutt-off.
The minister of his parish had a clubbe-foote
or feete (I think his name was Hugh). Said
he, 'Sir Hugh'—after his toes were cutt off—
'I must be acquainted with your shoemaker.'

† Mr. Dighton would oftentimes say that he generally observ'd in the Irish warres that those men that went to their wenches the day before the battayle either did dye upon the spott or came under his handes. *Digitus Dei!*

   Sir Robert Pye, attorney of the court of wardes, was his
neighbour, but there was no great goodwill between them—
Sir Robert was haughty. He happened to dye on Christmas day: the newes being brought to the serjeant, said
he 'The devill haz a Christmas pye.'

   * MS. Rawl. D. 727, fol. 95.

He was a very strong man, and valiant, and an early riser in the morning (scil., at four in the morning). He was black-eyed and had black hayre.

He lies buried under an altar monument on the north side of the choire of Dowr abbey in Herefordshire.

(In this abbey church of Dowre are two *frustum's* or remaynders of mayled and crosse-legged monuments, one sayd to be of a lord Chandois, th' other, the lord of Ewyas-lacy. A little before I sawe them a mower had taken one of the armes to whett his syth.)

On his monument is this inscription :—

Hoc tegitur tumulo totus quem non tegit orbis,
Hoskinus, humani prodigium ingenii,
Usque adeo excoluit duo pugnacissima rerum
Et quae non subeunt numina [a] pectus idem,
Pieridum Legumque potens, jucundus honesto
Mixtus, Liticulans Musa, forense melos,
Orando causas pariter pariterque canendo,
Captavit merito clarus utrumque sophos.
Sic dum jura tenens Solymorum et gentis Idumae,
Narratur cytharâ percrepuisse David;
* Talem Thebanas [b] struxisse Amphiona turres,
Sic indefessa personuisse chely,
Sic populos traxisse truces et agrestibus antris
Exutos homines consociasse lyrâ;
Sic magni pectus divinum arsisse Platonis,
Tum, cum deplorans Astera, jura daret;
Talem credibile est vixisse Solona poëtam
Et queiscunque datum est et sapere et furere [c].
Sed tu, magne, peris, dum lis certatur utrinque,
Te Astraea suum vultque Thalia suum.
Haec habitat coelis, sed et haec terrestribus oris,
Ipse tui judex poneris ante Deos;
Scilicet in partes se dividit Hoskinus ambo,
Haec coelo potitur particula, illa solo.

Obiit Aug. 27 1638

Canoro cineri jurisprudentissimi
Parentis pii, memoriae ergo,
hunc posuit cippum conscriptum marmoreum
flens Benettus, sequiturque Patrem
non passibus aequis.

[a] 'nomina' in MS.
* MS. Rawl. D. 727, fol. 95ᵛ.
[b] 'Thebanos' in MS.
[c] Subst. for 'vivere.'

This epitaph was made by Thomas Bonham, of Essex, esquier.

The serjeant's epitaph on his wife at Bowe church, Heriff. :—

> Hic Benedicta jacet, de qua maledicere nemo
> Cui genus aut virtus vel pia lingua potest:
> Bournii et Hoskinii conjux et prolis utrique
> Mater erat, Moyli filia, serva Dei.

On Mr. Bourne, his sonne-in-lawe[a], by him :—

> Nobilis innocuos transegit Bournius annos
> Multa legens, callens plurima, pauca loquens.
> Juridicus causis neque se ditavit[b] agendis
> Non in habendo locans sed moriendo lucrum.

* *Serjeant Hoskins* :—Serviens ad legem ; quaere, if ⟨he was⟩ a knight. His crest (I believe) granted for his bold spirit, and (I suppose) contrived by himselfe.

Amici ⟨included⟩ Egremund Thynne.

> Hic jacet Egremundus Rarus,
> Tuendis paradoxis clarus.
> Mortuus est, ut hic apparet:
> At si loqui posset, hoc negaret.

Was wont to say that all those that came to London were either carrion or crowes.

** ⟨Memorandum⟩ :—Hoskyns—to collect his nonsense discourse, which is very good.

Notes.

[1] Aubrey gives in trick the coat:—'parted per pale gules and azure, a chevron between 3 lions rampant or [Hoskyns]: the crest is a lion's head crowned or, vomiting flames.'

[2] John Hoskins, of 'Mownton' (Monnington on the Wye) in 'Lanwarne' parish, Hereford, was admitted probationer of New College June 22, 1584, and Fellow 1586. He was expelled in 1591 'propter dicteria maledica sub persona Terrae filii.' This was the Serjeant-at-Law.

John Hoskins, of 'Mownton in Lanwarne parish,' Hereford, was admitted probationer of New College, Aug. 24, 1599, and fellow Aug. 24, 1601, and resigned his fellowship in 1613. He took D.C.L. in 1613. He died in 1631 (buried at Ledbury, on August 9). This was 'the Doctor.'

[a] His step-son, more correctly.   * MS. Aubr. 8, fol. 15ᵛ.
[b] 'dicavit' in MS.   ** MS. Aubr. 21, p. 15.

[3] John Owen (the 'epigrammatist'), of Armon in Carnarvonshire, was admitted probationer of New College Oct. 20, 1582, and Fellow March 31, 1584. He resigned his fellowship in 1591.

[4] Aubrey, writing Oct. 27, 1671, in Wood MS. F. 39, fol. 142, says :—

'At Winton College is the picture of a servant with asses eares and hind's feet, a lock on mouth, etc., very good hi(er)oglyphick, with a hexastique in Latin underneath. . . . It was done by the serjeant when he went to school there; but now finely painted. It is at the fountain where the boyes wash their hands.'

Sir John Hoskyns (1634–1705).

* Sir John Hoskyns, knight, one of the Masters of the Chancery, borne at Morehampton in the countie of Hereford, A.D. . . .

Aug. 3rd, 1671, the native maryed.

Aug. 20, 1667, the native broke his thigh; Oct. 1671, the native had another fall which was no lesse dangerous then the former.

Sir John Hoskyns' eldest son John[1], borne at . . ., 14 die Novembr. 1673, 4^h 48' A.M. Obiit . . . 1684.

Mris Jane Hoskyns, daughter of Sir John Hoskyns of Morhamton, Hereff., borne at Harwood in com. praedict. March the 2nd, about 6 a clock in the morning, A.D. 167$\frac{7}{8}$.

** Gazette de Londres :—Jean Hoskins, esq., honoré du titre de chevalerie et l'un de maîtres ordinaires de la cancellerie 30 Janvier 1675.

Note.

[1] In MS. Aubr. 23, fol. 63, is a letter to Aubrey from Sir John Hoskyns, dated Nov. 15, 1673, announcing the birth of this son on Nov. 14, 4^h 48' A.M., and asking him to send to H. C., i.e. Henry Coley the astrologer.

Charles Howard (16– –16–).

*** Charles Howard, eldest son of the honourable Charles Howard of Norfolke, borne 1664 (old style) on a Thursday between 3 and 4 of the clocke in the morning, the last day of March, London. Obiit May 5th 1677, of the small pox.

Henry Howard, second son, borne 1668, between 8 and

* MS. Aubr. 23, notes in foll. 65, 65^v, 67, 67^v. ** MS. Aubr. 23, fol. 102. *** MS. Aubr. 23, slips at fol. 100^v.

9 in the morning, being Sunday 18 of Oct., St. Luke's day.

Thomas Howard, 3rd son, born 12 of July, between one and 2 in the morning, 1670, being Thursday. Obiit, All Saints ⟨day⟩, twelvemonth after his birth.

Elizabeth Teresa Howard borne the 6 of April, being Easter Eve, 22 minutes after 9 of the clock in the evening. Obiit August 12-moneth after her birth.

Robert Hues (1553–1632).

* My cosen Whitney, a parson, quondam Aeneinas., told me that Hues *de Globis* was of that house[a]; which I put downe in the margent of the Oxford book[b].

** Mr. Ashmole thinkes that Robert Hues was of Christ Church. Perhaps he might be of St. Mary Hall too—for so my old cosin Whitney told me by tradition.

*** Hues *de Globis* :—I have heard my old cosen parson Whitney say—an old fellow of Brasennose (dyed 12 yeares since, aetat. 78 or 9)—⟨that⟩ he was of St. Mary Hall.

Edward Hyde, earl of Clarendon (160⁸⁄₉–1674).

**** Edward Hyde, earl of Clarendon, Lord Chancellor of England, was borne at Dinton in com. Wilts., anno Domini 1608, Febr. 16, as this[c] earle thinkes. He told me he has his father's life written by himselfe, but 'tis not fitt so soon to publish it.

***** I thinke I told you that this earl of Clarendon told me his father was writing the history of our late times. He beginns with king Charles 1st and brought it to the restauration of king Charles II, when, as he was writing, the penne fell out of his hand: he took it up

---

* Aubrey in MS. Wood F. 39, fol. 234 : Nov. 15, 1673.

[a] Wood notes here, 'quaere': see the corrections in the next paragraphs.

[b] i.e. the Oxford 1663 edition of the *De globis*.

** Aubrey in MS. Wood F. 39, fol. 237 : Nov. 30, 1673.

*** Ibid., fol. 343ᵛ : Aug. 7, 1680.

**** MS. Aubr. 6, fol. 2.

[c] Henry, 2nd earl.

***** Aubrey in MS. Wood F. 39, fol. 366 : June 24, 1682.

again to write : it fell out again.   So then he percieved he
was attacqued by death, scilicet, the dead palsey.—They
say 'tis very well donne : but his sonne will not print it.

* I advertised you, in my last, of a booke printed
newly by . . . Royston, viz. ' A vindication of Dr. Stilling-
fleet against Dr. Cressy, writt by *a person of honour.*'   Mr.
Royston assures me the earl of Clarendon is the author.

** The place of the Lord Chancellor Hyde's birth
is Dinton, four miles from Chalke.

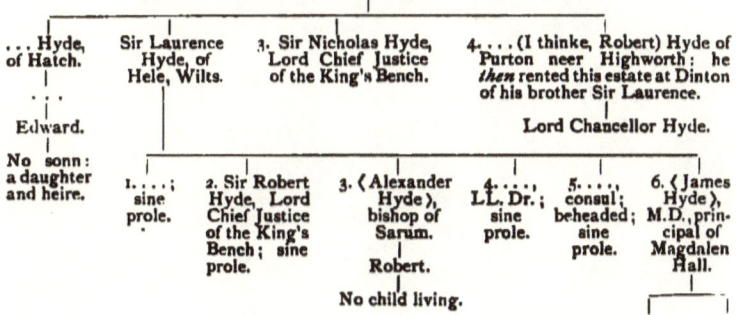

Laurence Hyde,
of Hatch (a hamlet), Wilts.; came out of Cheshire; the third son
of Robert Hyde, prout per inscription at Tisbury Church.

... Hyde, of Hatch.	Sir Laurence Hyde, of Hele, Wilts.	3. Sir Nicholas Hyde, Lord Chief Justice of the King's Bench.	4. ... (I thinke, Robert) Hyde of Purton neer Highworth : he *then* rented this estate at Dinton of his brother Sir Laurence.
Edward.			Lord Chancellor Hyde.
No sonn : a daughter and heire.			

1. ... ; sine prole.	2. Sir Robert Hyde, Lord Chief Justice of the King's Bench; sine prole.	3. ⟨ Alexander Hyde ⟩, bishop of Sarum.	4. ... , sine prole.	5. ... , consul; beheaded; sine prole.	6. ⟨ James Hyde ⟩, M.D., principal of Magdalen Hall.
		Robert.	LL. Dr. ;		
		No child living.			

* Ibid., fol. 250 : Jan. 1, 167¾.   ** Ibid., fol. 365 : June 24, 1682

OXFORD
PRINTED AT THE CLARENDON PRESS
BY HORACE HART, M.A.
PRINTER TO THE UNIVERSITY

www.ingramcontent.com/pod-product-compliance
Lightning Source LLC
Chambersburg PA
CBHW030941110726
47900CB00004B/1080